The Sackett Novels
of
Louis L'Amour

THE SACKETT NOVELS
OF
LOUIS L'AMOUR

VOLUME IV

Lonely on the Mountain
The Sky-Liners
The Man From the Broken Hills
Ride the Dark Trail

BANTAM BOOKS
TORONTO · NEW YORK · LONDON · SYDNEY

*This low-priced Bantam Book
has been completely reset in a type face
designed for easy reading, and was printed
from new plates. It contains the complete
text of the original hard-cover edition.*
NOT ONE WORD HAS BEEN OMITTED.

THE SACKETT NOVELS OF LOUIS L'AMOUR, VOLUME IV
*A Bantam Book
September 1980*

PRINTING HISTORY
Originally published as four separate works
LONELY ON THE MOUNTAIN
Copyright © 1980 by Bantam Books, Inc.
THE SKY-LINERS
Copyright © 1967 by Bantam Books, Inc.
THE MAN FROM THE BROKEN HILLS
Copyright © 1975 by Louis L'Amour
RIDE THE DARK TRAIL
Copyright © 1972 By Bantam Books, Inc.

*Bantam Books are published by Bantam Books, Inc. Its trademark,
consisting of the words "Bantam Books" and the portrayal of a rooster
is Registered in U.S. Patent and Trademark Office and in other countries.
Marca Registrada. Bantam Books, Inc., 666 Fifth Avenue, New York,
New York 10103.*

PRINTED IN THE UNITED STATES OF AMERICA

0 9 8 7 6 5 4 3 2

Contents

Foreword

If you wish to see the places I write about in my stories, they can be visited in most cases. Occasionally, however, a 4-wheel drive is necessary unless you want to walk or climb some distance on foot.

Those of you who saw the "60 Minutes" show about my work may recall the ending. It was filmed at around 11,000 feet and only a hundred yards or so from where Tell Sackett's father was killed. The cliff over which he almost stepped in the darkness lay in the direction I was walking. Flagan finally met his wolf on a mountain-top somewhat south of there, and almost as high.

Many of the places I write about were places discovered years ago. To hold a mining claim it is necessary to do at least $100 work on it each year. During my teenage years I discovered there were a lot of doctors, lawyers, merchants, etc., who had mining claims but did not relish the pick-and-shovel work, so when jobs were scarce I'd do their assessment work. It got me into all sorts of back corners in the mountains and deserts I'd never otherwise have found.

Usually, there was time to explore a little. On occasion, travelling across the country with some friend met in the mines, we'd stop to examine old mines (from the outside, they're very dangerous!), old town-sites, abandoned ranches, lumber-camps, ghost towns. In twenty years of "yondering" here and abroad one can see quite a lot.

Since then I've been back to some of these places, and I've also found new ones. Usually I try to find one or two old-timers who know the country well and take them along with me. They know who built what fallen-in cabin, who worked the claims, built the foot-bridges, etc.

Surprisingly, some of the places are unchanged. A few years ago I went to a place on Cascade Creek where an Army officer had gone in 1873, and it was much as he described it.

Trees fall and rot away, others grow, but the mountains change but little . . . usually. Yet there is a subtle change taking place all the time, and if one sits quietly in a wild place one can almost feel it happening.

Each year I spend some time in the desert or in the high country. I like to walk the old trails, to get up high where a man can look over a hundred miles of magnificent country or stand among the high, bare peaks where even the trees have stopped growing.

When you are up high that way you are not alone, you have the company of eagles.

LONELY ON THE MOUNTAIN

Chapter 1

There will come a time when you believe everything is finished. That will be the beginning.

Pa said that when I was a boy. There was a hot, dry wind moaning through the hot, dry trees, and we were scared of fire in the woods, knowing that if fire came, all we had would go.

We had crops in the ground, but there'd been no rain for weeks. We were scrapin' the bottom of the barrel for flour and drinkin' coffee made from ground-up beans. We'd had our best cow die, and the rest was ganted up, so's you could count every rib.

Two years before, pa had set us to diggin' a well. "Pa?" I asked. "Why dig a well? We've got the creek yonder and three flowin' springs on the place. It's needless work."

He lifted his head, and he looked me right in the eye and said, "Dig a well."

We dug a well.

We grumbled, but when pa said dig, you just naturally dug. And lucky it was, too.

For there came the time when the bed of the creek was dust and the springs that had always flowed weren't flowin'. We had water, though. We had water from a deep, cold well. We watered our stock, we watered our kitchen garden, and we had what was needful for drinkin' because of that well.

Now, years later and far out on the grass prairie, I was remembering and wondering what I could do that I hadn't done.

No matter which way you looked between you and anywhere else, there was a thousand miles of grass—and the Sioux.

3

The Sioux hadn't come upon us yet, but they were about, and every man-jack of us knew it. It could be they hadn't cut our sign yet, but cut it they would, and when they did, they would come for us.

We were seven men, including the Chinese cook, in no shape to fight off a bunch of Sioux warriors if they came upon us. Scattered around the cattle, we'd be in no shape at all.

"If it comes," I told them, "center on me and we'll kill enough cattle for a fort and make a stand."

Have you seen that Dakota country? It varies some, but it's likely to be flat or low, rolling hills, with here and there a slough. You don't find natural places to fort. The buffalo wallows offer the best chance if there's one handy. The trouble was, if the Sioux came upon us, it would be a spot of their choosing, not ours.

The buffalo-chip fire had burned down to a sullen red glow by the time Tyrel rode back into camp. He stripped the gear from his mount and carried his saddle up to the fire for a pillow. He took off his chaps, glancing over at me, knowing I was awake.

"They're quiet, Tell"—he spoke soft so's not to wake the others, who were needful of sleep—"but every one of them is awake."

"There's something out there. Some*thing* or some*body*."

"This here is Injun country." Tyrel shucked his gun belt and placed it handy to his bed. He sat down to pull off his boots. "We knew that before we started."

He went to the blackened, beat-up coffee pot and looked over at me. "Toss me your cup."

Well, I wasn't sleeping, nohow. I sat up and took the coffee. "It ain't Injuns," I said. "Least it doesn't *feel* like Injuns. This is something else. We've been followed, Tyrel. You know that as well as me. We've been followed for the last three or four days."

The coffee was strong enough to grow hair on a saddle. "Tye? You recall the time pa wanted us to dig that well? He was always one to be ready for whatever might come. Not that he went around expecting trouble. He just wanted to be ready for whatever happened. For anything."

"That was him, all right."

"Tyrel, something tells me I forgot to dig my well. There's something I should have done that I've missed, something we've got to think of or plan for."

Tyrel, he just sipped his coffee, squatting there in his sock feet, feeling good to have his boots off. "Don't know what it could be," Tyrel said. "We've got rifles all around and ammunition to fight a war.

At Fort Garry, Orrin will pick up some Red River carts and a man or two. He'll load those carts with grub and such." He pushed his hat back, sweat-wet hair plastered against his forehead. "The stock are fat—eleven hundred head of good beef, and we've gotten an early start."

"Don't make no difference, Tyrel. I've forgotten something, or somebody."

"Wait'll we meet up with Orrin. When he joins us at Fort Garry, he'll know right away if anything's wrong."

"I've been thinkin' about Fort Garry, Tyrel. Seems foolish to drive east even a little way when we've got to go back west."

Tyrel refilled his cup and held up the pot. I shook my head. "It's the boys," he said. "This here shapes up to be a rough, mean drive. Oh, we'll see some new country, an' mighty beautiful country, but any way you take it, it will be rough. We'd better give the boys a chance to blow off some steam."

"They'd better blow it careful," I said. "Some of those Canadians are mighty rough. Nice folks, but they can handle themselves."

Low clouds blotted out the stars; wind whispered in the grass. Sleep was needed, but I was wakeful as a man with three sparkin'-age daughters. "You were there when the word came, Tyrel. D'you figure there's more to this than Logan let on?"

"You know Logan better'n I do. He cut his stick for trouble before he was knee-high to a short hog, and you know any time Logan calls for help, there's no telling what's involved. There's mighty little in the way of trouble Logan can't handle all by himself."

"He never lied to us."

"He never lied to nobody. Nolan and Logan have done things here and there that you and me wouldn't, but they never broke their given word."

Tyrel bedded down, but I lay awake, trying to think it out, tired though I was.

We were pushing eleven hundred head of fat steers across the Dakota plains, headed for the gold mines in far western Canada. The Dakota country was new to us. Wide, wide plains but good grass so far, and we'd been lucky enough to come upon water when needed. Cap Rountree had been up this way before, but aside from Tyrel, who had been marshal of a gold-minin' town in Idaho, none of us had been so far north.

We'd put the herd together in a hurry because Logan was in need and started the drive short-handed, which meant extra work for all.

Orrin was coming up by steamboat and was to meet us at Fort Garry for the long drive west.

Those to whom we'd talked, who might or might not know what they were talkin' about, said there were no towns to the west. There were trading posts here and yonder, however, one of them being Fort Whoop-Up.

Even about that we heard two stories. Some said it was simply a trading post, but others said it was a hangout for rustlers, whiskey peddlers, and the like. If it was kin to such places as we'd known, it could be both.

We Sacketts had come west from the Tennessee-North Carolina country in search of new lands. Ours had been among the earliest folk to settle back yonder, but somehow we stuck to the high-up hills where the game was and let the good bottom lands slip away to latecomers. Most newcomers to the west found the life hard and the ways rough, but to mountain-bred folks it was no different from what we were accustomed to.

Any time a Sackett had meat on the table, it was likely to be meat he'd shot, and if pa was away from home, it was we youngsters who did the shootin'. Those who lived 'round about used to say that Sacketts and shootin' went together like hog meat an' hominy.

Stock driving had been our way of life since first we settled in the hills. It was old Yance Sackett who began it some two hundred years back, and he started it with turkey drives to market. After that, it was hogs, and, like turkeys, we drove them afoot, for the most part.

If you had turkeys or hogs to sell, you just naturally drove them to market or sold them to a drover.

Word came from Logan just after we'd sold nine hundred head of prime beef in Kansas. We'd actually sold fourteen hundred head, but some of the stock belonged to neighbors.

Cap Rountree, Tyrel, and I were at a table in the Drover's Cottage when that man with the green eye-shade came up to me and said, "Mr. Sackett? This here message come for you a day or two back. I reckon it's important, and I just now heard you were in town."

"Cap," I said, "if you and Tyrel will pardon me, I'll just see what this is."

"Shall I read it?" Tyrel asked me.

"You might," I said, and was glad for the offer. When it came to schoolin', I'd come up empty, and whilst I was learning to read and write, I was mighty short on words. There were still a good many I'd never driven into the corral to slap the brand of memory on.

Tyrel had only learned to read a short time back, but he could read handwritin' as easy as print, nigh as good as any schoolmarm.

He opened up that message like he'd been gettin' 'em every day. He looked over it at me. "Listen to this," he said.

William Tell Sackett,
Drover's Cottage,
Abilene, Kansas.

I taken money to deliver several hundred head of beef cattle before winter sets in. I got no cows. I got no money. I can't get away to help. Withouten they get them cows, folks will starve, and I'll be wearin' a rope necktie.

Logan

P.S. You can expect Higginses.

"Higginses?" Cap said. "I thought you'd done rolled up their carpet?"

"By 'Higginses' he means we can expect trouble. For some reason he didn't want to say that, but he knew we'd understand."

"Those Higgins boys were rough," Tyrel said, "and we sure didn't dust off all of them. They were good folks, only we just didn't get along."

"Fact is," he added, "there was one of those Higgins gals who used to give me the big eye back yonder in school. *Boy, was she something!* She'd give me a look out'n those big blue eyes, and I wouldn't know come hither to go yonder."

Cap, he was a-settin' there lookin' at me out of those wise old eyes. "He wants beef cattle, and we've just sold our stock. We got a piece of money, but we ain't got near enough to buy at these prices. So what do we do?"

"We've got to buy," I said.

"We haven't got enough to buy, let alone to feed ourselves from here to Canada. It's a far piece."

Whilst we ate, I did some studyin'. The thought of not doing it never entered our minds. We Sacketts just naturally stood by one another, and if Logan was in trouble, we'd help. Undoubtedly, he'd given his word to deliver cattle, and a Sackett's word was his bond. It was even more than that. Anywhere a Sackett was known, his name was good for cash in the hand.

This was going to take every cent we could put our hands on, and worst of all, we had to *move!*

Cap put down his cup. "Got me an idea," he said, and was gone from the table.

"This couldn't come at a worse time," Tyrel commented. "I need all I've got to pay debts back in Santa Fe."

"Me, too," I said, "but Logan's in trouble."

"You believe he meant that about hanging?"

"Logan is a man who takes hanging right serious, and he wouldn't joke about it. If he says hanging, he means just that." For a moment there, I paused, looking into my coffee. "From that remark about Higginses, we can expect trouble along the way."

"Sounds like Logan figures somebody doesn't want the cattle to get through"—Tyrel glanced over at me—"which doesn't make a lot of sense."

Cap was coming back into the room followed by a straw-hatted sod buster wearing shoes. Farmers were beginning to settle around, but a man didn't see many of them yet, and almost never in the Drover's Cottage.

"Set, Bob, an' tell them what you told me," Cap said.

Bob had wrinkles from squinting at the sun and wrinkles around his eyes from laughing. "My cousin's come down from the north. Lives up on the Missouri near Yankton. He was telling me about some Indian cattle, and Cap here, he overheard us."

"Indian cattle?"

"Well, some of them. Quite a few years back, two brothers brought some cattle into the Missouri River country. One of the brothers was gored by a steer, and by the time the other one found him, he was in bad shape. Blood poison, or whatever. He lasted a few weeks, then died.

"The brother took the body back home for burial, and when he came back, he was crossing a stream when his horse fell with him. Both of them lost—horse and man.

"So those cattle run wild. The Injuns around there are mostly friendlies, and they killed a steer time to time, but those cattle have run wild in some of the gullies leading back from the river. I'd say if anybody has claim on them now, it's those Injuns."

"But would they sell them?"

"Right now they would. They'd sell, and quick. You see, the Sioux have been raiding into their country some, and just now the Sioux learned about those cattle. They'll drive them off, leaving the friendlies with nothing. If you were to go in there and make 'em a decent offer, you'd have yourself a herd."

"How many head, do you figure?"

"Eight, nine hundred. Maybe more. There's good grass in those bottoms, and they've done right well. What you'll find is mostly young stuff—unbranded. What Texas folk call mavericks."

So that was how it began. We met the Injuns and sat down over a mess of bacon, bread, and beans, and we made our deal. They didn't want the Sioux to run off those cattle, and we paid them well in blankets and things they were needing.

There was a star showing here and there when I rolled out of my blankets and shook out my boots. The morning was cold, so I got into my vest and coat as quick as ever I could, and after rolling my bed, I headed for the cook fire and a cup of coffee.

Lin, our Chinese cook, was squatting over the fire. He gestured to the pot. "All ready," he said.

He dished up a plate of beef and beans for me, and when I'd taken a couple of swallows of coffee, almost too hot to drink, I started on the beans.

"These are good. What've you done to them?"

"Wild onions," he said.

My eyes swept the horizon. Far off to the west, I could see some black humps. "Buffalo," I commented.

He stood up to look. "I have never seen a buffalo. There will be more?"

"A-plenty. More'n we want, I expect."

Leaving the fire, I saddled up and then returned for another plate of the beef and beans. When a man rides out in the morning on a cattle drive, he never knows when he will eat again. Too many things can come up.

Whether it was the wild onions, I did not know, but his grub was the best I'd ever tasted in a cow camp. I told him so.

"I've never cooked but for myself." He glanced at me. "I go home now, to China."

"Isn't this the long way?"

"You go to British Columbia? I have a relative there, and ships leave there for China. I had no money, and when I heard you were going to British Columbia, I wished to go with you."

"It'll be rough."

"It often is." He looked at me, not smiling. "It can be rough in China, too." He paused. "My father was an official in the western desert country, in what we called the New Territories. It is a land where all people ride, as they do here."

A low wind moaned in the grass, and the long ripples ran over the far plain. It would be dawn soon. The cattle were beginning to get up, to stretch and to graze.

When I was in the saddle, I looked back at him. "Can you use a rifle?"

"Our compound was attacked several times by bandits," he said. "We all had to shoot."

"Before this is over, you may have another chance," I said.

Chapter 2

We were four hours into the morning when Cap Rountree stood in his stirrups, shading his eyes as he looked off to the north. Then he waved us west and came cantering back to meet me as I rode up from riding drag.

"There's been a prairie fire. There's no more grass."

"How about going east? We have to ride east, anyway, to hook up with Orrin."

"The fire came from the east. The way I figure, the grass back thataway is burned off. Westward we've got a chance because of that mite of rain we had night before last. That could have put out the fire."

That made sense. "Stay with the herd," I said, "and I'll scout off to the west."

"Keep your Winchester handy. I cut some Injun sign over yonder."

Sure enough, I'd not gone a quarter of a mile before I rode up to the edge of the burn. Far as the eye could see, the prairie was black. Turning west, I cantered along for a ways, studying the country. The raindrops had speckled the burned grass, and the chances were Cap's guess was right. Nobody knew more about handling cattle in rough country than Cap.

Several times, I came upon buffalo tracks, and they had turned off to the west just as we were doing. This was going to set us back a day or two, and it was time we could ill afford to lose. It was just spring, with the grass turning green, but we had a long drive ahead and must reach our destination before winter set in.

Every time I topped a rise, I studied the country around, but mostly what lay behind. There were always a few antelope in sight and usually buffalo, but in small bunches and afar off.

Just short of midday, we swung the herd into a shallow valley where there was a slough and some good grass. Lin went off to one side and put together a small fire.

Nobody takes a herd over two thousand miles of rough country without trouble. We'd have our share, and we were ready for it, but we didn't want more than we had to have.

Tyrel came in from the herd, and getting down from the bay he was riding, he whipped the dust from him with his hat, standing well back. When he came up to the fire for coffee, he looked over at me. "See anything?"

He'd seen me looking around when I topped those rises. "Nothing but buffalo," I said.

"I got a bad feeling," he said.

"You and me both," I said.

Cap rode in and dismounted, switching his saddle to a rat-tailed dun that looked like the wrath of God but was rougher than whalebone, a mustang born to the wide plains and the rough country.

When he came up to the fire, he glanced from one to the other. "If you want to know what I think—"

"I do," I said.

"We better skip that drive east. Allowin' there's good grass like we heard, we still lose time, and we just ain't got it to lose."

He filled his cup and came over, squatting on his heels. He took a stick and drew in the dust. "Right here's about where we are. Right over here is the Jim River—the James if you want to be persnickety about it. I say we drive west, then follow the Jim north, which gives us water all the way.

"Right here there's a mighty pretty valley where the Pipestem flows into the Jim. We can let the cattle have a day there, which will give Orrin a chance to gain on us.

"There's good grass in that valley, and there's a lot of elm, box elder, and some cottonwood along the rivers. There'll be firewood and shade for the stock if we have to wait, and it might pay to wait a couple of days for Orrin."

"We've been lucky on the grass," Tyrel said, "bein' so early in the year, but we're drivin' north."

"You're durned right." Cap sipped his coffee. "An' from here on, the new grass will be slower, and farther west it will be almighty scarce."

Well, now. That fitted in with my own thinking, but I studied on it a mite. Orrin was probably on the river right now, ridin' one of them steamboats up the Red River to Pembina. Once he got there, he'd have to find a couple of men, buy teams and a couple of Red River carts, then stock up with supplies for the westward drive.

He would need a day if he was lucky, three days if he wasn't, and then he would start west to meet us. We would be coming up from the south, and he would be driving west.

From Pembina there was a trail that led due west through the Pembina Mountains and skirting the Turtle Mountains on the north. If Orrin could make his arrangements in Pembina, he could strike west along that trail, and with luck we'd meet him somewhere close to the Mouse River. With horse-drawn carts, he should make about twenty miles a day, while we would make no more than twelve to fifteen. If he had to go on to Fort Garry, that would throw everything out of kilter, and we'd have to meet farther north.

We scratched around in the dirt, indicating trails and figuring how best to go. Here and there, we'd picked up word of what to expect. We'd stay with the Jim as far as we could, then strike west-northwest for the Canadian border.

"Wish we had more men," Cap said. "The Sioux can be mighty ornery."

"We'll have to chance it." I went out to the remuda and threw my saddle on a rangy buckskin.

It was a worrisome thing. The last thing I'd wanted was a cattle drive through country I'd never seen. Aside from Cap and Tyrel, the other men were strangers, picked up where we could get them. They seemed to be mighty good hands, but only time would show what they were made of, and any time you ride through Sioux and Blackfoot country, you're borrowing trouble.

We were short on grub, long on ammunition, and needful of a tie-up with Orrin. Worst of all, he'd be coming west with strangers, too, if he could recruit any help at all.

It was early spring, with patches of snow still holding on the shady side of the hills. The grass was growing, but mostly it was just like a green mist over the hills, although a lot of last year's grass, cured on the stem, was still out there.

Logan had said we could expect Higginses, and the name of Higgins, some folks with whom we'd had a long-running feud, was our name for trouble. Some of those Higgins boys could really shoot.

After I'd had a bite, I swung into the saddle and rode out to relieve one of the boys watching the cattle. He was a new boy we'd found riding south for Abilene, and he stopped at our fire. When we heard he was hunting a riding job, we told him he had one if he was a stayer.

"Never quit nothin' yet," he said, "until it was done."

"You got a name you want to use?"

"Isom Brand. Folks call me Brandy."

"All right. Now think on this. You hook up with us, you'll be riding into wild country, Injun country. You'll see mountains like you've never seen and wider plains than you can believe. You're likely to miss a meal or two, as we're short of grub until we hook up with my brother Orrin, but we don't want anybody who is likely to complain."

He just looked at me, that smooth-faced kid with the quick blue eyes, and he said, "You goin' to miss those meals, too?"

"We miss them together," I said.

"You hired a hand," he said. He hesitated then, flushing a little. "I ain't got much of an outfit. I give all I had left in cash money to my ma for her and sis afore I pulled out."

"Couldn't you find a job close to home?"

"No, sir. There just weren't none."

"They got enough money to last?"

"No, sir. I have to send some to them as soon as I can."

"You shape up," I said, "and I'll advance you some."

He was riding a crow-bait plow horse that was no good for our work, so we turned him into the remuda, and we roped a paint we bought off an Injun. Brandy topped him off all right, and we rode along.

He was walking a circle on the far side of the herd when I came up to him. "Better go in and get yourself a bite," I suggested, "and catch yourself some shuteye. We won't be moving out for about an hour."

There was water a-plenty and good grass, so we took some time. Meanwhile, keeping a watch out and seeing none of the cattle got to straying, I thought about Logan.

Logan and his twin brother Nolan were Clinch Mountain Sacketts, almost a different breed than us. They were rough boys, those Clinch Mountain Sacketts, right down from ol' Yance Sackett, who founded the line way back in the 1600s. He settled so far back in the mountains that the country was getting settled up before they even knew he was there.

Some of those Clinch Mountain Sacketts were Blockaders; least that's what they were called. They raised a lot of corn up in the mountains, and the best way they could get it to market was in liquid form. They began selling by the gallon rather than the bushel.

Pa, he would have none of that. "If'n you boys want to take a drink, that's your business, but buy it in town, don't make it. Maybe I don't agree with the government on all things, but we elected them, a majority of us did, and it's up to us to stand by them and their laws.

"From all I hear handed down," he added, "that Yance was a wild one, and his get are the same. Those boys are rougher than a cob, but if you're in trouble, they'll come a-runnin'. They'll build you a fire, lend you money, feed you, give you a drink from the jug, or he'p you fight your battles. Especially he'p you fight battles. Why, ain't one of them Clinch Mountain Sacketts wouldn't climb a tree to fight a bear.

"Why, there was a man over at Tellico whupped one of them boys one time. Sure enough, come Saturday night, here was that Sackett again, and the feller whupped him again. An' ever' Saturday night, there was Sackett awaitin' on him, an' ever' time he whupped that Sackett, it got tougher to do. Finally, that feller just give up and stayed to home. He was afraid to show his face because Sackett would be waitin' on him.

"Finally that feller from Tellico, he just taken out and left the country. Went down to the settlements and got hisself a job. He was a right big man, make two of Sackett, but it was years before he stopped jumpin' if you came up behind and spoke to him. 'Made a mistake,' he said after. 'I should have let him whup me. Then I'd of had some peace. Wust thing a man can do is whup a Sackett. They'll dog you to your dyin' day.'"

That was the way it was. If one of us was in difficulties, Logan would come a-runnin', and the least we could do was go see what we could do.

He said he needed beef cattle, so we'd take him beef cattle. I don't know what had him treed up yonder, but it must've been somethin' fierce, knowin' Logan.

So we'd spent all we had, barrin' a few dollars in pocket, and we were headed into wild, rough country with eleven hundred head of steers. But it wasn't only that Logan was in trouble. It was because a Sackett had given his word.

I hear tell that down in the towns some folks don't put much store in a man's word, but with us it was the beginning and the end. There were some poor folks up where we come from, but they weren't poor in the things that make a man.

Through the long afternoon, we plodded steadily west, the blackened earth only a few hundred yards off on our right. The low gray clouds broke, and the sky cleared. The grass was changing, too. We rarely saw the tall bluestem that had grown further east. Now it appeared only in a few bottoms. There was a little bluestem, June grass and needle grass.

Slowly, the herd was gettin' trail broke. Once in a while, some old mossyhorn steer would make a break to go home, and we'd have to cut him back into the herd, but generally they were holdin' steady. A rangy old brindle steer had taken the lead and held it. He was mean as a badger with his tail in a trap and would fight anything that argued with him, so mostly nobody did.

Cap rode back to me just about sundown as we were rounding the stock into a hollow near a slough. "Tell," he said, "better come an' have a look whilst it's light."

He led the way to the far side of the slough, and we studied the ground. The grass was pressed down here and there, the remains of a fire and the tracks of two travois.

"Six or seven, I'd say," Cap said, "but you're better at this than me."

Well, I took a look around. "Six or seven," I agreed. "Maybe eight. One of them travois leaves a deep trail, and I figure they've got a wounded man on it.

"They've had them a fight," I said, "and that's odd because there's at least two women along. It's no war party."

"There's a papoose, too," Cap said. "If you look yonder by that rock, you'll see where they leaned his cradle board."

I indicated a dirty piece of cloth lying in the trampled-down grass. It was very bloody. "Somebody is hurt," I said. "Probably the man on the travois."

Squatting, I sat on my heels and looked over the place where they'd camped and the ashes left from their fire. "Yesterday," I said, "maybe the day before."

"And they're headin' west, like us."

"We got to keep an eye out. We'll be comin' up with them maybe tomorrow night or next morning. They aren't going to make much time."

"What do you make of it?" Cap asked.

"A papoose in the cradle board, one walkin' about youngster, two women and four men. Two of the men are oldish, gettin' on in years. One's a youngster—fightin' age but young. Then there's the wounded man."

"I spotted 'em a while back." Cap put the butt of his rifle on the ground. "They've been keepin' to low ground. Looks to me like they're scared."

Well, I took my hat off and wiped the sweat off my forehead, then put my hat on and tugged her down tight. "Cap," I said, "we'd best sleep light and step careful because whatever's after them is comin' our way, too."

Chapter 3

We were taking it easy. We had a long way to go, but the season was early, and there was no use us gettin' so far north that the grass wouldn't have come yet. The country was greenin', but it would take time. We had come up to the Jim River just below Bear Creek.

Cap an' Tyrel scouted ahead, riding into the trees to see if company waited on us, but there was nobody. There was fair grass on the plain and mighty good grass in the creek bottom, so we swung our herd around and bedded them down.

Swingin' along the edge of the trees, I dabbed a loop on a snag and hauled it up for the fire. Lin was already down from the wagon and picking up some flat stones he could use to set pots on.

We hadn't any chuck wagon, and grub was scarce. Leavin' Brandy with the stock, Tyrel rode down to where I sat my horse. "Saw some deer back yonder." He gestured toward the creek. "Figured I'd ride out and round up some meat."

"Sure." As he turned his mount away, I said, "Keep your eyes open for those Injuns. I think they're somewhere about."

"Maybe so." He pulled up for a moment. "Night before last— maybe I was wrong, but I thought I smelled smoke." He let it rest for a minute, and then he said, "Tell? You know what I think? I think those Injuns are ridin' in our shadow. For protection, like."

He took out his Winchester and rode off into the trees, but what he said stayed with me. Those Indians were only a handful, and they'd seen trouble from somebody. Tyrel might be right, and they could be stayin' close to us with the idea that they'd not be attacked with us so close by.

By the time I started back for camp, the cattle had settled down. A few were still grazing on last year's grass, but most of them were full as ticks. I wasn't fooled by their good shape because I knew rough country lay ahead of us.

When I stepped down from the saddle and ground hitched my horse, the other two riders had come in and were drinkin' coffee. Gilcrist was a lean, dark man who handled a rope well and seemed to know something about stock but was obviously a gambler. He'd not had much luck getting up a game around camp because mostly when we bedded down the cattle, we were too tired to do anything but crawl into our blankets ourselves. The man traveling with him was a big, very heavy man but not fat. He was no taller than me, maybe even a mite shorter, but he was a good fifty pounds heavier, and it wasn't fat. Gilcrist called him the Ox, so we followed suit. Nobody ever did ask him his name, as folks just didn't ask questions. Whatever somebody named you or whatever you answered to was good enough.

Just as I was stepping down from my bronc, I heard a rifle shot. "We'll have fresh meat for supper," I said.

Gilcrist glanced around. "Suppose he missed?"

"That was Tyrel. He doesn't miss."

A few minutes later, Tyrel rode into camp with the best parts of a deer. He unloaded the meat at the fire and led his horse away to strip its gear. Nobody said anything, but when Tyrel came back into camp, I noticed Gilcrist sizing him up.

We ate, and Tyrel spoke quietly to me. "They're about, Tell. I spotted one of them watchin' me." He paused a moment. "I left them a cut of the meat."

"He see you?"

"Uh-huh. I laid it out nice and ready for him. I think they're hard up."

I turned to Gilcrist and the Ox. "When you finish, ride out and let Cap and Brandy come in."

The Ox wiped his hands on his pants. "Do the kid good to wait a mite. Teach him something."

I looked across the fire at him. "If he needs teaching, I'll teach him. You relieve him."

The Ox leaned back on his elbow. "Hell, I just got here. They can wait."

"Relieve him," I said, "now."

The Ox hesitated, then slowly got to his feet, deliberately prolonging the movements. "Oh, all right," he said. "I'll go let mama's little boy come in."

He mounted his horse and rode out. Gilcrist got to his feet, then commented, "Better go easy with him. He's a mighty mean man."

"Where I come from they're all mean if you push them," I said. "If he stays on this job, he'll do his work."

Gilcrist looked around. "Mighty big country out here. Looks to me like a man could do what he wanted."

"Boot Hill is full of men who had that idea." Tyrel spoke casually, as if bored. "It's a big country, all right, big enough for men who are big enough."

Gilcrist mounted up and rode out, and Tyrel threw his coffee on the grass. "Looks like trouble."

"I saw it when I hired them, but who else could I get? Nobody wanted to ride north into wild country."

"Maybe they wanted to. Maybe they had reason."

"That big one," I commented, "looks strong enough to wrassle a bull. Maybe I should save him for Logan. Logan likes his kind."

"Maybe. Maybe you won't be able to save him, Tell. Maybe he won't wait that long."

Cold winds blew down from the north, and there were occasional spitting rains. The scattered patches of snow were disappearing, however, and the trees along the river bottoms were green. There were pussywillows along the bottoms, too, and patches of crocus growing near the snow.

We moved north, day after day, following the course of the James River but holding to the hills on one side or the other.

As we came down the hill into the valley where the James and

Pipestem met, Tyrel rode over to where I was. "Cold," he said, meanin' the wind, "mighty cold!"

"There's wood along the river," I said, "and we'll rest up for a couple of days. It's needful that Orrin have time. No tellin' whether he'll find the men we need or not."

"Wish we could get rid of them two." Tyrel gestured toward the Ox and Gilcrist. "I just don't cotton to them."

"Nor me," I said, "an' old Cap is keepin' his mouth shut, but it's hard."

Turning to look at him, I said, "Tye, all day I've been thinkin' of the mountains back home. Must be I'm gettin' old or something, but I keep thinkin' of how it was back home with ma sittin' by the fire workin' on her patchwork quilt. Night came early in the winter months, and lookin' out the window a body could see pa's lanterns making patterns on the snow as he walked about. He'd be doin' the last of the chores, but when he came in, he always brought an armful of wood for the wood box."

"I recall," Tyrel said. "We sure spent some time climbin' around those mountains! All the way from Chunky Gal to Roan Mountain. I mind the time Orrin got lost over to Huggins Hell and was plumb out of sight for three days."

"I wasn't there then. I'd already slipped along the mountains and over the Ohio to join up with the Union."

"Nolan went t'other way. He rode down to Richmond and joined the Confederacy. We had people on both sides."

"It was that kind of a war," I commented, and changed the subject. "When we were talkin' about who'd been to the north, I clean forgot the drive I made right after the war. Went up the Bozeman Trail into Montana. I didn't stay no longer than to get myself turned around and headed back, although it was a different trail I rode on the return.

"It was on the way up I got my first taste of the Sioux. They're a rough lot, Tyrel. Don't you take them light."

Tyrel chuckled suddenly. "Tell? You mindful of an old friend of yours? The one we called Highpockets?"

"You mean Haney? Sure. Odd you should speak of him. Last time I heard tell of him, he was headed north."

"Mind the time he went to the sing over at Wilson's Cove? He fell head over heels for some visitin' gal from down in the Sequatchie and went at it, knuckle and skull, with some big mule skinner.

"I remember he come back, and he got out what he used to call his 'reevolver,' and he said, 'That ol' boy's give me trouble, so I'm a gonna take my ol' reevolver an' shoot some meat off his bones.' He done it, too."

We rounded up our steers in the almost flat bottom of that valley and let them graze on the stand of last year's grass. There was green showin' all about, but mostly what they could get at was cured on the stem. There was water a-plenty, and this seemed like a good time to rest up a mite.

Cap killed a buffalo, a three-year-old cow, on the slope above the river, so we had fresh meat. The boys bunched the cattle for night, and Cap said, "We'd best start lookin' for windy hills for campin'. The way I hear it, up north where there's all those rivers, lakes, and such, there's mosquitoes like you wouldn't believe. Eat a man alive, or a horse."

"Mosquitoes?" I said. "Hell, I've seen mosquitoes. Down on the Sulphur—"

"Not like the ones they have up north," Cap said. "You mind what I say, Tell. When you hear stories of them, you'll swear they're lies. Well, they ain't. You leave a horse tied out all night and chances are he'll be dead by morning."

Me, I looked over at him, but he wasn't smiling. Whether he knew what he was talkin' about, I didn't know, but he wasn't funnin'. He was downright serious.

There were mosquitoes there on the Pipestem, but we built a smudge, and it helped some. Nobody talked much, but we lazed about the fire, takin' our turn at watching over the cattle. The remuda we kept in close to camp where we could all more or less keep an eye on it. What Indians wanted most of all was horses, and without them we'd be helpless.

A time or two, I walked out under the stars, away from the campfire and what talk there was, just to listen.

There was no sound but the cattle stirring a mite here and there, rising or lying down, chewing their cuds, occasionally standing up to graze a bit. It was still early.

Later, when I was a-horseback on the far side of the head, I thought I caught a whiff of wood smoke that came from a different direction than our fire. Well, if they were riding in our shadow, they were no bother, and it was all right with us.

Gave a body a kind of restful feeling, just knowing he wasn't alone out there.

This was a lovely valley, already turning green with springtime, but it was a valley in a great wide open country where we rode alone, where we had no friends, and if trouble came, we'd have to handle it all by our lonesome. There wasn't going to be anybody coming to help. Not anybody at all.

Chapter 4

For two days, we rested where the Pipestem met the James, holding the cattle on the grass at the edge of the woods and gathering fallen limbs and dead brush for firewood.

"Pleasant place," Tyrel said. "I hate to leave."

Gilcrist glanced over at me. "We pulling out?"

"Just before daybreak. Get a good night's sleep."

Gilcrist finished his coffee and got up. "Come on, Ox, let's relieve mama's boy and the old man."

Tyrel glanced at me, and I shrugged. Lin straightened up from the fire, fork in hand. The Ox caught his expression. "Something you don't like, yellow boy?"

Lin merely glanced at him and returned to his work.

The Ox hesitated, glancing over at me where I sat with my coffee cup in my hands; then he went to his horse, mounted, and followed Gilcrist.

"If we weren't short-handed," I said to Tyrel, "he'd get his walkin' papers right now."

"Sooner or later," Tyrel agreed. Then he added, "The other one fancies himself with a gun."

By first light, we were headed down the trail, climbing out of the valley and heading north. A few miles later, I began angling off to the northwest, and by sundown we had come up with the Pipestem again.

The herd was trail broke now, and the country was level to low, rolling hills. We saw no Indians or any tracks but those of buffalo or antelope. The following day, we put sixteen miles behind us.

Each night, just shy of sundown, Tyrel, Cap, or I would scout the country around. Several times, we caught whiffs of smoke from another campfire, but we made no effort to seek them out.

Short of sundown on the third day, after our rest, I killed a buffalo, and the Ox came up to lend a hand. I never did see a buffalo skinned out faster or meat cut and trimmed any better. I said as much.

"Pa was a butcher, and I growed up with a knife in hand. Then I hunted buffalo on the southern plains."

"Take only the best cuts," I said, "an' leave the rest."

He was bent over, knife in hand. He turned his head to look at me. "Leave it? For varmints?"

"There's some Indians close by, and they're having a bad time of it. Leave some for them."

"Injuns? Hell, let 'em rustle their own meat. What d'we care about Injuns?"

"They're hungry," I said, "and their best hunter is wounded and laid up."

Obviously, he believed me crazy. "I never knew an' Injun worth the powder it took to kill him."

"Back in the mountains," I said, "I knew quite a few. Generally speakin', they were good folks.

"We had trouble with them a time or two and they're good, tough fightin' men. I've also hunted and trapped with them, slept in their lodges. They are like everybody else. There's good an' bad amongst them."

We left some meat on the buffalo hide, and I stuck a branch in the ground and tied a wisp of grass to it. Not that they'd need help findin' it.

Come daylight, when we moved out with the cattle, I took a look, and every last bit of meat was gone, and the hide, also. I counted the tracks of a boy and two women. They'd have read the sign and would know that meat was left a-purpose.

With Cap ridin' point, the cattle strung out along the trail, and I rode drag. Tyrel was off scoutin' the country. Pipestem Creek was east of us now, and the country was getting a mite rougher. Maybe it was my imagination. Off on the horizon, far ahead and a hair to the west, I could see the top of a butte or hill.

By noontime, that butte was showing strong and clear. It was several hundred feet high and covered with timber. When Tyrel came back to the drag, I rode ahead to talk to Cap.

"Heard of that place," he said. "They call it the Hawk's Nest. There's a spring up yonder—good water."

After a bit, he added, "Big lake off to the north. Maybe a mite east. Devil's Lake, they call it. Got it's name, they say, from a party of Sioux who were returning victorious from a battle with the Chippewa. Owanda, the Sioux medicine man, had warned them not to make the attack, but they were young bucks, eager for battle and reputation, and they didn't listen.

"Their folks were watching from the shore, saw them coming far out on the lake, and could tell from the scalps on the lifted lances that they'd been victorious.

"Well, some say that night came down. It had been dusk when they were sighted. Night came, but the war party didn't. That day to this, nobody's seen hide nor hair of them. Devils in the lake, the Injuns say."

"Owanda must have been really big medicine after that," I commented.

"You can bet he was. But the way I hear it, he was one of the most powerful of all medicine men. Lot of stories about him. First I heard of him was from the Cheyenne."

Cap went on to his flank position, and I took over the point, riding well out in front, studying the country as we moved. Wherever possible, I held the herd down off the skyline. We didn't want to get in the bottoms and among the trees but at least as low as we could move while handling the cattle. There were Indians about, and if they did not know of us now, they would very soon, but I wanted to attract as little attention as possible.

At the same time, I was studying our future. The grass was growing, and soon it would be high enough for grazing. Until then, the cattle would be eating last year's grass. We were getting a jump on the season, and that was why we were not pushing along. We had to stall until the grass was up.

By that time, we should have met with Orrin and his Red River carts. Or so we hoped.

Westward the drive was long. The camp for which we were headed was in rugged mountain country, and we had to make it before the snow started falling. Once the grass was up and we had Orrin with us, we'd have to push hard, even at the risk of losing flesh from those steers.

Tyrel and me, we didn't even have to talk to know what the other one was thinking. It was almost that way with Cap.

Gilcrist and the Ox were worrisome men. Tyrel was right when he said Gilcrist fancied himself with a gun, and while I'd never wanted the reputation of gunfighter, a reputation both Tyrel and me had, I kind of wished now Gilcrist knew something about us. Might save trouble.

Many a man thinks large of himself because he doesn't know the company he's in. No matter how good a man can get at anything, there's always a time when somebody comes along who's better.

It was Tyrel who worried me, too. Tyrel was a first-class cattleman, a good man with handling men, and he never hunted trouble, but neither did trouble have to look very far to find him. Orrin an' me, we might back off a little and give a trouble-huntin' man some breathin' space.

Not Tyrel—you hunted trouble with him, you'd bought yourself a packet. He didn't give breathing space; he moved right in on you. A man who called his hand had better be reaching for his six-shooter when he did it.

Worst of it was, he seemed kind of quiet and boylike, and a body could make a serious mistake with him.

Back in the high-up hills where we came from, fightin' was what we did for fun. You got into one of those shindigs with a mountain boy and it was root hog or die. Pa, who had learned his fightin' from boyhood and seasoned himself around trappers' rendezvous, taught us enough to get started. The rest we picked up ourselves.

The wind was picking up a mite, and there was a coolness on it that felt like rain, or snow. It was late in the season for snow, but I'd heard of snow in this country when it was summer anywhere else. When we were close to the Hawk's Nest, we bedded them down for the night.

"Lin, feed 'em as quick as ever you can," I said to the cook. "I think we're sittin' in for a spell of weather." I pointed toward the Hawk's Nest. "I'm going up yonder to have a look over the country before it gets dark."

The Hawk's Nest was a tree-capped butte rising some four hundred feet above the surrounding country, and when I topped out, I found a gap in the trees and had a good view of the country.

There was a smoke rising about a mile up the creek from where we were camped at the junction of the Pipestem and the Little Pipestem. Far ahead, I could see a line of green that showed the Pipestem curved around to the west. Somewhere off there was the Sheyenne.

The water in the spring was fresh and cold. I drank, then watered the line-back dun I was riding and swung into the saddle. Just as I was starting to come off the top, I glimpsed another smoke, only this one was to the west of us and seemed to be coming from a bottom along the Pipestems as it came from the west and before it began its curve toward the south.

It lay somewhat to the west of the route we should be taking on the morrow but not so far off that it wasn't cause for worry.

For a time, I just sat there under cover of the last trees and studied that layout. I brushed a big horsefly off the shoulder of the dun and said, "You know, Dunny, this here country is sure crowdin' up. Why, there's three smokes goin' up within a five-mile square. Gettin' so it ain't fittin' for man or beast."

Then I turned that dun down trail and headed for the beef and beans. Seemed so long since I'd eaten, my stomach was beginnin' to think my throat was cut.

By the time I reached the fire, Cap an' Brandy were just finishing up. Cap glanced over at me, and I said, "We've got neighbors."

"I seen some tracks," Cap said.

"How many?"

"Four, looked like. Shod horses. Big horses, like you find up here in the north where you have to buck snow in the wintertime."

"There's no way we're going to hide eleven hundred head of cattle," I said, "but we won't start westerin' for a bit. Come daybreak, we'll hold on the North Star."

"Back in Texas," Cap said, "when night came, we used to line up a wagon tongue on the North Star. Use it for a pointer."

Lin handed me a tin plate full of beans and beef, and I took a look at Brandy. He was settin' quiet, almighty serious for a boy his years.

"You havin' any trouble?" I asked him.

He gave me a quick look. "No, not really."

"Stand clear if you can," I said. "That's a mean lot."

"I can take care of myself."

"I don't doubt it. But right now I need every man, need 'em bad. Once we hook up with Orrin, it may be some better, but we don't know. Understand, I'm not puttin' any stake rope on you. A man just has to go his own way."

Brandy went out to throw his saddle on a fresh horse, and Cap looked up from his coffee. "He's makin' a fair hand, Tell, and he's got the makin's."

Well, I knew that. Trouble was I had to walk almighty careful not to step on his pride. No matter how rough it was, a man has to saddle his own broncs in this western country. Only I was afraid Brandy was goin' to have to tackle the big one before he'd whupped anybody his own size. It didn't seem fair, but then, a lot of things aren't. We take them as they come.

If I was around—

But who knew if I would be?

The Ox looked fat, but he wasn't. He was just heavy with bone and muscle, and his broad, hard-boned face looked like it had been carved from oak. He was a man of tremendous strength, with thick arms, massive forearms, and powerful hands. He gave me the feeling of a man who has never seen anything he couldn't lift or any man who could even test him.

I said as much to Tyrel. "Gilcrist told me he'd seen him break a man's back just wrasslin' for fun."

"I don't think he ever did anything just for fun," I said.

Tyrel nodded. "You be careful, Tell. That Ox ain't human. He's a brute."

"I want no part of him," I replied.

On most cow outfits, a man stands night guard about two hours at a time, but we were short-handed and in wild country. The Ox and Gilcrist were going to be on from six to ten, Cap and Brandy would take over from ten until two, with Tyrel and me closing out until morning when one of us would come in, get the fire started, and awaken Lin so's he could fix breakfast.

If we were going to be attacked by Indians, it would most likely occur just before daybreak, but nobody has any certainty of any such thing.

When Cap touched me on the shoulder, it was just shy of two, and I was up, tugging on my boots. Under a tree about thirty yards away, Tyrel was already on his feet. We made it a rule to sleep apart, so if somebody closed in on one of us, the other could outflank them. There were those who thought we'd be better off side by side, but we figured otherwise. Too easy for one man to hold a gun on us both.

All was quiet, the cattle resting. The stars were bright, here and there blotted by clouds. A body would see the darkness of the trees, the lumped bodies of the cattle, and hear the footfalls of a horse as it moved.

It was past three, closing in on four o'clock before it started to grow gray. The line-back dun was moving like a ghost toward a meeting with Tyrel. Suddenly, the dun's head came up, ears pricked. My Winchester slid into my hands, and at that moment I saw Tyrel.

He was sitting quiet in the saddle, his hands on his thighs, reins in the left hand.

Facing him were four Sioux warriors.

Chapter 5

Now I'd lay a hundred to one those Injuns had never seen a fast draw, but if one of them lifted a weapon, it would be the last thing they ever did see.

At that range, there was just no way he was going to miss, and that meant he would take out two for sure, and likely he'd get three. Time and again, I've seen him fire, and men would swear he'd fired once when actually he'd fired twice and both bullets in a spot the size of a two-bit piece.

They'd never seen a fast draw, but they were fighting men, and there was something about him, just a-settin' there quiet with his hand on his thigh that warned them they'd treed a bad one.

Their eyes were riveted on him, so I was within fifty feet and moving in before they saw me, and I was on their flank.

"Something wrong, Tyrel?" I asked.

He never turned his head, but he spoke easy. "Looks like I was about to find out."

One big Indian turned his pony to face me, and the minute he did, I recognized him. "Ho! I see my old friend, High-Backed Bull!" I said.

He looked to be as tall as my six feet and four inches, and he was heavier, but a lean, powerful man. He was darker than most, with high cheekbones and a Roman nose. He stared at me.

"I have no friend who is white eyes," he said.

Me, I pushed my hat brim back so's he could see my face a little better. "You and me, Bull, we had a nice run together. That was years back, down on the Bozeman Trail.

"You were a mighty strong man," I added, "a big warrior." I doubled my biceps and clapped a hand to it, then pointed at his. "Much strong!" I said. "Run very fast."

He peered at me. *"Sack-ETT!"* he shouted. "You *Sack-ETT!"*

I grinned at him. "Long time back, Bull!" Now I knew he had no liking for me. He'd tried to kill me then, not from any hatred of me but simply because I was a white man driving cattle over the Bozeman Trail, which the Sioux had closed to us. They'd caught me, stripped me, and had me set to run the gauntlet, only I'd started before they were ready and had broken free, taking off across the country. John Coulter had done it one time, and maybe there was a chance.

They came after me, the whole lot of them, only I'd been running in the mountains since I was a youngster, and I began putting distance between us. All but this one, the one they called High-Backed Bull. Soon it was just the two of us, him and me, and a good mile off from the rest, and he throwed a spear at me.

It missed by a hair, and then he closed in on me, running fast. Dropping suddenly, he spilled right over me, and he was up, quick as a cat, but I was up, too, and when he come at me, I throwed him with a rolling hip lock, as pa had showed me long ago. I throwed him, all right, and throwed him hard. He hit the ground, and I grabbed up his spear and was about to stick him with it.

He'd been stunned by the shock of hitting the ground, just for a moment, like. He stared up at me, and he was such a fine-lookin' man, I just couldn't do it. I just broke the spear across my knee, threw down the pieces, and I taken out across country.

Some of the Injuns had gone back for ponies, and they were coming at me when I made the trees atop a knoll. They come up, a-runnin', and I scrooched down behind a bush, and when this rider paused to swing his pony between two trees, I hit him across the small of the back with a thick branch I'd picked up.

It knocked him forward and off balance, and in a moment I was jerkin' him off the pony and swingin' to its back.

We ran those ponies, me ahead and them after me, until the sun went down, but I'd circled around and came back to where my outfit was camped. I went through patches of woods, across plains, down rocky draws, and finally I seen ol' Tilson's high-top sombrero against the sky, and I called out, "Don't shoot, Til! It's me! Sackett!"

Well, they'd give me up for dead. Two days the Injuns had me, and there'd been a third day of gettin' away from them.

"Where the hell you been? We're short-handed enough," Til said, "'thout you taken off a Sundayin' around over the hills whilst the rest of us work."

"I was took by Injuns," I said.

"A likely story!" he scoffed. "You've still got your hair."

He pointed toward camp. "Get yourself some coffee. You'll be standin' guard at daybreak."

Well, I walked down into camp, and ol' Nelson was standin' there by the fire. "You bring any company with you?" he asked.

"Tried to avoid it," I said, "but there might be one of them show up. I done some runnin'," I said, "and then I got this horse."

"You call that a *horse*. Won't weigh six hundred pound."

"Don't you miscall him. He can *run*."

Nelson took up a cup and filled it. "Have yourself something." He looked at me. "You et?"

"Oh, sure! Don't you worry none about me! Why, two, three days ago, I et at a cow camp run by Nelson Storey, who was takin' cows to Montana. I ain't had a bit since, but then what can a man expect? I didn't come up on no rest-too-rawnts, and them Injuns didn't figure to waste grub on a man who wasn't goin' to live long enough to digest it."

He pointed. "There's some roast buffalo, camp-baked beans, and some prunes. That should fix you up." He took out a big silver watch. "You got two hours to sleep before you stand guard."

"Nels," I said, "I lost my rifle, and—"

"One of the boys picked it up," he said. "It's in the wagon. Draw you a new knife there. I'll dock you for the time off."

Well, I knew he wouldn't do no such thing, but I was so glad to be back, I didn't care if he did. Only when I was a-settin' my horse out there by the cattle that night, I thought back to the hatred lookin' at me out of those fierce black eyes of High-Backed Bull, and I was glad I'd seen the last of him.

Until now—

He stared at me. "You *Sack-ETT*," he said.

Tyrel said, "You actually *know* this Injun?"

"I know him," I said, "from that trip I took up the Bozeman Trail after the War Between the States. We had us a little run-in back yonder. They had me fixed to run the gauntlet—fifty-sixty big Injuns all lined up with me to run down the aisle betwixt 'em and each one hittin' or cuttin' at me.

"Well, I recalled that story pa told us about John Coulter, so I done likewise. I just taken off across the country and not down their gauntlet. This big buck here, he durned near caught me."

"So Sack-ETT," Bull said, "it is again."

Smiling, I held out my hand. "Friends?" I said.

He stared at me. "No friend," he said. "I kill."

"Don't try it. I'm bad luck for you. Me," I said, "bad medicine for you, much bad medicine."

He stared at me, very cool and not at all scared. "Soon you hair here." He touched his horse's bridle where three other scalps, one of them obviously that of a white man, already dangled.

He changed the subject. With a wide sweep of his hand, he said, "This belong to Sioux. What you do here?"

"Crossing it, Bull. We're just driving across on the way to Fort Qu'Appelle." It was a Canadian fort, and the name just came to me. "Maybe we'll meet on the way back."

They turned and rode away, and Tyrel, he just sat there looking after them, and then he shook his head. "There was a time there when I figured I'd have to do the fastest shootin' I ever done."

Gilcrist and the Ox come ridin' up. They could see the four Sioux ridin' away. "What happened?" Gil asked.

"No trouble," I said. "Just a Sioux who tried to take my hair one time, thinkin' about another try."

"You *knew* him?"

"Some years back," I said. "I'd just come out of the Sixth Cavalry and—"

"The *Sixth?*" He was surprised. "Sackett? Were you *that* Sackett?"

"So far as I know, I was the only one in the outfit."

"I'll be damned," he said. "I'll be dee-double damned!"

"That was a long time ago," I said. "Let's get 'em movin'!"

We lined them out and pointed them north and prayed a little that we wouldn't meet any more Sioux, but after my meeting with High-Backed Bull, I knew they'd be back.

Cap rode up to see me at point. "Hustle 'em, Cap. I want distance."

"You know you ain't goin' to outrun any Injuns," he said. "If they come for us, they'll find us."

"They'll come," I said.

"You should've killed him when you had the chance."

Brandy had come up to us, wanting to hear. "I'd figure him grateful," Brandy said. "You let him live when you could've killed him."

"They don't figure that way, son," Cap remarked. "They figured him a coward for not followin' through. They don't think he had nerve enough.

"Injuns don't think the same as us, and we keep thinkin' they do. That's been the cause of most of the trouble. We think one way, they think another, and even when the words are the same, they mean different things.

"I've fought 'em here and there, lived with some of them, too. They're good people, mostly, but there's right-out bad ones, the same as with us.

"Folks get the wrong idea about Injuns. Somebody figured the Injuns thought the white man was somethin' special. Some easterner who'd never seen an Injun figured it that way. Nothing of the kind. The Injuns mostly looked down on the white man.

"Why? Because he was tradin' for furs, and the Injuns figured if he was any kind of a man, he'd go ketch his own. He traded for 'em because he didn't know how to hunt or trap.

"The Sioux, the Cheyenne, an' all them, they despised the white man, although they wanted what he traded. They wanted steel traps, guns, blankets, and whiskey."

Cap pushed a brindle steer back into the herd. "Some folks figured it was all wrong to trade the Injuns whiskey, and no doubt it was, but it wasn't meanness made 'em do it. They traded the Injuns whiskey because it was what most of those white men wanted themselves, so they figured the Injun wanted it, too."

We pushed 'em on into the evening and bedded down on Rocky Run, finding ourselves a little hollow down off the skyline. The mosquitoes were worse, but we were a whole lot less visible.

When we had a fire going, I roped a fresh horse and switched saddles. "I'll mosey around a mite," I told Cap. "You an' Tyrel, you keep a hold on things whilst I'm gone."

"We'll try," Cap said.

Rocky Run was a mite of a stream that probably fed into the James, but there'd been rains, and there was good water. Topping out on a ridge, I dropped over the edge far enough not to skyline myself and took a look around.

Mostly, I studied the country to the west. Come daybreak, we'd be lined out to the west, shaping a bit north for the James again.

How many Sioux were there and how far away?

There'd be a-plenty, no doubt, but I was hoping High-Backed Bull would have to go some distance to his village. There was no way to hide eleven hundred head of cattle and no way you could move them very fast. We'd have to do what we could.

Turning back toward camp, a movement caught my eye. Somebody was coming, somebody on a slow-walking horse that stopped now and again, then started on. But he was coming my way.

Shucking my Winchester, I taken my horse down off the low ridge, kind of angling toward that rider.

It was already almost dark, and there were stars here and yonder, but a body could make things out. This rider was all humped over in the saddle like he was hurt. I caught a momentary glint of metal, and I pulled up and waited.

When he was some fifty yeards off, I covered him with my Winchester and let him close the distance.

"Pull up there! Who are you?"

He straightened up then. "What? A *white* man? What're you doing out here?"

"Drivin' some cattle," I said. "What about you?"

"I been runnin'," the man said. "Sioux. I'm headed for Fort Stevenson, Army mail."

"Fort Stevenson? Hell, I didn't know there was a fort up this way. Come on into camp."

He was a fine-looking man, Irish, and with the bearing of a soldier. When I said as much, he said, "Some years back, in England and India." He threw me a quick glance. "Cattle, you say? Where to?"

"The gold mines," I said.

"It's a long drive," he said, "a very long drive. Strike north toward the South Saskatchewan. You can follow it part of the way. It won't be easy—and stay away from Fort Garry."

"What's wrong?"

"There's trouble brewing. When the Bay Company let go of Rupert's Land, which means most of western Canada, there was no government. It wasn't immediately apparent that Canada was going to take over, so a *métis* named Louis Riel has set up a provisional government."

"*Métis?*"

"It's a name for the French-Indian or sometimes Scotch-Indian buffalo hunters. Anyway, it looks like trouble, so I'd steer clear of Fort Garry."

"And Pembina?"

"The same."

By now, or very soon, Orrin would be there. He would be right where the trouble was, and he would be alone.

Chapter 6

Orrin Sackett boarded the stage at St. Cloud. Two women were already seated, a short, stout woman with a florid complexion and a young, quite pretty girl in an expensive traveling suit. Seating himself in a corner, Orrin watched the others as they got aboard.

There were three. The first was a square-shouldered, strongly built man in a dark, tailored suit with a carefully trimmed beard. He was followed by two men, roughly dressed and armed with pistols under their coats and rifles in their hands. Scarcely were they seated when, with a pistol-like crack of the whip, they were off.

The man with the trimmed beard glanced at him. Orrin knew he presented a good appearance in his planter's hat, his dark gray frock coat, and trousers of a lighter gray, his dark green vest sporting a fine gold watch chain.

"Fort Abercrombie?" The man asked. "Or are you going further?"

"Fort Garry," Orrin replied. "Or possibly only to Pembina."

"My destination, also. From Georgetown to the steamboat you may have to provide your own transportation. The stage often goes no further than Georgetown. Much depends on the condition of the roads and the disposition of the driver. And, I might add, on the mosquitoes."

Orrin lifted an eyebrow. "The *mosquitoes?*"

"If you have not heard of them, be warned. They are unlike any mosquitoes you will have seen. At least in number. Leave an animal tied out all night and by morning it may be dead. I am serious, sir."

"But what do you do?"

"Stay inside after sundown. Build smudges if you're out. Sleep under mosquito netting. They'll still get you, but you can live with them."

The young girl twisted her lips, obviously disturbed. The two men showed no concern, as if the story were familiar to them, but *what was wrong about them?* He did not wish to stare at them, but there was something, some little thing that disturbed him.

It was not that they were armed. He carried his own pistol in its holster and another, a derringer, in his vest pocket. His rifle was in the blanket roll in the boot. The man with the beard was also armed with a small pistol. Very likely, the women were also, although a woman could, in most cases, travel anywhere in the West in complete safety.

It was not that the two were roughly dressed that disturbed him. He had dressed no better, if as well, for the better part of his life, and in the West men wore whatever was available or what they could afford. Over half the greatcoats one saw were army issue, either blue or gray, and a good number of the hats came from the same source. Yet somehow these men seemed different. Their clothing did not seem to belong to them. They were old clothes and should have been comfortable, but neither man wore them with ease.

"You have been to Fort Garry before? And Pembina?"

The man with the trimmed beard nodded. "Several times, although I am not sure what my welcome will be like this time." He glanced at Orrin again. "They aren't very friendly to outsiders right now."

"What's the problem?"

"They've had an influx of outsiders. Some of them from Ontario but many from the States. Some are land grabbers, some are promoters. You see, when the Bay Company moved out, they left the country, Rupert's Land, they call it, high and dry and without a government."

He paused, peering from the window. The stage was slowing for a bad place in the road. "The *métis*, the French-Indian people who formerly worked for the company, have lived on their land for several generations. Now, suddenly, there's a question of title. The newcomers say the *métis* own nothing at all.

"Louis Riel has returned from Montreal and is reported to be forming a provisional government. I have met the man but once, in passing, and know nothing about him."

"He's a breed," one of the other men spoke suddenly. "He's part Indian."

His manner of speaking made the statement an accusation, and Orrin said mildly, "Could be in his favor. I've dealt with Indians. They know the country, and some of them are wise men."

The man was about to reply, but seeing the way the conversation was going, the man with the trimmed beard thrust out his hand. "I am Kyle Gavin, and a Scotsman, although I've spent a deal of time in both your country and Canada. We may be of service to each other."

"I am Orrin Sackett, of Tennessee. I have been practicing law in New Mexico and Colorado."

At the name, both the other men glanced up sharply, first at him, and then they exchanged a glance.

Darkness was crowding into the thick brush and trees along the trail, leaning in long shadows across the trail itself. Atop a small hill where some wind was felt, the stage pulled up, and the driver descended.

"I'd sit tight if I was you," he warned. "Keep as many mosquitoes out as you can. I'm lightin' the carriage lamps."

He did so, and then they moved on into the darkness. "There will be food at the next stop," Gavin commented. "I'd advise all to eat. The night will be long."

The road was a mere trace through towering trees, then across open prairies dotted with clumps of brush. Trees had been cut down, but the stumps remained, and occasionally a wheel would hit one of the stumps with a bone-jolting shock. There were strips of corduroy road across marshes, made by laying logs crosswise and covering them with brush and mud.

Inside the coach, all was dark. Orrin removed his hat and leaned his head back against the cushion. In that way, he could doze fitfully, jarred into wakefulness by getting a sharp rap on the skull when the stage passed a bad bump.

After a long time of endless bumping, jolting, and crackings of the whip, a bit of light flickered across his vision. He opened his eyes and, lifting the corner of the curtain, peered out. They had come to a settlement, and only a minute or two later the stage pulled up before a low-roofed building of logs.

The door opened and the stage driver said, "Grub on the table! Better eat up!"

Kyle Gavin got down and turned to offer his hand to the ladies, but the two other men pushed by him and stumbled toward the door.

Exasperated, he started to speak, but Orrin spoke first. "Let them go. It isn't worth the trouble." He waited until both women had been helped to the ground, then said, "Please, let me apologize. Western men are usually thoughtful of womenfolk."

"Thank you, young man," the older woman said. "I live west. I know what the men are like. Those two, they're trouble. I seen it when they got on."

Orrin escorted the two women to the one table, and several men promptly got to their feet, plates in hand. "Set here, ma'am," one of them said.

One of the others turned toward a harried man standing over a stove. "Joe? We've a couple of ladies."

"Yes, sir! Ma'am! Be right there."

Orrin glanced around the room. Several wagons were pulled up outside and at least three saddle horses. He saw no one whom he knew, but that was expected, for this was new country to him. Yet he searched the faces of the men. Some would be going on to Pembina or Fort Garry, and he badly needed at least two good men.

One was a short, stocky man with a thick neck and a bristle of tight blond curly hair atop his head. There was a deep dentlike scar under his cheekbone. He was one of those who had arisen quickly when he saw the women. He stood to one side now, plate in hand.

"How's the food?" Orrin asked.

The short man threw him a quick, measuring glance. "I've et worse. Matter of fact, it ain't bad."

"Cowhand?"

Shorty shrugged. "Whatever it takes to get the coon. I been a cowhand. I been a timber stiff, too, an' I've driven freight here and there."

"At Pembina or maybe Fort Garry, I'll need a couple of men. A couple who can handle cattle, drive a team, and make a fight if that's necessary."

"Where you goin'?"

"West, through the mountains. They call it British Columbia. I'll pay thirty a month, and the grub's good."

Shorty finished his food. "If you're eatin', you better get up there," he advised. "They don't set no second table."

Orrin Sackett moved up to the table and found a place near the girl who was traveling with them. Passing her a platter of beans and rice, he said, "If there is anything I can do, you have only to ask."

"Thank you."

LONELY ON THE MOUNTAIN

As she did not seem disposed to talk, he said nothing more but finished his eating and went outside. The two men with rifles were standing near the stage in deep conversation with a third man, pants tucked into his boots, a battered hat pulled low so little of his face could be seen.

Kyle Gavin strolled over and stood near. "Those men," Gavin commented, "something about them worries me."

"It's the clothes," Orrin replied. "The men don't look like they belonged in them."

"You mean a disguise?"

Orrin shrugged. "Maybe, or maybe just trying to fit into the country." Then he added, "They handle the rifles like they were used to them, though."

The stage rolled on, and again Orrin slept fitfully. Where were Tell and Tyrel? The letter received in St. Paul had stated only that their route would be up the valley of the James, and if they reached the Turtle Mountains first, they would proceed westward, leaving some indication behind.

They were going into wild country, a land unknown to them. Even now, they would be somewhere in Dakota, the land of the Sioux, a fierce, conquering people who had moved westward from their homeland along the Wisconsin-Minnesota border to conquer all of North and South Dakota, much of Montana, Wyoming, and Nebraska, an area larger than the empire of Charlemagne.

This land through which they traveled was that which divided the waters flowing south toward the Gulf of Mexico from those flowing north toward Hudson's Bay. There were many lakes, for this was the fabled "land of the sky-blue water," and soon they would be descending into the valley of the Red River of the north.

Orrin awakened suddenly, feeling a head on his shoulder. It was the young lady, who had fallen asleep and gradually let her head fall on his convenient shoulder. He held very still, not wishing to disturb her.

The coach was very dark inside, and he could see little but the gleam of light on the rifle barrels and light where the coach lamps let a glow in through a crack in the curtains. All the rest seemed asleep.

He was about to doze once more when he heard a drum of hoofs on the road behind them. Someone, a fast rider, was overtaking the coach. Carefully, he put his fingers on the butt of his six-shooter, listening.

He heard the rider come alongside and lifted the corner of the curtain but could see nothing, as the rider had already passed too far forward. The stage slowed, and he could hear conversation between the rider and the driver but could distinguish no words.

After a moment, he heard the rider go on, listened to the fading sound of hoof beats, but the stage continued at the slower pace.

A long time later, daylight began filtering through the curtains, and suddenly the girl beside him awakened. She sat up with a start, embarrassed.

"Oh! Oh, I am so sorry!" She spoke softly so as not to disturb the others. "I had no idea!"

"Please do not worry about it, ma'am," Orrin said. "My shoulder's never been put to better purpose."

She tucked away a wisp of hair. Her eyes were brown, and her hair, which was thick and lovely, was a kind of reddish-brown. He suddenly decided that was the best shade for hair, quite the most attractive he'd seen.

He straightened his cravat and longed for a shave. The stubble must be showing. He touched his cheek. Yes, it was. He touched his carefully trimmed black moustache.

Kyle Gavin was awake and watching him with a glimmer of amusement in his eyes. Orrin flushed.

He thought again of the short, blond man he had seen at the first stage stop. He looked to be a good man, and it might be hard to find men with all this Riel affair muddying up the waters.

Shorty had looked like the kind who would finish anything he started, and that was the kind of man they would need.

Orrin looked over at Gavin. "What about this Riel affair? What's going to happen?"

"Your guess is as good as mine. The Canadians are sending an army out, but that country north of the lakes is very rugged. We've heard some soldiers were lost. Forty of them, according to one story."

"If Riel wanted to make a fight of it," Orrin suggested, "he could defend some of the narrow rivers through which the army must come. Certainly, with all the woodsmen he would have at his command, that would be simple enough."

"That isn't my understanding," Gavin said. "I was under the impression he wished only to establish a temporary government until the Canadians could take over. But no matter what, we're arriving at a bad time. You, especially, if you want to get men or supplies. What supplies Riel doesn't have, the army will need. You'd better move fast."

"You'll find no men in Fort Garry"—one of the other men spoke up suddenly—"nor any supplies, either. They won't welcome strangers."

"Then you're arriving at a bad time," Orrin suggested, smiling, "aren't you?"

The man stared at him. "Maybe it'll be a bad time for you. I've got friends."

Orrin smiled. "Yes," he said gently, "I suppose everyone has one or two."

Chapter 7

By the evening of the second day, the stage rolled up to a stockade near the Ottertail River. Orrin stepped down and stretched, then extended a hand to the young lady and, after her, to the older woman.

"It isn't much of a place," Orrin said, "but let me look around. I will see what can be found."

"Not much," Gavin admitted. "Last time I was here, it was a good deal more comfortable to sleep in the haymow than inside."

"And the mosquitoes?"

"They'll find you either place. They call this place Pomme-de-Terre, but I can think of several other names for it. Tomorrow we should reach Abercrombie."

"Are there accommodations at the fort?"

"No, but there is in McCauleyville. A chap named Nolan has a fairly decent hotel there."

"And the boat?"

"Probably down river from there." Gavin was watching the two men with rifles. They had gone into the fort at once and disappeared behind some buildings. It was obvious they knew where they were going and what they were about.

Inside the fort, the man behind the bar shook his bald head and rubbed the back of his hand across a stubbled chin. "Mister, we sure ain't set up for ladies. Don't often get womenfolks hereabouts." He jerked his head toward an inner room. "Five beds yonder. Men will sleep three to a bed, mostly, and they ain't finicky."

He was honestly worried. "I seen 'em get off the stage, and I seen trouble. I mean, settin' 'em up. Such womenfolks are expectin' more'n we can offer."

"How about the barn? There's fresh hay, isn't there?"

"Hay? Plenty o' that. Say! Come to think of it, there's the tack room—harness room. Cavalry officers used to keep their horse gear in there."

"How about blankets? And mosquito netting?"

He shook his head. "I got 'em, but only for sale, not for use."

They would need blankets and mosquito netting, too.

"How much for six blankets and netting enough for four?"

He scratched his head, then worried at a piece of paper with a pencil. The figure was excessive but not so much as he'd expected. Nor was the tack room as much of a mess as it might have been.

"We had better eat," Orrin warned them, "and get bedded down before dark. The mosquitoes are coming now."

The younger woman suddenly put out her hand. "I am Devnet Molrone, Mr. Sackett. And this is Mary McCann. She is going to Fort Garry."

"And you?"

"I shall be meeting my brother. He will be at Fort Carlton."

Gavin was surprised. "At Fort Carlton? Is your brother with Hudson's Bay Company?"

It appeared, after some conversation, that her last letter from him had been from Fort Carlton, and she assumed he was located there.

Later, he said to Orrin, "Sackett, if you're going west, you'd best try to keep an eye on that girl. I am afraid she's in trouble." He paused. "You see, Carlton's a trading post, but there aren't too many white men there, and I know most of them. A good lot, on the whole, but unless her brother is employed by the company in closing up some of their operations, I can't see how he'd be there for more than a few days."

Later, over supper, Orrin said, "Tell me about your brother."

"Oh, Doug's older than I am, three years older. He always wanted to hunt for gold, and when he heard of the discoveries out west, nothing would hold him. He wrote to us, told us all about it, and it sounded very exciting. Then, when Uncle Joe died, well, there was nothing to keep him in the East, and Doug was the only living relative I had, so I decided to join him."

Orrin glanced at Gavin. "He knows you're coming?"

"Oh, no! He'd never approve! He thinks girls can't do anything! It's a surprise."

Her eyes were wide and excited. Obviously, she was pleased with her daring and thought he would be equally pleased and surprised.

"Ma'am—Miss Molrone," Orrin spoke carefully. "I think you should reconsider. If your brother was hunting gold, he'd be in British Columbia, and that's a long way, hundreds of miles, west of Fort Carlton.

"Fort Carlton isn't a town, exactly, it's a trading post with a stockade around it. There are a few buildings inside, mostly quarters for those who work there."

She was shocked. "But I thought—I—!"

"Fort Garry is only a small town," Kyle Gavin said, "but I'd suggest you stop there until you locate your brother.

"There's no regular mail, you know. Most of the gold camps are isolated, trusting to someone who brings mail in by boat, horseback, or snowshoes, depending on the situation. And only rarely is there a place where a decent young woman can stay. Your brother probably shares a tent or a small cabin with other men."

Her lip trembled. "I didn't know. I wanted to surprise him. I thought—"

"We can make inquiries at Fort Garry," Gavin suggested. "Some of the *métis* may know him. Or they may remember him."

Suddenly, the realization of what she had done came to her. She put her hand to her mouth. "Oh, my!" Pleadingly, she looked at Gavin, then at Orrin. "I wanted to surprise him. I'm all he's got, you know, now that Uncle Joe is dead."

"Does he know that?"

"How could he? I was going to tell him when I met him. You see, Uncle Joe didn't leave anything. He died very suddenly, and I was alone. I wanted to be with Doug, and so—"

"Don't worry about it," Orrin said. "We'll find him for you."

Later, Kyle Gavin exclaimed, "Sackett? Do you have any idea how tough that will be? To find one man among all those who came west?

God knows, he might be dead. There've been men lost in riding the rivers, men killed when thrown by horses or in falls from wagons. The worst of it is," Gavin added, "she's uncommonly pretty."

In the morning, Orrin heated water for her in a bucket and took it to her, then went back outside. The morning was cool, and there were no mosquitoes about. The stage was standing nearby, and the driver and a hostler were hooking up the trace chains.

From the driver Gavin learned the two men with rifles were brothers, George and Perry Stamper. They said they were buffalo hunters.

"Then they've much to learn," Gavin said dryly. "The *métis* have very controlled buffalo hunts. They all work together under rigid discipline. They don't care for the single hunter unless he's just hunting meat for himself or his family."

It was nearly noon when the stage rolled into McCauleyville, close to Fort Abercrombie. They stopped at Nolan's, and Orrin retrieved his blanket-roll and haversack from the boot.

He helped the ladies from the stage and escorted them into the hotel. Nolan's place was clean, the floors mopped as carefully as a ship's deck, curtains at the windows.

Nolan glanced at Gavin, suddenly wary, but said nothing.

"A room for the ladies," Sackett suggested, "and one for me, if available. If not, Mr. Gavin and I will make do."

After the women had been shown to their rooms, Orrin asked, "Know anything about a Douglas Molrone? Probably came through here several months back."

Nolan shook his head. "Night after night, the place is full. It isn't often I know the names of any of them. Going west, was he?"

"Gold hunting."

"Aye, like most of them. He'd be lucky to make it unless he was with a strong party. There's bunches of the Santee Sioux who didn't dare go home after the Little Crow massacre, and they're raiding, taking scalps, stealing horses, usually from the Crees or the Blackfeet, but they'd be apt to attack any small party."

There was, as it chanced, a room for him. Alone, Orrin removed his coat and hung it on a peg in the wall; then he checked his six-shooter. The action was smooth, easy. He hung the cartridge belt and holster over the back of a chair close at hand and, stripping to the waist, bathed as well as he could.

His thoughts skipped westward. Tell and Tyrel should be well into the northern part of Dakota by now and would be wondering about him.

Scowling, he considered Devnet Molrone. She was none of his business, yet could he leave her alone in such a place? He suspected she had little money, possibly only enough to get her to Fort Carlton.

There was nothing wrong with Carlton, but so far as he knew, it was a trading post and little else. No doubt some people had settled around, but they would be few. She would be treated like the lady she was, but no matter, a trading post was simply not equipped or planned to cope with unescorted females.

Would she be any better off in a Red River cart on a trip to nowhere? For the truth was they did not know their exact destination. They would be met—by whom? When? Where? And then what?

Drying himself with the rough towel provided, he slipped on a fresh shirt—somewhere along the line he must have some laundry done or do it himself—then he brushed his coat.

She *was* pretty. Damned pretty!

Nolan was behind the desk worrying over some figures. He pushed his hat back and looked up at Orrin. "Damn it! I never was no hand with figures! Only thing I can count is money, when it's laid right out before me!"

He looked up again. "Where'd you say you was headed, Sackett?"

"We're driving cattle to the gold fields. My brothers are already on the way. Somewhere in Dakota, right now."

"In Dakota? They got to be crazy! That's Sioux country, and those Sioux, they're fighters! Despise the white man, got no use for the Winnebagos, the Crees, or the Blackfeet. They'll fight anybody."

"We hope to have no trouble. We'll be trying to avoid them."

"Avoid them? Hah! I doubt if a bird could fly over Dakota without them knowin' it.

"That Molrone girl, huntin' her brother. Like lookin' for one pine needle. But don't you worry none! She'll find herself a husband! Women are almighty scarce, and the way I see it there should be at least one in every family!" He looked up at Orrin, smiling. "A man like you, you should latch onto her. Women that pretty are hard to come by. She's a right pert little lady, too! Gumption, that's what she's got! Took a sight of gumption to come all the way out here huntin' her brother."

He glanced at Orrin. "That feller with you. That Gavin feller, you know him long?"

"Met him on the stage."

"Well, I like you, young feller, and you watch yourself, d'you hear? You be careful."

"Why?"

"I'm just a tellin' you. Watch yourself. Things ain't always what they seem."

"What about this man Riel?"

"Don't know him. Knew his pa. A right good man. He spoke up for the *métis* a time or two. Honest in his dealin's, level-headed man. Owned a mill or something. Good man.

"The young man's just back from Montreal. He was studyin' to be a priest, I heard, then changed his mind, or they changed it for him.

"When those outsiders began to come in with their newfangled way of surveyin', his ma sent for him to come home. She seen trouble comin'.

"I ain't sure he's the right man for it. He's a thoughtful young feller. Seems reasonable. Been through here a time or two.

"Now away out west, the way you're a-goin', there's a man named Dumont, Gabriel Dumont. Captain of the buffalo hunts! Those *métis* would follow him through hell! Good man! A great man! Reminds me of that poem, writ by a man named Gray, somethin' in it about 'Cromwells guiltless of their country's blood' or some such thing. Well, I seen a few in my lifetime! Men who had greatness but no chance to show it elsewhere than here! I seen 'em! I seen a passel of them!"

Nolan glanced at him again. "You ever hear of Frog Town? Well, you fight shy of it. Rob you. Cheat you. Knock you in the head or knife you. That's a bad lot. Sometimes the steamer starts from there, dependin' on how high the water is.

"Steamboatin' on the Red ain't like the Mississippi. Mean. Mean an' cantankerous, that's what it is. River's too high some of the time, too low most of the time, and filled with sawyers, driftin' logs, and sandbars. No fit river for man or beast."

"But it flows north?"

"That it does! That it does!" Nolan put a hand on his sleeve. "Here she comes now, that Molrone girl. Say, is she the pretty one! If I was single—!"

Orrin turned toward her, smiling. She looked up at him. "Oh! Mr. Sackett! I am so glad you are here! They say we must go from here by oxcart, and I was wondering if—?"

"You can go with us. We would have it no other way. And we shall leave tomorrow morning, early."

"I'll be ready."

He paused. "The offer includes Mrs. McCann."

"You want her," Nolan whispered, "you'd better act fast, young feller! She's too durned pretty to be about for long!"

There was a pause, and Nolan pulled his hat brim down and started around the counter. "Don't envy you, young feller. Not one bit! You got a long road to travel, an' it can be mean. Oh, there's folks done it! Palliser done it, the Earl of Southesk, he done it, and, of course, folks like David Thompson, Alexander Henry, and their like, but the Sioux weren't around then, an' there wasn't all this trouble with the *métis*—"

"But you said Riel was a reasonable man?"

"I did, an' I still say it. Trouble is, both them and the army will need grub, they will need rifles and ammunition, and you'll have 'em— if you're lucky."

"You made a reference to Gavin?"

"I said nothing. Only"—he paused—"I like a careful man. I always did like a careful man, and you shape up like such. I said nothing else. Nothing a-tall!"

He started for the door, then turned and came back. "You get smart, young feller. You latch on to that girl. You'll travel a weary mile before you see her kind again. Ain't only she's pretty, she's game. She's got gumption! That's my kinda woman, boy. That there's my kinda woman!"

Chapter 8

It was cold and dark when he opened his eyes, holding himself still for a long minute, just to listen. There were subdued rustles from the next room where the women were, so they were already astir.

Rising, he bathed lightly and swiftly, then pulled on his pants and boots and began stropping his razor. The vague light in the room was sufficient until he wished to shave; then he lighted the coal-oil lamp. He shaved with care, and as he shaved, he considered the situation.

With luck they would be aboard the *International* before sundown, and if they hoped to miss the mosquitoes, they must be. Once aboard, he must settle down to some serious thinking, as well as the planning of his every move once he reached Fort Garry.

He rinsed his razor, stropped it once more for the final touch-up, thinking as he did so. It was a foolhardy venture at best, something not to be considered had not a Sackett been in trouble.

You can expect Higginses.

To any Sackett the phrase indicated trouble, but from whom? And why?

Folding his razor, he put it away in its case with his brush and soap, then completed dressing. He rolled his blankets, including his spare pistol, then put out the light.

Taking up his rifle, he stepped to the door, opening it a crack. The air was cool, and he inhaled deeply, waiting and listening.

The small lobby was empty and still. There was no one at the desk. Sitting near the door was a valise that belonged to Kyle Gavin, but the man himself was nowhere about.

As he put his things down near the door, he noticed part of a torn sticker on the valise . . . *toria*. He straightened up, considering that.

Victoria, B.C.? It could be.

So? Gavin could easily have been there. He was a widely traveled man.

Yet when they had talked of British Columbia, he had offered no information on the area, nor had he mentioned visiting there. Why had Nolan warned him against Gavin? Or about him?

He was opening the door to step outside when he heard a click of heels on the board floor and turned. Devnet Molrone looked fresh and lovely, as though she had not traveled a mile.

"The cart is coming," he said. Even as he spoke, it was pulling up at the door. He was surprised, although he should not have been. He had never seen a Red River cart before, although he had heard of them.

Each cart was about six feet long and three wide; the bottom was of one-inch boards; the wheels were seven and a half feet in diameter. The hubs were ten inches across and bored to receive an axle of split oak. The wood used was oak throughout. Each cart was drawn by a single horse and would carry approximately four hundred pounds. No nails were used. Oak pins and rawhide bindings held it all together.

Kyle Gavin followed the cart and gestured to the driver. "Baptiste, who will drive for us. The ladies will ride in the cart. You and I"—Gavin glanced at Orrin—"will ride horseback. You do not mind?"

Orrin Sackett shrugged. "I prefer to ride. I always feel better on a horse."

Orrin threw his gear into the cart, then placed Devnet's valise and a small trunk in the wagon. Mary McCann had only a valise.

The ungreased axle groaned as they moved out, Kyle Gavin leading off. Orrin slid his rifle into the boot and swung into the saddle.

The sun was not yet up when they moved out, heading north, parallel to the Red River. There was no sign of the Stampers. As the cart was lightly loaded, they moved out at a good pace.

There was no time for conversation but the route was plain before them. At noon, they pulled up under a wide-spreading elm, and Baptiste set about preparing a meal while the horse, after being watered, was picketed on the thick green grass.

Orrin sat down under the elm's shade, removed his hat, and mopped his brow, his rifle across his lap. His eyes looked off toward the west. "What's over there?" he asked.

Baptiste shrugged a shoulder. "Sand, much sand. Once a sea, I t'ink. Maybe so. Great hills of sand."

"Do you know Riel?"

"Aye, I know him. He is good man—great man. He speaks what we t'ink." He gestured. "We, the *métis,* our home is here. We live our lives on this land. All the time we work. We trap t' fur for Hudson's Bay Company. We have our homes, we raise our children, then the Comp'ny goes away.

"It iss here—*poof!* It iss gone! Then come others, strangers who say we have nothing. They will take our homes. Long ago we call upon Louis Riel, the father. He speaks for us. Now we call upon the son."

"I wish him luck," Orrin said.

Baptiste glanced at him slyly. "You do not come for land? Some mans say Yankees come with army. Many mans."

"That's foolish talk," Orrin replied brusquely. "We've problems of our own without interfering in yours. There are always some folks who make such talk for their own purposes, but the American people wouldn't stand for it."

He squinted his eyes toward the river, frowning a little. Had he seen a movement over there? "As for me, I'm going to buy a couple of carts and go west to help my brothers with a cattle drive."

Orrin leaned his head back against the tree and closed his eyes. It was cool and pleasant in the shade of the old elm. Kyle Gavin lay only a few yards away, his head pillowed on his saddle. Devnet, also in the shade, was fanning herself with her hat. He liked the way the sun brought out the tinge of red in her hair.

He liked women, and that might be his trouble. A good judge of men, he had proved a poor judge of women in his first attempt, a very poor judge. Yet what was he doing here, anyway? He should be back at home, building friendships before the next election.

He had been a sheriff, a state legislator, and they said he was a man with a future. Yet when a Sackett was in trouble, they all came to help. Old Barnabas, the father of the clan in America, had started that over two hundred years ago. It was a long, long time.

He awakened suddenly, conscious that he had actually slept. Baptiste was harnessing the horse again. Gavin was saddling his horse. Somewhat ashamed of being the last to awaken, he went to his horse, smoothed the hair on his back, and put the blanket in place. He saddled swiftly and from long habit drew his rifle from the scabbard.

He started to return it, to settle it more securely in place, but something held his hand. What was wrong? He glanced quickly around, but nobody seemed to be watching.

Then he knew. It was his rifle. The weight was wrong.

When a man has lived with guns all his life and with one rifle for a good part of it, he knows the weight and feel of it. Quickly, his horse concealing him from the others, he checked the magazine. It was empty. He worked the lever on his rifle. The barrel was empty, too.

Somebody had deliberately emptied his rifle while he slept!

Swiftly, he shucked cartridges from his belt and reloaded. He was just putting the rifle in the scabbard when Gavin appeared. "Everything all right? We're about to move out."

"I'm ready. I fell asleep over there; first time I've been caught napping in a long time." He smiled pleasantly. "But I'm awake now. Let's go!"

Gavin walked to his horse, and Orrin Sackett swung into the saddle.

Somebody wanted him defenseless. Who? Why? It could hardly be Logan Sackett's enemies, whoever they were. They were over a thousand miles away. Or were they?

Baptiste started the cart moving at a trot. The horse seemed fit enough to go all day.

Avoiding Gavin, Orrin rode wide of the cart, sometimes in advance, scouting, sometimes falling back. He rode warily, his eyes seeking out every bit of cover.

Why unload his rifle unless it was expected that he would need it at once? He thought suddenly of his pistol. He checked it. All secure, loaded, and ready. But, of course, there had been no way they could get to that.

Off to their right, only a short distance away, was the Red River with its thousands of windings through the low hills and between its green banks. Elm, box elder, occasional cottonwood, and much chokecherry or pussywillow crowded the banks and for about a quarter of a mile to a hundred yards on either side.

On the left and over a mile away, another line of trees marked another stream. He mentioned it to Baptiste.

"Wild Rice Creek," he said, "he flows into Red." He pointed with his whip in the direction they were traveling. "Not far."

"And the Sheyenne?"

"Far off—westward. He comes nearer." Baptiste pointed again with his whip to the north. "He comes to marry with Red. You see. Tomorrow, you see."

He rode on ahead, skirting a clump of trees, pausing briefly to let his horse drink at a small creek. He could hear the awful creaking and groaning of the wooden axle of the cart and occasionally a shout from Baptiste.

He listened, hearing the rustle of water in the creek, the scratching of a bird in the leaves, the whisper of the wind through the branches. Quiet sounds, the sounds of stillness, the sound of the woods when they are alone.

His horse, satisfied at last, lifted his dripping muzzle from the cool water, looking about, ears pricked. A drop or two of water fell from his lips. Then, of his own volition, he started on.

Orrin turned his mount suddenly and walked him downstream in the water, then went out on the bank and wove a careful way through a clump of trees, pausing before emerging into the sunlight.

He could see the cart afar off, perhaps a half mile. Suddenly, his horse's head lifted sharply, ears pricked. Orrin shucked his rifle and looked carefully about. Then he saw them.

Two men hunkered down, watching the cart. They were a good twenty yards off, and it was not the Stampers. These were strangers. One wore a black coat, the other a buckskin hunting jacket. Both had rifles.

Orrin stroked the horse's neck, speaking quietly to him, watching. The last thing he wanted now was to precipitate trouble, and what he needed most was information.

One of them started to lift his rifle, and Orrin slid his from the scabbard, but the other man put a hand on the other man's rifle and pushed it down. What he said, Orrin did not know, but they both withdrew into the brush. He waited, listening. After a short interval, he heard a distant sound of horse's hoofs, then silence. He rode back to the cart.

Kyle Gavin rode to meet him. "See anything?"

"There's been somebody around. Travelers, most likely."

How far could he trust Gavin? After all, he knew nothing about the man, and *somebody* had unloaded his rifle, which could have gotten him killed.

Had that somebody been expecting an attack? Perhaps by the two men? Was it his absence from the cart that caused the men to withdraw? Perhaps it was he they wished to kill, and if he was not present—?

Toward sundown, the wind began to pick up again. He scouted on ahead, watching for tracks, using cover. They crossed the Wild Rice, skirted a small settlement, and camped near the crest of a hill away from the river, to be at least partly free from mosquitoes.

Before daybreak, they moved on and by noon reached Georgetown.

"The *International?* She's tied to the bank about twenty mile downstream," a man informed them. "Water's too low here an' there. Wasn't much of a melt this year, so water's low."

The man peered at Orrin. "Name wouldn't be Sackett, would it? There was a feller around askin' after you. Least you come up to what he described. The way he made it out, you was a mighty mean man."

"Me?" Orrin widened his eyes. "I'm a reasonably mild man. Just a tall boy from Tennessee, that's all!"

"Tennessee? Ain't that where they make the good corn liquor? Folks tell me it's the finest whiskey in the world if it's aged proper."

"Kentucky, Tennessee, the Carolinas, they all have good corn whiskey, but as to age, I had a friend down in the Dark Corner who made first-rate whiskey, but he didn't hold much with aging. He said he kept some of it a full week and couldn't see any difference!"

There was a pause, and Orrin asked, "That man who was asking after me? Is he still around?"

"Ain't seen him in a couple of days. A big, tall man with a buckskin huntin' jacket."

"If you see him again," Orrin said mildly, "just tell him Sackett's in town, and if he's got any business with him, to hurry it up because Sackett can't afford to waste around waitin' for him."

"Mister, if I ain't mistaken, that man had killin' on his mind. Least that was the way it sounded."

"Of course. You tell him it's all right now. The frost is out of the ground."

"Frost? What's that got to do with it?"

Orrin smiled pleasantly. "Don't you see? It would be hard to dig a grave for him if the ground were still frozen, but we've had mild weather, and I reckon the digging would be right easy!"

Chapter 9

A tall man in a buckskin jacket? Could he have been one of the two men who were watching the cart?

Georgetown was little more than a cluster of shacks and log houses close to the river. Orrin Sackett wanted no trouble, but if trouble was to come, he preferred it here, now.

He walked the street, alert for a sight of the man in the buckskin jacket, but he saw him nowhere. The stores, he noticed, were well stocked, and it struck him that instead of waiting until he reached Pembina or Fort Garry, he might stock up here. There was a good chance that Riel or someone buying for the Canadian army would have bought out the stores.

For that matter, why not try to buy the Red River cart from Baptiste? Or to hire him to drive? Usually, he had learned, in the long caravans of carts, one driver took care of three carts, and he planned to have but two.

Transporting horses or carts on the *International* was no new thing, so arrangements were quickly made. In the store, he bought the staples he would need. Flour, bacon, beans, dried apples, coffee, tea, and several cases of hardtack, similar to the Bent's Hard-Water Crackers he had enjoyed as a boy.

He purchased powder, shot and cartridges as well, and four extra rifles.

"Better cache them good," the storekeeper advised. "Louis Riel needs all the guns he can get."

"Do you think there will be a shooting war?" Orrin asked.

The storekeeper shrugged. "Not if Riel can help it. I've done business with him, with his pa, too. They was always reasonable folks, but from what the newcomers are saying, they've got an idea back East that he's leading a rebellion, and they want to hang him."

Outside on the street, Orrin took a quick look around for the buckskin-shirted man but also for anyone else who might seem too interested or too disinterested.

He was worried, and not about what might happen here but what could happen to the north. Tell and Tyrel were depending on him not only for food and ammunition but for additional help, and the last thing he wanted was to get into the midst of a shooting fight in which he had no stake.

The way to stay out of trouble was to avoid the places where trouble was.

When a difficulty develops, unless one can help, it was far better to get away from the area and leave it to those whose business it was to handle such things.

Despite the wisdom of staying out of trouble, his route led right through the middle of it. The best thing he could do would be to get in and out as rapidly as possible.

He looked around the store, buying blankets, a couple of spare ground sheets, odds and ends that would be found useful on the way west where one could buy little or nothing. That was all right. All the Sacketts were used to "making do." It had been their way of life.

"Old Barnabas would enjoy this," he thought suddenly, and said it aloud, not thinking.

"Hey? What's that?"

Orrin smiled. "Just thinking about an ancestor of mine. Came over from England many a year ago, but he was always going west."

"Mine, too," the storekeeper said. "My grandpa left a mighty good farm and a comfortable business. Just sold out and pulled out. Pioneering was in the blood. I guess."

Orrin agreed. "I've got it, too," he admitted. "I'm a lawyer, and I've no business even being here."

"Well, luck to you." The storekeeper looked up. "You goin' west? To the gold fields, maybe?"

"That's right."

The storekeeper shook his head. "I'll talk to Jen about it. That there western country—well, I'd like to see it. I surely would. Wild country, they say, with mountains covered with snow, deep canyons—"

"I'll send my cart around for this," Orrin said.

"Better get you another cart. You got a load here. You got enough for two carts. I've got one I'll let you have reasonable, and a good, steady horse with it."

"The way you talk," Orrin said, "you may need it yourself."

"Up to Jen. I'll talk to her. But maybe—Jenny's got the feelin', too. I seen her lookin' off to the horizon now and again. After all, we was westerin' when we come here." He waved a hand. "Don't worry about the cart. I got a good man can build me one. I'll sell you cart, horse, and harness reasonable. When I come west—well, we may meet up sometime."

"Thanks." Orrin held out his hand. "That's decent of you. If you don't see me, and you hear the name of Sackett, you just go to them and tell him you were friendly to Orrin Sackett. You won't need more than that."

He returned to the street and walked back to the hotel. Baptiste was loaded and standing by his horse.

"You ever been to British Columbia, Baptiste?"

"I dream of it. But it is for young men. I am no longer young."

"It is for men, Baptiste, and you are a man. I have another cart. Will you get it for me?"

"I will. But British Columbia? He iss far off, I t'ink."

"We will cross the wide plains, Baptiste, and follow strange rivers until they are no more. Then we shall climb mountains. It will be cold, hard, and dangerous. You know what the western lands are like, and it is never easy."

Devnet Molrone came out on the street with Mary McCann. "Do we start so soon?"

"It is twenty miles, they say. We will have to hurry."

He glanced up the street. There was a tall man standing there, a tall man in a buckskin coat. Across the street, seated on a bench, was a man in a black coat. He smiled; it was so obvious.

"What is it?" Devnet asked.

"What?" He glanced at her. "Oh? Nothing, I was just—"

"You looked so stern there for a moment, and then almost amused. Somehow—"

"It is nothing," he replied. "It is just that some patterns are so familiar. The men who use them do not seem to realize the same methods have been used for centuries. Each seems to think he invented it."

"I don't believe I understand."

He leaned on the wagon. "Miss Molrone? Do you see those two men up the street? For some reason, they wish me harm. They have followed us here. When I go up the street, as they know I must, the man in the buckskin jacket will start trouble, somehow. Then, when he makes a move to draw a gun, the man across the street in the black coat will try to kill me."

"You're mad!" She stared at him. "That's utterly preposterous! People don't do such things."

"Not so often here as further south, nor so often where we are going. Nevertheless, it does happen. Trial by combat, Miss Molrone, has been a way of life since the beginning of time. A savage way, I'll admit, and dying out. But it is still with us."

"But that's ridiculous! Those two men—why, I saw one of them talking to Mr. Gavin just this morning!"

She turned to look at him. "You do not seem the type, somehow. You're so much the southern gentleman. I just—"

He smiled again. "Southern gentleman? It's just the hat and maybe the fact that I trim my moustache. I grew up in the mountains, ma'am, a-fightin' an' a-feudin', and I cut my western teeth roundin' up wild cows. I've been up the hill and over the mountain, as we Sacketts say."

"But you're a lawyer!"

"Yes, ma'am, and respectful of the law, only if one is to settle difficulties in court, it must be agreeable to both parties. I suspect those gentlemen up the street have already selected their twelve jurymen, and they are in the chambers of their pistols.

"Now," he said, "I must let them present their case, and I am wondering if they have become familiar with a new tactic the boys invented down Texas way?

"We will have to hope they have not heard of it." He unbuttoned his coat. "Miss Molrone, ma'am, would you mind going inside?"

"I will not! Besides, if what you say is true, it's not fair! There are two of them!"

"Please. Do go inside. I know where my bullets are going, but I don't know about theirs."

"Here—what is this?" It was Gavin. "What's going on?"

"It's those men up there. Mr. Sackett believes they will try to kill him."

"*Two* men? I see but one."

"The man in the black coat. Mr. Sackett believes when trouble develops with the one, the other will kill him."

Kyle Gavin's features showed nothing. "Oh? I scarcely think—"

"Gavin? Will you take Miss Molrone inside? I wish to ask that man why he has been following us. If there is anything he wants, I am sure he can have it. There's no need to go skulking about in the brush."

"Following us? I wasn't aware—"

"Perhaps not. I was aware."

"But *two* men? Surely, if you know there are two, or believe there are, I cannot see why you would walk into the trap."

Orrin shrugged a shoulder. "If one knows, it ceases to be a trap. And to an extent the situation is reversed. But that's the lawyer in me. I talk too much."

He turned to Devnet again. "And, Miss Molrone, do let Mr. Gavin take you inside. And please? Stay close to him, for my sake?"

Gavin glanced around. "Now what's that mean?"

"We want her to be safe, do we not?" Orrin's expression was bland.

"If there's a shooting here," Gavin warned, "you will be arrested. The Canadian—"

"We are still in Dakota Territory," Orrin reminded him. "Now will you take Miss Molrone inside?"

"He's right, miss," Mary McCann said. "When lead starts to flyin', anybody can get shot."

The tall man in the buckskin jacket leaned lazily against an awning post. The man opposite in the black coat was reading a newspaper.

Orrin Sackett did not walk toward the man in the buckskin coat, and he did not walk up the middle of the street. He started as if to do one or the other, then switched to the boardwalk that would bring him up behind the man in the black coat.

The tall man straightened suddenly, uncertain as to his move, and in that moment Orrin was behind the man with the newspaper, who had started to turn.

"Sit still now," Orrin warned, "and hang on to that paper. You drop it, and I'll kill you."

The man clutched the paper with both hands. "See here, I don't know what—"

"All right!" Orrin's voice rang clearly in the narrow street. "Unbuckle your gun and let it fall." He was speaking to the man across the street. "Easy now! I don't want to have to kill you."

"Hey? What's this all about?" The man in the buckskin coat rested one hand on his buckle. "What's going on?"

"Nothing, if you unbuckle that belt, nice and easy, and then let it fall."

The man across the street could not even see if Sackett had drawn his gun since he was standing directly behind the man with the newspaper.

The man with the newspaper said, "Better do what he says, Cougar. There's always another day."

Slowly, carefully, Cougar unbuckled his belt and let the gun slip to the ground along with belt and holster.

"Now walk away four steps to your left and stop." Orrin reached down and slipped the seated man's gun from its holster, then a derringer from a vest pocket. He gave the man a quick, expert frisk.

"Fold your paper and put it in your coat pocket," he suggested, "then walk over and join your friend."

As the man walked, Orrin moved across the street behind him and gathered up the gun belt and slung it over his shoulder. "Sit down, boys. Right on the edge of the boardwalk. We might as well be comfortable."

"What's going on?" Cougar demanded. "I don't even know this gent."

Orrin smiled. "You seemed to know each other pretty well when I saw you out in the brush today. I had you under my rifle several times out there, and I was tempted, gentlemen, tempted."

"We was just wonderin' where you was goin'," Cougar said.

"You could have asked us," Orrin said mildly. "No use to skulk in the brush and maybe get mistaken for a Sioux."

"We was just curious"—Cougar's eyes were bright with malice— "especially since you got no reason to go west no more."

Orrin's expression did not change, but within him something went cold and empty. "What's that mean?"

"Them others, with the cows. They're gone. Wiped out. Herd's gone, all of them massacred by the Sioux."

"That's right," the man in the black suit said. "We rode over the

ground. The Sioux stampeded buffalo into them an' then follered the
buffalo. We seen where a couple of bodies was trampled into prairie,
an' gear all over everywhere. They're dead—killed—wiped out."

Chapter 10

Orrin's expression did not change. Their faces were sullenly mali-
cious. Cougar hooked his thumbs in his belt. "You lost 'em all," he
said, "your family and the cows. The Sioux wiped 'em out. You got
nothin' left."

He smiled. It was not easy, but he did it. Were they lying? He
wanted to believe it, but he doubted they were.

"They was comin' north," Cougar said. "God knows how they got
that far, but they was west of the Turtle Mountains, between there an'
the Souris River, when the buffalo stampede hit 'em."

"You saw the bodies?"

"No, I never seen 'em. Hell, there wasn't nothing left. You ever
seen a buffalo stampede? Must have been three or four thousand of
them.

"We seen some bodies trampled into the torn-up ground. We seen
scattered stuff, torn clothing, a busted rifle. Whatever was left the Injuns
took, but it can't have been much. And the cattle was scattered to hell
and gone!"

Once started, Cougar seemed minded to talk, and Orrin kept still.
"There was a little creek comes along there. Don't amount to much,
but this time of year there might be water enough for a herd. Anyway,
they was in there on a small slope to catch what wind there was because
of the skeeters.

"Them Sioux, they'd prob'ly been follerin' them for days, watching for it to be right, and they sure did make it work."

"Why were you following me?"

Cougar shrugged insolently. "Just seen you, wondered what you was doin', then heard your name was Sackett. Figured to tell you what happened."

"All right," Orrin replied, "I'll leave your guns down at the store. But stay off my trail. If I catch you following me, you'd better make your fight because I will."

Abruptly, he turned and walked back to the hotel. Gavin was waiting with Mary McCann and Devnet. "What happened?" he asked.

As briefly as possible, he explained. When he had finished, Devnet said, "Then you won't be going west? You'll stop here?"

"I'll go west, ma'am, and if there's no other way, and you're mindful to travel along, I'll take you and Mrs. McCann. It will be rough, and you won't travel fast, but you can come."

"No," Devnet said, "we'll go to Carlton. We will find a way. But thank you." She paused. "But why will you go now? Everything is gone, finished."

"No, ma'am. Those cattle were stampeded, not killed. I'll round up what I can of them and go on west. If I can find anything left of my brothers, they'll have decent burial, and I'll read from the book over them.

"If not, they'll lie out there with their blood fed into the grass. Ma'am, neither of those boys would feel too lonely out there, for there's Indian blood in that grass. Good men died before them, and there's mighty few western trials that don't have a Sackett buried somewhere along the route. You don't build a country like this on sweat alone, ma'am."

"But there are Indians! And those cattle will be scattered for miles!"

"Yes, ma'am. I'll buy me some extra horses, and if I can find a man or two to help, I'll do it. We started to deliver a herd to the mines, and there's a Sackett yonder who's needful of our help. I reckon I'll go, ma'am, and if it be that I don't make it, well, there's more Sacketts where we come from."

The track lay along the Dakota side of the Red, and they moved at a good pace. Accustomed through long practice, the second horse followed the first cart, driven by Baptiste, without a driver. The afternoon waned, and the lead cart moved faster.

Orrin Sackett drew up to look back along the trail. He saw nothing, no sign of pursuit, no dust. His mount seemed nervous and eager to be off, so he turned and once more began following the carts, although his horse, without any urging, rapidly overtook them.

The carts were moving at a fast trot, and Baptiste kept looking around at the sky on all sides. "How far?" Orrin called out.

"Soon!" Baptiste replied.

The women rode in the carts, resting on the bedrolls and sacks of gear and equipment.

Kyle Gavin, seemingly indisposed to conversation, had ridden on ahead.

Again and again, Orrin looked about, watching the terrain. He was not about to trust Cougar or his companion, and he had neglected to find out who they represented or why they had an interest in him. Not that they showed any indication of being willing to tell him.

Suddenly, the old man yelled at him, gesturing. At the same time, he heard a long, weird moan rise from around or behind him. He had only time to reach up and pull down the mosquito netting from the brim of his hat, and then they were all about him.

He had seen mosquitoes before but nothing like this. They settled on the horse, five and six deep. Again and again, he swept them away, crushing many at a blow, sweeping others away only to have them return in thousands. Suddenly, ahead of them and through the leaves, they saw lights and a gleam of white. It was the *International!* The gangway was down, but there was no one in sight. Without hesitation, they drove aboard, and the women scrambled from the carts and rushed inside.

Kyle Gavin disappeared also, but Orrin remained behind, covering the horses with fly nets that helped only to a limited degree. Some deck hands appeared, and the gangway was hoisted inboard, and with a great amount of puffing, threshing, and groaning the *International* moved from the bank and started downstream.

To eat supper was impossible. Mosquitoes drowned themselves in the coffee, buried themselves in the melting butter, crawled into the ears and the eyes. Devnet Molrone and Mary McCann had already given up and disappeared. Orrin followed.

In his small stateroom, there were mosquitoes, too. He succeeded in driving many outside by waving a towel, then got under the netting on his bunk. Dead tired, he slept, awakening in the cool of morning to find no mosquitoes about.

Shaving was all but impossible, but he worried through it, swearing more than a little. From the porthole he could see green banks sliding past.

After a while, in a clean shirt, he emerged on deck. From the pilot he learned the *International* was one hundred and thirty-odd feet long but drew only two feet of water. There were few straight stretches on the river, for it persisted in a fantastic series of S curves that seemed without end. Some of the curves could barely be negotiated, and the longer Mississippi boats would have had no chance here.

Returning to his cabin after a quick, pleasant breakfast, Orrin checked his guns once more. Soon they would be in the little frontier post of Pembina. He must make new plans now. Without his brothers, he must do what needed to be done alone or with what help he could secure.

Tell and Tyrel gone! His mind refused to accept it.

William Tell Sackett, that older brother of his, the quiet, steady one, always so sure, so strong, so seemingly fearless.

Tyrel, younger than he as he was younger than Tell, but Tyrel was different, had always been different. And perhaps the best of them all with a gun.

Gone!

No, he'd not accept it, not until he found some tangible evidence of their death. Yet, at the same time, his experience told him the risk they had run, the dangers to be expected, the attraction of such a herd of cattle moving through Sioux country.

Nonetheless, he must plan as though they were gone. He must plan to round up the cattle, scattered though they might be, and deliver them himself.

He would, of course, need help. Baptiste seemed willing to go along, but he was only a cart driver. What he would need would be cowboys or some of the *métis*, who were handy men at anything. They, however, would be busy with Riel and the pending rebellion.

Pembina—he must see what could be done there. And there were a couple of men aboard the *International* who might be interested.

Devnet Molrone did not appear on deck, and Kyle Gavin seemed preoccupied. Orrin walked along the upper deck, watching the shoreline and the river ahead, although rarely could they see the river for more than a few hundred yards, if that far.

Twice he saw deer, once a small herd of buffalo. He saw no Indians.

There were few passengers aboard. Three men and a woman bound for Pembina and a tall, lean young man for Fort Garry. There was also a portly, middle-aged man in a tweed suit.

"This Riel," the latter said distastefully, "who does he think he is? How dare he? He's nothing but a bloody savage!"

"I understood he'd studied for the priesthood," the young man protested, "and worked for some paper in Montreal or somewhere."

"Balderdash! The man's an aborigine! Why, he's part Indian! Everybody knows that!"

"One-eighth," the young man said.

"No matter. Who does he think he is?"

"From what I hear," Orrin suggested mildly, "he simply stepped in to provide a government where there was none."

"Balderdash! The man's an egotistical fool! Well," he said finally, "no need to bother about him. The army will be here soon, and they'll hang him. Hang him, I say!"

The young man looked over at Orrin and shrugged. After a bit, he walked forward with him. "A man of definite opinions," Orrin said mildly.

"I know little enough about Riel except some poetry of his that I've read. Not bad at all, not bad. But he seems a reasonable man."

"If they give him time," Orrin commented. "It would seem some at least have already made up their minds."

"You're headed west, I hear?"

"British Columbia, but first I've got to round up some cattle and find, if I can, the bodies of my brothers, who are said to have been killed in a stampede."

"Dash it all! I am sorry! I heard something to that effect." He glanced at Orrin. "Going to the gold fields?"

"Eventually, if we get the cattle."

"I would take it as a favor if you permitted me to come along."

"You?" Orrin glanced at him. "I will carry no excess baggage. If you come with me, you will work and be paid for it. You will ride, round up cattle and drive them, and if necessary, fight Indians."

"I'm your man. It sounds like great fun."

"It won't be. It is brutally hard work, and a good chance to be killed."

"I understand Miss Molrone is going with you?"

So that was it? "She may change her mind. Right now she is headed for Carlton House and may go no further. If it is she whom you're interested in, I would suggest you go to Carlton House."

Pembina would soon be showing up around a bend. Once, there, he could begin recruiting, but instead of the two men he had hoped to get, now he would need at least four and preferably more. This young man—what was his name? He might prove to be just the man he needed.

Kyle Gavin came forward to stand beside him, watching the blunt bow part the river waters. Huge elms hung over the river, extending limbs out from either side until they almost met above the river. Here and there along the banks were clumps of willow, some grown into trees of some size.

"Dev—, I mean Miss Molrone tells me you've had bad news? About your brothers, I mean?"

"Yes, the man called Cougar told me they were dead. That they had been killed. I'll believe that when I see it."

"I *am* sorry! I must—well, I have to admit I heard the same story, but I just hadn't—I mean, I couldn't bring myself to tell you."

Orrin glanced at Gavin, his eyes cool. "I prefer to know such things. The sooner the better."

"You're still going west?"

"Why not? I still have a herd to deliver. Their death, if dead they are, changes nothing in that sense."

"But your cattle are gone! Scattered to the winds, and probably many of them have been killed. What can you do?"

"That we will see, Mr. Gavin. A cousin of mine is waiting for the delivery of those cattle. He will not be disappointed."

Gavin stared at him in obvious disbelief. "But you don't seem to understand! You're over two thousand miles from there! You have no cattle! You have nobody to help! The same Sioux who killed your brothers will be waiting for you, and further west there are Blackfeet! You don't have a chance!

"Even," he added, "if Riel does not requisition your carts and supplies. And if he does not demand them, the army certainly will. Such things are in short supply."

"We will manage."

Suddenly, there was a blast from the whistle. Orrin Sackett turned, pulling his hat brim down.

Pembina was just ahead.

Chapter 11

Pembina had little to offer. A customhouse, a trade store, and a scattering of cabins. The oldest settlement around, its fortunes had varied with travel and the fur trade, but now Fort Garry and the village of Winnipeg were attracting settlers that might otherwise have been drawn to Pembina.

Orrin Sackett wasted no time, for the *International* would be there for but a short stay. He walked up to the trading post and looked around quickly.

Only a few men were present, at least two of whom he immediately catalogued as drunks. He started to turn away when he stopped and looked again at the man at the end of the bar. He had his hat pushed back, and an impudent grin touched his lips. "Howdy!" he said. "You all still rustlin' for men?"

"How are you, Shorty? Yes, I am." He paused. "You travel fast."

"It's a mighty poor horse that ain't faster'n that steamboat, what with all the curves in that river. I beat you by a whole day." Shorty emptied his glass. "Word gets around that you won't be needin' any hands. They say your cattle were stampeded and your brothers killed. They say you're wiped out."

Orrin pushed his hat back. He glanced at the bartender. "A beer," he said, "and give Shorty whatever he's drinking."

He waited for the beer, took a swallow, and then said, "I never seen a herd so scattered that a man couldn't round up some of them, and as for Tell and Tyrel, they don't kill very easy. I've seen 'em shot at, I've seen 'em wounded, I've seen them days without food or water, and somehow they always came through.

"Regardless, we gave our word to deliver cattle, and deliver them I will if I have to round up a herd of buffalo and drive them through.

"I've got just one man, Shorty, an' old cart driver named Baptiste. We've got two cartloads of grub an' gear, and I'm rustling for men and horses.

"Out west there, they've got some mighty mean Sioux, some meaner Blackfeet, and some grizzlies that will stand higher than a horse and heavier than a bull. They've got mountains where nobody ever drove a cow critter before, and there may be some men along the trail who'd like to stop us. What d'you say?"

"Sounds like my kind of a deal." Shorty tossed off his drink. "Finish your beer. I know a man who's got some horses."

Two hours later, Orrin owned six new horses. Shorty stood back and watched him, an amused smile on his face. Orrin passed by dozens of horses to choose the six he finally bought.

"You done yourself proud," Shorty said. "You got yourself six of the best. But you get to roundin' up stock on the plains, and six horses won't last even two men no time at all."

"We'll have more. What I need right now is men."

"Tough. Usually, you could find all you wanted. These *métis* ain't cowpunchers by a long shot, but they can ride, and they can shoot, and you find quite a few who are fair hands with a rope. And they're workers, every durned one of them."

The steamboat whistled. "Shorty? You want to meet me in Fort Garry with these horses?"

"Surest thing you know. But you watch your step. That's a mighty touchy situation there."

He had no doubt of it, yet there was nothing to do but to go ahead and cope with the situations as they occurred.

He could not make himself believe that Tell and Tyrel were dead. If not dead, they might be lying somewhere, injured and suffering. Or they might be prisoners of the Sioux.

He made the *International* just as they were taking in the gangway.

Devnet met him on the upper deck. "It isn't far now, is it?" she asked.

"A few more hours. You are going to Fort Carlton?"

"Of course."

"Is Mrs. McCann going with you?"

"I think not. I do not know her well, you know. We just met while traveling, and all I know is that she wishes to go west, all the way to the Pacific."

"You should have no trouble."

She turned to him suddenly. "I am sorry about your brothers, so very sorry. Were you so very close?"

"We had our differences, but they never amounted to much. Yes, we were close. I left my law practice to help them."

"What will you do now?"

"Find their bodies, if possible, bury them, and then round up the cattle and go on west." He paused. "But I cannot believe they are dead. They were both so strong, so alive. They were survivors. They'd been through a lot."

He hesitated, then said, "Miss Molrone, I—"

"My friends call me Nettie. It is easier to say than Devnet."

"All right, Nettie. What will you do if you learn nothing of your brother at Carlton?"

"Go on west, I presume. He has to be there."

"You must realize there is no regular mode of travel to the west, only occasional groups of travelers. Someday there will be a railroad. They are talking of it now, and since this Riel trouble, I imagine there will be a serious effort made, but that's years away."

"I have to go—somehow."

"We will not be going by way of Carlton but will be going west from Fort Ellice. We will follow the Qu'Appelle River, more or less. If you could join us—of course, it will be rough, sleeping on the ground and all that."

"I could do it."

They talked the morning away but saw nothing of Kyle Gavin. Before the noontime meal, Mary McCann came up to join them. She said little, had blunt but not unattractive features, and Orrin noticed her hands showed evidence of much hard work.

Occasionally, now, there were breaks in the wall of trees on either bank, and they could catch glimpses of meadows and in one case of a plowed field. The country was very flat, and the river wound slowly through it. They saw many ducks and an occasional hawk.

A dozen men armed with rifles, whom he took to be *métis,* waited on the landing. One of them came forward as the carts were being driven ashore. His name, he said, was Lepine.

"I am Orrin Sackett."

Lepine nodded. "We have heard of you." He gestured to the carts. "These will be confiscated."

Briefly, Orrin explained. Lepine shrugged. "It will be up to Louis. He will decide."

It was arranged for him to be conducted to the fort where Riel had taken up his residence.

Riel came into the room wearing a black frock coat, vest and trousers, and moccasins, as did nearly everyone. He had quick, intelligent eyes, a broad forehead, and a shock of black hair.

He listened, his eyes roaming around the room, as Orrin explained. At the end, he nodded. "Of course. We will release your goods. I have heard of the attack you mention."

"And my brothers? Were they killed?"

"What we heard was little enough. There was a stampede, an attempt to scatter the cattle so the Sioux could take them when they wished.

"There was some fighting, which would imply somebody survived the stampede. The Sioux claim to have lost no one, but one of my men, who was in their camp shortly after, learned there were some losses, and the Sioux had but one fresh scalp that he saw."

He glanced at Orrin. "You must give me your word the rifles will not be used against me, nor the supplies given to those who consider themselves my enemies."

His restless eyes kept moving about the room. Suddenly, he asked, "How many men do you have?"

"Two—now. A cart driver named Baptiste—"

Riel smiled. "I know him. A good old man." He looked around at Orrin. "But only two? What can you do?"

"I hope to find more."

"Well"—he shook his head doubtfully—"you have a problem." He waved a hand. "Go! It is all right! You shall have your carts. I want trouble with no one. I began all this because I wanted peace. There were surveyors coming on our land, and I was afraid there would be a shooting."

Orrin turned to the door, and his hand was on the latch when Riel spoke again. "Wait! There is a man, an American like yourself. He is in jail here. I think he is a good man."

"In jail for what?"

"Fighting."

Orrin smiled. "All right. I will talk to him."

"If you hire him, the case will be dismissed." Riel smiled slyly, his eyes twinkling. "Just take him away from here. It needed four of my men to get him locked up."

Lepine unlocked the cell, and a man got up from the straw. He was at least two inches taller than Orrin's six feet and four inches but leaner. He had a handlebar moustache and a stubble of beard. One eye was black, fading to blue and yellow, and his knuckles were skinned.

"You want a job?" Orrin said.

"I want to get out of here."

"You take the job, you get out. Otherwise, they'll throw the key away."

"Don't look like I have much choice." He stared at Orrin. "What kind of a job is this, anyway?"

"Rounding up cattle stampeded by buffalo. It's in Sioux country."

"Hell, I'd rather stay in jail. They gotta let me out sometime."

He was watching Orrin, and suddenly he said, "What's your name, mister?" He paused. "It wouldn't be Sackett, would it?"

"It would. I am Orrin Sackett."

"I'll be damned! They call me Highpockets Haney. I thought you had the mark on you. You Sacketts all seem cut to the same pattern, sort of. I served in the army with a Sackett named William Tell."

"My brother."

"I'll be damned! All right, you got yourself a boy. On'y you got to get me a *wee*pon. They done taken my rifle gun an' my pistol."

A burly *métis*, sitting on a log with a rifle across his knees, looked up as they came out. "Take heem! Take heem far! He geef me a leep!" He touched his lip with tender fingers.

"Hell," Haney said, "look at the eye you gave me!"

"What we fight about?"

Haney chuckled. "You expect *me* to remember? More'n likely I wondered whether you was as tough as you looked." He chuckled again. "You're tougher!"

Shorty was at the customhouse with the six horses. He led the way to a place back from the river and on a grassy hillside under the spreading branches of some old trees. "Camped here before," he explained.

He watched Baptiste come up the rise with the two carts. "Ain't much of an outfit, but it's a start," he suggested. "We'll need at least two more men, and we should have six."

"We'll just have to look around," Orrin said, "but there's three of us now."

The next man was a volunteer. He approached Shorty, who was having a beer. "You look like a rider," he suggested. "I'm another, and I'm broke and rustlin' work."

His name was Charlie Fleming, and he was from Arkansas, he said. He had two horses of his own and knew where there were four more to be had.

"That's it," Orrin told them. "We'll move out tomorrow. The first thing is to find where that stampede took place and hunt for my brothers, or their bodies."

"You won't find much," Fleming said. "Not after a stampede. I lost a friend thataway, and all we found was his boot heels and some buttons. By the time several hundred head of buffalo run over you, there isn't much to find."

"We'll look," Haney said. "Tell Sackett was the best friend I ever had. We were in the Sixth Cavalry together."

Orrin walked back to the hotel. Studiously, he had avoided any thought of his brothers. His job was to get an outfit. When the time came to look, that would be another thing.

Three men riding and one on the carts. Four men riding, counting himself. It was too few, and he should have about ten more horses. Rounding up scattered cattle, if any were left, would be rough on the riding stock.

The first person he saw at the hotel was Nettie Molrone. "Oh, Mr. Sackett! I'm so glad to see you! I'm leaving in the morning for Fort Carlton!"

"Who's taking you?"

"I'm going with a group. Mrs. McCann is going, and there will be another lady whose husband is there. There are six trappers, Mr. Taylor from the Hudson's Bay Company, and Kyle Gavin."

"I wish you luck," he said. His expression was a little sour, and she noticed it. "I mean, I really do," he added. "I'll be leaving tomorrow, too."

"I know. I mean, Mr. Gavin said he believed you were leaving. He doesn't think you'll have much luck."

"We'll see." He hesitated, then said, "I hope you find your brother and that everything goes well for you. Remember, we'll be miles to the south of you, and once we get the cattle, we'll be driving west. We'll follow the South Saskatchewan."

"But aren't the cattle down in Dakota?"

"On the border," he said. "We'll need several days to round them up."

He was in his room and combing his hair before going down to dinner when the thought struck him. How did Kyle Gavin know he was leaving?

He didn't even have his outfit yet, not the men or stock he needed. Just a surmise, probably. A lucky guess.

Chapter 12

The morning was clear and bright with only a few scattered clouds. The wind sent ripples through the vast sea of grass before them, but the sound of it was lost in the screech and groan of the carts, which were entirely of oak and ungreased.

Highpockets Haney rode up beside Orrin. "You got your work cut out for you, Sackett," he said. "You ever rounded up cattle scattered by a buffalo stampede? They're likely to be scattered to hell an' gone."

"It won't be easy."

"We'll be workin' alone most of the time, just the way the Injûns like it."

"We'll work in pairs," Orrin suggested. "Takes less time to bunch them. If trouble comes, use your own judgment. Fight if that's necessary, but run if you can, just so long as you run together. I don't want any man left alone unless he's already dead."

Now he left them, riding out at least a mile in advance of the carts and the other riders. Since the news had come, there had been no time to be alone, no time to mourn, no time to think, only time for the immediate business, and first things must come first.

They had started to drive cattle to the gold fields because Logan Sackett had promised it. Therefore the job must be continued. Logan was still in trouble, and a Sackett had given his word.

Rumor had it his brothers were dead. He did not believe it, yet it could be. Men died every day, and his brothers were no more immune than their father had been.

It was his mission now to go to the area, accept the risks it entailed, round up the cattle if possible, and find and bury the bodies of his brothers.

Feeling sad was a luxury he could not afford at the moment. With resolution, he turned from sadness to the task at hand. Now, with all going forward, he could think, so he rode far out before his small party where he could ride alone.

He was alone, simply with his horse, the sound of his passing, and the wind in the grass.

Tell and Tyrel—gone! That he could not accept, even for the moment. Tell had always been the older brother, strong, quiet, and sure. He had been less talkative, even, than Tyrel, who was himself quiet. He, Orrin, had always been the easy-talking one, taking after the Welsh side of the family.

He remembered the day when Tell, still only a boy, had ridden off to war. They lived in the mountains of Tennessee and had kinfolk fighting for the Confederacy, but Tell had said, "Ma, I'm a goin' to war. I'm goin' to fight for the Union."

"For the Union, son?"

"Yes, ma. It's my bounden duty. Our folks fought to build this country, and I'll not turn my back on it. It's our country, all of it. Not just the South. And there's many a boy in Kentucky and Tennessee feels likewise."

He went in the night, using the old Indian trails, that only mountain folk knew, and somehow he got through to Ohio, and eventually he'd wound up in the Sixth Cavalry. He never said much about the war years, and if he met any kinfolk on the field of battle, he didn't say.

When it was over, he'd gone to fightin' Injuns and then quit the army and joined up with a cattle drive. He'd covered a far stretch of country before their paths crossed again in the western lands. So far as they knew, Tell had not been back to Tennessee, which was surprising because there'd been a girl back yonder that he'd been shinin' up to when the war started.

Tyrel was the youngest but already married and owner of a ranch, part of which his wife brought to him, but which he'd helped to save from renegades in the Land Grant fights. He was better off than any of them. He owned land and stock, but he owed money, and this trip was costing him.

This was wide-open country, yet there were unexpected hollows and valleys, and a man had to keep his wits about him. There were sloughs, small lakes usually surrounded by a thick stand of cattails. The hills were green now; only a few days had made a striking difference.

The grass was short but long enough to color the hills with springtime. Wild flowers were everywhere, harebell, silverberry, and blue-eyed grass as well as wild parsley and yellow violet.

Here and there were small herds of antelope, and occasionally they saw a buffalo.

That night by their small fire he warned them again. "This here's Sioux country, and they're first-class fighting men. You got to expect them all the time."

On the third day they killed a buffalo for fresh meat and skinned it out with the meadowlarks calling. Orrin's eyes kept roving, searching, watching, yet a part of his mind was far away, with Nettie Molrone, wondering where she was and how she fared.

Douglas Molrone—he must remember the name and listen for it, yet the gold fields had a way of devouring men, of chewing them up and spitting them out at the ragged ends of the world. It was whiskey and hard work that did them in, standing in cold streams, panning for the elusive gold.

So many times even the best discoveries somehow seemed to come to nothing. Tell had struck it rich in the mountains of Colorado only to have the vein play out. He had taken out a goodly sum, but part of it had gone back into searching for the lost vein. Sometime, somebody would discover it, broken off and shifted by some convulsion of the earth.

In the distance, they could see the flat-looking blue shadow that was the Turtle Mountains. Not mountains at all but a plateau of rolling country scattered with lakes and pretty meadows among the trees.

The dim trail they were following, probably made by *métis* buffalo hunters, skirted the Turtle Mountains on the north, but Orrin led the way south, skirting the plateau's eastern end and making camp near a slough almost in the shadow of the hills.

"Keep your rifles handy," he advised, "but be damned sure you see what you're shooting at. You boys know as well as I do that some or all of them might come through a stampede. If it takes place at night there'd likely be only two, three men on night herd, and they'd know you can't stop a buffalo stampede."

"So?" Fleming asked.

"It's likely they'd scatter. They'd take out an' run," Haney said. "That's what I'd do. A dead cowhand ain't no good to anybody."

"If my brothers or Cap come through this, they'd more than likely take to the hills. There's water there, and there are hideouts and small game."

They were camped in a small hollow with some low brush around, a few polished granite boulders left by a vanished glacier, and several tall cottonwoods. The slough where they watered their stock was about fifty yards below. Baptiste built a small fire and roasted buffalo steaks. Orrin could not rest but prowled about outside of the hollow, listening for any small sound.

He heard nothing but the expected sounds of the night.

It was very still. To the north loomed the bulk of the plateau; to the west the land fell gradually away into a vast plain, which he suspected was a prehistoric lake bed. Behind him there was a faint rustling of wind in the cottonwood leaves and a low murmur of voices.

Somewhere out in that great silence were his brothers and Cap, alive or dead, and he had to find them.

He walked out a few steps farther, listening. Overhead were the stars, and the sky was very clear. He moved out still farther, haunted by the feeling that something was out there, something vague that he could not quite realize.

He let his eyes move slowly all around the horizon, searching for any hint of a fire. He turned his head this way and that, trying for a smell of smoke.

Nothing!

Were they gone, then? Truly gone? After all, there is a time for each of us.

Faintly, something stirred. His gun came easily into his hand. He waited, listening. There was nothing more.

Some small animal, perhaps.

After a few minutes, he went back to the fire. In the morning, they would continue on to the westward. Then he would climb the plateau and see what he could see from that height. Certainly, he could see farther, and he might detect some movement out there. Also, he should check for tracks.

The trouble was there were, so he had heard, many lakes in the Turtles and no end to available water. It was not as simple as in the desert where waterholes were few.

"Charlie," he suggested, "you take the first watch. Give yourself an hour and a half, then awaken Shorty. The same for you, Shorty, and then call Haney and Haney will call me."

"You t'ink I am too old?" Baptiste asked.

"You have to get up early, anyway, and you'll have to watch the camp tomorrow. You get some sleep now."

Fleming took up his rifle. "Anything else?"

"Don't sit by the fire. Stay out on the edge somewhere."

He unrolled his bed and pulled off his boots, then his gun belt. Shorty was asleep almost as soon as he hit his blankets, and Haney followed suit. Baptiste stirred about a bit, then settled down.

Orrin lay still, listening. The fire had burned down to reddish coals. His six-gun was ready at his hand. He heard a brief stirring outside of camp, then stillness.

Haney touched his shoulder just as his eyes were opening. Haney squatted on his heels. "Quiet," he said, "but there's an uneasy feelin' in the air."

"Everybody asleep?"

"Sure, except maybe that Frenchman. I don't know if he ever sleeps."

Orrin sat up and tugged on his boots. For a moment he waited, listening and looking at the coals. If they were to keep the fire, he must add fuel, but he did not want it to flare up. He slung his gun belt around his hips as he stood up, then moved on cat feet over to the fire and with a stick pushed some of the charcoal into the redder coals. If there was a flare-up, it would be slight.

Moving back into the shadows, he retrieved his rifle, stood it against a tree, and shrugged into a buckskin jacket, then moved out to where the horses were. Their quiet munching indicated there was, for the moment, nothing to suggest trouble.

The stars were still bright overhead, but there were clouds in the northwest. After a circling of the camp, he sat down on a rock in the shadows of a larger one and began to consider the situation.

Except for what he had been told, he had no further evidence that his brothers had not continued on west. Knowing them as he did, he knew nothing would turn them from the way they had chosen. If they had been attacked and killed, he would know it within hours, for the battle site could not be far off.

Yet he must not lose time looking for them. He would look, but he would also round up what cattle he could find. It was likely that the cattle were scattered in bunches, for they would certainly try to find one another, and by this time they would have done so.

Soon he must awaken Baptiste and let him prepare breakfast for an early start, for today they would not only search for his brothers and their riders but would begin gathering cattle, if there were any to be found.

He got up suddenly and moved away, impatient with himself. This, of course, was a family matter and not to be avoided, but he had wasted time, too much time. No man knew how much or how little he had, but there were things that he, Orrin Sackett, wanted to do, wanted to become.

He had been admitted to the bar, had begun a practice of sorts, mixed with some political activity, but not enough of either. He had too much to learn to be losing any time. When this was over, he would get right back to Colorado and try to become the man he wished to be.

He remembered something pa said. Pa quoted it, rather, from a distant relative gone long before. "There's two kinds of people in the world, son, those who wish and those who will. The wishers wish to be rich, they wish to be famous, they wish to own a farm or a fine house or whatever. The ones who will, they don't *wish*, they start out and *do* it. They become what they want to or get what they want. They *will* it."

Well, he wasn't going to be a wisher. He'd been lucky. He'd begun to get himself an education. He'd not gone to school long, as there wasn't a school to go to most of the time. But there'd been books.

Suddenly, he was alert. Something was moving out there. He melded his shadow against a tree, listening. There was no further sound.

Orrin's rifle came up in his two hands, ready for a shot or a blow.

After a minute, with no further sound, he eased back close to where Baptiste lay. The old man was already sitting up, shaking out his boots.

"Somet'ing," he whispered, "somet'ing, he come. He come soon."

Standing back a little, Orrin threw several branches on the fire. It flared up, and he added some heavier wood.

When he stood up again, it was faintly gray. Baptiste was working over the fire, and Orrin went out to where the horses were and saddled his mount.

"Comes a man," Baptiste said. "You see?"

Highpockets Haney stood up on his bed, looking. Orrin walked closer.

Down on the flat, if it could be called that, there was a man, a big man who moved like a bear. He came on slowly, head down, plodding.

Some fifty yards away, he stopped and looked at them. "I'm the Ox," he said. "I'm coming in."

Chapter 13

Orrin waited, his hands on his hips while the big man lumbered closer. He was huge, not as tall as Orrin's six feet four inches but thicker and wider. He gave off a sense of shocking physical power, to such a degree that Orrin was irritated by it.

A civilized man with some sense of decency and proportion, he bristled at the sight of the man. He had the good sense to realize it was something of the same feeling two stallions must feel when first they met. He had had his share of fights, but he had never *wanted* to hit a man until now.

"All right," Orrin said, "you are called the Ox. What else are you? Who are you?"

The Ox knew who he was facing. He did not know the man or care, but he sensed a rival male beast and welcomed it. He was a creature nature had bred to destroy.

"There was a stampede, buffalo. Everything went with them. Men, horses, cattle, everything. There was nothing I could do."

"Where were you when it happened?"

"Off to one side. I was swinging wide around the herd. They came out of the night like—like an avalanche. And then it was all gone."

"Where's your horse?"

"Gone. He went crazy when the stampede came, and he threw me. He ran away following the herd."

"Get something to eat. You look all in." The trouble was that he did not, and Orrin sat down across the fire from him. Something here was wrong, completely wrong. The Ox did not look done in; he did not look tired or hungry. He had appeared so, coming up the slope from the flat, but no longer. His gun was still in its holster.

Orrin's sense of justice warred with his innate dislike of the man he was watching. He warned himself to dismiss his antagonism and judge fairly.

"Was this the Sackett herd?" he asked.

The big man was eating, not very seriously. A really hungry man did not gulp food, he savored it, he ate slowly. A truly hungry man cannot gulp food because his stomach has shrunk. He is more apt to eat in small bites. The Ox ate as one does who has already eaten his fill, which is a different thing altogether.

"It was. Gilcrist and me, we hired on some time back. The drive was headed west. All gone now, all gone."

"What happened to the Sacketts?"

"Dead, I reckon. They must be dead."

"But if you were off to one side, mightn't they have been, also?"

The Ox squinted his eyes. Orrin suspected he did not like the thought. "Maybe, but I ain't seen them."

"Where have you been since?"

"Hidin' from Injuns. I ain't seen any, but I think it was them started the stampede."

Orrin watched the Ox put down his plate. The man's movements were easy, perfectly controlled. There was much about him that was puzzling. He was, Orrin was sure, a much brighter man than he at first appeared and probably a better-educated one.

Orrin stood up. "All right, boys, as soon as you're through eating, let's move out. Work south and east, and stay together, two by two. I'll ride with Fleming.

"You"—he turned on the Ox, "help Baptiste—and tomorrow we'll start you riding for us."

The Ox started to speak, then turned away obviously irritated.

"Work south and east but not too far east. Anything you find, start this way. We'll try to bunch them on the flat down there."

"That's crazy!" the Ox exclaimed. "They're scattered to hell and gone!"

"Maybe," Orrin agreed, "but we'll find out, won't we?"

It was a long, hard day. Fleming and Orrin worked south and for some time saw nothing. Twice Orrin cut the sign of old Indian travels. Then they came upon three young steers and started them west.

"Take them along, Fleming," Orrin said. "They'll be a start, anyway, and I'll work on south."

"But I think—"

"It's all right," Orrin said blandly.

Fleming, none too pleased, rode off herding his three steers.

Orrin waited until he was some distance off and then turned back. In less than three hundred yards, he found what he had seen a few minutes before, the tracks of two shod horses and a trail obviously made that day. One of the horses had been carrying a very heavy man.

At a point where the trail would have brought them within sight of Orrin's camp, the two riders had suddenly turned south. Orrin followed, swinging along the trail in a wide circle. There, in the shade of some cottonwoods, one of the riders had dropped from the saddle and walked away.

The other rider had gone off to the west, leading a spare horse.

Orrin Sackett glanced off to the east where the rider had taken the spare horse and then turned in the saddle and glanced up at the plateau of the Turtles. "I'd lay a little bet," he muttered aloud.

He rode south, swinging in a wide circle toward the west, and in a little hollow found six head of cattle gathered around a small seep. He moved them out toward the northwest, picking up two more on the way. By the time he reached the gathering place, there were at least thirty head there, and Fleming was bringing in another.

Throughout the day, they worked, finding more and more of the scattered groups with occasionally a buffalo calf running with them. By sundown, they had gathered nearly three hundred head.

Baptiste had shifted camp farther west by a good five miles, with the Turtle Mountains still looming close on the north. He had a good fire going on some broiled buffalo steaks for all hands as well as more of his beans. He had made sourdough bread, and they ate simply but well.

The Ox was irritable and not talkative. It was obvious things had not gone as he expected. Baptiste was wary, watchful, and kept a gun handy, not trusting the Ox.

"There's a-plenty off to the southwest," Haney told them. "I saw maybe fifty, sixty head in one bunch and glimpsed several other scattered bunches.

"It won't be easy," he added. "They're scattered wide, and there's still a good many buffalo among 'em who will stampede again at the slightest excuse. If they do, most of those damn fool cows will go right along with them."

"We need more help," Orrin suggested, "but tomorrow we'll have the Ox helping us."

"I ain't in no shape to ride," the Ox muttered.

"If you want to eat," Orrin replied, "you'll ride. You can work with me. I think we understand each other mighty well."

The Ox glared but made no comment.

"We may be able to get some help," Shorty suggested. "This country isn't as empty as a body might think. I came on two sets of tracks today, both of them shod horses and none of them our horses."

Orrin knew he had been shying away from the thing that must be done. He had been avoiding the site of the stampede, and he knew why. If Tell and Tyrel were dead, he did not want to know it. Until he actually saw their bodies or some other evidence that proved them dead, he could still delude himself they were alive still.

"Tomorrow I am going over to check their last camp." Orrin glanced at the Ox. "You can show me where it was."

The Ox said nothing, sipping a cup of coffee, and Shorty smiled. "Ain't much to see," he said. "I was over there."

They waited, and he said, "I scouted that country some. The buffalo hit that camp goin' all out, and they just run everything right into the ground. But I don't think anybody was in the camp."

"What?" Orrin turned to stare. "Then where in God's name—?"

"They were with the cattle. They were moving them when the stampede hit them." He glanced at the Ox. "Wasn't that what you said? You were off on the flank?"

"I was." The Ox paused. "It was like I said. They were here, then they were gone, and the cattle with them. I heard one man scream. I've no idea who it was."

"Did you see any Indians?" Orrin asked.

The Ox hesitated. "Can't say I did. I heard whooping. I figured it was Indians, and I lit out."

"Haney, you and Shorty continue the roundup. The Ox and I will go over the site of the stampede before we settle down to rounding up cattle."

Orrin glanced at Baptiste. "You stay with the carts and keep your rifle handy. Any sign of trouble everybody closes in on the carts, do you hear? We need that grub."

It was a quiet night, and before daybreak they were in the saddle. Orrin, with the Ox beside him, rode down toward the site of the stampede.

The Ox turned in his saddle to look at Orrin. "You don't like me much, do you, Sackett?"

"No, I don't."

"When the right time comes, I'll take pleasure in beating your head in," the Ox said.

Orrin smiled. "Don't talk like a fool, man. You couldn't whip one side of me, and away down inside you know it."

The Ox was not amused. "Nobody ever whipped me," he said, "and nobody can."

"Keep that thought. I want you to have it when I prove you wrong."

Orrin drew up, looking over the terrain before them. The shallow valley, if such it might be called, sloped away toward the south. The earth was still torn by charging hoofs. He glanced around, taking in the situation. The Ox stared at it, then looked away. "You know, Ox," Orrin said quietly, "you're a liar. Your whole story is a tissue of lies, from start to finish. Now where's your partner?"

The Ox stared at him, an ugly expression in his eyes. "I don't know what you're talkin' about, but you just called me a liar."

"That's right. I did call you a liar." He put up a hand. "Now don't be a damned fool and go for your gun. I'm a whole lot faster than you and a much better shot, and you'd be dead before you cleared leather.

"You boys bought yourselves a packet, d'you know that? If you're going to try to get away with something, why don't you pick on some greenhorns?"

The Ox was wary. He did not believe Orrin Sackett was faster than he, but neither did he want to be mistaken. It was a simple case. If he was wrong, he was dead.

"My brothers, William Tell and Tyrel, are two of the fastest men alive when it comes to handling six-shooters. I'm only a shade less good.

"Just a moment ago, I had a notion to let you go ahead and draw so I could kill you."

The Ox stared at him. "Then why didn't you if you're so fast?"

Orrin smiled. "Because I'd miss the pleasure of whipping you with my fists," he said. Orrin rested both hands on the pommel of his saddle. "You see, Ox, you've always been big, you've always been strong, you've always been able to either frighten or outmuscle anybody whose trail you crossed. So the truth is, you've never really had to learn to fight. You've never had to get up after being knocked down. You've never had to wipe the blood out of your eyes so you could see enough to keep fighting.

"You're not really a fighter, Ox, you're just a big, abnormally strong man who has had it all his own way for too long."

The Ox smiled. "Maybe I don't have to know how to fight," he said. "I just take hold and *squeeze,* and they scream. You can hear the bones break, Sackett. I will hear yours break."

Orrin looked around again. "Now where were you when the stampede started?"

The Ox pointed across the plain. "Over there. Tyrel Sackett was riding drag. That's why I am sure he is dead."

"What d'you mean?"

"They hit us on the flank, more than halfway back, and there was no way Tyrel could get out of there."

"Then I've misunderstood. I didn't know it was that way." Orrin paused. "What kind of a horse was Tye riding?"

"It was that line-back dun he favored. I remember that because he let Brandy—"

"Who?"

"The kid—Isom Brand was his name. We called him Brandy. He wasn't much. Some farm kid they taken up with. Anyway, I remember Tyrel rode the dun because he let Brandy have that little black."

Orrin was thinking. If Tyrel was on the dun, there was a chance. That line-back dun was a cutting horse and as quick on his feet as a cat.

If any horse alive could get out of the way of that stampede, it would be the dun.

For an hour he rode back and forth across the grassy plain where the herd had been when the buffalo came. He found the remnants of a body churned into earth, but there was no way of telling who it had been.

By nightfall, working farther and farther to the west and south, they had rounded up nearly five hundred head, among them the old brindle steer who had been the leader of the herd.

"One more day," he said by the fire that night. "Just one more day, and then we leave. We've no more time."

"I wonder," the Ox said, "what become of the Indians? The ones who were, as Tell put it, ridin' in our shadow?"

Orrin reached for the coffee pot and filled his cup, then several others. He put the pot down and looked across the fire at the Ox. "Something new has been added," he said pleasantly. "What Indians?"

The Ox explained. "Tell, he left meat for them a time or two. I never saw them myself. I don't reckon he did, either."

"That dead man?" Shorty asked. "Could he have been an Indian?"

"No, he was a white man. He was wearing boots. We found the heels."

It had to be one of them. Which one?

Chapter 14

Orrin Sackett was a careful man. He knew what he had to do, and he wanted to be about it, although, even more, he wanted to hunt for his brothers. Yet whatever else he was, he was a Sackett, and the Sacketts finished the jobs they started. Also, Tyrel and Tell, if alive, would know what he was doing and where he would be.

It was that certainty of each other that had helped them through many difficulties. They had set out to deliver cattle, and he would persist in the delivery. If Tyrel and Tell could, they would follow on and join up, and they might even be on ahead somewhere, waiting.

The situation was puzzling. The Ox was here, and they had seen what were the remains of at least one other man. According to the Ox, there had been seven, including the Chinese cook, so where were the other five?

One man could disappear easily, two almost as easily, but five, widely scattered men?

He turned his horse and rode back to the carts. The Ox rode alongside, saying nothing.

The country around was pretty wide open, and scanning it as they rode, he could see herds of antelope, most of them a mile or more away, and a good many buffalo, moving as they usually did in small herds that made up the larger group, feeding as they moved.

He could see nothing else. The antelope and buffalo moved as if no man was near them, and he was sure there was no one out there.

The mountains, if such they could be called, had to be the answer. Before they left the country, he was going to make one sweep through those hills. He knew he could see little in that time, but there was a chance, particularly if he brought an extra man or two.

Baptiste was with the carts when they rode up, his rifle at hand. Nearby, the cattle were gathered, grazing peacefully, seemingly glad to be back together again. Across the herd he could see Charlie Fleming coming in with a small bunch of cattle. Highpockets and Shorty were at the carts, both hunkered down by the fire with cups of coffee in their hands.

Haney looked up as Orrin swung down. "We've about cleaned her up," he said, "unless you're of a mind to take the carts south, set up a new camp, and round up what went on south.

"I saw cow tracks down thataway, so we know some went on south with the buffalo." He paused. "Odd thing. Shorty an' me, we come down into a low place over yonder, and we came up on about three hundred head, all bunched and pretty, all wearin' the Sackett road brand."

Orrin was filling his cup. He sipped his coffee. "See any tracks?"

"Uh-huh. Two riders, one of them carryin' mighty light. Fresh tracks, Mr. Sackett, like those cattle had been bunched within the last few hours."

"Nobody around?"

"Nobody. It doesn't make sense. A body would think they had been bunched a-purpose and just left for us."

"No use looking gift horses in the teeth. You brought them in?"

"You're durned right! The way I figure it, we've got a shade over nine hundred head."

"Good enough. We'll move out for the northwest tomorrow. We've lost a couple of hundred head, but we will just have to take the loss and run."

"You aimin' to look for Tell an' them?"

"Something's wrong, Haney. Five, six men missing with no sign, but somebody bunched those cows for us.

"Yes," he added, "you and me are going to take a ride into the Turtles. We couldn't cover the place in a month or more, but we can scout for tracks. If we see anything, we'll check it out. Otherwise, we'll get on with the job."

Fleming left the herd, bunching them a bit more as he circled back to the fire. He stepped down from the saddle.

"See any tracks?"

He shook his head. "Nothing, and cows are scarce, mighty scarce."

"We pull out tomorrow," Shorty said.

Fleming went to the fire, squatted on his heels, and held his cup, staring into the fire for a long minute. Then he filled his cup, avoiding the eyes of the Ox, who was staring at him.

"Good bunch of cattle," Fleming commented. "Makes a man want to get into the cow business."

Orrin threw the dregs on the ground. "Fleming, you come with Haney and me. Shorty, you stay close to the wagons with Baptiste unless you see some of the stock straying too far. But keep a rifle handy."

Orrin led the way up a dim trail into the trees. Here and there were dense stands of forest, then scattered trees and meadows with frequent small lakes and pools. They scattered out, keeping within sight of one another but watching for tracks.

"Mr. Sackett?" Haney called out.

Orrin turned his horse and cantered over to where the tall man waited. Haney indicated the grass at his feet.

There was a place by a rotting log where a part of the grass was pressed down, and there were flecks of what appeared to be blood on the grass and the leaves. "Looks like somebody has been lyin' here, maybe a few days back."

"Horse tracks?"

"Don't see none. I reckon he was afoot. My guess would be he was bad hurt. He got this far an' just collapsed."

"Then what?"

"Well, there's a track." He pointed to their north. "I figure he came out of it and started on."

Leading their horses, they followed the tracks. Charlie Fleming was some distance away, and Orrin stood for a moment, watching him. He seemed to be studying the ground as he moved.

"Haney," Orrin said, "walk careful. If this is some of our boys, and they're hurt, they'll be wary of trouble."

"I soldiered with Tell, remember? He never shot at anything he couldn't see. He wasn't one of those damned fools who heard a noise and just blasted away."

The trail was dim and old. Whoever the wounded man was, he made over two hundred yards before he fell. They found the place where he went to his knees, then had fallen forward on his face. There had been a struggle to rise; then the fallen man had subsided and lay still for some time.

However, they found no blood on the grass. Orrin looked carefully around, searching the brush, the trees, and the grass for some indication of movement. He saw none. He looked around for Charlie Fleming, but the rider was nowhere in sight.

He moved on, taking his time, missing nothing. The wounded man had gotten back to his feet and was moving at a somewhat better pace.

"He's feelin' some better," Haney suggested.

"Either that or he suspects he's being followed and wants to hide," Orrin said.

He paused again, looking carefully around. Suddenly, he grunted and ran rapidly forward, stopping at a small cairn of three stones. Gently, he lifted off the first one, then the second.

There, placed neatly across the face of the second stone, were three parallel blades of grass.

"It's Tyrel," Orrin said.

Haney looked at the small pile of scarcely noticeable rocks. "I don't see how—!"

Orrin held up the three blades of grass. "He is the third son of my father. If there had been but one blade of grass, it would have been Tell."

"And two?"

"Me," Orrin said. "We started it when we were youngsters, playing and hunting in the woods. Tell began it when he was about nine so we boys could follow him in the woods and also so we could find our way back. Most of us have some such system, and it saves a lot of time and trouble."

"Don't tell you where he is, though."

"It will if he doesn't pass out."

"What if nobody ever comes along?"

Orrin merely glanced at him. "A Sackett always knows one of us will be along. He knows that sooner or later a Sackett will find the trail, and if at the end of it he finds a dead man, there will be some indication of who was responsible."

Haney swore softly. "I'll be damned!"

"No, but the man responsible will."

"How long's this been going on?"

"One way or another, for more than two hundred years. Oh, here and there somebody fails, but that's rare. Mostly they come through. Mostly they stick to the family tradition of helping one another.

"Tell started this system, but he had heard of it from pa. That is, he heard of something like it. This was his own idea. It doesn't have to be rocks and grass, it can be twigs, knots tied in grass, leaves, scratches on tree bark—ah!" he pointed.

At the side of a fallen branch was a sharp, triangular piece of slate, pointing off to the northwest.

"Could be an accident," Haney said skeptically.

"It could be. If so, we'll have to come back to this point and start over."

They hurried on, walking faster now. Haney was also alert, watching. It was he who saw the next mark, faint though it was. Simply three scratches on the bark of a tree.

Haney stopped. "Say! Where's Fleming?"

"He went off to the west. We'll find him later."

"I don't trust him too much," Haney said.

"Neither do I."

Orrin stopped abruptly. The tracks of three horsemen came down from the east and crossed the trail of Tyrel Sackett. Three hard-ridden horses, all shod.

"Be careful!" Haney lifted his rifle. "Those tracks are fresh!"

They faded into the brush, took the time to look around carefully, then followed the trail they had found.

Orrin stopped suddenly, studying the terrain ahead. The way seemed to lead along the side of a low hill that sloped down to a lake with a sandy shore. On the side of the hill were several clusters of trees. One of the clusters, a little higher and farther back, grew up among some rocks. There was a clump of brush and smaller trees, then two tall ones joined by a third somewhat smaller but close to the other two.

"We've found him," Orrin said.

Haney just looked, and they rode on, scrambling their horses up the bank to the clump of trees and brush.

They found him there, sprawled on fallen leaves, one hand still clutching a stick he had used to help him along. There was blood on the top of his shoulder near his neck where a bullet had cut through the muscle, and his right leg was swollen to almost twice its normal size. He had split the pants leg to ease the binding effect on the swollen leg, which showed black and blue through the gaping hole.

"Haney," Orrin said, "you ride back to the carts and get a spare horse. Keep your eyes open for Fleming on the way back, and tell the boys to sit tight and guard the cattle. I won't try to move him tonight. Bring the horse up in the morning."

When Haney had ridden off, Orrin cleared a place of leaves, scraping them well back, and then he put together a small fire of twigs and bits of bark. The flame was too small and too well hidden by the trunks of the trees and the brush to be seen. As for the smoke, it would be dissipated by rising through the foliage of the trees until spread so thin as to be invisible.

He made a bed of piled leaves, and with water from his canteen he bathed the wound. It was going to be troublesome but not dangerous, and from past experience he knew the dangers of infection were few in the fresh pure air of the western country.

When he had made Tyrel comfortable, he led his horse to water at the lake, then let him graze on a small patch of grass not far from the cluster of trees where he could watch both the horse and Tyrel. When it started to become dark, he led the horse into the brush, which was some protection from the mosquitoes, and settled down beside his small fire.

It was then he thought to check Tyrel's six-shooter. Four chambers had been fired; two remained loaded. He reloaded the empty chambers and thrust the gun back into its holster.

He might have been shooting to try to turn the stampede; if not, somebody was dead.

Darkness made a mystery of the forest and goblins of the trees.

He added a knot to the coals and dozed with arabesques of shadow-play upon his dark, hawklike features.

A whisper of sound, the faint crunching of a branch, and his eyes opened wide, and his gun slid into his hand. Something black and ominous loomed in the open space between two trees. His gun was up, his thumb ready on the hammer.

It was Tyrel's line-back dun.

Chapter 15

Highpockets Haney reached the group of trees before the first light, but Orrin already had Tyrel on the dun.

"See anybody?"

"Not a soul." He paused. "Fleming was in camp, wondering what had become of us. He brought in two, three head of young stuff he found in the brush."

"No sign of anybody else?"

"He says he saw nothing."

Tyrel was obviously suffering from a mild concussion, and when he became conscious, he showed no disposition to talk. When asked about Tell, he merely shrugged. The stampede had caught them scattered about the herd, and they had remained scattered.

Orrin rode ahead, scouting for trouble. He had a feeling they'd find it before the day was over.

"Shorty's starting the herd," Haney said. "Baptiste and his carts will bring up the drag. We should see them when we come out of the trees." They were skirting a small pond, and Tyrel's horse took a sudden turn, and he groaned.

"He's got a bad leg there," Orrin said. "It doesn't seem to be broken but bruised like you wouldn't believe. Horse must have fallen or something of the kind."

They sighted the herd as they came into the open. Shorty had them moving; Fleming was on the far side with the carts bringing up the rear. Baptiste stopped when he saw them, and with great care they loaded Tyrel into one of the carts, making a place for him among the sacks, his rifle beside him. They tied the dun behind the cart in which he was riding.

Haney fell into place with the herd, and Orrin stayed off to one side, watching the country around for some movement or sign of life. He saw nothing.

Somewhere out there was Tell or what was left of him. Somewhere were other hands, lost in the same stampede. The Ox he could see working alongside the herd, but what had become of *his* partner? The man Orrin had not yet seen?

Uneasily, Orrin rubbed the stubble of beard on his chin. Shaving every day had become a habit, and he had a dislike of going unshaven no matter where he was.

He was reluctant to leave the area without finding Tell, but Tell, had he been present, would have insisted they get on with the job. Wherever he was, if he was alive, Tell was doing what was needful.

Tyrel was sleeping when he rode by the carts, so there was no chance to try to learn more from him even if he knew more, which was doubtful.

Wide rolled the prairies before their roving eyes, and steadily the cattle moved on, pointing the way to the northwest. All day they walked, and the day following and the next. Somewhere, Orrin supposed, they had reached or would reach the border and pass into Canada. There was no marker, and he looked for none.

They camped by small creeks, near a slough, or in some small meadow where the cattle could feed. They saw no Indians and no wildlife but flocks of antelope, always within view, or buffalo. Prairie wolves hung on their flanks, watching for the animal who might trail too far behind.

Ten miles that first day because of the late start, fifteen and sixteen on the days following. On the third day, Tyrel spent part of the day in the saddle. At night, they sat beside the campfire.

"They came right out of the prairie," he explained. "Suddenly, we heard the thunder of hoofs, and they came over the rise like a black thunder cloud.

"We were all scattered out; there was no chance or time to do anything but try to get out of the way, and that's just what we did. The cattle turned ahead of that herd and began to run with them. There was nothing anybody could do, and even the cattle had no choice but to run. Otherwise, they'd have been trampled into the ground. I heard a scream, but, Orrin, I doubt if it was one of our boys. I don't recall anybody being where that scream came from."

"We found some remains, but they were so trampled we could only tell it had been a man and more than likely a white man."

"I doubt if he was one of ours. Brandy was within sight when the buffalo came into sight, and I had time to wave him out of there. Lin— he was our Chinese cook—he was out behind the herd somewhere, and I think it missed him altogether."

"Who shot you?"

"That happened later. There were three of them, and they were hunting me, or maybe just any survivors.

"A big buffalo bull tossed the dun and me, and when we went down, he came in with his head down to gore us. He hooked, but his horn hit my saddle and so saved the dun. Then I stuck my six-shooter in his ear and squeezed her off.

"That bull just naturally rolled over, and the dun scrambled up, and I started to. Seemed that buffalo bull rammed his head into my leg just about the time I was sticking my gun barrel in his ear.

"I got the dun over to me and grabbed a stirrup and pulled myself up. By that time my leg was hurting.

"Well, I taken a look around. The cattle were scattered to kingdom come, and there was nobody in sight but some buzzards."

Tyrel refilled his cup. "Being one who is apt to accept the situation and take it from there, I considered.

"Here I was out in the middle of nowhere and maybe the only one left alive. You were on a steamboat or maybe in a cart coming west. I had me a good horse, although he was some irritated at being knocked over, and I had fifteen hundred pounds of buffalo meat, hide, and bone.

"So I gathered me some buffalo chips and put together a fire. Then I cut out some buffalo steak and broiled about four or five pounds of it. When that was done, I cut myself some more meat, tied it up in some buffalo hide, and climbed into the saddle.

"It was when I tried to get into the saddle that I realized I was in trouble. It durned near killed me."

"You ain't told me about those empty chambers."

"Comin' to it. I'd ridden a far piece, but my leg was givin' me what for, and I rode in under the trees, grabbed hold of a limb, and pulled myself up from the saddle and then kind of lowered myself down to the ground.

"Next thing I knew, they come up on me. I was backed up to a tree, and the dun had walked off, grazin', and there was three of them. Right away I spotted them for what they were. They were goin' to kill me, all right, but first they were going to tell me how awful mean and tough they were.

"You know the kind. We've met them before. They were talkers.

They just had to run off at the mouth awhile before they did anything.

"There were three of them, and they didn't know me from Adam's off-ox. They knew I had been with the cattle and contrary to what we'd figured, it had been them who started the stampede and not the Sioux.

"They started tellin' me about it. And they started to tell me what they were going to do.

"Me, I listened to them a mite, and then I said, 'What did you fellows come up here for?'

"'We're goin' to kill you!' This big redhead was saying that, with a nasty grin on his face.

"'So you're going to kill me? Then what the hell is all the talk for?'

"That kind of took the wind out of them, and as I spoke, I just fetched my piece.

"Didn't seem to me like they'd ever seen a fast draw before. Two of them went down, and the third one taken off, or maybe his horse ran off with him. Anyway, you couldn't see him for dust."

"And you saw nothing of Tell?"

Tyrel shook his head. He was obviously tired, and Orrin asked no more questions. The night was quiet, and the herd had bedded down.

Baptiste had added to his duties the care of Tyrel's injured leg. The flesh wound gave no particular trouble, and with Baptiste caring for it, the swelling in the leg reduced slowly.

Orrin forded the cattle across the Mouse and pointed the herd toward Pipestone Creek, some distance off to the northwest by the route they were following.

"We've got to figure it this way," Orrin said over a campfire. "The stampede was not caused by Indians but apparently by white men.

"Now who would want to do such a thing? Thieves who wished to steal our cattle? Maybe. Some of the 'Higginses' Logan spoke about? That's more likely.

"Somebody, for some reason we do not know, wishes to prevent our cattle from reaching their destination. So far they've done us some damage, but they haven't stopped us, so it's likely they will try again.

"From what Tyrel says, at least two of them won't be showing up again. That may make them back off completely, but we can't depend on that. We will have to take it for granted they will come again, and soon.

"We've got some extra rifles. I want them loaded and ready, and every camp must be a fort."

Orrin glanced over at the Ox, who was simply listening and offering no comment or even an acknowledgement that he heard.

Yet, in the days that followed, all their preparations seemed for nothing. The mornings came one after another, each crisp and clear, and the days warmed. The grass was green on all the hills now. There were several light showers and a thunderstorm that brought a crashing downpour that lasted for less than an hour.

The Qu'Appelle River lay somewhere before them and off to the west the Moose Mountains.

Orrin found himself thinking of Nettie. She should be well on her way to Fort Carlton now, far away to the north. He would probably not see her again. The thought made him melancholy, yet there was nothing to be done. Their way lay west, and if Tell were alive, he would be coming on to join them if by some chance he was not already there before them.

Occasionally, they saw the bones of buffalo, once the antlers of a deer. Occasionally, there were other bones, unfamiliar to a quick glance, but there was no time to pause and examine them. They pushed on, accompanied by the creaking, groaning wheels of the Red River carts.

Tyrel's bruised leg remained sore and stiff, but his flesh wound healed rapidly, as wounds usually did on the plains and in the mountains. He took to riding a little more each day, usually scouting wide of the drive and only returning to it occasionally.

"Something's not right," he commented once. "I can smell trouble."

"The Ox is worried," Orrin added. "He's got something on his mind. That partner of his, I guess. Gilcrist, his name was. Or so he said."

"Good a name as any," Tyrel said. "Out here, if a man doesn't like his name, he can choose his own, and a lot of folks have."

"He never talks to Fleming," Orrin said. "At least, I haven't seen them even near one another for days."

A brief but violent thunderstorm came with the afternoon. Fort Qu'Appelle was nearby, but there was no need to stop, and when the storm passed, he led the drive on past the fort. However, he had gone but a mile or less when a party of riders appeared. Several Indians, Crees by the look of them, rode up. While the cattle moved on, Orrin waited with Baptiste and the carts.

The Indians were friendly, curious as to where the cattle were being taken and about the Sioux, with whom they were only occasionally friendly.

Tyrel rode to meet them when they finally caught up.

"Picked up some sign," he said. "Something you should see, Orrin."

"Trouble?"

"Maybe."

Orrin glanced at the sun. "We've got a few miles of driving ahead of us. All right, let's go look!"

The tracks were two miles ahead of the herd. At least five riders had come up from the southwest and had met a half-dozen riders coming down from the northeast. They had dismounted, built a small fire, and made coffee. The coffee grounds had been thrown out when they emptied their pot for packing.

"Maybe a dozen men riding well-shod horses," Tyrel said, "and they rode off to the west together."

Orrin nodded. He had been poking around the campfire and looking at tracks.

"Just for luck, Tye," he said, "let's turn due north for a spell."

"Toward Fort Carlton?" Tyrel asked, his eyes too innocent.

Orrin flushed. "Well, it seems a good idea."

Chapter 16

When first it come to me that I was alive, I was moving. For what seemed a long time, I lay there with my eyes closed and just feeling the comfort of lying still. Then I tried to move, and everything hurt, and I mean everything.

Then I got to wondering where I was and what was moving me and what was I doing flat on my back when there was work to be done?

When I tried to move my right arm, I could, and my hand felt for my gun, and it was gone. So was my gun belt and holster. Yet I wasn't tied down, so it must be that I was with friendly folks. About that time, I realized I was riding on a travois pulled behind an Indian pony.

After a bit, I closed my eyes and I must have passed out again because the next thing I knew we were standing still. I was lying flat out on the ground, and I could hear a fire crackling and smell meat broiling.   .

Now when a body has been around as long as me, he collects a memory for smells, and the smells told me even without opening my eyes that I was in an Indian camp.

About that time, an Indian came over to me, and he saw my eyes were open, and he said something in an Indian dialect I hadn't heard before, and an Indian woman came over to look at me. I tried to sit up, and although it hurt like hell, I managed it. Didn't seem I had any broken bones, but I was likely bruised head to foot, which can be even more painful sometimes.

She brought me a bowl with some broth in it, and whatever else was wrong with me hadn't hurt my appetite. The man who had found me awake was a young man, strongly made but limping.

A youngster, walking about, came over and stared at me with big round eyes, and I smiled at him. When I had put away two bowls of broth, an old Indian came to me with my gun belt and holster. My six-shooter was in it, and he handed it to me. First thing, I checked the loads, and they were there.

The old man squatted beside me. "Much cows, all gone," he said. He gestured to show they'd scattered every which way.

"Men?" I asked.

He shrugged and pointed across the way, and I saw another man lying on the ground a dozen feet away. I raised up a bit and looked. It was Lin, the Chinese cook.

"How bad?"

"Much bad. Much hurt." He looked over at Lin and then said, "White man?"

"Chinese," I said.

The word meant nothing to him, so I drew a diagram in the dust, showing where we now were, the south Saskatchewan and the mountains of British Columbia. That he grasped quickly. Then I made a space and said, "Much water." Beyond it, I drew a coast and indicated China. "His home," I said.

He studied it, then indicated British Columbia and drew his eyes thin to seem like Lin's. "Indian," he said, "here."

It was true. A long time since I had been told by a man in the Sixth Cavalry that some of the Indians from the northwest coast had eyes like the Chinese.

After a while, I went to sleep and was only awakened when they were ready to offer me food; it was daybreak.

The young Indian who had been wounded and on the travois when first we encountered them carried a rifle of British make. The older men were armed only with bows. We were heading northwest, but I asked no questions, being content to just lie and rest. What had happened to me, I did not know, but I suspected a mild concussion and that I had fallen and been dragged. My shoulders were raw, I discovered, and had been treated with some herbs by a squaw.

On the following day, I got up and could move around. Then one old Indian, who seemed to be in authority if anyone was, showed me my saddle, bridle, saddlebags, and rifle, carefully cared for on another travois. I left the riding gear where it was but took up the rifle, at which the old man showed approval. Seemed to me they expected grief and were glad to have another fighting man on his feet.

Lin had a broken leg. He was skinned up and bruised not unlike what happened to me, but he had the busted leg to boot. They'd set the bone, put splints on the leg, and bound it up with wet rawhide, which had dried and shrunk tight around the leg.

"Where are the others?"

I walked beside him as we moved. "No tellin'. Dead, maybe. Scattered to the winds, maybe. All you've got to do is get well."

Well, I was a long way from being a well man. Before the day was over, I was so tired I could scarce drag. They made camp in a tree-lined hollow with a small waterhole and a bunch of poplars.

We'd lost all track of time, Lin an' me. We'd both been unconscious, and we didn't know how long. I'd no idea what had become of my horse or the remuda stock we had, and we'd lost all our cattle.

Only thing I could say for us was that we were headin' in the right direction and we were alive.

What I needed was a horse. This was the first time I'd been caught afoot in a long time, and I didn't like it. I should be scouting the country, hunting for Tyrel and roundin' up cows.

Lin was feeling better. As for me, I limped along with a head aching something fierce and a disposition that would frighten a grizzly. Not that I let those Indian folks see it, but, believe me, I was sore.

Meanwhile, a way out in the western mountains, Logan was in trouble and wishful of our coming.

As to Tyrel, he might be killed dead, but I misdoubted that. Tyrel was just too downright ornery to be killed that easy. If he ever went down to death, there'd be bodies stacked all about, you could bet on that.

One thing about a Sackett, he finishes what he starts if it is a good thing to start. All of us knew that whatever else was happening, we'd be pushing on west. West was where I was going, and if I arrived there with no cows, I'd round up a buffalo herd and drive it in, or try.

If that failed, I'd have to get a rattlesnake for a whip and drive a flock of grizzlies. Right now I was mad enough to do it.

It so happened that at the time of the stampede these Indians were a way off to one side where they'd had to go to camp on water. The stampede went right by, an easy half mile off.

"Where do you go?" I asked the old man.

He gestured to the northwest. They were going back to some place; that was all I could gather. His English was limited, and I spoke none of the Indian tongues that made sense to him. It was a rare thing to find an Indian who spoke any language but his own, although some had picked up some French or English because of trade.

Their direction was our direction, so we stayed with them. Besides, they needed us. The young warrior was still not able to travel far when hunting, and neither of the old men had much luck with hunting. Their food was mostly small game or roots picked hither and yon.

The meat I'd left them had been a godsend.

Soon as I was fit, I scouted around some of an evening. First evening I had no luck; never even saw anything worth shooting until the second day when I spotted a buffalo calf.

It was a week before Lin could walk, even a little, and by that time we'd traveled most of a hundred miles. It was that night by the fire that Little Bear came to me. He was the youngster walking about, and me and him had talked a good deal, neither understanding too much except that we liked one another.

He had been out setting snares, and he came to me by the fire. "A horse!" he said.

"That's it, son. That's what I need."

He pointed off to the east. "A horse!" he repeated.

"You mean you've seen a horse?"

When he said yes, I went to my saddle and took my rope from it. "You show me," I said.

Our horses had been scattered when the stampede took place, and it might just be one of our own. Not that it would be any easier to catch.

We walked maybe a mile, and he pointed. Sure enough, feeding along the shadow of some poplars was a dun horse.

Now Tyrel and me, we both rode line-back duns, probably get of the same sire, as we'd caught them out of a wild bunch who ran with a powerful old dun stallion. The stallion was no horse to catch. He'd run wild too long; he was too strong and too mean. A horse like that will never stop fighting, and he'll either kill somebody or himself.

At that distance, I couldn't make out whether that was Tyrel's dun or mine. But he'd been riding his when the stampede hit us, so this one must be mine. There was a shadow from the trees, or I might have guessed which one it was.

Anyway, we moved toward him.

His head came up sharp, and he looked at me with ears pricked and he let me come on.

When I was within fifty yards, he shied away a mite, but he didn't run, and I called to him. He walked toward me then, and I rubbed his neck a little, and he seemed glad to be back with folks again. I rigged a hackamore and led him back to camp. Next morning, when we started out, I was in the saddle and felt like a whole man again.

The wind began to pick up, the grass bending before it, and I was scouting ahead looking for game when I came on some tracks.

Little Bear looked at them and pointed toward the direction they'd taken. "You cattle," he said. "Two mans!"

Maybe thirty head of cattle and two riders, and we set off after them.

We found them bedded down near a slough alongside a capful of fire with some meat broiling.

"'Light an' set!" Cap said, like he'd seen me only that morning. "Brandy an' me got a few of your cows."

It was good to see them. They had six horses, two of them strange, wearing a Lazy Y brand.

"You don't look the worse for wear," I said.

"Pure-dee luck! We was out in front, and we run for it. We had fast horses, an' after a mile or two, we managed to cut away to the side. Seen anybody else?"

"Lin's alive. He's with the Indians."

Little Bear rode off to get his people, and we set by the fire explainin' to each other what happened.

"All we can do," I said, "is head north to meet Orrin. He'll have grub, and if there's anybody else alive, they'll come to that rendezvous."

"That's how I figured it." Cap glanced over at me. "You see the tracks? It wasn't Sioux."

"We know."

"I wonder what Logan's tied into, anyway?"

The smell of the wood fire was almighty nice, and I felt right just having a horse again. I've spent so much time sittin' on the hurricane deck of a horse that I ain't at home anywhere else.

Little Bear's folks came in shy of midnight, and we all bedded down close together, with Cap, Brandy, an' me sharin' time with the cows.

Cap an' Brandy were sure enough hungry. They'd been eatin' squirrel, rabbit, and skunk most of the time since the stampede, when they ate anything at all.

"There's hills up ahead," Cap said. "Maybe we'll run into Orrin an' his carts. Those are the Thunder Breeding Hills. If he didn't find anything west of the Turtles, he'd keep on west, wouldn't he?"

"He would. Or I think he would."

Yet I was worried. We were a long way from the mines, we had only thirty head or so, we were short on riding stock, and we had no grub or ammunition. We'd lost the biggest part of our outfit, and we were riding strange country.

There were Sioux around, and there were the white renegades who'd attacked before. Yet it felt good to be back with Cap. Brandy and Lin were new men, but Cap I knew from way back. Any kind of a stir-up, be it work or fight, Cap would stand his ground.

The cattle had lost weight. A stampede can run a good many pounds off a critter, and these had been driven hard since.

The way we drove them was across a prairie with islands of brush and occasional swamps. Time or two we had to stop and rope some old mossyhorn out of the bog. Those islands of brush worried me because a body could get close to a man before he realized. And they did.

All of a sudden, Cap ups with his hand and outs with his Winchester, and we saw three men ride into view from behind a clump of brush.

I had no idea who they were but had a mighty good idea they weren't friendly.

Chapter 17

The sun lay bright upon the land ahead and bright upon the three horsemen who rode to meet us.

Cap glanced around. "Good boy," he said. "Brandy's facin' the other way. So's Lin."

The Indians were behind us and to the right, concealed from the riders by the brush.

"There will be more of them," Cap said.

"There will," I agreed, and glanced at the small lake that lay ahead and to the right. It was likely they would attack from the left and try to drive us toward the lake. The three riders were too obvious.

"Howdy, boys! Huntin' for something?"

"Lookin' to buy cattle." The speaker was a big, bearded man in a buckskin coat worked with blue and red beads. He had a rifle in his hand and a fur cap.

"Sorry. These are not for sale."

"Make you a good offer?" His horse was sidling around, and I saw him throw a quick glance toward left rear.

"Not for sale, boys," I said. I rode out from the herd a little and toward the right, outflanking them a little, and I could see they didn't like it.

Cap had promptly shifted a little to the left, and I said, "Better move, boys. We're coming through!"

"Sell 'em," the big man repeated, "or we'll take them!"

"All right, *Brandy!*" I yelled, and he let out a whoop and started the cattle.

They were headed that way, and cattle like to go where they're pointed, so they started moving. Brandy let out another whoop, and one of the steers turned right at the nearest horseman.

The sudden rush of cattle split the three riders. Two went one way and one the other, and the nearest one was coming my way, so I headed right at him. In trying to swing wide of a head-on collision, he put his horse into the soft ground at the lake's edge, and his horse floundered in the mud, his rider swearing.

Wheeling the dun, I raced along the flank of the moving cattle, heard two quick shots from behind, and saw Lin on the ground, his horse beside him; he was shooting across a fallen log.

A half-dozen riders had come from behind one of those clumps of brush, and Lin, being on the ground, had the advantage.

I saw a horse stumble and go down, pitching his rider over his head. Mud leaped in front of another rider, and his horse swerved sharply, and a third bullet had him dropping his rifle and grabbing for a mane hold as his horse went charging away, cutting across the front of the other riders.

It all happened in seconds. Two men were down, a horse running wild and the cattle charging. The big man with the beard threw up his rifle to shoot at me, but Cap burned him with a quick shot, and my bullet burned his hand. What other damage it did, I couldn't see, but I did see a splash of blood on the buckskin coat and on the saddle.

Lin was back in the saddle and riding up the flank of the small herd, and we swung the cattle past the lake and into the open toward some sand hills looming ahead.

Brandy closed in behind the herd, and we moved them out of there.

Cap Rountree closed in toward me. "Pilgrims," he said contemptuously. "They haven't burned the powder we have."

"We were lucky. Next time, we may not get the breaks."

We pushed the cattle on, keeping a lookout on all sides. What Cap said was obviously true. The men who had attacked us were tough men and hard but not seasoned fighting men.

Any man can take a gun in hand and go out to use it, and often enough he is braver because of that gun. But fighting is like playing poker. You have to pay to learn, and you only learn with the cards in hand and money on the table. Cap and me, well, we had been through more fights in any one year of our lives than most men get in a lifetime.

Me? Well, I'd been fightin' one way or another all my life. Cap had begun as a mountain man, and he'd fought Sioux, Cheyenne, Blackfeet, Comanches, Kiowas, and Apaches, and he still had his hair.

"That youngster," Cap said, "he'll do to take along. He was almighty cool."

"So was Lin," I added. "Don't discount that heathen Chinee."

"Heathen? Hell!" Cap spat. "He knows more than both of us. Why we was talkin' the other night, and he come up with some of the damndest stuff you ever heard!"

We were not through with fighting, and we knew it, so we moved the cattle along faster than we should have to keep the weight on them. We wanted to get to some place where we could make a stand. We'd got by them, but they still outnumbered us, and we could expect trouble.

"Maybe we should take it to them," Cap suggested. "Discourage them. I'm a pretty good horse thief when need be."

"Good idea," I suggested, "but let's try for distance."

"How you fixed for ca'tridges?"

"Short," I said. "We've got to avoid a fight if we can."

"Wished Orrin would show up."

"Or Tyrel and the boys with those packhorses. We're going to need them, Cap. Need them bad."

Spotting a long, sandy draw, I turned the herd down it, as the sand was deep and left few tracks. There was small hope that it would help, but we needed every advantage.

Toward nightfall, we turned up another draw, crossed a gravely hill, and camped on a knoll close to a small grove. We built our fire for coffee inside the grove where the glow of the fire was hidden. The cattle, exhausted from the drive, grazed only a little before lying down.

"One man on guard," I said. "We all need rest. Stay on the ground and don't skyline yourself."

After they were settled and we had eaten, I walked out from the camp. Nothing could be seen but the darkness of the trees and brush. The cattle merged with the darkness.

While the others slept, I took count as well as I could without disturbing them. I could see fourteen cartridges in Cap's belt, eight in Brandy's. Lin had no belt but might have some in his pockets. How many were in their rifles I could not guess. My rifle was fully loaded as was my six-shooter. Nine bullets remained in my belt. We'd be lucky to survive any kind of an Indian fight or any other.

Shortly before daybreak, we drove off the hill, found a small stream, and walked the cattle in the water for over a mile. That such tactics would delay them more than a little was unlikely, yet at least some of the attackers had been greenhorns.

Who, then, were they? There had been no attempt of which I knew to steal our cattle. They seemed more interested in stopping or delaying us.

Leaving the water, we found where a herd of buffalo had passed and followed in their tracks, losing our trail in theirs.

We watered that night in the Qu'Appelle River. It had been named, so we heard, because an Indian, dropping down the river in a canoe, thought he heard a call from the bank. He waited, listening, then called out himself. There was no reply, so he went on, but since then it has been the Who Calls River. At least that was the story Kootenai Brown told me one night by the fire.

Cap and me looked for cart tracks but found none. There could be other carts, of course, but we knew ours had not passed.

We crossed the river where there were no bluffs and bedded our few cattle on the far bank. It was not a good place, and Cap grumbled a good bit.

Wolves prowled close around the camp, and we did not wish to attract attention by firing a shot. Several times, we took flaming sticks from the fire and charged at them, but they soon came back.

Between mosquitoes, sand flies, and wolves, we had little sleep. When morning came, I was up early and in a bad mood. There was little to eat, and nobody talked much.

There was crisp grass and sand with occasional swamps. Several times steers went into the swamps to escape the flies, and we had to throw a loop around their horns and drag them out. It made nobody any happier. By the time nightfall arrived, I was almost hoping for a fight, being that irritable.

Yet it was pretty country. There were bluebells and wild roses everywhere and a few small tiger lilies growing here and there. At one place, we came upon acres of bluebells.

In camp, Brandy sat opposite me nursing a cup of coffee, one of the last we'd have if Orrin didn't find us.

"What month is it?" Brandy said. "I lost track of the days. Now I'm not even sure of the month."

"June," I replied, and the thought made me no happier. Time was a getting on, and we'd a far piece to go before snow fell, and at the end we had to find our way through mountains we didn't know and where trails were, we had heard, mighty few.

Looking at the cattle gave me no pleasure. They'd started out in fine shape, but due to long drives and the necessity to keep moving, they'd lost weight.

We had seen no buffalo or even an antelope for days. "We can always kill a beef," Cap suggested.

"We may have to," I said.

Come to think of it, Cap was looking gaunt himself, and Brandy, too. Lin, he never seemed to change, grub or no. His leg, despite the fall, was better.

"We'll lay up tomorrow," I suggested. "Maybe we can catch us a mess of fish."

The horses, too, were in bad shape. The rest, little as it was, would do them good, and they did not have to worry about food. There was grass enough to pasture half the stock in Canada.

It was almighty hot. We let the stock feed, and we let them drink. When we moved on, there was going to be none too much water.

Cap was the fisherman amongst us. Him and Lin. Both of them caught a mess of fish, but Brandy and me couldn't catch cold.

We had fish for supper, and we had fish for breakfast, and nothing tasted any better, seasoned a mite with wild garlic.

We were riding out to start the cattle when I saw our Indian friends. One of them rode up to where we were with a chunk of fresh venison. We took a look at each other and got down from the saddle and broiled and ate it right on the spot.

Little Bear waited, and then he said, "White man comes."

"A white man? Where?"

"I see him, alone."

Something about his manner bothered me. It seemed he wanted to tell me more than he knew how, but he just said, "He ride here."

"You mean he's coming here?"

"He comes here. He rides here."

Cap got up and wiped his hands on his chaps. "I think he's tryin' to tell you this gent rides for you."

We looked back toward the river. "Let him come on," I said. "We've miles to go."

We started them out and hadn't gone fifty yards when we saw a lone buffalo calf. When he saw us, he bawled.

"Lost his ma," Cap said. "Shall we take him along?"

"Why not?"

Cap rode wide and started the calf toward the herd. He did not take to being driven, but the herd had its attractions. Finally, he galloped off and joined the cattle.

We were a good half mile into the sand hills under a blistering sun when the rider caught up with us. We heard him coming, and I turned in the saddle.

"Well," Cap said, "we can use every hand we can get."

He should have been having a hard time of it, but he didn't look like hard times. He looked fat and sassy like he'd been eating mighty well. He rode up and said, "Howdy! I've missed you boys!"

It was Gilcrist.

Chapter 18

"You come out alive," Gilcrist said.

"All of us," I said. "Where've you been?"

"Huntin' for you. Livin' off the country."

"Must've been good country," Cap commented.

Gilcrist turned sharply, but Cap's features were bland and innocent. Gilcrist turned back to me. "Lost some cattle, I see. Ain't much use in goin' on with this little bunch."

"Beef is beef," I said. "I never knew a mining camp to turn down good beef cattle."

He started to speak, then changed his mind. He turned his mount to ride away, and I watched him drop back to where Lin was riding.

"Notice that?" I said to Cap. "He never asked about the Ox. You'd think a man would at least want to know what happened to his partner."

"Maybe he knows," Cap commented. "Maybe he knows just a whole lot that we don't. If that man's been livin' off the country, he's the luckiest hunter I ever did see."

They rode on for a short distance, and Cap said, "He's right about the cattle, though. What are all of us doin' drivin' this little ol' bunch of cows? Even sayin' they need beef, this is a mighty small bunch."

"We taken a contract to deliver beef," I said, "and we're going to deliver beef if there's only one cow left when we get there, but I've a hunch we'll have a sight more.

"Where's Tyrel? Where's Orrin? Those boys are somewhere, and if they're alive, they'll have some stock. I'd bet on it.

"Orrin now, he's turned lawyer, but he can still read more'n law books. He can read sign. He's comin' along a trail where he knows we're supposed to be. He's going to be lookin' for sign, and he will learn as much from what he doesn't see as what he does. If he doesn't find cattle sign where he expects to find it, he will start hunting for it.

"Orrin's a good hand on a trail, and he will know as much of what happened as if we'd left a written-out guide for him.

"What we've got to study on is what's wrong at the other end? What happened to Logan? Why can't he help himself? Who's threatening to hang him? What's he need the cattle for?"

"Seems plain enough," Cap said. "If he can't help himself, he must be sick, hurt, or in jail. Knowin' something of Logan, I'd say he's in jail. He's too mean and tough to be hurt."

"You may be right. Some of those Clinch Mountain boys are rough. Nice folks, but don't start nothing unless you want trouble."

"What's he need the cattle for?"

"God only knows! The folks up there need them for beef, that's plain enough. They've probably hunted the country until all the game's been killed off or fled, and minin' men have to eat."

"You thought about gettin' cattle in over the trails?" Cap asked. "You an' me, we've covered some rough country, but mostly we just walked or rode over it. We never tried to move no cattle along those trails.

"There's trails up yonder where if a man makes a misstep, he can fall for half a mile. Same thing goes for a cow."

We were in the sand hills now, and water was scarce. Somewhere ahead of us was the elbow of the Saskatchewan or what the Indians called "The River That Turns." The cattle began to labor to get through the sand; at times, some of them stopped, ready to give up. We found no water, and the heat was almost unbearable.

Cap came to me, mopping his brow. "We got to find water, Tell. We've got too few horses, and they're about played out. On a drive like this, we should have three or four horses per man, at least."

"I wish we had them."

All day they struggled through the sand hills, and only as dark was closing in did they find a small lake that was not brackish. Many of the cattle walked belly deep in the water to drink.

Lin had a fire going when they bunched the cattle on a nearby flat. Leaving Cap and Brandy with the cattle, I headed in for camp with Gilcrist riding along. The boys had done a great job with the cattle, and they deserved credit. Even Gilcrist had done his part, and I said so.

He glanced at me. "Didn't know you noticed."

"I don't miss much," I said. "You did your share."

"You've got some good hands."

"Cap's worth two of any of the rest of us. He's forgotten more than the rest of us will ever know."

They were pulling up at camp, and as I swung down, Gilcrist asked, "You serious about goin' all the way through?"

"Never more serious."

"You'll never make it, Sackett. Nobody's ever taken cattle into that country. Nobody can."

A moment there, I stopped, my hands on the saddle, and I looked across it at him. "There's some folks who hope we won't make it, and they want to keep us from making it, but they don't know what they're up against."

"Maybe you don't."

"We had a run-in with some of that outfit. Let me tell you something, Gilcrist. If they want to stop us, they ought to stop sending a bunch of tenderfeet to do it. Just because a man can shoot, it doesn't turn him into a fightin' man. If we had started to fight back, there wouldn't be a man of that bunch alive. It scares me to think what would happen if that bunch of thugs happened to run into a war party of Blackfeet!"

Gilcrist dismounted. He started to speak, then changed his mind. Walking along, I picked up sticks for the fire, then walked around gathering what fuel I could.

Lin glanced at me when I dropped the fuel. "The Indian boy came in. He says there is somebody following us. A big outfit."

Lin was picking up the western lingo. He started slicing meat into a pan for frying, and he said, "The Indians had not seen the outfit, just heard them and seen their dust."

"Dust?"

"A lot of it."

Gilcrist came in and sat down. "You say somebody was coming?"

"Indians," I told him. "Somebody saw some Indians."

I surely wasn't lying about that. How much he'd heard, I didn't know. Soon the boys started coming in.

Gilcrist was looking across the fire at me. "I'd no idea you were the Sackett who rode with the Sixth. They used to say you were good with a gun."

"You hear all sorts of stories."

Cap spat into the fire. "Them ain't stories. You can take it from me, Gil, an' I've seen 'em all! There ain't anybody who is any better!"

Gilcrist started to speak, stopped, then said, "You ain't seen 'em all. You ain't seen me."

"I hope I never do," Cap said dryly.

Gilcrist stared at him. "I don't know how to take that."

Cap smiled. "I just hate to see a man get killed," he said. "You or anybody else."

"I ain't goin' to get killed."

Cap smiled again. "I helped bury twenty men who thought the same thing."

It was a quiet night. We ate and turned in, all of us dog tired. The stars were out, bright as lanterns in the sky, but nobody stayed awake long. Those days, when a man works from can see to can't see, he just naturally passes out when he hits the bed. It was long days of hard work and no chance for daydreaming when the cattle were dry and wanting water.

Only Cap and me, we set late by the fire. I was thinking of what was to come. As for him, I didn't know what he was thinking about. Or didn't until he said, "You want me to ride back and see who that is? It may be trouble."

"Not you. Anybody but you. A body can always find another cowhand but a good cook? No way you can find another cook without a miracle."

There was a-plenty to consider. We were down to our last coffee, and as for other grub, we'd been making do on what we could rustle for days. Looked to me like we would have to strike north for Fort Carlton and lay in a stock of grub. It was going to throw us back, but I saw no way out of it.

Carlton was due north. Thinking of that, I wondered, but not aloud, about trying to go west from there. Traveling in strange country like this, where I knew nothing of the rivers. If there was a practical route west from Fort Carlton, we might lose no time at all.

"All right," I said to Cap, "we'll swing north."

"You want I should have a look at who that is comin' up the line?"

"I'll go."

"You're tired, man. You need rest."

"Why, you old buffalo chaser, you say I'm tired? What about you?"

"You lose me, you ain't lost much. You get lost, and we're all up the creek."

Well, I got up and roped me a horse. "Stand by for trouble, Cap," I told him. "I think we've got it coming."

With that I rode off west. It was dark when I started, but that was a good night horse I had between my knees, and we found a trail that left the creek and went up on the bluffs. Off to the east, I spotted a campfire.

Down a trail through the forest, winding down where darkness was, winding among the silent trees. Only the hoof falls of my horse, only the soft whispering of night creatures moving. Now I was riding where danger might be. I was riding where a man's life might hang in the wind, ready to be blown away by the slightest chance, yet I will not lie and say I did not like it.

That horse was easy in the night, moving like a cat on dainty feet. He knew we were riding into something, he knew there might be the smell of gunpowder, but he liked it, too. You could sense it in the way he moved. A man riding the same horse a lot comes to know his feelings and ways, for no two are alike, and I was one to make companions of my horses, and they seemed to understand. They knew we were in this together.

Time and again, I drew up to listen. A man can't ride careless into wild country. The banks of the river had an easier slope below the elbow, and some grassy tongues of land pushed into the river. There was a rustling of water along the banks and a dampness in the air near the river. My horse pricked his ears, and we walked slowly forward. I heard no unnatural sound, smelled nothing until I caught a faint smell of wood smoke, and then a moment later an animal smell.

Cattle! I drew up again. There was much brush, almost as high as my head, but scattered. Suddenly, sensing something near, I drew rein again.

There were cattle near, and a large herd. I could smell them and hear the faint sounds a herd will make at night, the soft moanings, shiftings, click of horn against horn when lying close, and the gruntings as one rose to stretch.

Well, right then I had me a healthy hunch, but what I wanted was to locate the fire. I reined my horse over and rode him around a bush, speaking softly so's not to startle the cattle, which, after all, were longhorns and wild animals by anybody's figuring.

The fire was off across the herd, and I glimpsed a faint glow on the side of some leaves over yonder, on a tree trunk. So I let my horse fall into the rhythm of walking around the herd, just as if we were riding night herd ourselves, which we'd done often enough.

From the way my horse acted, I didn't figure these were strange cattle, so when I saw the fire ahead, I rode over and let my horse walk up quiet.

Tyrel, he was a-settin' by the fire, and he never even raised up his head. He just said, "Get down, Tell, we've been a-missin' you."

So I got down and shook his hand, and we Sacketts was together again.

Chapter 19

"**Y**ou got yourself some cows," I said.

"Seems as though. We've had some losses. Right now we're a few shy of having nine hundred head. We lost cattle in the stampede, and we lost a few head in the sand hills. All of them are worn down and beat."

"We've got thirty-two head, last count," I told him. Then I asked, "How you fixed for grub?"

"A-plenty. Orrin came along with his carts. Trouble was we underguessetimated the size of the carts and the appetites of the boys. We'd about decided to go into Fort Carlton to take on more grub."

"Suits me. We've been wishful for coffee the last couple of days, and as for grub, we've been fixin' to chaw rawhide."

"Come daylight," Tyrel said, "we'll move the herd on some fresh grass and go into camp. Give you boys a chance to catch up on your eating."

"How you fixed on ammunition? We've been ridin' scared of a fight."

"We've enough."

The coffee tasted good. We sat by the fire, comparing what had happened to each of us, and we studied some about what Logan's trouble could be.

"Whoever it is that wants our hides," Tyrel said, "is from below the border. At least, those I've talked to. Looks to me like ol' Logan stumbled into something and he's thrown or is about to throw some trouble their way."

When I finished my coffee, I went to my horse and mounted up.

We'd picked a place for meeting that he'd scouted the day before, and I rode back to our camp.

Brandy was standing guard, and I told him of the morning move. "All quiet here," he said. Then he said, "Mr. Sackett? I ain't been punchin' cows long, but there's something that puzzles me. Most of what we've got here are steers, so why do you call them cows?"

"Just a manner of speaking, Brandy. Lots of places you never hear cattle called anything else but cows."

Well, I went in and bedded down, resting easy for the first time in days. Tyrel and Orrin were alive and close by, and tomorrow we'd join up with them. Most of my years I'd lived alone and rode alone; even when I was with other folks, I was usually a man alone. Now my brothers were close by, and it was a comfort.

They'd come a long way. Tyrel had married well and had him a nice ranch.

Orrin's marriage hadn't worked out, but he had studied law, been admitted to the bar, and had been making a name for himself in politics. He was the best educated of us all, and he'd never let up on learning.

We bunched our cattle on a flat among some low hills, and our boys all got together. I noticed Gilcrist had headed for the Ox as soon as the two outfits stopped, and they had them a long talk. Fleming rode nearby a couple of times but did not stop, yet I had an idea they spoke to him.

We started on at daybreak and pushed the cattle at their usual gait. For the first couple of hours, we let them take their time, kind of spread out and grazing; then we moved them along at a steady gait until noontime.

We rested them at noon while we took our turn at coffee and some beef; then we started again with two to three hours of grazing and two to three hours of steady travel until we bedded them down. Driving that way was good for twelve miles a day or better, and we could still keep them in good shape. Naturally, we varied the drives and the grazing in relation to the grass and water.

Me, I was worried. It was unlikely whoever wanted us stopped was going to give up, and the chances were we'd find some tougher men next time.

Also, the country ahead, according to old Baptiste, who had covered it, was rougher and wilder. So far, we had seen few Indians and had no trouble since our meeting with High-Backed Bull, far away in Dakota.

Yet Indians know no borders and roamed where they would, although each tribe had an area it conceived as its own hunting grounds until pushed out by some stronger tribe.

Fort Carlton, or as some termed it, Carlton House, was several days to the north. Leaving there, we must strike westward for the mountains, moving as rapidly as possible considering the condition of the cattle. All this had once been known as Prince Rupert's Land, a vast and beautiful area now in dispute because of Louis Riel's move to set up a provisional government.

We knew little or nothing of the dispute, having learned but the barest details, and had no wish to become involved in something that was clearly none of our business. We had heard there were a few Americans, and no doubt some Canadians as well, hungry for land for themselves or land to sell, who hoped to somehow profit from depriving the *métis* of their lands.

Lin was now the cook, and Baptiste handled the carts and helped with the cooking.

"Have care!" he warned me. "Blackfeet and Cree are fighting, and this is the way they come! They will steal your horses!"

It was a good warning, and we took care, for we had too few horses as it was. We hoped to get more at Carlton, but Baptiste shook his head to indicate doubt.

"Few horse! Many no good!" He paused a minute, then glanced at me. "You ride ver' good. There is a place where some wild horses run, but grizzly bear, too! Much big grizzly! Ver' mean! A place called Bad Hills!"

Day by day, we edged farther north, the length of our drives depending on the grass. In some places, rains had fallen, and the grass grew tall, but we found stretches where grass was poor and water hard to find. There were salt swamps and bare, dry hills. Buffalo we saw in plenty, and there was no question about meat. We found buffalo and occasionally a deer or bighorn sheep.

There were wolves always. They clung to our drive, watching for the chance to pull down any straggler, and several times they succeeded. One of the younger steers went into a swamp to test the water—it was salt—and became mired. Before its frightened bawling could bring us to help, the wolves were upon it.

Tyrel heard and came in at a dead run. His first shot caught one wolf atop the luckless steer and another fled, yelping wildly and dragging its hind quarters. We were too late to help the steer, and Cap put it out of its misery with a bullet.

* * *

We were camped at the Bad Hills when trouble erupted suddenly. Brandy had come in for coffee, and Gilcrist sat by the fire with the Ox, preparing to go on night guard.

Brandy was still limping from the fall he had taken during the stampede. Orrin an' me had come in from scoutin', and Orrin was on the ground stripping the gear from his horse. We were back under the trees and out of sight of the camp. Lin was at the fire, and Baptiste was repairing a lariat.

Cap and Haney were coming in; Tyrel, Fleming, and Shorty were with the cattle.

Brandy was limping a little. He'd been thrown and hurt during the stampede but said nothing of it, and we'd never have known except that once in a while, when he'd been in the saddle for a long time, you'd see him favoring the bad leg. Most of us were banged up more or less, but we taken it as part of the day's work, as he did.

It was the Ox who started it. "What's the matter, mama's boy? Tryin' to make somebody think you're hurt?"

"Nothing of the kind. I do my share."

The Ox took up a stick from the pile gathered for the fire. "Where's it hurt, boy? There?" He hit him a crack just below the hip bone.

Brandy turned on him. "You put that stick down, Ox. And you lay off, d'you hear?"

"Or else what?" The Ox sneered.

Orrin came out of the trees. "Or else you settle with me, Ox."

"This is my fight, Mr. Sackett," Brandy said. "I will fight him."

The Ox was twice the size of Brandy and several years older. Orrin walked forward. "Yes, Brandy, you have a prior claim, but this man is working for me, and he has chosen to ignore my suggestions. I'd take it as a favor if you'd let me have him."

"Ha!" The Ox stood up. "Forget it, kid. I'd rather whip this smart lawyer-man. I'll show him something he'll never learn in books!"

He started around the fire, and Orrin let him come. Now I came out of the woods. Cap and Haney rode up, and we saw the Ox start for Orrin, swinging a ponderous right fist. Orrin took a short step off to the left and let the right go over his shoulder. At the same instant, he whipped up his right into the Ox's belly.

It was a jolting punch, but the Ox turned like a cat, dropping into a half crouch. Orrin's left took him in the mouth, but the Ox lunged, grabbing for Orrin to get hold of him. Orrin evaded the clutch, hooked a right to the body, and then walked in quickly with a one-two to the face.

The Ox ducked a left and grabbed Orrin, heaving him from his feet to hurl him violently to the ground. Charging in to put the boots to him, the Ox missed his first kick, and Orrin lunged against the leg on which the Ox was standing. The big man went back and down but came up like a rubber ball. A swinging fist caught Orrin beside the head and he staggered; a left dug into his midsection, and Orrin clinched with the Ox.

The Ox gave a grunt of satisfaction and wrapped his powerful arms around Orrin and began to squeeze. He was enormously powerful, with arms as thick as the legs of most men, and he put the knuckles of a fist against Orrin's spine; then he spread his legs and brought all his power to bear. Orrin gasped, then hooked a left to the Ox's face, then a right; they had no effect. He started to bend Orrin back, trying literally to break his spine, but Orrin was a veteran of too many mountain and barge fights. He threw up his legs and fell back to the ground, bringing the Ox down atop him. The fall broke the grip the Ox had, and Orrin was too fast. Like an eel, he was out of the bigger man's grasp and on his feet. The Ox lunged and met a stiff left that split his lips. He ducked and tried to get in close, but Orrin put the flat of his hand on the Ox's head and spun him away, then deftly tripped him as the Ox went forward, off balance.

The Ox got up slowly. Orrin, knowing the bigger man was better on the ground, stood back and allowed him to get to his feet. "What's the matter, Ox? Is something wrong?"

Cautious now, the Ox moved in, arms spread wide for grappling. Orrin waited on the balls of his feet, feinted a move to the left, then stepped in with a straight left and a right. The blows jolted the Ox but did not stop him. He landed a light left to Orrin's chest, then a smashing right to the head that made Orrin's knees buckle. Lunging close the Ox's head butted Orrin on the chin, knocking Orrin's head back like it was on a hinge.

Orrin went down. The Ox lunged close, kicking for Orrin's head, but a swift movement partially evaded the kick, taking it on the shoulder. It toppled him over again, and the Ox rushed in, booting Orrin viciously in the ribs. Orrin, gasping with pain, lunged to his feet and swung a left that missed and a right that didn't.

Moving around, neither man showing any sign of weariness, they circled for advantage. Orrin stabbed another left to the Ox's bleeding lips and crossed a right that the Ox ducked under. He smashed a right to the ribs that jolted Orrin, who moved back, stabbing a left to the Ox's face.

The Ox rushed, and instead of trying to evade the rush, Orrin turned sidewise and threw the Ox with a rolling hip lock. The bigger man hit the ground hard but came up fast, and Orrin threw him again with a flying mare.

Jolted, the Ox got up more slowly, and Orrin moved in, stabbing a left three times to the mouth, then slipping away before the Ox could land.

The Ox was breathing hard now. There was a swelling over his right eye, and his lips were puffed and split. He was learning that he must evade the left that was stabbing at his face. He moved his head side to side with his swaying body, then lunged to come in, lost balance, and as he fell forward, Orrin lifted a knee in his face.

The Ox went to his knees, blood dripping from his broken nose and smashed lips.

There was an awesome power in his huge arms and shoulders, but somehow those fists were always in his face, and Orrin's evasiveness left him helpless. He got up slowly, of no mind to quit. As his hands came up, Orrin's left hit him again, and the right crossed to his chin.

He ducked under another right and hooked a right to Orrin's ribs that seemed to have lost none of its power. Orrin stabbed a left that the Ox evaded. Another left missed and then another. Orrin feinted the same left and landed a jolting right cross. He feinted the left again and repeated with the right. The Ox moved in; Orrin feinted the left and then followed through with a stiff jab to the mouth.

The Ox circled warily waiting for the chance he wanted. He knew his own strength and knew what he could do. He had never fought anyone as elusive as Orrin Sackett, nor anyone who could hit as hard. He was learning there were times when strength was almost useless, but he was in no way whipped. He was getting his second wind, and he was ready. Above all, Orrin seemed to be slowing down.

He no longer could be content with whipping Orrin Sackett. He wanted to maim or kill him. Get hold of an arm or a leg and break it. Break his neck if he could. *Kill him!*

The Ox held his hands low, inviting the jab. Could he grab that darting fist, so like a snake's tongue? If he could—

The fist darted, and he caught it in his open palm. The other palm smashed upward at Orrin's elbow, but instead of resisting, Orrin went with the power and fell forward to his knees. Before he could turn, the Ox booted him in the ribs. He felt a wicked stab of pain, and he lunged to his feet.

Orrin moved carefully. That he had at least one broken rib he was sure. He had narrowly evaded a broken arm or shoulder. The Ox was learning, and he was dangerous. He had to get him out of there, and now.

There could be no delay.

The Ox, suddenly confident, was coming in now, ready to destroy him. Orrin feinted a left, and the Ox smiled. Orrin backed off slowly, and the Ox, sure of himself, came on in. Orrin feinted a left, and the Ox blocked it with almost negligent ease but failed to catch the right that shot up, thumb and fingers spread.

It caught him right under the Adam's apple, drew back swiftly, and struck again just a little higher.

The Ox staggered back, gagging, then went to his knees, choking and struggling for breath.

Orrin backed off a little, then said to Gilcrist, "Take care of him."

He sat down, mopping his brow; then he looked around at me. "They don't come much tougher."

"No," I said, "they surely don't. Better soak those hands in some warm water with some salts in it. It will take the soreness out."

I walked over to the fire and filled my cup. We had made a good start, but we had a long way to go.

And we were losing two hands.

Chapter 20

We gulped black coffee in the cool, crisp air, then saddled our broncs for the drive. We roused our cattle from their resting place and moved them out on the trail. There were wild, shrill calls from the cowboys then and whoops to hurry them on. There was a click of horns and a clack of hoofs and the bawling of an angry steer, but the cattle bunched up, and old Brindle took the lead and we headed toward Carlton.

We hung their horns on the Northern Star, and the pace was good for an hour, and then we let them graze as they moved.

"Don't bother with Eagle Creek," Baptiste advised. "The water is brackish, although the grass is good. There's a wooded glen beyond, a place of trees and springs. But much grizzlies, too."

By late afternoon, we were crossing a long, gently sloping flat; then we pushed the cattle through Eagle Creek and moved on toward the Bad Hills.

It was one long hill, really, and not so much of one at that, cut with many deep, wooded ravines. I did not wonder there might be bears, for the country suited them. It reminded me somewhat of the canyons in the mountain range back of the Puebla de Los Angeles, in California. I'd been there once, long since, and there were grizzlies there, too.

We saw none of the wild horses Baptiste had told us would be there. Orrin came in with a story of old horse tracks on the far side of the herd and added, "This is Blackfoot country."

Fort Carlton was about a quarter of a mile back from the river, a palisaded place with bastions at each of the corners. We bunched our cattle on a flat and a hillside not far from the fort, and with Tyrel remaining with the herd, Orrin and I rode in.

We had come some distance from the Bad Hills, a place we were glad to be free of, as we lost two steers there to grizzlies, both of them found in the morning, one half eaten, the other dragged some distance and covered with brush.

There were a good many Indians, all friendly, in the vicinity of Carlton. At the store, where many things were on sale, we arranged to buy a small amount of ammunition and some supplies. More, they suggested, might be available if we talked to the man in charge.

We were coming out of the store when Orrin stopped short. A girl in a neat gray traveling suit came toward him, hands outstretched. "Why, Mr. Sackett! How nice!"

He flushed and said, "Tell, let me introduce you to Devnet Molrone."

"Howdy, ma'am!"

She turned. "And this is Mrs. Mary McCann, Mr. Sackett!"

"Well, well! Howdy, Mrs. McCann!"

Mary McCann had flushed. Nettie glanced at her, surprised, then at me. I hoped my expression showed nothing but pleasure at the meeting.

"Rare pleasure, Mrs. McCann," I said. "Womenfolks to a man on the trail—well, we surely see almighty few of them. I've got a friend along with me who would be right happy to shake your hand, ma'am, if you was so inclined. I reckon he ain't seen a woman in weeks, maybe months."

Mary McCann looked right at me and said, "Now that's interestin'. I haven't seen many men, either. Just what would his name be?"

"Mr. Rountree? We call him Cap. He's seen most everything a man can see an' been most everywhere, but I d'clare, ma'am, he'd be right proud to meet you!"

Nettie Molrone put her hand on Orrin's sleeve. "Mr. Sackett? My brother is not here, and they are not sure they even remember him! They think he passed through on his way west."

"I was afraid of that, ma'am."

"Mr. Sackett? You're going on west. Could you take me? Take us?"

Orrin glanced at me, hesitating. Now the last person I wanted on a cattle drive was a young, pretty woman. As far as that goes, Mary McCann was a handsome woman, considering her age and poundage.

"Please? There's no other way west, and I *must* find my brother! I have to find him!"

"Well—" I hesitated, trying to find a way out, and I couldn't see one. After all, I was the oldest brother, and officially, I suppose, I was the boss. Not that I wanted the job or cared for it.

All the time, I was wondering what Cap would say and wondering also how Mary McCann got her name and what made her change it. Not that a change of names was anything unusual west of the Mississippi, and especially west of the Rockies. The last time I'd run into Mary McCann was down New Mexico way.

"Ma'am," I said, "it's a far land to which we go, and the way will be hard. Nothing like what you see here. So far as I know, there's but one fort betwixt here and the mountains. The land is wild, ma'am, with Injuns, with wolves and grizzlies.

"We may be long periods without water, and the grub may not be of the best. We can stop for nothing, man, woman, or beast, once we start moving again. We've taken a contract to deliver these cattle before winter sets in, and we're bound an' determined to do it.

"If you come with us, we'll play no favorites. You'll stand to the drive as the men do, and at times you may be called upon to help. It is a hard land, ma'am, and we'll have no truck with those who come with idle hands."

Her chin came up. "I can do my share! I will do my share!"

Well, I looked at her, the lift to the chin and the glint in her eyes, and I thought of Orrin there beside her, and I remembered the failure of his first marriage. If this girl stood to it, she was a woman to ride the river with, and Orrin wanted it, and her. Surely, no woman would have a harder time of it.

"All right," I said, "but no whining, no asking for favors. You'll be treated like a lady."

"You need have no fears." She stood straight and looked me in the eye. "I can stand as much as any man."

"Can you ride, ma'am? And can you shoot?"

"I can ride. I can shoot a little."

"Come along, then, and if your brother is alive, we will find him."

"What became of Kyle Gavin?" Orrin asked.

She frowned a little. "Why, I don't know. He was very attentive, and then suddenly he was there no longer. I don't know when he left or how."

When I went outside, Cap was riding in through the gate with Highpockets Haney. "Cap," I said, "if you see any familiar faces don't call them by name."

He looked at me out of those wise old eyes, eyes wiser and older than the man himself, and he said, "I learned a long time ago that a name is only what a person makes it."

He stepped down and said, "What about those womenfolks?"

"We're takin' them with us, Cap. One of them is tough enough and strong enough to charge hell with a bucket of water. The other one thinks she is."

Cap hesitated, one hand resting on his saddle. "Tell, you and me know better than any of them what lies ahead."

"We do," I said.

We had ridden the empty trails with a hollow moon in the sky and the bare peaks showing their teeth at the sky. We'd seen men die and horses drop, and we'd seen cattle wandering, dazed from thirst and heat. The leather of our hides had been cured on the stem by hot winds and cold, by blown dust and snow and hail falling. We knew what lay ahead, and we knew that girl might die. We knew she might go mad from heat and dust, and we knew I'd no business in letting her come. Yet I'd seen the desperation in her eyes and the grim determination in her mouth and chin.

"Orrin's taken with her, Cap," I said, "and I think she'll stay the route."

"If you say so," he said. He tied his horse. "That person you thought I might put a name to?"

"Mary McCann," I said, "and she's a damned fine cook." I looked at him slyly. "An' for much of her life she's been in love with a miserable old mountain man turned cownurse who drifts where the wind takes him."

"I wouldn't know anybody like that," he said, and went inside.

We got the pemmican and other supplies we needed, including the ammunition, but we couldn't buy them for money. They needed cattle. When we started out of Fort Carlton, we were thirty head short of what we brought in. They wanted the beef, we needed the supplies, and lucky it was because none of us were carrying much money. We'd spent a good bit and were running shy of cash money.

We went over the bluffs and into higher, beautiful pasture land, and we let the cattle graze. God knew what lay before us, but the best advice we got was to fatten our stock whilst we could.

Many a time those days I wished I had the words of Orrin, who could speak a beautiful tongue. It was the Welsh in us, I guess, coming out in him, but it left me saddened for my own lack. I hadn't no words with which to tell of the land, that beautiful green land that lay before and around us. Some didn't like the cottonwoods. Well, maybe they weren't just that for folks up here called them poplars, and maybe that's what they were. Only they were lovely with their green leaves rustling.

Westward we marched, short-handed by two, for we'd left the Ox and Gilcrist behind.

It had all come to a head when we were fixing to leave Carlton. Gilcrist had come to me with the Ox at his shoulder. "We want our time," Gilcrist said.

When he had his money in his hand, Gilcrist said, "Someday I'm goin' to look you up, Sackett. Someday I want to find out if you can really handle that gun."

"Follow me back to the States," I said, "and choose your time."

"To the States? Why the States?"

"I'm a visitor here," I said, "and a man has no call to get blood on a neighbor's carpet."

Westward we went following the route north of the North Saskatchewan through a country of hills and poplars with many small lakes or sloughs. There was no shortage of firewood now, for at every stop we found broken branches under the trees. It was a lovely, green, rolling country even now in the latter days of July.

Anxiously, we watched the skies, knowing that cold came soon in these northern regions and that we had but little time. The nights were cool and the mornings crisp; the campfires felt good.

"A good frost would help us," Cap said, nursing a cup of coffee by the fire, "kill off some of these mosqueeters an' flies."

We were camped by Bear Lake, a place I could have stayed forever. How many times I have found such campsites! Places so beautiful it gave a man the wistfuls to see or to think back on. So many times we said, "We've got to come back some time!" an' knowin' all the while we never would.

That night, we heard the wolves howl, and there were foxes barking right out by the cattle. In the night, we heard a squabble, an' Tyrel an' me came out of our sleep, guns in hand. Then the noise quieted down, and we went back to sleep, only to be awakened again with a wild bawling of a cow, the crack of a whip, and the yelp of a wolf.

Come daylight, we learned some wolves had jumped a steer; he'd been scratched in some brush earlier and had blood on him. Orrin had come in with that Spanish whip he carried on his saddle, a long, wicked lash that could take the hide off. He'd used it on wolves before, and he could flick a fly from a steer's hide without touching the steer. I'd seen him do it.

The steer the wolves had attacked was so badly hurt it had to be shot.

We were breaking camp when we heard some yells, then a sound of galloping horses. In a moment, we had our rifles, but Baptiste gestured wildly and waved us back.

It was a party of *métis* wearing brass-buttoned capots, calico shirts in a variety of colors, and moleskin trousers. Their belts were beaded in red and white or blue and white, and most of them wore cloth caps, only a few having hats and one a coonskin cap.

They were a friendly, cheerful lot, talking excitedly with Baptiste whom they obviously knew well.

"They go to Fort Pitt," he explained. "They are hunters, and they have been to another camp, feasting."

Tyrel indicated their horses. "Wish we had some of them. That's some of the best horseflesh I've seen."

When Baptiste suggested it, they agreed to show us some stock when we reached Fort Pitt. After drinking an enormous amount of coffee, they swung to their saddles and dashed off, whooping and yelling, at top speed.

After they had gone, Baptiste stopped me as I was mounting. "Bad!" he whispered. "Ver' bad! They speak of many mans, maybe ten, twelve mans near Jackfish Lake. They wait for somebody, or somet'ing. Today, they say the mans move back into woods, hide horses."

Haney came in for coffee at the nooning. "Seen some tracks. Two riders, keepin' out of sight. I caught a flash of sunlight on a rifle and slipped around and taken a look. They're scoutin' us."

"White men?"

"You betcha! Well mounted, Tell, well mounted an' well armed."

Well, we had known it was coming. Now we were in wild country. If we vanished out here, who would know? Or care?

Chapter 21

Wolves hung on our flanks as we moved out, nor would they be driven off. We had no wish to shoot and attract undue attention, nor would the waste of ammunition have done any good, for their ranks were continually added to by other wolves.

We pushed on over some flat country dotted by trees and groups of trees, crossing several small streams.

It was the thought of a stampede that worried me. "If they scatter our stock, we lose time in the gather," I said. "Cap? Why don't you scout on ahead and try to find us a camp in the woods? Some place where we can fall some trees to make a so-so corral?"

"I can look," he said.

"Ride easy in the saddle," I said. "This is an ugly bunch. I don't think much of them as fightin' men, but they'll kill you."

He rode off through the scattered trees, and we came on. Fleming was doing a good day's work, but I still had no trust in the man. There had seemed to be something between him an' Gilcrist.

Nettie was proving herself a hand. She caught on to what was necessary, and she rode well. I'd no doubts about Mary McCann. She might be no youngster, and she might be carrying some weight, but she could still ride most anything that wore hair.

We pushed on, and I had to smile at Haney and Shorty. Both of them were pretty handy with the cussing, but since the girls showed up, there was none of that. It must have been a strain, but they were bearing up under it.

Cap had us a camp when we came to it, a small meadow near a stream with trees and brush all around. We watered them, got them inside, and dragged some deadfalls across the openings. Then we scouted the brush and trees on both sides to see how an attacker might approach us.

Cap an' me, we went back in the trees and rigged some snares and deadfalls, traps for anybody who might come sneaking up.

If they wanted to come up on us in the night, they were asking for whatever they got. Come daylight, we'd dismantle the traps so's they wouldn't trap any unwary man or animal after we'd gone.

Lin fixed us a mighty nice supper, having a mite more time. Nettie came to me while we were eating. "Why can't we stand watch? You men need the rest."

"Let them," Cap was saying.

None of us had been around when Cap finally met Mary, and none of us asked any questions, although I was curious as to what made her change her name and leave that place she had back in New Mexico. But it was her business. By the position of the Big Dipper, it was maybe two o'clock in the morning when Nettie touched me on the shoulder. "There's something moving in the brush," she said, "several some-things."

She and Mary had been riding herd, and I rolled out, shook out my boots, and stuck my feet into them. Haney was already moving, and so were Orrin and Tyrel.

Taking up my Winchester I followed her to her pony. He was standing head up, looking toward the woods, his ears pricked. At just that moment, there was a sudden crash in the brush and a grunt, then an oath.

"Sit tight, boys," I said. "Don't go into the woods."

Somebody called for help in a low voice, but there was no answer; then there was some threshing about, we all just awaiting to see what would happen.

Nothing did until suddenly there was a louder crash and some swearing.

"Nettie," I whispered, "you and Mary might as well get some sleep."

"And miss all the fun?"

Me, I taken a long look at her. "Ma'am," I said, "if anything happens, it won't be fun. It will be hard times for somebody, probably them. You get some sleep whilst you've the chance."

Turning to Orrin, I said, "You an' Tye go back to sleep. Me an' Highpockets can handle this here."

"You figure we caught something?"

"By the sound, we caught two somethings," I said, "and I suspect we've persuaded them that crawlin' in the brush ain't what they want to do."

When day was breaking, we stirred up the fire for Lin and Highpockets and me; we decided to see what we'd caught and whether it needed skinning or not.

We come to a snare, and there we had a man hangin' head down by one ankle, and he was some unhappy. He'd been hangin' there several hours, and he had been mad; now he was almost cryin' to be set loose.

Me an' Haney, we looked at him. "The way I figure it, Haney," I said, "anything catched in a trap has fur, and when something has fur, you skin it for the hide."

"I know," he said. "That's the way we always did it in the mountains, but this one's kind of skimpy on the fur." He took the man by his hair and tilted his face up. "He's got fur on his lip. Maybe we should skin that like I hear you done to somebody down New Mexico way."

I reached over and taken him by the end of his handlebar moustache. I held his head up by it while he swung wildly with his arms. Haney hit one of the wrists a crack with the barrel of his pistol, and the swings stopped.

Holding him by the end of his moustache I turned his head this way and that.

"No," I said, "I don't think it's worth skinning. I figure we should just let him hang. Maybe somebody will come for him."

"Nobody has," Haney said. "Give him a few days and he'll dry out some."

The man's pistol had fallen to the ground, and Haney picked it up, then unstrapped the man's cartridge belt. "Would you look at this here, Tell? This man's been walkin' in the dark woods with a pistol in his hand. Why, he might have hurt somebody!"

"Or tripped over something and shot hisself. We'd better carry that gun with us so's he won't get hurt."

Haney walked around the hanging man, looking him over. "How long d'you think a man could hang like that?"

"Well"—I pushed my hat back and scratched my head—"depend on how long before some bear found him, or maybe the wolves. If they stood on their hind legs, they could sure enough reach him.

"Man smell would bother them for a while," I suggested. "Then they'd get over that and start jumpin' for him. Sooner or later, one of them would get hisself a piece of meat—"

"Hey! You fellers goin' to let me hang here, or are you goin' to turn me loose?"

"It talks," Haney said, "makes words like it was almost human. How d'you think anything got caught in a trap like that?"

"Must've been sneakin' in the woods," I said. "We'd better let this one hang an' see what else we got."

"Aw, fellers! Come on now! Turn a man loose!"

"So you can come huntin' us again?" Haney asked. "No way."

We walked off through the woods toward the deadfall.

There was no game in that trap, but there had been. There was a hat lying on the ground, but the victim had been carried away. We could see tracks where two men had helped a third away. "Busted a leg, most likely," Haney suggested cheerfully. "Lucky it wasn't his skull."

Our other traps were empty, so we dismantled them and went back to camp. "They don't know much," Haney said, "but they'll learn from their troubles. Or maybe they'll recruit some all-out woodsman who could make trouble for us."

He paused. "Shall we just forget about that other feller?"

"We don't want him hangin' around," I suggested, "so let's turn him loose."

We done so. And when he had his feet on the ground, I told him to take off his boots.

"What?"

"Take off your boots," I said, "and your pants. We need something for the fire."

"Now see here! I—!"

"Give him a short count," I said to Haney, "and if he ain't got his boots off, shoot him."

He stared at me, wild-eyed, then hit the ground and tugged off his boots. "Now your pants," I said.

He took off his pants. I shook my head at him. "You ought to wash them long johns. Ain't decent, a man as dirty as that." I pointed off through the woods. "Your friends, if you've got any, are off thataway. You get started."

"Now look here," he protested, "that's a good set of spurs! I wish—"

"Beat it," I said. "You take off through those woods and don't you ever come back. If I see you out here again, I'll hang your hide on the nearest deadfall."

"Those are good spurs," Haney said.

"Hang 'em on a tree," I said. "Somebody will find them."

We bunched our cows and started them west, and we swung south to avoid the traveled trails. We found fair pasture and moved them along. The wolves taken a steer here and there, and we lost one to a grizzly. Shorty nailed the grizzly but not before he'd killed a good-sized steer.

The grass was sparse, and we crossed some sandy plains with occasional low hills. We had to scout for patches of good grass, but it looked like forest was taking over from the plains. On the third day after the mix-up in the trees, we saw a party of riders coming toward us, but Baptiste told us they were *métis*, and sure enough they were.

Some of them were the same crowd we'd met, and they brought some horses for trading. We had them with us all night and most of the next day, but when we split up, we had nine good horses and a couple of fair ones, and they had some odds and ends of truck as well as some cash money.

We swapped them a rifle we'd picked up and the pistol we'd taken from our hanging man, among other things. The Canadian army had come to Fort Garry, they said, and Riel had disappeared before they could lay hands on him.

The *métis* wanted sugar, salt, and tobacco, and I had an idea they were hiding out themselves, although they were a far piece from Fort Garry now. Evidently, they planned to stay out of sight for a while. With salt, coffee, and tobacco, they could live off the country. It was their country, and they understood it well.

They warned us we were going into wild country where there was little grass and no trails for cattle.

We pushed on regardless, and for the first time our worn-down saddle stock got a rest.

Before they parted from us, one of the *métis* who was a friend to Baptiste and had become my friend, also, took me aside and warned me.

"Two mans, ver' bad. They come to Fort Garry and ride to Carlton. They are sent for by a bearded man, and they meet two other mans who come from the States who are brothers, also. They hunt for you."

"The first two men? Do you know who they are?"

"*Oui*. Ver' bad! Polon is their name. Pete and Jock Polon. If the Hudson's Bay Company was here, they would not come back! They are thieves! They killed trappers! They killed some Cree! And in the woods they are superb! Have a care, *mon ami!* Have a care!"

We drove on another seven miles before we camped after watching the *métis* ride away.

Orrin looked across the campfire at me that night. "Tell, we aren't going to make it. We can't make it before snow flies."

"What d'you think, Cap?"

"Orrin's right. We've got to push them, Orrin, even if we run beef off them. After all, it's cattle we are supposed to deliver. Nobody said nothing about fat cattle!"

That night, two men, headed east, rode into our camp. "You're takin' *cattle* out there?" They stared at me. "You must be crazy!"

"You mean there's no market?"

"Market? Of course, there's a market! It's gettin' 'em there. There's no decent trails; there's rivers to cross, grizzlies a-plenty, and wolves—you ain't seen any wolves yet!"

One of them, a tall man named Pearson, indicated the carts. "You won't be able to use those much longer. The trails are too narrow. Put your stuff on pack horses."

"My old horse will carry a pack," Brandy suggested. "He's done it before."

We sat long with the two travelers, getting as much advice as we could. They drew the trail in the dirt for us, indicating the passes.

"How are things up there?" I asked. "Peaceful?"

"Generally speaking. Some of the boys get a mite noisy now and again. There's brawls and such and once in a great while a shooting. Mostly, they're just noisy."

"The best claims are all taken," the other one said. "If you're figuring on staking claims, forget it."

"We'll just sell our beef and get out," Orrin commented. Then, tentatively, he added, "We promised delivery to a man named Sackett, Logan Sackett."

They stared at him. "Too bad about him, and I'm afraid you're too late. He's dead."

"What?"

"I'll say this for him. He was a man. Party got trapped in the passes last year, and he went up and brought 'em out. Saved seven men and a woman. He brought 'em through snow like you never saw. Avalanche country."

"You say he's dead?" I asked.

"He went north. There were rumors of a strike up in the Dease River country. Story was that he was killed in a gun battle up there with some outlander."

"Big man?"

"Your height," Pearson said to Orrin, "but heavier by twenty pounds. Come to think of it, he favored you somewhat."

"Who killed him?"

"That was a bad outfit. They'd been in some trouble in Barkerville. Don't recall what. Five or six of them, and smart, tough men. The one who seemed to be the leader was named Gavin."

"Gavin?" I glanced over at Nettie, who was listening.

"Kyle Gavin?"

"No, this one's called Shanty. Shanty Gavin, and he's as mean and tough as he is smart."

Pearson looked over at me. "It was Shanty Gavin who killed Logan Sackett. Shot him dead."

Chapter 22

Logan Sackett dead? I didn't believe it. He was too durned ornery to die. Besides, I'd seen him come through cuttings and shootings and clubbings like he was born to them.

Shanty Gavin? Any relation to Kyle Gavin?

Who was Shanty, and what did he want? For that matter, who was Kyle Gavin?

Pearson and his partner headed on east, back to the fleshpots and away from the gold fields. Fraser River gold was too fine, and the Cariboo was played out, or so they said, but we'd learned long ago to discount anything anybody said who was either going to or coming from a gold field.

"Any way you look at it," Cap said, "we're drivin' these cows right into trouble."

"I never seen any trouble a cow couldn't handle," Haney said wryly. "What I'm wonderin' about is us. What are we gettin' into?"

"Move 'em along," I said. "The time's gettin' short, and if we don't hurry, there'll be frost on the punkin before we get where we're going."

"I want to get there," Shorty said, "so's we can get out before the snow settles down. I'm a warm-weather man myself, born for the sunny side of the hill."

That was the night we left our carts behind. We divided what they contained into packs for four horses.

"We can burn them," Fleming said. "They'll make a hot fire for cooking."

"We'll leave them," I said. "Somebody may come who needs a cart. We'll push them back under the trees and leave them for whoever comes. Good hands made them, and I'll not destroy honest work."

Again we moved out, pointing our way into the darker hills. The forest was changing now, and ahead of us we saw peaks that were bare of growth, and some were covered by snow. Grass was scarce, and we watched for meadows where the cattle could stop and feed. Our travel was arranged to make the most of grass when we found it. There were firs among the poplars now and sometimes groves of stunted pine. We skirted a forest blown down by winds where the dead trees lay in rows like mowed grain.

Orrin was riding point when we met the grizzly. We'd been coming along a forest trail, the cattle strung out for a couple of miles or more and Orrin riding quiet, making no sound. Suddenly, the grizzly arose from the brush and stood tall in the trail. Startled, Orrin's horse reared, and Orrin kept his seat, drawing his pistol as he did so.

The first we knew of trouble was the sharp bark of his pistol, then three times more, rapid fire. Tyrel, Haney, Cap, an' me, we lit out for the front of the column.

Ever try to get through a trail jammed with cattle? It took time, too much time.

Cattle began bucking and plunging, trying to get into the woods and brush on either side of the trail, and we could hear the roaring and snarling of what was obviously a mighty big bear. We fought our way through, but getting there was tough.

We heard two more shots, and we broke through to find a big grizzly lying in the trail, crippled but still full of fight.

Orrin was just getting up off the ground. His hat was gone, and his buckskin jacket was ripped, and there was blood on his shoulder. He made it to his feet, staggered, and commenced jamming loads into his pistol. Me, I took my rifle from the scabbard and killed that grizzly with two good shots.

He would have died from Orrin's shots, we later saw. Two of them had hit him in the neck, and after going down, Orrin got two more shots into his spine, fired as the bear was turning. They had crippled him in the hindquarters, which kept him from getting at Orrin. He'd hit him one glancing swipe, knocking him tail over teakettle into the brush.

It taken us the rest of the evening to skin out that grizzly and get the best cuts of meat; then we had to get the cattle around the blood in the trail. The carcass we hauled off with that old plow horse of Brandy's.

Scouting ahead, Shorty found a long meadow along a winding stream, and we turned the cattle in there for a good bit of grass and water. We rounded up some of the cattle that got away into the trees, but there was a few of them we never did find and didn't take the time to hunt. One old steer came up the trail after us when we started the next morning.

All the following day we struggled through bogs, the cattle floundering and plunging, our horses doing no better, and the trail when it could be found at all was wide enough for one animal only. During the whole day, we made scarcely four miles, yet the next morning we climbed a low hill and then another and emerged in a forest of huge old poplars, scattered but with no undergrowth. Here and there, the cattle found a bite of something, usually a clump of wildflowers. We made good time and by nightfall had twelve miles of easy travel behind us.

We broke out into a plain at sundown, and the cattle scattered on the good grass there, and we found a camp up against some willows and near a small stream.

We were dead beat, and me an' Shorty were taking the first guard. I slapped a saddle on a dusty red roan and cinched up. I was putting my rifle in the scabbard when suddenly there was a thunder of hoofs, wild shrill whoops, and we saw a party of Indians swooping down upon us.

I grabbed my rifle back out of the scabbard, saw Tyrel hit the dirt behind a log, and heard Haney's pistol barking, and then they were gone and with them about fifty head of our cattle.

Well, I done some cussing, then apologized to Nettie, who came up from the campfire to see what had happened.

"Blackfeet," Cap said. "Count yourself lucky they wasn't war minded."

"Let's go get 'em!" Shorty suggested.

Cap just glanced at him, but that glance said more than a passel of words. "Blackfeet, I said. You don't chase Blackfeet, Shorty. You just count your blessings an' let 'em go.

"Those were young braves, just out for a lark. They wasn't huntin' scalps, but you go after them, and they will. We lost some cows. Let's move out of here."

"To where?"

"Any place but here. They might get to thinkin' on it and come back."

Tired as we were, we put out our fire, loaded our gear, and headed off up the trail. We found a meadow three miles farther on and bedded them down.

Nobody set by the campfire that night; nobody wanted a second cup of coffee. Everybody crawled into his bed, and only the night guard was left.

Day after day, we plodded on; we had lost cattle one way or another until at least a third of them were gone. Old Baptiste killed a mountain sheep, and we dined well, but it had been weeks since we had seen a buffalo. There was little talk now during the day. Fleming looked sour and discontented. He seemed to have been expecting something that did not happen.

"Overlanders have come this way," Cap said, "but it's been a while."

All the tracks we found were old, and we were getting more and more worried.

"Beats me where we're to meet Logan, if he's alive."

"That feller said he was dead," Fleming said, "that he'd been killed."

"He's a hard man to kill."

"A bullet will do it for anybody," Fleming said. "If he's hit in the right place, one man is no tougher than another."

"Seems like we've been pushin' these cows forever," Shorty said. "I wouldn't mind standin' up to a bar for a drink."

"Be a while," Tyrel said. "You boys set easy. Goin' back will be easy as pie."

"If we ever," Fleming said.

Nettie and Mary had been keeping out of the way. They knew this was a trying time, and they had done their best to help. Both of them had become good hands, although Mary—well, she'd been *born* a hand.

"If my brother is out here," Nettie asked Orrin, "where do you think he would be?"

Orrin shrugged. "There's Barkerville, and there's Clinton. I don't know many of the towns, but I can tell you this. If he's in this country or has been, some of those folks will know. This is a big country, but she's right scarce of people. A body can be away up yonder at the forks of the creek, and somebody will have seen him. There's nothing happens up here somebody doesn't know about."

Fleming chuckled. It was a dry, rather unpleasant, skeptical chuckle. Nobody said anything.

We'd been keeping our eyes open for sign. All three of us Sacketts expected it, and we knew the sort of sign one Sackett was apt to leave for another.

We found nothing.

We waded rivers, fourteen crossings in one day, and wove our way through some fir trees whose wet branches slapped us wickedly as we passed. The horses were game. They struggled through the muskeg, and finally we topped out on some reasonably solid ground.

Supplies were running low, and game was scarce. All day we had seen nothing. Ducks flew over, the Vs of their flight pattern pointing south. In the morning when we awakened, there was a chill in the air.

"Wonder what become of those Injuns we had followin' us?" Cap asked one day. "I kind of miss 'em?"

"Little Bear," I said, "now there was a lad."

"If we don't get something to eat soon," Lin suggested, "we'll have to slaughter a beef."

Now there's little goes more against the grain of a good cattleman than killing his own beef. But we'd left buffalo country behind, and we were fresh out of bear. Me, I was of no mind to tackle a grizzly unless he came hunting trouble, which they often did. A grizzly has been king in his own world for so long, he resents anybody coming around. Only man threatens his world, and whether he avoids or fights men depends pretty much on his mood at the moment.

Down San Francisco way during the gold rush, some of the gamblers used to pit bears in cages with lions, tigers, and most anything that would fight. The grizzly almost always won in quick time. In one particular case, a full-grown African lion lasted less than three minutes.

There were a lot of grizzlies in these mountains, but mostly they kept out of the way, not because they were afraid, but because they simply did not want to be bothered.

Orrin, who reads a lot, was reading me a piece in a magazine, *Century* or *Atlantic,* I think, about some explorers coming back from some foreign country where they'd been hunting şome wild creature. They were busy hunting for a few weeks and came back saying there was no such thing. Now I've lived in panther or mountain lion country most of my life and never seen but one or two that weren't treed by hounds. Wild animals don't want to be seen, and it's sheer accident if you see them.

We were climbing all the while, getting higher and higher, and the nights were getting colder. Then, one morning, Tyrel come to me. "Tell," he said, "there's a fringe of ice on the lake, yonder."

Well, that sent a chill through me. A fringe of ice—and we had some distance to go. I wasn't sure how much.

Now we were moving up some magnificent valleys, green and lovely with great walls of mountain rising on either side; often these were sheer precipices of bare rock, or with an occasional tree growing from some rock a body could no way get to. We caught fish, and one night I got three ducks in three shots with a rifle, two sitting, one just taking off. They were needed, as grub was getting low. We had flour, salt, and the like, but we needed meat.

Every morning now there was frost. The sky was gray often enough, and one night, when there were no clouds, we saw the Northern Lights, a tremendous display brightening the whole heavens. I'd heard of it but seen it but once before, in Montana, but never like this.

It was late afternoon, and Tyrel was riding point. It was an easy trail, across some green meadows and up along a trail through huge boulders and scattered clumps of fir. Me, I was riding on the flank when I saw Tyrel pull up short.

Well, my rifle snaked into my hands, and I saw Cap Rountree out with his, but Tyrel wasn't drawing. He was looking at a big gray boulder beside the trail.

Coming down off the slope, I rounded the head of the herd and pulled up alongside him. I started to say, "What's wrong, Tye?" and did say it before I looked past him and saw the mark on the face of the boulder.

Scratched on the face of the rock was **CLINCH-S-Dease-?**

"Well," Orrin had come up, "he isn't dead then."

"Who isn't dead?" It was Fleming.

Orrin an' Tyrel glanced at me, and I said, "We're losin' time, boys. We've got a far piece to go."

Fleming stared hard at the scratching on the rock. "What's that mean?" he wondered. "It don't make no sense!"

"Doesn't, does it?" Tyrel said mildly. He turned his mount. "Hustle them along, Charlie. We've a ways to go."

Reluctantly, Charlie Fleming turned away.

Nettie Molrone rode up with Mary McCann. "What is it, Orrin?"

"Just some scratching on a rock," he said. "We were wondering about it, that's all."

She looked at him quickly, her eyes searching his. She glanced at the rock. "It doesn't make sense. Except"—she paused, studying it—"there's a Dease River up here somewhere and a Dease Lake."

"There is?" Orrin looked surprised. "What d'you know about that?"

She looked at him again, half angry.

In the morning, Charlie Fleming was gone.

Chapter 23

Fleming was gone, and a light rain was falling that froze as it reached the ground. We drank our coffee standing around the hissing fire in our slickers.

"I'd like to know where he went," Orrin said, "but it's not worth following him."

"D'you think he made sense out of Logan's message?"

"If he did," Shorty said, "he's smarter than me."

"We've been passing messages around for years," Orrin said. "Started back in the feuding days, I reckon. The 'Clinch S' just means he's a Clinch Mountain Sackett, which is one branch of the family, descended from old Yance. 'Dease?' simply means we should head for the Dease River, and the destination after that is in doubt."

"Unless you were one of the family," Tyrel commented, "it's unlikely you'd guess."

"Why'd you say he was still alive? That message might have been written days ago."

"Could be, but it's scratched on there with some of that chalk rock he picked up, and had it been more'n a few days old, it would have washed away."

Cap came riding in as they were mounting. "Took a look at the trail," he said. "There's a marker there. Could be by one of you boys, but that trail is one thin cow wide, and with this ice—"

"Think we can make it?"

"Maybe. There's no tellin' the luck of a lousy cow. Anyway, it doesn't seem like we have much choice."

"It's up to me, then," I said, and rode out with old Brindle falling in behind.

When we started up the trail, old Brindle hesitated, not liking it. His horns rattled against the wall, but as I was going on, and he was used to following, he sort of fell in behind.

"Hope I don't let you down, old boy," I said. "It looks bad to me, too!"

We wound steadily upward, the trail narrowing, then widening, occasionally opening to a small space of an acre or more covered with stunted trees, then narrowing again. The sleet continued to fall, and the air was cold. Far below, we could see the spearlike tops of trees, and the silver ribbon of a stream.

The trail grew steeper. At times, I had to dismount and lead my mount over the icy rocks. At one point, I came to a bank of last year's snow, a dirty gray shelf of the stuff, which I had to break off to make a way for my horse and the following cattle.

It was slow, hard work. All day long, we climbed. There was no place to stop and rest; there was not even a place to stop.

Suddenly, the trail dipped down around a steep elbow bend, and the rock of the trail slanted toward the outer edge. Walking along the wall as tightly as possible, I led the roan around the corner.

The cattle came on. Glancing back when several hundred yards farther along, I was in time to see a steer suddenly slip and, legs flailing, plunge off into space headed for the tops of the trees five hundred feet below. Even as I looked, another fell.

Swearing softly, I plodded on, feeling for footholds around the edge. Suddenly, as it had begun, the narrow trail ended and gave out into a thick forest. Ahead, there was a meadow and beyond a stream, already icing over.

There was room enough, and there was but little undergrowth. Tying the roan, I went to a deadfall and from under it tried to gather some scraps of bark that had not been soaked by the rain. From inside my shirt, I took a little tinder that I always kept for the purpose, and breaking a tuft of it free, I lit a fire. As it blazed up, I hastily added more fuel.

Walking back into the woods, I broke off some of the small suckers that grew from the tree trunks and died. They had long been dead and were free from rain. By the time the cattle began to wander out on the meadow and the first rider appeared, I had a fine fire blazing and was rigging a lean-to between two trees that stood about ten feet apart.

The trees had lower limbs approximately the same height above the ground, and selecting from among the fallen debris, broken limbs, and dead branches one of the proper length I rested it in the crotches of the limbs selected, and then I began gathering other sticks to lean slant-wise from the pole to the ground.

From time to time I stopped to add fuel to the fire, well knowing the effect the fire would have on the tired men and the two women.

Across the poles, I put whatever lay to hand. I was not building anything but a temporary shelter, and I used slabs of bark from fallen trees, fir branches and whatever was close by.

By the time Lin and Baptiste reached the fire with the pack horses, I had a fairly comfortable shelter and was starting on another. Haney was first to reach the fire, and he began gathering fir boughs from nearby trees.

Orrin helped Nettie from her horse, and for a moment she swayed and fell against the horse. She straightened up. "I'm sorry," she said, "I guess I'm tired."

One by one, the men came in, carrying their gear, which they dropped under the second shelter. Several of them went to the fire. Cap walked out and began gathering boughs, and after a minute Shorty went to help.

Highpockets Haney held his hands to the fire. He looked around at me. "Tell Sackett I been a lot of places with you, but if you think I'm goin' back over that trail in the snow, you got another think a-comin'."

"We lost some stock, Cap?"

Rountree looked at me. Tired as he had to be, he looked no different than always. He had degrees of toughness nobody had ever scratched. "That we did!"

Shorty looked over at me. "Fourteen, fifteen head, Tell. I'm sorry."

"This weather's rough," Haney added. "We'll lose some more if we've far to go."

We huddled about the fire, and soon the smell of coffee was in the air. Tyrel went back to the edge of camp, and soon he came in with several chunks of meat. "Big horn," he said. "I nailed him back on the other side of the mountain."

Soon the smell of broiling meat was added to that of coffee. Outside, the falling sleet rustled on the fir boughs and on the meadow. The cattle ceased to eat, and one by one took shelter under the trees.

"Ain't nothin' like a fire," Cap said, "and the smell of coffee boilin'."

"How far you reckon it is?" Shorty asked.

Nobody answered because nobody knew. Me, I leaned my forehead on my crossed arms and hoped there would be a marker on this side of the pass we'd come over. We would surely need it because I had no idea which way to turn.

The Dease was someplace off to the northwest. Beyond that, anybody's guess was as good as mine, and I was ramrodding this outfit.

We had fire, and we had shelter, and we had a bit of meat, and good meat at that. Yet I was uneasy.

Where had Charlie Fleming gone?

Surely, as we drew closer and closer to our destination, we drew closer to his also, so why hadn't he waited a bit longer where he could have coffee and grub on the way?

Maybe, just maybe, because we were closer than we thought.

Certainly, even though he could not interpret the message, he would know there had been a message, and that would mean that Logan Sackett was not only alive but free—or probably free.

Had he fled to warn someone of our coming? Or was he afraid of Logan?

Orrin got up and moved over to where Nettie Molrone was. I could hear the murmur of their voices as they talked. "I'll ask about for your brother," he said, "as soon as we meet anybody. There'll be a town," he added, "or something of the kind."

The sleet still fell, but it was changing into snow, which would be worse, for beneath the snow there would be ice on the trails. Beyond the reach of the fire shadows flitted wolves.

Now stories came to me, stories told me when I was a small boy by my father. My father had trapped these very lands; he told us much of animals and their habits and of how the wolves would work as a team to drive an animal or a group of animals into a position where they could easily be killed. To drive an elk or moose out on the ice where he would slip and fall was one trick often used. Sometimes they herded them into swamps or drove them off cliffs.

These tricks were often attempted with men, and the unwary were trapped by them.

The snow continued to fall throughout the night, and when morning came, the ground and the trees were covered with it. We got out of bed under the lean-tos, and Baptiste had a fire built up in no time. It had burned down to coals during the last hours of the morning.

It was good to hear the crackle of the fire and to smell the wood burning. Tyrel saddled up, and him and me took a turn through the woods, bunching the cattle a little. They'd had tolerable shelter under the trees, but it was right cold that morning, and they were in no way anxious to move. Some of the horses had pawed away the snow to get at the grass. These were mustangs, used to wild country and to surviving in all kinds of weather.

We were slow getting started because everybody rolled out a mite slower than usual. Nettie's face looked pinched and tight, and she held her hands to the fire.

Orrin said, "We're gettin' close. This is the kind of country you'll find your brother in."

"How can he stand it? I mean even if there's gold."

"Gold causes folks to do all manner of unlikely things, ma'am," Tyrel said. "Sometimes even folks a body has figured were right good people have turned ugly when gold's in the picture."

"Kyle Gavin did not want me to come looking for my brother," Nettie said. "He offered to lend me the money to start home."

"It's a rough country, ma'am. He knows that. He probably didn't want you to get trapped in a place you couldn't get out of."

We came down to a deep canyon before we'd gone more than a few miles and wound down a narrow switchback trail to the water's edge. The river flowed past the road a whole lot faster than we liked, so we pointed the herd upstream and started them swimming across somewhat against the current. They held to it only a little, but by that time they were well on their way, and when they turned a bit on the downstream side, they were pointed toward the landing. We got most of them across and started up the trail opposite. Shorty was in the lead, and as he topped out on the ridge, we heard a sharp report that went echoing down the canyon, and we saw Shorty whip around in his saddle and fall.

At least two hundred cattle were on the trail, and there was no way to get past them. We urged them on, and they began to boil over the edge, running. We crowded the rest of them across and Tyrel an' me, we went hightailing it up the trail after those cows.

We went over the edge, running, but saw nothing but an empty meadow scattered with the arriving cattle. Shorty's horse stood a short distance off, and Shorty was on the ground. Tyrel rode hellbent for election across the meadow and into the trees, and I swung my horse around and rode to Shorty. He was on his face, and there was a big spot of blood on his back, and I turned him over easy.

His eyes were open, and he said, "Never saw him, Tell. Not even a glimpse. Sorry."

He was hit hard, and he knew it. Nettie came up over the rim followed by Mary, and they went right to him.

"I did my part, Tell. Didn't I?" He stared up at me.

"All any man could, Shorty. We rode some rivers together."

"It ain't so bad," he said. "There's nobody to write to. I never had nobody, Tell."

"You had us, Shorty, and when we ride over the rim, we'll be lookin' for you. Keep an eye out, will you?"

There were low clouds, and the place where he lay was swept clean of snow. Nettie and Mary, they came to him, trying to ease him some, as womenfolk will.

"Can't you do something, Tell?" Nettie said to me.

"Nothin' he can do, ma'am," Shorty said. "Just don't try to move me."

Tyrel came back from the woods, and Orrin rode up, and we squatted near Shorty. "Highpockets and me," Shorty said, "we were headin' for the Jackson Hole country. You tell him he'll have to go it alone, will you?"

"He's comin', Shorty. He'll be here in just a moment."

"He better hurry. I got my saddle on something I can't ride."

Highpockets loomed over them. "See you down the road a piece, Shorty. You be lookin' for me. You'll know me because I'll have a scalp to my belt."

Nettie brushed the hair back from his brow, and Shorty passed with his eyes on her face.

"He was a man loved high country," I said. "We'll bury him here."

"Smoke over yonder," Cap said. "Might be a town."

"Bunch the cattle," I said. "We're going on in."

Chapter 24

Of the cattle with which we started less than half remained, and they were lean and rangy from the long drive.

"Nettie," Orrin advised, "you and Mrs. McCann had better hang back behind the herd. We're going to have trouble."

"What's this all about, anyway?" Mary McCann demanded.

"We'll know when we meet Logan, and that should be soon."

"Is that a town down there?"

"It is no town," Baptiste said. "Once there was fort. A man named Campbell had fort here back in 1838 or '39. Sometimes trapper mans camped here."

"There's somebody here now," Haney said, "and somebody killed Shorty."

Sitting my roan horse, I listened to what was being said with only a bit of my attention. What was worrying me was what we'd find down below. Shorty had been killed. Shot right through the chest and spine and shot dead. He had been shot deliberately, and to me it looked like they were trying to warn us to stay out.

"Baptiste? Why here? Why don't they want us there? Why would anybody want a herd of cattle here? There isn't enough grass to keep a herd of this size alive."

"You say he say 'before winter comes.' They want beef. They want food. No game comes in winter. Ver' little game. People could be much hungry.

"Winter comes an' nobody here. Nobody goes out. I t'ink somebody wish to stay here through the winter."

140

"He could be right, Tell," Orrin said. "What other answer is there?"

"Whoever it is, they mean business. The shooting of Shorty was deliberate. It was a warning. *Stay out or be killed.*"

Suddenly, I made up my mind. My impulse was to go right on in, but into what? "We'll camp," I said. "We'll camp right here on the mountain."

Tyrel turned to stare at me. "I say let's go on in. Let's get it done."

"Get what done, Tye? Who is the enemy? Who are we hunting? Where's Logan? If he's free, he may not even be down there. If he's a prisoner, we'd better know where he is.

"There may be ten men down there, and there may be fifty. They've already showed us they are ready to fight, and to kill. According to what we heard, they've got the Samples down there and those Polon brothers.

"Go into camp," I said, "right back at the edge of the trees, and let's get set for a fight."

We moved the cattle into a kind of a cul de sac at the edge of the forest. Dragging a log into place here and there and propping them against trees, we made a crude sort of a fence. It wouldn't stop a determined steer but might stop a casual wanderer.

We found a place at the edge of the trees where a fire might safely be built without being seen from too great a distance. "Fix us a good meal, Lin," I suggested. "We may need it tomorrow."

"What's on your mind, Tell?"

"I'm going down there tonight. I'm going to see what's going on."

"They will expect somebody."

"Maybe."

"If Logan didn't leave that marker himself," I said, "somebody did it for him, somebody who could get out and come back in."

"I didn't see any tracks."

"You didn't look close enough. There were tracks, most of them wiped out and with leaves scattered over. Back in the brush a few steps I found some—woman's tracks."

"That sounds like Logan. He never got himself in trouble yet there wasn't some woman tryin' to get him out of it."

There was grass enough to keep the cattle happy, and we settled down to study what lay ahead of us. During the night, there could well be an attack. We had been warned in about the worst way, and we knew they would not hesitate to kill. The worst of it was that we did not know what was at stake except that Logan Sackett was somehow involved.

My night horse was fresh, and I shifted the saddle. Right now I wasn't sure whether I'd ride or walk, and I was thinking the last way might be best. Usually, I carried some moccasins in my outfit, and they were handy today.

Tyrel and Orrin stood with me at the last. "We'll handle things here. If there's shootin', don't worry yourself. We'll hold the fort."

Baptiste came to me. "A long time back there is a path down the mountain." He drew it in the dust. "The old fort is gone—only some stones here. This is grass. There is the river. I do not know what is here.

"The smokes—is ver' much smoke. Two, three fires, maybe." He hesitated. "A man who was at the fort, he tell me they find gold. Maybe—"

That could be the answer. But why threaten Logan with hanging? Why did he need cattle? Who was trying to prevent our arrival?

When darkness came, there were stars over the Cassiar Mountains, and I found Baptiste's trail and went down quietly to the water and crossed to the point where the old fort had stood. Some of the snow had melted, but there were patches which I avoided, not wanting to outline myself against the white or to leave tracks that could be found.

A straight dark line against the sky told me a building was there.

Where would Logan be? If I could find Logan, he could explain it all. Slowly, taking infinite care, I circled the area at the edge of the woods. I found a sluice, heard a rustle of running water in it. Somebody had been placering for gold.

A tent, and another tent. A canvas-walled house, a shedlike place, a log cabin with light shining from some cracks. A dug-out door with a bar across the outside—the *outside?*

For a moment, I held still in the shadows. Now why a bar across a door from the outside? Obviously not to keep anybody from getting in, so it must be to keep somebody from getting out.

Logan?

Maybe. There was a larger log cabin close by and light from a window made of old bottles, a window I could not see in, and nobody inside could see out. Beyond it, there was a corral. Easing along in the shadows, I counted at least twelve horses, and there were probably more.

There was a building with a porch in front of it, steps leading up to the door, and no light at all. It could be a store. In all, there were not more than five or six structures and a scattering of tents and lean-tos.

Nobody was moving around, and there seemed to be no dogs, or my presence would have been discovered. A door of a cabin opened, and a woman stood revealed in the door, a light behind her. She stood there for several minutes, and the night wind stirred her skirt. She brushed back a wisp of hair and went back inside, leaving the door open.

There was a fireplace in view, a homemade chair, a table, and some firewood piled by the fireplace. Suddenly, she came to the door again singing softly, "Bold, brave and undaunted..."

"Rode young Brennan on the moor!" I finished the line for her.

She ceased singing, swept off the door step, and then she spoke softly. "I shall lower the light and leave the door ajar."

She took a few more brushes with the broom, then stepped back inside and partly closed the door; then she lowered the light.

I hesitated. It might be a trap, but "Brennan on the Moor," about an Irish highwayman, was a favorite song of Logan's, and mine, for that matter.

I crossed the open space swiftly, flattened against the wall of the cabin to look and listen; then, silent as a ghost, I slipped inside.

She was waiting for me, her back to the table, her eyes wide. A surprisingly pretty girl with a firm chin and a straight, honest look to her.

"You will be William Tell," she said.

"I am."

"He described you to me, and Tyrel and Orrin as well. Even Lando, for we did not know who would come. He promised me that somebody would. I could not believe it."

"Three of us came, with some friends."

"I heard." There was something ironic in her voice. "I heard that you did not come alone."

"There's a girl with us who is looking for her brother, Douglas Molrone."

"He is here."

"Here?"

"Of course."

"And Logan?"

"He's here. He's getting over a broken leg. It should be almost healed by now, but I think he's prolonging it."

"If you are his nurse, I can understand why."

"He has no nurse. They permit no one near him."

"Who," I asked, "are 'they'?"

"There's gold here. Quite a lot of it, we believe. Some of us began finding it, first just a little, then more. We built a cabin or two and settled down to work.

"Then those others came. They saw what we were doing, and then they began to go to the store for supplies. At first, they bought a little as we did, then they returned for more. Nobody thought anything of it until my father went in to the store and found they had sold out. Everything was gone.

"John Fentrel, the storekeeper, sent a man out for supplies. He did not return.

"Then Logan Sackett came along. He came down the river in a canoe and tried to buy supplies at the store. Then he tried to buy from us, but we were down to almost nothing.

"He found out what had happened, and he offered to drive in a herd of beef cattle for us. He collected money from us, all we had. We managed to kill a little game, and we waited.

"Apparently, he had known of a small herd that had been driven part way here. Actually, I think the drover was headed for Barkerville and got hung up somewhere inland.

"Logan said he bought the herd from him and started back here. His men deserted him, but he kept on; then his cattle were stampeded, and his leg was broken."

"We got word somebody wanted to hang him."

"Some of us did. We thought he had taken our money and tried to get away with it. Some of us did not believe there had ever been any herd. Some of us thought he had lied. He promised us that if he could get a message out, he'd get cattle here before snow fell. There wasn't much else we could do, so we sent his message, and we've waited."

"Did you believe him?"

"Sort of. We sent a man out for supplies, and he got back, traveling at night with a canoe. He was going again, but his canoe was stolen.

"All the time those other men just loafed around, eating very well and just waiting. They mined very little and cut just enough wood for themselves and waited for us to starve.

"The man they called Cougar taunted us. He said if we were smart, we'd get out while we could, that Logan had lied and there was no herd. He said even if there was, there was no way cattle could reach us.

"They brought in more supplies, but they would sell none of them, and every man we sent out either failed to come back or had his supplies stolen.

"They wanted the gold for themselves, all of it, and they were trying to force us out. We put some fish traps in the river, Indian style, and that helped until they discovered what we were doing. They destroyed our traps as fast as we built them."

"How many of you are there?"

"Eight. There are four men and three women." She paused. "And there's a boy. Danny is about ten."

"And them?"

"There was just five of them. Now there are at least a dozen. Two of them were gone for quite a while, and when they came back, there were some other men with them. The two who left were George and Perry Stamper."

"We've met them."

He was listening. Several times he thought he heard faint sounds outside. He glanced at her. How far could he trust her? Was she one of *them?*

"Can you put names to the others?" he asked.

"Shanty's their leader, or he seems to be. That's Shanty Gavin. Then there's Doug Molrone—"

"He's one of them?"

"Yes, he is. He was one of the first ones. He came in with Shanty and the Stampers and that man Cougar. Oh, it's simple enough! If we leave, they will simply take over all the claims and have the gold to themselves! All they want to do is starve us out so we have to leave. Then they can say we abandoned the claims."

"Mind sitting in the dark?"

"What? Oh? No, not really. If you mean am I afraid of you, I'm not. Not in the least. I'm not afraid of any man."

"Put the light out, will you? There'll be the glow from the fireplace."

She glanced at me, then blew out the light. "Did you hear something?"

"I thought I did."

The fire had died to red coals. I liked the glow of it on her face. Her hair was dark, as were her eyes, and her skin deeply tanned.

"Where is your father?"

"He went away. He went overland to try to find supplies. He has not returned."

"You know who I am," I suggested.

She hesitated, then turned her eyes to me. "I am Laurie Gavin," she said.

Chapter 25

"**G**avin?"

"Shanty is my stepbrother," she explained.

"And Kyle?"

Surprised, she looked around at me. "What do you know of Kyle? But how could you know him? He is in Toronto!"

"He is on his way here, I believe."

"Kyle is my brother. My real brother."

I drew my gun. "Someone is coming, I think. Are you afraid?"

"Of course. I know them. On the surface, they are very quiet, very smooth, very soft-spoken, but do not trust them, William Tell Sackett, for they lie, and they will kill."

"Shanty, too?"

"He is the worst of them. Remember this. He is no blood brother of mine. My father married his mother, and he took our name. He preferred it to Stamper."

I returned the gun to its holster. There was a tap on the door. She glanced at me, and I said, "Answer it."

She went to the door. "Yes?" she said.

"Open the door, Laurie. You've a man in there we want."

She opened it, and Cougar and another, larger, more powerful man with a shock of blond hair stepped in.

"I am Tell Sackett," I said. "Are you looking for me?"

Cougar stepped aside. "Be careful, Shanty. This one's tough."

"Knowing that," I said, "might save us all some trouble."

Shanty had a nice smile. "But we've got you," he said. "There's no way you can get away."

I smiled back at him. "Then take me," I said. "I'm here."

Shanty hesitated. It worried him that I was not afraid, and he was a cautious man. I did not doubt his courage, but there is a time to be brave and a time not to be a damned fool.

"We've got your brother," he said. "We can kill him whenever we wish."

"Logan? He's not my brother, just a sort of distant cousin, but there are a lot of Sacketts, Shanty. If you step on the toes of one, they all come running."

"You came," he admitted. "I never thought you'd make it."

"There are two more up on the mountain, and by now they're beginning to miss me. They're getting lonely on the mountain, Shanty, and they'll come down."

"We will handle them."

"And there are more of us where we came from. Be smart, Shanty. Cash in your chips while you still can. Walk away from here now. Just lay down your hand."

He laughed, and there was real humor in it. "You know, Sackett, I like you. I'm going to hate to kill you."

"We've brought the cattle through, Shanty. In spite of all your boys could do, they are here. There's beef enough to last the winter through, and we might get in some other supplies before the cold sets in.

"As far as that goes, we can let them have what's left of our supplies. You played a strong hand, but when the showdown came, you just didn't have it."

Out on the mountain, I heard a wild, clear yell in the night, and I knew what it was. The boys were bringing the cattle down. They'd be here soon; no doubt some of them already were.

"He's right." It was a voice behind me, a voice I knew. It was Logan. He appeared from behind the curtain covering the door to Laurie's bedroom.

"Sorry, Laurie, but I had to use your window. It isn't quite shut."

Shanty looked from one to the other. "He's yours, Cougar. You always thought you could take him."

Logan was leaning on a crutch, but suddenly he dropped it and stood on his two feet. "That bar of yours," he said, "I just poked a stick through a crack and worked it loose. I tried it a week ago and found it would work." He smiled. "I was waitin' for the Sacketts. I knew they'd come. They always come."

Laurie stepped back.

Shanty's expression had changed. The humor was gone now. His eyes were large. I knew he was ready. I knew he was a dangerous man. Cougar had eyes only for Logan, who was smiling widely.

Outside in the town, I could hear the stir of cattle, a rattle of spurs on the porch of the store.

Then I heard Orrin speak. "Up to you, George. You and Perry can take a canoe and go down river. There's lots of new country waiting." He paused. "All your boys can just ride out, walk out, or paddle out, but all of you are leaving."

It was quiet in the room where we stood. We were listening.

"Not Doug!" That was Nettie. "He's my brother! He wouldn't—"

"He did," somebody else said. "He was one of the worst of them. Some men will do anything for gold."

"Not Doug!" she protested.

"I was in it, Sis. I was in it all the way! It was a chance to get rich! To get rich all at once! To get rich without all that slavin', standing in icy water, panning out gold! I could sell the claim! I could—!"

"And now you can't," Tyrel said.

"It was worth a try," Shanty said, and went for his gun.

Only the red glow of the fire, then a moment of crashing thunder, the brief stabs of gun lightning in the half light.

Outside in the street, the sound was echoed. There was a sound of running, a scream, a pound of racing hoofs.

Tell and Logan Sackett stood alone in the red glow from the fire. Behind them, on the edge of a bench, Laurie sat, horror stricken, gripped fast in shock.

Shanty Gavin stared up at them. "Damn it! Damn it to hell! It looked so good! We had it all! They'd starve out and pull out, and we'd work and then sell! It was a cinch! We had a pat hand!"

Me, I was reloading my gun, and Logan looked down at him. "You had a pat hand, all right, Shanty. You've still got it. Five of a kind, right in the belly!"

Laurie stood up. "Tell—please! Take me out of here."

"We can go out the easier way," Logan said, "down to the Stikine River and out to Wrangell and the sea. Then a ship to Frisco."

Cap looked over at Mary McCann. "If this was where you was comin', you got here too late. You want to go out with me?"

Nettie was standing there alone, and Orrin went to her.

"He ran," she said. "Doug ran away."

"The Stampers didn't," Tyrel said, "and look where they are."

"It's getting light," Orrin said. "What's the matter with this country?"

"That's because it's morning," Tyrel said. "The sun's comin' up."

"Mr. Sackett?" It was John Fentrell. "This may seem a bad time and all, but with you and your boys talking of leaving, I think you should come into the store and we'll settle up."

Laurie was walking down toward the gravel point where the old landing had been. "I'll be along," I said, and went inside.

Fentrell looked old and tired. He removed a loose board and lifted out some sacks of gold. "If they knew where it was," he said. "They'd have taken it all."

The gold was there on the counter. It was not enough, but it was all they had. We would have debts to pay and hard work to do to make up for the time.

So I taken the gold and walked outside into the morning sun and looked toward the shore where the rest of them had gathered by the boats.

"Mr. Fentrell," I said, "we left one man up yonder." I gestured toward the trail down which we had come. "Walk up there and see him sometime."

Shorty was a good man, and he'd come a far piece, and I hoped he wouldn't be lonely on the mountain.

THE SKY-LINERS

Chapter 1

Everybody in our part of the country knew of Black Fetchen, so folks just naturally stood aside when he rode into town with his kinfolk.

The Fetchen land lay up on Sinking Creek, and it wasn't often a Sackett got over that way, so we had no truck with one another. We heard talk of him and his doings—how he'd killed a stranger over on Caney's Fork, and about a fair string of shootings and cuttings running back six or seven years.

He wasn't the only Fetchen who'd worked up to trouble in that country, or down in the flat land, for that matter. It was a story told and retold how Black Fetchen rode down to Tazewell and taken some kin of his away from the law.

James Black Fetchen his name was, but all knew him as Black, because the name suited. He was a dark, handsome man with a bold, hard-shouldered way about him, as quick with his fists as with a gun. Those who rode with him, like Tory Fetchen and Colby Rafin, were the same sort.

Me and Galloway had business over in Tazewell or we'd never have been around those parts, not that we feared Black Fetchen, or any man, but we were newly home from the western lands and when we went to Tazewell we went to pay off the last of Pa's debts. Pa had bad luck several years running and owed honor debts we were bound to pay, so Galloway and me rode back from the buffalo plains to settle up.

We had taken off to the western lands two years before, me twenty-two then and him twenty-one. We worked the Santa Fe Trail with a freight outfit, and laid track for a railroad mountain spur, and finally went over the trail from Texas with a herd of steers. It wasn't until we went buffalo hunting that we made our stake.

About that time we heard some kinfolk of ours, name of William

Tell Sackett, was herding up trouble down in the Mogollon, so we saddled up and lit out, because when a Sackett has trouble his kin is just bound to share it with him. So we rode down to help him clean things up.*

This debt in Tazewell now was the last, and our last cent as well. After two years we were right back where we started, except that we had our rifles and hand guns, and a blanket or two. We'd sold our horses when we came back to Tennessee from the hunting grounds.

We walked across the mountain, and when we got to town we headed for the town pump. Once we'd had a drink we started back across the street to settle our debt at the store that had given Pa credit when times were bad.

We were fairly out in the middle of the street when hoofs began to pound and a passel of folks a-horseback came charging up, all armed and loaded for feudin' or bear-fightin'.

Folks went high-tailing it for shelter when they saw those riders coming, but we were right out in the middle of the street and of no mind to run. They came a-tearing down upon us and one of them taken a cut at me with a quirt, yelling, "Get outen the street!"

Well, I just naturally reached up and grabbed a hold on that quirt, and most things I lay a hand to will move. He had a loop around his wrist and couldn't let go if he was a mind to, so I just jerked and he left that saddle a-flying and landed in the dust. The rest of them, they reined around, of a mind to see some fun.

That one who sat in the dust roosted there a speck, trying to figure what happened to him, and then he came off the ground with a whoop and laid at me with a fist.

Now, we Sacketts had always been handy at knuckle-and-skull fighting, but Galloway and me had put in a spell with Irish track-layers and freighting teamsters who did most of their fighting like that. When this stranger looped a swing at my face, I just naturally stepped inside and clobbered him with a short one.

I fetched him coming in on me, and his head snapped back as if you'd laid the butt end of an axe against it. He went into the dust and about that time I heard Galloway saying, mild-like, "Go ahead, if you're a mind to. I'm takin' bets I can empty four, five saddles before you get me."

Me, I'd held my own rifle in my left hand this while, so I just flipped her up, my hand grasped the action, and I was ready. The two

---

*The Sackett Brand.

of us stood there facing the nine of them and it looked like blood on the ground.

Only nobody moved.

The big, handsome man who had been riding point for the outfit looked us over and said, "I'm Black Fetchen."

Galloway, he spoke over to me. "Black Fetchen, he says. Flagan, are you scared?"

"Don't seem to be, now that I think on it. But I've been scared a time or two. Recall that Comanche out there on the short grass? There for a minute or two I figured he had me."

"But you fetched him, Flagan. Now, what all do you figure we should do with this lot?"

"Well, he made his confession. He owned up fair and honest who he was. He never tried to lie out of it. You got to give credit to a man who'll confess like that."

"Maybe"—Galloway was almighty serious—"but I think you're mistaken in this man. He owned up to the fact that he was Black Fetchen, but there wasn't the shame in him there should have been. I figure a man who can up and say 'I'm Black Fetchen' should feel shame. Might at least hang his head and scuff his toe a mite."

Black Fetchen had been growing madder by the minute. "I've had enough of this! By the—!"

"Hold off, Black." That was Colby Rafin talking. "I seen these two before, over nigh the Gap. These are Sacketts. I heard tell they'd come home from the buffalo range."

Now, we Sacketts have been feuding up and down the country with one outfit or another for nigh on to a hundred years, and nobody could say we hadn't marked up our share of scalps, but nobody could say that we hunted trouble.

When Rafin said that, we could just sort of see Black Fetchen settling down into his saddle. We weren't just a pair of green mountain boys putting on a show. He was a brave man, but only a fool will chance a shot from a Winchester at forty feet. Knowing who we were, he now knew we would shoot, so he sat quiet and started to smile. "Sorry, boys, but a joke is a joke. We've come to town on business and want no trouble. Shall I say we apologize?"

That was like a rattlesnake stopping his rattling while keeping his head drawn back to strike.

"You can say that," I agreed, "and we'll accept it just like you mean it; but just so's there's no misunderstanding, why don't you boys just shuck your artillery? Just let them fall gentle into the street."

"I'll be damned if I will!" Tory Fetchen yelled.

"You'll be dead if you don't," Galloway told him. "As to being damned, you'll have to take that up with your Lord and Maker. You going to shuck those guns, or do I start shooting?"

"Do what he says, boys," Black said. "This is only one day. There'll be another."

They did as ordered, but Galloway is never one to let things be. He's got a hankering for the fringe around the edges.

"Now, Gentlemen and Fellow-Sinners, you have come this day within the shadow of the valley. It is well for each and everyone of us to recall how weak is the flesh, how close we stand to Judgment, so you will all join me in singing 'Rock of Ages.'"

He gestured to Black Fetchen. "You will lead the singing, and I hope you are in fine voice."

"You're crazy!"

"Maybe," Galloway agreed, "but I want to hear you loud and clear. You got until I count three to start, and you better make sure they all join in."

"Like hell!" Tory was seventeen, and he was itching to prove himself as tough as he thought he was . . . or as tough as he wanted others to think he was.

Galloway fired, and that bullet whipped Tory's hat from his head and notched his ear. "Sing, damn you!" Galloway said; and brother, they sang.

I'll say this for them, they had good strong voices and they knew the words. Up in the mountains the folks are strong on goin' to meetin', and these boys all knew the words. We heard it clear: *Rock of ages, cleft for me, Let me hide, myself in thee."*

"Now you all turn around," Galloway advised, "and ride slow out of town. I want all these good people to know you ain't bad boys—just sort of rambunctious when there's nobody about to discipline you a mite."

"Your guns," I said, "will be in the bank when it opens tomorrow!"

So James Black Fetchen rode out of town with all that rowdy gang of his, and we stood with our rifles and watched them go.

"Looks like we made us some enemies, Flagan," Galloway said.

"Sufficient to the day is the evil thereof," I commented, liking the mood, "but don't you mind. We've had enemies before this."

We collected the guns and deposited them in the bank, which was closing, and then we walked across the street and settled Pa's account.

Everybody was chuckling over what happened, but also they

warned us of what we could expect. We didn't have cause to expect much, for the fact was we were going back to the buffalo prairies. Back home there was nothing but an empty cabin, no meat in the pot, no flour in the bin.

We had done well our first time west, and now we would go back and start over. Besides, there were a lot of Sackett kinfolk out there now.

We started off.

Only we didn't get far. We had just reached the far end of town when we sighted a camp at the edge of the woods, and an oldish man walked out to meet us. We'd talked with enough Irish lads whilst working on the railroad to recognize the brogue. "May I be havin' a word wi' you, boys?"

So we stopped, with Galloway glancing back up the street in case those Fetchen boys came back with guns.

"I'm Laban Costello," he said, "and I'm a horse-trader."

More than likely everybody in the mountains knew of the Irish horse-traders. There were eight families of them, good Irish people, known and respected throughout the South. They were drifting folk, called gypsies by some, and they moved across the land swapping horses and mules, and a canny lot they were. It was in my mind this would be one of them.

"I am in trouble," he said, "and my people are far away in Atlanta and New Orleans."

"We are bound for the buffalo lands, but we would leave no man without help. What can we do?"

"Come inside," he said, and we followed him back into the tent.

This was like no tent I had ever seen, with rugs on the ground and a curtained wall across one side to screen off a sleeping space. This was the tent of a man who moved often, but lived well wherever he stopped. Out behind it we had noticed a caravan wagon, painted and bright.

Making coffee at the fire was a girl, a pretty sixteen by the look of her. Well, maybe she was pretty. She had too many freckles, and a pert, sassy way about her that I didn't cotton to.

"This is my son's daughter," he said. "This is Judith."

"Howdy, ma'am," Galloway said.

Me, I merely looked at her and she wrinkled her nose at me. I turned away sharp, ired by any fool slip of a girl so impolite as to do such as that to a stranger.

"First, let me say that I saw what happened out there in the street, and you are the first who have faced up to Fetchen in a long while. He is a bad man, a dangerous man."

"We ain't likely to see him again," I said, "for we are bound out across the plains."

Personally, I wanted him to get to the point. It was my notion those Fetchens would borrow guns and come back, loaded for bear and Sacketts. This town was no place to start a shooting fight, and I saw no cause to fight when nothing was at stake.

"Have you ever been to Colorado?"

"Nigh to it. We have been in New Mexico."

"My son lives in Colorado. Judith is his daughter."

Time was a-wasting and we had a far piece to go. Besides, I was getting an uneasy feeling about where all this was leading.

"It came to me," Costello said, "that as you are going west, and you Sacketts have the name of honorable men, I might prevail upon you to escort my son's daughter to her father's home."

"No," I said.

"Now, don't be hasty. I agree that traveling with a young girl might seem difficult, but Judith has been west before, and she has never known any other life but the camp and the road."

"She's been west?"

"Her father is a mustanger, and she traveled with him."

"Hasn't she some folks who could take her west?" I asked. Last thing I wanted was to have a girl-child along, making trouble, always in the way, and wanting special treatment.

"At any other time there would be plenty, but now there is no time to waste. You see Black Fetchen had put his mind to her."

"Her?" I was kind of contemptuous. "Why, she ain't out of pigtails yet!"

She stuck out her tongue at me, but I paid her no mind. What worried me was that Galloway wasn't speaking up. He was just listening, and every once in a while he'd look at that snip of a girl.

"She will be sixteen next month, and many a girl is wed before the time. Black Fetchen has seen her and has told me he means to have her . . . in fact, he had come tonight to take her, but you stopped him before he reached us."

"Sorry," I told him, "but we've got to travel fast, and we may have a shooting fight with those Fetchens before we get out of Tennessee. They don't shape up to be a forgiving lot."

"You have horses?"

"Well, no. We sold them back in Missouri to pay up what Pa owed hereabouts. We figured to join up with a freight outfit we once worked with, and get west to New Mexico. There's Sacketts out there where we could get some horses until time we could pay for them."

"Suppose I provide the horses? Or rather, suppose Judith does? She owns six head of mighty fine horses, and where she goes, they go."

"No," I said.

"You have seen Fetchen. Would you leave a young girl to him?"

He had me there. I wouldn't leave a yeller hound dog to that man. He was big, and fierce-looking for all he was so handsome, but he looked to me like a horse- and wife-beater, and I'd met up with a few.

"The townsfolk wouldn't stand for that," I said.

"They are afraid of him. As for that, he says he wishes to marry Judith. As far as the town goes, we are movers. We don't belong to the town."

It wasn't going to be easy for us, even without a girl to care for. We would have to hunt for what we ate, sleep out in the open, dodge Indians, and make our way through some of the worst possible country. If we tied on with a freight outfit we would be with rough men, in a rough life. Traveling like that, a girl would invite trouble, and it appeared we would have a-plenty without that.

"Sorry," I said.

"There is one other thing," Costello said. "I am prepared to give each of you a fine saddle horse and a hundred dollars each to defray expenses on the way west."

"We'll do it," Galloway said.

"Now, see here," I started to protest, but they were no longer listening. I have to admit that he'd knocked my arguments into a cocked hat by putting up horses and money. With horses, we could ride right on through, not having to tie up with anybody, and the money would pay for what we needed. Rustling grub for ourselves wouldn't amount to much. But I still didn't like it. I didn't figure to play nursemaid to any girl.

"The horses are saddled and ready. Judith will ride one of her own, and her gear will be on another. And there will be four pack horses if you want to use them as such."

"Look," I said. "That girl will be trouble enough, but you said those horses of hers were breeding stock. Aside from the geldings you'll be giving us, we'll have a stallion and five mares, and that's trouble in anybody's country."

"The stallion is a pet. Judith has almost hand-fed it since it was a colt."

"Ma'am," I turned on her. "That stallion will get itself killed out yonder. Stallions, wild stock, will come for miles to fight him, and some of them are holy terrors."

"You don't have to worry about Ram," she replied. "He can take care of himself."

"This here girl," I argued, "she couldn't stand up to it. West of the river there ain't a hotel this side of the Rockies fit for a lady, and we figure to sleep under the stars. There'll be dust storms and rain-storms, hail the like of which you never saw; and talk about thunder and lightning . . ."

Costello was smiling at me. "Mr. Sackett, you seem to forget to whom you are talking. We are of the Irish horse-traders. I doubt if Judith has slept under a roof a dozen times in her life, other than the roof of a caravan. She has lived in the saddle since she could walk, and will ride as well as either of you."

Well, that finished me off. Ride as well as me? Or Galloway? That was crazy.

"Look," I said to Galloway, "we can't take no girl!"

"Where else are we going to get horses and an outfit?" he interrupted.

He was following Costello out the back way, and there were eight horses, saddled, packed and ready, standing under the poplars. And eight finer animals you never did see. Nobody ever lived who was a finer judge of horseflesh than those Irish traders, and these were their own stock, not for trading purposes.

Right off I guessed them to be Irish hunters with a mite of some other blood. Not one of them was under sixteen hands, and all were splendidly built. The sight of those horses started me weakening almighty fast. I'd never seen such horses, and had never owned anything close to the one he'd picked for me.

"Irish hunters," he said, "with a judicious mixture of mustang blood. We did the mustanging ourselves, or rather, Judith and her father and his brother did. They kept the best of the mustangs for breeding, because we wanted horses with stamina as well as speed, and horses that could live off the country. Believe me, these horses are just what we wanted."

"I'd like to," I said, "but—"

"Fetchen wants these horses," Costello added, "and as they belong to Judith and her father, they would go with her."

"That makes sense," I said. "Now I can see why Fetchen wanted her."

She was standing close by and she hauled off and kicked me on the shin. I yelped, and they all turned to look to me. "Nothing," I said. "It wasn't anything."

"Then you had better ride out of here," Costello said; "but make no mistake. Black Fetchen will come after you. Today was the day Fetchen was coming after Judith."

When I threw a leg over that black horse and settled down into the leather I almost forgave that Judith. This was more horse than I'd ever sat atop of. It made a man proud. No wonder Fetchen wanted that fool girl, if he could get these horses along with her.

We taken out.

Galloway led the way, keeping off the road and following a cow path along the stream.

When we were a mile or so out of town, Galloway edged over close to me. "Flagan, there's one thing you don't know. We got to watch that girl. Her grandpa whispered it to me She thinks highly of Black Fetchen. She figures he's romantic—dashing and all that. We've got to watch her, or she'll slip off and go back."

Serve her right, I thought.

Chapter 2

Now, there's no accounting for the notions of womenfolks, particularly when they are sixteen. She came of good people. We Sacketts had dealt with several generations of Irish horse-traders, and found them sharp dealers, but so were we all when it came to swapping horseflesh. There were several thousand of them, stemming from the eight original families, and it was a rare thing when one married outside the clans.

I thought about Black Fetchen. To give the devil his due, I had to admit he was a bold and handsome man, and a fine horseman. He was hell on wheels in any kind of a fight, and his kinfolk were known for their rowdy, bullying ways. Judith had seen Fetchen ride into town, all dressed up and flashy, with a lot of push and swagger to him. She knew nothing of the killings behind him.

We rode a goodly distance, holding to mountain trails. Judith rode along meek as a lamb, and when we stopped I figured she was plumb wore out. She ate like a hungry youngster, but she was polite as all get out, and that should have warned me. After I banked the fire I followed Galloway in going to sleep. Judith curled up in a blanket close by.

The thing is, when a man hunts out on the buffalo grass he gets scary. If he sleeps too sound he can lose his hair, so a body gets fidgety in his sleep, waking up every little while, and ready to come sharp awake if anything goes wrong.

Of a sudden, I woke up. A thin tendril of smoke lifted from the banked fire, and I saw that Judith was gone. I came off the ground, stamped into my boots, and grabbed my pistol belt.

It took me a minute to throw on a saddle and cinch up, then I lit out of there as if the devil was after me. The tracks were plain to see. There was no need to even tell Galloway, because when he awakened he could read the sign as easy as some folks would read a book.

162

She had led her horse a good hundred yards away from camp, and then she had mounted up, held her pace down for a little bit further, and then started to canter.

At the crossing of the stream the tracks turned toward the highroad, and I went after her. For half a mile I let that black horse run, and he had it in him to go. Then I eased down and took my rope off the saddle and shook out a loop.

She heard me coming and slapped her heels to her horse, and for about two miles we had us the prettiest horse race you ever did see.

The black was too fast for her, and as we closed in I shook out a loop and dabbed it over her shoulders. The black was no roping horse, but when I pulled him in that girl left her horse a-flyin' and busted a pretty little dent in the ground when she hit stern first.

She came off the ground fighting mad, but I'd handled too many fractious steers to be bothered by that, so before she knew what was happening I had her hog-tied and helpless.

For a female youngster, she had quite a surprising flow of language, shocking to a man of my sensibilities, and no doubt to her under other circumstances. She'd been around horse-trading men since she was a baby, and she knew all the words and the right emphasis.

Me, I just sat there a-waiting while she fussed at me. I taken off my hat, pushed back my hair, settled my hat on my head again, all the time seeming to pay her no mind. Then I swung down from the saddle and picked her up and slung her across her horse, head and heels hanging. And then we trotted back to camp.

Galloway was saddled up and ready to ride. "What all you got there, boy?" he called to me.

"Varmint. I ketched it down the road a piece. Better stand shy of it because I figure it'll bite, and might have a touch of hydrophoby, judgin' by sound."

Wary of heels and teeth, I unslung her from the saddle. "Ma'am, I'm of no mind to treat anybody thisaway, but you brought it on yourself. Now, if you'll set easy in the saddle I'll unloose you."

Well, she spoke her piece for a few minutes and then she started to cry, and that done it. I unloosed her, helped her into the saddle, and we started off again, with her riding peaceable enough.

"You just wait," she said. "Black Fetchen will come. He will come riding to rescue me."

"You or the horses," I said. "I hear he's a man sets store by good horseflesh."

"He will come."

"You'd best hope he doesn't, ma'am," Galloway suggested. "We promised to deliver you to your pa in Colorado, and that's what we aim to do."

"If he really loves you," I said, "he'd think nothing of riding to Colorado. Was I in love with a girl, that would seem a short way to go."

"You!" she said scornfully. "Who would ever love *you?"*

Could be she was totally right, but I didn't like to think it. Nobody ever did love me that I could remember of, except Ma. Galloway, he was a rare hand with the girls, but not me. I never knew how to sit up and carry on with them, and likely they thought me kind of stupid. Hard to find two brothers more alike and more different than Galloway and me.

Both of us were tall and raw-boned, only he was a right handsome man with a lot of laughter in him, and easy-talking except in times of trouble. Me, I was quieter, and I never smiled much. I was taller than Galloway by an inch, and there was an arrow scar on my cheekbone, picked up on the Staked Plains from a Comanche brave.

We grew up on a sidehill farm in the mountains, fourteen miles from a crossroads store and twenty miles from a town—or what passed as such. We never had much, but there was always meat on the table. Galloway and me, we shot most of our eatin' from the time I was six and him five, and many a time we wouldn't have eaten at all if we couldn't shoot.

Ma, she was a flatland schoolma'am until she up and married Pa and came to live in the mountains, and when we were growing up she tried to teach us how to talk proper. We both came to writing and figuring easy enough, but we talked like the boys around us. Although when it came right down to it, both of us could talk a mite of language, Galloway more than me.

Mostly Ma was teaching us history. In the South in those days everybody read Sir Walter Scott, and we grew up on *Ivanhoe* and the like. She had a sight of other books, maybe twenty all told, and one time or another we read most of them. After Ma died, me and Galloway batched it alone until we went west.

Galloway and me were Injun enough to leave mighty little trail behind us. We held to high country when possible, and we fought shy of traveled roads. Nor did we head for Independence, which was what might have been expected.

We cut across country, leaving the Kentucky border behind, and along Scaggs' Creek to Barren River, but just before the Barren joined the Green we cut back, west by a mite south, for Smithland, where the Cumberland joined the Ohio. It did me good to ride along Scaggs' Creek, because the Scaggs it was named for had been a Long Hunter in the same outfit with one of the first of my family to come over the mountains.

We bought our meals from farms along the way, or fixed our own. We crossed the Mississippi a few miles south of St. Louis.

No horses could have been better than those we had. They were fast walkers, good travelers, and always ready for a burst of speed when called upon.

Judith was quiet. Her eyes got bigger and rounder, it seemed to me, and she watched our back trail. She was quick to do what she ought and never complained, which should have been a warning. When she did talk it was to Galloway. To me she never said aye, yes, or no.

"What is it like out there?" she asked him.

"Colorado? It's a pure and lovely land beyond the buffalo grass where the mountains r'ar up to the sky. Snow on 'em the year 'round, and the mountains yonder make our Tennessee hills look like dirt thrown up by a gopher.

"It's a far, wide land with the long grass rippling in the wind like a sea with the sun upon it. A body can ride for weeks and see nothing but prairie and sky . . . unless it's wild horses or buffalo."

"Are the women pretty?"

"Women? Ma'am, out in that country a body won't see a woman in months, 'less it's some old squaw or an oldish white woman . . . or maybe a dancing girl in some saloon. Mostly a man just thinks about women, and they all get to look mighty fine after a while. A body forgets how mean and contrary they can be, and he just thinks of them as if they were angels or something."

We saw no sign of Black Fetchen nor any of his lot, yet I'd a notion they were closing in behind us. He didn't look like a man to be beaten, and we had stood him up in his own street, making him lose face where folks would tell of it, and we had taken his girl and the horses he wanted.

There was more to it than that, but we did not know it until later.

From time to time Judith talked some to Galloway, and we heard about her pa and his place in Colorado. Seems he'd left the horse-trading for mustanging, and then drifted west and found himself a ranch in the wildest kind of country. He started breeding horses, but kept on with the mustanging. Judith he'd sent back to be with his family and get some education. Only now he wanted her out there with him.

Now and again some of the family went west and often they drove horses back from his ranch to trade through the South. But now he wanted his daughter, and the stock she would bring with her.

Back of it all there was a thread of something that worried me. Sizing it up, I couldn't find anything that didn't sound just right, but there it was. Call it a hunch if you like, but I had a feeling there was something wrong in Colorado. Galloway maybe felt the same, but he didn't speak of it any more than me.

We camped out on the prairie. It was Indian country, only most of the Indians were quiet about that time. Farmers were moving out on the land, but there were still too many loose riders, outlaws from down in the Nation, and others no better than they should be. This was a stretch of country I never did cotton to, this area between the Mississippi and the real West. It was in these parts that the thieves and outlaws got together.

Not that Galloway or me was worried. We figured to handle most kinds of trouble. Only thing was, we had us a girl to care for . . . one who would grab hold of a horse any time she saw a chance and head for home . . . and Black Fetchen.

One night we camped on the Kansas prairie with a moon rising over the far edge of the world and stars a-plenty. We could hear the sound of the wind in the grass, and stirring leaves of the cottonwoods under which we had camped. It was a corner maybe half an acre in extent, at a place where a stream curled around a big boulder. There was a flat place behind that boulder where we shaped our camp; here there was a fallen tree, and firewood from dead limbs.

We built up a small fire, and after we'd eaten our beef and beans we sat about and sang a few of the old songs, the mountain songs, some of them reaching back to the time when our folks came across the water from Wales.

Judith was singing, too, and a clear, fine voice she had, better than either of us. We liked to sing, but weren't much account.

The horses moved in close, liking the fire and the voices. It was a mighty fine evening. After Judith turned in, Galloway did likewise. I had the first watch. Taking up my rifle, I prowled around outside the trees of the small woods.

Second time around I pulled up short over on the west side. Something was moving out yonder in the dark, and I squatted down to listen, closer to the ground, to hear the rustle of the grass.

Something was coming slow . . . something hurt, by the sound of it. The sound was a slow, dragging movement, and a time or two I heard a faint groan. But I made no move, for I was trusting no such sound.

After a bit, I made him out, a crawling man, not many yards off. Carefully, I looked all around at the night, but I saw nothing.

I slipped back to camp. "Galloway," I whispered, "there's a man out yonder, sounds to be hurt bad. I'm going to bring him in."

"You go ahead. I'll stand by."

If it was a trick, somebody would wish it wasn't. I walked out there, spotted the man again, and spoke to him quiet-like, so's my voice wouldn't carry.

"What's the trouble, *amigo?*"

The crawling stopped, and for a moment there was silence. Then the voice came, low, conversational. "I've caught a bad one. Figured I glimpsed a fire."

"You bein' sought after?"

"Likely."

Well, I went up to him then and picked him up and packed him into camp. He was a man of forty or so, with a long narrow face and a black mustache streaked with gray. He had caught a bad one through the body and he looked mighty peaked. The slug had gone on through, for he was holed on both sides. Whilst I set to, plugging him up, Galloway he moved out to keep an eye on the prairie.

Judith, she woke up and set to making some hot broth, and by the time I'd patched him up she was about ready with it. I figured he'd lost blood, so I mixed up some salt water and had him drink that. We had been doing that for lost blood for years back, and it seemed to help.

He was game, I'll say that for him. Whilst Judith fed soup into him, I had a look at his foot.

"Wagon tongue fell on it," he said. "Rider jumped his horse into camp and knocked the wagon tongue over and she hit me on the instep."

His foot was badly swollen, and I had to cut the boot off. He stared at me between swallows of soup. "Look at that now!" he worried. "Best pair of boots I ever did have! Bought 'em a month back in Fort Worth."

"You a Texan?"

"Not reg'lar. I'm an Arkansawyer. I been cookin' for a cow outfit trailin' stock up from the Neuces country. Last evenin' a man stopped by our wagon for a bite of grub. He was a lean, dark, thin sort of man with narrow eyes. He was rough-dressed, but he didn't look western." He glanced up, suddenly wary. "Fact is, he talked somewhat like you boys."

"Don't be troubled. There's no kin of ours about here."

"He wore a sort of red sash and carried a rifle like he was born to it—"

"Colby Rafin!" Judith said.

"You called it, I didn't," I said.

"Anyway, he et and then rode off. About the time we'd been an hour abed, they come a-hellin' out of the night. Must've been a dozen of them or twenty. They come chargin' through camp, a-shootin' and a-yellin' and they drove off our herd, drove them to hell off down the country."

"You'd better catch some rest. You look done in."

He looked straight at me. "I ain't a-gonna make it, *amigo*, an' you know it."

Judith, she looked at me, all white and funny, but I said to him, "You got anybody you want us to tell?"

"I got no kin. Bald-Knobbers killed them all, a long time back. Down Texas way my boss was Evan Hawkes, a fine man. He lost a sight out there this night—his herd, his outfit, and his boy."

"Boy?"

"Youngster . . . mebbe thirteen. He had been beggin' the boss to let him ride north with us instead of on the cars. We were to meet Hawkes in Dodge."

"Are you sure about the boy?"

"Seen him fall. A man shot right into him, rode over him. If any of our outfit got away it was one of the boys on night herd."

He sat quiet for a while, and I stole a glance at Judith. She was looking almighty serious, and she had to realize that bunch of raiders that stole the herd and killed the boy had been the Fetchen outfit. Colby Rafin was never far from Black.

"They know they got you?"

"Figured it. They knew I was knocked down by the wagon tongue, and then one of them shot into me as he jumped his horse over."

As carefully as I could, I was easing the biggest sticks away from the fire so it would burn down fast. One thing was sure. That Fetchen outfit had followed us west. But this was no place or time to have a run-in with them.

The man opened his eyes after a bit and looked at Judith. "Ma'am? In my shirt pocket I got a gold locket. Ain't much, mebbe, but my ma wore it her life long, and her ma before her. I'd take it kindly, if you'd have it as a present."

"Yes . . . thank you."

"You got tender hands, ma'am, mighty gentle hands. Been a long time since a woman touched me . . . gentlelike. It's a fine thing to remember, ma'am."

I'd moved off to the edge of the darkness, listening for trouble riding our way, but I could faintly hear him still talking. "That tall man here," he said, "he carries the look of an eagle. He'll make tracks in the land, ma'am. You better latch onto him, ma'am, if you ain't spoke for. His kind run mighty scarce."

After a moment, he opened his eyes again. "You knowed that man come to my camp?"

"Colby Rafin." She was silent for a moment, and then she said, "They were looking for us, I think."

"For *him?*" he half-lifted a hand toward me. "They're crazy!"

Galloway came in out of the dark, and I whispered to him about Rafin and how the herd was lost.

"It's like them—outlaws always. Now they've turned cattle thieves."

Neither one of us had much to say, because we were both thinking the same thing. The Fetchens had come west, all right, and they had come a-hunting us. The trouble was they had us outnumbered by a good bit, and running off this herd showed they'd taken the full step from being rowdies and troublemakers to becoming genuine outlaws. From now on it would be a fight to the death against an outfit that would stop at nothing . . . and us with a girl to watch out for.

That Colorado ranch began to look mighty far away, and I was cursing the hour when I first saw Costello or Judith.

Not that we minded a fight. We Sacketts never had much time for anything else. If we weren't fighting for our country we were fighting men who still believed in rule by the gun, and no Sackett I ever heard of had ever drawn a gun on a man except in self-defense, or in defense of his country or his honor.

Right then I was glad Galloway stood beside me. Nobody ever needed an army when they had Galloway, and maybe one other Sackett . . . it didn't make much difference which one.

Chapter 3

We hit trail before sunup, keeping off the skyline as much as possible, but always moving westward, riding sidewise in the saddle so as we could look all around, Galloway facing one way, me the other.

There was a look to the sky that spelled a weather change, but we didn't pay it no mind, figuring only to get distance behind us.

Short of noon a man came up from the south riding a paint pony and hazing about thirty head of cattle. When he put eyes on us he rode his pony around the cattle and came up to us, keeping his Winchester handy and studying us careful-like.

"You pass anybody back yonder? I'm huntin' my outfit."

The brand on his pony and those cattle spelled the story for me—a Half-Box H. "You got stampeded a while back," I said, "and one of your outfit died in our camp."

"Which one?"

"Said he was the cook. Come to think on it, he never did give us his name. Said he rode for Evan Hawkes, and he told us Hawkes's boy got killed in the stampede."

The man's face showed shock. "The boy's dead? That'll go hard on the boss. He set store by the lad."

Me, I curled one leg around the pommel and pushed my hat back. "Mister, looks to me like your herd was scattered hell to breakfast. We covered some miles back yonder and seen nobody. What you figure to do?"

"Drive these cattle into Dodge an' report to Evan Hawkes. All I can do."

He told me his name was Briggs. "Might as well ride with us," I said to him. "It's one more gun for each of us."

"What's that mean?"

170

"That was James Black Fetchen's outfit from Tennessee who jumped your herd. They're hunting us. If we meet up with them there'll be shooting, and you can lay to it that if they see you're alive they'll be after you, too."

"I'll ride along," he said.

During the next hour we picked up thirteen head of scattered cattle wearing the Hawkes brand. By nightfall we had close to fifty head more. We'd scarcely made camp when we were hailed out of the night . . . in those days no man in his right mind rode up to a strange camp without giving them a call.

"That'll be Ladder Walker," Briggs said. "I know the voice."

Walker was an extra tall, extra lean man, which was why they called him Ladder. He was driving six head of steers, and he had a lump on his skull and a grouch over what happened. "You catch sight of any of that bunch?" he asked Briggs. "All I ask is a sight down a gun barrel at them."

"You stand easy, friend," Galloway said. "That's a mean outfit. If they can help it you'll not get a shooting chance."

The upshot of it was that of the herd of fifteen hundred cattle the Half-Box H sent up the trail, we drove into Dodge with a hundred and twenty, picked up along the way. No doubt a few more riders could have combed twice that number out of the breaks along the creeks and the coulees, scattered stuff left behind from the stampede.

Now, we Sacketts carried a name known in Dodge. Tyrel, Orrin, and some of the others had come into Dodge long before, Tyrel and Orrin being there when the town was mighty young. They were the first Sacketts to go west to settle. Their pa had come west earlier than that, riding and trapping fur along with Bridger, Carson, and Joe Meek. He'd never come back from his last trip, so it was always figured that some Blackfoot had raised his hair, back up in Montana. We'd heard the story as youngsters, but had never known any of that branch of the family until we bumped into Tyrel and Orrin down in the Mogollon, where they'd gone to lend a fighting hand to their brother Tell.

Knowing that if the other riders had come through the stampede alive, they would head for Hawkes at his hotel, we went along with Walker and Briggs. Three other riders had already come in, which left seven missing.

Evan Hawkes was a tall, broad-shouldered but spare-built man with darkish red hair. The build of him and the way he combed his hair reminded a body of Andy Jackson, and he had a pair of gray eyes that advised a man he'd make a better friend than an enemy.

"They've got that herd to sell," Hawkes said, "and we will be there when they try. I'll pass the word around."

"Mr. Hawkes," I said, "you got to remember that Fetchen is no fool. From all I hear, he's mighty shrewd, as well as mean. He may not sell that herd at all."

"What do you mean?"

"From what I've seen of those we gathered, you had quite a bit of young breeding stock. Fetchen could push that herd west into Wyoming, peddle the steers to Indians or the army or some beef contractor. Then he could use the young stuff to start his own outfit."

"You believe he has come west to stay?"

"I've been wondering about that. It doesn't seem reasonable they'd all come west without reason. I figure something happened back there after we left."

Judith had been standing by getting madder by the minute, and now she let go at all of us. "You've no right to suppose anything of the kind! And you've no evidence that Black Fetchen stole that herd!"

Hawkes looked at her, kind of surprised. "It seems to be there's a difference of opinion among you."

"The little lady doesn't think Black is all that mean," Galloway said.

"I certainly do not!"

"The way we figure it," Galloway went on, "what happened to you is mostly our fault. You see, the Fetchens came west hunting us. Black wants the little lady here, and he wants her horses, some of the finest breeding stock you ever did see. Back there in Tazewell—"

"Tennessee?" said Hawkes. "I know it well. I'm from Kentucky."

"Well, we had a run-in with those boys, sort of calmed 'em down when they were about to show their muscle. They been used to having things their own way."

Leaving Hawkes with his riders, the three of us went downstairs to the dining room. Judith had her nose up, and her cheeks were flushed and angry. When we'd found seats at a table she said, "You have no right to talk that way about Mr. Fetchen. He is an honorable man."

"I hope so," Galloway commented, "because if he wasn't, and you went to him, you'd be in a kind of a fix, wouldn't you? This far from home, and all."

We ordered, and then she started to look around some, and so did we. Neither me nor Galloway had been to many towns. We had seen Sante Fe, Dodge, Abilene, and Sedalia, Missouri, and both of us liked to see folks around us.

There were cattle buyers, land speculators, officers from the army post, cattle drivers, gamblers and such like around. All of them were dressed to the nines, and were looking almighty fancy. Galloway and me had taken time before coming in to brush up a little, but somehow we didn't shape up like these folks. We looked like a pair of mountain boys still, and it shamed me. As soon as we got some money, I thought, we'd buy us some proper clothes.

"You been to big towns, Judith?" Galloway asked her.

"I have been to Atlanta and Nashville, and to New Orleans, Mobile, and Louisville . . . oh, lots of towns. My folks traded in all of them."

I'd had no idea she was such a traveled girl, but it followed. The Irish traders were folks that got about a good bit. There for a few minutes she forgot all about Black Fetchen and took to telling us about the big towns, and believe me, we listened to every word.

The restaurant door opened while she was talking and I turned my head. It was Black Fetchen.

He had surely changed. He wore a brand-new black broadcloth suit, a white shirt, and black tie. His boots were polished like all get out, and he carried a new black hat in his hand. His hair was all slicked down with bear grease or the like, and I'll have to admit he was a handsome sight. Tory came in behind him, with Colby Rafin and another one of their outfit known as Ira Landon.

Fetchen walked right over to our table, the others sitting down across the room with their backs to us.

"Why, Judith! How nice to see you!" Then he turned to me and said, "I hope you boys carry no grudge against us. We're certainly not about to hunt trouble with you. Back there we were just a-funnin'—we didn't mean no trouble."

Judith was beaming. It made me mad to see so much sparkle in her eyes over such a no-account rascal. Me, I didn't buy that flannel-mouth talk, and he knew it. All the time he was talking I could just see the taunting in his eyes; but Judith, she was all excited and happy.

"Why, sure!" Galloway was the smooth-talking one of the two of us. "Why don't you pull up a chair and set? We'd enjoy talking a while. Maybe you could tell us something about a herd of cattle somebody stampeded and run off back down the trail."

Judith's face went white and her lips tightened up. She was both mad and scared . . . scared something was going to happen.

"Cattle? Since when did you two go into the cattle business?"

"They weren't our cattle," Galloway said as smooth as silk. "They

belong to a friend of ours, name of Evan Hawkes . . . a good man. His·
herd was stampeded by some rustlers . . . murderers, too, because they
killed his boy, and some of his men."

Fetchen never batted an eye. Oh, he was a cool one! He just smiled
and said, "Come to think of it, we did see a few stray cattle. We even
drove in half a dozen and turned them over to the marshal."

He pulled back a chair and sat down, easy as you please. "As a
matter of fact, I didn't just come over to say howdy to some old friends
from the home state. I came over to see Judith. Seems you boys aren't
going to give me a chance to be alone with her, so I'll have to speak
my piece right here before all of you."

Judith's eyes were shining and her lips were parted. I didn't like
it to see her getting so flustered. Before I could say anything, Black
Fetchen, still smiling like the cat sizing up the canary, says, "Judith,
will you marry me?"

And before either of us can say aye, yes, or no, she ups and says,
"Yes, James—yes, I will!"

"I'm honored, ma'am, right honored." Then he says, "I don't think
it is really the right thing for a man's betrothed to be spending so much
time with two men, single men who are no kin to her, so I've taken
a room for you here at the hotel until we're married."

We sat there, caught flat-footed. This here was something we
hadn't expected, nor did we know what to do. It was Galloway who
spoke first. "That's right nice, Black," he said, "but her grandpa asked
us most particular·to take her to her pa in Colorado. Now, it ain't so
many miles from here, so why don't you two figure on being married
there where her pa can attend? After all, she's his only daughter."

Fetchen never stopped smiling. "Mr. Sackett, I wouldn't expect
you to understand, but I am in love. I do not want to wait."

"Nor do I!" Judith said. "We can be married right here in Dodge."

Galloway didn't show any ire, even if he felt it. He just said, "It
would be nice if your pa knew, Judith. Do you care so little for him?"

That got to her, and she sobered up, suddenly so serious I thought
she might cry.

"It's a noble sacrament," I said, "and a rare thing for a man to see
his daughter wedded to the man of her choice."

She looked up at Fetchen. "James . . . maybe we should wait. After
all, it isn't very far."

Black's lips tightened and his eyes squinted just a mite. I'd always
heard he carried a fearful temper, liable to burst out whenever he was
thwarted, and it was edging toward the surface now. Maybe if she saw

him in a rage it would help. Me and Galloway must have been thinking the same thing. Only trouble was, I up and made a damn fool of myself. I said the wrong thing.

"Besides," I said, "Judith is only a youngster. She's not old enough to marry."

Judith ran up her flag and let go with all her guns, she was that mad. "Flagan Sackett, you wouldn't know a woman if you saw one! I am so old enough! We'll just show you how old I am! James, if you're ready we can be married tomorrow morning."

Fetchen straightened up. Of course, that was all he wanted all the time. He threw me a look that was what a body might call triumphant. "I would be honored, Judith. If you'll come with me I'll show you to your room."

Judith got up and turned her back squarely to me. I started to speak, but what could I say?

Fetchen turned and looked back at us. "Gentlemen, I'll send a couple of the boys over for my fiancée's clothing and her horses—all of them."

"What do you mean, all of them?"

"I mean those you two have been riding. They are Costello horses."

"For which we have a bill of sale," I said calmly, but I was fighting mad underneath.

"That's right, James," Judith said. "Those horses belong to them."

"We will look into that a bit further," Fetchen replied. "I do not think those bills of sale, as you call them, will stand up in court."

They walked away together and left us sitting there, and of a sudden I no longer had any appetite. Youngster she might be, but I had no wish to see any girl in the hands of Black Fetchen.

"Galloway, we can't let him do it. We got to stop him."

"You tell me how. She wants to marry him, and we can't prove a thing against him."

"Do you suppose he really drove in some Half-Box H cattle?"

"I'd lay a bet on it. Oh, he's a smart one! If anybody saw him with cattle of that brand, he's now got himself an alibi. Also, it makes him look good with the other cattlemen around."

"What's he see in her, do you suppose?"

Galloway, he gave me an odd look. "Why, you damn' fool, that's a right pretty little girl. Shapes up like pretty much of a woman. And in case you forget, Ma was no older when she married Pa."

He was right, only I didn't like to admit it. That Judith seemed like a youngster . . . all those freckles and everything. Only when I started reminding myself of that everything, I got to remembering that what Galloway had been saying was right. She was nigh to being a woman, even if she wasn't one yet . . . in my judgment, anyway.

"Flagan, what are we going to do?"

Upshot of it was, we went to see the marshal, Wyatt Earp, but he said he could do nothing. "Sorry, boys." He was kind of abrupt. "Mr. Fetchen brought in some of the Hawkes cattle and turned them over at the corral. That certainly doesn't make him seem a thief. Also, there seems to be no evidence that he had anything to do with running off the herd. As for the girl, she is old enough to marry, and she wants to marry him. I am afraid I can do nothing."

Bat Masterson was sheriff of Ford County, and we went next to see him. He was a right handsome young man about twenty-four or -five years old, wearing a dark suit and a black derby hat. You had to be quite a man to wear a hard hat in those days; it was such a temptation for some half-drunk cowpoke to try to shoot it off your head. Bat's didn't carry any bullet marks that I could see.

He listened to what we had to say, then shook his head. "Sorry, boys, there's nothing I can do. The girl has a right to marry, and there's no warrant out for any of that crowd." He paused a minute. "Although I've got some good ideas of my own."

"Anything we can tie to?" Galloway asked.

"No. But a man who rode in the other day said he saw the Fetchen outfit driving about fifty head of cattle. They didn't turn in but half a dozen scrubs."

"Ain't that evidence?"

"Not exactly. Rufe was drunk when he saw them. Now, I'd take his word for how many head he saw, drunk or sober—Rufe's an old cowhand. But I doubt if you could make it stick in a court of law."

"What can we do?"

Masterson tipped back in his chair and considered the question. "I'd say you might wire her grandfather. Get authority from him to hold up the wedding. And wire her father too."

Well, now. Neither one of us had even thought of that, because we'd had no truck with telegraph wires. We'd heard about them, and seen the wires along the railroad tracks, but the idea of sending a message to Costello never occurred to us.

"If you'd write us out a message, we'd be obliged," I said, "and you'd be helping a mighty nice girl from a bad marriage."

So Bat taken up a pen and scratched out the message. I had figured a body would have to write it some special way, but nothing of the kind.

He wrote it out, slick as you please: *Fetchen here. Proposed marriage, Judith accepted. Wire authority to stop marriage.*

"If we get a wire from Costello saying he refuses permission," Masterson said, "I'll stop it."

When we had sent the message we stood on the boardwalk in front of the Long Branch and considered the situation. Of a sudden, Galloway had an idea. "This sort of town," he said thoughtfully, "I wonder how many preachers it's got?"

"Three, four, maybe."

He was looking at me kind of funny-like and I began to read the sign of what he was thinking. "Now, that there," I said, "is what comes of contemplating. I think we better ask around."

"Ladder Walker, Harry Briggs, and them," Galloway said, "they owe us a favor, and Hawkes told me this morning that they were holding what cattle they'd found about fifteen miles north of here. I figure one of those boys should talk to a preacher. Ladder, f'r instance. If he was dyin' he would surely want a preacher."

About that time Bat came walking down the street headed for the Long Branch, carrying the cane from which he had taken his name.

"Mr. Masterson," I said, "how many preachers in Dodge?"

Bat's eyes started to twinkle. "You're lucky," he said. "They're all out of town but one." And then he added, "Don't forget the justice of the peace."

Galloway, he rounded up his horse and headed for the camp on the run to set up the deal at that end. Me, I mounted up, taken my horse out of town for a good run, and brought him back into town and up to the preacher's house, all lathered up.

"Reverend," I said, "there's a man in a bad way out to a cow camp, and he's bound to make his peace with the Lord. Will you ride out to him?"

Now, that sky pilot was a right fine gentleman who put down his coffee cup, wiped his mouth, and harnessed his team. I hooked up the traces whilst he slipped into his coat. In less time than it takes to tell about it, he was ready.

"One more thing," I said, "he wishes to make a will, and he said the man he wanted to draw it up for him was the justice of the peace. Said he didn't know whether the J.P. was a proper lawyer or not, but he doesn't care. He believes he's an honest man."

Well, with me riding alongside the buckboard we made it to the J.P.'s house and he was quick enough to go. It looked like a good fee and he was ready. They went dusting out of town in that buckboard, riding on their mission of mercy, and I tailed behind them.

When we rode up to the camp it was nothing but a corral, a spring, and a sod shanty that was half dugout. Ladder Walker was a-lying on his back with a blanket pulled up over him, and he looked sicker than anybody I ever did see. Those others cowpokes were all standing around with their hats off, talking in low voices.

As soon as all was going well, Galloway and me slipped out and rode back to Dodge. It looked to me as if Ladder was shaping up to one of the longest death scenes in history.

Although the preacher said he was a Protestant, and confession was not necessary, Ladder couldn't miss a chance like that. So he started off by confessing to several hours of the most lurid sinning a body ever heard tell of. He had confessed to all he had done, which was a-plenty, all he had wanted to do, which was a sight more, and then he began inventing sins the like of which you never heard. I'll say one thing for him. He had him an audience right from the word go. They never even looked up when we went out.

"You can bet your bottom dollar," Galloway said, "they'll never get out of there tonight."

The thing that worried us, suppose one of those sky pilots who had been out of town should return?

Only they didn't.

Chapter 4

Galloway and me, we rode up to the hitch rail in front of the Lady Gay and stepped down from our saddles. We were hungry and tired, and it was coming on to storm. As we stood on the boardwalk sizing up the town, lightning flashed out over the prairie.

"Looks to be a gully-washer," Galloway said. "I've been watching those clouds all the way in."

"You go ahead. I'll put up the horses." I hesitated there a moment, then added, "You might look to see if Judith has switched her gear over to that room Fetchen got for her."

The street was empty. I could hear boots on the walk down half a block or so, but could see nobody. The saloons were all lit up, going full blast, but there were few horses or rigs around because of the storm a-coming.

Leading both horses, I walked across the street and went on down to the livery stable. On the corner I held up for a moment, watching a tumbleweed rolling down the street and thinking of that Judith. Of all the contrary, ornery, freckle-faced . . . Trouble was, I missed her.

There was a lantern over the livery stable door, the flame sputtering in the wind. Nobody was around, so I led the horses back to their stalls and tied them, then went up a ladder into the loft and forked hay down to both of them. I was finishing off the last fork of hay when I thought I heard a step down below, a slow, careful step.

The loft where I was covered the whole top of the barn, and there were three ladders up to it—three that I'd seen, two on one side, one on the other. Come to think of it, there should be a fourth ladder, but if there was it must come down in an empty stall at the back of the barn where the liveryman hung spare bits of harness, tools, and suchlike.

All the time I was thinking of that, I was listening. Had somebody followed me in? Or was it some drunk hunting a place to sleep away from the storm? Or maybe somebody coming to get his horse?

The way those footsteps sounded made me think it was surely not one of the last two. My Winchester was down there beside my saddle and my slicker, waiting to be picked up before I went to the hotel. Likely that man down there had seen them and was just a-playing 'possum, waiting for me to come down and pick them up. And whatever lead he could throw at me.

Now, some folks might think me a suspicious man, and they'd be right. Many's the time I've suspected something when I was wrong; but there were other times I'd been right, and so I was still among the living.

Slipping the rawhide thong off the hammer of my six-shooter, I put that pitchfork down as easy as I could. Then I straightened up to listen. If he knew I was up here I'd best stir around a mite, or he'd be suspicious.

Many a cowpoke slept in a livery stable, and that was the idea I hoped to give him. What I figured on was getting him to come up that ladder, instead of him catching me coming down.

All the same, I started figuring. Seems to me a man can most usually take time to contemplate, and if he does it will save him a lot of riding and a lot of headaches.

Now, suppose I was down there and wanted to shoot a man on one of those ladders? Where would I take my stand so's I could watch all three to once?

It didn't leave much choice. Two ladders were on one side of the loft, opposite to him; the other ladder he knew of was on his side of the loft, up toward the front. If the man below wanted to keep all of them under cover, he had to be somewhere on the right side of the stable, toward the rear. If there was another ladder, which went up from that empty stall, one long unused, it would be behind the watcher.

If I made a try at coming down any one of the three ladders now, I'd be climbing down with my back to the gunman—if that was what he was.

The first thing I did was to sit down on some hay. I fluffed some of it around as if I was shaping a bed, and not being careful about noise; then I took off my boots and dropped them on the floor. After that I picked them up, tied them together with a piggin string, and slung them around my neck. Then, just as carefully as I could, I stood up in my sock feet. The floor was solid and not likely to squeak, so I eased across, soundlessly as I was able. And I waited.

There was not a sound from below. Near me was a bin full of corn, unshelled corn waiting to be fed to some of the local horses. I tossed an ear of that corn over to where I had taken off my boots, and it hit the boards near the hay. I hoped he would believe I'd dropped something, or something had slipped from my pockets. Then I eased along the side of the loft till I was over that empty stall. Sure enough, there was an opening there, with a ladder leading down.

It was well back in the stall and in a dark corner. The chances were that few of the stable's customers had any idea that this ladder was there.

Crouching by the opening, I listened, but heard no sound. I drew my Colt and carefully lowered my head until I could see into the lower level. . . . Nothing.

Swinging my feet down, my Colt gripped in my right hand, I felt for the first rung of the ladder, found it, and then the second. Lowering myself down, clinging to the ladder, I searched for him but could see nothing. I came down a step further, and heard a shout.

"Got you, damn it!" A gun blasted not over thirty feet away. The bullet smashed into the frame of the ladder, stabbing my face with splinters, and I fired in return, my bullet going slightly above and left of the flash. I realized even as I fired that my shot was too high, and I triggered a second shot lower down.

At the same instant I let go and dropped, landing on the balls of my feet, but I tumbled forward with a crash of harness and a breaking chair; and then came the bellow of a gun, almost within inches of me. Rolling over, I fired again.

Outside I heard a shout, heard running feet, and I sprang up. Down the far side of the stalls near the horses a man was staggering. He was bent far over, clutching at his stomach, and even as I saw him he stumbled forward and fell on his face.

The running feet were coming nearer.

Ducking out the back door of the barn, I slid between the corral bars and, still in my sock feet, ran lightly along the area back of the buildings until I was close to the hotel. I paused for just a moment and got my boots on, and then I went up the back stairs of the hotel, and along the hall.

Several heads appeared from doorways, and one of them was Judith's. She saw me, and for a moment I thought I saw relief on her face. "Flagan, what is it? What's happened?" she asked.

"Some drunken cowhand," I said. "You've got to expect that in Dodge."

She still stood there in the door of her room. She was fully dressed, although it was very late. "I will be married tomorrow," she said, almost tentatively.

"I wish you luck."

"You don't really mean that."

"No, ma'am, I don't. I think you're doing the wrong thing, and I know it isn't what your grandpa wanted . . . nor your pa, either, I'm thinking."

"Mr. Fetchen is a fine man. You'll see."

We heard voices from down below, and then boots on the stairs. Colby Rafin was suddenly there, Black Fetchen behind him, with Norton Vance and Burr Fetchen coming up in the rear.

"There he is!" Colby yelled.

He grabbed for his gun, but I had him covered. Back in Tennessee those boys never had to work at a fast draw, and the way that gun came into my hand stopped them cold.

"I don't know what you boys are looking for," I said, "but I don't like being crowded."

"You killed Tory!" Burr shouted.

Before I could open my mouth to speak, Judith said, "How could he? He's been standing here talking to me!"

That stopped them, and for the moment nobody thought to ask how long I'd been there. After that moment they never got the chance, because the marshal pushed by them.

"What happened down there?" he asked me.

"Sounded like some shooting. These boys say Tory Fetchen got killed."

Just then Bat Masterson came up the steps. "Everything all right, Wyatt?" Then he saw me standing there at Judith's door. "Oh, hello, Sackett."

Earp turned on him. "Do you know this man, Bat?"

"Yes, I do. He brought Evan Hawkes's cattle in, and helped round up some strays. He's a friend of mine."

Earp glanced down at my boots. "Mind if I look at your boots? The man who did the shooting had to come along behind the buildings. It's muddy there."

I lifted one boot after the other. Both were as slick as though they'd never stepped on anything but a board floor.

Colby Rafin was sore. He simply couldn't believe it. "He's lying!" he shouted. "It had to be him! Why, Tory was—"

"Tory was what?" Masterson demanded. "Laying for him? Was that it?"

It was Burr who spoke up. "Nothin' like that," he protested, "Tory just went after his horse."

"At this hour?" Earp asked. "You mean he was riding out of town this late, with a storm brewing?"

"Sure," Burr replied easily. "He was riding out to join some of our outfit."

"Gentlemen," Earp said coldly, "before we ask any further questions or you give any more answers, let me tell you something. Your friend Tory Fetchen wore new boots, boots with a very distinctive heel pattern. He left enough tracks down there at the stable for a man who was doing a lot of waiting, a man crouched down or standing beside one of the support posts. From those tracks, I'd say he was waiting for somebody and trying to keep out of sight. He was either nervous or he waited a long time. In any case, his gun was fired twice, and he was hit twice . . . looked to me like a third shot cut the top of his coat's shoulder. We've no case against the man who shot him. Both men were armed, both were shooting. It's nothing but a matter of clearing up the details."

"Just a question, gentlemen," Masterson said. "You came up here, apparently headed for Sackett's room. Did you have some idea of finishing the job Tory tried to do?"

"Aw, it was nothing like that!" Burr Fetchen waved a careless hand. "Only we had some trouble back in Tennessee, and—"

"Then I suggest you go back to Tennessee and settle it," Earp interrupted. "I won't have shooting in Dodge."

"I give you my word, Marshal," I said, "I won't shoot unless I'm shot at."

"That's fair enough, Sackett. All right, you boys go about your business. If there's any more trouble I'll lock you up."

When they had gone, I said, "Judith, I'm sorry I got you into this."

"You were standing here with me!" she insisted. "Why, I must have come out of my door just as those shots died away."

She had been quick enough. The trouble is that a running man can cover a good distance, and folks just never calculate time as well as they think. In any event, she had stopped a nasty shooting in a crowded place where she or others might have been hurt, and for that much I was glad.

"They didn't tell the truth," she said then. "Tory wasn't going out of town. He was going to have dinner with James and me."

"Late for dinner, isn't it?"

"James said he would be busy. He wanted to eat late. He said the restaurant would not be so crowded."

"I'd better go," I said. I backed off a few steps. "If you change your mind, you can always come back and join us. We'll take you on to your pa."

She smiled a little. "Flagan, I shall not change my mind. I love James, and he loves me."

"You keep telling yourself that. Maybe after a while you'll come to believe it," I said.

"Flagan Sackett, I—"

Maybe it isn't right for a gentleman to walk away whilst a lady is talking, but I did. This was an argument where I was going to have the last word, anyway . . . when they found no preacher in town.

There was a corner at the head of the stairs where a body couldn't be seen from above or below, and I stopped there long enough to reload my gun.

Galloway was sitting in the lobby holding a newspaper. He looked up at me, a kind of quizzical look in his eyes. "Hear there was a shooting over to the livery," he said.

"Sounded like it," I agreed, and sat down beside him. In a low tone I added, "That Tory laid for me whilst I was putting hay down the chute. He come close to hangin' up my scalp."

"Yeah, and you better start pullin' slivers out of your face. The light's brighter down here than in that hallway upstairs."

Something had been bothering my face for several minutes, but I'd been too keyed up and too busy talking to notice it much. Gingerly, I put my hand up and touched the end of a pine sliver off that post. Two or three of them I pulled out right there, getting them with my fingers, but there were some others.

We walked down the street to the Peacock, just to look around, and Bat was there. He came over to us, glanced at the side of my face and smiled a little. "I hope you had time to change your socks," he said. "A man can catch cold with wet, muddy socks on."

Me, I had to grin. "Nothing gets by you, does it?"

"I saw you go into the barn. I also saw Tory follow you. I saw the track of a sock foot just back of the barn. I kicked straw over it."

"Thanks."

"When I take to a man, I stand by him. I have reason to believe that you're honest. I have reason to believe the Fetchens are not."

But, no matter how good things looked right at that moment, I was worried. Black Fetchen was not one to take Tory's shooting lying down, and no matter what anybody said, he would lay it to me or Galloway. I'd had no idea of killing anybody; only when a man comes laying for you, what can you do? The worst of it was, he'd outguessed me. All the time, he knew about that other door from the loft, and he figured rightly that I'd find it and use it. That he missed me at all was pure accident. I'd been mostly in the dark or he'd have hit me sure, and he'd been shooting to kill.

After a bit Galloway and me went back to the hotel and crawled into bed. But I slept with a Colt at my hand, and I know Galloway did, too.

Tomorrow two things would happen, both of them likely to bring grief and trouble. First would be Tory's funeral, and second would be when they tried to find somebody to marry Judith and Black Fetchen.

Anybody could read a funeral sermon, but it took a Justice of the Peace or an ordained minister to marry somebody.

Chapter 5

There was a light rain falling when we went down to the restaurant for breakfast. It was early, and not many folks were about at that hour. The gray faces of the stores were darkened by the rain, and the dust was laid for a few hours at least. A rider in a rain-wet slicker went by on the street, heading for the livery stable. It was a quiet morning in Dodge.

We stopped at the dining-room door, studying the people inside before we entered, and we found a table in a corner where we could watch both doors. Galloway had the rawhide thong slipped back off his six-shooter and so did I, but we were hunting no trouble.

Folks drifted in, mostly men. They were cattlemen, cattle buyers, a scattering of ranch hands, and some of the business folks from the stores. A few of them we already knew by sight, a trick that took only a few hours in Dodge.

There were half a dozen pretty salty characters in that room, too, but Dodge was full of them. As far as that goes, nine-tenths of the adult males in Dodge had fought in the War Between the States or had fought Indians, and quite a few had taken a turn at buffalo hunting. It was no place to come hunting a ruckus unless you were hitched up to go all the way.

We ordered scrambled eggs and ham, something a body didn't find too much west of the Mississippi, where everything was beef and beans. Both of us were wearing store-bought clothes and our guns were almost out of sight. There was a rule about packing guns in town unless you were riding out right off, but the law in Dodge was lenient except when the herds were coming up the trail, and this was an off season for that. Evan Hawkes had been almost the only one up the trail right at that time.

186

Nowhere was there any sign of the Fetchen crowd, nor of Judith.
"You don't suppose they pulled out?" Galloway asked.

" 'Tisn't likely."

Several people glanced over at us, for there were no secrets in
Dodge, and by now everybody in town would know who we were and
why we were in town; and they would also know the Fetchen crowd.

It was likely that Earp had figured out the shooting by this time,
but as had been said, Tory was armed and it was a fair shooting, except
that he laid for me like that. He'd tried to ambush me, and he got what
was coming to him. Dodge understood things like that.

We ate but our minds were not on our food, hungry as we were,
for every moment we were expecting the Fetchens to show up. They
did not come, though. The rain eased off, although the clouds remained
heavy and it was easy enough to see that the storm was not over. Water
dripped from the eaves and from the signboards extending across the
boardwalk in some places.

We watched through the windows, and presently a man came in,
pausing at the outside door to beat the rain from his hat and to shake
it off his raincoat. He came on in, and I heard him, without looking
at us, tell Ben Springer, "They had their buryin'. There were nineteen
men out there. Looked to be a tough lot."

"Nineteen?" Galloway whispered. "They've found some friends,
seems like."

We saw them coming then, a tight riding bunch of men in black
slickers and mostly black hats coming down the street through the mud.
They drew up across the street and got down from their horses and went
to stand under the overhang of the building across the street.

Two turned and drifted down the street to the right, and two more
to the left, the rest of them stayed there. It looked as if they were
waiting for us.

"Right flatterin', I call it," Galloway said, picking up his coffee
cup. "They got themselves an army yonder."

"Be enough to go around," I commented. Then after a minute I
said, "I wonder what happened to Judith?"

"You go see. I'll set right here and see if they want to come a-
hunting. If they don't, we'll go out to 'em after a bit."

Pushing back my chair, I got up and went into the hotel and up
the stairs. When I got to her door, I rapped . . . and rapped again.

There was no answer.

I tried rapping again, somewhat louder, and when no answer came
I just reached down and opened the door.

The room was empty. The bed was still unmade after she'd slept in it, but she was gone, and her clothes were gone.

When I came back down the stairs I came down moving mighty easy. Nothing like walking wary when a body is facing up to trouble, and I could fairly smell trouble all around.

Nobody was in the lobby, so I walked over to where I could see through the arch into the dining room.

Galloway was sitting right where I'd left him, only there were two Fetchens across the table from him and another at the street door, and all of them had guns.

The tables were nigh to empty. Chalk Beeson was sitting across the room at a table with Bob Wright; and Doc Halliday, up early for him, was alone at another table, drinking his breakfast, but keeping an eye on what was happening around.

Black Fetchen was there, along with Burr and a strange rider I didn't know, a man with a shock of hair the color of dead prairie grass, and a scar on his jaw. His heels were run down, but the way he wore his gun sized him up to be a slick one with a shootin' iron, or one who fancied himself so. A lot of the boys who could really handle guns wore them every which way, not slung down low like some of the would-be fast ones.

"It was your doing," Black was saying, "you and that brother of yours. You got that preacher out of town. Well, it ain't going to do you no good. Judith is ridin' west with us, and we'll find us a preacher."

"I'd not like to see harm come to that girl," Galloway commented calmly. "If harm comes to her I'll see this country runs mighty short of Fetchens."

"You won't have the chance. You ain't going to leave this room. Not alive, you ain't."

About that time I heard a board creak. It was almost behind me, and it was faint, but I heard it. Making no move, I let my eyes slant back. Well, the way the morning sunlight fell through the window showed a faint shadow, and I could just see the toe of a boot—a left boot.

Just as I sighted it, the toe bent just a mite like a man taking a step or swinging a gun to hit a man on the head. So I stepped quickly off to the right and back-handed my left fist, swinging hard.

When he cut down with that six-gun barrel he swung down and left, but too slow. My left fist smashed him right in the solar plexus, right under the third button of his shirt, and the wind went out of him as if he'd been steer-kicked. His gun barrel came down, his blow wasted, and by that time my right was moving. It swung hard, catching him full in his unprotected face, smashing his nose like a man stepping on a gourd.

The blood gushed out of his nose and he staggered back, and I walked in on him.

Now, there's a thing about fighting when the chips are down. You get a man going, you don't let up on him. He's apt to come back and beat your ears down. So I reached out, caught him by one ear and swung another right, scattering a few of his teeth. He turned sidewise, and I drove my fist down on his kidney like a hammer, and he hit the floor.

Now, that all amounted to no more than four or five seconds. A body doesn't waste time between punches, and I wasn't in anything less than a hurry.

Nor was I making much noise. It was all short and sharp and over in an instant, and then I was facing back toward that room.

Galloway was sitting easy. Nobody ever did fluster that boy. He was a soft-talking man, but he was tough, and so rough he wore out his clothes from the inside first. There were Fetchens ready to fire, but Galloway wasn't worried so's a body could see, and I was half a mind to leave it all to him. It would serve them right.

One time when he was short of thirteen we were up in the hills. We'd been hunting squirrels and the like, but really looking for a good razor-back hog, Ma being fresh out of side-meat. Well, Galloway seen a big old boar back under the brush, just a-staring at him out of those mean little eyes, and Galloway up and let blast at him. That bullet glanced off the side of the boar's shoulder and the hog took off into the brush. We trailed him for nigh onto two miles before he dropped, and when we came upon him there was a big old cougar standing over him.

Now, that cougar was hungry and he'd found meat, and he wasn't figuring on giving up to no mountain boy. Galloway, he'd shot that wild boar and we needed the side-meat, and he wasn't about to give it up to that big cat. So there they stood, a-staring one at the other.

Galloway was carrying one load in that old smooth-bore he had, and he knew if he didn't get the cat with one shot he would be in more trouble than he'd ever seen. A wounded cougar is something nobody wants any truck with, but if that cougar'd known who he was facing he'd have taken out running over the hills.

Galloway up and let blast with his gun just as that cougar leaped at him. The bullet caught the cat in the chest but he was far-off from dead. He knocked Galloway a-rolling and I scrambled for a club, but Galloway was up as quick as the cougar, and he swung the smooth-bore and caught that cat coming in, with a blow on the side of the head. Then before the stunned cougar could more than get his feet under him, Galloway outs with his Arkansas toothpick and then he and that cat were going around and around.

Blood and fur and buckskin were flying every which way, and then Galloway was up and bleeding but that cat just lay there. He looked at Galloway and then just gave up the ghost right there before us.

Galloway had his ribs raked and he carries the cougar scars to this day. But we skinned out the cougar and toted the hide and the side-meat home. We made shift to patch Galloway up, and only did that after he lay half naked in a cold mountain stream for a few minutes.

What I mean is, Galloway was nobody to tackle head-on without you figured to lose some hide.

Galloway, he just sat there a-looking at them, that long, tall mountain boy with the wide shoulders and the big hands. We two are so much alike we might be twins, although we aren't, and he's away the best-looking of the two. Only I can almost tell what he's thinking any given time. And right then I wouldn't have wanted to be in the shoes of any Fetchen.

"I'm going to leave this room, Fetchen," he said, "and when I please to. If I have to walk over Fetchens I can do it. I figure you boys are better in a gang or in a dark barn, anyway."

Black came to his feet as if he'd been stabbed with a hat pin. "It was you, was it?"

"Don't push your luck." Galloway spoke easy enough. "The only reason you're alive now is because I don't figure it polite to mess up a nice floor like this. Now, if I was you boys I'd back up and get out of here while the getting is good. And mind what I said, if one hair of that girl's head is so much as worried, I'll see the lot of you hang."

Well, they couldn't figure him. Not one of them could believe he would talk like that without plenty of guns to back him. He was alone, it seemed like, and he was telling them where to get off, and instead of riding right over him, they were worried. They figured he had some sort of an ace-in-the-hole.

Burr glanced around and he saw me standing back from the door, but on their flank and within easy gun-range—point-blank range, that is. I was no more than twenty or twenty-five feet away, and there was nothing between us. Not one of them was facing me. For all they knew, there might be others, for they'd seen us around with some of the Half-Box H outfit.

Black got up, moving easy-like, and I'll give it to him, the man was graceful as a cat. He was a big man, too, bigger than either Galloway or me, and it was said back in the hills that in a street fight he was a man-killer.

"We can wait," he said. "We've got all the time in the world. And the first preacher we come upon west of here, Judith and me will get married."

They went out in a bunch, the way they came in, and then I strolled over from the door. Galloway glanced up. "You have any trouble?"

"Not to speak of," I said.

We walked out on the street, quiet at this hour. Somewhere a chicken had laid an egg and was telling the town about it. A lazy-looking dog trotted across the street, and somewhere a pump was working, squeaking and complaining—then I heard water gush into a pail.

A few horses stood along the street, and a freight wagon was being loaded. Right then I was thinking of none of these things, but of Judith. It seemed there was no way I could interfere without bringing on a shooting. She'd consented to marry James Black Fetchen, and we'd had no word from her folks against it. The law couldn't intervene, nor could we, but I dearly wished to and so did Galloway.

We knew there'd be more said about Tory Fetchen. That was no closed book. The Fetchens were too canny to get embroiled in a gun battle with the law when the law is such folks as Wyatt Earp, Bat Masterson, and their like. West of us the plains were wide, and what happened out yonder was nobody's business but theirs and ours. We all knew that west of here there'd be a hard reckoning some day.

We saw them coming, riding slow up the street in that tight bunch they held to, Judith out in front, riding head up and eyes straight ahead, riding right out of town and out of our lives, and they never turned a head to look at us, just rode on by like a pay car passing a tramp. They simply paid us no mind, not even Judith.

She might at least have waved good-bye.

When they disappeared we turned around and walked back inside. "Let's have some coffee," Galloway said gloomily. "We got to contemplate."

We'd no more than sat down before Evan Hawkes came in. As soon as he spotted us he walked over.

"Have you boys made any plans? If not, I can use you."

He pulled a chair around and straddled it. "If we are correct in assuming that the Fetchen crowd stampeded and stole my cattle, it seems to me they will be joining the herd somewhere west of here. No cattle have been sold that we know of, beyond a possibility of some slaughtered beef at Fort Dodge. We now have about three hundred head rounded up that I was planning on pushing to Wyoming, but I mean to have my herd back."

"How?"

"Why not the same way they got it?"

Well, why not? Fetchen had stolen his herd, so why not steal it back? There was sense to that, for nobody wants to have nigh onto fifty thousand dollars' worth of cattle taken from under his nose.

"We're riding west," I told him. "We figured to sort of perambulate around and see they treat that girl all right."

"Good! Then you boys are on the payroll as of now—thirty a month and food."

He sat there while we finished our coffee. "You boys know the Fetchens better than I do. Tell me, do they know anything about the cattle business? I mean *western* cattle business?"

"Can't see how they could. They're hill folk, like we were until we came west the first time. Howsoever, they might have some boys along who do know something . . . if they dare show their faces."

"What's that mean?"

"I figure they've tied in with some rustlers."

"That's possible, of course. Well, what do you say?"

Me, I looked at Galloway, but he left such things to me most of the time. "We're riding west, and we'd find the company agreeable," I said. "You've hired yourselves some hands."

We moved out at daybreak, Evan Hawkes riding point, and ten good men, including us. He had Harry Briggs and Ladder Walker along, and some of the others. A few, who were married men or were homesick for Texas, he paid off there. In our outfit there were, among others, two who looked like sure-fire gunmen. Larnie Cagle was nineteen and walked as if he was two-thirds cougar. The other was an older, quieter man named Kyle Shore.

Wanting to have our own outfit, Galloway and me bought a couple of pack horses from Bob Wright, who had taken them on a deal. Both were mustangs, used to making do off prairie grass, but broken to saddle and pack. Evan Hawkes was his own foreman, and I'll say this for him: he laid in a stock of grub the like of which I never did see on a cow outfit.

He had a good, salty remuda, mostly Texas horses, small but

game, and able to live off the range the way a good stock horse should in that country.

The outfit was all ready to move when we reached the soddy where his boys had been holed up, so we never stopped moving.

Hawkes dropped back to me. "Flagan, I hear you're pretty good on the trail. Do you think you could pick up that outfit?"

"I can try."

There were still clouds and the weather was threatening. A little gusty wind kept picking up, and the prairie was wet without being soggy. Galloway stayed with the herd and I cut out, riding off to the south to swing a big circle and see what I could pick up.

Within the next hour I had their sign, and by the time a second hour had gone by I had pegged most of their horses. I knew which one Judith rode and the tracks of all her other horses, and I also knew which one was Black Fetchen's. It had taken me no time at all to identify them.

This was wide-open country, and a body had to hang back a mite. Of course, they were well ahead of me, so it was not a worrisome thing right away, but it was something to keep in mind. Of course, a man riding western country just naturally looks at it all. I mean he studies his back trail and off to the horizon on every side. Years later he would be able to describe every mile of it. As if it had been yesterday.

First place, it just naturally had to be that way. There were no signposts, no buildings, no corrals, or anything but creeks, occasional buttes, sometimes a bluff or a bank, and a scatter of trees and brush. As there wasn't much to see, you came to remember what there was. And I was studying their sign because I might have to trail the whole outfit by one or two tracks.

There was one gent in that outfit who kept pulling off to one side. He'd stop now and again to study his back trail, plainly seen by the marks of his horse's hoofs in the sod. It came to me that maybe it was that new rider with the scar on his jaw. Sure enough, I came upon a place where he'd swung down to tighten his cinch. His tracks were there on the ground, run-down heels and all. Something about it smelled of trouble, and I had me an idea this one was pure poison.

And so it turned out . . . but that was another day, and farther along the trail.

Chapter 6

The land lay wide before us. We moved westward with only the wind beside us, and we rode easy in the saddle with eyes reaching out over the country, reading every movement and every change of shadow.

Now and again Galloway rode out and took the trail and I stayed with the herd, taking my turn at bringing up the drag and eating my share of dust. It was a job nobody liked, but I didn't want those boys to think I was forever dodging it, riding off on the trail of the Fetchens.

Of a noon, Galloway rode in. He squatted on his heels with those boys and me, eating a mite, drinking coffee, then wiping his hands on a handful of pulled brown grass. "Flagan," he said, "I've lost the trail."

They all looked up at him, Larnie Cagle longest of all.

"Dropped right off the world," Galloway said, "all of a sudden, they did."

"I'll ride out with you."

"Want some help?" Larnie Cagle asked. "I can read sign."

Galloway never so much as turned his head. "Flagan will look. Nobody can track better than him. He can trail a trout up a stream through muddy water."

"I got to see it," Cagle said, and for a minute there things were kind of quiet.

"Some day you might," I said.

We rode out from the herd and picked up the trail of that morning. It was plain enough, for an outfit of nineteen men and pack horses leaves a scar on the prairie that will last for a few days—sometimes for weeks.

Of a sudden they had circled and built a fire for nooning, but when they rode away from that fire there wasn't nineteen of them any longer.

The most tracks we could make out were of six horses. We had trouble with the six and it wasn't more than a mile or two further on until there were only three horses ridden side by side. And then there were only two . . . and then they were gone.

It made no kind of sense. Nineteen men and horses don't drop off the edge of the world like that.

In a little while Hawkes rode over with Kyle Shore. Shore could read sign. Right away he began casting about, but he came up with nothing.

"The way I figure it, Mr. Hawkes," I said, "those boys were getting nigh to where they were going, or maybe just to those stolen cattle, so they had it in their mind to disappear. Somebody in that lot is almighty smart in the head."

"How do you think they did it?" Shore asked.

"I got me an idea," I said. "I think they bound up their horses' hoofs with sacking. It leaves no definite print, but just sort of smudges ground and grass. Then they just cut out, one at a time, each taking a different route. They'll meet somewhere miles from here."

"It's an Apache trick," Galloway said.

"Then we must try to find out where they would be apt to go," Hawkes suggested.

"Or just ride on to where they'll likely take that herd," Shore added. "Maybe we shouldn't waste time trying to follow them."

"That makes sense," I agreed.

"Suppose they just hole up somewhere out on the plains? Is there any reason why they should go farther?"

"I figure they're heading for Colorado," I said. "I think they're going to find Judith's pa."

They all looked at me, probably figuring I had Judith too much in mind, and so I did, but not this time.

"Look at it," I said. "Costello has been out there several years. He has him a nice outfit, that's why he wanted Judith with him. What's to stop them taking her on out there and just moving in on him?"

"What about him? What about his hands?"

"How many would he have on a working ranch? Unless he's running a lot of cattle over a lot of country he might not have more than four or five cowboys."

They studied about it, and could see it made a kind of sense. We had no way of telling, of course, for Fetchen might decide to stay as far from Judith's pa as possible. On the other hand, he was a wild and lawless man with respect for nothing, and he might decide just to move in on Judith's pa. It would be a good hide-out for his own herd, and unless Costello had some salty hands around, they might even take over the outfit.

Or they might do as Hawkes suggested and find a good water hole and simply stay there. In such a wide-open country there would be plenty of places.

The more I contemplated the situation the more worried I became, and I'm not usually a worrying man. What bothered me was Judith. That girl may have been a fool about James Black Fetchen; but she was, I had to admit, a smart youngster. I had an idea that, given time and company of the man and his kin, she'd come to know what he was really like. The more so since he would think he had everything in hand and under control.

What would happen if she should all of a sudden decide she was no longer inclined to marry Black Fetchen?

If she could keep her mouth shut she might get a chance to cut and run; but she was young, and liable to talk when she should be listening. Once she let Black know where he stood with her, the wraps would be off. She would have to cut and run, or be in for rough treatment.

"They don't want to be found," I told Hawkes. "They've buried the ashes of their fires. And I trailed out two of them today, lost both trails."

"What do you figure we can do?"

"Let me have Galloway, Shore, and maybe one or two others. You've got hands enough. Each one of us will work out a different trail. Maybe we can come up with something."

"You mean if the trails begin to converge? Or point toward something?"

"Sooner or later they've got to."

So it boiled down to me an' Galloway, Shore, Ladder Walker, and an old buffalo hunter named Moss Reardon. We hunted down trails and started following them out. They were hard enough to locate in the first place.

The idea didn't pan out much. By the end of two days Walker's trail petered out in a bunch of sand hills south of us. Galloway lost his trail in the bed of a river, and Shore's just faded out somewhere on the flat. Only Reardon and me had come up with anything, and that was almighty little. Both of us lost the trail, then found it again.

When we'd joined up again with the others, I drew on the ground with a bit of stick and tried to point out what I'd found. "Right about here—and there was no trail, mind you—I found a place where the grass was cropped by a horse. It's short grass country, but the horse had cropped around in a circle, so figuring on that idea and just to prove out what I'd found, I located the peg-hole that horse had been tied to. It had been filled up, and a piece of grass tucked into the hole—growing grass."

Hawkes sort of looked at me as if he didn't believe it.

"Only there wasn't one of them, there were three. I sort of skirted around, looking for another cropped place and I found two more, further out from camp."

"You found their *camp?*"

"Such as it was. They'd dug out a block of sod, built their coffee fire in the hole, then replaced the sod when they got ready to move."

Hawkes sat back on his heels and reached for the coffeepot. He studied the map I had drawn, and I could see he was thinking about all we had learned.

"What do you think, Moss? You've hunted buffalo all over this country."

"Sand Creek," he said, "or maybe Two Buttes."

"Or the breaks of the Cimarron," Kyle Shore suggested.

Moss Reardon threw him a glance. "Now, that might be," he said. "It just might be."

We moved westward with the first light, keeping the small herd moving at a good pace. As for me, just knowing that Judith was out there ahead of us gave me an odd feeling of nearness. Up to now we hadn't been exactly certain which way she was taking, but now I had the feeling that if I was setting out to do it I could come up to them by sundown.

That night we camped on the north fork of the Cimarron, and scarcely had coffee boiling when a rider hailed the fire. In those days, as I've said before, nobody just rode up out of the dark. If he wanted to live to see grandchildren he learned to stop off a piece and call out.

When he was squatting by the fire and the usual opening talk was over, such as how did he find the grass, and how beef prices were, or had he seen any buffalo, he looked across the fire at me and said, "You'll be Flagan Sackett?"

"That I am."

"Message for you, from Bat Masterson."

He handed me a folded paper. Opening it, I found another inside. The first was a note from Bat: *If we had known this!*

The second was an answer to our telegram sent to Tazewell: *J.B.*

LOUIS L'AMOUR

Fetchen, Colby Rafin, Burr Fetchen and three John Does wanted for murder of Laban Costello. Apprehend and hold.

"So they killed him," Galloway said. "I had a thought it might be so."

"We got to get that girl away from them, Galloway," I said.

"If what you surmise is true," Hawkes said, "they might want her for a bargaining point with the old man. Look at it this way. They've got a big herd of cattle and no range. They could settle on free range most anywhere, but there will be questions asked. Mine is a known brand, so if they haven't altered it, they must."

"They ain't had the time," Walker said. "Takes a spell to rope and brand that many head."

"We're wastin' time," Larnie said. "Let's locate the herd and take it from them."

"There's nineteen of them," Briggs objected. "Taking a herd from such an outfit wouldn't be that easy. A man's got to be smart to bring it off."

"Larnie's right about one thing," Hawkes said. "We've got to find the herd."

In a wide-open land like this where law was a local thing and no officer wanted to spread himself any further than his own district, a man could do just about what he was big enough to do, or that he was fast enough with a gun to do. The only restraint there was on any man outside of the settled communities was his own moral outlook and the strength of the men with him.

Black Fetchen and his kin had always ruled their roost about as they wanted, and had ridden rough-shod over those about them, but they had been kind of cornered by the country back there and the fact that there were some others around that were just as tough as they were.

The killing of Laban Costello had made outlaws of them and they had come west, no doubt feeling they'd have things their own way out here. They started off by stealing Hawkes's herd, killing his son, and some of his men as well, and seeming to get away with it.

They had been mighty shrewd about leaving no tracks. Galloway and me were good men on a trail, and without us Hawkes might never have been on to them. That's not to say that Kyle Shore and Moss Reardon weren't good—they were.

But the West Fetchen and his men were heading for wasn't quite what it had been a few years before, and I had an idea they were in for a surprise. Circumstances can change in a mighty short time where the country is growing, and the West they had heard about was, for the most of it, already gone.

For instance, out around Denver a man named Dave Cook had gotten a lot of the law officers to working together, so that a man could no longer just run off to a nearby town to be safe. And the men who rode for the law in most of the western towns were men who weren't scared easy.

James Black Fetchen was accounted a mighty mean man, and that passel of no-goods who rode with him could have been no better. I had an idea they were riding rough-shod for grief, because folks in Wyoming and Colorado didn't take much pushing. It's in their nature to dig in their heels and push back.

This was an uncomplicated country, as a new country usually is. Folks had feelings and ideas that were pretty basic, pretty down to earth, and they had no time to worry about themselves or their motives. It was a big, wide, empty country and a man couldn't hide easy. There were few people, and those few soon came to know about each other. Folks who have something to hide usually head for big cities, crowded places where they can lose themselves among the many. In open western country a man stood out too much.

If he was a dangerous man, everybody knew it sooner or later; and if he was a liar or a coward that soon was known and he couldn't do much of anything. If he was honest and nervy, it didn't take long for him to have friends and a reputation for square-dealing; he could step into some big deals with no more capital than his reputation. Everybody banked on the man himself.

Once away from a town, a man rode with a gun at hand. There were Indians about, some of them always ready to take a scalp, and even the Indians accounted friendly might not be if they found a white man alone and some young buck was building a reputation to sing about when he went courting or stood tall in the tribal councils.

A rustler, if caught in the act, was usually hung to the nearest tree. Nobody had time to ride a hundred miles to a court house or to go back for the trial, and there were many officers who preferred it that way.

Now, me and Galloway were poor folks. We had come west the first time to earn money to pay off Pa's debts, and now we were back again, trying to make our own way. And the telegram from Tennessee had changed everything.

We had made no fight when Black Fetchen claimed Judith, because she had said she was going to marry him, and we had no legal standing in the matter. But the fact that he had killed her grandpa changed everything, and we knew she'd never marry him now, not of her own free will.

"We got to get her away from them, Flagan," Galloway said, "and time's a-wasting."

But things weren't the way we would like to have them around the outfit, either. That Larnie Cagle was edgy around us. He had heard of the Sackett reputation, and he reckoned himself as good with a gun as any man; we both could see he was fairly itching to prove it.

Kyle Shore tried to slow him down, for Kyle was a salty customer and he could read the sign right. He knew that anybody who called a showdown to a Sackett was bound to get it, and Shore being a saddle partner of Cagle's, he wanted no trouble.

Half a dozen times around camp Larnie had made comments that we didn't take to, but we weren't quarrelsome folks. Maybe I was more so than Galloway, but so far I'd sat tight and kept my mouth shut. Larnie was a man with swagger. He wanted to make big tracks, and now he had a feeling that he wasn't making quite the impression he wanted. A body could see him working up to a killing. The only question was who it would be.

Like a lot of things in this world, it was patience that finally did it for us. Galloway and me were riding out with Moss Reardon. We had followed a faint trail, picking up where we'd left off the day before, as it had run along in the same direction we were taking. On that morning, though, it veered off, doubled back, turned at right angles, switching so often it kept Galloway and me a-working at it.

All of a sudden we noticed Moss. He was off some distance across the country but we recognized that paint pony he was riding; we hung to our trail, though, and so did he. And then pretty soon we found ourselves riding together again.

"I think we've got 'em," Moss said. "As I recall, there's a hole in the river yonder where water stays on after the rest dries up. There'd be enough after a rain to water the herd."

We left the trail and took to low ground, keeping off the sky line but staying in the same direction the trail was taking. Every now and again one of us would ride out to see if we could pick up track, and sure enough, we could.

Moss Reardon's bronc began to act up. "Smells water," he said grimly. "We better ride easy."

We began to see where the grass was grazed off in the bottoms along the river. Somebody had moved a big bunch of cattle, keeping them strung out in the bottoms, which no real cattleman would do because of the trouble of working them out of the brush all the while.

Only a man whose main idea was to keep a herd from view might try that.

We found a place in the river bed where there had been water, all trampled to mud by the herd, but now the water had started to seep back. We pulled up and watered our horses.

"How far do you figure?" Galloway asked.

Reardon thought a minute or two. "Not far . . . maybe three, four miles."

"Maybe one of us ought to go back and warn Hawkes."

It was coming on to sundown, and our outfit was a good ten miles back. Nobody moved. After the horses had satisfied themselves we pulled out.

"Well"—I hooked a leg around the saddlehorn—"I figure to Injun up to that layout and see how Judith is getting along. If she's in trouble, I calculate it would be time to snake her out of there."

"Wouldn't do any harm to shake 'em up a mite," Moss suggested, his hard old eyes sharpening. "Might even run off a few head."

We swung down right there and unsaddled to rest our horses, giving them a chance to graze a little. Meanwhile we sort of talked about what we might do, always realizing we would have to look the situation over before we could decide. The general idea was that we would Injun up to their camp after things settled down and scout around. If the layout looked good we might try to get Judith away; but if not, we'd just stampede that herd, or a piece of it, and drive them over to join up with the Hawkes outfit.

All the while we weren't fooling anybody. That outfit had acted mighty skittish, and they might be lying out for us. They had men enough to keep a good guard all the while, and still get what sleep they needed.

After a while we stretched out to catch ourselves a few minutes of sleep. Actually, that few minutes stretched to a good two hours, for we were beat.

Me, I was the first one up, as I am in most any camp. There was no question of starting a fire, for some of their boys might be scouting well out from camp.

I saddled up and then shook the others awake. Old Moss came out of it the way any old Indian fighter would, waking up with eyes wide open right off, and listening.

We mounted up and started off, riding easy under the stars, each of us knowing this might be our last ride. Lightly as we talked of what we might do, we knew we might be riding right into a belly full of lead.

It was near to midnight when we smelled their smoke, and a few minutes later when we saw the red glow of their fire. We could make out the figure of a man sitting on guard, the thin line of his rifle making a long shadow.

Chapter 7

We had come up to their camp from down wind so the horses wouldn't get wind of us. The cattle were bedded on a wide bench a few feet above the river, most of them lying down, but a few restless ones still grazing here and there.

There would be other guards, we knew, and without doubt one was somewhere near us even now, but we sat our horses, contemplating the situation.

About midnight those cattle would rise up, stretch, turn around a few times and maybe graze for a few minutes, and then they would lie down again. That would be a good time to start them.

We figured to start the stampede so as to run the cattle north toward our boys, which would take it right through the camp Fetchen had made, or maybe just past it. And that meant that we had to get Judith out of there before the cattle started running.

The upshot of it was that I cut off from the others and swung wide, working toward the camp. I could see the red eye of the dying fire all the while. Finally I tied my horse in a little hollow surrounded by brush. It was a place where nobody was likely to stumble on the horse, yet I could find it quickly if I had to cut and run.

Leaving my rifle on the saddle, I started out with a six-shooter, a spare six-gun stuck down in my pants, and a Bowie knife. Switching boots for moccasins, which I carried in my saddlebags, I started easing through the brush and trees toward the camp.

Now, moving up on a camp of woods-wise mountain boys is not an easy thing. A wild animal is not likely to step on a twig or branch out in the trees and brush. Only a man, or sometimes a horse or cow, will do that, but usually when a branch cracks somewhere it is a man moving, and every man in that camp would know it.

Another distinctive sound is the brushing of a branch on rough clothing. It makes a whisking-whispering sound the ear can pick up. And as for smells, a man used to living in wild country is as keenly aware of smells as any wild creature is. The wind, too, made small sounds and, drawing near to the camp, I tried to move with the wind and to make no sudden clear sound.

The guard near the fire could be seen faintly through the leaves, and it took me almost half an hour to cover the last sixty feet. The guard was smoking a corncob pipe and was having trouble keeping it alight. From time to time he squatted near the fire, lifting twigs to relight his pipe, and that gave me an advantage. With his eyes accustomed to the glow of the fire, his sight would be poor when he looked out into the darkness.

The camp was simple enough. Men were rolled up here and there, and off to one side I could see Judith lying in the space between Black Fetchen and Burr. At her head was the trunk of a big old cottonwood, and Fetchen lay about ten feet to one side, Burr the same distance on the other. Her feet were toward the fire, which was a good twenty feet away.

There was no way to get her without stepping over one of those men, or else somehow getting around that tree trunk. Unless . . . unless the stampede started everybody moving and for the moment they forgot about her.

It was a mighty big gamble. But I thought how out on the plains a man's first thought is his horse, and if those horses started moving, or if the cattle started and the men jumped for their horses, there might be a minute or so when Judith was forgotten. If, at that moment, I was behind that tree trunk . . .

We had made no plans for such a thing, but I figured that our boys would take it for granted that I'd gotten Judith, so they would start the stampede after a few minutes. The best thing I could do would be to slip around and get back of that tree trunk, so I eased back from where I was, and when deep enough into the woods I started to circle about the camp.

But I was uneasy. It seemed to me there was something wrong, like maybe somebody was watching me, or laying for me. It was a bad feeling to have. I couldn't see anybody or hear anything, but at the same time I wasn't low-rating those Fetchen boys. I knew enough about them to be wary. They were such a tricky lot, and all of them had done their share of hunting and fighting.

When I was halfway to where I was going I eased up and stayed quiet for a spell, just listening. After a while, hearing no sound that seemed wrong, I started circling again. It took me a while, and I was getting scared they'd start those cattle moving before I could get back of that tree trunk.

Of a sudden, I heard a noise. Somebody had come into their camp. By that time I was right in line with the tree trunk, so I snaked along the ground under the brush and worked my way up behind it.

I could see Black Fetchen standing by the fire, and Burr was there too. There were three or four others with them, and they were all talking together in low tones. Something had happened . . . maybe they had seen the boys, or maybe some of their lot had seen our outfit off to the north.

About that time I saw Judith. She was lying still; her eyes were wide open and her head was tilted back a mite and she was looking right at me.

"Flagan Sackett," she whispered, "you go right away from here. If they find you they will kill you."

"I came for you."

"You're a fool. I am going to marry James Black Fetchen."

"Over my dead body."

"You stay here, and that's the way it will be. You go away."

Was I mistaken, or did she sound less positive about that business of marrying Black? Anyway, it was now or never.

I had no idea whether anything had gone wrong or not, but that stampede should have begun before this. It was unlikely I'd ever get this close again without getting myself killed, so I said, "Judith, you slip back here. Quiet now."

"I will do no such thing!"

"Judith," I said, for time was slipping away and I'd little of it left, "why do you think the whole Fetchen outfit came west?"

"They came after me!" she said proudly.

"Maybe . . . but they had another reason, too. They ran because the law wants them for murder!"

The Fetchen boys were still standing together, talking. Another man had gotten up from his blankets and gone over to join them. About that time one of the group happened to move and I saw why they were all so busy.

Standing in the center was someone who didn't belong with them, but someone who looked familiar. He turned suddenly and walked off toward his horse. I couldn't see his face, but I knew that walk. It was Larnie Cagle.

"I don't believe you!" Judith whispered.

Me, I was almighty scared. If Cagle was talking to them he would have told them we were close by, for from the way they welcomed him you'd have thought he was one of the family.

"I've got no more time to waste. Black Fetchen, Burr, and them killed your grandpa, and I've got a telegram from Tazewell to prove it."

She gasped and started to speak; then suddenly she slipped out of her blankets, caught up her boots, and came into the brush. And I'll give her that much. When she decided to move she wasted no time, and she made no noise. She came off the ground with no more sound than a bird, and she slid between the leaves of the brush like a ghost.

We scrambled, fear crawling into my throat at being scrooched down in that brush. Suddenly behind us somebody yelled, "Judith! . . . Where's that fool girl?"

Behind us I heard them coming, and we got to our feet and started to run. Just at that moment there was a thunder of hoofs, a wild yell, a shot; then a series of yells and shots and we heard the herd start.

Glancing over my shoulder to get my direction from their fire, I could see the clearing where they were camped. Everybody had stopped dead in their tracks at those yells, and even as I looked they ran for their horses. And then the cattle hit the brush in a solid wall of plunging bodies, horns, and hoofs, . . . maddened, smashing everything down before them.

My horse was safely out of line, but we had no chance to reach him. I jumped, caught the low branch of a cottonwood and hauled myself up, then reached and grabbed Judith, pulling her up just as a huge brindle steer smashed through beneath me, flames from the fire lighting his side.

Behind us at the camp there were shots and yells as they tried to turn the herd, then I heard a scream, torn right from the guts of somebody trampled down under churning hoofs. Then the cattle were sweeping by under us, and I could feel the heat of their bodies as they smashed through.

It could have been only a few minutes, but it seemed a good deal longer than that.

As the last ones went by, I dropped to the ground, caught Judith by the hand, and she jumped down beside me. We ran over the mashed-down brush where the cattle had passed. Running, it taken us no time at all to reach my horse, and he was almighty glad to see me. I swung up, and took Judith with me on the saddle. She clung to me, arms around my waist, as I hit out for our camp where we'd planned to meet.

Yet all I could think of at the moment was Larnie Cagle. He had sold us out.

It was nigh on to daylight when I met Moss and Galloway. They came riding up, leading one of the Costello mares and a pinto pony.

Judith switched to the mare's saddle and we headed north for Hawkes's camp, rounding up what cattle we saw as we rode. By the time we reached the camp we had at least five hundred head ahead of us. The four of us had spread out, sweeping them together and into a tight bunch. Here and there as we rode, other cattle came out of the gray light of morning to join the herd.

Kyle Shore was the first man out to meet us, and right behind him came Ladder Walker.

I looked over at Shore, measuring him, and wondering if he had sold us out too. Or how far he would go to back his partner.

We walked the cattle up to the camp. Evan Hawkes, in his shirt-sleeves and riding bareback, came to meet us, too.

He glanced from the cattle to Judith. What he said was, "You boys all right?"

"Yeah," I said. "But the Fetchens may be hurting. The stampede went right through their camp."

"Serves them right," Walker said.

The cattle we'd brought moved in with our herd, and we swung our horses to the fire. When I got down I stood back from the fire where I could see them all. "Who's with the herd?" I asked.

"Cagle, Bryan, and McKirdy. Briggs just rode in to build up the cook fire."

"You sure?"

They looked at me then, they all looked at me. "Anybody seen them?" I asked.

Briggs looked around from the fire. "Everybody's all right, if that's what you mean."

"Did you talk to any of them, Briggs?"

"Sure. Dan McKirdy and me passed by several times. What are you getting at?"

There was a sound of singing then, and Larnie Cagle rode in. "How about some coffee?" he said. "I'll never make no kind of a night hawk."

I stepped forward, feeling all cold and empty inside. "I don't know about that," I said. "You did a lot of riding tonight."

Of a sudden it was so still you could almost hear the clouds passing over.

He came around on me, facing me across the fire. Nobody said anything for a moment, and when one of them spoke it was Kyle Shore.

Even before he spoke I knew what he would say, for I knew other men who had ridden other trails, men like Shore who were true to what they believed, wrong-headed though it might be.

"Larnie Cagle is a friend of mine," he said.

"Ask him where he was tonight, and then decide if he is still your friend."

"You're talking," Cagle said. "Better make it good."

"Before we start talking," I said, "let every man hold a gun. The Fetchens are coming for us, and they know right where we are. They should be here almost any minute."

Harry Briggs turned suddenly from the group. "I'll tell Dan and the boys," he said, and was gone.

Kyle Shore had been looking at me, only now he was turning his eyes upon Cagle. "What's he mean, Larnie?"

"He's talkin', let him finish it."

"Go ahead, Sackett," Shore said. "I want to hear this."

"Larnie Cagle slipped away from night-herding and rode over to the Fetchen camp. He told them all they wanted to know. He told them about Galloway, Moss, and me, and if we hadn't made it sooner than expected, we'd have been trapped and killed. They'd have followed with an attack on this camp."

Cagle was watching me, expecting me to draw, but he was stalling, waiting for the edge.

"Nobody is going to believe that," he said, almost carelessly.

"They will believe it," Judith said suddenly. It was the first thing she had said since coming into camp. "Because I saw you, too. And that wasn't the first time. He had been there before."

Suddenly all the smartness had gone out of him. Cagle stood there like a trapped animal. He had not seen Judith, and had no idea she was in camp.

"What about it, Cagle?" Hawkes's tone was cold.

"Mr. Hawkes," Kyle Shore said, "this here is my deal. I rode into camp with him, we hired on together."

He turned to Cagle. "Larnie, when I ride, I ride for the brand. I may sell my gun, but it stays sold."

Briggs rode up to the edge of the firelight. "They're comin', Mr. Hawkes. They're all around us."

"You ain't got a chance!" Cagle said with a sneer in his voice. "You never had a chance."

"You've got one," Kyle Shore said. "You've got just one, Larnie, but you got to kill me to get it."

They looked at each other across the fire, and Shore said, "I never rode with no double-crosser, and never will. I figure you're my fault."

Cagle gave a laugh, but the laugh was a little shrill. "You? Why, you damn' fool, you never saw the day you—"

He dropped his hand, and he was fast. His gun cleared the holster and came up shooting. The first shot hit the dirt at Shore's feet and the second shot cut a notch from his hat brim.

Kyle Shore had drawn almost as fast, but his gun came up smoothly, and taking his time he shot . . . just once.

Larnie Cagle took a teetering step forward, then fell on his face, dead before he touched the ground.

"Damn' fool," Shore said. "He surely fancied that fast draw. I told him he should take time. Make the first shot count. He wouldn't listen."

Out upon the plains there was a shot, then another. We ran for our horses, bunching them under the trees. Galloway dropped to one knee near a tree trunk and fired quickly at a racing horse, then again. Taking Judith by the hand, I pushed her down behind a big fallen tree. Then I knelt beside her, rifle up, hunting a target.

There was a flurry of hammering shots and then the pound of racing hoofs, and they were gone. When Black saw there was no surprise, he just lit up the night with a little rifle fire and rode off, figuring there'd be another day . . . as there generally is.

Daylight took its time a-coming, and some of us waited by the fire nursing our coffee cups in chilly fingers, our shoulders hunched. Others dozed against a fallen log, and a few crawled back into their blankets and catnapped the last two hours away.

Me, I moved restlessly around camp, picking up fuel for the fire, contemplating what we'd best do next. Evan Hawkes would be wanting to get the rest of his cattle back; but now that we had Judith again, it was our duty to carry her west to her pa.

There was a sight of work to do, and some of the cattle would be scratched or battered from horns or brush, and unless they were cared for we'd have blow-flies settling on them. A cowhand's work is never done. He ropes and rides before sunup and rarely gets in for chow before the sun is down.

Judith, she slept—slept like a baby. But she worried me some, looking at her. She didn't look much like a little girl any more, and looking at a girl thataway can confuse a man's thinking.

My fingers touched my jaw. It had been some time since I'd shaved, and I'd best be about it before we got to riding westward again.

Kyle Shore wasn't talking. He was sitting there looking into the fire, his back to the long bundle we'd bury, come daybreak. I had Shore pegged now. He was a good, steady man, a fighter by trade, with no pretense to being a real gunman. He was no fast-draw artist, but his kind could kill a lot who thought they were.

Thinking about that, I went for coffee. It was hot, blacker than sin, and strong enough to float a horseshoe. It was cowboy's coffee.

Chapter 8

Morning, noon, and night we worked our hearts out, rounding up the scattered herd, and when we had finished we still lacked a lot of having half of what Evan Hawkes had started with when he left Texas. The Fetchen outfit had made off with the rest of them.

After a week of riding and rounding them up we started west once more.

Judith was quiet. She pulled her weight around camp, helping the cook and generally making herself useful, and when she was on the range she showed that she not only could ride the rough string but that she could savvy cattle.

Much as I wanted to pay her no mind, it was getting so I couldn't do that. She was around camp, stirring pots, bending over the fire, and looking so pretty I wondered whether I'd been right in the head when I first put eyes on her back yonder in Tazewell.

Nonetheless, I kept my eyes off her as much as I could. I rode out from camp early, and avoided sitting nigh her when it was possible. Only it seemed we were always winding up sitting side by side. I never talked or said much. First off, I'm simply no hand with women. Galloway now, he had half the girls in the mountains breathing hard most of the time, but me, I was just big and quiet, and when I was seated by womenfolks all the words in me just lost themselves in the breaks of my mind. No matter how much I tried, I couldn't put a loop over even one sentence.

Besides, there was the land. A big, grand, wide country with every glance lost in the distance. There was a special feeling on the wind when it blew across those miles of grass, a wind so cool, so deep down inside you that every breath of it was like a drink of cool water. And we saw the tumbleweeds far out ahead of us, hundreds of them rolling south ahead of the wind, like the skirmish line of an army.

At first they made the cattle skittish, but they got used to them, as we did. I never knew where they came from, but for three days the wind blew cool out of the north and for three days they came in the hundreds, in the thousands.

Trees grew thicker along the streams, and the grass was better. From time to time we saw scattered buffalo, three or four together, and once a big old bull, alone on a hilltop, watching us pass. He followed us for two days, keeping his distance—wanting company I suppose.

Twice we saw burned-out wagons, places where Indians had rounded up some settlers. Nobody would ever know who they were, and folks back home would wonder about them for a while, and then time would make them become dimmer.

Like Galloway and me. We had no close kinfolk, nobody keeping account of us. If we were to get killed out here nobody would ask who, why, or whatever. It made a body feel kind of lonesome down inside, and it set me to wondering where I was headed for.

Once, far ahead of the herd, I heard a galloping behind me, and when I turned in the saddle I saw it was that Judith girl. She rode sidesaddle, of course, and looked mighty fetching as she came up to me.

"You'd be a sight better off with the rest," I said. "If we met up with Indians, you might get taken."

"I'm not afraid. Not with you to care for me."

Now, that there remark just about threw me. I suppose nobody had ever said such a thing to me before, and it runs in the blood of a man that he should care for womenfolk. It's a need in him, deep as motherhood to a woman, and it's a thing folks are likely to forget. A man with nobody to care for is as lonesome as a lost hound dog, and as useless. If he's to feel of any purpose to himself, he's got to feel he's needed, feel he stands between somebody and any trouble.

I'd had nobody. Galloway was fit to care for himself and an army of others. He was a man built for action, and tempered to violence. Gentle, he was most times, but fierce when aroused. You might as well try to take care of a grizzly bear as of him. So I'd had nobody, nor had he.

"I'd stand up for you," I said, "but it would be a worrisome thing to have to think of somebody else. I mean, whilst fighting, or whatever. Anyway, you'd take off after that Fetchen outfit if they showed up."

"I would not!"

She put her chin up at me, but stayed alongside, and said nothing more for a while.

"Mighty pretty country," I ventured after a bit.

"It is, isn't it? I just can't wait to see Pa's ranch." She sobered down then. "I hope he's all right."

"You worried about the Fetchens?"

"Yes, I am. You've no idea what they are like. I just never imagined men could be like that." She looked quickly at me. "Oh, they were all right to me. James saw to that. But I heard talk when they didn't think I was listening." She turned toward me again. "The happiest moment in my life was when you came from behind that tree trunk. And you might have been killed!"

"Yes, ma'am. That's a common might-have-been out here. There's few things a man can do that might not get him killed. It's a rough land, but a man is better off if he rides his trail knowing there may be trouble about. It simply won't do to get careless. . . . And you be careful, too."

A pretty little stream, not over eight or ten inches deep, but running at a lively pace, and kind of curving around a flat meadow with low hills offered shelter from the north, and a cluster of cottonwoods and willows where we could camp . . . it was just what we needed.

"We'll just sort of camp here," I said. "I'll ride over and get a cooking fire started."

"Flagan!" Judith screamed, and I wheeled and saw three of them come up out of the grass near that stream where they'd been laying for me.

Three of them rising right up out of the ground, like, with their horses nowhere near them, and all three had their rifles on me.

Instinctively, I swung my horse. He was a good cutting horse who could turn on a dime and have six cents left, and he turned now. When he wheeled about I charged right at them. My six-shooter was in my hand, I don't know how come, and I chopped down with it, blasting a shot at the nearest one while keeping him between the others and me.

Swinging my horse again, I doubled right back on my heels in charging down on the others. I heard a bullet nip by me, felt a jolt somewhere, and then I was firing again and the last man was legging it for the cottonwoods. I taken in after him as he ran, and I came up alongside him and nudged him with the horse to knock him rolling.

I turned my horse again and came back on him as he was staggering to his feet. I let the horse come alongside him again, and this time I lifted a stirrup and caught him right in the middle with my heel. It knocked him all sprawled out.

One of the others was getting up and was halfway to his horse by the time I could get around to him, but I started after him too. He made it almost to the brush before I gave him my heel, knocking him face down into the broken branches of the willows.

Judith had now ridden up to me. "Are you hurt?" she asked.

"Not me. Those boys are some upset, I figure." I looked at her. "You warned me," I said. "You yelled just in time."

Three riders had come over the hill, riding hell bent for election. They were Galloway, Kyle Shore, and Hawkes himself, all of them with rifles ready for whatever trouble there was.

There was only blood on the grass where the first man had fallen. He had slipped off into the tall grass and brush, and had no doubt got to his horse and away. One of the others was also gone, but he was hurting—I'd lay a bit of money on that. The last man I'd kicked into the brush looked as if he'd been fighting a couple of porcupines. His face was a sight, scratched and bloody like nothing a body ever saw.

"You near broke my back!" he complained. "What sort of way is that to do a man up?"

"You'd rather get shot?"

He looked at me. "I reckon not," he said dryly, "if given the choice."

"You're a Burshill by the look of you," I said.

"I'm Trent Burshill, cousin to the Fetchens."

"You might be in better comp'ny. But I know your outfit. You folks have been making 'shine back in the hills since before Noah."

"Nigh to a hunert years," he said proudly. "No Burshill of my line never paid no tax on whiskey."

"You should have stayed back there. You aren't going to cut the mustard in these western lands. Now you've mixed up in rustling."

"You got it to prove."

Kyle Shore looked hard at him. "Friend, you'd best learn. Out here they hold court in the saddle and execute the sentence with a saddle rope."

"You fixin' to hang me?"

"Dunno," Shore said, straight-faced. "It depends on Mr. Hawkes. If he sees fit to hang you, that's what we'll do."

Trent Burshill looked pretty unhappy. "I never counted on that," he said. "Seemed like this was wide-open land where a man could do as he liked."

"As long as you don't interfere with no other man," Shore said. "Western folks look down on that. And they've got no time to be ridin' to court, maybe a hundred miles, just to hang a cow thief. A cottonwood limb works better."

Trent Burshill looked thoughtful. "Should be a way of settling this," he said. "Sure, I lined up with Black, him being my cousin an' all."

"Where's Black headed for?" I asked.

He glanced around at me. "You're one of them Tennessee Sacketts. I heard tell of you. Why, he's headed for the Greenhorns—some mountains westward. He's got him some idea about them."

Burshill looked at me straight. "He aims to do you in, Sackett. Was I you, I'd be travelin' east, not west."

The rest of the outfit were trailing into the bottom now with the herd. I spotted a thick limb overhead. "There's a proper branch," I said. "Maybe we ought to tie his hands, put the noose over his neck, and leave him in his saddle. Give him a chance to see how long his horse would stand without moving."

Trent Burshill looked up at the limb over his head. "If you boys was to reconsider," he said, "I'd like to ride for Tennessee. These last few minutes," he added, "Tennessee never looked so good."

"That puncher with the scar on his face," I said to him, "that newcomer. Now, who would he be?"

Burshill shrugged. "You can have him. I figure he deserves the rope more than me. Personal, I don't cotton to him. He's snake-mean. That there is Russ Menard."

Kyle Shore looked at me. "Sackett, you've bought yourself trouble. Russ Menard is reckoned by some to be the fastest man with a gun and the most dangerous anywhere about."

"I knew a man like that once," I said.

"Where is he?"

"Why, he's dead. He proved to be not so fast as another man, and not so dangerous with three bullets in him."

"Russ Menard," Shore said, "comes from down in the Nation. He killed one of Judge Parker's marshals and figured it was healthier out of his jurisdiction. He was in a gun battle in Tascosa, and some say he was in the big fight in Lincoln, New Mexico."

Evan Hawkes, who had ridden over to locate his chuck wagon and crew, now came back. Judith Costello rode beside him. Harry Briggs and Ladder Walker drifted along, leading a horse.

"Found his horse," Hawkes said.

"Tie him on it," Walker said, "backwards in the saddle, and turn him loose."

"Now, see here!" Burshill protested.

"Then take his boots off and let him walk back. I heard about a man walked a hundred miles once, in his bare feet!"

"Way I heard it," Burshill said, "was there would be land and cattle and horses for the taking. A man could get rich, that's what Black said. I never figured on no rope."

"The land's for the taking," Hawkes said, "but the cattle and the horses belong to somebody. You have helped in rustling, and you were about to dry-gulch my men. What have you to say for yourself?"

"I made good whiskey. It was 'shine, but it was good whiskey," Burshill said. "I wouldn't want to grieve my kinfolk back in Tennessee."

"I'll let you have your horse," Evan Hawkes said, "but if we see you west of here we'll hang you."

"Mister, you let me go now, and you'll have to burn the stump and sift the ashes before you find me again."

"All right," Hawkes said, "let him go."

Trent Burshill let out of there as if his tail was afire, and that was just as well. I wasn't strong on hanging, anyway.

When the night fire was burning and there was the smell of coffee in the air, I went to Evan Hawkes.

"Mr. Hawkes, Galloway and me, we figure we'd best light out of here and head for Costello's ranch in the Greenhorns. If the Fetchens come on him unprepared they might ride him down. We can make faster time free of the herd."

"All right. I'm sorry to lose you boys, but we're heading the same way." He paused. "I'm going to get my herd back, so you boys figure yourselves still on the payroll. When you get that girl back to her father, you roust around and locate my cattle for me."

By daylight we had the camp well behind us. The horses we rode were good, fast ones with a lot of stamina. Judith was a rider, all right, and we stayed with it all day, riding the sun out of the sky, and soon we could see the far-off jagged line of mountains. The stars came up.

We slept in a tiny hollow under some cottonwoods, the horses grazing, and the remains of a small fire smoking under the coffeepot. Me, I was first up as always, putting sticks and bark together with a twist of dried grass to get the flame going, but keeping my ears alert for sound. At times I prowled to the edge of the hollow and looked around.

Back at camp Galloway still slept, wrapped in his blanket, but Judith lay with her cheek pillowed on her arm, her dark hair around her face, her lips soft in the morning light. It made a man restless to see her so, and I turned back to my fire.

Judith Costello . . . it was a lovely name. But even if I was of a mind to, what could I offer such a girl? Her family were movers, they were horse-traders and traveling folks, but from all I'd heard they were well-off. And me, I had a gun and a saddle.

My thoughts turned to the ranch in the Greenhorns. The Fetchens had killed Judith's grandpa back in Tennessee, more than likely in anger at Judith and because of the loss of the horses. But suppose there was something more? Suppose the Fetchen outfit knew something we did not even surmise?

First of all, it was needful for us to ride west to that ranch, and not come on it unexpected, either. It was in my mind to circle about, to look the place over before riding right in. I had no idea what sort of a man Costello was, or how much of an outfit he had, but it would do no harm to sort of prospect around before making ourselves known.

We put together a breakfast from provisions we'd brought from Hawkes's outfit, then saddled up and rode west, keeping always to low ground.

The Greenhorns were a small range, a sort of offshoot of the towering Sangre de Cristos. It was Ute country, and although the Utes were said to be quiet, I wasn't any too sure of it, and I was taking no chances.

First off, we had to locate Costello's ranch, for all we had in the way of directions was that it was in the Greenhorns. The nearest town I knew of was Walsenburg, but I wanted to avoid towns. Sure as shootin', the Fetchens would have somebody around to let them know of us coming. North of there, and about due west of us, was a stage stop called Greenhorn, and at the Greenhorn Inn, one of Kit Carson's old hangouts, we figured it was likely we'd hear something.

Big a country as it was, most everybody knew of all the ranchers and settlers around, and the place was small enough so we could see about everything in it before we rode into town—if town it could be called.

We made our nooning on the Huerfano River about ten miles east of Greenhorn, and made a resting time of it, for I wanted to ride into the place about sundown.

Galloway was restless, and I knew just what he felt. There was that much between us that we each knew the other's feelings. He could sense trouble coming, and was on edge for it. We both knew it was there, not far off, and waiting for us like a set trap.

There was a good deal of hate in the Fetchens, and it was in Black most of all; and they would not rest until they'd staked our hides out to dry, or we had come it over them the final time.

When noon was well past, we mounted up and pushed on to

Greenhorn. The mountains were named for an Indian chief who had ruled the roost around there in times gone by. It was said of the young buck deer when his horns were fresh and in velvet that he was a "greenhorn," for he was foolishly brave then, ready to challenge anything. The chief had been that way, too, but the Spanish wiped him out. So the name greenhorn was given to anyone young and braver than he had right to be, going in where angels fear to tread, as the saying is.

The Greenhorn Inn was a comfortable enough place, as such places went—a stage stop and a hotel with sleeping quarters and a fair-to-middling dining room. We rode up, tied our horses out of sight, and the three of us checked the horses in the stable, but we saw none we recognized as Fetchen horses.

The place was nigh to empty. One old codger with a face that looked as if it was carved out of flint was sitting there, and he looked at us as if he'd seen us before, although I knew no such face. He was a lean, savage-looking old man, one of those old buffalo hunters or mountain men, by the look of him—nobody to have much truck with.

The man behind the bar glanced at Judith and then at us. We found a table and hung our hats nearby, then sat down. He came over to us.

"How are you, folks? We've got beans and bacon, beans and bear meat, beans and venison. You name it. And we've got fresh-baked bread . . . made it my ownself."

We ordered, and he brought us coffee, black and strong. Tasting it, I glanced over at Judith. For a girl facing up to trouble, she looked bright and pretty, just too pretty for a mountain boy like me.

"This here," I said to her, "is right touchy country. There's Indians about, both Utes and Comanches, and no matter what anybody says there's angry blood in them. They don't like white men very much, and they don't like each other."

"I can't think of anything but Pa," she said. "It has been such a long time since I've seen him, and now that we are so close, I can hardly sit still for wanting to be riding on."

"You hold your horses," Galloway advised. "We'll make it in time."

Even as he spoke, I had an odd feeling of foreboding come over me. It was such a feeling as I'd never had before. I looked across at Galloway, and he was looking at me, and we both knew what the other felt.

What was going to happen? What was lying in wait for us?

When the man came back with our food I looked up at him and

said, "We're hunting the Costello outfit, over in the Greenhorns. Can you tell us how to get there?"

He put the dishes down in front of us before we got an answer. "My advice to you is to stay away from there. It will get you nothing but trouble."

Judith's face went pale under the tan, and her eyes were suddenly frightened.

When I spoke, my voice was rougher than I intended, because of her. "What do you mean by that?"

The man backed off a step, in no way intimidated, simply wary. "I mean that's a tough outfit over there. You go in there hunting trouble and you're likely to find it."

"We aren't seeking it out," I said, more quietly. "Costello is this lady's pa. We're taking her home."

"Sorry, ma'am," he said quietly. "I didn't know. If I were you, I'd ride careful. There's been trouble in those hills."

It was not until we had finished eating that he spoke to us again. "You boys drop around later," he said, "and I'll buy you a drink."

At the door, hesitating before going to her room, Judith looked from Galloway to me. "He's going to tell you something, isn't he? I mean that's why he offered to buy you a drink, to get you back there without me."

"Now, I don't think—" Galloway interrupted.

She would have none of it. "Flagan, you'll tell me, won't you? I've got to know if there's anything wrong. I've simply got to! After all, I haven't seen Pa in a long time."

"I'll tell you," I said, though I knew I might be lying in my teeth, for I figured she'd guessed right. That man had something to relate, and it was likely something he didn't want Judith to hear.

She turned and went to her room, and we stayed a minute, Galloway and me, hesitating to go back.

Chapter 9

We stood there together, having it in our heads that what we would hear would bring us no pleasure. The night was closing in around us, and no telling what would come to Greenhorn whilst we were abed. Whatever it was, we could expect nothing but grief.

"Before we go to bed," Galloway suggested, "we'd better take a turn around outside."

"You sleep under cover," I said. "I'll make out where I can listen well. I'd not sleep easy otherwise."

"I ain't slept in a bed for some time," Galloway said, "but I'm pining to."

"You have at it. I'll find a place where my ears can pick up sound whilst I sleep."

We walked back into the saloon, two mountain boys from Tennessee. The old man still sat at his table, staying long over his coffee. He shot a hard glance at us, but we trailed on up to the bar.

The bartender poured each of us a drink, then gestured toward a table. "We might as well sit down. There'll be nobody else along tonight, and there's no sense in standing when you can sit."

"That's a fine-looking young lady," he said after we were seated. "I'd want no harm to come to her, but there's talk of trouble over there, and Costello is right in the midst of it."

We waited, and there was no sound in the room. Finally he spoke again, his face oddly lighted by the light from the coal-oil lamp with the reflector behind it. "There's something wrong up there—I don't know what it is. Costello used to come down here once in a while . . . the last time was a year ago. I was over that way, but he wouldn't see me. Ordered me off the place."

"Why?"

"Well, it was his place. I suppose he had his reasons." The bartender refilled the glasses from the bottle. "Nevertheless it worried me, because it wasn't like him. . . . He lives alone, you know, back over on the ridge."

He paused again, then went on, "He fired his hands, all of them."

"He's alone up there now?"

"I don't think so. A few days back there were some men came riding up here, asked where Costello's layout was."

"Like we did," I said.

"I told them. I had no reason not to, although I didn't like their looks, but I also warned them they wouldn't be welcome. They laughed at me. One of them spoke up and said that they'd be welcome, all right, that Costello was expecting them."

"They beat us to it, Flagan," Galloway said. "They're here."

The bartender glanced from one to the other of us. "You know those men?"

"We know them, and if any of them show up again, be careful. They'll kill you as soon as look at you . . . maybe sooner."

"What are you two going to do?"

"Go up there. We gave a fair promise to see the young lady to her pa. So we'll go up there."

"And those men?"

Galloway grinned at him, then at me. "Why, they'd better light a shuck for Texas before we tie cans to their tails."

"Those men, now," I said, "did they have any cattle?"

"Not with them. But they said they had a herd following." He paused. "Is there anything I can do? There's good folks in this country, and Costello was a good neighbor, although a man who kept to himself except when needed. If it comes to that, we could round up a goodly lot who would ride to help him."

"You leave it to us. We Sacketts favor skinning our own cats."

The old man seated alone at the table spoke up then. "I knowed it. I knowed you two was Sacketts. I'm Cap Rountree, an' I was with Tyrel and them down on the Mogollon that time."

"Heard you spoken of," Galloway said. "Come on over and set."

"If you boys are ridin' into trouble," Rountree said, "I'd admire to ride along. I been sharin' Sackett trouble a good few years now, and I don't feel comfortable without it."

We talked a spell, watching the night hours pass, and listening for the sounds of riders who did not come.

Black Fetchen must have sent riders on ahead, and those riders must have moved in fast and hard. He might even have gone on ahead himself, letting the herd follow. We would have ridden right into a trap had we just gone on ahead without making inquiries, or being a mite suspicious.

"Hope he's all right," I said. "Costello, I mean. It would go hard with Judith to lose her pa as well as her grandpa all to once, like that."

"Well, I'll see you boys, come daylight," Rountree said. "I'm holed up in the stable should you need me."

"I'll be around off and on all night," I told him. "Don't shoot until you see the whites of my eyes."

Cap walked outside, stood there a moment, and then went off into the darkness.

"I like that old man," Galloway said. "Seems to me Tyrel set store by him."

"One of his oldest friends. Came west with him from eastern Kansas, where they tied up on a trail herd."*

"We'll need him," Galloway added. "We're facing up to trouble, Flagan."

"You get some sleep," I advised. "I'll do the same."

Outside it was still. Off to the west I thought I could see the gleam of snow on the mountains. I liked the smell of the wind off those peaks, but after a minute I walked tiredly across the road, picked up my blanket and poncho, and bedded down under a cottonwood where I could hear the trail sounds in the night. If any riders came up to the Greenhorn Inn I wanted to be the first to know.

Tired as I was, I didn't sleep, my thoughts wandering, just thinking of Galloway and me, homeless as tumbleweeds, drifting loose around the country. It was time we found land, time we put down some roots. It did a man no good to ride about always feathered for trouble. Sooner or later he would wind up dead, back in some draw or on some windy slope, leaving his carcass for the coyotes and buzzards to fight over. It doesn't matter how tough a man becomes, or how good he is with a gun, there comes the time when his draw is a little too slow, or something gets in the way of his bullet.

We were rougher than cobs, Galloway and me, but in this country many a tough man had cashed in his chips. It wasn't in me to think lightly of Black Fetchen. He was known throughout the mountains for his fist fighting and shooting, a man of terrible rages and fierce hatreds . . . we weren't going to come it over him without grief.

---

*The Daybreakers

Suddenly, I came wide awake. I had no idea just when I'd dozed off, but my eyes came wide open and I was listening. What I heard was a horse walking . . . two horses.

My hand closed on my gun butt.

There was no light showing anywhere in any of the four or five buildings that made up Greenhorn. The inn was dark and still.

The first thing I made out was the shine of a horse's hip, then the glisten of starlight on a rifle barrel. Two riders had pulled up in the road right in front of the inn. A saddle creaked . . . one man was getting down.

Our horses were out back, picketed on a stretch of meadow. Unless those riders scouted around some they'd not be likely to find them, for the meadow was back beyond the corral and stable.

Noiselessly I sat up, keeping the blanket hunched around my shoulders, for the night was chill. I held my .45 in my hand, the barrel across my thigh.

After a bit I heard boots crunching and the rider came back. By now I could almost make him out—a big man with a kind of rolling walk. "Ain't there," I heard him whisper. "At least, their horses aren't in the stalls or the corral."

He stepped into the saddle again and I listened as they walked their horses down the road. Beyond the buildings they stepped them up to a trot, and I wondered where they figured to lay up for the night. It seemed to me they might have a place in mind. Come daylight, if they didn't find our tracks on the trail, they might just hole up and wait for us.

I dozed off, and when next I awakened the sky was getting bright. I rolled my bed and led the horses in, gave them an easy bait of water, and had all three horses saddled before Galloway came out of the inn.

"They're a-fixing to eat in there," he said. "It smells almighty nice."

Cap Rountree came from the stable, leading a raw-boned roan gelding, under a worn-out saddle packing two rifle scabbards. He glanced at me and I grinned at him.

"I take it your visitor wasn't talking much," I said.

"Didn't see me," Cap said, "an' just as well. I had my old Bowie to hand, and had he offered trouble I'd have split his brisket. I don't take to folks prowlin' about in the dark."

"Fetchen men?" Galloway asked.

"I reckon. Leastways, they were hunting somebody. They went on up the road."

Rountree tied his horse alongside ours. "You boys new to this country? I rode through here in the fall of 1830, my first time. And a time or two after that." He nodded toward the mountains. "I brought a load of fur out of those mountains two jumps ahead of a pack of Utes.

"Ran into Bridger and some of his outfit, holed in behind a stream bank. I made it to them, and those Utes never knew what hit 'em. They'd no idea there was another white man in miles, nor did I. . . . Good fighters, them Utes."

He started across the street toward the inn. "Point is," he stopped to say, "I can take you right up to Costello's outfit without usin' no trail."

Judith was waiting for us, looking pretty as a bay pony with three white stockings. We all sat up, and the bartender, innkeeper, or whatever, brought on the eggs and bacon. We put away six eggs apiece and most of a side of bacon, it seemed like. At least, Galloway and me ate that many eggs. Judith was content with three, and Cap about the same.

An hour later we were up in the pines, hearing the wind rushing through them like the sound of the sea on a beach. Cap Rountree led the way, following no trail that a body could see, yet he rode sure and true, up and through mountains that reminded us of home.

Presently Cap turned in his saddle. "These Fetchens, now. You said they rustled the Hawkes herd. You ever hear talk of them hunting gold?"

"We had no converse with them," Galloway said, "but I know there was some talk of a Fetchen going to the western mountains many years back."

"Fetchen?" Cap Rountree puzzled over the name. "I figured I knowed most of the old-timers, but I recall no Fetchen. Reason I mentioned it, this here country is full of lost mines. The way folks tell it, there's lost mines or caches of gold all over this country."

He pointed toward the west and south. "There lie the Spanish Peaks, with many a legend about them of sun gods an' rain gods, and of gold, hidden or found.

"North of here there's a cave in Marble Mountain, called the Caverna del Oro, where there's supposed to be gold. I never did hear of gold in a natural cave unless it was cached there, but that's possible. Those old Spanish men rode all over this country.

"There's a man named Sharp lives over there yonder," he went on. "Got him a place called Buzzard Roost Ranch and he's made friends with the Utes. He probably knows more about those old mines than anybody, although I don't rec'lect him wastin' time a-huntin' for them."

Half a mile further he drew up to let the horses take a blow. "I was thinkin' that maybe the Fetchen outfit knew something you boys don't," he said. He threw a sharp glance at Judith. "You ever hear your grandpa talk of any gold mines or such?" he asked her.

Then he said to us, "You told me the Fetchens murdered him. D' you suppose they wanted something besides this here girl? Or the horses?"

He grinned slyly at Judith. "Meanin' no offense, ma'am, for was I a younger man I might do murder myself for such a pretty girl."

"That's all right," Judith said. "I'm used to it." After a moment, she shook her head. "No, there's nothing that I can recall."

"Now, think of this a mite. Yours is a horse-tradin' family, and they stick together. I know about the Irish traders—I spent time in country where they traded. Seems unusual one of them would cut off from the rest like your pa done. D' you suppose he knew something? Maybe when he got to swappin' around, he took something in trade he didn't talk about."

The more I considered what Cap was saying the more I wondered if he hadn't made a good guess. That Fetchen outfit were a murdering lot by all accounts, but why should they kill Costello? What could they hope to gain?

It was possible, trading around like they had done, that one of the Costellos might have picked up a map or a treasure story in trade. Maybe thrown in as boot by somebody who did not believe it themselves.

Now here was a new idea that would account for a lot.

"You consider it," I said to Judith. "Come morning, you may recall something said or seen."

There were a lot of folks scattered through the East who had gone west and then returned to the States—some to get married, some because they liked the easier life, some because they figured the risk of getting their hair lifted by a Comanche was too great. It might be that one of them had known something; or maybe some western man, dying, had sent a map to some of his kinfolk.

We had been following Rountree up an old Indian trail through the high country, but now we saw a valley before us, still some distance off. He drew up again and pointed ahead.

"Right down there is Sharp's trading post, the Buzzard Roost. Closer to us, but out of sight, is the town of Badito.

"Some of the finest horseflesh you ever did see, right down in that valley," he added.

"Costello's?"

"His an' Sharp's. Tom Sharp went back to Missouri in seventy-one and bought himself about thirty, forty head o' stock, a thoroughbred racer among them. Then he sent north into Idaho and bought about two hundred head of appaloosa's from the Nez Percé. He's bred them together for some tough, hardy stock."

"That's what Pa and Grandpa were doing," Judith said.

Well, I looked over at her. "Judith, was your pa in Missouri in seventy-one? I mean, it might have been him or some of his kinfolk who made a deal with Sharp. The tie-up might be right there."

"I don't know," she said doubtfully. "I was just a little girl. We were in Missouri in that year or the next, I think, but I never paid much attention . . . we were always moving."

We camped in the woods that night, smelling the pines, and eating venison we'd killed ourselves. It was a good night, and we sat late around the fire, just talking and yarning of this and that. Galloway and me, we sang a mite, for all we mountain boys take to singing, specially those of Welsh extraction like us.

It was a fine, beautiful night, and one I'd not soon forget, and for once we felt safe. Not that one or the other of us didn't get up once in a while and move away from the fire to prowl around and listen.

Tomorrow we were heading down into the valley, for we had decided to talk to Tom Sharp. Cap knew him, and he had been a friend to Costello. If there was anything to be found out, we would learn it from him.

But I was uneasy. I'd got to thinking about that girl too much, and it worried me. When a man gets mixed up in a shooting affair he'd best keep his mind about him, and not be contemplating a girl's face and a pair of lovely lips.

When we tangled with the Fetchens again they would be out for blood. They had got where they were going, but we had won several hands from them . . . now they would try to make us pay for it. We were few, and there was nowhere about that we could look for help.

Cap gestured off toward the western mountains. "Just over there Tell Sackett an' me had quite a shindig a while back. Believe me, they know the name of Sackett in that country."*

I knew about Tell. I'd heard all that talk down in the Mogollon. The trouble was, mostly we Sacketts were noted for our fighting ways,

---

*Sackett

except maybe for Tyrel, who had become a rancher, and Orrin, who was in politics. It was time some of us did something worthwhile, time we made a mark in the country for something besides gunplay.

A man who rides a violent road comes to only one end—up a dry creek somewhere, or on Boot Hill.

Chapter 10

Tom Sharp was a fine-looking man, the kind you'd ride the river with. He was pushing forty. He had been wounded in the War Between the States, had come west, hunted meat for the mining camps, and cut telegraph poles on contract for the Union Pacific. Finally he'd traveled up the old Ute trail to Huerfano River and opened a trading post in the valley in a big adobe building.

Right off, he started to improve both his horses and cattle by bringing in blooded stock from the States. He was not one of those who came west to get rich and get out; he came to stay and to build. The town of Malachite grew up around his trading post.

As we came riding up to the trading post, he came outside and stood on the steps to meet us, giving us a careful study. All I needed was one glimpse of Sharp to know that he was a man who would stand for no nonsense, and he certainly would not cotton to the likes of Black Fetchen.

"Mr. Sharp?" I said. "I'm Flagan Sackett, this here is my brother Galloway, and our friend, Cap Rountree. The young lady is Judith Costello."

Now, mayhap that wasn't just the way to introduce folks, but I wanted Tom Sharp to know who we were right off, for if a lot of tough strangers had been coming into the country, he would not be in a trusting mood.

He ignored me, looking first at Judith, for which I didn't blame him. "How are you, Judith? Your father has spoken of you."

"Is he all right? I mean . . . we haven't heard, and those men . . ."

"He was all right the last I saw of him, but that's been over a month ago. Will you get down and come in? The wife will be wanting to talk to you, and I'm sure you could all do with some food."

Whilst the rest of them went in, I led the horses to water. After a bit Tom Sharp came out, and gave a look at the horses. "Fine stock," he said. "Is that some of the Costello brand?"

"Yes, it is. We've taken the responsibility of bringing Judith out here to her pa, but there's been trouble along the way. With the Fetchens."

"I have heard of them," Sharp said grimly, "and nothing good. And it isn't the first time."

I gave him a surprised glance. "You've run into them before? You surely ain't from Tennessee?"

"From Missouri. No, it wasn't back there. A few years ago we had a sight of trouble over east and north of here with the Reynolds gang, and one of the gang was a Fetchen. They were some connection of the Reynolds outfit, I never did know what it was. The Reynolds outfit were wiped out, but Fetchen wasn't among those killed."

"Which one was he?"

"Tirey Fetchen. He'd be about my age now. He was a wanted man even before he tied up with the Reynolds gang. I'd had wanted circulars on him when I was a deputy sheriff up in Wyoming, maybe twelve years back, and I recall they listed killings back before the war. He was with the Reynolds gang during the war."

We stabled the horses, and then I went inside. The rest of them were gathered around a table eating, and that food surely smelled good.

"We've seen them come in," Sharp told us over coffee, "but not to stay around. They'd show up, then head for the hills." He looked around at me. "If they've gone up to Costello's place, he may be in real trouble."

"If Judith can stay here," I suggested, "we'll ride up and look around."

"I'll not stay!" Judith exclaimed.

"Now, ma'am," Sharp protested.

"I mean it. I have come all the way to see my father, and I won't wait any longer. I'm going with you." Then she added, looking right at me, "If you don't take me I'll go by myself."

Well, I looked over at Galloway and he shrugged, and that was all there was to it. Both of us knew there was no time to be gained arguing with a woman, and we'd both had a try before this at arguing with Judith.

She went off with Mrs. Sharp, and Sharp sat down with us. "You boys better ride careful," he said. "That's a bad outfit."

So we told him about the trip west and the loss of the Hawkes herd, the Half-Box H.

Sharp was thoughtful. When he looked up at us he said, "I'd better warn you, and when Hawkes comes along you'd better warn him. Fetchen registered a brand in his own name, the JBF Connected."

Cap chuckled. "Ain't takin' him a while to learn. A JBF Connected would fit right over a Half-Box H, fit it like a glove. If Hawkes ain't right careful he'll find all his herd wearin' the wrong brand."

I looked at Sharp. "How are folks hereabouts? Are they understandin'?"

"That depends."

"Maybe the only way we can get those cattle back is to rustle them," I said. "If he can misbrand cattle, we can just brand 'em over."

"What about that?" Galloway said. "What would cover a JBF Connected?"

"When we were ridin' through Texas," I suggested, "we saw a man down there who had a Pig-Pen brand. And I heard tell of one with a Spider-Web. They would cover most anything you could dream up."

"You would have to be careful," Sharp said. "And if you will forgive me, I would have to see Hawkes's papers on the herd."

"He's got 'em, and he'll be showing up right quick." I paused a minute, giving it thought. "What we figured, would be to sort of let the word get around. I mean, about Hawkes's herd and what he figures to do about it."

Sharp chuckled. "Now, that could be right amusing. But you'd have to move fast. It is about roundup time."

"So much the better. A lot of things can happen during a roundup. Only thing we want is to have it understood this is strictly between us and the Fetchen crowd."

"Serve them right," Sharp said. "You just wait until word gets around. You'll have the whole country on your side."

Nevertheless, I was worried. We had to get back into the hills and scout around the Costello outfit, and we had to see Costello himself, but Galloway and me, we knew that every step of the way would be a step further into trouble. Whatever the Fetchens were up to, they were also laying a trap for us, and we were riding up there, maybe right into the trap.

The more we learned, the more we had to worry about. Evan Hawkes was still far behind us, whilst the Fetchens were here, and in considerable strength. Along the line they had picked up more men, outlaws and the like.

But what was it that Black Fetchen was really after? What lay behind their move west? Had it been simply because of their killing of Laban Costello? And for revenge on us? Or was there some deeper cause that began even before we showed up? Was it something they wanted even more than Judith, more than the horses, more than Costello's ranch, if that was what they aimed for?

The thing that stuck in my mind was that Tirey Fetchen had stirred about in these parts before any of us came west, and with the Reynolds gang. Now, there was something about that . . . I couldn't recall what it was, but something I'd heard about that Reynolds outfit.

They had been a gang of outlaws who passed it off that they were robbing to get money for the Confederacy, or that was the tale I'd heard. They had been caught up with, and some of them had been tied to a tree and shot. I had nothing to say about that part of it to anybody, because I wanted to recall what it was about the Reynolds gang that made me remember them . . . some item I'd forgotten.

We went into the hills, climbing high up by an old Ute trail that Sharp told us of, and we skirted about to reach the valley where Costello's outfit lay.

No horse tracks showed on the trail we rode. No sound came from anywhere near. There were, of course, birds talking it up in the bushes, and a slow wind that stirred the trees as we rode along. Nothing else but once in a while the rattle of a spur or the creak of a saddle as a horse took strain in climbing, or a rider shifted weight in the saddle. Sunlight dappled the trail with leaf shadows.

We did not talk. We listened as we rode, and from time to time we paused to listen more carefully.

Cap, who was riding point, drew up suddenly, and we closed in around him. Before us was an opening among the branches of the trees lining the trail. Several miles away we could see a green valley, perhaps five hundred feet lower down, and from it sunlight reflected from a window.

"That will be it," Cap commented. "The way Sharp told it, we will be ridin' Costello range at almost any minute."

We pushed on, circling the smaller valleys that made a chain through the hills. Now, from time to time, cattle tracks showed among those of deer and elk.

The ranch, when we came upon it, lay cupped in the hills, a small but comfortable house set back on a green meadow where a stream curled through. There was slow smoke rising from the chimney, and a good lot of horses in the corrals. Sitting on the stoop in front of the house was a man with a rifle across his knees. We saw no other folks around.

In the meadow a dozen or so head of horses were grazing, the sun gleaming from their smooth flanks. It made a handsome sight, but the man on the stoop looked mighty like a guard.

Galloway sat his horse, giving study to the place, and I did likewise. "Looks too easy," Galloway said after a bit. "I don't like it."

"It's a nice morning," Cap commented. "They might just be idling about."

"Or hid out, waiting for us," I said.

We waited, but Judith was impatient. "Flagan, I want to go down there. I want to see Pa."

"You hold off," I said. "You'll see him soon enough . . . when we know it's safe."

"But he may be in danger!" she protested. "They killed my grandfather, you told me so yourself."

"Yes, but it won't ease your pa's mind to have you in their hands, too. You just wait."

The valley where the ranch lay opened into another, wider valley that we could see as we moved along. There were a few cattle in the first one, and we could see more beyond. The grass was green and rich, and running down the streams there was all the snow water that any rancher could want for his stock. Costello had found a good place.

"They're hid out," Galloway said finally. "I have it in mind they're expecting us. No ranch is quiet like that, this time of day. Not with so many men somewhere about."

We had moved along to a lower bench among the trees, a place not forty feet from where the mountain dropped off into the valley. We saw a man come from the ranch house, saw the screen door shut behind him. From where we were, we could hear it slam.

This man, after a few minutes of talk, seated himself on the steps, while the first man went inside, apparently relieved from guard duty.

"Your pa," Cap surmised, "must be in the house. Certain sure, there's something or somebody down there to be watched over."

Nobody was saying what we had been thinking, that it would make little sense to keep Costello alive . . . unless they were worried for fear some neighbor might insist on seeing him. By this time the Fetchens would know about Tom Sharp, a man not likely to be put off, nor one to trifle with. Yet time would be running out.

They might hold Costello as they had planned to hold Judith, one to be used in controlling the other. If Black Fetchen could get hold of

Judith, marry her, and so establish legal claim to the Costello ranch, then Costello might be made to disappear, leaving them in control. It was a likely thing, but there was much that was puzzling about the whole affair, and about their possible connection with the Reynolds gang.

We waited under the trees, moving as little as possible, and keeping wary for fear we would be discovered. The whole thing was growing irksome, and Judith had my sympathy. Her pa was down there, and it was natural she should want to see him. Only we needed to know a few more things before we could act against them. We needed to know if Costello was alive, and how they were holding him, and we needed to know what they were after.

By now we were all pretty sure that the cattle had been incidental. They had the Half-Box H herd, and they would try to hold it, but I felt certain there was more to it than the herd, or even the ranch.

We had to wait them out. I knew they were not patient men and would soon tire of lying around in the brush, doing nothing.

"We've got to know more about this setup," I said. "Cap, do you know the story of the Reynolds outfit?"

"No more than everybody hereabouts knows. They gave it out that they were Confederate sympathizers, and began robbin' some gold trains and the like, letting it be known they were gettin' the gold to hold for the South. But most folks thought they had no such idea—not after the gold started pilin' up. They figured they planned to use it for themselves."

"What happened to the gold?"

"I can't say as I ever heard, although no doubt folks who lived round here could tell you."

"Sharp would know," Galloway suggested.

In the fading afternoon the Costello ranch looked mighty pretty. Shadows were stretching out, but down there the light was mellow and lovely. I could see why a man, even a mover like Costello, would like to settle in such a place. And there was good grazing in the hills around.

But we saw nothing of Costello, nor of anyone else at all.

The stars came out and the wind grew cool. Restlessly, I walked out to a place where the valley could be seen in more detail. There were lights in the ranch house, and shadows moved before some of the windows. Suddenly the door opened and someone went in. It was open long enough to admit two or three men.

Judith came up beside me. "Do you think Pa is down there, Flagan?"

"Uh-huh."

She said nothing more for some time, and then wondered out loud, "Why did this happen to us?"

"I reckon folks have wondered that always, Judith. In this case it's no accident, I'm thinking. Your pa or your grandpa knew something somebody else wanted to know, or else for some reason they need this ranch."

"Flagan, I've been thinking about what you wanted to know . . . you know, if Pa had been in Missouri in seventy-one. I am sure he was, because I've just remembered something."

"What?"

"Pa had an uncle who wasn't much good. He'd gone off and left us after he got into some trouble with the family, and he went out west. Nobody would talk about him much, but he got into more trouble . . . in Denver, I think it was."

"And so?"

"He came back one night. I remember I woke up and heard talking in a low voice, in Pa's side of the tent. I heard another man's voice, a man who sounded odd . . . as if he was sick or something."

That was all she remembered right then, but it was enough to start me thinking.

Maybe what the Costellos knew was nothing they picked up in trade. Maybe it was something that renegade told them that night in Missouri.

That renegade had been in or around Denver. So had Tirey Fletchen. And so had the Reynolds gang.

Chapter 11

We rode away down the mountain to a hollow in the hills, sheltered by overhanging cliffs and a wall of pines, and made camp there where we could have a fire.

"I figure if we go down to the ranch we'll get so shot full of holes our hides wouldn't be worth tanning," Galloway said. "That outfit's all laid out for an ambush, so let's leave 'em wait."

"Seems to me a likely time to be thinkin' of them cattle," Cap suggested.

"Now, there's a good thought. Let's dab a loop on some and check out the brand."

So we settled down over coffee and bacon to consider. It stood to reason that if most of their crowd were waiting for us to show up, there would be only a few watching the cattle, if any at all. In these mountain valleys, with plenty of grass and water, cattle needed no watching.

The upshot of it was that when the sky lightened with another day coming, we saddled up and went off. The only one who was upset by our decision was Judith.

"This isn't taking me any closer to Pa!" she objected. "I wish I could find a man like Ivanhoe or the Black Knight! He would ride right down there and bring Pa back!"

"You know," I said, "I don't carry any banners for the Fetchen boys, but if the Black Knight was to ride down amongst them in his tin suit he'd have a sieve for an overcoat. Those Fetchens may run short on morals, but morals don't win no turkey-shoots! I know those boys, and they could part your hair with the first bullet and trim around your ears with the next two.

"If you want to choose up heroes to help you, you'd be a sight better off to pick on Robin Hood or Rob Roy. My pa always said you should never walk into a man when he's set for punching. Better to go around him and work him out of balance.

"Well, while they're waiting for us to come down on 'em, we'll simply round up and drive off a few head of cattle. Then we might sort of scout around down to Sharp's place at Buzzard Roost. I'll lay a bet Fetchen has somebody staked out down there to bring him word."

By the time the sun was high we were at Buzzard Roost and sitting alongside the stove eating crackers and sardines, and I mentioned the Reynolds outfit. I'd scarcely said the name before Sharp was giving us the story.

The Reynolds gang had buried a treasure, some said, somewhere near the Spanish Peaks. They were right over there to the south of us, only a few miles away.

Contrary to what some folks said, they hadn't been a very bloody outfit. Fact was, it was claimed they'd killed nobody in their robberies. Reynolds had some reputation as an outlaw before the war began, and then supposedly he was recruited by the South to loot Colorado of its gold and silver shipments. "There's been a lot of talk about how much he stole," Sharp said, "and how much they buried when the law caught up with them; but no matter what anybody says there's small chance they had over seventy thousand dollars."

"That's a lot," Galloway said, kind of dryly. "That's more money than I'm likely to see in this lifetime."

"Do you think it's there?" Cap asked.

Sharp shrugged. "It's certain they hadn't anything on 'em when they were caught, and they hadn't much time to hide it unless they hid it very soon after taking it—which could be."

Judith wasn't talking, she was just sitting there looking solemn and kind of scared too, yet knowing her I had a feeling she was scared less for herself than for her Pa. It came to me that I should try, by some trick, to get him away from the ranch.

That was easy said, but the little valley was bounded by pretty high mountains, and getting in and out of such a guarded place would be next to impossible.

Cap drifted off somewhere, and Galloway did, too, while I sat with Judith. I said to her, "Don't you worry. He's all right, and we'll have him out of there in no time."

"Flagan, I just couldn't imagine he would be like this—James Fetchen, I mean."

For a minute I couldn't place James Fetchen, we were so used to

calling him Black. Then I said, "How could you know? All you'd seen
of him was a tall, fine-looking man riding by on a horse. Believe me,
you can't always tell a coyote by his holler. But that Fetchen outfit
was known all over the mountains by the trouble they caused, by the
shootings and cuttings they'd been in."

Judith left me, to talk with Sharp's wife, and I walked out on the
stoop, looking about for Galloway and Cap, but I saw neither one of
them. I don't know what made me do it, but I reached my fingers back
and slipped the rawhide loop off my six-gun, freeing it for quick use,
if need be.

There's times when nothing is more companionable than a six-
shooter, and I had an uneasy feeling, almost as if somebody was walking
on my grave, or maybe digging one for me.

The sunlight was bright on Buzzard Roost, and on the mountains
all around. A dog trotted lazily across the dusty road, and far up the
valley I could see cattle feeding on the grass on the lower slopes of
Little Sheep. Everything looked peaceful enough.

There seemed no particular reason why I should feel this way just
now. Black Fetchen and his kin had reason for wanting to stake out
my hide, but it seemed to me they were in no hurry. That outfit was
sure of itself. They'd been in shooting scrapes before and they had
come out on top, and they figured they could again. Winning can make
folks confident . . . or it can make them cautious.

Here and there I'd come out ahead a few times, but it only made
me careful. There's too much that can happen—the twig that deflects
your bullet just enough, the time you don't quite get the right grasp on
the gun butt, the dust that blows in your eyes. . . . Anyway, there's
things can happen to the fastest of men and to the best shots. So I was
cautious.

And then there's the gun itself. No man in his right mind will play
with a gun. I've seen show-offs doing fancy spins and all that. No real
gun-fighter ever did. With a hair-trigger, he'd be likely to blow a hole
in his belly. The gun-fighter knows enough of guns to be wary of them.
He treats them with respect. A pistol was never made for anything
except killing, and a gun-fighter never draws a gun unless to shoot,
and he shoots to kill. And he doesn't go around trying to gun up a
score. That's only done by tin-horns. Nor does he ever notch his gun,
another tin-horn trick.

All the while these thoughts were sort of in the back of my mind,
I had my eyes searching for a lookout, if there was one. It seemed
likely that the Fetchens would have somebody around who could keep

a watch on Buzzard Roost, for anybody coming or going in that country just naturally rode by there, or stopped off.

I gave a thought to where I'd hole up if I was to keep a watch on the place. It would be best to find a place on a hillside, or somewhere a man could keep out of sight while seeing all who came and went. That naturally cut down on the possibilities.

I began to feel that somebody was watching me—I could feel it somehow in my bones. Judith, she came out and walked up to me. "Flagan—" she began, but I cut her off.

"Go back inside," I said. "Take your time, but you get inside and stay there till I come."

"What's wrong?"

"Judith! Damn it, get inside!"

"Flagan Sackett, you can't talk to me like that! Who do you think—"

Sunlight made a slanting light on a gun barrel in the brush not a hundred and fifty feet away. It was a far shot for a six-gun, but I'd hit targets at a greater distance than that.

With my left hand I swept Judith back toward the door, and my right went down for my gun just as the other gun muzzle stabbed flame. It was the movement to push Judith out of the way that saved my bacon, for that bullet whipped by my ear, stinging me as it went.

My six-gun was up and hammering shots. I was holding high because of the distance, and I let three bullets go in one roll of sound, as fast and slick as I could thumb back the hammer and let it drop.

Then I ran forward three steps, and took one to the side and fired again, holding a mite higher because he might be up and running. I was firing at the place I'd seen the flare of the gun muzzle, but was scattering my shots to have a better chance of scoring a hit.

The battering explosion of the shots died away, leaving a sudden silence, a silence in which the ears cried out for sound. I stood there, gun poised, aware that it was empty, but hesitating to betray the fact to my enemy, whoever he was.

Slowly I lowered the gun muzzle, and as unobtrusively as possible I opened the loading-gate with my thumb and worked the ejector, pushing the empty shell from the cylinder. Instantly, I fed a cartridge into place, then ejected another, and repeated this until the gun was reloaded. In all that time there was no sound, nor was there any movement in the brush.

Unwilling to take my eyes from the brush, I wondered where Cap and Galloway might be.

And had Judith been hit? I felt quite sure she had not, but a body never knew, when there was shooting taking place.

Warily, I took a step toward the brush, but nothing happened.

Off to my right Galloway suddenly spoke. "I think you got him, boy."

Walking slowly toward the brush, I had to make several climbing steps as I got close to it. There was an outcropping of rock, with thick, thorny brush growing around and over it, and several low trees nearby. The whole clump was no more than thirty or forty yards across, and just about as deep.

First thing I saw was the rifle. It was a Henry .44 and there was a fresh groove down the stock, cut by a bullet. There was blood on the leaves, but nothing else.

Gun in hand, I eased into the brush and stood still, listening. It was so quiet I seemed to be hearing my own heart beat. Somewhere off across country a crow cawed; otherwise there was silence. Then the door of the trading post opened and I heard boot heels on the boards.

My eyes scanned the brush, but I could see no sign of anyone there. Parting the branches with my left hand, I stepped past another bush. On a leaf there was a bright crimson spot . . . fresh blood. Just beyond it was a barely visible track of a boot heel in the soft earth. I was expecting a shot at any moment. It was one of those places where a man figures he's being watched by somebody he can't see.

Then I saw a slight reddish smear on the bark of a tree where the wounded man had leaned. He was hit pretty good, it looked like, although a man can sometimes bleed a good bit from a mighty inconsiderable wound.

I could tell that the man I hunted had gone right on through the brush. I followed through and suddenly came to the other side.

For about fifty yards ahead the country was open, and a quick glance told me that nothing stirred there. Standing under cover of the brush, I began to scan the ground with care, searching every clump of grass or cluster of small rocks—anywhere a man might be concealed.

The ground on this side of the knoll sloped away for several feet, and this place was invisible from the trading post. A man might slip down from the mountain, or come around the base and ease into the brush, leave his horse and get right up to that knoll without anybody being the wiser.

Pistol ready, I walked slowly toward the further trees, my eyes scanning the terrain all around me. Twice I saw flecks of blood.

Beyond the trees, on a small patch of grass, I saw where a horse had been tied on a short rope. By the look of the grass he had been tied there several times, each time feeding close around him. Whoever tied the horse had allowed him just enough rope to crop a little grass without giving him more rope than a man could catch up along with the reins, in one quick move.

Whoever had been watching there must have suddenly decided to try his shot. It must have seemed like a copper-riveted cinch, catching me out like that. Only my move in getting Judith out of the way had saved me.

Galloway had come up behind me. "You're bleedin', Flagan," he said.

I put my hand to my ear, which had been smarting some, and brought it away bloody. From the feel of it, the bullet had just grazed the top of the ear.

We followed the rider back into the hills a short way, then lost his trail on a dusty stretch. We found no more blood, and from the way he'd moved in going to his horse I figured he hadn't been hurt more than I had been.

When we got back to the trading post, Evan Hawkes was there, making plans with Tom Sharp for the roundup.

It turned out they had friends in common, stock-buyers and the like. There were eight or ten other cattlemen around the country who were all close friends of Sharp, and all of them had come to be wary of the Fetchen boys.

"One thing I want understood," Hawkes said. "This is our fight. They opened the ball, now we're going to play the tune and they'll dance to our music."

"Seems to me you're outnumbered," said Dobie Wiles. He was the hard-bitten foreman of the Slash B. "And it seems to me that JBF Connected brand will cover our brand as well as yours."

"They left blood on the Kansas grass," Galloway said, "blood of the Half-Box H. I figure Hawkes has first call."

He gave a slow grin. "And that includes us."

Chapter 12

The cattle came down from the hills in the morning, drifting ahead of riders from the neighboring ranches. They moved out on the grass of the bottom land and grazed there, while the riders turned again to the hills.

At first only a few riders were to be seen, for the land was rough and there were many canyons. The cowboys moved back into the hills and along the trails and started the cattle drifting down toward the valley.

The chuck wagon was out, and half a dozen local cattlemen, all of whom rode out from time to time only to return and gather near the wagon. James Black Fetchen himself had not appeared, although several Fetchens were seen riding in the hills. Once, Evan Hawkes roped a young steer and, with Tom Sharp as well as two other cattlemen beside him, studied the brand. It was his Half-Box H worked over to a JBF Connected.

"They do better work down in Texas," Breedlove commented. "There's rustiers down there who do it better in the dark."

Rodriguez looked around at Hawkes. "Do you wish to register a complaint, Senōr?"

"Let it go. That steer will be wearing a different brand before this is over."

"As you will."

"When this is over, if there is any steer you want to question we can either skin him and check the brand from the reverse side, or turn him into a pool for it to be decided. I want no cattle but my own, and no trouble with anyone but Fetchen."

"And that trouble, Senōr—when does it come?"

"I hope to delay it until after the roundup. There's a lot the Fetchens

241

don't know about cattle and rustling. If I figure it right, they're going to come up short and never know what hit them." He glanced around at them. "Gentlemen, this is my fight, mine and the Sackett boys'. There's no reason to get mixed up in it if you don't have to."

"This is our country," Sharp replied, "and we don't take to rustlers. We'll give you all the room you want, but if you need a hand, just lift a yell and we'll be coming."

"Of course, Senōr," Rodriguez said mildly, "but there may have to be trouble. A rider from the Fetchen outfit was drinking in Greenhorn. It seems he was not polite to one of my riders. There were seven Fetchens, and my man was alone. At the roundup he will not be alone."

Hawkes nodded. "I know . . . I heard some talk about that, but shooting at a roundup might kill a lot of good men. Let's take it easy and see what happens when the tally is taken."

I listened and had no comment to offer. It was a nice idea, if it worked. It might work, but there were a few outsiders riding with the Fetchen gang now, and they might know more about brand-blotting than the Fetchens did. That scar-faced puncher with the blond hair, for example. What was his name again? . . . Russ Menard.

I spoke the name out loud, and Rodriguez turned on me. *"Russ Menard?* You know him?"

"He's here. He's one of them."

The Mexican's lips tightened, then he bared his teeth in a smile that held no humor. "He is a very bad *hombre*, this Menard. I think no faster man lives when it comes to using the pistol. If he is one of them, there will surely be trouble."

The cattle had scattered so widely in the hills that it was brutally hard work combing them out of the brush and canyons. This was rugged country—canyons, brush, and boulders, with patches of forest, and on the higher slopes thick stands of timber that covered miles. But there was water everywhere, so most of the stock was in good shape. Aside from Hawkes's rustled herd, there were cattle from a dozen other outfits, including those of Tom Sharp. By nightfall several hundred head were gathered in the valley.

Most of the riders were strangers, men from the ranches nearby, good riders and hard-working men. They knew the country and they knew the cattle and so had an advantage over us, who were new to the land. Most of them were Mexicans, and they were some of the best riders and ropers I ever did see. Galloway and me were handy with ropes but in no way as good as most of those around us, who had been using them since they were knee-high to a short pup.

Most of the stock was longhorn, stuff driven in from Texas over the Goodnight Trail. The cattle from New Mexico were of a lighter strain when unmixed with longhorn blood; and there was a shorthorn or whiteface stock brought in from Missouri or somewhere beyond the Mississippi. Both Costello and Sharp had been driving in a few cattle of other breeds, trying to improve their stock to carry more beef.

The longhorn was a good enough beef critter when he could get enough to eat and drink, but in Texas they might live miles from water, drinking every two or three days, in some cases, and walking off a lot of good beef to get to water.

But in these mountain valleys where there was water a-plenty, there was no need to walk for it and the eastern stock did mighty well. And nowhere did we see the grass all eaten down. There was enough feed to carry more stock than was here.

The only two Fetchens I saw were men I remembered from that day in Tazewell. Their names I didn't learn until I heard them spoken around the roundup fire.

Clyde Fetchen was a wiry man of thirty-five or so with a narrow, tight-lipped look about him. He was a hard worker, which was more than I could say of the others, but not a friendly man by any way of speaking. Len Fetchen was seventeen or eighteen, broad-shouldered, with hair down to his shoulders. He didn't talk at all. Both of them fought shy of Galloway an' me—no doubt told to do so by Black.

Others came to the fire occasionally, but those were the only two I saw. Them and Russ Menard.

Meanwhile we were doing a sight of work that a body couldn't see around the branding fire. We were doing our work back in the hills, wherever we could find Half-Box Hitch cattle. All their brands had been altered by now, some of the changed brands so fresh the hide was still warm, or almost. Wherever we found them we dabbed a loop over their horns, threw them, and rebranded with a Pig-Pen, which was merely a series of vertical and horizontal lines like several pens side by each. A brand like that could cover everything we found, but we were only hunting stolen Hawkes cattle. We took turn and turn about bringing cattle to the fire, and the rest of the time we roamed up and down the range, sorting out Hawkes cattle.

Russ Menard spent mighty little time working cattle, so he didn't notice what was going on. The Fetchen boys brought in cattle here and there, mostly with their own brand. At night Briggs and Walker could usually manage to cut out a few of them and brand them downwind from the wagon, out of sight in some creek bed or gully.

By the third day half the hands on the range had fallen in with the game and were rebranding the rustled cattle as fast as we were. On the fifth day, James Black Fetchen came riding down from the hills with Russ Menard and six of his riders.

Evan Hawkes was standing by the fire, and when he saw Fetchen coming he called to Ladder Walker. The tall, lean Half-Box H puncher looked up, then slid the thong off his six-gun. The cook took another look, then slipped his shotgun out of his bedroll and tucked it in along his dried apples and flour.

Cap Rountree and Moss Reardon were both out on the range, but it so happened I was standing right there, taking time out for coffee.

Fetchen rode on up to the fire and stepped down, and so did Menard and Colby. Fetchen turned his hard eyes to me, then to Walker at the fire. The cook was busy kneading dough. Tom Sharp was there, and so were Rodriguez and Baldwin, who was repping for a couple of outfits over on the Cucharas.

"I want to see the tally list," Fetchen said.

"Help yourself." Hawkes gestured to where it lay on a large rock, held down by a smaller rock.

Fetchen hesitated, and looked hard at Hawkes.

Russ Menard was looking across the fire at me. "You one of them gun-fighting Sacketts?" he asked.

"Never paid gun-fighting no mind," I said. "Too busy making a living. Seems to me a man's got mighty little to do, riding around showing off his gun."

He got kind of red in the face. "Meaning?"

"Meaning nothing a-tall. Just commenting on why I don't figure myself a gun-fighter. We Sacketts never figured on doing any fighting unless pushed," I added.

"What do you carry that gun for?" he demanded.

I grinned at him. "Seems I might meet somebody whose time has come."

Black Fetchen had turned around sharply, his face red and angry. "What the hell *is* this? You've only got thirty-four head of JBF cattle listed."

"That's all there was," Hawkes said quietly, "and a scrubby lot, too."

Fetchen stepped forward, the color leaving his face, his eyes burning under his heavy brows. "What are you trying to do? Rob me? I came into this valley with more than a thousand head of cattle."

"If you have a bill of sale," Sharp suggested, "we might check out the brands and find out what's wrong. Your bill of sale would show the original brands, and any stolen cattle would have the brands altered."

Fetchen stopped. Suddenly he was cold, dangerous. Me, I was watching Menard.

"You can't get away with this!" Fetchen said furiously.

"If you have any brand you want to question," Sharp said, "we can always shoot the animal and skin it. The inside of the hide will show if the brand has been altered."

Fetchen glanced at him, realizing that to check the brand would reveal the original alteration, the change from Hawkes's Half-Box H to his JBF Connected. Frustrated, he hesitated, suddenly aware he had no way to turn.

Hawkes, Sharp, and Rodriguez were scattered out. Baldwin stood near the chuck wagon, and all of them were armed. Ladder Walker had released the calf he had been branding and was now standing upright, branding iron in his left hand.

And there was me.

To start shooting now would mean death for several men, and victory for nobody. Fetchen started to speak, then his eye caught the dull gloss of the shotgun stock, inches from the cook's hand.

"While we're talking," I suggested, "you might tell Costello he should be down here, repping for his brand. We have business to discuss with him."

"He's not well," Fetchen replied, controlling his anger. "I'll speak for him."

"Costello is a very good friend of mine," Sharp said, "and a highly respected man in this country. We want to be sure he stays well. I think he should be brought down to my place where he can have the attention of a doctor."

"He's not able to ride," Fetchen said. He was worried now, and eager to be away. Whatever his plans had been, they were not working now. His herd was gone, taken back by the very man from whom it had been stolen, and the possibility of his remaining in the area and ranching was now slim indeed.

"Load him into a wagon," Sharp insisted. "If you don't have one, I'll send one up, and enough men to load him up."

Fetchen backed off. "I'll see. I'll talk to him," he said.

Right at that moment I figured him for the most dangerous man I'd ever known. There'd been talk about his hot temper, but this man was cold—cold and mean. You could see it in him, see him fighting down the urge to grab for a gun and turn that branding fire into a blaze of hell. He had it in him, too, only he was playing it smart. And a few moments later I saw another reason why.

Moss Reardon, Cap Rountree, and Galloway had come up behind us, and off to the left was Kyle Shore.

Fetchen's gang would have cut some of us down, but not a one of them would have escaped.

Russ Menard looked at me and smiled. "We'll meet up, one of these days."

"We can make it right now," I said. "We can make it a private fight."

"I ain't in no hurry."

James Black Fetchen looked past me toward the chuck wagon. "Judith, your pa wants you. You comin'?"

"No."

"You turnin' your back on him?"

"You know better than that. When he comes down to Mr. Sharp's, at Buzzard Roost, I'll be waiting for him."

The Fetchens went to their horses then, Russ Menard taking the most time. When he was in the saddle, both hands out in plain sight, he said, "Don't you disappoint me, boy. I'll be hunting you."

They rode away, and Tom Sharp swore softly. With the back of his hand, he wiped sudden sweat from his forehead. "I don't want to go through that again. For a minute there, anything could have happened."

"You sleep with locked doors," Galloway said, riding up. "And don't answer no hails by night. That's a murdering lot."

The rest of the roundup went forward without a hitch. The cattle were driven in from the hills and we saw no more of the Fetchens, but Costello did not come down from the hills. Twice members of the gang were seen close to the Spanish Peaks. Once several of them rode over to Badito.

The roundup over, Rodriguez announced a fandango. That was their name for a big dancing and to-do, where the folks come from miles around. Since no rider from the Fetchen crowd had come down to claim the beef that still wore their brand over the Half-Box H, it was slaughtered for a barbecue . . . at least, the three best steers were.

Rodriguez came around to Galloway and me. "You will honor my house, Senõres? Yours is a name well known to me. Tyrel Sackett is married to the daughter of an old friend of mine in New Mexico."

"We will come," I said.

Nobody talked much of anything else, and Galloway and me decided we'd ride down to Pueblo or up to Denver to buy us new outfits. Judith was all excited, and was taking a hand in the planning.

We rode off to Denver, and it was two weeks before we got back, just the night of the big shindig. The first person we saw was Cap Rountree.

"You didn't come none too soon," he said. "Harry Briggs is dead . . . dry-gulched."

Chapter 13

It had been a particularly vicious killing. Not only had Briggs been shot from ambush, but his killers had ridden over his body and shot into it again and again.

There could be no doubt as to why it had been done. Briggs was a hard-working cowhand with no enemies, and he carried no money; of the little he could save, the greater part was sent to a sister in Pennsylvania. He had been killed because he rode for the Half-Box H, and it could just as easily have been any of the other hands.

And there was no doubt as to who had done it, though there didn't seem to be any chance of proving it. It was the Fetchen crowd, we knew. There was no other possibility. From the fragments of tracks found near the body, they could tell that more than one killer was involved; he had been shot with at least two different weapons—probably more.

"We've done some scoutin' around," Reardon told us. "The Fetchen riders have been huntin' around the Spanish Peaks. We found tracks up that way. Sharp figures they're huntin' the Reynolds treasure."

Ladder Walker was glum. "Briggs was a good man. Never done harm to nobody. I'm fixin' to hunt me some Fetchens."

"Take it easy," Reardon warned. "Those boys are mean, and they ain't about to give you no chance. No fair chance, that is."

Judith was standing on the porch when I rode up. "Flagan, I'm worried about Pa. All this time, and no word. Nobody has seen him, and the Fetchens won't let anyone near the place."

I'd been giving it considerable thought, and riding back from Denver, Galloway and me had made up our minds to do something about it. The trouble was, we didn't know exactly what.

Nobody in his right mind goes riding into a bottlenecked valley

248

where there's fifteen to twenty men waiting for him, all fixing to notch their guns for his scalp. And the sides of that valley allowed for no other approach we knew of. Yet there had to be a way, and one way might be to cause some kind of diversion.

"Suppose," I suggested, "we give it out that we've found some sign of that Reynolds gold? We could pick some lonely place over close to Spanish Peaks, let out the rumor that we had it located and were going in to pick it up."

"With a big enough party to draw them all away from the ranch?"

"That's right. It wouldn't do any harm, and it might pull them all away so we could ride in and look around."

We finally picked on a place not so far off as the Spanish Peaks. We rode over to Badito—Galloway, Ladder Walker, and me—and we had a couple of drinks and talked about how we'd located the Reynolds treasure.

Everybody for miles around had heard that story, so, like we figured, there were questions put to us. "Is it near the Spanish Peaks?" one man asked.

"That's just it," Galloway said. "Everybody took it for granted that when Reynolds talked about twin peaks he meant the Spanish Peaks. Well, that was where everybody went wrong. The peaks Reynolds and them talked about were right up at the top of the Sangre de Cristos. I mean what's called Blanca Peak."

"There's three peaks up there," somebody objected.

"Depends on where you stand to look at them. I figure that after they buried the loot they took them for landmarks—just looked back and saw only two peaks, close together."

"So you think you've found the place?" The questioner was skeptical. "So have a lot of others."

"We found a knife stuck into a tree for a marker, and we found a stone slab with markings on it."

Oh, we had them now. Everybody knew that Reynolds had told of thrusting a knife into a tree to mark the place, so we knew our story would be all around the country in a matter of hours. Somebody would be sure to tell the Fetchens, just to get their reaction.

"We're going up there in the morning," Walker said, making out to be drunker than he was. "We'll camp in Bronco Dan Gulch, and we'll be within a mile of the treasure. You just wait. Come daylight, we'll come down the pass loaded with gold."

Now, Bronco Dan was a narrow little gulch that headed up near the base of Lone Rock Hill, only three or four miles from the top of the rim. It was wild country, and just such a place as outlaws might choose to hide out or cache some loot. And it wasn't but a little way above La Veta Pass.

Anyway a body looked at it, the place made a lot of sense. La Veta Pass was the natural escape route for anybody trying to get over the mountains from Walsenburg to Alamosa, and vice versa.

Of course, they knew about the knife. That was the common feature of the stories about the Reynolds treasure—that he had marked the place by driving a knife into a tree. The stone marker was pure invention, but they found it easy to accept the idea that Reynolds might have scratched a map on a slab of rock.

That night Cap Rountree went up the mountain and hid in the brush where he could watch the Costello place, and when we arrived shortly after daybreak he told us the Fetchens had taken out in a pack just before daylight.

"They took the bait, all right. Oh, yes, I could see just enough to see them ride out."

"How many stayed behind?"

"Two, three maybe. I don't know for sure."

Galloway went to his horse, and I did the same. You can lay a couple of bets I wasn't anxious to go down there, but we had set this up and this was the chance we'd been playing for.

Cap started to follow along, but I waved him back. "You stay here. No use all of us getting boxed in down there. If you see them coming back, give a shout."

Ladder Walker was along with us—there was no leaving him out of it. So the three of us went down the mountain, following the trail where cattle had crossed a saddle, and we came into the valley within two hundred yards of the ranch, just beyond the corral.

"Stay with the horses, Ladder," I said. "And keep an eye on the opening. I don't like this place, not a bit."

"You figure it for a trap?"

"Could be. Black Fetchen is a wily one, and we've had it too easy so far. We've had almost too much luck."

Galloway and me, spread apart a little, walked toward the house.

We played it in luck this time too. Nobody seemed to be around until we stepped up on the porch. Then we could hear voices coming from the back of the house.

"Don't get any ideas, old man. You just set tight until the boys come back. Then maybe Black will let you go. If'n he can find that

gold and them Sacketts all to once, he might come back plumb satisfied."

"He won't find the Sacketts," I said, stepping from the hallway
into the room where they sat. It was the kitchen, and on my sudden
entrance one of the men stood up so quick he almost turned over the
table.

"Get your hat, Mr. Costello," I said. "We've come to take you
to Judith."

I hadn't drawn my gun, being of no mind to shoot anybody unless
they asked for it. There were two of Fetchen's men in the room and
our arriving that way had taken the wind out of them. They just looked
at us, even the one who had stood up so quick.

Costello, who was a slim, oldish man with a shock of graying
hair, got up and put on his hat.

"Here, now!" The Fetchen man standing up had gotten his senses
back, and he was mad. "Costello, you come back and set down! The
same goes for you Sacketts, unless you want to get killed. Black Fetchen
is ridin' up to this ranch right now."

"We needn't have any trouble," I said calmly.

"I'll get a horse," Galloway said, and ducked out of the door,
Costello following him.

"Black will kill you, Sackett. He'll fill your hide with lead."

"I doubt if he's got the guts to try. You tell him I said that."

"I hear tell you're a fast man with a shootin' iron." I could just
see the gambler stirring around inside him, and it looked as if it was
gettin' the better of his common sense. "I don't think we need to wait
for Black. I'd sort of like to try you on myself."

"Your choice."

Meanwhile I walked on into the room, and right up to him. Now,
no man likes to start a shooting match at point-blank range, because
skill plays mighty little part in it then, and the odds are that both men
will get blasted. And anyhow, nobody in his right mind starts shooting
at all unless there's no other way, and I wasn't planning on shooting
now, if I could help it.

So I just walked in on him and he backed off a step, and when
he started to take another step back, I hit him. It was the last thing he
was expecting, and the blow knocked him down. It was one quick
move for me to slip his gun from its holster and straighten up, but the
other man hadn't moved.

"You shuck your guns," I told him. "You just unbuckle and step back, and be careful how you move your hands. I'm a man mighty subject to impressions, and you give me the wrong one and I'm likely to open you up like a gutted sheep."

"I ain't figurin' on it. You just watch it, now." He moved his hands with great care to his belt buckle, unhitched, and let the gun belt fall.

The man on the floor was sitting up. "What's the matter, you yella?" he said to his companion.

"I'm figurin' on livin' a mighty long time, that's all. I ain't seen a gray hair yet, and I got my teeth. Anyway, I didn't see you cuttin' much ice."

"I should've killed him."

"You done the right thing, to my thinkin'. Maybe I ain't so gun-slick as some, and maybe I ain't so smart, but I sure enough know when to back off from a fire so's not to get burned. Don't you get no fancy notions now, Ed. You'd get us both killed."

Well, I gathered up those guns and a rifle I saw in the corner by the door, then I just backed off.

Galloway and Costello were up in their saddles, holding my horse ready.

There wasn't any move from the house until we were cutting around the corral toward the trail down which we had come, and then one man ran from the house toward the barn. Glancing back, I was just in time to see him come out with a rifle, but he took no aim at us; he just lifted the rifle in one hand and fired two quick shots, a space, and then a third shot . . . and he was firing into the air.

"Trouble!" I yelled. "That was a signal!"

Ladder Walker, who had hung back, wanting a shot at anyone who had helped to kill Briggs, now came rushing up behind us. The trail to the saddle over which he had come into the valley was steep, and a hard scramble for the horses, but much of it was among the trees and partly concealed from below.

We heard a wild yell from below and, looking back, I saw Black Fetchen, plainly recognizable because of the horse he rode, charging into the valley, followed by half a dozen riders.

Even as I looked, a man ran toward him, pointing up the mountain. Instantly there was firing, but shooting uphill is apt to be a tricky thing even for a skilled marksman, and their bullets struck well behind us. Before they had the range we were too far away for them, and they wasted no more shots.

But they were coming after us. We could hear their horses far below, and saw the men we had caught in the house catching up horses at the corral, ready to follow.

Deliberately, Galloway slowed his pace. "Easiest way to kill a horse," he said, "running it uphill. We'll leave that to them."

Riding close to Costello, I handed him the gun belt and rifle I'd taken from the cabin. When I'd first run out I had slung the belt over the pommel and hung onto the rifle.

Up ahead of us we heard the sudden boom of a heavy rifle . . . Cap Rountree and his buffalo gun. A moment later came a second shot. He was firing a .56 Spencer that carried a wicked wallop. Personally, I favored the Winchester .44, but that big Spencer made a boom that was a frightening thing to hear, and it could tear a hole in a man it hit so that it was unlikely a doctor would do him much good.

Cap was in the saddle when we reached him, but he made us pull up. "Flagan," he said, "I don't like the look of it. Where's the rest of them?"

There were six or seven behind us, that we knew, but what of the rest?

"You figure we're trapped?" I asked.

"You just look at it. They must know how we got up here, and they can ride out their gap and block our way down the mountain before we can get there."

I was not one to underrate Black Fetchen. Back at the Costello place that man had said Fetchen was due to come riding in at any moment, and at the time I gave it no credit, figuring he was trying a bluff, but then some of the outfit had showed up.

Ladder Walker turned his mount and galloped to a spot where he could look over part of the trail up which we had come in first arriving at our lookout point. He was back in an instant. "Dust down there. Somebody is movin' on the trail."

"Is there a trail south, toward Bronco Dan?"

Cap Rountree chewed his mustache. "There's a shadow of a trail down Placer Creek to La Veta Pass, but that's where you sent some of this outfit. Likely the Fetchens know that trail. If you try it, and they're waitin', it's a death trap."

I gave a glance up toward those peaks that shut us off from the west, and felt something like fear. It was almighty icy and cold up there against the sky, up there where the timber ran out and the raw-backed ridges gnawed the sky. My eyes went along the east face of those ridges.

"What about west?" I asked.

"Well," Cap said reluctantly, "there's a pass off north called Mosca Pass. It's high up and cold, and when you come down the other side you're in the sand dunes."

"We got a choice?" Galloway asked.

"Either run or fight," Walker said, "and if we fight we'll be out-numbered three or four to one."

"I like the odds," Galloway said, "but somebody among us will die."

I looked over at Costello. "Do you know that pass?"

"I know it. If there's any trail there from here, it's nothing but a sheep trail."

"Let's go," I said. Below us we could hear them coming—in fact, we could hear them on both trails.

Costello led off, knowing the country best. Cap knew it by hearsay, but Costello had been up to the pass once, coming on it from the ancient Indian trail that led down Aspen Creek.

We started up the steep mountainside covered with trees, and followed a sort of trail made by deer or mountain sheep.

Mosca Pass had been the old Indian route across the mountains. Later it had been used by freighters, but now it was used only by occasional horsemen who knew the country, and sheepherders bringing their flocks to summer grazing.

Beyond the pass, on the western side, lay the great sand dunes, eighty square miles of shifting, piled-up sand, a place haunted by mystery, avoided by Indians, and a place I'd heard talk of ever since entering Colorado, because of the mysterious disappearances of at least one train of freight wagons and a flock of a thousand sheep, along with the herder.

We didn't have any choice. Black Fetchen undoubtedly had gone himself or had sent riders to look into the story of the Reynolds gold, but at the same time he'd kept riders close to Costello's place to move in if we tried to rescue him. I thought the only thing they hadn't guessed was the trail down the mountain from the saddle. Their missing that one was enough to get us a chance to free Costello; but now they were pushing us back into the mountains, leaving us mighty little room in which to maneuver.

The ridge along which we now rode was a wall that would shut us in. We had to try for one of the passes, and if we succeeded in getting across the mountain we would be on the edge of the sand dunes.

Suppose Black could send those riders who had gone to Bronco Dan Gulch on through La Veta Pass? They could close in from the south, and our only way of escape would be into the dunes. It began to look as if we were fairly trapped, cornered by our own trick, trying to get rid of the gang for a few hours.

From time to time we had to shift our trail. Sometimes it simply gave out, or the ground fell away too steep for any horse to travel. There was no question of speed. Our horses sometimes slid down hill as much as ten to twenty feet, and at times the only thing that saved us were outcroppings of rock or the stands of pine growing on the slope.

But most of the way was under cover and there was no chance of dust, so anybody trying to track us could not be sure exactly where we were.

"We could hole up and make a stand," Walker suggested.

"They'd get above us," Galloway said. "They'd have us trapped on a steep slope so we couldn't go up or down."

Once, breaking out of the timber, we glimpsed the smoke rising from the trading post near the Buzzard Roost Ranch. It was miles away, and there was no chance of us getting down there without breaking through a line of guns. We could make out riders below us, traveling on the lower slopes, cutting us off.

Suddenly there was a bare slope before us, a slope of shale. It was several hundred yards across and extended down the mountain for what must be a quarter of a mile.

Galloway, who was in the lead at the moment, pulled up and we gathered near him. "I don't like it, Flagan," he said. "If that shale started to slide, a man wouldn't have a chance. It would take a horse right off its feet."

We looked up, but the slope above was steep and rocky. A man afoot could have made it with some struggling here and there, but there was no place a horse could go. And downhill was as bad . . . or worse.

"Ain't much of a choice," Cap said.

"I'll try it," I said. Even as I spoke I was thinking what a fool a man could be. If we tried going back we'd surely run into a shooting match and somebody would get killed—maybe all of us—but if my horse started to slide on that shale I'd surely go all the way; and it was so steep further down that the edge almost seemed to break off sharply.

Stepping down from the saddle, I started toward the edge of the slope, but my horse wanted no part of it. He pulled back, and I had to tug hard to get him out on that shale.

At my first step I sank in over my ankle, but I didn't slide. Bit by bit, taking it as easy as I could, I started out over the slide area. I was not halfway across when I suddenly went in almost to my knees. I struggled to get my feet out of the shale, and felt myself starting to slide. Holding still, I waited a moment, and then I could ease a foot from the shale and managed a step forward. It was harder for my horse, but a good hold on the reins gave him confidence and he came on across the stretch. It took me half an hour to get to the other side, but I made it, though twice my horse went in almost to his belly.

It was easier for the next man, who was Cap Rountree. Cap had been watching me, and I had found a few almost solid places I could point out to him. Before he was across, Walker started, then Costello. All told, that slide held us up a good two hours, but once across we found ourselves on a long, narrow bench that carried us on for over a mile, moving at a good gait.

The top of the pass was open, wind-swept and cold. The western side of it fell steeply away before us. Hesitating, we looked back and glimpsed a bunch of riders, still some miles off, but riding up the pass toward us.

Black Fetchen had planned every move with care. Now we could see just how he must have thought it out, and it mattered not at all whether he went to Bronco Dan or not, he could have trapped us in any case. I was sure they had sent up a smoke or signaled in some manner, and that when we reached the foot of the pass he would have men waiting for us.

The others agreed, so we hunched our shoulders against the chill wind and tried to figure a way out.

It looked as if we either had to fight, facing enemies on both sides, or we had to take our chances in the waterless waste of the sand dunes.

Black Fetchen had taken setbacks and had waited; and then, like a shrewd general, he had boxed us in.

Harry Briggs was dead . . . murdered. And now it would be us, trapped in the dunes where the sand would cover our bodies. And then Fetchen could go back to get the others . . . to get Evan Hawkes and his men.

To get Judith. . . .

Chapter 14

Galloway urged his horse close to mine and pointed down the mountain. "Riders coming!" he said.

There were two of them, out in the open and coming at a good clip, considering they were riding uphill. We could not make out who they were, but they came on, and no shots were fired.

When they topped out on the ridge we saw they were Kyle Shore and Moss Reardon.

"There's been a shooting over at Greenhorn," Kyle said. "Black Fetchen killed Dobie Wiles in a gun battle—an argument over cattle."

"You boys have ridden right into a trap," Walker told them. "The Fetchens have us boxed in."

They looked around, seeing nobody. "You sure?"

"We'd better get off the ridge," Galloway advised. "Here we're sitting ducks."

"We didn't see anybody," Reardon said doubtfully.

"Try going back," Cap told him. "They're out there, all right."

So now Dobie, foreman of the Slash B, and an outspoken enemy of the Fetchens, was dead. Whatever had brought the Fetchens into this country, it was an all-out war now.

Pushing my horse to the lead, I rode over the rim and started down the steep trail toward the dunes. As I rode, I was trying to figure some way out of this corner without a fight. Not that I was dodging a fight with the Fetchens. That had to come, but right now the odds were all against us and nobody wants to begin a fight he stands to lose. What I wanted was to find a place we could fight from that would come close to evening things up.

"Keep your eyes skinned," I said over my shoulder. "Unless I've got it wrong, there'll be more Fetchens coming in from the south."

Galloway looked back up the mountain. "They're up there, Flagan," he said, "right on the rim."

Sure enough, we could count eight or nine, and knew there were twice that many close by.

"Flagan," Cap said, "look yonder!"

He pointed to a dust cloud a couple of miles off to the south, a dust cloud made by hard-ridden horses.

It looked to me as if we were up the creek without a paddle, because not far below us the trees scattered out and the country was bare all around, with no kind of shelter. We'd have to stand and fight, or run for the dunes. Well, I just pulled up, stopping so short they all bunched in around me.

"I'll be damned if we do!" I said.

"Do what? What d'you mean?"

"Look at it. He's heading us right into those dunes. We could get boxed in there and die of thirst, or maybe he's got a couple of boys perched on top of one of those dunes with rifles. Just as we get close to them, they'd open fire."

Riders were now on the trail behind us, but some distance back.

"What do you figure to do?"

"We've got to get off this trail. We've got to make our own way, not ride right down the trail he's got set for us."

We walked our horses on through the trees, searching for some kind of way we could take to get off the trail. Knowing the ways of wild game, we figured there might be some trail along the mountainside. Of course, a man on horseback can't follow a deer trail very far unless he's lucky, the way we had been earlier. A deer will go under tree limbs, over rocks, or between boulders where no horse could go. We scattered about as much as the trail and the terrain would allow, and we hunted for tracks.

We were under cover now, out of view from both above and below, but that would not last long.

Ladder Walker came back up the trail from where he had scouted. "They're closin' in, Flagan. They'll be under cover an' waitin' when we show up."

The forest and the mountains have their own secret ways, and in the changing of days the seemingly changeless hills do also change. Fallen snow settles into crevices in the rock, and expands in freezing, and so cracks the rock still further. Wind, rain, and blown sand hone the edges of the jagged upthrusts of rock, and find the weak places to hollow them away.

In the passing of years the great cliffs crumble into battlements with lower flanks of talus, scattered slopes of rock, and debris fallen from the crumbling escarpment above.

There upon the north side of the trail I saw a fallen pine, its roots torn from the earth and leaning far over, exposing a narrow opening through the thick timber and the rocks into a glade beyond. It might be no more than a dead end, but it was our only chance, and we took it.

Swiftly, I turned my horse up into the opening, scrambling around the roots, and down through the narrow gap beyond into the glade.

"Cap, you and Moss fix up that trail, will you? We're going to need time."

Maybe we had run into an even worse trap, but at least it was a trap of our own making, not one set and waiting for us. A blind man could sense that Black Fetchen was out for a kill. He did not want just Galloway and me, although no doubt we topped his list: he wanted us all.

While we held up, waiting for Cap and Moss to blot out our trail, I scouted around.

There was a narrow aisle among the pines that followed along the slope toward the north. A body could see along it for fifty or sixty yards. When Cap and Moss came up, we pushed on.

We rode on no trail except one we made, and we found our way with difficulty, weaving among trees and rocks, scrambling on steep slopes, easing down declivities where our horses almost slid on their hindquarters. Suddenly we came upon a great slash on the mountain, came upon it just where it ended.

A huge boulder had torn loose hundreds of feet up the mountain and had come tumbling down, crushing all before it, leaving a steep but natural way toward the higher slopes.

Costello glanced up the mountain. "We'll never make it," he said, seeing my look. "It's too steep."

"We'll get down and walk," I said. "We'll lead our horses. It's going to be a scramble, but it'll be no easier for those who follow, and we'll have the advantage of being above them."

Swinging down, I led off. Mostly it was a matter of finding a way around the fallen trees and rocks, scrambling up slopes, pushing brush or fallen trees out of the way. In no time at all we were sweating, fighting for breath from the work and the altitude.

We were topping out at the head of our long corridor when Ladder kind of jerked in the saddle and gave an odd grunt. Almost at the same instant, we heard the shots.

We saw them at once. They were below us, in the open beyond

some trees. They had lost our trail until we came into sight on the slope, and they had fired . . . from a good four hundred yards off.

Scrambling into the trees, I swung around on Ladder. "You hurt?"

"I caught one. You boys keep going. I can handle this."

"Like hell." I got down.

Cap and Galloway had already moved to the edge of the trees and were returning the searching fire the Fetchens were sending into the trees. We had bullets all around us, but most of them were hitting short . . . shooting up or down hill is always a chancy thing.

Ladder Walker had caught a .44 slug on the hip bone—a glancing shot that hit the bone and turned off, tearing a nasty gash in the flesh. It was not much more than a flesh wound, but he was losing blood.

We made a sort of pad with a patch of moss ripped from a tree trunk, binding it in place with his torn shirt.

We were under cover now, and our return fire had made them wary, so with Walker sitting his saddle, we worked our way along the slope and across Buck Creek Canyon.

There was nothing about this that a man could like. We had broken the trap, but we were far from free. They were wasting no shots, moving in carefully, determined to make an end of us. We had them above and below us, others closing in, and no doubt some trying to head us off.

Pulling up suddenly, I stood in my stirrups and looked off down through the trees toward the sand dunes. If they tried to follow along the side of the mountain below us, we might be able to drive them into the dunes.

Cap rode up beside me. "Flagan, there's a creek somewhere up ahead that cuts through the mountain, or nearly so. I figure if we could get up there we could ride up the creek and cross the mountain; then we could come down behind the Buzzard Roost Ranch."

We moved along, taking our time, hunting out a trail as we rode. There was a good smell of pines in the air, and overhead a fine blue sky with white clouds that were darkening into gray, sort of bunching up as if the Good Lord was getting them corralled for a storm.

The traveling was easier now. We wound in and out amongst the fallen trees, most of them long dead, and the boulders that had tumbled down from the mountain higher up. The ground was thick with pine needles or moss, and there were some damp places where water was oozing out.

For about half a mile we had cover of a sort. We couldn't see any of the Fetchen gang, nor could they shoot at us, but there was no chance to make time. Had we slipped from their trap, maybe only to get into a worse one, I wondered. We all rode with our Winchesters in our hands, ready for the trouble we knew was shaping up.

On our right the mountains rose steeply for more than two thousand feet, their peaks hidden in the dark clouds. The air grew still, and the few birds we saw were flying low, hunting cover. A few scattering drops of rain fell.

There came a puff of wind, and then a scattering shower, and we drew up to get into our slickers. The grass on the mountain slope seemed suddenly greener, the pines darker.

Glancing at Ladder Walker, I saw he looked almighty drawn and pale. He caught my eyes and said, "Don't you worry your head, Sackett. I'm riding strong."

It was no easy place to travel. Because the mountainside was so steep we had to pick our way carefully, stopping from time to time to give the horses a breathing spell. We were angling up again now, hunting for the cover of scattered trees that showed higher up. Thunder rumbled back in the peaks, sounding like great boulders tumbling down a rocky corridor. Lightning flashed, giving a weird light.

Galloway, who was riding point at the moment, caught the move-ment of a man as he was lifting his rifle, and Galloway was not one to waste time. He shot right off his saddle, his rifle held waist-high . . . and nobody ever lived who was better at off-hand shooting than Galloway.

We heard a yelp of pain, then the clatter of a rifle falling among rocks; and then there was a burst of firing and we left our saddles as if we'd been shot from them. We hit ground running and firing, chang-ing position as we hit grass, and all shooting as soon as we caught sight of something to shoot.

They'd caught us in the open, on the slope of a rock-crested knoll crowned with trees. We were short a hundred yards or so of the trees, but Cap and Galloway made the knoll and opened a covering fire. Costello helped Walker to a protected spot, whilst Moss and me gath-ered the horses and hustled them behind the knoll.

We stood there a moment, feeling the scattering big drops before an onrush of rain. The back of that knoll fell away where a watercourse made by mountain runoff had cut its way. There was shelter here for the horses, but there was a covered route down to the next canyon.

"They aren't about to rush us," I told Moss. "You stay here with the horses. I'm going down this gully to see if we can get out of here."

"You step careful, boy," Reardon said. "Them Fetchens have no idea of anybody getting home alive."

The Fetchens were going to be wary, and all the more so because they probably figured they'd either killed or wounded some of us when we left our saddles like that. Now they were getting return fire from only two rifles, with occasional shots from Costello, so they would be sure they were winning and had us nailed down.

Rifle in hand, I crept down that gully, sliding over wet boulders and through thick clumps of brush. All the time I was scouting a route down which we could bring our horses as well as ourselves.

Suddenly, from up above, a stick cracked. Instantly I froze into position, my eyes moving up slope. A man was easing along through the brush up there, his eyes looking back the way I had come. It seemed as if the Fetchens were closing in around my friends, and there wasn't much I could do about it.

Going back now was out of the question, so I waited, knowing a rifle shot would alert them to trouble up here. When that man up there moved again . . . He moved.

He was a mite careless because he didn't figure there was anybody so far in this direction, and when he moved I put my sights on him and held my aim, took a long breath, let it out, and squeezed off my shot. He was moving when I fired, but I had taken that into account, and my bullet took him right through the ribs.

He straightened up, held still for a moment, and then fell, head over heels down the slope, ending up within twenty feet of me.

Snaking through the brush, I got up to him and took his gun belt off him and slung it across my shoulders. Also taking up his rifle, I aimed it on the woods up above, where there were likely some others, and opened fire.

It was wild shooting, but I wanted to flush them out if I could, and also wanted to warn my folks back there that it was time to get out.

There were nine shots left in the Winchester, and I dusted those woods with them; then I threw down the rifle and slipped back the way I had come. A few shots were fired from somewhere up yonder, fired at the place from which I'd been shooting but I was fifty yards off by that time and well down in the watercourse where I'd been traveling.

Waiting and listening, it was only minutes until I heard movement behind me and, rifle up, I held ready for trouble.

First thing I saw was Moss Reardon. "Hold your fire, boy," he said. "It's us a-comin'."

Me, I went off down the line and brought up on the edge of a small canyon; it was no trouble to get down at that point. When the others bunched around, I pointed down canyon. "Yonder's the dunes. And there seems to be a creek running along there. I take it we'd better reach for the creek and sort of take account of things."

"Might be Medano Creek," Cap said.

"What's that amount to?"

"If it's Medano, we can foller it up and over the divide. I figure it will bring us out back in the hills from Buzzard Roost."

Once more in the saddle, I led off down the canyon, and soon enough we were under the cottonwoods and willows, with a trickle of water at our feet. There was a little rain falling by then, and lightning playing tag amongst the peaks.

Ladder seemed to be in bad shape. He was looking mighty peaked. He'd lost a sight of blood, and that crawling and sliding hadn't done him any good.

The place we'd come to had six-foot banks, and there was a kind of S bend in the stream that gave us the shelter of banks on all sides. Just beyond were the dunes. From a high point on the bank we could see where the creek came down out of the Sangre de Cristos.

"We might as well face up to it," Galloway said. "We're backed up against death. Those boys are downstream of us and they're up on the mountain, and they surely count us to be dead before nightfall."

"One of them doesn't. I left him stretched out up yonder. This here's his gun belt."

"One less to carry a rifle against us," Moss said. He leaned back against the bank. "Gol durn it. I ain't as young as I used to be. This scramblin' around over mountains ain't what I'm trimmed for. I'm a horse-and-saddle man myself."

"I'd walk if I could get out of here," Galloway said.

Costello was saying nothing. He was just lying yonder looking all played out. He was no youngster, and he'd been mistreated by the Fetchens. So we had a wounded man and one in no shape to go through much of this traveling, and we were a whole mountain away from home.

That Medano Creek might be the way, but I didn't like the look of it. It opened up too wide by far for safety.

"Make some coffee, somebody," I suggested. "They know already where we are."

Moss dug into his war-bag for the coffee and I poked around, picking up brush and bark to build us a fire. It took no time at all to have water boiling and the smell of coffee in the air. We had a snug enough place for the moment, with some shelter from gunfire, and water as we needed it.

Galloway and Cap had gone to work to rig a lean-to shelter for Ladder Walker.

There were willow branches leaning out from the bank and they wove other branches among them until they had the willows leaning down and making a kind of roof for those who would lie down. Where the creek curved around there were two or three big old cottonwoods and we bunched the horses there.

We sat around, shoulders bent against the rain, gulping hot coffee and trying to figure what we were going to do.

The Fetchens had us bunched for the kill. They were good mountain fighters, and they had herded us right into a corner. Maybe we could ride up Medano Creek and get clean away, but it looked too inviting to me. It would be a death trap if they waited for us up there where the cliffs grew high.

If we got out of this alive we'd have to be lucky. We'd have to be hung with four-leaf clovers—and I couldn't see any clover around here.

Chapter 15

The worst of it was, we weren't getting much of a look at those boys. They were playing it safe, slipping about in the trees and brush as slick as Comanches.

"Galloway," I said, "I'm getting sort of peevish. Seems to me we've let those boys have at us about long enough. A time comes when a man just can't side-step a fight no longer. We've waited for them to bring it to us, and they've done no such thing, so I figure it's up to you and me to take it to them."

"You give me time for another cup of coffee," Galloway said, "and I'll come along with you."

Cap Rountree looked at us thoughtfully. "What you expect *us* to do . . . mildew?"

Me, I just grinned at him. "Cap, I know you're an old he coon from the high-up hills, but the fewer we have out there the better. You boys can stay right here. They'll be expecting us to move on pretty quick, and they'll be settled down waiting for it. Well, me and Galloway figure to stir them up a mite.

"Anyway," I went on, "Ladder's in no shape to travel more'n he's going to have to, getting out of here. Costello's in pretty bad shape, too. I figure you and Moss can hold this place if they try to attack you, which I doubt they will."

Galloway and me, we picked up our rifles and just sort of filtered back into the brush. "You thinking the same thing I am?" I said.

"Their horses?"

"Uh-huh. If we set them afoot we've got a free ride . . . after we get through that valley yonder."

We'd been timber-raised, like most Tennessee mountain boys, so when we left our horses we swapped our boots for moccasins, which we always carried in our saddlebags.

The weather was clouded up again and it was likely to rain at any moment. We found no sign of the Fetchens until I came upon a corn-shuck cigarette lying on the moss near the butt end of a fallen tree. It was dry, so it must have been dropped since the last shower. After scouting around we found tracks, and then we worked our way up the mountain, moving all the quieter because of the rain-soaked ground.

Suddenly, high up on the mountain, there was a shot.

A voice spoke so close we both jumped in our skins. "Now what the hell was *that?*"

Galloway and me froze where we stood. The speaker couldn't be much more than twenty feet off from us.

"Do you s'pose one of them slipped out?" another man said.

"Naw! That's gotta be somebody else. Huntin', maybe."

"In this rain?"

We eased up a step, then another. In a sheltered place in the lee of a rock stood two of the Fetchen outfit. I knew neither one of them by name, but I had seen them both before. In front of them was a grassy slope that fell gradually away for about fifty feet, then dropped off sharply.

The two stood there, their rifles leaning against the rock wall, well to one side, and out of the wet. They were sheltered by the overhang, but could watch a good distance up and down the canyon. One man was rolling a cigarette, the other had a half-eaten sandwich in his hand.

Taking a long step forward, rifle leveled, I turned squarely around to face them. Galloway stepped up beside me, but several feet to my right. One of them noticed some shadow of movement or heard some sound and started to turn his head.

"Just you all hold it right where you stand," I said. "We got itchy fingers, and we don't mind burying a couple of you if need be."

Neither of them was in shape to reach for a gun fast, and they stood there looking mighty foolish. "Go up to 'em, Galloway," I said, "and take their hardware. No use tempting these boys into error."

Galloway went around behind them, careful to keep from getting between my rifle and them. He slipped their guns from the holsters, and gathered their rifles. Then we backed them into the full shelter of the slight overhang and tied them hand and foot.

"You boys set quiet now. If any of the Fetchens are alive when this is over, they can come and turn you loose. But if we should happen to see you again, and not tied—why, we'd just naturally have to go to shootin'."

"If I ever see you two again," one of them said, "I'll be shootin' some my own self!"

So we left them there, scouted around, found their horses, and turned them loose. Then we went on up the mountain, careful-like. It wasn't going to be that easy again, and we knew it.

Suddenly, from up the mountain there came another rifle shot, and then a scream of mortal agony. And then there was silence.

"What's going on up there, Flagan?" Galloway said. "We got somebody on our side we don't know about?"

He pointed up the hill. Three men were working their way down the hill toward us, but their attention was concentrated on whatever lay behind them. Once one of them lifted his rifle to fire, then lowered it, as if his target had vanished.

Again he lifted his rifle, and as he did so I put my rifle butt to my shoulder. If we had a helper up yonder he was going to find out it worked both ways.

"Hold your fire!" one of them called.

It was Colby Rafin, and with him was Norton Vance and two other men. They had us covered, and were close upon us.

This was no time to be taken prisoner, so I just triggered my shot and spun around on them. Galloway knew I wasn't going to be taken, and he hadn't waited. He had his rifle at his hip and he fired from there. It was point-blank range and right into the belly of Norton Vance.

He snapped back as if he'd been rammed with a fence post, then sat down and rolled over, both hands clutching his midsection.

A bullet whipped by my ear, burning it a little, but I was firing as fast as I could lever the shots. I missed a couple even at that range, for I was firing fast into the lot of them with no aim, and I was moving so as to give them no target, but I scored, too.

I'd shot at Rafin and missed him, the bullet taking the man who stood behind and to his right, and Rafin dived into the brush with lead spattering all around him. As soon as Colby Rafin got turned around he'd have us dead to rights, so we scrambled out of there and into the brush.

We moved in further, then lay still, listening.

For a time we heard no sound. Then behind us we heard a groan, and somebody called for Rafin, but he wasn't getting any answer.

We moved on, angling up the hill toward the edge of the pass.

Then a burst of firing sounded below us where we'd left the rest of our party, and we stopped to look back down the hill. We could see nothing from where we were, but the firing continued. It made a body want to turn and go back, but what we had to do was what we'd started to do— clean up the pass.

They hit us just as we started to go on. During those distracting moments, few as they were, they had somehow moved down on us, and they weren't asking questions. They just opened fire.

A bullet caught me on the leg and it buckled, probably saving my life, for there was a whipping of bullets all around me, and another one turned me sideways. I felt myself falling and tucked my shoulder under so I could roll with it, and I went over twice on the slope before I stopped.

What had happened to Galloway, I didn't know. I did know that I'd been hit hard, and more than once, and unless I moved from where I was I'd be dead within minutes. Somehow I'd clung to my rifle—I'd needed to hang onto something. Now I began to inch my way along the steepening face before me.

Instinctively, for I surely can't claim to much thinking just then, hurting the way I was, I worked back toward those hunting me. They would be off to my right, I was sure, and would think I'd try to get away, which was the smart and sensible thing. But I wanted to stay within shooting distance at any cost, and my best chances of getting away free would be to work right close to them.

But then I almost passed out. For a moment there consciousness faded, and when I snapped out of it I knew I couldn't risk that again. I had to find a place to hole up.

Crawling on, I'd gone no more than a dozen feet before I saw what I wanted, maybe sixty feet further along. It was at a steep place on the mountainside where a boulder had jarred loose and tumbled off down the slope into the pass below, leaving a great empty socket overgrown by brush that had once hung over the boulder. If I could only get into that hollow . . .

Hours later I awakened, shaking with chill. I was curled up in that hollow and I still had my rifle. I had no memory of getting there, no idea how long it had taken me. It was nighttime now, and I was cold and hungry, and hurt.

There was room to sit up. Easing myself around, I touched my leg gingerly, feeling for the wound. One bullet had gone through my leg about five or six inches above the knee and had come out on the other side.

In here I had a hole about six feet either way, and though it was raining outside it was snug and dry here. The branches in front hung almost to the ground and, breaking off some of those on the underside, I wove them into a tighter screen. There was some bark and dry wood around the base of the tree back of the hole, but I didn't want to chance a fire.

Try as I might, there was just no way I could get comfortable. Hour after hour I lay there, huddled in the cold and the damp, trying to see my way out of this trouble. Come daylight, those Fetchen boys would be hunting my hide, and unless the rain washed out the mess of tracks I must have laid down by crawling and losing blood, they'd have me for sure.

The night and the rain are often friendly things to fugitives, but it gave me small comfort to sit there with my teeth rattling like ghost bones in a hardwood cupboard, and a gnawing pain in my thigh and another in my side.

After a time I dug out a mite more of dirt with my hands, made a hollow for my hipbone, and snuggled down on my unwounded side. I must have slept then, and when I woke up it was still dark but there was no rain—only a few drops falling from leaves. I felt that I was living on short time.

But the thing that worried me most was Galloway. Had they killed him right off? That I couldn't believe. But where could he have gotten to?

Right then I taken out my six-shooter and checked every load. I did the same with my Winchester, and added a few rounds to bring her up to capacity. If the Fetchen boys found me they were going to lose scalps rooting me out of here.

Then I sat back to wait. I would have liked a cup of coffee . . . four or five cups, for I'm a coffee-drinking man. But all I could do was wait and think.

That Judith girl, now. She was a mighty pretty thing, come to think of it. How could I have been so dumb as not to see it . . . Mighty contrary and onery, though. And those freckles . . . She was pert, too pert. . . .

Other thoughts were in my mind, too. How long could those boys hold out down below—Moss, Cap, and the others?

I had to hand it to Black Fetchen. He was a general. We seemed to be winning a round or two, but all the while he was baiting trap for us.

I wished I knew what had happened to Galloway. He might be

dead, or he might be lying up somewhere, worse off than me. Far down the slope I heard a long "halloo"—no voice I knew. All right, let them come.

I twitched around and studied my layout by the coming daylight. They couldn't get at me from behind, and nobody was coming up that slope in front of me. What they had to do was come right along the same way I had. Taking sight down the trail, I figured I had it covered for fifty yards; then there was a bend which allowed them cover. I had the side of the canyon for a hundred yards further along.

It started to rain again, a cold drizzle that drew a sheet of steel mesh across the morning. The grass and the trees were greener than I had ever seen them, the trunks of the trees like columns of iron. For a long time I saw no movement. When I did see it down the trail I saw it half asleep, but I was startled into wakefulness by it.

On a second look I saw nothing, yet something had moved down there, something black and sudden, vanishing behind a bend in the trail even as it registered on my consciousness.

I lifted my rifle muzzle, and rested it on my half-bent knee. My hand was on the action as I watched the trail. My ears were alert to catch any sound, and I waited for what would come. . . .

Supposing I could get out of this jam—and all the time I knew how slight my chances were—what could I do with my future? Well, Tyrel had no more when he came west, and now he was a well-off man, a respected man, with a fine wife and a ranch.

My eyes had not wandered from the trail, and now a man came into view down there. He was following some sort of a trail, although mine must have washed out long since, and he was edging closer. From his manner, it seemed to me that he fancied he was close upon whatever he was hunting.

Once, while my rifle held him covered, he paused and started to lift his own weapon. He was looking at something above and back of me, but evidently he was not satisfied with his sight picture or else he had been mistaken in his target, for he lowered the rifle.

He came on another step, seemed then to stagger, and he started to fall even as the sound of a shot went booming down the canyon, losing itself in the rain.

The man went down to the ground, his rifle still gripped in his hand, and he lay there sprawled out not sixty yards away from me. I could see the bright stain of blood on his skull and on the trail beside him.

Who had fired?

Waiting for a minute, I saw no one, but suddenly I knew I could not stay where I was. I had taken time to plug and bind my wounds as best I could, but I desperately needed help. So, using my rifle for a crutch, I crawled from my shelter and hobbled into the cold rain.

For a few moments I would be invisible to whoever was up there. With care I worked around and started to go on up the narrow trail. I could not see anybody, but visibility was bad; I knew that shot could not have come from far off.

The trail became steeper. Hobbling along, I almost fell, then I pulled up under some trees.

"Flagan?" came the voice.

It was Judith.

She was standing half behind the black trunk of a spruce, partly shielded by its limbs. She wore a man's hat and a poncho. Her cheeks glistened in the rain and her eyes seemed unnaturally large. She must have been out on the mountain all night long, but I never saw anybody look so good.

"Be careful," she warned. "They are all around us."

"Have you seen Galloway?" I asked.

"No."

I moved up toward her, but stopped to lean against a tree. "I've been hit, a couple of times," I said. "How is it above us?"

"They are all along the ridge. I don't know how I managed to slip through," she said.

Looking up toward the ridge through the branches, I could see nothing but the trees, the rain, and the low rain clouds.

"I've got a place," she said. "We'd better get to it."

She led the way, and before she'd taken half a dozen steps I could see she knew what she was about, holding to cover and low ground, taking no chance of being seen. It was obvious she had used the route before, and that worried me. With a canny enemy against you, it never pays to go over the same ground twice. Somebody is likely to be waiting for you.

"How do you happen to be over here?" I asked her.

"Nobody came back, and we were worried. Finally I couldn't stand it any longer, so I slipped away and came in this direction."

The place she had found wasn't much more than a shelter from the rain. A lightning-struck tree had fallen almost to the ground before being caught between two others. Wedged there, it formed a shelter that she had improved by breaking off small branches on the underside and weaving them into the top.

The steep bank behind and the trees kept it dry, and she could enter it without being seen. The trees lower down the slope screened it in front, and we felt we could even have a small fire without it being seen or the smoke attracting attention.

"Flagan?" She was on the ground beside the fire, waiting for coffee water to boil.

"Yes?"

"Let's just ride away from here. I don't want to fight any more. I don't want trouble."

"Your pa's down there." I gestured toward the base of the mountain, almost within view from here. "He's almighty tired, but when I left them they were holed up in a good spot."

"I want to see him, but I'm scared for you. Black will never rest until he's killed you, Flagan. You and Galloway."

"We don't kill easy."

When the coffee was ready, we drank some, and nothing ever tasted so good. But I was worried. The Fetchens were close around somewhere on this mountain, and I knew I wasn't going to get another chance. The next time we met, it had to be all or nothing. Hurt as I was, I knew I couldn't last very long.

Putting down my coffee cup, I checked my guns. Just then somewhere up the slope a branch cracked, and we both heard it.

Taking up my cup again in my left hand and keeping my six-gun in my right hand, I looked over at her. "You get down behind that mess of branches. This here is going to be a showdown."

"You scared, Flagan?"

"I guess I am. I'm not as sharp as I should be, this here wound and all." I finished my coffee. "That tasted good."

With my rifle I pushed myself up, holstered my gun, and wiped off the action of my rifle, flicking the water away. Standing on a small mound of dirt pushed up by the roots of the fallen tree, I looked down the slope.

They were coming all right. I counted five of them. And there were others up the slope, too, closing in. There must have been fourteen or fifteen in all.

"This here's going to be quite a fight," I said. "You got a pistol besides that rifle?"

She tossed it to me and I caught it left-handed and put it back of my belt.

"What are you going to do?"

"Wait until they get closer. They want a showdown, they'll have it. When they get up close I'm going to step out and go to shooting."

There wasn't anything else to do. I wasn't able to go any further, and I wasn't of a mind to. Right here we would settle it, Black and me and the rest of them.

Right here, on this wet ground we were going to fight . . . and some of us would die.

Chapter 16

At a time like that you don't count the odds, and I had the odds against me, no matter what. It wasn't as if I had a choice. This was one time when there was no place to run. It was root hog or die, and maybe both.

But seeing them coming at me, I didn't feel like dying, and I wasn't even feeling that the odds were too great. I'd come to a place and a time where it no longer mattered, and I was only thinking about how many I could take, just how I ought to move, and which targets I should choose first.

My eyes searched for Black. He was the one I most wanted to get into my sights. And in the back of my mind I was thinking: Where was Galloway?

Judith waited there behind me, and I could feel her eyes upon me. "Flagan?" she said.

"Yes."

"Flagan, I love you."

Turning my head, I looked at her. "I love you, too," I said. "Only we haven't much time. . . . When this fuss begins, Judith, you stay out of it, d' you hear? I can make my fight better if I know you're out of harm's way."

"All right." She said it meekly enough, and I believed her.

They came on, carrying their rifles up, ready to throw down on anything that moved.

It gave me time to pick my targets—to figure my first shot, and to see just how much I'd have to move my rifle for a second. The way I figured, I had two shots before they could get me in their sights, and if I fired those two and then threw myself down I could move along the ground and get at least one more before they located me. What

274

followed would depend on how they came up shooting, and whether they took shelter or came on.

There was no way of telling whether they had located us yet or not, only they knew we were somewhere along that slope. At first I'd been ready to step out and go to shooting as soon as they got within easy range, but then I began to figure if there wasn't some way to make the situation work for me. So much of any fight depends on the terrain and how a body uses it.

They were coming up from below and coming down from above, and we had the canyon behind us and no way out that we could see. But there was a dip of low ground running diagonally down the mountainside. It was shallow, and partly cloaked with brush, but it was deep enough so a crouching man might slip along it unseen.

If I did step out and go to shooting, I could start downhill, fire my shots, then drop into that hollow and go back up the mountain on an angle, under cover. From where they were, I doubted if they could see that low place, which had likely been scooped out by a rock slide with a lot of snow and weight behind it. With luck, I might make the hollow, get under cover, and come out where they least expected me.

All the time my thoughts kept shifting to Galloway. Common sense told me he must be dead, but there was something in me that refused to accept it. I knew Galloway, who was a tough man to kill.

The men below were well out in the open now, and they were coming along slow. Looking up, I could see the line of the ones above, spaced at intervals and coming down slope, but they could not see each other yet.

"I want to come with you," Judith said.

With my rifle, I pointed the way. "See that long gouge? If there's a way out, it will be up that way. When I shoot, or anybody else does, you hit the ground and scramble. Just keep going up that low place—there's brush all around it and they may not realize it's there. I'll be right behind you."

The time was now.

Rifle up and ready, I stepped out. Judith scooted by me and was into that shallow place before they could glimpse her. I took another quick step, brought up my rifle just as they saw me, and caught a man in my sights who wore a gray Confederate coat. The rifle jumped in my hands, the report came smashing back, and I was already shifting aim. My timing was right, and my second shot was following the first before the report died away; and then, with lead flying all around me, I took a running dive into the brush.

Branches tore at my face. I hit rolling, came up in a crouch, and made three fast steps before I caught a glimpse of an opening and a Fetchen with his rifle on me. There was no time for aiming, so I simply turned my body slightly and fired from the hip. A rifle bullet hit the tree near me and splattered my face with bark, but my bullet scored a hit . . . not a killing hit, but it turned that man around in his tracks, and I was off and running, going uphill with great leaps. Twice I fell, once I lost hold of my rifle, grabbed it again, and ran on. My breath tore at my lungs . . . it was the going uphill and the altitude. I slipped and fell again, felt the hammer of bullets in the earth ahead of me, rolled over under a bush, and wormed out on the other side.

That time I made three steps, but they were closing in on me. Half raised, I fired blind, left and right, and drew a smashing hail of bullets; I was just hoping they would kill each other.

Somebody hollered, and the shooting eased off. I heard them calling back and forth. They had me located, but I kept on squirming along the hollow. It seemed almost like a deer or varmint trail.

A rifle blasted somewhere up ahead, somebody cried out, and I slid across a wet boulder, hit a stretch of sand in the watercourse beyond, and managed four plunging steps before I fell, mouth open—my lungs seemed to be tearing apart.

Fear had wiped out the pain from my wounded leg, but I realized it was bleeding again. My pants leg was soaked and I could feel the squishing in my shoe, although a part of it was rain water.

There was a lot of shooting now. Judith must have opened fire from some place above me. Bleeding or not, exhausted or not, I knew it was death to stay where I was, so I scrambled. I could hear them all around me.

As I squirmed between two boulders, one of the Fetchen men reared up right before me and I hit him with my rifle butt. It wasn't much of a blow, because I held the rifle one-handed and I just swung it up from where it was.

He grabbed the rifle with both hands. But instead of trying to pull it away, I held it hard against him and swung my foot and kicked him under the chin. He went over backwards and I jerked the rifle away. He looked up at me for one black, awful instant, but it was kill or be killed, and I gave him the rifle butt in the face with both hands.

Holding up there, gasping for breath, I fed a few cartridges into the magazine of my rifle. My belt was running shy, so I reached down and ripped the belt off the Fetchen man.

Rain was pouring down, and the firing had let up. Nobody seemed to be moving, and I worked my way slowly ahead, nearing the crest of the ridge. Here and there the bottom of the gouge was choked with brush, and there were many rocks, polished by running water and the abrasion of other tumbling stones.

Once, crawling through the brush, I suddenly felt myself growing weaker, and almost blacked out. I fought against the dizziness for a moment, and then somehow I came out of it, and crawled on.

They had come in behind me now, closing off the way back, even if I had been willing or able to take it. I could hear them coming on, taking their time, checking every clump of brush or rocks.

There was no longer any question of running. I could pull myself up, and by using the rocks and brush I could remain erect long enough to move forward a few feet.

Then the ridge was close above me. I could see the bare wet rocks, the stunted cedars, and the occasional bare trunks of pines shattered by lightning.

At that moment I looked around. Four men were standing not much more than fifty feet away, aiming their rifles at me. Desperately, I threw myself to one side and fired my rifle at them. Fired, worked the lever, and fired again.

Bullets smashed into the ground around me. My hat was swept from my head, blood cascaded into my eyes, and my rifle was struck from my hand. I grabbed for it, and through the haze of blood from a scalp wound I saw that the action was shattered and useless.

Throwing the rifle down, I grabbed my six-shooter. Somehow, in throwing myself to one side, I had gotten into the cover of a rock.

A man came running down the gully, but the earth gave way and he slid faster than he expected, stones and rubble crashing down before him. I shot at point-blank range, my bullet striking the V of his open shirt and ranging upward through him.

He fell forward. I grabbed at his rifle, but it slipped away and fell down among the rocks.

Up ahead of me there was a shattering burst of gunfire—it sounded like several guns going. They must have caught up with Judith.

I could hear the ones close by talking as I waited. They were hunting me out, but they could not see me, a fact due more to the rocks where I lay than to any skill on my part. After the sudden death of the man who had slid down among the rocks they were wary, hesitant to take the risk . . . and I was just as pleased.

Right about then I must have passed out for a minute. When I opened my eyes again I was shaking with cold. The wind had come up, and was blowing rain in on me. I didn't have what you'd call shelter, just the slight overhang of a slab of fallen rock.

My hands felt for my guns. I had both pistols, and I reloaded the one right there. All the time I was listening, fighting to keep my teeth from chattering, and the knowledge growing in me that it would be almighty cold up here at night.

Nothing moved; only the rain whispered along the ground and rattled cold against the rocks. Even if I couldn't get out of this, I had to find a safer place.

On the downhill side there was a scattered stand of pine, stunted and scraggly, along with the boulders and the low-growing brush. On the uphill side there was even less cover, but the gouge up which I'd been crawling ran on for sixty yards or so further, ending just off the ridge.

It stood to reason that if they wanted me they could get me crossing that ridge. All they had to do was hold their fire and let me get out on the bare rock.

But Judith, unless she was dead or captured, was up there somewhere.

So I crawled out of shelter, over a wet boulder and along the downhill side of a great old deadfall, the log all turned gray from the weather. Maybe I made fifteen feet before I stopped to catch my breath and breathe away the pain; then I went on.

I was nearing the end of the gouge. The only thing for me to do now was break out and run for it. And I couldn't run.

Only I had to. I had to make it over that ridge. Lying there shivering in the cold rain, I studied that ridge and the ground between. Thirty steps, if I was lucky.

There was no sense in waiting. I came off the ground with a lunge, stabbing at the ground with my good leg, but hitting easy with the wounded one. I felt a shocking pain, and then I was moving. I went over the ridge and dropped beside a rock, and there they were, the lot of them.

There was Judith too, her hands held behind her, and a man's dirty hand clasped tight over her mouth so she couldn't call out to warn me. There were six of the Fetchen gang, with Black right there among them—Black and Colby Rafin.

At times like that a man doesn't think. There's no room for thought. I was soaked to the hide, bedraggled as a wet cat, bloody and sore and hurt and mad, and when I saw that crowd I did the last thing they expected.

I went for my gun.

Oh, they had guns on me, all right! But they were too busy feeling satisfied with themselves at setting the trap, and there's such a thing as reaction time. A man's got to realize what is happening, what has to be done, and he has to do it, all in the same moment.

My right hand slapped leather and came up blasting fire. And almost at the same instant my left hand snaked the other Colt from my waistband.

There was no time for anything like choosing targets. I shot into the man right in front of me, shifted aim, and blasted again. I saw Judith twisting to get free, and pulling Rafin off balance.

Somebody else was shooting, and I saw Galloway, leaning on a crutch and his gun leaping with every spout of flame. And then, as suddenly as it began, it was over. There was a scrambling in the brush, then silence, and I was stretched out on the rocks and the rain was pounding on my back.

It seemed like hours later that I got my eyes open and looked around.

There was a fire in a fireplace, and Judith was sitting in front of it, watching the flames. I never saw anything so pretty as the firelight on her face, and catching the lights of her hair.

I was stretched out in a bunk in some sort of a low-roofed cabin, and the floor was littered with men, all apparently sleeping. Coffee was on the fire, and by the look of the coals we'd been here quite a spell.

I felt around for my gun and found it, but the rustling drew Judith's attention. She came over to me. "Ssh! The others are all asleep."

"Was that Galloway that showed up? Is he all right?"

"He's been hurt. He was shot three times, and has a broken foot. Pa's here, and so are Cap and Moss."

"Walker?"

"He's dead. He was killed, Flagan."

"Black?"

"He got away. He was hurt, I know that. You hit him once at least. He ran, Flagan. He turned and ran."

"That ain't like him."

"He was a coward," she insisted bitterly. "For all his talk, he was a coward."

"I don't believe it," I said. And I didn't believe it either. He was a lot of things, that James Black Fetchen, but he was no coward in a fight. He hated too much for that. He might have turned and run—she said he had, and she would tell me the truth—but I was sure there was more to it than that.

The old prospector's cabin where we had found shelter was on the eastern slope, not more than half a mile from where the fight had taken place.

We stayed right there a day and a half, until Evan Hawkes and Tom Sharp brought a wagon up Medano Pass. They built stretchers, and three of us came off the mountain that way.

Two weeks later I was able to sit on the porch outside the trading post and watch folks go by. Galloway was still laid up, but he was coming along fine. Though Costello was still sick, he was looking better. Cap and Moss, like the tough old-timers they were, looked about the same.

We got the news bit by bit. Three of the Fetchens had pulled out for Tennessee. Tirey was dead . . . he'd been killed up on the mountain. And they hadn't found the Reynolds treasure. Like a lot of folks who've looked for it before and since, they just couldn't locate it. They had all the landmarks and they had a map, but they found nothing.

"I've seen four maps of that Reynolds treasure," Sharp told me, "and no two of them alike."

Nobody saw any of the Fetchens around, but after a few days we heard they were camped over at the foot of Marble Mountain, with several of them laid up, and at least one of them in bad shape.

Galloway limped around, still using the crutch he had cut for himself up on the mountain. Costello filled us in on all that happened before we got there.

The Fetchens had just moved in on him and he had welcomed them as guests, although mistrusting their looks. Well, they were hunting the Reynolds treasure, all right, but they wanted his ranch and Judith as well.

Costello had had a lead on that treasure himself, but it didn't pan out, and so he had settled down to hunting wild stock and breeding them to horses brought from the East, the way Tom Sharp was doing.

"Reynolds buried some loot, all right," Costello said, "but whoever finds it will find it through pure dumb luck. I don't trust any of those maps."

"They aren't cured," Moss Reardon said. "There's supposed to be treasure in a cave on Marble Mountain too. I'd lay a bet they're huntin' it now."

For the first time in my life I was pleased just to sit and contemplate. I'd lost a lot of blood and used myself in a hard way, and so had Galloway. As I looked around that country it made me wish I had a place of my own, and I said as much to Galloway.

"We get up and around," I said, "we ought to find us a place, some corner back in the hills with plenty of green grass and water."

James Black Fetchen seemed to me like somebody from another world. After a week had passed we never mentioned the big fight on the mountain, nor any of that crowd. One thing we did hear about them. The Fetchens had buried another man somewhere up on Grape Creek.

My appetite came back, and I began thinking about work. Galloway and me had used up the mite of cash we'd had left and had nothing but our outfits. I mentioned it to Tom Sharp.

"Don't worry about it," he said. "You just eat all you're of a mind to. Those men would have caused plenty of trouble for us if you hadn't taken their measure."

The next morning we heard about the stage holdup over on the Alamosa trail.

Four men, all masked, had stopped the stage and robbed the passengers. There was no gold riding the boot on that trip, and the passengers were a hard-up lot. The robbery netted the outlaws just sixty-five dollars.

Two days later there was another holdup in the mountains west of Trinidad. That netted the thieves about four hundred dollars. There had been six of them in that lot, and one of the passengers had ridden the other stage and said they were the same outfit. One of them had been riding a big blaze-faced sorrel that sounded like Russ Menard's horse.

Sitting around waiting to get my strength back, I hadn't been idle. I'd never been one to waste time doing nothing, so while I sat there I plaited a rawhide bridle for Sharp, mended a saddle, and fixed some other things.

Costello rode out to his ranch. His place had been burned, even his stacked hay, and all the stock in sight had been driven off.

Galloway had taken to wearing two guns, one of them shoved down behind his waistband.

Then there was a holdup near Castle Rock, to the north; and word came down that Black Fetchen had killed a man at Tin Cup, a booming mining camp.

Meanwhile, Galloway and me were beginning to feel spry again, and we helped Tom Sharp round up a few head of cattle and drive them down to Walsenburg. There we heard talk of the Fetchen outlaws.

Those days Galloway and me were never far apart. We knew it was coming. The trouble was, we didn't exactly know what to expect, or when.

Costello hired two new hands, both on the recommendation of

Rodriguez and Sharp. One was a Mexican named Valdez, a very tough man and a good shot who, as a boy, had worked for Kit Carson; and the other was Frank White, a one-time deputy sheriff from Kansas. Both were good hands and reliable men.

Judith was riding with me one day when she said, "Flagan, you and Galloway be careful now. I'm scared."

"Don't worry your pretty head. We'll ride loose and careful."

"Do you think he'll come back?"

Now, I was never one to lie or to make light of trouble with womenfolks. There's men who feel they should, but I've found women stand well in trouble, and there's no use trying to make it seem less than it is. They won't believe you, anyway.

"He'll come," I said. "He wasn't scared, Judith. He just wanted to be sure he lived long enough to kill Galloway and me. I've got an idea he's just waiting his chance."

By now Galloway and me were batching it in a cabin on Pass Creek. We had built up the corral, made some repairs in the roof, and laid in a few supplies bought on credit at the trading post. Work was scarce, but we disliked to leave the country with Black Fetchen still around . . . and of course, there was Judith.

We had talked about things, even made some plans, but I had no money and no immediate way of getting any. Evan Hawkes had sold out and gone back to Texas. The loss of the boy had hurt him more than he had ever showed. We were just waiting, shooting our meat out in the hills and occasionally prospecting a little.

The showdown came all of a sudden, and by an unexpected turn.

A short, stocky man came riding up to the place one day, and he had a big, black-haired man with him. Both of them were dressed like city folks, except they wore lace-up boots.

"Are you the Sacketts? Flagan and Galloway?" the short man asked.

Now, I didn't take to these men much, but they were all business. "Understand you've had trouble with the Fetchen outlaws? Well, I've got to ride the stage to Durango, and I'll need some bodyguards."

"Bodyguards?" I said.

"I'll be carrying twenty thousand dollars in gold, and while I can use a gun I am no gun-fighter, nor is my partner here. We'd like to hire you boys to ride with us. We'll pay you forty dollars each for the ride."

Now, forty dollars was wages for a top hand for a month, and all we had to do was sit up on the cushions in that stage and see that no harm came to Mr. Fred Vaughn and his money. His partner was made known to us as Reed Griffin.

We taken the job.

Chapter 17

Walsenburg was quiet when we rode in and stabled our horses. We had come up a day early, for we both needed a few things and we hadn't been close to a town since the fight. The trading post at Buzzard Roost had most things a body could wish for, but we both figured to buy white shirts and the like to wear in Durango.

We found a table in a back corner of the restaurant and hung our hats on the rack. The food was good, and the coffee better. We were sitting where we could look out the window and down the street, and we were sitting there when we saw Reed Griffin come out of a saloon down the street.

"Might as well let him know we're here," I said, but when I started to get up, Galloway stopped me.

"Plenty of time for that," he said.

Griffin walked across the road and went down a passage between two buildings and disappeared.

It was quiet where we were, and we continued to sit there, talking possibilities. We figured to prospect around Durango a mite and see what jobs were available, if any. If there were none, we would use what cash we had to outfit ourselves and go wild-horse hunting. There was always a good market for saddle stock that had been rough-broken, and while many of the wild horses were scrubs there were always a few good ones in every herd.

Later in the afternoon we went across the street to the hotel and hired ourselves a room on the second floor, in back. Pulling off our boots, we stretched out for a rest. When I woke up it was full dark, but there was a glow coming through the windows from the lights in the other buildings.

Without putting on my boots I walked across the room and poured cold water into the bowl and washed my face and combed my hair by the feel of it. I had picked up my boots and dropped into a chair by the window when I happened to look out.

The door of a house on the street back of the hotel was standing open and there were two men seated at a table over a bottle. One of those men was Colby Rafin. The other was Reed Griffin.

"Galloway?" I said, not too loud.

He was awake on the instant. "Yeah?"

"Look."

He came over and stood beside me and we looked out of our dark window and into that open door. Reed Griffin was on his feet now, but as he turned away from Rafin he was full in the light.

"Now, what d' you know about that?" Galloway said softly. "I'd say we've got to move quiet as mice."

We ate at the restaurant that night, but we fought shy of the saloons, and in the morning, right after breakfast, we were waiting at the stage stop.

Mr. Fred Vaughn was already there. He had a carpetbag and a iron-bound box with him. The stage driver loaded the box as if it was heavy, then Vaughn got in and Griffin came out and joined him. We loitered alongside, watching folks come up to the stage. There was another man, a long-geared, loose-jointed man with a big Adam's apple and kind of sandy hair. He carried a six-shooter in a belt holster, and a Winchester.

The last man to enter was lean and dark-haired. He shot us a quick, hard look, then got in. His boots were worn and his pants looked like homespun. We had never seen him before, but he had a Tennessee or maybe Missouri look about him.

The stage driver was a fat, solid-looking man with no nonsense about him, and he was obviously well known to everybody else, if not to us. We got in last and sat down facing Griffin and Vaughn, with the Tennessee man beside us; the sandy-haired man was across the way. The stage took off, headed west.

We both carried Winchesters and our belt guns, but each of us had a spare six-shooter tucked behind our waistbands. Griffin and Vaughn wasted no time talking, but made themselves comfortable as possible and went to sleep. The sandy man settled down too, although he kept measuring us with quick looks, and the man beside us as well.

The road was rough. The stage bounced, jolted, and slid over it, and every time we slowed the dust settled over us in a thick cloud.

Both of us were thinking the same thing. Why hadn't Vaughn

taken the train? It ran west as far as Alamosa now, and much of our route by train ran parallel to it. In fact, the stage line was going out of business soon. This made no sense. . . . Unless there was something that could be done on the stage that could not be done on the train.

La Veta lay ahead. Once, not long ago, it had been the end of the railroad tracks, and a wild, wild town. Now the end-of-the-line boys had moved to Alamosa, although a couple of dives still remain there. To most people in this part of the country it was still simply the Plaza.

The hunch came to me suddenly, and my elbow touched Galloway ever so gently. I had noticed that Reed Griffin did not seem to be really asleep, though his eyes remained closed. My eyes went to Vaughn. He was also shamming sleep. The Tennessee man beside me was unfastening a button on his coat. Sandy was completely awake. He was watching me with bright, hard eyes, and his hand stayed close to his pistol butt.

When we got to the Plaza we changed horses, and I noticed that the Tennessee man disappeared into the stable there. Shortly after he returned, a man came from the stable, mounted a horse, and rode off down the road along which we would soon travel.

The stage driver stood by with a cup of coffee in his hands, watching the teams being switched. Strolling over to him, I said, "You size up like an honest man."

"I am that," he said cooly, "so don't make any mistakes."

"I won't, but some others will. Mister, if you hear a shot or a Texas yell from inside the stage, you let those horses run, d' you hear?"

He gave me a quick look. "What do you know?"

"I'm Flagan Sackett. That there's my brother. I think the Fetchen gang plan to take us, or kill us. And probably rob your stage in the process."

"Now I'm told. There's no law at the Plaza now."

"We'll handle it. You just run the legs off that team."

"All right," he said.

Indicating the sandy man, I asked, "Do you know him?"

"El Paso to Denver, Durango to Tucson. That's all I know. My guess is that he's a Ranger, or has been one."

He walked back inside with his coffee cup and the Tennessee man strolled over and got into the stage. Vaughn and Griffin followed. The sandy man threw down his cigarette and rubbed it out with his toe. I took one step over so he had to come up close to me, and when he drew abreast I said, "Stay out of it. The trouble's ours."

He turned his eyes on me. "You're a Sackett, aren't you? That's why you are familiar. I rode with McNelly at Las Cuevas. Orlando Sackett was there. He was a good man. I won money on him once when he fought in the ring."

"They've set us up," I said. "Everybody in that stage but you and us is safe enough," I said. "They'll stop us on the grade, I think, near Muleshoe."

The stage rolled out again, and the climb before us was a long one. Gradually the team moved slower and slower. Taking my hat from my head, I lowered it into my lap, and as I did so I drew out my waistband gun and eased it down beside my leg and out of sight, then I put my hat on again.

We went on, climbing steeply. The men across from me appeared to sleep again.

The switchback was behind us, and the stage leveled out, then suddenly I heard the driver hauling on the lines, and I lifted my Colt and looked at the men across from me.

"Sit tight, if you want to live," I said.

Galloway had lunged against the Tennessee man and I saw him strip his gun from him. The Tennesseean started up, but Galloway laid the barrel of the gun alongside his skull and he fell across our knees. We pulled our legs back and let him go to the floor of the stage.

Vaughn and Griffin both started to complain, but I shut them up. "Unless you want a cracked skull," I said.

From outside we heard a familiar voice. "All right, pull up there!"

To the Texan I said, "You want to hold these boys for me? I've got some shooting to do."

"A pleasure!" he said, and meant it.

Catching the top of the door I drew myself out of the open window on my side, hesitated an instant, and dropped to the road on the balls of my feet.

Rafin walked up to the door of the stage on the other side. I could see his boots. "All right, boys," he said. "Trot them out!"

Galloway shoved the door open, knocking him back, and leaped into the road. At the same moment I stepped around the back of the stage.

Russ Menard was the first man I saw. He was on his horse, and he had a gun resting easy in his hand. Galloway had hit the dirt and, dropping into a crouch by the wheel, was shooting into Rafin. I shot over him and my bullet crossed that of Menard, who had been taken by surprise.

He shot quickly, his bullet hitting the edge of the stage-door window, and mine knocked his shoulder. Stepping wide of the door, I shot at him again. I felt the whiff of a bullet and, turning slightly, I saw Black Fetchen taking dead aim at me.

The muzzle of his gun wasn't three feet from my head and I dived at him, going under his outstretched arm. My shoulder sent him crashing into the side of the stage. I pushed my gun against him and fired three blasting shots, and felt his body jerk with every one, then whip free.

Menard had held his fire for fear of hitting Black, but now he fired, the bullet striking my gun belt such a blow that I was knocked staggering, and it exploded a cartridge in my belt that cut a groove in my boot toe. His horse had turned sharply, and for an instant his gun couldn't bear. When it could, I was ready and shot first, Galloway's bullet crossing mine.

Menard went off his horse, hit ground on the other side, and tried to get up. He had been hit hard, but his eyes were blazing with a strange white light and his grip on his gun was steady. I shot into him again and he backed up and sat down again.

Somewhere off to my right I heard the stage driver saying, "Careful now, you with the itchy finger. This shotgun will cut you in two. Just stand fast."

Menard was sitting there looking at me, one knee sort of drawn up, his gun lying across his leg. He had been hit twice in the lungs and every time he drew breath there was a frothy burst of blood from the front of his vest.

"I told him he should leave you alone," he said, "but he wouldn't listen. I told him nobody could beat a man's luck, and you had it."

"So this is all for you," I said quietly.

"Looks like it. Pull my boots off, Sackett, and bury me deep. I don't want the varmints after me."

Not being a trusting man, I still held my gun on him while I tugged his boots free.

"You take the gun," he said. "It brought me nothing but trouble."

Galloway had come up to me. "Fetchen's dying," he said. "You tore him apart."

Taking Menard's gun, I backed off from him.

James Black Fetchen was not dying; he was dead, and there were two others besides him, one of them the man I'd seen at the stable.

The stage driver rolled his tobacco in his cheeks. "If you boys are through, we might as well bury 'em and get on. I got a schedule to keep."

*   *   *

At the placer-mining camp of Russell the stage pulled up and we got down. We took Reed Griffin and Fred Vaughn out on the street. "We agreed to see you safe to Durango. You had us set up for killing. Now, do you figure we've earned our money, or do we take you all the way?"

"You going to let us go?"

"Forty dollars each," I said, and he paid it.

"Ride out with the stage," I said, "and keep going."

So we let them go, the Texan riding along to see them on their way.

"Galloway," I said, "we'd better find some horses and ride back to that cabin on Pass Creek."

"You figure we should stay there?"

"Well, there's Judith. And that's pretty country."

"Hey, did you see that niece of Rodriguez' do the fandango? Every time I looked at her my knees got slacker'n dishwater."

We had come a far piece into a strange land, a trail lit by lonely campfires and by gunfire, and the wishing we did by day and by night. Now we rode back to plant roots in the land, and with luck, to leave sons to carry on a more peaceful life, in what we hoped would be a more peaceful world.

But whatever was to come, our sons would be Sacketts, and they would do what had to be done whenever the call would come.

THE MAN FROM
THE BROKEN HILLS

To Art Jacobs,
with appreciation

Chapter 1

I caught the drift of woodsmoke where the wind walked through the grass.

A welcome sign in wild country . . . or the beginning of trouble.

I was two days out of coffee and one day out of grub, with an empty canteen riding my saddle horn. And I was tired of talking to my horse and getting only a twitch of the ears for answer.

Skylining myself on the rimrock, I looked over the vast sweep of country below, rolling hills with a few dry watercourses and scattered patches of mesquite down one arroyo. In this country, mesquite was nearly always a sign that water was' near, for only wild mustangs ate the beans, and if they weren't bothered they'd rarely get more than three miles from water. Mesquite mostly grew from horse droppings, so that green looked almighty good down there.

The smoke was there, pointing a ghost finger at the sky, so I rode the rim looking for a way down. It was forty or fifty feet of sheer rock, and then a steep slope of grass-grown talus, but such rims all had a break somewhere, and I found one used by run-off water and wild animals.

It was steep, but my mustang had run wild until four years old, and for such a horse this was Sunday School stuff. He slid down on his haunches and we reached bottom in our own cloud of dust.

There were three men around the fire, with the smell of coffee and of bacon frying. It was a two-bit camp in mighty rough country, with three saddle-broncs and a packhorse standing under a lightning-struck cottonwood.

"Howdy," I said. "You boys receivin' visitors, or is this a closed meetin'?"

They were all looking me over, but one said, "You're here, mister. Light and set."

He was a long-jawed man with a handlebar mustache and a nose that had been in a disagreement. There was a lean, sallow youngster, and a stocky, strong-looking man with a shirt that showed the muscle beneath it.

The horses were good, solid-fleshed animals, all wearing a Spur brand. A pair of leather chaps lay over a rock near the fire, and a rifle nearby.

"Driftin'?" the stocky fellow asked.

"Huntin' a job. I was headed east, figurin' to latch onto the first cow outfit needin' a hand."

"We're Stirrup-Iron," the older one commented, "an' you might hit the boss. We're comin' up to roundup time and we've just bought the Spur outfit. He's liable to need hands who can work rough country."

Stepping down from the saddle I stripped off my rig. There was a trail of water in the creek, about enough to keep the rocks wet. My horse needed no invitation. He just walked over and pushed his nozzle into the deepest pool.

"Seen any cattle over west?" the handlebar mustache asked.

"Here an' there. Some Stirrup-Irons, HF Connected, Circle B . . . all pretty scattered up there on the caprock."

"I'm Hinge," the handlebar said, "Joe Hinge. That long-legged galoot with the straw-colored hair is Danny Rolf. Old Muscles here is Ben Roper.

"The boy there," he added, "is all right. Seein's he ain't dry behind the ears yet an' his feet don't track."

Rolf grinned. "Don't let him fool you, mister. That there ol' man's named Josiah . . . not Joe. He's one of them there pate-ree-archs right out of the Good Book."

I collected my horse and walked him back onto the grass and drove in the picket pin, my stomach growling over that smell of bacon. These were cowhands who dressed and looked like cowhands, but I knew they were doing some wondering about me.

My rope was on my saddle and I was wearing fringed shotgun chaps, a sun-faded blue shirt, army-style, and a flat-brimmed hat that was almost new but for the bullet hole. I also wore a six-shooter, just as they did, but mine was tied down.

"Name's Milo Talon," I said, but nobody so much as blinked.

"Set up," Hinge suggested, "we're eatin' light. Just a few biscuit and the bacon."

"Dip it in the creek," I said, "and I'll eat a blanket."

"Start with his," Ben Roper gestured to Rolf. "He's got enough wild life in it to provide you with meat."

"Huh! I—!"

"You got comp'ny," I said, "five men, rifles in their hands."

Roper stood up suddenly, and it seemed to me his jaws turned a shade whiter. He rolled a match in his teeth and I saw the muscles bulge in his jaws. He wiped his hands down the side of his pants and let them hang. The kid was up, movin' to one side, and the oldster just sat there, his fork in his left hand, watching them come.

"Balch an' Saddler," Hinge said quietly. "Our outfit an' them don't get along. You better stand aside, Talon."

"I'm eatin' at your fire," I said, "and I'll just stay where I am."

They came on up, five very tough men, judging by their looks—well-mounted and armed.

Hinge looked across the fire at them. " 'Light an' set, Balch," he offered.

Balch ignored him. He was a big man, rawboned and strong with a lantern jaw and high cheekbones. He looked straight at me. "I don't know you."

"That's right," I said.

His face flushed. Here was a man with a short fuse and no patience. "We don't like strange riders around here," he said flatly.

"I get acquainted real easy," I said.

"Don't waste your time. Just get out."

He was a mighty rough-mannered man. Saddler must be the square-shouldered, round-faced man with the small eyes, and the man beside him had a familiar look, like somebody I might have seen before.

"I never waste time," I said. "I thought I'd try to rustle a job at the Stirrup-Iron."

Balch stared at me, and for a moment there we locked eyes but he turned his away first and that made him mad. "You're a damn fool if you do," he said.

"I've done a lot of damn fool things in my time," I told him, "but I don't have any corner on it."

He had started to turn his attention to Hinge, but his head swung back. "What's that mean?"

"Read it any way you like," I said, beginning not to like him.

He did not like that and he did not like me, but he was not sure of me, either. He was a tough man, a mean man, but no fool. "I'll make up my mind about that and when I do, you'll have my answer."

"Anytime," I said.

He turned away from me. "Hinge, you're too damn far west. You start back come daybreak and don't you stop this side of Alkali Crossing."

"We've got Stirrup-Iron cattle here," Hinge said. "We will be gathering them."

"Like hell! There's none of your cattle here! None at all!"

"I saw some Stirrup-Irons up on the cap-rock," I said.

Balch started to turn back on me, but Ben Roper broke in before he could speak. "He saw some HF Connected, too," Roper said, "and the major will want to know about them. He will want to know about all of them."

Balch reined his horse around. "Come daybreak, you get out of here. I'll have no Stirrup-Iron hand on my ranch."

"Does that go for the major, too?" Roper asked.

Balch's face flamed with anger and for a moment I thought he would turn back, but he just rode away and we watched them go, then sat down.

"You made an enemy," Hinge commented.

"I'm in company," I replied. "You boys were doing pretty well yourselves."

Hinge chuckled. "Ben, when you mentioned the major I thought he'd bust a gut."

"Who," I asked, "is the major?"

"Major Timberly. He was a Confederate cavalry officer in the late difficulty. Runs him some cattle over east of here and he takes no nonsense from anybody."

"He's a fair man," Hinge added, "a decent man . . . and that worries me. Balch an' Saddler aren't decent, not by a damn sight."

"Saddler the fat one?"

"It looks like fat, but he's tough as rubber, and he's mean. Balch is the voice and the muscle, Saddler is the brain and the meanness. They come in here about three, four years ago with a few head of mangy cattle. They bought a homestead off a man who didn't want to sell, and then they both homesteaded on patches of water some distance off.

"They've crowded the range with cattle, and they push . . . they push all the time. They crowd Stirrup-Iron riders and Stirrup-Iron cattle, and they crowded the cattle of some other outfits."

"Like Spur?" I suggested.

They all looked at me. "Like Spur . . . crowded him until he sold his brand to Stirrup-Iron and left the country."

"And the major?"

"They leave him alone. Or they have so far. If they crowd him, he'll crowd back . . . and hard. The major's hands don't scare like

some of the others. He's got a half dozen of his old Confederate cav-
alrymen riding for him."

"What about Stirrup-Iron?"

Hinge glanced at Roper. "Well . . . so far it's been kind of a hands-
off policy. We avoid trouble. Just the same, come roundup time we'll
ride in there after our cattle, calves and all."

We ate up. The bacon was good and the coffee better. I ate four
rolls dipped in bacon grease and felt pretty good after my fifth cup of
coffee. I kept thinking about that third man. The others had been
cowhands, but the third man . . . I knew him from somewhere.

Most of the last three years I'd been riding the the outlaw trail.
Not that I was an outlaw. It was just that I liked the backbone of the
country, and most of the outfits I'd worked for since leaving the home
ranch had been along the outlaw trail. I'd never crossed the law at any
point and had no notion of it, but I suspect some of the outlaws thought
I was a cattle detective, and more took me for some kind of a lone
hand outlaw. It was simply that I had a liking for rough, wild country . . . the high-up and the far-out.

My brother Barnabas . . . named for the first of us ever to come
across from England . . . he took to schooling and crossed the ocean to
study in England and France. While he learned the words of Rousseau,
Voltaire and Spinoza, I was cutting my educational teeth on the plains
of the buffalo. While he courted the girls along the old Boul' Miche,
I busted broncs on the Cimarron. He went his way and I mine, but we
loved each other none the less.

Maybe there was a wildness in me, for I had a love for the wind
in the long grass blowing, or the smell of woodsmoke down some rocky
draw. There was a reaching in me for the far plains, and from the first
day that I could straddle a bronc it was in me to go off a-seeking.

Ma held me as long as she could, but when she saw what it was
that was choking me up with silence she took down a Winchester from
the gunrack and handed it to me. Then she taken a six-shooter, holster,
belt and all, and she handed them to me.

"Ride, boy. I know it's in you to go. Ride as far as you've a mind
to, shoot straight when you must, but lie to no man and let no man
doubt your word.

"It is a poor man who has not honor, but before you do a deed,
think how you will think back upon it when old age comes. Do nothing
that will shame you."

She saw me to the door and when I started to saddle my old roan,
she called after me. "No son of mine will go forth upon a horse so old

as that. Take the dun . . . it's a wicked one he is, but he'll go until he drops. Take the dun, boy, and ride well.

"Come back when you're of a mind to, for I'll be here. Age can seam my face as it can the bark of an oak, but it can put no seams in my spirit. Go, boy, but remember you are a Sackett as well as a Talon. The blood may run hot, but it runs strong."

They were words I still remembered.

"We'll ride home in the morning," Hinge said. "We will talk to the major, too."

"Who's your boss? Who runs the Stirrup-Iron?"

Danny Rolf started to speak, but shut up at a look from Roper. It was Hinge who replied. "An old man," he said, "and a kid girl."

"She ain't no kid," Danny said, "she's older'n me."

"A girl-kid," Roper added, "and the old man is blind."

I swore.

"Yeah," Roper said, "you'd better think again, mister. You ain't in this like we are. You can ride on with a clear conscience."

"If a man can ever leave a pair like Balch and Saddler behind and still have a clear conscience. No," I said, "I ate of your salt, and I'll ride for the brand if they'll take me on."

"What's that mean?" Danny asked. "That about the salt?"

"Some folks think if you eat of somebody's bread and salt it leaves you in debt . . . or something like that," said Hinge.

"That's close enough," I said. "Are you boys quitting?"

There was no friendly look in their eyes. "Quittin'? Who said anything about quittin'?"

"Goin' against a tough outfit for a blind man and a girl," I said, "just doesn't make sense."

"We ain't about to quit," Roper said.

I grinned at them. "I'm glad I ate that salt," I said.

Chapter 2

The ranch house on the Stirrup-Iron was a low-roofed house of cottonwood logs chinked with adobe, its roof of poles covered with sod where grass had sprouted and some flowers grew.

Nearby were three corrals of peeled poles, and a lean-to barn with an anvil at one end, as well as a forge for blacksmithing.

It was a common enough two-by-twice outfit with nothing special about it. Others of its kind could be found in many parts of Texas and other plains states. Only when we rode down the long, gradual slope toward the house did we see a man standing in the yard with a rifle in the hollow of his arm.

He must have agreed with what he saw, for he turned on his heel, seeming to speak toward the house. Then he walked back to the bunk-house which lay across the hard-packed yard facing the shed.

A thin blonde girl stood on the steps, hair blowing in the wind, shading her eyes to see us.

Joe Hinge said, "Ma'am, I brought you a hand."

"He's welcome, and when you've washed, come up for supper."

She looked after me as we rode to the corral and stripped the gear from our horses.

"Who was that with the rifle?" I asked.

"You'll see," Danny cautioned, "but step light and talk easy. He's a neighbor."

"How many hands do you have?"

"We're them," he explained. "Harley comes over to help, some-times. He's got him a rawhide outfit over east against the break of the hills."

The bunkhouse, also of logs, was long and narrow with bunks along the sides and a sheet-iron stove at the end. There was a pile of dusty wood near the stove with somebody's socks drying on it, and a fire-blackened coffeepot atop the stove.

Four of the bunks had rumpled bedding and four had no bedding at all, only cowhide for springs, lashed to each side of the bed frame with rawhide strings.

Coats and slickers hung on pegs along the wall, and there were a couple of benches and a table with one slightly short leg. A kerosene lamp stood on the table, and there was another in a bracket on the wall near the stove. There were two beat-up lanterns sitting along the wall.

The floor was scuffed and dusty, not looking like it had been swept in a while, but I'd grown up with Ma watching and knew that wouldn't last. Outside the door there was a washstand with a broken piece of mirror fastened to the log wall with nails, and a roller-towel that had been used forty or fifty hands too long.

Rinsing the basin I washed my hands and combed my hair, looking in the mirror at the man I was: a man with a lean, dark face and sideburns and a mustache. It was the first time I'd seen myself in anything but water for three or four months, but I didn't seem to have changed much. The scar where a bullet cut my hide near a cheekbone was almost gone.

Danny came out and slicked back his hair with water. A cowlick stuck up near the crown of his head. "The grub's good," he said. "She's a mighty fine cook."

"She does the cooking?"

"Who else?"

I whipped the dust from my clothes with my hat, drew the crease a mite deeper and started toward the house, my eyes sweeping the hills around, picking out the possible places for anyone watching the place. They were few, as the hills were bare and lonely.

There was a picket fence around a small bare yard in front of the house and a few pitiful, straggly flowers. A stone-flagged walk led to the door, and the table inside was spread with a red and white checked cloth. And the dishes were kind of blue enamel and a chipped enamel coffeepot.

There was a fine looking beef stew steaming on the table, and an apple pie on the sideboard . . . dried apples, of course, but it looked good. There was also a pot of beans, some crab-apple jelly and slices of thick white bread looking fresh from the oven.

She was even thinner than I'd thought, and her eyes were bluer. "I am Barby Ann." She gestured to the head of the table. "And this is my father, Henry Rossiter."

He had the frame of a once-big man, and the hands and wrists of one who must have been powerful. Now he was grizzled and old, with a walrus mustache and white hair that was too long. There was no sight to his eyes now, but I'd have known him anywhere.

"Howdy," I said at the introduction, and his head came up. He looked down the table at me, his eyes a blank stare, yet with an intentness that made me uneasy.

"Who said that?" His voice was harsh. "Who spoke?"

"It's a new hand, Father. He just rode in with the boys."

"We had us some words with Balch and Saddler," Hinge explained. "He stood with us."

Oh, he knew, all right! He knew, but he was shrewd enough to ask no more questions . . . not of me, at least.

"We can use a hand. You ready for war, son?"

"I was born ready," I said, "but I ride peaceful unless crossed."

"You can ride out if you're of a mind to," Rossiter said, "and if you ride west or north you'll ride safe. You ride south or east in this country and your chances of getting through are mighty poor . . . mighty poor."

Hinge explained what had happened with Balch and Saddler in a slow, casual tone that made enough of it but no more, leaving nobody in doubt.

Barby Ann ate in silence. Twice she looked at me, worried-like, but that was all. Nobody talked much, as it was not the way of ranch folk to talk much at supper. Eating was a serious business and we held to it. Yet at my home there'd been talk. Pa had been a man given to speaking, an educated man with much to say and all of us had the gift of gab. We talked, but amongst ourselves.

When we were down to coffee and had the pie behind our belts, Rossiter turned his dead eyes toward Hinge. "There will be trouble?"

"Reckon so. I just figure he aims to keep us this side of the caprock, no matter whose cattle run up yonder. Unless we're ready to fight, we just ain't a-going to get 'em."

Rossiter turned his eyes in my direction, and he wasn't off-center one whit. "Did you see any Stirrup-Iron cattle?"

"I wasn't keeping count. I'd guess fifteen, maybe twenty head along where I rode. Probably twice that many Spur."

"There will be trouble then. How many hands does he have?"

"Hinge was careful. He thought a minute, then shrugged. "No tellin'. He had eight, but I hear he's been hirin', and there was a man with him I'd never seen before."

The boys finished off and headed for the bunkhouse but Danny lingered, sort of waiting for me. I held on, then gave it up and stood.

"You," Rossiter said. "You set back down. You're a new hand and we'd better talk." He turned his head. "Good night, Danny."

"Good night," Danny said grudgingly, and went out.

Barby Ann went to the kitchen, and he said, "What did you say your name was?"

"You know what it is," I said.

"Are you hunting me?"

"No, I was just drifting."

"Seven years . . . seven years of blindness," Rossiter said. "Barby Ann sees for me. Her an' Hinge. He's a good man, Hinge is."

"I think so."

"I've got nothing. When we've made our gather and drive, there won't be much. Just what I owe the hands, and supplies for a new year . . . if we can round up what we have and get to the railhead with the herd."

He put his hand to the table, fumbling for his pipe and tobacco. Just when I was about to push it to him, his hand found it. He began loading his pipe.

"I never had anything. It all turned sour on me. This here is my last stand . . . something for Barby Ann, if I can keep it."

"She'd be better off in some good-sized town. There's nothing here for a girl."

"You think there is in them towns? You know an' I know what's in them towns, and her with nothin' put by. This here is all I got, an' it's little enough. You could take it all away from me right now, but you'd still have a fight on your hands."

"You borrowed trouble, Rossiter. I don't want your outfit. You cheated your friends and you've only got what you asked for."

"Ssh! Not so loud! Barby Ann don't know nothing about them days."

"I'll not tell her."

"Your ma? Is Em still alive?"

"Alive? Em will die when the mountains do. She runs the outfit since Pa died, and she runs it with a tight hand."

"She scared me. I'll admit to that. I was always afraid of your ma, and I wasn't alone. She put fear into many a man. There was steel in that woman . . . steel."

"There still is." I looked across the table at him. He was still a

big old man, but only the shell remained. I remembered him as he was
when I was a boy and this man had come to work on the Empty.

He had been big, brawny and too handsome, a good hand with
a rope. And he knew stock. We had been short-handed and he did the
work of two men. But the trouble was, he was doing the work of three,
for at night he'd been slipping away from the ranch and moving cattle
to a far corner of the range.

Pa had been laid up with a badly injured leg, and Ma was caring
for him, and this big young man had been always willing to help, but
all the while he was stealing us blind. Yet he had helped us through
a bad time.

He left suddenly, without a word to anyone, and it had been two
days before we knew he was gone and almost a week before we knew
anything else was wrong. It was Ma who got suspicious. She took to
scouting, and I was with her when we found the corral where he'd been
holding the stock. By that time he had been gone nearly two weeks.

It was a box canyon with a stream running through it, and Henry,
as we knew him then, had laid a fence of cottonwood rails across the
opening.

There were indications there had been four men with Henry when
he drove the cattle away. We knew the hoof tracks of Henry's horse,
and they were all over the place. Ma sent me back to the house after
Barnabas and one of our hands, as well as a pack horse.

"Tell your pa we're going after the cattle. It may take us a while."

When we got back, Ma was long gone down the trail, so we taken
off after her. Them days, she mostly rode a mule, so her tracks were
mighty easy to follow.

We found where the four extra men had camped, while waiting
for Henry to tell them to come in and drive the herd. Judging by the
tracks, they had five or six hundred head. It was a big steal, but on a
place the size of ours—and us shorthanded—it hadn't been so difficult.
All he'd done was to move a few head over that way each time he rode
out, and then gradually bunched them in the canyon.

On the third day we caught up with Ma, and on the fifth day we
caught up with them. We'd no cattle to drive, so we'd come along fast.
Ma was from Tennessee mountain stock, nigh to six feet tall and raw-
boned. She was all woman, and where she came from women were
women. She could ride as well as any man and use a rifle better than
most, and she'd no liking for a thief. Especially one who betrayed a
trust like Henry had done.

She wasted no time. We came up on them and Ma never said aye, yes, or no, she just cut loose. She had left her Sharps .50 at home but she had a Spencer .56, a seven-shot repeater, and she let drive. Her first shot emptied a saddle.

Coming down off the hill, we stampeded the herd right into them.

Henry, he lit a shuck out of there. He knew Ma would noose a rope for him and he lit out of there like somebody had lit a brushfire under his tail.

The other two taken off up a canyon and, leaving a hand to gather the stock, we taken out after them. We run them up a box canyon and Ma, she throwed down on them with that Spencer and she told it to them.

"You can throw down those guns an' come out with your hands up, or you can die right there. An' I don't care a mite which it is. Also, you might's well know. I ain't missed a shot since I was close on five year old and I ain't about to start now."

Well, they'd seen that first shot. She was nigh three hundred yards off and in the saddle when she pulled down on that moving rider, and she'd cut his spine in two. They only had their six-shooters and there was Ma with her Spencer, and Barnabas an' me with our Winchesters.

Where they stood, there wasn't shelter for a newborn calf, whilst we were partly covered by the roll of the hill and some brush. They decided to take a chance on the law, so they dropped their guns.

We brought them out and hustled them to the nearest jail and then went to the judge. We were a hundred miles from home then, and nobody knew any of us.

"Cow thieves, eh?" The judge looked from Ma to me. "What you think we should do with 'em?"

"Hang 'em," Ma said.

He stared at her, shocked. "Ma'am, there's been no trial."

"That's your business," Ma said quietly. "You try them. They were caught in the act with five hundred of my cattle."

"The law must take its course, ma'am," the judge said. "We will hold them for the next session of court. You will have to appear as a witness."

Ma stood up, and she towered above the judge, although he stood as tall as he was able. "I won't have time to ride back here to testify against a couple of cow thieves," she told him. "And the worst one is still runnin'."

She walked right down to the jail and to the marshal. "I want my prisoners."

"Your prisoners? Well, now, ma'am, you—"

"I brought them in, I'll take them back." She took up the keys from his desk and opened the cell doors while the marshal, having no experience to guide him, stood there jawing at her.

She rousted them out of their bunks and, when one started to pull on his boots, she said, "You won't need those," and she shoved him through the door.

"Now, ma'am! You can't do this!" The marshal was protesting. "The judge won't—"

"I'll handle this my own way. I'm the one who made the complaint. I am withdrawing it. I'm going to turn these men loose."

"Turn them loose? But you said yourself they were cow thieves!"

"They are just that, but I haven't the time to go traipsing across the country as a witness, riding a hundred miles back home, then a hundred miles up here and maybe three or four such trips while you bother about points of law. These are my prisoners and I can turn 'em loose if I want."

She herded them down to the horse corral in their long johns, where she picked out two rawboned nags with every bone showing. "How much for them?"

"Ma'am," the dealer shook his head, "I'd not lie to a lady. Those horses got no teeth to speak of, an' both of them are ready for the bone yard."

"I'll give you ten dollars apiece for them, just as they stand."

"Taken," he said quickly, "but I warned you, ma'am."

"You surely did," Ma agreed. Then she turned to the cow thieves, shivering in the chill air. "You boys git up on those horses . . . *git!*"

They caught mane-holts and climbed aboard. The backbones on those old crow-baits stood up like the tops of a rail fence.

She escorted them out of town to the edge of the Red Desert. We rode a mite further and then she pulled up. "You boys steal other folks' cows, but we ain't a going to hang you . . . not this time. What we're goin' to do is give you a runnin' start.

"Now my boys an' me, we got rifles. We ain't goin' to start shootin' until you're three hundred yards off. So my advice is to dust out of here."

"Ma'am," the short one with the red face pleaded, "these horses ain't fit to ride! Let us have our pants, anyway! Or a saddle! Those backbones would cut a man in two, an'—"

"Two hundred and fifty yards, boys. And if he talks any more, one hundred yards!"

They taken out.

Ma let them go a good four hundred yards before she fired a shot, and she aimed high. That old Spencer bellowed, and those two gents rode off into the Red Desert bare-footed and in their underwear on those raw-backed horses, and I didn't envy them none a-tall.

That was Ma, all right. She was kindly, but firm.

Chapter 3

We drove our cattle home, but Ma never forgave or forgot the man we knew as Henry. He had betrayed a trust, and to Ma that was the worst of sins. Now he was here, across the table from me, blind and only a shell of the fine-looking big man we remembered.

Without a doubt, his hired hands had no idea of the kind of man he had been and still might be. As cowhands they were typical. When they took a man's wages, they rode for the brand, for loyalty was the keynote of their lives. They would suffer, fight and die for their outfit at wages of thirty dollars a month . . . if they ever got them.

They did not know him, and could be forgiven their ignorance. I did know, so what was I going to do?

It was a question I did not consider. It was Balch who had made my decision for me, back there at our first meeting. For there was something about such a man, prepared to ride roughshod over everybody, that got my back up.

There was range enough for all, and no need to push the others off.

"I'll stick around, Rossiter," I said. " Hinge tells me you're going to round 'em up soon?"

"We are. There are only six ranches in the Basin, if you want to call it that, but we're going to round up our cattle, brand them, and drive to the railhead. If you want to stay, we can use you. We'll need all the hands we can get."

There was a checker game going in the bunkhouse when I walked in. There were not enough checkers, so Hinge was using bottle corks— of which there seemd to be an ample supply.

Hinge threw me a quick, probing glance when I came in, but

307

offered no comment. Roper was studying the board, and did not look up.

Danny was lying on his back in his bunk with a copy of a beatup magazine in his hands. "You stayin' on?" he asked.

"Looks like it," I said, and opened up my blanket roll and began fixing my bed on the cowhide springs.

Hinge made his move, then said, "You'll take orders from me then, and we'll leave the stock west of here until the last.

"We've got one more hand," he added. "He's away over east tonight, sleepin' in a line-shack." He glanced at me. "You got any objections to ridin' with a Mexican?"

"Hell, no. Not if he does his work. We had four, five of them on my last outfit. They were good hands . . . among the best."

"This man is good with stock, and a first-class man with a rope. He joined up a couple of weeks back, and his name is Fuentes."

Hinge moved a king, then said, "We start rounding up in the morning. Bring in everything you see. We'll make our big gather on the flat this side of the creek, so you'll just work the breaks and start them down this way.

"There's grub at the line-shack, and you and Fuentes can share the cooking. You'll be working eight to ten miles back in the rough country most of the time."

"How about horses?"

"Fuentes and Danny drove sixteen head up there when he went, and there's a few head of saddle stock running loose on the range."

Hinge paused. "That's wild country back in there, and you'll run into some old mossyhorn steers that haven't been bothered in years. You're likely to find some unworked stuff back there, too, but if you get into thick brush, let Fuentes handle it. He's a brush-popper from way back. Used to ride down in the big thicket country."

At daybreak the hands scattered, but I took my time packing. Not until I had my blanket roll and gear on a packhorse and my own mount saddled did I go to the house for breakfast.

Henry Rossiter was not in sight, but there was movement in the kitchen. It was Barby Ann.

"You weren't in for breakfast, so I kept something hot."

"Thanks, I was getting my gear ready."

She put food on the table, then poured coffee. She filled two cups.

"You're going to the line-cabin?"

"Is there only one?"

"There were two. Somebody burned down the one that was west of here, burned it down only a few weeks ago."

She paused. "It's very wild. Fuentes killed a bear just a few weeks ago. He's seen several. This one was feeding on a dead calf."

"Probably killed by wolves. Bears don't kill stock as a rule, but they'll eat anything that's dead."

She had curtains in the windows and the house was painfully neat. There must have been at least three more rooms, although this seemed to be the largest.

"You met Mr. Balch?"

That 'mister' surprised me, but I nodded.

"He's got a fine big ranch, he and Mr. Saddler. He brought lumber in from the eastern part of the state to build the house. It has shutters and everything."

It seemed to me I detected a note of admiration, but I could not be sure. Women-folks set store by houses and such. Especially houses with fixings.

She should see our house up in Colorado, I thought. It was the biggest I'd ever seen, but Pa had been a builder by trade and he designed it himself—and did most of the work himself. With Ma helping.

"Roger says—"

"Roger?" I interrupted.

"Roger Balch. He's Mr. Balch's son. He says they are bringing in breeding stock from back east, and they will have the finest ranch anywhere around."

Her tone irritated me. Whose side was she on, anyway? "Maybe if you're so friendly you should tell him to leave your father's hands alone, and to let us gather our cattle where they happen to be."

"Roger says there's none of our cattle up there. His pa won't have anybody coming around his place. I've told father that, and I've told Joe, but they won't listen."

"Ma'am, it's none of my business yet, but from the way your Mr. Balch acted, I'd say your pa and Joe Hinge were in the right. Balch acted like a man who'd ride roughshod over everything or anybody."

"That isn't true! Roger says that will all change when he tells his father about—"

She stopped.

"About you and him? Don't count on it, ma'am. Don't count on it at all. I've known such men here and there, and your Mr. Balch doesn't shape up like anyone I'd want any dealings with. And if he has any plans for that son of his, they won't include you."

She went white, then red. I never saw a woman so angry. She stood up, and her eyes were even bigger when she was mad. And for a moment I thought she'd slap me.

"Ma'am, I meant nothing against you. I simply meant that Balch wouldn't want his son tying up with anybody he could ride over. If he wants somebody for his son, it will be somebody big enough to ride over him. The man respects nothing but money and power."

Riding away from there I figured I'd talked out of turn, and I'd been guilty of hasty judgment. Maybe I'd guessed wrong on Balch, but he seemed like he didn't care two whoops for anything, and had I not been there to more or less even things up he might have been a whole lot rougher.

I wondered if Hinge and the boys knew that Barby Ann was seeing Roger.

Somehow, I had an idea they knew nothing about it, nothing at all.

Riding over the country, I could see they'd had a dry year, but this was good graze, and they had some bottoms here and there where a man could cut hay.

Riding over country I was going to have to work, I took my time, topping out on every rise to get the lay of the land. I wanted to see how the drainage lay, and locate the likely spots for water. Fuentes would fill me in, but there was nothing like seeing the land itself. Terrain has a pattern and, once the pattern is familiar, finding one's way about is much easier.

As I went east, the hills grew steeper and more rugged. Turning in the saddle I could see the cap-rock far off against the sky. What lay behind me was what was loosely called the Basin, and far off I could see the tiny cluster of buildings that was Stirrup-Iron headquarters.

It was midafternoon before I sighted the line-shack. It lay cupped in a hand of hills with a patch of mesquite a few yards off and a pole corral near the cabin.

A rider's trail came down off the hill into the trail to the cabin—a trail that looked fresh. In the corral were a number of horses, yet not more than a half dozen, one of them still damp from the saddle.

The cabin was of logs that must have been carted some distance, for there were no trees around. They had been laid in place with the bark on, and now, years later, the bark was falling off. There was a washstand at the door and a clean white towel hanging from a peg.

Tying my horses to the corral bars, and with my Winchester in my right hand and my saddlebags and blanket roll in the left, I walked up to the cabin.

Nothing stirred. A faint thread of smoke pointed at the sky. I tapped on the door with the muzzle of my rifle, then pushed it open.

A lean Mexican with a sardonic expression was laying on his back on a bunk, with a six-shooter in his hand. "*Buenos dias, amigo . . .* I hope," he said smiling.

I grinned at him. "I hope, too. I'm in no mood for a fight. Hinge sent me up to watch you work. He told me he had a no-account Mexican up here who wouldn't do any more work than he could help."

Fuentes smiled, rolling a thin cigar in his fine white teeth. "Of all he might say, that would not be it. I was sent to gather cattle. Occasionally, I gather them, and occasionally I lie down to contemplate where the cattle might be—as well as the sins of men. More often I just look for cattle to gather. I am trying to figure out," he swung his boots to the floor, "the number of miles to catch each cow. Then if I figure the wages they pay me, the expense of keeping horses for me to do the work, I should be able to figure out whether it is good business to catch cows."

He paused, brushing the ash from his cigar to the floor. "Moreover, some of these steers are *big*, very, very big, and very, very mean. So I lie down to contemplate how to get those steers out of the canyons."

"No problem," I said, "no problem at all. You send back to the ranch for one of those screw jacks. If they don't have one there, go to town. If you go to town you can always have a drink and talk to the senoritas.

"You get one of those screw jacks . . . You know, the kind they lift buildings with when they wish to move them? All right. You get one of those. Better yet, get several. You go back of the east rim of the country, and you stick them under the edge and you start turning. You turn and turn and turn, and when you get the country tilted high enough, the cattle will just tumble out of the canyons. And you wait here with a big net and you bag them as they fall out. It is very simple."

He picked up his gunbelt. "I am Tony Fuentes."

"And I am Milo Talon, once of Colorado, now of anywhere I hang my hat."

"I am of California."

"Heard of it. Ain't that the land they stacked up to keep the ocean from comin' in over the desert?"

Fuentes pointed toward the coals of a dying fire, and the blackened pot. "There are beans. There are also a couple of sage hens under the coals, and they should be ready to eat. Can you make coffee?"

"I'll give it a try."

Fuentes stood up. He was about five-ten and had the easy movement of a bullwhip. "Did they tell you anything down there? About Balch?"

"Met him . . . along with Hinge and some others. I didn't take to him."

We ate, and he filled me in on the country. The water was mostly alkali or verging on it. The country looked flat, but was ripped open by deep canyons in unexpected places. Some of these canyons had grassy meadows, some thickets of mesquite. There was also a lot of rough, rocky, broken country.

"There are cattle back in those canyons that are ten years old and never been branded. There's even a few buffalo."

"About Balch," I said.

"A bad one . . . and some other bad ones with him."

"I'm listening."

"Jory Benton, Klaus, Ingerman and Knuckle Vansen. They get forty a month. His regular hands get thirty, and Balch has passed the word that any of his hands who prove themselves will also get forty."

"Prove themselves?"

Fuentes shrugged. "Rough stuff against anybody who gets in the way . . . like us."

"And the major?"

"Not yet. Saddler doesn't think they are strong enough. Besides, there are other considerations. At least, that is what I think, but I am only a Mexican who rides a horse."

"Come daylight you can show me. Want to tackle some of the big stuff?"

"Why not?"

The mosquitos were getting bad so we moved indoors. Besides, it was cooling off. At the door I turned to look around.

It was a nice little hollow, undistinguished but nice. The sun was setting behind us, leaving a faint brushing of pink along the clouds. Somewhere an owl hooted.

The cabin floor was hard-packed but it had been swept. The fireplace was obviously little used. It too was neatly swept, with a fire laid. No doubt it was pleasant to cook outside.

"Balch has a son? Roger, I think his name is?"

Fuentes features became bland. "I think so. I see him here and there."

"Big man?"

"No . . . not big. Small. But very strong, very quick . . . and how do you say it? Cruel."

Fuentes sat silent, considering the subject. "He is very good with his hands. Very good. He likes to punish. The first time I see him is in Fort Griffin. He has beaten a woman there, a woman of the dance halls. He has beaten here badly, and her man comes after Balch . . . a big man, ver' strong.

"Roger Balch moves in very fast. He bobs his head to get in close and then he hits short and hard to the belly. He beats that big man, but finally they pull him off, and in Fort Griffin they do not stop a fight for nothing. It was bad, senor, bad."

Fuentes took out another of the cigars and lighted it. He waved the match out with a gesture. "You have reason for asking, amigo? Some particular reason?"

"Oh . . . not exactly. Heard some mention of him."

Fuentes drew on his cigar. "He rides . . . wherever he will. Rides very much. And he seeks trouble. I think he tries to show himself better than anyone else. He likes to fight big men, to beat them."

It was something to remember. Balch bobbed his head, threw short punches from in close. Probably he had done some boxing, learned how to fight big men, and that would give him an advantage. For most men knew only about fighting what they had learned by applying it. So a man who knew something of boxing would have little trouble.

It was a thing to remember.

Chapter 4

We rode into the broken hills before the sun rose, across thin, scant pasture drawn tight over cracked white rock. It was high country with no edge but the sky until we rode into the canyons, but here and there were bones, bleached by wind and sun, grass growing through the rib cages where once had been beating hearts. Among other bones, some burned-out wagons.

"Some pioneer," I said, "played out his string."

Rusted rims of wagon wheels, the solid oak of a hub, scattered bolts and charred wood. It was not much for a man to leave behind.

Fuentes indicated the bones. "You and me, amigo . . . sometime."

"I'm like the Irishman, Fuentes. If I knew where I was going to die, I'd never go near the place."

"To die is nothing. One is here, one is no longer here. It is only that at the end one must be able to say 'I was a man.'"

We rode on. "To live with honor, amigo. That is what matters. I am a vaquero. They expect little of me, but I expect much of myself.

"What is it a man wants? A few meals when he is hungry and, at least once in his lifetime, a woman who loves him. And, of course, some good horses to ride."

"You have forgotten two things: a rope that does not break, and a gun that does not hang when one starts to draw."

He chuckled. "You ask too much, amigo. With such a rope and such a gun a man might live forever!"

We began to see cattle. I swung out toward four or five that were feeding nearby and started them drifting. They would not go far, but they would move easier when we came back with more cattle. Ours was to be a slow job and a dusty one, to roust out these cattle and start them toward the flat country.

This was rough, broken country, and the mesquite thickets were mixed with prickly pear, some of the largest I'd ever seen. I wished for a leather jacket, or one of heavy canvas. Fuentes had a tight buckskin jacket that was some help to him. We plunged into the brush, rousting out the cattle. Some of the old mossyhorn steers were as quiet as cougars in the thick brush, moving like ghosts.

When we got them out of the brush, they'd circle and make a dash to get back. We both rode good cutting horses, but they had to work. We kept the cattle moving.

Sweat trickled down my back and chest, under my shirt, and my skin itched from the dust. When we paused there were the black flies. I'd worked cattle all my life, but this was some of the roughest.

Often the draws were empty. We would follow them to where they ended and find nothing. In others there were little gatherings of cattle, four or five, sometimes more. By noon we had started fifty or sixty head down toward the flat with only a little young stuff.

The sun was past the midmark when Fuentes topped out on a rise and waved his sombrero at me. It was a magnificent hat, that one. I envied the Mexicans their sombreros.

When I joined him, he said, pointing with his hat, "There is a spring down there, and some shade."

We walked our horses along the slope and into a pocket of hills. Two huge old cottonwoods grew there, and some willows. Further downstream there was much mesquite.

It was a mere trickle of water from the rocks, and a small pool where the horses could drink. A stream that ran a mere seventy yards before vanishing into the ground.

We stepped down and loosened the girths a little, and let the horses drink. Then we drank, ourselves. Surprisingly, the water was cold and sweet, and not brackish like most of the springs and water holes.

Fuentes lay down on the grassy slope in the shade, his hat over his eyes. After a few minutes, he sat up suddenly and lit the stub of one of his cigars. "You see something, amigo?"

"There isn't much young stuff, if that is what you mean."

"It is what I mean. There should be calves. There should be yearlings. We've seen nothing under two years old, almost nothing under three."

"Maybe," I said, too seriously, "these cattle go over to Balch and Saddler to drop their calves. Or maybe these cows just don't have calves."

"It is a thing," Fuentes agreed. He looked at the glowing end of his cigar. "I will be unhappy, senor, if we find that Balch's cows have twins."

Fuentes went to the spring for another drink. It was very hot, even there in the shade. "Amigo, I am suddenly hungry. I am hungry for beef. There's a nice fat steer that carries a Balch and Saddler brand. Now if we—"

"No."

"No?"

"It might be just what they want, Tony, so they could say we were rustling their beef. You mark that steer in your mind—and all the steers with doubtful brands."

"And then?"

"At the roundup. We'll peel a hide at the roundup. Right in front of witnesses. We'll be sure there are witnesses, sort of accidental-like on purpose, so when we take that hide off we'll have a lot of people watching."

Fuentes stared at me. "You would skin that steer right in front of Balch? You'd do that?"

"You or me . . . one to skin, one to watch so nobody stops him."

"He will kill you, amigo. He is good with a gun, this Balch. I know him. He has men who are good with guns, but none so good as him. They do not know this, but I know it. He will not shoot unless he must. He will let others do his shooting, but if he must—"

"He'll either shoot or ride," I said quietly, "because once we peel a hide wearing his brand, and they see it has been worked over, he'll either leave or have his neck stretched."

"He is a hard man, amigo. He does not believe anybody would dare, nor will he let them dare."

I got to my feet and put on my hat. "I'm a mighty narrow-minded man. These folks hired me to ride in their roundup. They hired me to round up their cattle . . . all their cattle."

We split up again, and each went into the canyons. We saw nobody, nor did we see tracks except those of cattle. Twice we came upon buffalo—once a group of five, the other time a lone bull. He was in no mood to be disturbed so I circled and went my way, leaving him pawing the earth and rumbling in his huge chest.

Once I put a loop over the horns of a big steer who promptly charged. My horse was quick, but tired, and just barely dodged the charge. And then we raced for a tree with the steer after us, and we did a flat-out turn around the tree and I snubbed him tight.

He snorted and blew, tugged and crashed one horn against the tree, but it was sturdy and held its place. Wild-eyed, he peered up at me, undoubtedly thinking of all he would do if he got free. I walked my horse into the shade and wondered why we had come so far without additional horses, when Fuentes came through the brush riding a short coupled bay, with black mane and tail and leading a roan.

"Meant to get the horses before nooning," he said. "I got to worrying about those brands."

We moved into the slight shade of some mesquite clumps and I switched my saddle. "I'll take your horse back." He pointed. "There's a corral . . . an old one . . . over there."

"Water?"

"*Si* . . . good water. It is an old place. A Comanchero place, I think."

He glanced at the steer. "Ah? So you have the old devil? Three times I have chased that one!"

"I wish you'd caught him. He nearly got me."

Fuentes chuckled. "Remember the bones, amigo! Nobody lives forever!"

I stared after him as he rode away, leading my horse. "Nobody lives forever," he said, "and nobody does . . . but I want to!"

The horse was a good one, and he put in a hard afternoon. By the time Fuentes had come along, he was played out.

Now he was leading a big old ox, heavymuscled and slow. "Amigo, this is Ben Franklin Ox. He is old and slow, but very wise. He will tie him together with your wild one, then we will see what happens!"

A good neck-ox—which Ben Franklin Ox certainly was—could be worth his weight in gold to an outfit with wild steers to bring out of the brush, and Ben Franklin knew his job. We tied them together and left them to work it out. Of course, unless the wild one died, Ben would bring him in a few days from now, right to the home corral at the ranch. If the steer died, we'd have to track them down and release Ben.

We fell into bed that night too worn-out to talk, almost too tired to eat. Yet at daybreak, I was outside washing in ice-cold water when Fuentes came out, rubbing his eyes.

"How many head, do you think?"

"Hundred . . . more probably, along with what we've got on the trail."

"Let's take them in."

He got no argument from me. Fuentes was a good enough cook, better than me, but the food Barby Ann put out was better. We'd ride in, deliver our stock, catch a fast meal and start back.

"The old corral?" He squatted on his heels and drew a map in the dust. "It is here? You see? I will cook something, you take our horses and bring back mounts for us. Better bring our own horses, too, so we can leave them at the ranch."

Saddling up, I lit out, leading his horse. It was only a few miles, and I did not relish leaving the dun out there so far from home. Ma gave me that dun, and it was a fine horse who understood my ways.

The way he had shown was closer than the way we had gone while rounding up steers, so it was no more than a half hour before I topped out on a rise in thick brush and glimpsed the corral not more than half a mile off. Suddenly, I pulled up, standing in my stirrups.

It looked to me like somebody . . .

No, I must be mistaken. Nobody would be at the corral. After all . . .

Yet I rode cautiously, and came down into the clearing smelling dust . . . My own? Or had somebody been there? The horses had their heads up, looking over the corral bars toward the east, where the old trail led off toward the once-distant settlements. I thought I had seen somebody, but had I? Was it just a trick of the eyes? Of the imagination?

Slipping the thong from my pistol, I walked on up to the corral and glanced toward the old cabin. Keeping a horse between me and it, I stripped my gear, roped a fresh horse and then called the dun to me.

As I worked, my eyes swept the ground. Tracks . . . fresh tracks. A shod horse, and well-shod at that.

Saddling the fresh horse, an almost white buckskin with black mane and tail and four black legs, I listened and looked, without seeming to.

Nothing.

Turning my horse into the corral, I checked the trough through which the spring had been guided to be sure there was water.

There was . . . but there was something else, too. There were a couple of green threads caught in the slivers at the edge of the trough—the sort of thing that might happen if a man bent over to drink from the pipe and his neckerchief caught on the slivers.

I took them in my hand, then tucked them away in my shirt pocket.

Somebody had been at the corral. Somebody had drunk here, but why had they not come by the line-shack? In cattle country, even an enemy would be welcomed at mealtime, and many a cattleman in sheep country had eaten at sheep wagons. In a country where meals and food might be many miles apart, enmity often vanished at the side of the table.

Balch had not hesitated to come to our fire, nor would his men be likely to. Yet somebody had come here and had ridden swiftly away, somebody who had deliberately avoided our line-shack, which everybody in the country was sure to know.

Leading my horse and that of Fuentes, as well as a fresh horse for him, I started back.

Fuentes had suggested that Roger Balch was a trouble hunter, so it was unlikely that he would hesitate to stop by. Nor Balch, either, for that matter.

Saddler? I had an idea Saddler spent little time out on the range. What of that other man? The one who seemed somehow familiar?

Irritably, I rode back. There was a lot going on that I did not like. One thing I had done before leaving the corral, and that was to look to see how the tracks had pointed, and they had gone east, a man riding a horse with a nice, even stride . . . a horse more carefully shod than many a western horse I'd seen.

"Balch leaves the major alone?" I asked suddenly.

Fuentes glanced at me. "Of course. You do not think—" He broke off and then he said, "Balch may have other ideas. You see, the major has a daughter."

"A daughter?" The thought made no connection and Fuentes saw it, smiling tolerantly.

"The major has a daughter, and the largest outfit anywhere around. And Balch has a son."

"Then—?"

"Of course . . . And why not?"

Why not, indeed, But where did that leave Barby Ann?

Chapter 5

As we moved back what cattle we had, our work was cut out for us. Most of the stock had kind of settled down, but there were two or three hardheaded old mossyhorns who would keep cutting back and trying to head for the breaks, and the worst of all was a lean old cow with one horn growing across, in front of her skull, and one perfectly set for hooking, and she knew it.

We'd had unusually good luck. Time and again I've combed the breaks for cattle on one outfit or another and come up with nothing, or only a few head. Of course, this was the beginning, and it would get tougher as we went along, and the cattle more wary.

Right now, most of them hadn't decided what was happening. Hopefully, by the time they did they'd be at the ranch and mixing with the growing herd on the flat.

It was sundown before we got in. Danny and Ben Roper were down on the flat with about sixty head. I scanned their gather and then looked over at Fuentes, who had cut in close to me. "Same thing here," I commented. "No young stuff."

Joe Hinge was in front of the bunkhouse with a man I hadn't seen before, a lean, hungry-looking man with no six-shooter in sight but a rifle in his hand. He had careful blue eyes and an easy way about him.

"Talon, this here's Bert Harley. He's a neighbor of ours, helps out once in a while."

"Pleased," he said, bobbing his head a little. Seemed to me there was a kind of a stop in his eye movement when Hinge said my name, but it could have been imagination.

"He'll help with the night herding. And we'll need all the help we can get."

Harley strolled over to the corral and flipped out a loop to catch up a horse. I poured water into the tin basin and rolled up my sleeves.

"Looked that bunch over?" I said to Hinge.

"You mean the size of it? You an' Tony must've worked your tails off."

"Look at 'em."

"I got to see the Old Man. What is it, Milo? What's wrong?"

"No young stuff."

Hinge had taken a couple of steps toward the house. Now he turned back. His eyes were haunted as he looked toward the cattle.

"Talon, we just got to find them. Those folks need ever' cent they can get. That girl . . . Barby Ann . . . she'll have nothing when the old man dies. Not unless we can make it for her. You know what that means? A girl like her? Alone and with nothing?"

"It's no accident," I told him, washing my hands. I splashed water on my face and looked hopefully at the roller towel. I was in luck . . . this one hadn't been up more than two days and I found a clean spot. "I've worked a lot of country and never seen so few calves. Somebody's been doing a mighty sly job of rustling."

"Balch!" Hinge's face tightened with anger. "That—!"

"Take another look at it," I said. "We've got no evidence. You brace Balch with something like that and you'll be shootin' the next minute. I'll admit he's an unpleasant sort of character, but we don't know nothing."

I paused. "Joe, do you know of anybody who might have been over our way today? A man on a nice-moving, easy-stepping horse with a long, even stride . . . almost new shoes."

He frowned, thinking. "None of our boys were over that way, and the only horses I know of that move like that belong to the major."

"You see somebody?" He looked at me. "It might have been the major's girl. She rides all over the country. You're liable to run into her anywhere. That girl doesn't care where she is as long as she's in the saddle."

"Be careful what you say about Balch," I warned. "I don't think Barby Ann would like it."

"What?" He had started off again. "What's that?"

"She's been talking to Roger. I think she's sweet on him."

"Oh, my God!" Hinge spat. "Of all the damn fool—!" He turned on me again. "That's nonsense! She wouldn't even—"

"She told me herself. She's serious about him, and she thinks he is."

He swore. Slowly, violently, impressively. His voice was low, bitter and exasperated.

"He's bad," Hinge said slowly, "a really bad man. His pa is rough, hard as nails, and he'll ride roughshod over everybody, but that son of his . . . he does it out of sheer meanness."

He walked on up to the house and I stood there. Maybe I should have kept my mouth shut, but that girl was walking into serious trouble. If Roger was thinking of the major's daughter . . .

But what did I know? And the one thing I did know was that there was no figuring out what went on in a woman's mind. Or a man's either, for that matter. I could handle horses, cattle, and men with guns, but when it came to human emotions I was a poor excuse for a prophet.

A girl like her, growing up in a place like this, would meet few men, and fewer still that would cause her to start dreaming. Roger Balch, whom I'd not met, was obviously young, not too far from her own age, and he was a rancher's son . . . Class had more to do with such things than most folks wanted to admit.

Fuentes and me, figuring to start back as soon as we could, were first at the table. First, that is, except for Harley. He was going to be riding night-herd on the stuff we had gathered in, so he was eating early.

"You boys made you a good day of it," Harley said when we sat down. "That's a mighty lonely country over there . . . or so I hear."

"You haven't been over there?"

"Off the track for me. My place is south of here. When a man's batching it, and workin' his own place, he doesn't have much time to get around."

"You runnin' cows?"

"A few scrubs. I'll get me some good stock someday. Takes a man a while to get started."

He wasn't joking about that. I had seen a number of men start from nothing and build ranches, and it was anything but easy. If a man had good water, and if there was plenty of open range, he had a chance. I'd seen many of them start, and a few who lasted.

"If I was going to try it," I commented, "I'd try Wyoming or Colorado. The winters are hard but there's good grass and plenty of water. That is, in the mountain country."

"Heard of it," Harley admitted, "but this here's where I'll stay. I like a wide open country where I can see for miles . . . But a man does what he can."

"Had a friend who favored Utah," Ben Roper commented. "There's country where no white man has ever seen. Or so he told me."

"Them Blues," Harley began, then cut himself off short, "them

Mormons . . . I hear they're a folk likes to keep among their own kind."

"Good folks," I said. "I've traveled among 'em, and if you mind your ways you'll have no trouble."

We talked idly, and ate. Barby Ann was a good cook, and Roger Balch was missing a bet if that was what he wanted. I had an idea his father was thinking about an alliance. The major was the one man who made Balch and Saddler hold their fire, but if they could marry him into the family . . .

Harley rode off to begin his night watch on the cattle, and we finished our supper, taking our time. We'd decided to start back that night, and not wait for morning.

Joe Hinge hadn't a word to say, all through supper, but when it was over he followed me outside. "Ben tells me you're a gunfighter."

"I've ridden shotgun a few times, but I wouldn't call myself a gunfighter."

"Balch has some tough men working for him."

I shrugged. "I'm a cowhand, Joe, jut a cowhand. I'm a drifter who's just passin' through. I'm not hunting any kind of trouble."

"I could use a man who was good with a gun and didn't mind usin' it."

"I'm not your man. I'll fight if I'm pushed, but a man would have to push pretty hard."

We stood there in the dark. "You an' Fuentes gettin' along?"

"He's a first-class hand," I said, "and a better cook than me. Why shouldn't I like him?" I paused, then asked, "Harley stayin' here or his place?"

"Back an' forth. He's got stock to take care of. Lives away back in the breaks of the hills. I don't wonder he likes to work around . . . Lonely place."

"You've been there?"

"No, but Danny was once. He rode over there after Harley one time. Had himself a time locatin' him. But that's Danny. He's a fair hand but he couldn't find a church steeple in a cornfield."

It was moonlight when we started back, loaded up with grub for a good long stay. Fuentes was an easy-riding man, and working with him was as I liked it, no strain.

And for the next four days we worked ourselves to a frazzle and had little to show for it. Where there had been cattle a few days ago, now there were none. Fuentes was a brush-popper who knew his business, and riding the brush was both an art and a science. None of your big, wide loops would work here. You saw a steer, and then you didn't, if you got him in the open at all, it was in a clearing your horse could cross in three or four jumps. And if you got a rope on him, you had to send it in like a bullet, and just wide enough to take him. In among the ironwoods, prickly pear and mesquite, you had no chance to build a loop . . . it was like casting for fish, only your fish weighed from a thousand to fifteen hundred pounds—and some of them would run heavier.

Fuentes could do it. And he had done it, and carried the scars of a lifetime in the brush. It was a business that left scars. You wore heavy leather chaps, a canvas or leather jacket and you had tapaderos on your stirrups so a branch wouldn't run through your stirrup and dump you or stab your horse.

We worked hard, and in four days we rounded up just nine head, and it didn't make sense.

"There's tracks, Tony," I said, "lots of tracks. It doesn't figure." We were eating.

He put his fork down, staring out the door, thinking. "There is one I am thinking of," he said, "a little red heifer. Maybe two years old, very pretty, but very wise for one so young. Every day I saw her, every day she eluded me, every day she was back, but since we have come back, I do not see her."

"Maybe she found herself somebody else to chase her," I said, amused. "They all do sooner or later."

He took up his fork again. "I think maybe you have said something, amigo. I think tomorrow we will not hunt cows."

"No?"

"We will hunt . . . maybe a little red heifer. Maybe we find her . . . maybe we find something else. I think we will take our rifles."

We went out at daybreak, and I rode the bay with the black mane and tail. It was a cool, pleasant morning, and we ate a quick breakfast. Fuentes led the way toward our hidden spring, and as he neared it he began casting back and forth, suddenly to draw rein and point: "See? Her track. Two days . . . maybe three days old."

She had drunk at the pool below the spring, and then had moved off, browsing, as cattle will, along with several others. We followed them out of the hollow and up on the high country beyond, yet it was almost noon before there was a change.

"Amigo? Look!"

I had seen it. Suddenly the wandering ceased and the little red heifer took on direction. She was going straight along now, hurrying occasionally, and she was with several others whose browsing had been interrupted. The reason was immediately obvious:

The track of a horse!

Now more cattle, brought in from the north, more cattle being driven east toward the hills. Another rider.

"If they see us," I suggested, "they will see we follow a trail. Let us spread out, as if searching for strays, but let us keep within sight of one another."

"*Bueno,* amigo." He cut off from me, occasionally standing in his stirrups as if looking. But we kept on, first one and then another cutting the trail of the small herd . . . at least thirty head now . . . perhaps more.

It was no wonder we had found no cattle. Somebody was deliberately driving them away from us.

Occasionally they let the cattle drift while they rounded up more, until at the end of what was obviously several days' work they had made a gather of at least a hundred head.

"They drive them far," Fuentes said, "but I am puzzled. If they wish to steal them, why not drive south, no?"

A thought came to me. "Maybe they do not plan to steal them, Fuentes. Maybe they just hope to keep us from sellin' them. If we don't get them to the roundup, they won't be sold."

"And if they are not?"

"Then Rossiter won't have as much money as he may need. Maybe then he will lose the ranch, and maybe then somebody will buy it who knows there are more cattle than Rossiter thinks he has."

"It is a thought, amigo, a very likely thought, and it is another way of stealing, no? Senor Rossiter believes he has few cattle left, he is in trouble, he sells for little, when there are truly many cattle."

"There's one thing wrong, I think. Aside from your little red heifer, I didn't see the tracks of much young stuff. These are steers, some cows . . . their hoofs are a little sharper . . . but very few young ones."

We made dry camp in the hollow atop a ridge, a sheltered hollow that allowed us to have a fire after the darkness came, by using buffalo chips for fuel. It was a high ridge, with a good view, and after we had eaten we left the coffeepot on the coals and went out on the ridge to look over the country. Above was a vast field of stars, but we scarcely saw them. We looked for another kind of light . . . a fire.

"You know this country best," I said. "Where do the ranches lie from here?"

He thought about that for an instant. "We are too far east, amigo. This is wild country where no man rides, only the Comanches or the Kiowa sometimes, and for them we must be wary.

"Back there lies the major's place . . . It is the closest. Away to the horizon yonder is where Balch and Saddler are."

"And Harley?"

"He has no ranch, amigo, only a homestead, I think, a very small place. He is there." He pointed at a place nearer, yet still some distance off.

"Tony?" I pointed. "Look there!"

It was—and not more than a mile away—a fire. A campfire in wild country!

Chapter 6

This country was wild and lonely, and there was reason for it. East of us, the ranches were pushing west from Austin and San Antonio; and west of us, a few venturesome ranchers were trying to settle in the Panhandle country. But this area where we were was a hunting ground and traveling route of the Kiowas and the Comanches who raided into Mexico.

It was Apache country, too, mostly Lipans, I believed, but I was no expert on this area of Texas. Most of what I knew was campfire talk . . . An army patrol had been massacred south of us two years before, and a freighter trying a new route toward Horsehead Crossing had been attacked, losing two men and all of his stock.

A rider for one of the Panhandle outfits had cut loose to go on his own and had tried settling down in this country. He lasted through one hardworking spring, fighting sleet, dust storms and late frost. The country killed his crops and the Indians got his cattle. When he tried riding out, leaving in disgust, they got him.

His cabin was somewhere south and east of us. Everybody had heard of it, but nobody knew exactly where it was. There were also rumors of some big caves in the country, but those we had yet to see.

Neither Fuentes nor me had any great itch to ride any closer to that campfire, although we were curious. If it was Kiowas, it was a good chance to lose hair, and the same for Lipans or Comanches. Anyway, we could ride down there tomorrow and, if they had pulled out, as seemed likely, we could put almost as much together by studying the remains of camp as if we actually saw it alive from close up.

A greenhorn might have tried slipping up on that camp. And if he was a good man at outguessing Indians, he might get close and get away . . . but he might not either.

It never seemed wise to me to take unnecessary chances, and Fuentes was of the same mind. We were way past that kid stage of daring somebody, or doing something to show how big and brave we were.

That was for youngsters not dry behind the ears. We moved when we thought it right to move, and we fought when the chips were down, but we never went around hunting trouble.

After studying that fire we went back and turned in, letting our horses keep watch for us.

We'd been lyin' there a while when I spoke out. "Tony, there's something wrong about this."

"*Si?*" His voice was sleepy, yet amused. "Somebody stealing cows, no?"

"Maybe . . . All we've got is some idea that cows have been moved, and the cows that were moved are a mixed lot. On the other hand, the cattle that are missing are young stuff.

"The old stock somebody might try to steal. But the young stuff? It's mostly too young to sell with profit, which means that whoever has the young stuff intends to hold it a while . . . And of course the young stuff hasn't been branded."

Fuentes said nothing and he was probably asleep, but it kept me awake a while, thinking about it. If all they wanted was young stuff, why had they broken the pattern and stolen older stock?

At daybreak we rolled out and had coffee over a buffalo-chip fire. We ate a little jerky and biscuit and then crawled into the saddle and left out of there. We taken a roundabout route and cut down into the bottom where we'd seen the cattle.

There was quite a bit of timber down there, and some rough, broken country. We saw no cattle at first, then a scattering of stuff, most of it wearing Stirrup-Iron brands. There was a sprinkling of Spur stuff, too, and we started them drifting toward home . . . knowing a few of them might keep going, but that we'd have to round up and push most of them.

We taken our time, scouting around as if hunting strays, but working closer to where the campfire had been. It was nigh onto two hours after sunrise when we came up on the camp.

It was deserted. A thin feather of smoke stood above the coals, which had been built with care not to let the fire get away. Two people had been in the camp, and they'd had two packhorses. One of the men carried a rifle with a couple of prongs on the butt plate that would kind of fit over the shoulder at the armpit. I'd seen another such gun some years back, and some fancy boys had them. I never cared for them myself, but it was easy to see that was his kind of gun, because wherever he put it down he left that mark in the ground.

Fuentes saw them too. "We'll know him when we see him," he commented, dryly. "It isn't likely there's more than one like that in the country."

Two men, and they had camped here at least two days and possibly longer. There were other signs of camping, too, so the place had been used more than once. We saw a big old brindle steer with a white nose that would weight eighteen hundred easy. There were a couple of others with him, one an almost white longhorn cow with a splash of red along one hip.

Fuentes was starting to haze them back when I had an idea. "Tony, let's leave them."

"What?"

"Let's leave them and see what happens. You'd know that brindle steer or white cow anywhere, so let's just see where they show up."

He nodded. "*Bueno,* I think that's a good idea."

The truth was that we'd know every head we saw that day. A man working cattle develops a memory for them—and the crowd they run with, so when we started back we had more than twenty head for our ride. It took some doing, like always, but it helped that they were headed back to their home range . . . even though their range was nowhere as good as what we were leaving.

Riding gives a man time to think—and to look. A man riding wild country has busy eyes if he hopes to stay alive, but a cowhand has them naturally. He learns to spot trouble before he comes close to it, and his eyes can pick out a bogged steer or one with screwworms. A good horse will smell screwworms when a man can't see the steer for the brush, and he will locate cattle where a man can't see them.

It was hot, dusty riding, and the black flies hung about us in a swarm. We picked up two three-year-old steers on the drive back. They just saw our cattle and joined up, as cattle will, and Fuentes and me, knowing they would be spooky, kept clear of them.

We were almost back to the line-shack when we saw a rider.

"Ah!" Fuentes grinned. "Now you will see her!"

"Her?"

He gestured at the rider. "The major's daughter. Be careful, senor. Sometimes she thinks she is the major."

She came riding toward us on as pretty a gray gelding as you ever saw, riding sidesaddle on something I'd never seen before, a black patent-leather saddle. She wore a kind of riding habit in checkered black and white—a fine check—and a black hat, black polished boots and a white blouse.

She gave me a quick glance that missed nothing, I'd guess, and then nodded to Fuentes. "How are you, Tony?" She glanced at the cattle. "Any T Bar T stuff in there?"

"No, senorita, only Stirrup-Iron and Spur."

"Mind if I have a look?"

"Of course not, senorita."

"Just don't spook those two speckled three-year-olds," I suggested. "They're edgy."

She threw me a glance that would have cut a wide swath at haying time. "I've seen cattle before!"

She rode around our gather, studying them, and mostly they paid her no mind. Then she cut in close to those steers and they taken one quick look at the sun shining off that patent-leather sidesaddle and they taken off, and it took some hot fast work by Tony an' me to hold our bunch together.

I pulled in close to her. "Ma'am, you go tell your papa to wipe behind your ears before you come out on the grass again, will you?"

Her face went white, and she took a cut at my face with her quirt. It was one of those woven horsehair-handled quirts in green and red, a pretty thing. But when she cut at my face with it, I just threw up my hand, caught the quirt and jerked it out of her hand.

She had a temper, that one did. She lost hold of the quirt, but she didn't stop. She grabbed for her rifle in its scabbard, and I pushed my horse alongside hers and put my hand over the butt of the gun so she couldn't draw it.

"Just take it easy," I said coolly. "You wouldn't shoot a man over something like this, would you?"

"Who the hell said I wouldn't?" she flared.

"You'd better also tell your papa to wash your mouth out with soap," I said, "That's no word for a lady to use."

She was sashaying around, trying to get away from me, but that little bay I was riding knew its business and was staying right close to her gray gelding. For three or four minutes we kicked up dust, sidling around on the prairie until she saw it was no use.

Maybe she cooled down a little. I don't rightly know, but she called over to Fuentes, who was sitting his saddle watching. "Fuentes, come and get this man away from me."

Tony walked his horse over and said, "I do not want you to shoot him, senorita. He is my compadre."

"I'll say this for you," I said. "You may have the devil of a temper, but you sure are pretty."

Her eyes narrowed a little. "The major will have you hung for this," she told me, "if the boys don't get to you sooner."

"Why don't you fight your own battles?" I asked. "You're a big girl now. No need to call on your papa to help you, *or* the big boys at the ranch."

"Stop calling him my papa!" she said angrily. "He's 'the Major!'"

"Oh, I'm sorry," I said, "I didn't know he was still in the army."

"He's not in the army!"

"Then he isn't a major, is he? I mean, he's a used-to-be major, maybe?"

She didn't know what to say to that. Defensively, she said, "He's the major! And he was a major . . . in the Civil War!"

"Well, good for him. I knew a couple of them, up north. There was one used to clerk in a hotel where I stayed, and then I punched cows with a colonel up Wyoming way. Nice fellas, both of them."

My face was smooth, my voice bland. Suddenly she said, "I don't think I like you!"

"Yes, ma'am," I said politely, "I gathered that. When a girl comes after me with a quirt . . . well, I sort of get the feeling she doesn't care for me. I'd say that wasn't really the romantic approach."

"Romance?" Her tone was withering. "With *you?*"

"Oh, no, ma'am! *Please!* Don't talk about romance with me! I'm just a drifting cowboy! Why, I'd never even think of romance with a daughter of the major!"

I paused. "Anyway, I never start courting a girl the first time I see her. Maybe the second time. Of course, that depends on the girl.

"You—," I canted my head on one side. "Well, maybe the third time . . . or the fourth. Yes, I think so. The fourth time."

She swung her horse around, glaring at me. "You! You're impossible! Just wait! Just you wait!"

She dashed away, spurring her horse. Fuentes pushed his sombrero back on his head and looked woeful. "I think you are in big trouble, amigo. This one . . . she does not like you, I think."

"I think, too," I said. "Let's get on with the cattle."

The two three-year-olds were gone, and neither of us were of a mind to follow or try to recover them. Besides, they'd be skittish now, and we'd be lucky to even get close.

We drifted along behind our cattle. Several times I thought I heard movement in the brush, as though the young ones were following along, but soon we were out on the open plain and they did not appear.

So she was the major's daughter? The one Roger Balch was supposed to be trying to round up . . . or so the talk went. Well, he could have her.

Still, she was pretty. Even when she was mad, she was pretty—very pretty. I chuckled. And she had been mad.

We bunched the cattle in a corral and bedded down for the night.

"Those steers," I suggested, "maybe they'll come up during the night."

Fuentes shrugged, and then he said, "It is Friday tomorrow."

"There's one most every week," I said.

"On Saturday there is a, what you call it, social at the schoolhouse."

"A box social?" I asked skeptically.

"*Si* . . . and I think of these cattle that they need to be with the herd. They will be restless and they might get away . . . somehow. It is in my mind that we should drive them in."

"Well," I agreed thoughtfully, "I do think they should be with their kinfolk. Of course, while we're over yonder we might's well stop by and see how they run that social affair."

"*Bueno*," Fuentes agreed seriously. "And you will see a dozen, maybe two dozen head of the finest looking girls in Texas."

"And that's pretty fine lookin' by any man's standards," I agreed. "You been to these box socials before? Here, I mean?"

"Often . . . whenever there is one."

"Who makes the best box?"

He shrugged. "Ann Timberly . . . the major's daughter."

"Next best?"

"Maybe Dake Wilson's daughter . . . maybe China Benn."

"China Benn? That's a girl?"

He kissed his fingers. "Ah! And such a girl!"

"She and Ann Timberly friends?"

"*Friends?* But no, senor! The major's daughter does not like her! Not one little bit! China is too . . . too . . ." he made gestures to indicate a rather astonishing figure.

"Good!" I said. "I know whose box I'm bidding for."

Fuentes just looked at me and shook his head. "You are a fool, a very great fool, but I think I shall enjoy this social."

He paused. "China Benn is beautiful. She is also the girl Kurt Floyd likes."

"If she's as pretty as you say, there must be a lot of men who like her."

His smile was tolerant of my ignorance. "Not as long as she is Kurt's girl." We were making camp in the lee of a low hill, a little way from the corral. We were hoping those steers would come up during the night and they might . . . if we weren't too close. "Floyd is *mucho grande*, amigo. How you say? He is *big!* He is also strong. He does not fight with a gun, like a gentleman, but with his fists. We Texans do not like to fight with fists. It is what we call 'dog-fighting,' you see?"

"You're a Texan? I thought you were from California?"

He shrugged. "When I am in Texas, I am a Texan. On the other side of the border I am a Mexican. It is political, you see?"

"All right, I see your point. Has this Floyd ever really beaten anyone?"

"There was One-Thumb Tom, there was George Simpson . . . a hard fight, that one. There was Bunky Green . . . only two punches, I think."

"You will introduce me to China?"

"Of a certainty. Then I shall stand back and watch. It will be so sad . . . you are so young! To see one so young demolished. Well, so be it."

"If you were a true friend," I suggested, "you'd offer to fight him while I get away with the girl."

"Of course. And I am a true friend. Up until I introduce you to China Benn . . . Then I shall be an observer, amigo, a spectator, an interested spectator, if you will, but a spectator only. Any man who endeavors to court China Benn in the presence of Kurt Floyd needs only sympathy."

"In the morning then," I said, "we will drive those steers to the home ranch. We will bathe, wash behind the ears, brush the dust from out boots and join the rush to . . . where is this fandango, anyway?"

He chuckled. "At Rock Springs Schoolhouse. And Rock Springs Schoolhouse is on the Balch and Saddler range, and Kurt Floyd is the Balch and Saddler blacksmith. And remember this, amigo. You will get no sympathy from the major's daughter. She detests China Benn."

"I remember now. You told me that before. Now I wonder how I ever forgot!"

Chapter 7

Henry Rossiter went with Barby Ann in a buckboard with Ben Roper and Danny— Fuentes and me riding a-horseback alongside.

The schoolhouse was built on a low knoll with the spring from which it took its name about twenty-five yards off. There must have been a dozen rigs around the place, mostly buckboards, but there was one Dearborn wagon, a surrey and an army ambulance among them.

As for riding stock, there looked to be forty or fifty horses under saddle. I wouldn't have believed there were that many people in the country but, as I was to discover, it was just like other western communities and some of the folks had been riding all day to get there. Parties, dances and box dinners were rare enough to draw a crowd at any time.

Saddler was just pulling up. On the seat beside him was a thin, tired-looking woman whom I discovered was his wife. Also beside him, a lean but heavy-shouldered man was dismounting. "Klaus," Fuentes whispered. "He gets forty a month."

When opportunity offered, I glanced at him. He was no one I knew, but he was wearing a gun and, unless I was mistaken, had another under his coat but tucked behind his belt.

Somebody was tuning up a fiddle, and there was a smell of coffee on the air.

Suddenly, somebody said, "Here comes the major!"

He came in a surrey, spanking new, polished and elegant, surrounded by six riders. In the surrey itself were Ann, beautifully but modestly gowned, and the man who had to be the major . . . tall, square-shouldered, immaculate in every sense.

He stepped down, then helped his daughter to the ground. With them was another couple, equally well-dressed, but whose faces I could not see in the dim light. I knew none of the riders with them, but they were well set-up, square-shouldered men with the look of the cavalry about them.

Standing back in the shadows as I was, Ann Timberly could not see me as she went in, and I was just as pleased. I'd dug out an expensively tailored black broadcloth suit I had, and was wearing my Sunday-go-to-meetin' boots, polished and fine. I also wore a white shirt and a black string tie.

Ann was beautiful. No getting around it, she was beautiful and composed, and as she swept into the shoolhouse you had no doubt that Somebody had arrived. Her manner, I decided, would have been neither more nor less had she been entering the finest home in Charleston, Richmond or Philadelphia.

Yet she was only in the door when somebody let out a whoop in the near distance and there was a rush of hoofs. A buckboard wheeled up, coming in at a dead run and skidding to a halt with horses rearing. And as the buckboard halted, a man leaped from a horse and caught the driver as she dropped from her seat.

The man caught her and swung her around before putting her down, but immediately, and without looking back at either man or rig, she strode for the door.

I caught a glimpse of dark auburn hair, of green, somewhat slanted eyes, a few freckles over a lovely nose, and I heard somebody inside say, "Here's China!"

She swept into the schoolhouse, only a step behind Ann Timberly, and I followed, pushing among the crowd, taking my time. Somebody, I noticed, was caring for her team, but the big man who had lifted her from the buckboard was right behind me.

As he started to push me aside, I said over my shoulder, "Take it easy. She'll still be there when you get there."

He looked down at me. Now I am two inches over six feet and weigh usually about an even one-ninety, although my weight is often judged to be less, but beside this man I was a shadow. He was at least four or five inches taller, and he weighed a good fifty pounds more. And he was not used to anybody standing in his way.

He looked again, and started to push me aside. I was half-facing him now and as he stepped quickly forward, my instep lifted under his moving ankle and lifted the leg high. Off-balance, he tottered and started to fall. It needed only a slight move toward him to keep him off-balance. He fell with a thud, and instantly I bent over him. "Sorry. Can I help you?"

He stared up at me, uncertain as to just what had happened, but I was looking very serious and apologetic, so he accepted my hand and I helped him up. "Slipped," he muttered. "I must've slipped."

"We all do that occasionally," I said, "if we've had one too many."

"Now, see here!" he broke in. "I haven't been— "

But I slipped away into the crowd and walked down the length of the room. As I reached the end I turned and found myself looking into the eyes of China Benn.

She was across the room but she was looking at me, suddenly, seriously, as if wondering what manner of man I was.

Fuentes moved over beside me. "What happened, amigo?"

"He was shoving too hard," I said, "and I guess he slipped."

Fuentes took out a cigar. His eyes were bright with amusement. "You live dangerously, amigo. Is it wise?"

On a long table at the end of the room were stacked the box lunches the girls had packed, their names carefully hidden. It was simple enough. A box would be held up by an auctioneer and the bidding would begin, the box going to the highest bidder. And the buyer of the box would then eat dinner with the girl who prepared it.

Naturally, there was a good deal of conniving going on. Some of the girls always succeeded in tipping off the men they wished to buy their boxes as to just which ones they were. Knowing this, other cowhands, ranchers or storekeepers from the town would sometimes deliberately bid up a box to raise more money . . . the proceeds always going for some worthy cause . . . or simply to worry the man who wanted the box.

There was also a good deal of pride in having one's box bring a high price.

Fuentes whispered. "The biggest bids will be for the major's daughter or China Benn, although there's a plump blonde over by the door who'll do pretty well . . . And some of the older women have the best dinners."

The room was crowded. The desks and chairs had been taken out and stored in the barn for the evening, and the benches pulled back along the walls. A number of the men usually spent most of the evening outside, just talking. There were a good many youngsters of all ages running around underfoot, probably having more fun than any of us.

The girls seated themselves on the benches, some of them surrounded by friends.

Barby Ann came in, looking frail, pale and lovely. She looked quickly around. For Roger Balch, no doubt.

A small, pretty girl came in, a girl with large dark eyes wearing a somewhat faded but painfully neat gingham dress. She was, I realized after a second look, really not that pretty. Some might have thought she was quite plain, yet there was something about her, some inner spark of strength that appealed.

"Who is that?" I asked Fuentes.

He shrugged. "I never saw her before. Seems to be alone."

Looking around, my eyes met those of Ann Timberly. Deliberately, she turned her back on me. I chuckled, feeling suddenly better.

Everybody here knew everybody else, apparently. At least, most of them knew each other. Only a few knew me.

Balch came in suddenly, with Saddler and his wife beside him, and a slender, wolfish man whom I knew instantly. Why had not the name struck me when it was first mentioned by Fuentes?

Ingerman . . . one of Balch's men, and a gunman. Did he know me? I doubted it, although I had seen him Pioche and again in Silver City.

Ingerman was no working cowhand. He could do the work, and would, but only when he was drawing fighting wages. Balch and Saddler evidently meant business.

It needed only a few minutes of standing around and watching to see that the belles of the evening were Ann Timberly and China Benn, and if there was to be high bidding for boxes they would be the chief rivals. As for me, I was out for fun, as well as to show Ann Timberly that there were other girls about.

Fuentes had drifted off with some Mexican girls he knew, and Ben Roper was having a drink with some friends. So I was alone, just standing there, looking the crowd over, and I could see some of them looking me over, too.

After all, I was a stranger. The black suit I wore was tailored, and I was somewhat better turned out than most of the men around me. I'd had a liking, picked up from my father and carried on by brother Barnabas, for the better things of life, and so I indulged myself whenever my finances would allow. Though the mere fact of being a stranger at such a time was enough to attract attention.

The music began, and for the first two dances I merely watched. Both China Benn and Ann Timberly danced beautifully, but when on the third dance I decided to take part, I asked Barby Ann. She danced well enough, but her attention was elsewhere. She kept turning her head and looking about, and obviously she was alert for the coming of Roger Balch.

He came in suddenly, flanked by two men whom I judged from descriptions to be Jory Benton and Knuckle Vansen, two of Balch and Saddler's fighting men. They came in, led by Balch, who was a well-built man of not over five feet five, which was only an inch or so below the average. He also wore a dark suit, a gray shirt, black tie and he wore black gloves, which he did not remove. He also wore two guns, which though done occasionally, was far from customary. It was something I'd never seen at a dance.

He stopped, feet wide apart, his fists resting on his hips.

"That is Roger Balch?" I asked.

"Yes." I could sense that she wanted the dance to be over. It was not flattering, but I minded not at all, and knew how she felt.

"Why two guns?" I asked mildly.

She stiffened defensively. "He always wears them. He has enemies."

"He does? I hope those aren't for your father. He does not even carry a gun anymore, and he doesn't hire gunfighters."

She looked up at me suddenly. "What about you? I have heard you are a gunfighter?"

Now where had she heard *that?* "I've never hired out as a fighting man," I replied.

Something else had her attention. She looked up at me again. "What did you mean when you said my father did not wear a gun anymore? You spoke as if you had known him before."

"I merely assumed that before he lost his eyesight he had carried one. Most men do."

Fortunately, the music ended before she could ask any more questions, and I left her at the edge of the floor, near where her father sat. I was turning away when I was stopped. It was Roger Balch.

"You the man riding the MT horse?"

"I am."

"You want to come to work for Balch and Saddler?"

"I am working for Stirrup-Iron."

"I know that. I asked if you wanted to work for us. We pay fighting wages."

"Sorry. I like it where I am." I smiled. "And I am not a fighter. Just a cowhand."

Before he could say more, I strolled away from him and suddenly found myself face to face with Ann Timberly. She was all prepared for me to ask her to dance, and was ready to say no. It showed in every line of her. I looked at her, smiled, but I walked by her to China Benn.

"Miss Benn? I am Milo Talon. May I have this dance?"

She was a striking girl, vibrant and beautiful. Her eyes met mine and she was set to refuse. Then suddenly her manner changed. "Of course." She glanced over her shoulder. "Do you mind, Kurt?"

I got only a glance at the startled eyes of the big man, and then the music was playing. And China Benn could dance.

She could really dance, and the musicians knew it. Suddenly the tempo changed to a Spanish dance, but I'd spent some time below the border in Sonora and Chihuahua, and liked dancing Spanish style. In a moment we had the floor to ourselves . . . and she was good.

I caught one flashing glimpse of Ann Timberly, her lips tightly pressed with what I hoped was anger or irritation. When the dance ended, there was a round of applause and China looked up at me. "You dance beautifully, Mr. Talon. I did not think anyone here but Tony Fuentes could dance Mexican style so well."

"I used to ride down Sonora way."

"Well," she said "evidently you did more than ride. Let's do it again later, shall we?"

Leaving her, I glanced across the room and met the eyes of the girl in the faded gingham dress. Turning in midstride, I walked over to her. "Would you dance? I am Milo Talon."

"I know who you are," she said quietly, rising with just a touch of awkwardness. "Thank you for asking me. I was afraid no one would."

"You're a stranger?"

"I live here, but I've never come to a dance before, and I can't stay much longer."

"No? That's too bad."

"I . . . I have to get back. I am not supposed to be away."

"Where do you live?"

She ignored the question. "I just had to come! I wanted to see people, to hear the music!"

"Then I am glad you came."

She danced stiffy, holding herself with care, each step a little too careful. I did not think she had danced very much.

"Did you come with your father?"

She looked at me quickly, as if to wonder if there might be some knowledge in the question. "No . . . I came alone."

Every other girl here had come with someone, if not a man friend, then with her family or other girls, and there were no houses close by.

"You'd better find somebody to take you home," I suggested. "It's very dark out there tonight."

She smiled. "I ride every night . . . alone. I like the night. It is friendly to those who understand it."

I was surprised, and looked at her again. "You knew my name," I said then. "Not many here know it."

"I know more about you than any of them," she said quietly, "and if they knew who you really were they'd be astonished, all of them."

Suddenly, her manner changed. "Sometimes they seem so stupid to me! They are so pompous! So impressed with themselves! The major! He's really a nice man, I think, if he would drop that foolish title! He doesn't need it. Nor does she."

"Ann?"

She turned sharply and looked at me. "You know her?"

"We've met. I am afraid the meeting was not friendly."

She smiled, a little maliciously, yet I did not think there was any malice in her. "If they only knew who you were! Why, the Empty is larger than all their ranches! You run more cattle on your ranch than Balch and Saddler and the major combined!"

Now I was startled. "Now how did you know that? Who are you, anyway?"

"I am not going to tell you." She paused, and the music ended with us on the other side of the floor from where she had been. "It would mean nothing to you, anyway. I mean, you would not know the name."

"You aren't married?"

There was just a moment of hesitation. "No," she said then, "I am not." Then bitterly she said, "Nor likely to be."

Chapter 8

Fuentes drifted around the room. "Didn't know you knew our dances," he said. Then he said, more quietly, "Don't get too far away. There may be trouble."

Across the room, I saw Ben Roper walk over to stand near Danny Rolf. They were only a few steps from where Rossiter sat with Barby Ann. So far, Roger Balch had not approached her.

"What is it?"

Fuentes shrugged. "I don't know what nor where, but I've got a feeling."

My eyes swept the room. I knew nothing about Danny, but was not worried about either Fuentes or Roper. They would stand.

"On the boxes," I asked. "How do the bids usually run?"

"Ten dollars is mighty high. Mostly they start at a dollar, run up to three or five dollars. A five dollar bid will usually be high. I've only seen one go to ten . . . and that's a lot of money.

"Nobody but Roger Balch can afford a price like that, or maybe the major."

"What about Balch himself?"

Fuentes smiled. "You joke, amigo. Balch would not spend dollars on such a thing. He'll bid for a box, more than likely, but he will not go over three dollars."

"How about Ann Timberly's box?"

He glanced at me. "You are reckless, amigo. But it will bring three, probably as much as five."

"And China Benn?"

"The same."

"Tony?"

"*Si?*"

341

"The little one, the strange one. She came alone. She must go early, and she knows some things about me that nobody else knows . . . nobody here, at least."

He glanced at her, then at me. "I have said it. I do not know her, nor did I see her come. She knows something about you? Maybe she comes from where you do?"

"No . . . I know she does not. At least, she is no one I have ever known or known of. And there are no girls within fifty miles of our home ranch whom I do not know."

He chuckled. "I would place a bet upon that. You have a ranch, then?"

"We do . . . my mother, my brother and I."

"Yet you are here?"

"There's a promised land somewhere beyond the mountain. I was born to look for it."

"I, also. But we will never find it, amigo."

"I hope not. I was born for the trail, not for the journey's end." I paused. "We were born to discover and to build, you and I, for the others who will come after us. They will live in a richer, sweeter land, but we will have made the trails. We go where the Indian goes, and the buffalo. We will ride far lands where the only companions are wind and rain and sun."

"You talk like a poet."

I smiled wryly. "Yes, and work like a dog, often enough, but it's the poetry that keeps us going. It's my blessing or my curse, according to the way you believe, to live with awareness.

"All of them," I gestured at the room, "are living poetry, living drama, living for the future, only they do not know it, they do not think of it that way. Most of them heard stories when they were youngsters, stories told by men who had been over the mountain or had dreamed of it, and those who did not hear the stories read them in books.

"I talked to an old gunfighter once who told me he'd been a farm boy in Iowa when one day a man on a fine black horse rode into the yard. A man wearing buckskins and a wide hat. The man had a rifle and a pistol, and he wanted only to stop long enough to water his horse.

"The gunfighter talked him into staying for supper and spending the night. And he listened to the stories the man told of Indians and buffalo, but mostly it was the land itself, the far mountains and the plains, with long grass blowing in the wind."

Fuentes nodded. "It was so with me also. My father would come down from the hills and tell us of the bears he saw, or the lions. He would ride in dusty and tired, his hands stiff from the rope or the branding iron, from twenty hours of work in a single day, but he had the smell of horses and woodsmoke about him. And one day he did not come back."

"You and me, Fuentes. Some day we will not come back."

"With him it was Apaches. When his ammunition was gone, he fought them with a knife. Years later I lived among them and they told me of him. They were singing songs of him, and how he died. It is the way of the Indian to respect a brave man."

"We talk very seriously, Fuentes. I think I will bid for a box."

"I, also. But be careful, my friend, and do not get too far away. I have a bad feeling about tonight."

Folks were beginning to come in from outside and gather on benches and chairs where they could see the small platform from which the boxes would be offered. We could see them all there, in neat piles, some of them decorated with paper bows, some tied with carefully hoarded colored string, and you can bet most of the boxes were intended for somebody special.

It was Ann Timberly's box I wanted, but she didn't want me to have it, and probably wouldn't talk to me if I got it. But there's more than one way of doing things, and I had my own ideas.

China Benn . . . now there was a girl! But if I bid for her box I might tangle with Kurt Floyd, and on a night when the whole outfit might have trouble there was no time for private arguments. Anyway, I knew what I was going to do.

The bidding started. And from the first box it was animated. The first one to go was a buxom ranchwoman of forty-odd, her box going to an oldster, a onetime cowboy with legs like parentheses, his thin shoulders slighty stooped, but a wry twinkle in his eyes. He bought the box for a dollar and fifty cents. A second box went a moment later for two dollars, a third for seventy-five cents.

Often, other men deliberately avoided bidding, so that a certain man might buy a box at a price within his grasp. Others just as deliberately built up the price to tease some ambitious would-be lover, or somebody who'd be joshed about it later.

The auctioneer knew all the bidders, and usually knew which boxes they wanted, although there was much bidding just for amusement.

I watched, enjoying it, until suddenly a box I was sure was Ann Timberly's box was put up. From the comments by the auctioneer I was doubly sure, so when he asked for bids, I bid twenty-five cents.

Ann stiffened as if struck, and for a moment there wasn't a sound. Then somebody countered with a bid of fifty cents and the moment was past, but our eyes met across the room. Her face was white, her chin lifted proudly, but the anger in her eyes was a joy to see. I should have been ashamed of myself, but I was remembering how she had tried to hit me with a quirt, and her arrogance.

The box went to Roger Balch for five dollars and fifty cents.

China Benn's box went up, and somebody opened the bidding at a dollar. I countered with two dollars, and saw Ann turn to look at me. I did not bid again, and China's box finally went to Kurt Floyd for four dollars, largely because nobody wanted to bid against him and run into trouble. I'd have done it, but I had other ideas.

There was that quiet little girl in the faded gingham dress. I had a notion nobody might bid for her box, and I could see she had that notion, too. She was edging a bit toward the door, wishing she had not even come, afraid of being embarrassed and having to eat her dinner alone. No doubt it took a lot of nerve to come alone, and it began to look like her nerve had just about petered out.

Her box came up. I knew it was hers by the frightened way she reacted and the sudden move she made toward the door. Nobody knew her, and that counted against her, and also the fact that so many of the cowpunchers present, despite their loud talk, were really very shy about meeting a new girl.

Finally the auctioneer, seeing there would be no bidding, opened the bid with one of his own. He bid fifty cents and I came up with a bid of a dollar.

I saw her eyes turn to me, and she stopped moving toward the door. And then something happened.

Jory Benton bid two dollars.

Jory was young, good-looking in a kind of a flashy, shallow sort of way, and he was tough. I knew a little about him. He'd stolen a few head of stock here and there, had carried a gun in a couple of cattle wars. He wanted to be considered a bad man, but was nowhere nearly as tough as Ingerman, for example. That girl was nowhere and no way the type who should be with him, and being alone, he'd surely want to take her home. And there was nobody to tell him no.

And she knew it.

"Two-fifty," I said, casually.

Fuentes had drifted away, now he started back toward me, stopping a few feet away.

Jory had had a few drinks, but I was not sure if it was that, or if he really wanted the girl, or whether it was a deliberate matter of policy by Balch and Saddler, who were watching.

"Three dollars!" Jory said instantly.

"Three-fifty," I replied.

Jory laughed and said "Four dollars!"

The room was silent. Suddenly everybody knew something was happening. The girls's face was white and strained. Whoever she was, wherever she came from, she was no fool. She knew what was happening, and she could see it meant trouble.

"Five dollars," I said, and saw Danny Rolf turn away from the girl he was with and face toward the front of the room.

Jory laughed suddenly. He glanced right and left. "Let's get this over with," he said loudly. "*Ten* dollars!"

Even at forty dollars a month fighting wages, that was a strong bid, and he had no idea it would go any further.

"Fifteen dollars," I said quietly.

Jory's face tightened and for the first time he glanced at me. He was a little scared. I did not know how much money he had, but doubted whether he had more than that in his pocket, at least not much more.

"Sixteen dollars!" he said, but from his manner I figured he had about reached the end of it.

Suddenly from behind me there was a whisper. It was Ben Roper. "I got ten bucks you can have."

Keeping my manner as casual as possible, I said, "Seventeen."

Roger Balch pushed through the crowd behind Jory, and I saw him taking some coins from his pocket. He whispered something to Benton and Jory put a hand back for money.

He glanced quickly at what was in his hand. "Twenty dollars!" he said triumphantly.

"Twenty-one," I replied.

For a moment there was silence. The auctioneer cleared his throat. He looked hot and worried. He glanced at Roger Balch, then at me.

"Twenty-two," Jory said, but with less assurance. Roger had his feet apart staring at me. I suppose he was trying to bluff me.

"Twenty-three," I said casually. Deliberately, I put my hand in my pocket and took out several gold pieces. I wanted them to realize they were going to have to spend to win. At least, I'd know how badly they wanted to win, or if it was just an attempt to assert themselves.

Jory saw the gold pieces. They were twenty-dollar pieces and I had a handful of them. What I held in my hand was a good year's pay for a cowhand, and they could see it.

"Twenty-three dollars has been bid! *Twenty-three!* Twenty-three once! Twenty-three twice! Twenty-three three times!"

He paused, but Roger Balch was turning away and Jory was just standing there.

"Going . . . going . . . *gone!* Sold to the gentleman from Stirrup-Iron!"

The big groups broke up and scattered around the room, gathering into smaller groups. I crossed to the auctioneer to get my box.

Jory Benton was staring hard at me. "I'd like to know where you got all that money," he said belligerently.

I took the box with my left hand, smiling at him. "I worked for it, Jory. I worked hard."

With the box in hand, I crossed to the girl in the gingham dress. "This is yours, isn't it?"

"Yes." She looked up at me. "Why did you do that? All that money?"

"I wanted your box," I said.

"You don't even know me."

"I know you a little . . . And I know a good deal about Jory Benton, and I know you came alone."

"Thank you." We found a bench corner and sat down together. "I shouldn't have come," she said then, "but . . . but I was lonely! I can't stay much longer."

"We'll eat then," I said, "and I'll ride you home."

She was genuinely frightened. "Oh, no! You mustn't! I can't let you do that!"

"Are you married?"

She looked startled. "Oh, no! But I just *can't!* You must understand."

"All right . . . part way, then? Just to be sure you're safely on the way?"

"All right." She was reluctant.

"I've told you my name. Milo Talon."

"Mine is Clarisa . . . call me Lisa." She mentioned no other name and I didn't insist. If she did not tell me, she had her own reasons.

Her box dinner was simple, but good. There were some doughnuts that were about as good as any I'd ever eaten, and Ma made the best, yet my eyes kept straying across the room to where Ann Timberly sat.

Fuentes crossed to me with Ben Roper. I introduced them, and Fuentes said, "I think we ride together tonight, *si?*"

"I've got to ride along with Lisa," I said, "but only partway."

"We'll follow," Ben said, "an' you watch your step. Roger Balch didn't like his man bein' beat. He just didn't want to spend that much to win."

They drifted off a ways, and after a bit Danny Rolf joined them. The Balch and Saddler riders were bunching a little, too.

Dancing started again, and I danced with Lisa, then left her talking to Ben and crossed the room to Ann.

She turned as I came up and was about to refuse my suggestion of a dance when she suddenly changed her mind.

She danced beautifully, and I did all right. I'd danced more in better places than most cowhands have a chance to, and I could get around pretty good out there, even without a horse. Mostly cowhands don't dance too well, but they don't mind and neither do the girls. The cowhands can always hold the girl while she dances.

Everybody was having a good time. I kept my eyes open, but nowhere did I see a badge. If there was law anywhere about, it wasn't at this dance, which was something to remember.

"Who is she?" Ann asked suddenly.

"Lisa? She's a nice girl."

"Have you know her long?"

"Never saw her before."

"Well! She evidently makes quite an impression!"

"She didn't cuss me out," I said.

Ann looked up at me suddenly. "I am sorry about that. But you made me very angry!"

"So I figured. And when you get angry, you really get angry."

"That was mean, what you did."

"What?"

"Bidding a quarter for my box. That was just awful."

I grinned at her. "You had it coming."

"That girl . . . Lisa. How did you know which box was hers?"

"Saw her bring it in, and then when they were putting it up for bidding, she started to leave. She was afraid nobody would bid on it. I could see she was scared and embarrassed."

"So you bid on it?"

"Why not? You've got lots of friends. So has China."

"Oh . . . China. She's the most popular girl around here. All the boys want her box, and most of the older men, too. I don't see what they see in her."

"You do, too," I said, grinning at her, "and so do I. She's got a lot of everything, and she's got it where it matters." Suddenly I wondered. I had been so preoccupied with the bidding and the conversation that followed.

"The man who got your box," I said, "was the lucky one."

She ignored that, then commented, "Roger Balch usually gets what he wants." Then she added, with a touch of bitterness. "Nobody was bidding against him . . . at least, not for long."

"You cuss at people. How can you expect them to."

"I wouldn't want you to bid against him," she said seriously. "He's very mean and vengeful. If you won over him he would hate you."

"I've been hated before."

Suddenly, I thought of Lisa. She would be wanting to go, and she would be very apt to go alone.

Fortunately, the music stopped and at that moment Fuentes was at my elbow. "If you want Jory Benton to take that girl home, say so."

"I don't," I said. Then I said to Ann. "Maybe we'll be riding the same country again. And anyway, wherever I ride, I'll be looking for you."

"She went out," said Fuentes. "Jory followed."

She was tightening her cinch and Jory was standing by, leaning against a post. What he had been saying, I did not know. But as I walked up, he straightened.

"Just wait a minute," I said to her. "I'll get my horse."

"You don't need to bother," Benton said. "I was just telling the lady. I am talking her home."

"Sorry," I smiled. "I bought the box, don't you remember?"

"I remember, but that was inside. We were inside then. This here's different."

"Is it?"

There was a faint stir in the shadows nearby. My friends or his? Or bystanders?

"You got to go through me to take her," Benton said belligerently.

"Of course," I said, and knocked him down.

He wasn't ready for it. He wasn't ready for that at all. He might have been trying to pick a fight, or maybe just running a bluff, but I'd long ago discovered that waiting on the other man could get you hurt.

My hand had been up, sort of adjusting my tie, so I just took a short step to the left and forward and threw my right from where it was. The distance was short. He had no chance to react. He hit the ground hard.

"Better get up in the saddle, Lisa. I'd help you but I'd rather not turn my back."

Benton sat up slowly, shaking his head. It took a moment for him to realize what had happened to him. Then he got up quickly, staggered a little, still feeling the effects of the blow.

"I'll kill you for that!" he said hoarsely.

"Please don't try. If you go for a gun, I'll beat you to it, and if you shoot, I'll shoot straighter."

"Does that go for me, too?" It was Ingerman.

"If you ask anybody from the Roost to the Hole, Ingerman, they'll tell you I'm always ready."

He had been poised and ready, but now there was a sudden stillness in him. From Robber's Roost to the Hole-in-the-Wall, Brown's Hole or Jackson's Hole . . . all hideouts on the Outlaw Trail. Not many here knew what I had said, but Ingerman did, and suddenly he was wary . . . Who was I?

Yet there was still a need to keep him from losing face.

"We've nothing to fight about, Ingerman. Maybe the time will come, but not here, not about this."

Ingerman was no crazy, wild-eyed kid with a gun. He was ice-cold. He was a money fighter, and there was no money in this. And from the way I spoke, I was trouble. Nobody had told him to kill me . . . not so far.

"Just wanted to know where we stood," he said quietly. "Don't push your luck."

"I'm a careful man, Ingerman. Jory, here, was about to get himself hurt. I was trying to keep him from it."

There was a crowd around now, and two of them were Danny Rolf and Fuentes. Just the other side of Ingerman was Ben Roper.

"Mount up, Talon," he said. "We're all goin' home."

Ingerman heard the voice behind him, and he knew Ben Roper by sight and instinct. He turned away, and Jory Benton followed.

The night was cool and clear, there were many stars, and the wind whispered in the sage-brush. We started riding, and I had no idea where we were going.

Chapter 9

At first we did not talk. Behind us Ben Roper, Fuentes and Danny Rolf were riding, and I wished to listen. Nor did Lisa wish to talk, so we rode to the soft sound of our horses' hoofs, the creak of our saddles and the occasional jingle of a spur.

When we had several miles behind us, I left Lisa for a moment and rode back to the others. "This may be a long ride. No use for you boys to follow on."

"Who is she, Milo?" Ben asked.

"She hasn't told me. She came alone, and I somehow don't think her people knew she was gone . . . I don't understand the situation."

We were talking low, and Lisa, some distance off, could not overhear us.

"You watch your step," Danny warned. "It don't sound right to me."

When they took off and I rode back to her, we started on without comment. The country was growing increasingly rugged, with many patches of timber and brush that grew thicker as we rode.

"You came a long way," I commented, at last.

The trail, only a vague one, seldom used, dipped down into a narrow draw that led to a creek bottom sheltered by giant oaks and pecans. At a stream, Lisa drew up to let her horse drink.

"You have come far enough. I want to thank you very much, both for riding with me and for buying my box. And I hope there is no trouble with that man."

"There would be trouble anyway. He rides for Balch and Saddler."

"And you for Stirrup-Iron?"

"Yes."

Her horse lifted his head, water dripping from his muzzle. My own was drinking also.

350

"Do not be quick to judge," she said quietly, "I do not know either Balch or Saddler, but I know they are hard men. Yet I think they are honest men."

I was surprised, yet I said, "I haven't formed an opinion. Somebody is stealing cattle, however."

"Yes, I think so. I do not think it is Balch and Saddler, nor do I think it is Stirrup-Iron."

Again I was surprised. "You mean somebody thinks *we* are stealing?"

"Of course. Did you think you were the only ones who could be suspicious? Be careful, Mr. Talon, be very careful. It is not as simple as you think."

"You are sure I should not ride further with you?"

"No . . . please don't. I haven't far to go."

Reluctantly, I turned my horse. "Adios, then." And I rode away. She did not move, and I could still see the dark patch in the silver of the water until I went into the arroyo. When I topped out on the rise, I drew up and thought I heard the pound of hoofs fading away, the hoofs of a running horse.

I glanced at the stars. I must be southeast of the ranch, some distance away. Taking a course by the stars I started across country, dipping down into several deep draws and skirting patches of brush and timber.

Just as I rounded one patch of brush, maybe three or four acres of it, I saw my horse's head come up. "Easy, boy!" I said softly. "Easy, now!"

I drew up, listening. Something was moving out there, a rustle of hooves in the grass, a vague sound of movement, a rattle of horns. "Easy, boy!" I whispered.

At my voice and my hand on its neck, my horse lost some of his tension, and I shucked my Winchester from its scabbard and waited. Somebody out there was moving cattle, and in ranch country honest men do not move cattle by night . . . not often, anyway.

They were no more than a hundred yards off, but I could not make them out, moving them southeast. I waited, and the sound dwindled. A small bunch. I was sure. Not more than thirty or forty head at most. To move in on them now would just result in getting somebody killed, and that somebody could be me—a thought I viewed with no great pleasure. And the trail would still be here tomorrow.

A thought came to me then . . . Why ride all the way back to the ranch? True, I had my work to do, and there was a lot of it, but if I could find out where those missing cattle were going, it would make up for the time lost. So when I started on I was hunting a camp, and I found it, a small place alongside a stream, probably the same stream, or a branch of it, where I'd left Lisa. The place was thick with huge old oaks and pecans, and fortunately the night was cool without being cold. I'd no blanket roll with me, nothing but my slicker and a saddle blanket. But I found a place with plenty of leaves and I bunched up more of them, then spread my slicker on the leaves and put the saddle blanket over my shoulders.

I put my Winchester down beside me, muzzle toward my feet, and my six-shooter I took from its holster and laid it at hand. I made no fire, as I had no idea how far off those cattle had been taken or whether the rider might come back by.

It was a cold, miserable night. But there had been many of those, and it was not the first time I'd slept out with nothing but a slicker and a saddle blanket . . . Nor would it be the last.

Daybreak came and I got up.

Usually I carried some coffee in my saddlebags but I had none now. Going to a box supper a man usually figures there'll be coffee, and there had been. A lot of good it did me now!

At the creek I washed my face in cold water and dried it on my shirt. Then I put the shirt back on, took a long drink from the stream, watered my horse, and mounted up.

The trail was there, and I picked it up, noticed the general way it led, and rode off to the south of it. After a bit, I cut back north as if hunting for strays, and crossed the trail again.

It was getting almost to noontime when the trail led around the roll of a hill into a gap beyond which I could see more oaks and pecans, with some willows and a few cottonwoods. That gap was green, pleasant to see, and promised water. Both my horse and I were thirsty, with no drink since daybreak, but I didn't like the looks of that gap . . . It just looked too good, and I'm a skeptical man.

So I kept back in the brush and reined my horse around to the north. And I worked my way up the slope, with frequent stops to listen and look, until finally I saw a place where there were trees and brush atop the hill. The trees were scrub oak and didn't look like much, but they could cover a man's approach.

Shucking my rifle, I worked up the slope, weaving in and out among the trees until I reached the top of the hill.

Beyond was a valley, a pretty little place, all hid away like that, with a couple of pole corrals for horses, and a lean-to, and maybe a hundred head of young stuff. I stepped down from the saddle and hunkered up against a busted-down oak tree and gave study to what lay below.

There was no smoke . . . no movement beyond the cattle, and there were no horses in the corrals. The valley was well-watered and the graze was good . . . but not adequate for a hundred head for very long. The cattle were in good shape, but I had a hunch this was just a holding place until they could be moved on.

To where? A good question.

The day was warm. I was tired and so was my horse. Moreover, I was hungry. There might be food down there, but I wasn't going to tip my hand by leaving tracks all over the place. Whoever hid those cattle here thought his hideout was unknown and secure, so I'd better leave it thataway.

I gave study to the cattle. Mostly three-year-olds or younger.

All of which brought me back to a thought I'd had before. Whoever was stealing cattle was not stealing them for a quick sale, but to hold and fatten. Give stock like this two to three years, even four, and they'd fatten into real money. And the chances were good that most— if not all—of this stock was unbranded.

I swore softly. I had work to do and they'd be wondering what happened to me. Moreover, my boss had been a thief himself . . . how did I know he wasn't a thief now? That's the trouble with a bad reputation, folks are always likely to be suspicious.

A thought came to me and I studied the hills around the valley with care. If this was a holding station these cattle would have to be moved, as others had probably been moved before them. So where did they go?

A couple of places in the hills that surrounded the valley gave me some ideas, so I led my horse back a ways, mounted up and rode down the slope, still holding to cover and alert for any movement. The man who drove those cattle was probably long gone, but I couldn't be sure.

Keeping far out, I skirted around the hills. It took me better than an hour to get around to the other side of the valley. But, sure enough, what I was looking for was there.

A trail, probably weeks old, made by sixty to seventy head, a trail pointing off to the southeast. Obviously it was a ride of a day or more— perhaps several days—to their destination.

No use thinking of that. I had to get back. I swung my horse suddenly and at the same instant heard the sharp *whap* of a bullet pass my skull.

My spurs touched the flanks of my horse, and he was off with a bound. A good cutting-horse, he was trained to go from a standing start into a sharp burst of speed, and it was well he did, for I heard the sound of another bullet and then I was dodging behind a clump of mesquite. Circling quickly about the end, I turned at right angles and rode straight-away, knowing the rifleman would expect me to appear at the other end. Before he could adjust his aim, I was behind another clump and my horse was running flat-out.

One more shot sounded, and then I was down into an arroyo. The arroyo headed straight back for the hills where I wanted to go, and from where I'd come when trailing the cattle, but I had an idea the hidden marksman knew more about that arroyo than I did. So I watched for a way up, glimpsed a steep game trail, and put my horse up the trail and over the rim and into the rocks.

Slowing down, I studied the country. Somebody had shot from cover, somebody who missed killing me only by the sudden move I'd made. Somebody who could shoot!

My way led west and north, but mostly west. I rode north, putting distance between myself and the man who had been shooting, and utilizing every bit of cover I could.

It was almost midnight when I finally walked my weary horse into the yard at the line-cabin.

A low voice spoke from the door of the dark cabin. "Where did she live, amigo? On the moon?"

Tired as I was, I chuckled. "I stumbled on some cattle moving at night. Made me sort of curious."

"I've coffee on the fire."

Fuentes struck a match and lit the coal-oil lamp. He put the chimney back in place. At the fireplace he dug a pot of beans from the coals and went to the cupboard for biscuits.

"You have something extra, amigo," he said, looking very serious. "How many were they?"

"Who?"

"The men who shot at you."

I had picked up the coffeepot and a cup, but now I stopped, half turning toward him. "Now how the hell would you know that?"

Fuentes shrugged a shoulder. "I do not think, amigo, that you would put bulletholes in your own hat . . . So I think somebody has been shooting."

I removed my hat. There was a bullet through the crown on the left side. That one had been close . . . very, very close!

As briefly as possible, I explained the events of the day and of the previous night, my trailing of the cattle, finding the herd of young stuff and turning away from the trail.

He chewed on a dead cigar and listened. Finally, he said, "How far away would you say? I mean, how far off was he when he shot?"

I had not thought of that, but recalling the terrain and what cover there had been, I said, "Not less than three hundred yards."

· "My advice, amigo, is do not wear that shirt again, not for a long time. You rode one of the Stirrup-Iron horses, so we will turn it loose. At three hundred yards he might not have recognized you. He might not even know you. So do not ride that horse again, and do not wear that shirt. You have others? If not, you may have one of mine, although I am afraid it would be tight, very tight."

That made sense, a lot of sense, for nobody could be more vulnerable than a working cowhand, riding after cattle in wild country, his mind intent on his business . . . And punching cows is a business that requires attention. When a roped steer hits the end of that rope, if your fingers are in the way, you have one or two less fingers. A quick turn around the horn with your rope at the wrong moment . . . I knew a lot of cowhands who had lost pieces of their fingers.

Of course, there was every chance that whoever shot at me had known exactly who he was stooting at. If he did, there was no help for it. If he did not, we could hope to confuse him. I'd no desire to have a good shooter rimrocking me as I went about my business.

Long before daybreak we were in the saddle. It was rough country, and some of those big old steers were elusive as ghosts. We'd glimpse them in the brush, but when we got there they'd be gone.

Shortly after sunup, the wind started to blow, and the sand stung our eyes. The cattle went into the thickest brush, and we worked hard rousting them out. A long, brutal day, and at the end of it we had but three head, seven or eight-year-olds no more friendly than as many Bengal tigers. They'd stalk you along the bars and hook, if you came too close.

"Seen Ol' Brindle today," Fuentes commented, as we walked our horses toward the cabin. "I was hoping he was dead."

"Old Brindle?"

"*Si* . . . a big one, amigo, maybe eighteen hundred pounds. About nine years old, I think, and horns like needles . . . and long . . . like so." He held out his arms to show me. "He killed a horse for me last year, treed me and kept me up a tree until long after sundown. Then, when I got away, he picked up my trail and came after me. Very bad, amigo . . . You watch! Very bad! I think he killed somebody."

"Stirrup-Iron?"

"Spur," Fuentes said, "and he hates me . . . All men. You be careful, amigo. He will kill. He will hunt you. He was born hating, born to kill. He is like a Cape buffalo, amigo, and a bad one."

I'd seen them before. Maybe not as evil as this one, but the longhorn was a wild animal, bred in the thickets and the lonely places, fearing nothing on earth. To those who have seen only domestic cattle, he was unbelievable . . . and no more to be compared to them than a Bengal tiger to a house cat.

We ate, and we fell into our bunks and slept like dead men, for morning was only hours away, and our muscles were heavy with weariness.

As if we had not troubles enough, with men stealing our cattle, with a mysterious girl who belonged we knew not where—nor to whom—and now this . . . a killer steer.

Chapter 10

Ben Roper came by the line-cabin bringing six head of horses to turn into our corral. "Figured you'd need 'em," he said. "How's the coffee?"

"Help yourself," I said.

We walked inside where it was out of the wind. Fuentes looked up from a job of mending a riata. "You findin' any cows?"

"Young stuff seems to have left the country," Ben said, and I told him what I'd found. "Southeast, you say?" He frowned, filling his cup. "That's rough country. Kiowa country."

He looked at my hat. "That wasn't no Kiowa," he commented. "If it had of been, he'd a-kept comin'. Chances are, there'd have been more of them."

"The tracks I saw were shod horses."

"This here's a white man," Ben decided. "One that doesn't want to be seen."

"Brindle's around," Fuentes commented.

"Leave him be," Ben said. "Joe told me to tell you that, if Brindle showed up. He ain't worth a ruined horse or a busted leg."

"I'd like to put a rope on him," I said. "Be something to tie on to."

"You leave him alone. Be like ropin' a grizzly."

"We used to do that in California," Fuentes said. "Five or six of us. Put two or three ropes on him, snag him to a tree and let him fight a bull. Makes quite a scrap."

"You leave Brindle alone," Ben got up. He glanced over at me. "You want to trail those cattle?"

"When there's time. I've got a feeling they aren't far off, and that the thief is somebody around here."

"Balch?"

I shrugged. "I don't know anything about Balch other than he's hard to get along with, and seems to want to have the range all to himself."

Ben Roper got up. "Got to get back. We're pullin' 'em in. But like you say, it's mostly old stuff."

He rode off toward the home ranch and Fuentes and me crawled into the saddle. Both of us had our Winchesters, because even if they were in the way sometimes, you'd better have one in case of Kiowas.

We cut off due south into a wide plain, bunches of mesquite here and there, with enough catclaw and prickly pear to keep it interesting. We found a few head, all pretty wild. "They've been hustled," I told Fuentes. "Somebody has been down here hunting calves."

Several times we saw tracks . . . cow-pony tracks, a shod horse. We rounded up eight or ten head and started them back toward the ranch, adding a couple more, who joined the drive of their own free will. I'd cut off into some rocks to see if any cattle were holed up in the breaks along the foot of a cliff, and suddenly come into a little hollow, wind-sheltered from three sides by the cliff and partly sheltered by mesquite on the other. It was a nice, cozy little spot, and like all other such spots, somebody else thought so, too.

There was a seep . . . nothing very much . . . and the ashes of old fires. When I saw the ashes, I pulled up and stopped my horse where he was, not wishful of leaving more tracks. From the saddle, I could see that somebody had left a pile of wood back under the overhang of a rock, where it would stay dry. So whoever had been here expected to come back.

"Makin' himself to home," Fuentes said, grinning at me.

We drove on. I rousted an old steer out of the brush, and a couple of range cows in surprisingly good shape. We corraled the cattle and it was shading up to dark when we rode up to the cabin.

There was a saddled horse tied to the corral bars, and a light in the cabin.

Fuentes glanced at the brand. Balch and Saddler. We both stepped down. "I'll have a look," I said. "Be right back to care for my horse."

"Watch yourself."

It was Ingerman. He had a fire going and had made fresh coffee. He looked up from under light eyebrows whitened even more by the sun. His old gray hat was pushed back, and he had a cup in his hand.

"You sure stay out late," he said. "Figured you'd developed cat eyes to see in the dark."

"We're shorthanded," I said. "Everybody works hard."

He tried a swallow. "Better have some. I make a good cup of coffee."

Taking a cup from the shelf, I filled it. He watched me, a hard humor in his eyes. "Milo Talon," he said. "Taken me a while to place you."

I tried the coffee. "It is good. You want a job as cook? We can't pay much but the company's good."

"You got a name along the Trail," he commented, looking into his cup. "They tell me you're pretty handy."

"Just enough," I said, "I don't hunt trouble."

"But you've handled some boys who did." He took another swallow. "Sure you don't want to work for us?" He looked at me, his eyes hard and measuring. "You may not know it, but there's some boys noosing a rope for the Stirrup-Iron riders."

"Be a long time using it," I said, casually. "What they upset about?"

"Losing cows . . . Losing too many cows."

Fuentes came in the door and looked at Ingerman, then at me. "He makes a good cup of coffee," I said. "Have some."

"Losing cattle," I said. "All young stuff?"

Ingerman nodded. "Somebody wants to get rich three or four years from now. Balch figures its Rossiter."

"It isn't," I told him. "We're losing stock, too. I don't think there's anything on the place younger than three years. What did you come over for, Ingerman?"

"First, because I remembered you. Want you riding with us." He grinned at me. "I could kill you if I had to, but you're good. You'd probably get some lead into me and I'd rather not have it. We'll pay you more than you'll get here, and you'll have better horses to ride."

He wiped the back of his hand across his mouth. "And you'll be on the right side when the hanging starts."

"How about Fuentes?"

"Roger Balch doesn't take to Mexicans. Never seen any harm in them, myself."

"Forget it. I ride for Stirrup-Iron. You might tell Balch he should have a talk with me before he starts swinging that loop of his. If hanging starts and the shooting begins, we'll take Balch and Saddler first, but there need be no shooting. Something's going on here, but it isn't us, and I don't think it's your outfit."

"Then who is it?"

I shrugged. "Somebody else."

He emptied his cup. "You been told." Then he added, "You watch your step. Jory Benton wants your hide."

"His knife isn't big enough to take it," I said. "If he says that again, you tell him to go to Laredo."

"Laredo? That where you bury your dead?"

"No," I replied, "that's where I tell men to go whom I don't want to bury. It's a nice town, and he'd like it."

When he had gone, Fuentes sliced some bacon into a pan. "What do you think, amigo?"

"I think somebody steals their cows, somebody steals our cows, and somebody plans on the two of us killing each other off. I think somebody wants both outfits, and all the range. And in the meantime he's gathering stock for his ranch to have when the shootin's done."

Fuentes left me in the morning to work a small valley north of us by himself. The wind had died down and I took a cold bath in the water tank, then shaved and dressed, and all the while I knew I was stalling. For my mind kept returning to the trail, and mixed with it were thoughts of Lisa.

Who was she? Where did she live, and with whom? I was not in love with her, but she offered a puzzle that kept gnawing away at my mind. Maybe there was more of Barnabas in me than I had thought. He was the scholar of the family, but we shared some traits in common.

Which brought me around to thinking of myself and just where I was headed. Barnabas seemed to *know*. He had gone to school in Europe, living part of the time with relatives we had in France. I'd been content with wild country and lonely trails, but I kept asking myself if that was going to be enough?

Just being a good cowhand took a hell of a lot of man. It also took a lot out of a man, and I was too restless to stay put. As a cowhand I wasn't as good as either Fuentes or Ben Roper. They knew things by instinct that I'd never learn, and the best thing I had going for me was uncommon strength, endurance and some savvy about stock. And most of all, the willingness to get in there and work.

Maybe the thing wrong with me was that back there in Colorado we had the Empty . . . the MT outfit that had more cattle, more water and better grass than any of the outfits since.

This was good country, and I liked it. But two weeks of riding would put me right back on land that belonged to me, and that made a difference in my thinking.

Rossiter knew who I was, and so did Lisa, whoever she was, but

I didn't want anybody else to know. Henry Rossiter wasn't apt to talk, and somehow I didn't think Lisa would either.

Just for luck I threw a saddle on a buckskin, tied him to the corral and then, taking my rifle, I walked up on the highest knoll around.

A man can ride a lot of country without really knowing until he gets up high and gets a good picture of how it lays. There are always some areas that will fool him by their position in relation to others. I'd noticed that when I was a youngster back at the Empty, and recalled how surprised I'd been when I first saw an accurate map of the ranch layout.

What I was looking for now was cattle. If I could see a few head I could save a lot of riding, and I'd combed too many likely spots to be confident. Also, I had some thinking to do.

There were too many things that made me uneasy. In the first place, blind or not, Henry Rossiter had stolen cattle before and might be doing it again, with help.

In the second place there was that girl Lisa. Where did she belong? Who was she? Nobody at the dance and box social seemed to have any idea of who she was, and strangers didn't stay strangers very long in the western lands.

Suddenly I caught a flicker of movement and saw a big steer come up out of a draw, followed by several others. I watched, waiting until six had appeared. The big steer was in the lead, and they were a good half mile away. They paused to sniff the air, then moved on into a hollow I remembered visiting a few days before. There was grass there, but no water.

Walking back to the corral I stepped into the saddle. The weather was changing. The air was still, yet great black thunderheads were looming up along the horizon. Rain? It seemed doubtful. Too often in this west Texas country I'd seen the clouds pile up and just hang there, sometimes with lightning, but not a drop of rain.

Riding out of the hollow, I cut across the slope of the hill toward the brush where I'd seen the cattle. Now there's some stock that will drive easy enough. You get them headed the right way and maybe one or two will try to cut out, but generally speaking that bunch will walk right along. There's others you couldn't herd for sour apples. No matter which way you try to head them, they decide that isn't the way they want to go. With luck this bunch would be of the first kind.

The closer I got, the more I began to wonder about that big steer who'd been leading them. Even at that distance he'd looked mighty big . . . too big.

Brindle? Maybe . . . and if so I wanted no part of him. When an outift is in a rush to gather cattle, there's no need to cripple a horse or a man trying to get one mean steer. He isn't worth the trouble, and no doubt that was why Ol' Brindle had gotten along so far . . . he was just too mean to handle.

I wanted no part of him.

So I eased down into that tree-filled draw where I'd seen those cattle go, and right away spotted several of them. I sat my horse a bit, studying the layout. There was no sign of the big steer. Once I thought I detected a spot of color back in the brush, but sunlight on a tree trunk seen through the brush might look like a steer. They'd seen me, but I was bothering them none at all, and they paid me no mind. Finally, I walked my horse kind of angling toward them with an idea of taking them up the draw and onto the plain behind it.

An old, half-white range cow started away from me, and that buckskin I was riding knew what he was about. He already knew what I had in mind, and we started that cow toward the draw. We camp up on another and another, and they started off, pretty as could be. They got right to the mouth of the draw before one of them suddenly cut left, and another right, and the seven head we had by that time scattered, going everywhere but up the draw where I wanted them to go.

My buckskin took out after the first one and we cut her back toward the draw. Slowly we began to round them up again, but they had no notion of going up that draw at all. Well, there was another down the creek a ways, and there was a chance I could ease them up on the plain without them knowing it, so I commenced pushing them down-creek, ever so easy.

I'd made a couple of hundred yards with them when something spooked that old half-white cow and she cut out, running, and the others after her. Before I finally got them rounded up again, my buckskin was worn to a frazzle and so was my patience, but I did get them together and headed for the plain.

There was a place where the creek bed narrowed down between some bluffs, with maybe fifty yards between them—with a lot of dead-falls and brush in there, some of it blackened by an old fire. Off to one side there were several big old cottonwoods, one pecan and a lot of willow brush mixed with catclaw and wait-a-bit. I was right abreast of it when I happened to glance right, and there was Ol' Brindle.

He was standing in thick brush, his head down a little, looking right at me. It had been said he weighed maybe eighteen hundred, but whoever said that hadn't seen him lately. He was bigger . . . and standing there in that brush he looked as big as an elephant and meaner than anything you ever did see.

I don't know what possessed me but I said, "Hi, fella!" And his head came up like he'd been stuck with a needle. He glared at me, showing the whites of his eyes, and those horns of his were needle-sharp.

If he charged me in among those deadfalls, that dry creek bed and the brush, I'd have no more chance than a hen at a hoboes' picnic. But he didn't. He just stood there glaring at me, and I turned my head to watch my stock. And for the second time I got the break of my life. As I turned my head there was a flash, a sharp concussion, and the echoes of a shot racketing away against the bluffs.

I hit the ground hard, automatically kicking free of the stirrups as I fell. I hit the ground, rolled over, and then felt a blinding pain in my skull. For a moment I thought that steer had rushed me. I could hear the pound of my horse's hooves as he raced away, and then I just faded out.

When I opened my eyes again, I thought I was sure enough crazy. A few drops of rain were falling, and something was snuffling around me. I heard a snort as it smelled blood, and out of the tail of my eye I saw a hoof within inches of my side, part white, and a big, scarred hoof.

Ol' Brindle was standing right over me. He pushed at my side with his nose—curiously, I thought—but the drops of rain continued to fall and he rumbled down low in his chest, and then went away from me. I heard his steps, heard him pause, probably to look back, and then he went on. I let the air out of my lungs then.

I'd been shot.

Shot by somebody lying up on those bluffs and not more than a hundred yards off, I figured.

How long ago I did not know.

I lay perfectly still. It might have been minutes, it might have been a half hour to an hour. I tried to think how long it would have taken those rain clouds to get from the horizon to me, but my skull throbbed heavily and my mouth was dry.

He might be still up there, waiting to see if I was alive. He probably hadn't come any closer because of Ol' Brindle. He must have seen him right away, and the chances were the big steer was still not far off.

If I got up and started to move, I might get shot. If not that, Ol' Brindle might charge me, and in my shape I'd play hell getting away from him. And I still didn't even know how badly I was hurt.

Now the rain was falling faster. I lay very still, only half aware, only half conscious. Again I must have faded out, for when my eyes opened again I was soaked to the skin and the rain was pouring down upon me.

With an effort, I pushed myself up from the ground. My skull was bursting and my side hurt, but I raised myself enough to see all around and I saw nothing but muddy ground, a trickle of water in the once dry creek bed, and the wet trees and dripping leaves.

Under the big cottonwoods the rain was a little less. I pulled myself to one and sat with my back against the trunk and looked around.

Nearby, another cottonwood had fallen, and under it lay a great trough of bark that had fallen from the underside. Another piece of loosened bark, all of six or seven feet long, lay atop the trunk.

My hat was gone, back near the creek bed, I supposed. My fingers touched my wet hair. There was something of a cut on my scalp, but I did not think it was from a bullet. More likely my head had hit something when I fell from my horse, and I was suffering from concussion.

The only wound I could find was on my hip where I'd been creased just below my belt. When hit, my body must have jerked and my horse swerved, so I fell, hitting my head when landing. That I'd lost blood there was no doubt, for the dark stain of it covered my pants on that side. Often a flesh wound would bleed more profusely than something really serious.

Desperately, I wanted a drink, and the few drops I could catch in my opened mouth helped not at all. Yet it was too far to the creek and I wanted only to rest and be still.

This was the second time somebody had tried to kill me. Jory Benton? Somehow, I doubted that. This must be the same man who had fired at me before, and who was now stalking me to kill.

He might return.

Obviously, he was a man who liked to make sure of his work. He had fired from cover, from ambush, no doubt. He had also shown the ability to hit what he shot at. Yet in each case I'd lucked out through no effort of my own. How many times could I be lucky?

The rain fell steadily. Somewhere off to the south, thunder rumbled. Occasionally, there was a flash of lightning. I could hear the creek now. It was running a fair head of water.

My hand reached to feel for my pistol. It was there. My belt, I remembered, had only two empty loops.

My horse was gone.

This place where I now was couldn't be more than a mile, maybe a mile and a half from our line-cabin. I'd guessed the big steer that led this bunch had been a half mile off, but after reaching the bottom I'd worked along it a ways, rounding up stock, and then I'd tried to get them out of the creek bottom . . . not more than a mile and a half. Yet I was in no shape for walking, and wasn't wishful of being caught in the open by a man with a rifle. And he might still be around.

Crawling to that dead cottonwood tree, I got those two lengths of bark. I lay down in one and pulled the other over me and I just lay there. After a while, I went to sleep.

Those two slabs of bark kept me off the ground and covered me, just like a hollow tree. Only I remember one of the last thoughts I had before I dropped off was that it was mighty like a coffin.

When that thought came to me, I almost got up and out, but I simply was too weak, too tired, and my head ached too much.

If anybody came looking for me now, I was helpless. A man had only to walk up and shoot me full of holes.

Chapter 11

Fitfully, I slept. I awakened, slept again, and awakened. When I tried to turn over, water leaked in from the sides where the two slabs of bark met, so turning over was an ordeal.

Finally, after an endless night of rain, day came. A day of rain.

My eyes opened to a dripping world. My head throbbed heavily and my side was sore, my muscles cramped. For a long time I simply lay still, listening to the rain on the bark, hearing the running of the creek. To hear it now one would never believe that yesterday it had lain dry and empty.

The line-cabin . . . I must get back to the line-cabin.

Pushing off the top slab of bark, I struggled to sit up, made it, and rolled over to my knees on the muddy ground. I pushed myself up, got to my feet, tottered, and fell against the trunk of a tree.

For a moment I clung there, trying to get the cramps from my legs. I felt for my pistol . . . It was in place.

A drink. I desperately needed a drink. Tottering on my injured leg, I got to the creek, lay down on the sand and drank. I drank and drank. Getting up, I saw my hat. It lay on the rain-heavy branches of a clump of mesquite near the stream. I retrieved it and shook some water from it, then put it on.

Clinging to a branch of a tree, I looked carefully around. The clouds were lowering and gray; the trees and the brush dripped with water. All was dark and gloomy, yet I saw no movement, no stir of life. No wild animal would be about on such a day, and probably no man.

I'd lost blood, and was therefore weak, yet I would get no better here. And the nearest chance was the line-cabin. It was near, but terribly far in my present condition. Most of all, I dreaded the thought of that open plain I must cross for most the distance to it. Once I stepped out on that plain, I was a target for any rifleman who might lie in comfortable shelter and take his own time to make the shot good.

Still clinging to the branch, I reached down and picked a length of dead branch long enough for a staff from the ground. Taking a deep breath, I started toward the bank. Only then did I realize what faced me. The banks I must climb to get away from the creek bed were in all places steep, and the few places that offered a route a man might take were slippery with mud.

When I had gone some fifty-odd feet, I paused to gasp for breath, to ease the pain of my hip and stiffened leg, and to study what lay before me.

There was no way I was going to get up that bank by walking. I must get down and crawl.

Onward I limped. At the foot of the bank I dug in with my stick and hobbled up a step, then two. Trying a third, my foot slipped under me and I came down hard in the mud, gasping with the agony of a suddenly wrenched leg. After a long time of lying in the mud, I pushed myself up, but it was no use. I sank down again and crawled on my hands and knees.

At last I topped out on the edge of the plain. A little scattered brush, and then the open grassland, level as a floor. Beyond it loomed the low hills, and just over those hills, the line-cabin.

A dry place, a warm fire, hot food . . . a cup of coffee. At that moment, no paradise I could imagine needed any more than that.

For a time I stood still, muddy and wet, looking carefully around. But again I saw nothing. No horesman, no cattle, no Brindle. No doubt Ol' Brindle was in some snug thicket, laying out the rain. At least, I hoped he was.

A step with my good left leg, then hitching my right forward with the aid of the staff, and then the good leg again. It was slow, and it was painful. My leg not only hurt, but the wound at my hip was bleeding again. The ache in my skull had subsided to a dull, heavy pounding to which I had grown accustomed.

Twice I fell. Each time I struggled up. Several times I stood still for a long time trying to wish myself across the plain. But wishing did no good, so I plodded on.

At last I reached the trail up the hill, and this was not steep. At the crest I looked down at the line cabin. Two horses were in the corral . . . No cattle in the corral beyond. No smoke from the cabin.

Where then was Fuentes?

There was a flat rock near a mesquite bush. I lowered myself down, stretching my stiff leg out carefully. From that point I could see the cabin. Everything I wanted was inside, yet I did not want to die to get it.

Fuentes should be there with a fire going. But suppose he was not, and somebody else was? Suppose the unknown marksman who had twice tried to kill me was down there instead?

He might believe me dead, but he might also realize that if I was not dead, and needed a horse, that I would surely come to this place where horses awaited me. I had struggled too much, suffered too much to want to walk through that door into a belly full of lead.

For a long time I watched the windows. At this distance I could see little, but hoped I would catch movement past them. I saw nothing.

Struggling to my feet, I hobbled slowly down the path to the cabin. Approaching it, I slipped the thong from the hammer, leaned my staff against the building and drew my gun.

With my left hand, ever so gently, I lifted the door latch. With the toe of my stiff leg, I pushed the door open.

"*Milo!*"

Swiftly, I turned. The stable! I'd forgotten! My pistol came around, the hammer eared back.

The only thing that saved her was my years of training—never to shoot unless I could see what I was shooting.

It was Ann Timberly!

Cold sweat broke out on my forehead, and slowly I lowered my gun muzzle, easing the hammer down ever so gently.

"What in God's world are you doing *here?*" I demanded, irritated by the fact that I might easily have shot her.

"I found your horse, and I remembered your saddle. I tried to backtrack him, but the rain washed out the trail, so I brought him here. I was just unsaddling when I saw you."

She helped me inside and I slumped down on my bunk, holstering my gun. She stared at me, shaking her head "What in the world has happened to you?"

Explanations could be long, I made it short. " Somebody shot me. I fell and got this," I touched my head. "And that was yesterday . . . I think."

"I'll get a fire started," she turned quickly to the fireplace. "You need some food."

"Get my rifle first."

"What?"

"It's still on my horse, isn't it? My rifle and the saddlebags. Somebody wants to kill me, Ann, and I want that rifle."

She wasted no time talking, and in a moment she was back with the rifle and the saddlebags. I had another fifty rounds of ammunition in that saddlebag.

She was quick and she was efficient. Rich girl she might be, but she'd grown up on a ranch and she knew what to do. In no time she had a fire going, coffee on, and was telling me to get out of my wet clothes.

"And into what?" I asked wryly.

She whipped the blanket from Fuentes' bed. "Into that," she said, "and if you're bashful, I'm not."

It was a problem getting out of my shirt, which was soaked and clung to my back. She helped me.

"Well," she said critically, "you've got nice shoulders, anyway. Where'd you pick up all that muscle?"

"Wrestling steers, swinging an ax," I said. "I've worked."

Fortunately, she could get a look at my hip just by me loosening my belt and turning down the edge of my pants, which were stiff with blood. It was a nasty-looking wound, an ugly big bruise around the top of my hipbone and a gash you could lay a finger in.

"You'd better start for home," I said, as she dressed the wound. "The major will be worried."

"He stopped worrying about me a long time ago. I can ride a horse and shoot, and he stopped arguing with me when I was sixteen."

I didn't like her being there, nonetheless. Folks will talk, given provocation or none, and a woman's good name was of first importance. Argument did no good at all. She was a stubborn girl, with her own notions about things, and I could see the major must have his problems.

Still, she could ride and she could shoot, and it was a big, wide-open country where a woman was safer than almost anything else a body could mention.

Wrapped in Fuentes' blanket, I relaxed on the bed while she fixed us a meal with what she could find. Meanwhile, we talked about the situation.

"There's nobody I can think of who'd want to shoot me," I commented, "unless it was whoever was driving those stolen cattle. I figure he must've seen me on his trail."

"Possibly," she agreed, but she did not seem too sure.

"Do you think Balch and Saddler are stealing cattle?"

She hesitated over that, then shook her head. "I don't know.

Neither does Pa. We've lost . . . we've lost a good many but not like you have. Balch claims they've lost young stuff, too. It doesn't make any kind of sense."

She turned to look at me. "There's been talk about you, Milo. I thought I'd better tell you. People are saying no cowboy has the kind of money you spent at the box social."

I shrugged. "I saved some money ridin' shotgun for Wells Fargo, then I hit a pocket of stuff placer-mining up in northern New Mexico."

"Most cowhands would have spent it."

I shrugged. "Maybe. I'm not much of a drinker. I carry a gun, and a good many folks know I've ridden shotgun. Besides, I've covered the Outlaw Trail, Canada to Mexico. A man riding that kind of country has to be careful."

"Is this what you're going to do the rest of your life? Just ride up and down the country?"

Smiling, I shook my head. "No, one day I'll settle down to ranching. Maybe I will. Barnabas says I was born for it, liking stock and the country and all."

I paused. "You'd like Barnabas," I added, "he's traveled in Europe, and he reads. He thinks a lot, too. He's planning to import some breeding stock from Europe, mix it with longhorns. The way he figures, the day of the longhorn is short. They'll do well in rough graze like this, but they walk too much and don't cary enough beef. Although," I added, "I've seen some mighty fat longhorns, given the graze."

It was mighty pleasant, sitting there talking to Ann but somewhere along the line I just dozed off. I'd lost blood, I was feeling sick, and I was tired from my struggle through the mud while ailing.

When I awakened again, the cabin was still, and only coals lay on the hearth. Ann was asleep on Fuentes' bed.

Hearing a stir, I raised up on an elbow and saw Fuentes sitting up. He grinned at me and put a finger to his lips. He'd been sleeping on the floor with his blanket-roll gear.

He went out, and I heard him washing beside the door. He automatically threw the water from the pan where it would usually help settle dust, although on this morning after the rain there was none. Then he came in. And moving silently, except for the tinkle of those big Spanish spurs he wore, he made coffee, stirred up the fire and added fuel.

Favoring my bad hip, I sat up.

Ann had put my rifle on the bed beside me—and my six-shooter, too. She'd forgotten to bar the door, and that was probably because she hadn't intended going to sleep.

She awakened suddenly. She stared at Fuentes and, when he bowed slightly, she smiled. "I must have fallen asleep. I am ashamed. Anyone could have come in."

"You were tired, senorita. It was best that you slept. But the major will be worried."

"Yes," she admitted, "this is the first time I've been gone all night."

She looked delightful, and in a matter of minutes she had washed, done something to her hair, and had taken over the cooking from Fuentes.

"I rode to talk to Hinge," he explained. "When I told him you were missing, he was very angry. He was worried, too. I had ridden to look, but your tracks were gone under the rain."

We ate and talked, then Ann was gone. My fever seemed to have disappeared during the night, although I still felt kind of used up. It gave me a cold twinge when I thought of both of us asleep and somebody out there who wanted to kill me. Yet Ann could not long have been asleep before Fuentes rode in.

Joe Hinge rode in. "Get well," he told me after we'd talked some. "We're goin' to need you. We got the west range to ride, an' that's where Balch says we can't go."

"Give me three, four days," I said.

"Take you longer than that," he said, "you surely look peaked." He changed the subject abruptly. "Both times you were shot at you were southeast of here?"

At my nod, he took off his hat and scratched his head thoughtfully. "You know, some things a body can figure. There's no way it could be Balch or Saddler . . . Roger, maybe. Jory Benton was riding away off north of here, and so was Knuckles Vansen."

He paused. "It's mighty easy for somebody to think that way out on the plains nobody would ever figure who shot you, but look at it. All the men we know of got jobs. They have to be somewhere. You locate those who were where they were supposed to be and you've trimmed down the list."

Hinge continued. "I can account for most of Balch's hands, and the major's as well. I know where ours were, and most of the major's."

"Harley?" I asked.

"Him? He wouldn't shoot nobody. He's got no cause to. Anyway, he never goes anywhere but our place and home. He'd have been home when you were shot at and that's a good distance off."

"Is he friendly to Balch? I'm only asking because I don't know him."

"Balch?" said Hinge. "Hell, no! They had words a while back over a horse, but Harley, he keeps to hisself. Doesn't want any truck with anybody. Does his job, draws his money and keeps that place of his."

The thing that worried me was: there was no logical suspect except the unknown cattle thief, and there was a good chance he—or they— would be unknown around here. Chances are, it was somebody laying up in the hills, taking cattle when nobody was around.

Hinge rode off with Fuentes, and I laid back on the bed. They had to get back, and I couldn't yet ride.

I could see the sunlight through the open door, and bees buzzing around the house. And somewhere, I could hear a mockingbird singing.

It was almighty quiet and pleasant, and it was a good time to think.

One by one I began thinking over every aspect of the problem.

First, Barnabas used to say, you've got to state your problem. A problem clearly stated is often a problem already half solved.

Somebody wanted me dead.

Who? And why?

Chapter 12

All my thinking got me nowhere at all. Somebody wished me dead—that was all I knew. I almost dozed off along there, just thinking about it, and then suddenly I was wide awake and scared.

I was alone. I was wounded and in bed.

And somewhere out yonder was a man with a rifle who was hunting me!

That was enough to wake anybody up.

To my way of thinking, he either figured me dead or still down there in that bottom somewhere. But suppose I was wrong? Suppose even now he was up there in the brush somewhere waiting a chance to get a shot at me?

Supposing he had watched Fuentes, Hinge and Roper ride away? Supposing he had seen Ann leave earlier?

Then he surely knew I was alone.

What he couldn't know was that, though I was weak from loss of blood and in no shape to straddle a horse, I was still able and willing to shoot.

Nobody lives long low-rating an enemy. You've got to give the other fellow credit for having as much savvy as you have, and maybe a little more.

Suppose he knew I was here, and was waiting for me to drift off to sleep, like I had almost done? Suppose—another thought came—just suppose he didn't have any plan of coming in on me, but just decided to wait up on the knoll, just waiting for me to come out?

Yet, me being sick and in bed, he couldn't expect me to come out and give him a target. Unless something drove me out.

Fire!

That was foolish. I was just imagining things. No doubt, whoever

373

it was who'd shot at me was miles away with his stolen cattle. He had wounded me, put me out of action, and I wouldn't be trailing him for a while. If I was the kind who scared easy, he might figure I'd never try.

What sleep had been coming over me had disappeared. I was wide awake now, and scared. The trouble was, I was in no shape to move quick, no shape for a running battle—or for a battle of any kind.

I could get out of the cabin if I was lucky, I could get into the brush. But I knew what brush fighting meant. A man has to be ready to move, and if he moves too slow he's dead. He has to be alert, too, and I was kind of foggy. I could think, all right, but could I think fast enough? React with enough speed?

The door stood open, for the air was fresh and clear. There were two windows, one on each side of the cabin, but only that one door. And the windows were high as a man's shoulder. A body could hoist himself up and crawl through one, but there was no easy way to do it and no way that wouldn't, for a minute or so, leave a man helpless. And going through a window would be sure to break what scab had started healing over my wound.

Yet I was only easily visible from one window. The bed was close against the wall and hard to see except from the door or one window.

It was very still. I strained my ears for the slightest sound, and heard nothing.

One hand was on my Winchester, but I withdrew it and slid my Colt from its scabbard. I needed a gun I could move quickly, easily, to cover any point.

Minutes passed . . . Nothing.

Whoever was out there . . . if anybody *was* out there . . . might be waiting for me to move.

So I would not move.

Yet I was being almighty foolish. I was getting scary as a girl alone in a house. I'd no reason to believe anybody would be coming after me here—except for my imagination.

The trouble was, I was a sitting duck and I didn't like the idea.

No sound, no movement.

My horse was in the corral. If I heard a sound, it would probably be that horse, yet I heard nothing.

I dozed. Scared as I was—and worried, I dozed. That was what weakness would do for a man.

What snapped me out of it was a noise. It was a very small noise and maybe it was just inside my own head. Gun in hand, I rolled up on one elbow and tried to look out the open door, but I could see nothing but the gradually drying earth beyond the door, a distant hillside and a corner of the corral.

What had I heard? Had it been a step? No . . . A step had a different sound? A horse bumping a trough, or something? No.

It had been a small sound, a kind of *plink*. It might have been anything. The handle of the coffeepot lay against the side of the pot, and it might have been raised a little, and just finally settling down against the side of the pot as the lessening of heat cooled the metal.

It might have been that, but I didn't believe it was. I lay back on the bed, staring up at the ceiling. Somebody wanted me dead . . . The problem was still there. If I could figure out who, I might know why, and even figure how he—or they—would try to kill me.

Here I was, worried and all on edge just at the idea that somebody might be out there.

The sound . . . What had it been? Carefully, I mentally sorted familiar sounds and tried to discover what it was I'd heard. In any event, I hadn't heard it again.

It had been a very small sound, anyway.

Yet I could not relax. My muscles were tense, my nerves on edge. Something was wrong . . . Something was about to happen. I forced myself to lie still, telling myself I was being silly. I could see out the door and all was quiet, and the one horse I could now see was browsing quietly on some wisps of hay left about the corral. What I needed was rest . . . just rest. I had to calm down and relax.

I turned on my side, facing the wall.

For a moment I lay absolutely still, petrified into immobility.

For as I turned on my side to face the wall, I found myself staring into the muzzle of a gun pushed through a crack where the chinking between the logs had been picked out. I stared, and then I came off the bunk with a lunge that sent a shock of agony through my wounded hip. I fell sprawling on the floor, the blast of the shot ringing in my ears. There was smoke in the room and the smell of singed wood and wool, and then I was on my feet, gun in hand, hopping toward the door.

Outside my horse had his head up, ears pricked, looking off to my right, I turned around the door post, gun poised . . . and saw nothing.

I could feel the blood running down my side from my reopened wound, but I waited, clinging to the doorjamb with my left hand, my right gripping the gun, poised for a shot.

Nothing . . .

For several minutes I waited, and then I turned myself around and fell into a chair, back to the wall, looking at my bunk.

Somebody had picked the dried clay from the cracks between the logs, using a stick or a knife blade, perhaps, and then had thrust the muzzle through. Had I remained lying where I'd been, I would now be dead, for that bullet would have taken me right through the skull.

Again I got up, peering from the windows, but there was nothing to see.

That faint, first sound I had heard was probably the dried mud falling to the ground, striking against a rock or something.

Whoever had tried to kill me had been in this cabin. Whoever had tried had known exactly where the bed was, exactly where my head would be laying on the pillow. He had known exactly the spot at which to pick away the plaster.

Whoever it was wanted to kill *me*. Not just a cowhand who happened to trail a horse thief, but *me*, a particular person.

It might be one of the Balch and Saddler outfit. For there was no doubt that my presence among the Stirrup-Iron riders stiffened their backs, and my death would weaken them considerably.

I limped along the wall. I looked out . . . nothing, nobody. Now I must be very careful. I dared not trust myself anywhere without being careful.

Impatiently, I looked around. I had to get out of here. The cabin was a trap. As long as I was here, I was available to the planning of the would-be killer, and I had to get out. Yet how to escape with him out there? And he would be, I was sure, somewhere right outside, awaiting a chance.

In my present condition, moving swiftly was out of the question. I would have to get to the corral, get a saddle and bridle on a horse, get the corral bars down and mount up, then ride out. And during every movement I would be sitting there like a duck in a shooting gallery, waiting for the shot.

After a moment, I took a chunk of wood from the fireplace and placed it in front of the hole in the wall. Then I lay down again, heaving a great sigh of relief.

I *was* tired. I lay back, exhausted. All my life I'd been a loner, but at that minute I wanted desperately for somebody to come. Somebody . . . anybody . . . Just somebody who could watch while I slept, if only for a few minutes.

I strained my ears for the slightest sound, and heard only the birds, the slight movements of my horse. I closed my eyes . . .

Suddenly they opened wide.

If I slept I would die.

Rolling over, I sat up. Fumbling with a cup and the coffeepot, I poured coffee. It was no longer hot, for the untended fire had gone down. I tasted the lukewarm coffee, something I'd never liked, then knelt before the fire and coaxed some flame from the coals with slivers of wood.

Would no one friendly ever come?

Hopefully, I continued to listen for the sound of a rider, and heard nothing. I could fix myself something to eat. That would keep me awake and busy. Again I pushed myself up off the bed, my hands trembling with weakness. At the cupboard, I got out a tin plate, a knife, fork and spoon.

In a covered kettle, I found some cold broth Ann had fixed for me, and I moved the kettle to the fire, stirring the broth a little as it grew warm. Again I looked from the windows, careful not to show my head.

What I needed more than anything was rest, yet to rest might be to die. Had I my usual speed of movement and agility, I would have gone outside and tried to hunt down whoever was trying to kill me, but my movements were too slow, I was too tired, and too weak.

Suddenly, I heard hoofbeats. A rider was approaching. Gun in hand, I moved cautiously toward the door, and peered beyond it. A moment later the rider appeared.

It was Barby Ann.

She rode right up to the door and swung down, trailing her reins.

She walked right in, then stopped, seeing me and the gun in my hand. "What's the matter?"

"Somebody took a shot at me. A little while back. Right through a crack in the wall."

When I showed her, she frowned. "Did you see him?"

"No," I said, "but it's likely the same one who tried to kill me twice before, and he'll try again. You'd better not stay."

"Joe Hinge said you were hurt. You'd better get back into bed."

"*That* bed?"

"You've covered the hole, so why not? He can't shoot through that wall. You need some rest."

"Look," I said, "would you stay here for an hour or so? I do need the rest, need it the worst way. If you'll stay, I'll try to sleep."

"Of course I'll stay. Go to bed."

She turned her back on me and walked outside the door, leading her horse to the corral trough for water.

Sitting on the edge of the bunk, I watched her go. She had a neat, if too thin figure, and she carried herself proudly. It was in me to ask her about Roger Balch, but it would not do. After all, it was none of my business. I was only a cowhand working for her father.

She tied her horse to the gate, then turned to come back to the line-cabin.

Inside the door, she looked at me, sitting there. "You'd better lay down," she said. "I can't stay too long."

Easing back on the bunk, I stretched out with a great sigh of relief. Slowly, I felt the tension ease from my muscles. I let go then, letting myself sink into the bed, just giving myself up to the utter exhaustion I felt.

The last I remembered was her sitting by the door staring out into the afternoon.

It was shadowed and still when I opened my eyes, but even before they opened I heard the low murmur of voices—of more than one voice. Danny Rolf and Fuentes were in the room. There was no sign of Barby Ann.

Fuentes heard me move. "You sleep," he said, chuckling. "You sleep ver' hard, amigo."

"Where's Barby Ann?"

"She rode back when we came. Or rather, when Danny got here. Then I came in. You've really slept. It is two hours since I came."

I lay still for a few minutes, then sat up. "You wish to eat? I have some stew . . . very good . . . and some tortillas. You like tortillas?"

"Sure. Ate them for months, down Mexico way."

"Not me," Danny said. "I'll take hot biscuits!"

Fuentes waved at the fireplace. "There it is. Make them."

Danny grinned. "I'll eat tortillas." He looked over at me. "Barby Ann said you'd been shot at?"

Indicating the chunk of stove wood I'd laid over the crack, I told them about it. Fuentes listened, but had no comment to offer.

"I'll not ride with you!" Danny said. "He might shoot the wrong man."

"Finding any cattle?" I asked.

"We rounded up sixteen head today, mostly older stuff. We got one two-year-old heifer, almost the color of Ol' Brindle."

"Seen him?"

"He's around. We saw his tracks along the bottom. He stays to the brush during the day, feeds mostly at night, I think."

We talked of horses, cattle and range conditions, of women and cards and roping styles, of riders we had known, mean steers and unruly cows. And after a while, I slept again, pursued through an endless dream by a faceless creature, neither man nor woman, who wished to kill me.

I awakened suddenly in a cold sweat. Danny and Fuentes were asleep, but the night was still and the door was open to the cool breeze.

A horse moved near the corner of the corral, and I started to turn over. Then like a dash of icy water I knew. *That was no horse!*

I'd started to turn over and I did, right off the bed and onto the floor. And for the second time that day a bullet smashed into the bed where I'd just been.

Fuentes came off the floor with a gun in his hand. Rolf rolled over against the wall, grabbing around in the darkness for his rifle. I lay flat on the floor, my side hurting like the very devil, with a bruised elbow that made me want to swear, but I didn't. This was one time when a single cuss word might get a man killed.

All was still, and then there was a pound of hoofs from some distance off, a horse running, and then the night was still.

"If I was you," Danny said, "I'd quit."

"Maybe that is it," Fuentes said. "Maybe they want you to quit. Maybe they want all of us to quit, starting with you."

He struck a match and lighted the lamp, then replaced the chimney. I pointed to the rolled-up blanket I'd been using for a pillow. There was a neat bullethole there, neat and round and perfect, despite the fuzzy material.

"He doesn't want me to quit," I said, "he wants me dead."

Chapter 13

Headquarters ranch lay warm in the sunlight when I came down the slope, walking my horse. Fuentes and Danny rode with me, because three men can watch the country easier than one, and I was almighty tired when we reached the bunkhouse.

Barby Ann came out on the porch. "What's the matter, boys?"

Danny went up to the porch and told her, while Fuentes saw that I got safely inside. "You will be better off here, I think." The Mexican squatted on his heels near the door. " Joe will be here, and Ben Roper."

"I'm better," I said. "The fever's gone, all right, and now I'm only tired from the walk. Give me a couple of days and I'll be working again."

"You staying on?"

"Somebody shot at me. I'd like to find him and see if he'll shoot at me face to face. If I ride away now, I'd never know."

For two days I rested at the ranch. On the second day I walked outside into the sunlight, and when chow time came I went up to the house rather than have food brought to me. Nothing in me was cut out for laying abed, and I was itching to get into a saddle again. I'd been thinking, and I had some ideas.

There was nobody in the ranch house except Barby Ann. When I got to the table, she came from the kitchen. "I was just coming down to see how you felt."

"I felt too good to have you walking all the way down there."

She brought two cups and the coffeepot, then went back for some other food. She was still in the kitchen when I heard somebody coming. I slid the thong off my sixshooter. It was probably Rossiter, but after a man has been shot at a few times, he gets jumpy.

Suddenly Rossiter loomed in the doorway, stopping abruptly. "Barby? Barby Ann? Is that you?"

"It's me," I said. "It's Milo Talon."

"Oh?" He put out a hand, feeling for a chair. I jumped up and took his hand and led him to a place near me at the table. "Talon? Are you the one who's been having trouble?"

"I've been shot at, if that's what you mean."

"Who? Who did it? Was it some of the Balch crowd?"

Barby Ann came in from the kitchen, looking quickly from her father to me. "Pa? You want coffee?"

"Please."

Barby Ann hesitated. "Pa? Milo's been shot. He was wounded."

"Wounded? You don't say! Are you all right, boy? Can you ride?"

"I'll be back at work in a couple of days," I said cautiously. Something in his manner irritated me, but I was not sure what it was. And I had to remember that, due to my own discomfort, I was more easily irritated.

We drank coffee and talked while Barby Ann got something on the table. "Hope this won't make you leave us, son. Barby Ann and me, well, we'd like to have you stay."

"I'll finish the roundup. Then I'll be drifting, I think."

"Hear you bid for some girl's box at the social. Paid a good sum for it." He paused. "Who was she?"

"As a matter of fact, I don't know. She never told me her whole name, and she wouldn't let me ride all the way home with her."

Rossiter frowned, drumming on the table with his fingers. "Can't imagine that. Everybody around here knows everybody." He turned his head toward Barby Ann. "Isn't that so, honey?"

"They didn't know her, Pa. I heard talk. Nobody had any idea who she was or where she came from. She was . . . well, kind of pretty, too."

After a while he turned and went into the next room. I sat over my coffee, half dozing. Yet my mind kept going back to those shots. Whoever had dug that hole between the logs in the cabin wall had known where to dig. Yet that might not be surprising, for line-cabins were often used by any passing cowboy who might stop overnight. The chances were good that every rider within fifty miles of the North Concho knew the place.

"How's the gather?" I asked Barby Ann.

"Good . . . We've nearly four hundred head down there now."

"Seen Roger lately?"

She flushed, and her lips tightened. "That's none of your business!"

"You're right. It isn't." I got up slowly, carefully, from the table. "Just making conversation. I think I'll go lay down."

"You do that." She spoke a little sharply. No doubt what I'd said had irritated her, and she was right. I'd no business asking a personal question, yet I couldn't help but wonder if Henry Rossiter knew his daughter was meeting Roger Balch.

For those two days I rested, slept, and rested. My appetite returned, and it became easier to walk around. On the third day, I got Danny to saddle up for me, as I still hesitated to swing a saddle on a horse for fear of opening the wound. I rode down to where the herd was gathered.

Harley was there, rifle in hand. It was a very good rifle, and well cared for.

"Nice bunch," I commented.

"They'll do," he said shortly. "Should have enough to drive."

He moved off to check a big cow that was showing an inclination to move toward the hills. The grazing was good, and they were close to water and showed little inclination to wander off. I could see another rider, Danny Rolf, I believed, on the other side.

It felt good to be back in the saddle, and I was riding my own horse with his easy way of moving. Harley seemed in no mood to talk, so I drifted on around the herd and into the edge of the hills. Yet I rode with care.

As I turned away from the herd to start back toward the ranch, I saw Joe Hinge coming down the slope from the west with a mixed lot of cattle. As they neared me, I drew up and helped guide them toward the main herd. With one or two exceptions they were Spur branded.

Joe pulled up near me, removing his hat to mop his brow. Despite the coolness of the air, he was sweating. And I didn't wonder. "How're you feelin'?" he asked me.

"So, so. Give me another day."

"Sure . . . But I can use you." He glanced at me. "You up to working out west?"

"Anytime," I said casually.

I decided against saying anything about a hunch I had.

"Good . . . But watch your step."

After a bid I rode back toward the bunkhouse, and unsaddled my horse when I got there. Doing the casual things that a man does all the time gives him time to think, and I was doing some thinking then.

Somebody wanted me dead . . . Why?

Another day I slept, loafed, and was irritable with myself for not being back on the job. The following morning I saddled up the bay with the black mane and tail, a short-coupled horse—and a good horse from which to rope.

The line cabin was empty but there was a note written on a slab of wood with charcoal: WATCH OUT FOR BRINDLE.

Well, I would. I'd no notion of tangling with that one if it could be avoided.

All day I worked the bench and a couple of long, shallow arroyos, and rounded up eight head, then struck a dozen atop the mesa and started them back down toward the ranch.

At noon I was near the line-cabin and rode in to swap horses. Fuentes had just come in. We both switched our saddles, mine to a steel-dust that I'd never ridden, and then we went inside for coffee.

Fuentes was quiet. Suddenly he broke his silence. "Balch . . . He rode this way. Two, three times I see him. He keeps out of sight."

"Balch himself? Alone?"

"*Si.*"

That was something to study about, for this was in an area where few of his cattle would be found. Those of his we did find we were drifting back down to the holding ground, just like the others. For they could all be separated during the roundup, as was usual.

Puzzles didn't suit me. I'd hired on to handle stock, and I was ready to do just that, but I'd no idea of getting myself killed when I didn't even know what was going on. Balch was a man likely to ride roughshod over anything that got in his way, and Saddler was no better. Roger Balch had a problem with himself, trying to prove to everybody what a tough man he was. The major seemed able to take care of himself. And as for Henry Rossiter . . . what could a blind man do?

Rossiter had some loyal hands, and Joe Hinge was a good cattleman.

"Take it easy," Fuentes suggested. "You look tired."

I shrugged. "What the hell? Should I leave it all for you to do?"

When we went outside, Fuentes warned me. "Don't tie onto anything with the steel-dust. That's one of the fastest horses on the place, and a good cutting horse—but skittish on a rope."

We split up and I turned off toward the southeast, riding right where I'd gotten into trouble. Which shows how much I've got in the way of brains. Yet the pickings were good. I found a half dozen head in the first few minutes, broke them out and started them back. I cut wider and brought in several more, then moved the lot down on the better grass en route to the ranch.

Circling back, I looked for signs. No horse tracks anywhere. Suddenly, I came upon several head of cattle, and had turned them, when I heard a crackling in the brush. The steel-dust started nervously and rolled his eyes. Sure enough, it was Ol' Brindle standing there with his head up, looking at me.

I'd no bones to pick with him. In fact, he'd probably saved my bacon there a while back. So I just waved a hand and worked away from him. When I turned to look back, he was still there. He had his head up and he was watching me.

The truth of the matter was that I had a warm feeling for the old boy. He was tough and mean, and someday he might kill a cowhand, even me. But he was wild and free and full of fight, and I liked that. And he had ruled the roost there in his own corner of the country for a long time.

There never was a fiercer animal than a big longhorn who had run wild in the plains or the brush. They'd tackle anything that walked, even a grizzly. Nonetheless, I think most of the riders in that part of the country wanted to get a rope on him. It was a challenge to see him there. A challenge, because you knew when you dabbed a loop on Ol' Brindle you had tied onto a cyclone, and you'd have to win or get smashed up or killed. You give a cowhand a rope and, sooner or later, he'll dab it on anything that's running loose. He'd rope wolves, coyotes, mountain lions and bears . . . And I knew of one even roped an eagle.

But as far as I was concerned, Ol' Brindle could make his own way and he'd get no trouble from me . . . unless he started it.

Which he might.

Topping out on a rise, I pulled up short. Down in the hollow before me, a man with his back to me had roped a steer and was kneeling on its side.

His horse looked up at us, ears pricked, but the stranger was too busy with what he was doing to know we were there.

Branding? I saw no fire.

Slowly I walked my horse down the hillside, shucking my Winchester as I went.

The steer was dead. The man had cut its throat, and now he was cutting a piece of hide from the hip. And I knew that steer. It was one of those we'd pushed out of the brush the first day I was back.

"Is this a one-man party," I said, "or can anybody get in?"

He turned swiftly, his hand dropping to his gun.

It was Balch.

Chapter 14

His face flushed even redder, then seemed to pale slightly. "Look," he said, "this isn't what you think."

"Take your hand off your gun and we'll talk about it," I said mildly. And very carefully he let go of his gun and lowered his hand.

"Seems to me," I said, "that you've killed one of our steers, on our range. I've seen men hung for less."

The stiffness and harshness had gone out of him. He measured me carefully. "Talon, this looks bad, mighty bad. The worst of it is, it *is* your steer, and he's wearing my brand."

"Your brand?" I was startled. To tell the truth, I'd seen that steer around and hadn't noted the brand, something a cowhand does naturally as he rides about his business. But this one had been pushed in among other cattle, and somehow I hadn't noticed.

"*Our* steer? Wearing *your* brand?" I repeated.

"Talon, this brand's two or three years old. And you can believe it or not, but I'm no rustler. I want every cow critter I can latch on to, but *honestly* latch on to. I'd steal from no man."

He paused. "Rossiter may believe different, an' you boys, too, but it's a fact. I never stole a beef from any man except for range eating . . . which we all do when we're out from home."

He continued. "A couple of years back I saw this steer following one of your cows. Now that'll happen now and again, when a calf loses its ma early and just takes after some cow that happens to be close by. But I paid it no mind until something else showed up a while back. Then I started to get curious, almighty curious."

Balch held out the patch of hide he had cut from the steer's hip. When a brand has been reworked, with another brand burned over it, it may look all right from the outside, but a look at the back side of the hide shows plainly what has been done.

385

"Been altered, all right," I agreed. "Ours to yours. There's evidence for a hanging, Balch."

He nodded. "Talon, I'll take an oath I didn't do it, and I'll speak for my boys, too. I'll admit, I've hired on some rough men lately, but the boys I had two years ago—and most of them are still with me—were honest as the day is long."

Balch paused again. "And why should I check the brand on a steer that reads to be mine? Talon, there's something goin' on here. I don't know what it is, or why, but somebody has been misbranding stock. Somebody has branded your cattle to look like mine, and they've done it the other way, too."

Now I didn't like Balch. He was a rough, hard-shouldered man who'd walk right over you if he could, but right now I believed him.

"Looks like somebody might be trying to stir up trouble," I said. "Maybe somebody wants us to fight."

"I thought of that."

"Maybe somebody wants to fall heir to all this range and what cattle are left, somebody who figures he's got a lot of time."

"Maybe . . . But who?"

Oddly, at that moment I thought of Lisa. I did not like mysteries or puzzles, not when they concerned my life or my work. And now we had two.

Might they be solved the same way?

After all, who *was* Lisa? Where was her family? Where was her home?

You'd think, in a big, wide-open land like this, that people wouldn't know each other. But a ranch community is tightly knit and everybody knows everything about each other . . . or thinks they do. A stranger is spotted at once, and nobody's quite satisfied until the stranger has been fitted into a place in the scheme of things. Yet nobody knew anything about Lisa.

Which meant two things, at least. Lisa was new to the country, and she lived in some remote place.

Who else was there?

The major . . . obviously out of the question. He had all he wanted, lived exactly like he wanted, was the most important man in the area, both in his own mind and that of others.

"Take some thinking," I said, after a bit. "Balch, let's keep this under our hats. If you come up with any ideas, let me know."

Suddenly, on an inspiration, I told him how I'd been shot. Of somebody hunting me down.

"Why you?" he was puzzled.

"Some of our boys thought it was your outfit. It seems some of the folks around have heard I was good with a gun, and they figure your boys would like to have me out of it."

"No . . . I doubt that." He looked up at me. " Talon, my boys aren't afraid of you . . . or anybody else. They've offered to brace you, bring matters to a showdown, and I've put my thumb down on it. Talon, if somebody shot at you, it was not one of our bunch."

"All right," I agreed. "You keep your lot and I'll try to keep ours. Meanwhile, let's say nothing and see what develops. When it begins to appear that we aren't going to fight, whoever it is may try something more drastic."

Balch held up his hand. "All right, Talon. I'll ride with that."

He rode out of the hollow and, not being a wasteful man, I stepped down and cut myself a few steaks before turning back to the cabin.

Now I had to talk to Joe Hinge. Fortunately, none of the Stirrup-Iron outfit were trouble hunters. There must be no trouble with Balch and Saddler.

All the way back to the new corral that had been put together in the brush while I was laid up, I thought about the situation. But I came no closer to seeing an answer.

Joe Hinge, Roper, Fuentes and Harley had done some work. Using a wide clearing in some brush, they had fenced in the few openings and had them an easy corral for holding stock, until it could be drifted down to the ranch. It was a rawhide job, but it was all we needed. There were a dozen places the cows might get out if they knew it, but we'd not leave them in there long enough for them to make any discoveries, or even to realize they were penned.

Fuentes showed up with some cattle and we bunched them, and got them into the corral. When we had the bars up on the crude gate, I told him about Balch.

"Say nothing . . . not to anybody," I said. "You'll see that steer, anyway, and you should know. Something stinks to high heaven, and I want to know what it is."

He rolled his cigar in his white teeth and gave me an amused look. "You do not think I am a thief, eh? You do not think I steal cows?"

"Well," I said, "I don't know about that. I'm just bettin' you wouldn't steal the cows of a man you worked for." I grinned. "To tell you the truth, I don't think you'd steal any cows. And I don't want you to shoot anybody without reason."

He looked at the end of his cigar. "I think, amigo, you be careful.

I think something happen soon. I think maybe these thieves, I think they find out what you know. They try to kill you."

"They've already tried," I said.

We rode back to the cabin and stripped our horses of their gear and went to the line-cabin and washed up. I was putting on my shirt when a horse came over the rise, coming fast.

It was ridden by Ann.

Fuentes was standing by the doorjamb with a Winchester. She gave him a quick look. "You all forted up? What's happened?"

"Nothing," I said. "We just don't want it to happen to us."

"Pa wants to see you," she said to me. "You're invited for dinner."

"Sorry," I said. "I've got nothing but my range outfit with me."

"That's all right." She glanced at Tony. "Sorry, he wants to talk to Milo . . . confidentially."

Fuentes shrugged. "Both of us could not be away, but if he goes, keep him all night. He is not strong, senorita. He works, but he is still weak. I see it."

"Who's weak?" I blustered. "I can down you anytime!"

He grinned at me. "Perhaps, amigo. Perhaps. But I think the night air on a long ride, I think it not good for you, eh?"

I knew what he was getting at, and he had a point. But I wasn't the only one. "Night air isn't good for you, either," I said. "I'm scared to leave you alone. The boogers might get you."

"Me?" He looked surprised.

"Even you. Boogers get funny ideas. They might think you know as much about them as I do."

"Will you two stop the nonsense?" Ann said impatiently. "You talk like a couple of children."

"He is always the joker, this one," Fuentes said. "Only sometimes does he make the sense."

Luckily, I had a clean shirt in the line-cabin. It took me no time to get into it, and I'd just washed and combed my hair, so we lit out. Fortunately, she wanted to get to the ranch and she was in a hurry. We rode fast and I liked that, because a fast-riding man makes a poor target.

What I'd expected I was not sure, but what I found was certainly unexpected. The major's house was big, white and elegant, with white columns across the front, four of them, and a balcony between the two on each side of the door. There was a porch swing and some chairs, a table, and three steps up to the porch.

For a moment, I hesitated. "Are you sure he wants me in there? And not out at the bunkhouse?"

"I am sure."

We walked in, and the major looked around from the big chair in which he sat, removing his glasses as he did so.

"Come in, come in, son!" He got to his feet. "Sorry I had to send Ann for you, but she had a horse saddled."

"It was a pleasure, sir."

He looked at me again, a puzzled measuring look. He gestured toward a chair opposite his. "Something to drink? A whiskey, perhaps?"

"Sherry, sir. I'd prefer it . . . unless you have Madeira."

He looked at me again, then spoke to the elderly Chinese who came in at that moment. "Fong, brandy for me, and Madeira for this gentleman." He glanced at me again. "Any particular kind?"

"Boal or Rainwater . . . either will do."

Major Timberly knocked the ashes from his dead pipe and sucked on it thoughtfully. Several times he glanced at me from under his thick brows. Then he began to pack his pipe with tobacco. "I don't quite place you, young man."

"No?"

"You are working cattle for a neighbor, and from what I hear you are known as a man who is good with a gun. Yet you have the manners of a gentleman."

I smiled at him. "Sir, manners do not care who wears them, no more than clothes. Manners can be acquired, clothes can be bought."

"Yes, yes, of course. But there is a certain style, sir, a certain style. One knows a gentleman, sir."

"I've not noticed that it matters to the cattle, sir, if a man has a good horse and knows how to swing a rope. I don't believe they have any preference as to whether a man is a gentleman or not . . . And in these days all manner of men come west."

"Yes, yes, of course." Major Timberly lit his pipe. "I understand you've been shot at?"

"More than that, sir. I've been hit."

"And you've no idea who did it?"

"Not at present, sir."

"Talon, I need men. Especially, I need a man who is good with a gun. It looks to me like this country is headed for a war . . . I don't know why, or how, or when . . . I don't know who will begin it, but I want to win." He puffed strongly on the pipe. "Furthermore, I intend to win."

"What do you hope to gain, sir?"

"Peace . . . Security. For a little while, at least."

"Of course, sir. They are things we never have for long, do we, sir?" I paused. "If you are wanting to hire me as a warrior, don't waste your time. I am a cowhand, that's all."

"Is that why Rossiter hired you?" the major spoke sharply, his irritation showing.

"I suspect I was hired because Joe Hinge said he needed a hand. They had no idea I could use a gun. I do not advertise the fact. Furthermore, I see no need for trouble here. I believe nothing is at stake that you, Balch, Saddler and Henry Rossiter cannot arrange between you. If you go to war, you'll play right into the hands of whoever is stirring this up."

He was very quiet. For a moment he smoked, and then he asked very gently, "And who might that be?"

"I do not know."

"And who could it be but one of us three? We are all there is."

The Madeira was good. I put my glass down and said, without really believing it, "Suppose it was an outsider? Someone safely away, who causes certain things to happen that arouse your suspicions?"

I waved my hand at the surroundings. "Several hundred thousand acres of range are at stake, Major." Suddenly, I changed the subject. "How is your gather progressing?"

He threw me a quick look. "So, so . . . Yours?"

"The same," I paused ever so briefly. "And your young stuff?"

He put his glass down hard. "Now what do you mean by that, young man? What do you know about my cattle?"

"Nothing at all, but I've a suspicion you are losing stock. I've a suspicion that you aren't finding much that is three years old or less."

He glared at me. "You're right, damn it! Now how did you know that?"

"Because it is the same with us, and the same with Balch and Saddler." I took up my glass. "We've found very little under four years old."

He put his glass down and wiped the back of his hand across his mouth. "It's damnable! Damnable, I say!" He gestured around him. "I live well, young man. I *like* to live well. But it costs money, damn it. It costs a lot of money, and I need every head of stock I can get. Believe me, young man, I'd say this to nobody else but you, but you're a gentleman, sir. I don't care what your job is, you're a gentleman, and you'll hold what I say in confidence."

He paused. "I *need* that breeding stock! I owe money. A lot of money. Folks believe me to be a rich man, and if the cattle I should have are out there, I am. But if they are not, and they do not seem to be, I'll lose all this. Every bit of it. And if you fail me and say I said that, I'll call you a liar, sir, and I'll call you out, gunfighter or no."

. "You may be sure I'll not speak of it. Does your daughter know?"

"Ann? Of course not! Women have no head for business, sir. Nor should they have. Women have beauty, graciousness and style, and that is why we love them and why we work for them. Even a poor man, sir, wants those qualities in a woman, and his wife should have them in his eyes. Ann knows nothing of this, and shall know nothing."

"And if something happens to you? What then? How will she manage?"

Major Timberly waved a hand. "Nothing will happen." He got up suddenly. "Balch and Rossiter have lost young stock, too? That puts a different look on it. Unless . . ." he paused and turned to look at me, "unless one of them is stealing from himself, too, to appear innocent. My boy, if what we assume is true, those cattle have been stolen over a period of years, stolen very carefully so their disappearance would not be noted."

My thoughts were running upon what he had said about women not understanding business. He should have known my mother. Em Talon was a quarter of an inch under six feet, a tall, rawboned mountain woman. She had been handsome as a young woman, yet I doubt if she had ever been what one would call pretty . . . striking, perhaps.

Even while my father lived, she had been the one who operated the ranch. A shrewd judge of stock as well as of men, she was strongly a Sackett, which was her family name. She was a strong woman, a woman fit to walk beside a strong man, which pa had been. Yet he was a builder, and only half a rancher.

Major Timberly and I talked long, and finally when it was time for bed, he said, "Young man, if you learn anything new, come quickly to me. If you have to take action to stop this rustling, do so, and I will back you."

"That's just it, sir. It must not be stopped."

"Not stopped? Are you daft?"

"No, sir. First we must find out what is being done with the cattle. I believe they are being held somewhere, in some hidden place, some distance off. If we put pressure on the rustlers now, they'll just get off with the herd and drive to Mexico. And that will be the end of it.

"Leave it to me, Major. I think I have an idea. If you wish to get in touch with me again, I'm at the line-cabin. If I'm not there, tell Fuentes."

"The Mexican?"

"He's the best hand on the Stirrup-Iron, Major, and a solid man."

"Of course. I meant no offense. I know Fuentes well, and he can go to work for me anytime he's of a mind to."

When I was at breakfast the following morning, the major did not appear, but Ann did.

She came in, looking bright and sunny in a starched gingham dress of blue and white with a kind of blue scarf at her throat.

"You and Pa talked a long time," she said brightly. "Did you ask him for my hand?"

"As a matter of fact," I said, "we talked about cattle. Didn't get around to you."

"You mean he didn't give you his little oration on women not knowing anything about business? I am surprised. He always enjoys that subject. He's a dear, but he's silly. I know more about the business of this ranch than he does, and have . . . since I was twelve. Ma told me I'd have to look after him."

I chuckled. "Does he know that?"

"Oh dear, no! He'd be very upset. But he's very bright about cattle and horses, Milo. He can make money, but he can also spend it . . . far too well. Even at that, we'd be doing well if it wasn't for the stock we've lost."

"Much?"

"Over half our young stuff . . . and some of the best six-year-olds are gone."

Over half? Balch and Rossiter had lost almost *all*. Was there a clue here? Actually, the major's stock was better than that of Stirrup-Iron or Balch and Saddler. He'd brought in a couple of excellent bulls, and was breeding more beef on his young stuff, so why only half or a bit more?

That needed some thinking, but when I rode out that morning I put the idea out of my mind. The first few miles led over a wide prairie where nobody could get within two miles of me without being seen. There were a few scattered cattle wearing the Stirrup-Iron, and I started them off ahead of me. But nearing the low rolling hills I grew cautious.

Such hills are deceptive, and they offer hiding places that do not seem to be there. I had cut wide to bring back a cow with a notion for the high country when I saw the tracks—several fresh tracks, clearly defined, of a fast-moving, smooth-stepping horse.

The tracks pointed toward the hills on my left, so my eyes swept the grassy crests but saw nothing that looked to be out of place. The steel-dust moved of his own volition to head a steer to the right, and I held my place there.

Suddenly, I let out a whoop and started the cattle running through the draw, yet once I had them started I swung the gray and went up the left slope at a run.

The gray topped out on the crest just as a bullet clipped past my ear, and then I saw a flurry of movement, somebody scrambling into a saddle, and a horse leaving at a dead run.

The gray was a runner, and it liked to run. Despite the quick scramble up the slope it was off and running without a word from me. I shucked my rifle, sighted on the bobbing figure ahead, and tried a shot.

I missed.

At the distance and at a bobbing target, it would have been a miracle had I not missed, but suddenly the rider whipped his horse over and vanished!

The rider was now two hundred yards off, and by the time I reached the place and saw the narrow slide that led into a wooded valley below, he was through the gap and gone. I went down it, and then pulled up.

Before me stretched a good half mile of thick brush ending in some broken hills. There was a scent of dust in the air, nothing more. The man I pursued might be in there anywhere, might be waiting for me to come on and be killed. Nonetheless, this was as close as I'd come and—

Tracks . . . The earth was dusty but I found a partial one and, taking that direction, picked up another. In a moment I was in the dense thicket, dodging prickly pear and mesquite.

Another track, a broken mesquite twig, leaves just coming back into place after something had pushed through them. I followed carefully, keeping a sharp lookout to left and right. Yet an hour of search brought me nothing.

Whoever had fired at me had gotten away again. I had a hunch my luck was running out. After all, how many times can a man miss?

Granted, he'd not had many good chances, but luck had saved my bacon, and such luck does not last. The odds were against me.

Dropping down in the arroyo, I rode on after my cattle, which had drifted on through a small, scattered thicket and were now beginning to spread out to graze. Once more I made my gather and started on, picking up two more head as I moved.

Fuentes was gone when I came in, but Danny Rolf was there.

He was seated at the table with a cup of coffee in his hand, yet I had the sudden impression that he had not been there long.

He looked up sharply, guiltily, I thought. Then put his cup down. "Howdy," he said. "Wondered where you was."

Chapter 15

Taking my cup, I went to the coffeepot and filled it. My eyes caught a bid of mud, still damp, near the hearth. I looked at it, suddenly every sense alert.

Mud? Where around here was there mud? I glanced out the door toward the water trough. It had not overflowed, and the earth around it was dry.

Straightening up, I took a swallow of coffee, taking the opportunity to look past the cup at Danny Rolf's boots.

Mud.

Dropping into a chair across the table, I glanced out the door again. His horse was tied on the far side of the corral, a curious thing in itself. The sort of thing a man might do who wanted to approach the cabin unseen, yet not to actually sneak up to it.

"Any luck?"

"Huh?" He was startled, obviously worried by something else. "Luck? Oh, no. Found a few head, but they're gettin' flighty. Hard to round up now, they've been drove so much."

He looked at my hat. "You're sure gettin' a good hat ruined. Better buy you a new one."

"I was thinking of that, but it's a far piece to where I can get one. Not many places this side of San Antone."

He looked at me suddenly. "San Antone? That's the wrong direction. Why, there's places north of us . . . I don't think they're so far off."

Neither of us said much, each busy with his own thoughts. Danny's clothes were dusty—except for those boots. He'd been working or riding . . . But where?

"Danny," I said, "we've got to go easy. Lay off the Balch and Saddler outfit."

"What's that mean?" He shot me a straight, hard look.

"They've been losing stock, too. There may be somebody else who wants trouble between us so he can pick up the pieces."

"Ah, I don't believe it," he scoffed. " What are they hiring gun-fighters for? You know damn well Balch would ride roughshod over anybody got in his way. And as for that son of his—"

"Take it easy. We don't have a thing to go on, Danny. Just dislike and suspicion."

"You ain't been around long. You just wait and see." He paused. "You been workin' south of here?"

"Some . . . Mostly east."

"Joe Hinge said you're needed over on the other side. He's fixin' to start cleanin' out our cattle from the Balch and Saddler stuff. If you're really good with that gun, that'll be the place for you."

"It needn't come to shooting."

He looked at me slowly, carefully. "That Ingerman, he shapes up pretty mean. An' Jory Benton . . . I hear he's gunnin' for you."

He seemed to be trying to irritate me, so I just grinned at him and said, "Ingerman is tough . . . I don't know about Benton, but Ingerman is a fighter. He's tough and he's dangerous, and any time you go to the mat with him, you'd better be set for an all-out battle. He takes fighting wages, and he means to earn them."

"Scared?"

"No, Danny, I'm not, but I'm careful. I don't go off half-cocked. When a man pulls a gun on another man, he'd better have a reason, a mighty good one that he's mighty sure of. A gun isn't a toy. It's nothing to be worn for show or to be flashed around, showing off. When you put a hand on a gun you can die."

"You sound like you're scared."

"No. I sound like what I am, a cautious man who doesn't want to kill a man unless the reason demands it. When a man picks up a gun he picks up responsibility. He has a dangerous weapon, and he'd better have coolness and discretion."

"I don't know what that means."

"He'd better have judgment, Danny. That other man who wears a gun also has a family, a home, he has hopes, dreams, ambitions. If you're human, you must think of that. Nobody in his right mind takes a human life lightly."

He got up, stretching a little. The mud on his boots was drying. He had gotten it somewhere not too far from here, but where? There were other waterholes . . . the springs Fuentes had showed me and a

couple we'd found, but they were over east. Of course, there was also
the creek over there.

"Seen Ol' Brindle?" I asked him suddenly.

"Brindle? No. Hope I never do."

"Better stay away from the creek," I said casually. "That's where
I saw him last."

"What creek?" he demanded belligerently. "Who says I been
around any creek?" He stared at me suspiciously, his face flushed and
guilty.

"Nobody, Danny. I was just telling you that's where Brindle is.
Joe Hinge doesn't want any of us getting busted up by him."

He walked toward the door. "I better be gettin' back." He lingered
as if there were something else on his mind, and finally he said, "That
girl whose box you bought. You sweet on her?"

"Lisa? No. She just seemed to be all alone, and I didn't know
anybody very much, so I bid on her box."

"You spent a lot of money," he accused. "Where'd you get that
kind of money?"

"Saved it. I'm no boozer, Danny, and I'm a careful man with a
dollar. I like clothes and I like horses, and I save money to spend on
them."

"You fetched a lot of attention to her," he said. "You brought
trouble to her, I'm thinkin'."

"I doubt it, but if I did it was unintentional."

He still lingered. "Where at did she say she lived?"

"She didn't tell me."

He thought I was lying. I could see it in his face, and I had a
hunch, suddenly, that Danny had been doing his own thinking about
her. Ann Timberly was out of his class, and so was China Benn. Barby
Ann was thinking only of Roger Balch, and Danny was young, and he
was dreaming his own dreams, and here was a girl who might fit right
into them. If he had taken a dislike to me, which was possible, she
might be the reason.

"If she didn't tell me, it's because she didn't want me to know.
It was my feeling she didn't want anybody to know. I think she's got
a reason for keeping herself unknown."

"You sayin' there's something wrong about her?" He stared at me,
hard-eyed and eager to push it further.

"No, Danny. She seemed a nice girl, only she was scared about
something. She did tell me that nobody knew she was there and she
had to get right back."

We talked a little longer to no purpose, and he went out and rode away. I walked to where his horse had been tied. There were several lumps of dried mud that had fallen from his horse's hooves.

If he had come far, that mud would have been gone before this. The mud had been picked up somewhere not too far off . . . But where?

I was stirring up the fire for cooking when Fuentes came in. He stripped the gear from his horse, noticed the tracks Danny had left and glanced toward the cabin.

Standing in the door, I said, "It was Danny. Had something on his mind, but he didn't say what. Said he saw Hinge. He wants us to come in. He's going to work west of here, up on the cap-rock. He's afraid there'll be trouble."

After a moment, I said, "I don't think there will be. I think Balch will stand aside."

"What about Roger?"

Well, what about him? I thought about Roger, and those two guns of his, and the itch he had to prove himself bigger than he was. I'd ridden with a number of short men, one time and another, and some of them the best workers I'd ever come across . . . Good men. It wasn't simply that he was short that was driving Roger. There was some inner poison in the man, something dangerous that was driving him on.

Fuentes changed the subject. "Found some screw-worms today. We had better check every head we bring in."

"Danny wants to work this part of the range."

Fuentes looked around at me. "Did he say why?"

"No, but I've got an idea it's Lisa. That girl at the box supper."

Fuentes grinned. "Why not? He's young, she's pretty."

All true enough, but somehow the idea worried me. Danny was young and impressionable, and Lisa had been frightened of what she had done. She had slipped away secretly to go to the box supper, and that implied that somebody at her home did not want her to go?

A mother? A father? Or was it somebody else? For some other reason?

It was not logical that a family could be in that country long and be completely unknown. So . . . chances were, they had not been here long.

They were living off the beaten track, which didn't mean too much because nearly everything out here lived far apart.

Still, there was considerable riding around. I thought about her clothes. They had been good enough—simple, and a bit worn here and there but clean, ironed, and prepared for wearing by a knowing hand.

Even if Lisa had only been here a short time, it was obvious she did not want to be found . . . For her own reasons? Or because of that someone who did not want her away from home?

"Tony," I paused, "I don't want to leave here."

He shrugged. "Joe needs us. He expects trouble with Balch."

"There will be none."

"You think, amigo, that because of your talk, he will say nothing?"

"Yes, I do . . . But lord knows, I can be wrong."

We packed up what gear we had around the place and saddled up with fresh horses, yet I still did not wish to go. What I wanted was time to ride further south, further east. There were a lot of canyons in the Edwards Plateau country, a lot of places where cattle could be hidden.

Suddenly, I began to wonder. How many head had been stolen? I asked Fuentes.

"Five hundred . . . Maybe twice that many. After all, whoever is stealing is taking from all three ranches, and has been taking for maybe three years. "

"He's got to think about Indians."

"*Si* . . . Maybe he doesn't have to think about them, amigo. Maybe they are friends, you think?"

"Or he's found some hiding place where they won't look."

Fuentes shook his head. "The Apache won't look? An Apache would look into the gates of hell, amigo. So would a Kiowa or a Comanche."

We rode on, not talking. Organized roundups were a new thing in this neck of the woods. Usually a man, with two or three neighbors, would make their gather, sort out the brands and start a trail drive. When they got to the end of the track, they would sell the cattle they had, keeping an account of any brands from their part of the country, and when they got home they'd straighten up.

Unbranded stuff was usually branded according to the brand its mother was wearing—if there was a mother around. And if the rancher was honest. Otherwise, any strays were apt to collect his own brand, and often enough there were a good many cattle that wore no brand at all . . . mavericks . . . To be branded in any way that pleased the round-up crew or the man in charge.

Years ago, down in east Texas, a man named Maverick had traded for a bunch of cattle, and never bothered to either count or brand them. Then when an unbranded cow crittur was seen on the range, somebody would be sure to say, "Oh, that's one of Maverick's!" Hence, the name for unbranded stock.

All was quiet at the ranch when we rode in. We had brought few cattle, as we wished to move right along, and those few we turned in with the lot on the flat.

Joe Hinge was in the bunkhouse when we walked in. He looked up, his surprise obvious. "Wasn't expectin' you fellers? What happened?"

"Didn't you tell Danny to have us come down? He said you were ready to move west after those cattle?"

"Well, I am . . . just about. But I surely didn't send Danny for you, nor nobody else. I figured the first of the week—"

Well, I looked at Fuentes, and he at me. "Danny said you wanted us," Fuentes commented. "He must have misunderstood you."

Ben Roper came in. "Seen anything more of Ol' Brindle?"

"He's over there. You want him, you can have him. He's got a few friends scattered around in that brush just about as mean and ornery as he is."

Irritated, I walked to the door. What was Danny up to? I heard Fuentes make some comment about it to Hinge, but my thoughts worried at the problem like a dog over a bone. He had given us . . . or so it seemed . . . misinformation, so he could have the field to himself. I had wanted a few days more over there.

Well, I swore a little, thinking of the ride I'd been planning over to the east and south. I wanted to find those missing cattle, and I had a hunch. Now it would be days, perhaps weeks, before I got over there again.

Ben Roper came out, rolling a cigarette. "What's up?"

I told him.

"Ain't like Danny," he said. "That's a pretty good lad. Good hand . . . works hard. Maybe you're right about the girl. He's been talkin' about her ever since the dance." He grinned at me. "No tellin' what a young bull will do when he's got somethin' on his mind."

He lit the cigarette. "Anyway, you'll get some good grub. Barby Ann's upset, too, and when she's upset, she cooks."

He looked at the glowing end of the cigarette. "That there Roger Balch was by . . . Stopped a while at the house. She's been upset ever since."

"How far is it to San Antone?" I said, changing the subject.

"Ain't never been there from here," he said doubtfully. "Maybe a hundred mile. Could be more." He glanced at me. "You goin' to light a shuck? Hell, man, we need you!"

"Just thinking."

Squatting on my heels, I took up a bit of rock and drew a rough outline of the cap-rock in the sand, as I thought it was . . . over west of us.

San Antone was the nearest big town, but it was a long way off . . . several days' ride.

Between here and there was a lot of rough country, and some plains—rolling hills and the like. There were streams, enough for good water even if a man didn't know where other waterholes lay. But a drive of young stuff over that route . . . stuff as young as some of it was . . . was unlikely. A man would be apt to lose half his gather, one way or another.

Wherever those cattle were, it was between here and there, and I'd bet it wasn't more than twenty miles off, somewhere down there in the Kiowa country. He would need water . . . Young stuff will drink a lot while growing . . . And he'd need somebody just to hold those calves . . . unless he had a lot of water and mighty rich graze.

I looked at what I'd drawn, but it wasn't enough. It told me nothing. There were several blank spaces I had to fill in. I needed to talk to somebody who knew the country, somebody who wouldn't be curious as to why I wanted to know. Better still, somebody from whom I could bleed the information without him even being aware I was trying.

Straightening up, I hitched up my gunbelt and was turning back toward the bunkhouse when there was a call from the house.

"Looks like you're wanted," Ben Roper said.

Barby Ann was on the steps, and I walked toward her. Ben went on into the bunkhouse.

She looked white and strained. Her eyes were unnaturally bright and her hands trembled a little. "Talon," she said, "do you want to make five hundred dollars?"

Startled, I stared at her.

"I said five hundred dollars," she repeated. "That's more than you'd make in a year, even at fighting wages for Balch and Saddler."

"That's a lot of money," I agreed. "How do I do it?"

She stared at me, her lips tightening. At that moment she looked anything but pretty. "You kill a man," she said. "You kill Roger Balch."

Chapter 16

Well, I just stood there. Barby Ann didn't look to be the same woman. Her skin was drawn tight, and there was such hatred in her face as I'd rarely seen on any man's, and never on a woman's.

"Kill him," she said, "and I'll give you five hundred dollars!"

"You've got me wrong," I said. "I don't kill for hire."

"You're a gunfighter! We all know you're a gunfighter. You've killed men before!" she protested.

"I've used a gun in my own defense, and in defense of property. I never hired my gun and never will. You've got the wrong man. Anyway," I said, more gently, "you're mad now, but you don't want him dead. You wouldn't want to kill a man."

"Like hell, I wouldn't!" Her eyes were pinpointed with fury. "I'd like to see him dead right here on the floor! I'd stomp in his face!"

"I'm sorry, ma'am."

"Damn you! Damn you for a yellow-bellied coward! You're afraid of him! Afraid! It's just like he says, every damn one of you is scared of him!"

"I don't think so, ma'am. None of us have any reason to jump Roger Balch. I don't think anybody likes him too well, but that's no reason to kill him."

"You're scared!" she repeated contemptuously. "You're all scared!"

"You'll have to excuse me, ma'am." I backed away. "I'm no killer."

She swore at me, then turned and went into the house. Fuentes came to the door of the bunkhouse as I went in. "What was that all about?" he asked, curiously.

I told him.

He looked at me thoughtfully, then shrugged. "I guess he told her he was through. Or that he was marrying Ann Timberly."

402

"Marrying *who?*" I turned on him.

"He's been courting her. Going to call, setting out with her . . . Everybody knows that. I guess Barby Ann found out and faced him with it."

Joe Hinge had been listening. "She'll get over it," he said, carelessly.

"I don't think so," I said, after a minute. "I think we'd better tie down for squalls. The way she feels now, if she can't get somebody to kill him, she'll do it herself."

Hauling my dufflebag from under my bunk, I got out a shirt that needed mending and started to stitch up a tear in it. Most cowhands have a needle and thread somewhere, but this was a buckskin shirt, and I was stitching it with rawhide.

Hinge watched me for a minute. "Hell," he said, "you do that like you was a tailor!"

"Me? I learned watching Ma," I said. "She was handy."

He looked at me thoughtfully. "Where you from, Talon? You never said."

It was a question rarely asked in western country. So I just said, "That's right, I never did."

He flushed a little, and started to rise and, not minding, I said, "Up north a ways . . . Colorado."

"Good country," he commented, and went outside.

Fuentes was stretched out on his bunk. Now he sat up and tugged on his boots. "I've got a bad feeling," he said. "I feel like a mossyhorn steer with a storm comin' up."

I looked at him, then forked out my knife and cut the rawhide, tucking in an end and drawing it tight. "Me, too," I agreed.

Ben Roper rode into the yard and stepped down, stripping the gear from his horse. Then he shook out a loop and roped a fresh one. "Now where'd you suppose he's goin'?" I asked Tony.

"He feels it, too," Fuentes said. "He's just gettin' ready."

Barby Ann came out from the house and called to Ben. "I forgot. Harley wants one of you boys should spell him. He's got to ride over home."

Fuentes started to rise but I waved him back. "I'll do it."

Outside, I told Ben. "Long's you got that rope in your hands, fish out one for me. That gray gelding will do. I'll take over for Harley."

"You just come in," he protested.

"Who didn't?" I grinned at him. "I got to get out of that bunkhouse. I'm gettin' cabin fever."

He put a loop on the gray, who quieted down when he felt the rope. It was a good horse, one I'd never ridden but had seen around. I threw my saddle on him and cinched up.

Ben stood by, coiling his rope. He kept looking at me, and finally he said, "Joe tells me you had words with Barby Ann. That she wanted you to kill Roger Balch."

"Uh-huh."

"How much did she offer?"

"Five hundred."

"Whew!" he glanced at me. "She's really mad!"

"Mad enough to do it herself." I glanced around. Nobody was close to us. "I wonder if her pa knows?"

Ben Roper finished coiling the rope. "He don't miss much," he commented. "Seems like he would, but he knows everything, seems like. "

Harley was waiting by the herd when I came down. "Took you long enough," he said.

"She just told me." I didn't like his attitude very much.

He just turned his mount and rode out of there, not toward the ranch, but south toward where his place was, I guess. I walked my horse around the herd, bunching them a little. They had fed well, and watered, and now they were settling down for the night, although it was just evening. A bit later one of the other boys would be out to help, but the cattle were quiet enough, liking the holding ground. Usually of a morning they were drifted a mite to fresh grass, then brought in closer where the ranch and the hills helped to corral them.

As I rode around, I tried to spot the restless ones, the trouble-makers. There's always a few ready to jump and run, or to cut up a mite.

Sitting a horse on night-herd can give a man a chance to dream. It was just dusk, the sun out of the sky, but night had not blacked things out. Here and there a star hung up there, advance agent for all those yet to come. Later on, the cattle might become restless, but now with the quiet of evening on them, they were laying down or standing, just chewing their cuds and letting time pass. Even the few calves born since we had them on the holding ground had stopped jumping about.

Turning the gray, I rode partway up the slope of the hill where I could see the entire herd. I curled one leg around the saddle horn, shoved my hat back on my head and went to contemplating.

First it was Ann . . . She was quite a girl, when you came right down to it, lots of fire there, but stamina, too. She'd stepped right in when I was hurt.

Aside from stiffness and a care how I wore my belt, my wound was much better. I'd lost blood, but the place had scabbed over, and unless I got to wrestling some steer it would stay that way. I tired fast, and would until I got my strength back, but in this wide-open plains country the air was fresh and clean and wounds healed fast.

From Ann my thoughts went to China Benn . . . We had danced together, and there for a moment all seemed right with the world.

My thoughts veered to the box social, and Lisa. Now I'd no romantic notion about her, yet the mystery of who she was, and where she went to, worried me.

She was in a hurry to get home, which spoke of a strict father or a husband . . . although she'd denied there was a husband.

When it was full dark, Ben Roper rode out. "Get some coffee," he advised. "You've got a long night ahead."

"All right," I said, but I sat my horse. "You know the country south of here?"

"A mite. South and east, that is. We used to ride over to San Antone now and again. If there's four, five in a bunch, it's safe enough. Although Rossiter told me there'd been news of Apaches raiding down thataway."

"Any settlers?"

He shook his head. "Not unless they keep themselves hid. Oh, there's some German folks, moved over from around Fredericksburg . . . But they just run a few cows down that way from time to time."

"Has Danny showed up?"

"He's up at the line cabin, I reckon." He glanced at me. "You ready to go up against Ingerman an' them?"

"There won't be any trouble."

Ben Roper turned his hat in his hands, then replaced it on his head. I'd noticed this was a way he had when he was thinking. "All right," he said, doubtfully, "but I'll be there and I'll be armed."

"Ben? You're a good man, Ben. There's nobody I'd rather have behind me. I think this time they will try for an easy way out and save face, but we've got to be ready for trouble from Jory. If they're as smart as I hope, they'll have him somewhere else. He's got a quick trigger, and he's anxious to prove he's a big boy now."

"That's the way I see it," Ben turned his horse. "Get your coffee," he said. And I turned my horse and cantered back to the ranch.

All was quiet at the ranch. A few stars hung in the the sky, others were appearing. There was a light in the bunkhouse, and two rooms were lighted in the ranchhouse. Turning my horse into the corral, I roped and saddled my night horse and tied him at the corral, then walked to the bunkhouse.

Joe Hinge was reading a newspaper, Fuentes was asleep. "Danny show up?" I asked.

"At the line-cabin, I reckon," Hinge said. "How're the cattle?"

"Quiet. Ben's out there."

From a pair of spare saddlebags I took cartridges and filled a few empty loops. Hinge put his paper down and took off the glasses he used for reading.

"You ain't expecting trouble over west?"

"I had a talk with Balch. If we take it light and easy, I think they will. It'll be touchy . . . especially with Jory Benton."

"Three, four days should do it."

"Joe? You've been around here a spell. What's off southeast of here?"

"San Antonio," he smiled a little, "but that's some way . . . more'n a hundred mile, I reckon."

"I meant in that Kiowa country."

"That's what's there. Kiowas, Comanches, often enough Apaches. It's a raiding trail when they ride up from Mexico or from the Panhandle. Comanches have themselves a hideout in the Panhandle somewhere. I've heard tell of it."

"I meant closer by."

"Nothin' I know of. Few good waterholes yonder, but folks fight shy of them because of Kiowas."

For a moment I stood there, wondering about Danny and thinking of Lisa . . . Now where the hell did she come from? And where did she go?

It was darker when I went outside. My horse turned to look at me, but I walked up to the house and went in.

The kitchen was lighted by one coal-oil lamp, and the table was set for breakfast with a blue and white checkered cloth. I got the coffeepot and a cup and went to the table. Several doughnuts were on the sideboard and I latched onto a couple of them, then straddled a chair and started to look at that tablecloth, but I was not seeing it. I was seeing the country southwest of here toward the Edwards Plateau country. There were a lot of canyons and brakes in there, room enough to hide several armies, and rough country with plenty of water if a body knew where to look . . . and nobody riding that way because of Kiowas.

Was there some tie-up between Lisa and whoever was stealing those cattle? I didn't like to think it, but it could be. And who had shot at me? Someone I knew? Or someone totally unknown to any of us?

Slowly my thoughts sifted the names and faces through the sieve of recollection. But it came up with nothing.

I heard a faint stir from the adjoining room, and a shadow loomed in the door. It was Rossiter.

"Joe?" His tone was questioning.

"It's Talon," I said. "Ben just relieved me for coffee."

"Ah!" He walked to the table, putting out a hand, feeling for the corner. "I hear you've had some trouble."

"Nothing I can't handle," I replied, with more confidence than I felt. "I've been shot at, but he can't always get away."

"How about you? He can't always miss, either."

"If that happens, there's always Barnabas," I said, "and the Sackett boys."

"*Sackett!* What have you to do with them?"

"Didn't you know? Ma was a Sackett. She was a mountain woman, living in Tennessee until Pa found her there."

"Well, I'll be damned! I should have guessed it. No," he was suddenly thoughtful, "I never knew." He drummed on the table with his fingers as I sipped coffee. "You mean that whole outfit would come if you needed them?"

"I reckon. Only we figure each of us can handle what comes our way. It's only when a man is really outnumbered that the clan gathers . . . or when one of us is dry-gulched. Whoever is trying to kill me doesn't realize what would happen if he did. There's only one of me, but you get seven or eight Sacketts and Talons in the country and they'll find whoever did it."

"If there's anything to find."

The doughnuts were good, and so was the coffee, yet Rossiter sat there after eating, obviously with something on his mind.

"Have you talked to Barby Ann?"

"Now and again," I said.

"She's a fine girl . . . a fine girl. Right now she's very upset about something, but she won't tell me what it is." He turned his face toward me. "Is it someting between you two?"

"No, sir, it isn't."

"You could do worse. She's a fine girl, Talon, and there isn't a better cook or baker in the country. She'll make some man a fine wife."

Now I was getting uneasy. I didn't like the sound of what he seemed to be leading up to. I grabbed the last doughnut and took a bite, then a swallow of coffee. I got up hastily. "Ben's waitin' out there. I'd better go."

"All right," he sounded irritated, "but you think on it."

I took another swallow of coffee and went out the door, but paused a moment on the stoop to eat the last of that doughnut. As I stood there in the dark I heard Barby Ann's voice, and it sounded just like her face had looked that other day.

"Pa? What you trying to do? Marry me off to that no-good cowhand?"

"Nothing of the kind. I thought—"

"Well, don't think about it. When I marry I'll choose my own man. In fact, you might as well know. I already have."

"Have *what?* Married?"

"No, pa. I've picked my man. I'm going to marry Roger Balch."

"Roger *Balch?*" His voice was a shade louder. "I thought his pa was figurin' on him marrying that Timberly girl."

Her voice was cold, a shade ugly. "That will change, Pa. Believe me, that will change."

"Rober Balch?" His tone was thoughtful. "Why, Barby, I hadn't given that a thought. Roger Balch . . . of all things!"

Back at the herd I watched Ben Roper ride off with my thanks, and then I started around the bunch. Most of them were laying down, settled down to rest until their midnight stretch.

Yet my thoughts kept going back to that talk I'd overheard. Not that anybody had said anything wrong, but it was the tone I detected . . . or thought I detected . . . in their voices.

I'd have sworn that Roger Balch had told her he was through with her, and that was the reason she had wanted me to kill him. Now she had changed her mind and was going to marry him.

Now just what did that mean?

Riding night-herd when things are quiet is a mighty easy time for thinking. It's almighty still out there and the cows are companions enough. You just set your horse, letting the natural habit of your mind listen and notice anything wrong with the herd, and then your thoughts go where they will.

Barby Ann, mad clean through, wanted me to kill Roger Balch. Yet now she told her father she was going to marry him?

A cover-up? Or a change of mind? Or . . . and the thought chilled me . . . had she thought of death for somebody else?

Like Ann Timberly. . . .

Chapter 17

Joe Hinge sat his horse and looked at us. There were Ben Roper, Tony Fuentes and me, all mounted and ready to go, and it not daybreak yet.

"Take it easy," Joe advised. "Don't run no cattle. Roust out what you find of Stirrup-Iron or Spur and get them back here. Steer clear of Jory Benton or any of that outfit. He'll be on the prod, maybe. Talon thinks they'll lay off, and we got to hope he's right, but don't you boys scatter out more'n you have to. Three quick shots, and you come together."

"Where?"

"Right where we first met up with Talon the first time. Right there. But if you have to, hole up and make a fight of it. You boys are all grown men, and you know what you have to do. Do it easy as you can an' get out. We don't want trouble if we can help it. First place, it don't make no sense. Second place, we're out-numbered and out-gunned."

He paused. "Not that we can't fight. We can. I rode with Jeb Stuart. Fuentes grew up fightin' and Ben, here, he was in the Sixth Cavalry. If need be, we can do our share."

I glanced at Ben. "Sixth Cavalry? Ever run into a long-geared Tennessee boy named William Tell Sackett?"

He laughed. "I should smile. Right out of the mountains and didn't know from nothin', but he sure could shoot!"

"He's a cousin of mine."

Ben Roper glanced at me. "I'll be damned. You're cousin to Tell? I figured Talon for a French name."

"It is. My ma was a Sackett."

We rode out, not talking. We had a few miles to go before we reached the Balch and Saddler range, but their riders could be anywhere about and we hoped to see them first.

It was short-grass country, with scattered patches of mesquite. We spotted a few cattle, most of them Balch and Saddler.

We were coming up a cliff from the lowlands when we saw three riders coming toward us. One of them was Ingerman, another was Jory Benton, and the third was Roger Balch.

"Ride easy now!" Hinge warned. Then he added, angrily, "Just our luck to have that young hothead along!"

We pulled up and let them come to us. I reined my horse off to one side a mite, and Fuentes did the same.

Roger was in the lead. "Where the hell d' you think you're goin'?" he demanded.

"Roundin' up cattle," Hinge said. "We're after anything with a Stirrup-Iron or a Spur brand."

"You were told there were none around!" Roger said. "Now back off and get out of here!"

"A few weeks back," I said quietly, "I saw Stirrup-Iron and Spur cattle up yonder. Those are the ones we want, and nothing else."

He turned on me. "You're Talon, I take it. I've heard of you." He looked again. "At the social! You were the one bought the box!"

"I've been around," I said.

"All right," he said, "now move. Or we move you!"

"If I were you," I said quietly, "I'd talk to my pa first. Last time I talked to him, he didn't have any objection to us rounding up cattle."

"Get off!" he said. Then the gist of my comment seemed to reach him. "You talked to Pa? When was this?"

"Few days back, over east of here. Seemed like we understood each other. Had a right friendly talk. Somehow I don't think he'd like trouble where there need be none."

Jory Benton broke in, roughly. "Hell, Rog, let me take him! What's all this talk for? I thought you said we were going to run them off?"

Hinge spoke quietly. "There's no need for trouble here. All we want is to drive our cattle off your range, just as your boys will want to drive some of yours off ours."

"Unless you want to make an even swap," Roper suggested. "You keep what you've got of ours, and and we'll keep what we've got of yours."

"The hell with that!" Roger declared. "How do we know how many head you've got?"

"The same way we know how many you've got," Roper said.

Jory Benton was edging off to one side. There was a gnawing

tension in him, a kind of driving eagerness to prove himself. "You told 'em to go, Rog," he said suddenly. "Let's make 'em!"

Roger Balch was uncertain. The mention of his father having a talk with me disturbed him. Arrogant he might be, and trouble-hunting he might be, but none of the trouble he hunted was with his father.

What might have happened I didn't know. My own pistol was resting easy in its holster and my rifle was in its scabbard. I was dividing my attention between Jory Benton and Roger, when suddenly Ingerman spoke. "Hold it up. Here comes Balch."

My eyes never left Benton, but I could hear horses approaching . . . more than one.

Balch rode up, two riders with him. "Pa? This man says you and him had an understanding. That he can gather cattle."

Balch glanced at me. "What else did he tell you?"

"Nothin' else."

Balch reined his horse around. "Gather your cattle," he said to me, "but don't mess around. I don't want my stuff all spooked."

"Thanks," I said, and rode right past Benton.

"Another time," he said.

"Anytime," I replied.

The wind was picking up and turning cool. We rode on, found some Stirrup-Iron stock and began working the mesquite to round out the cattle.

We scattered, working carefully through a couple of square miles of rough, broken country. We saw many Balch and Saddler cattle, of course, but by nightfall we had thirty-seven of Spur and nine of Stirrup-Iron. We bunched them in a canyon and built us a fire. By that time it was downright cold, a real Texas norther blowing.

For three days of cold, miserable weather we worked that corner of the range, collars turned up, bandanas over our faces except for Joe, whose hat had no chin strap. He tied his bandana over his hat to keep it from blowing away.

There was a good bit of mesquite wood in that canyon, and toward each nightfall we'd gather more to keep the fire going. Long ago somebody had grubbed out nearly an acre, probably figuring on building a house, and the roots lay piled nearby.

On the third day, Balch came riding with Ingerman. He looked over our cattle. "I'm going to cut them," he said.

I was standing at the fire, warming my hands. "Have at it," I said.

He needed little time to scan that herd. He rode through it several times and around it, then came up to the fire. "There's coffee," I said. "We're running short of grub."

"Send you some?" he offered.

"No, we've about got it. We'll drive 'em out come daylight."

"You made you a good gather." He glanced up at me. "No young stuff."

"No." I was squatting by the fire. "Balch, I'm going to take a few days off and do some snooping around, southeast of here."

"You'll lose your hair. I lost a rider down thataway maybe a year back . . . a good man, too. Feller named Tom Witt. Rode off there, huntin' strays, he said. I never seen him again but his horse showed up, blood all over the saddle. It rained about then and we found no trail."

"Balch," I said, "you've got you some gunhands. Ingerman is good . . . one of the best . . . but somebody needs to ride herd on Benton."

"Rog will do it."

I took a swallow of coffee and made no comment. He looked at me as if expecting something, but I'd nothing to say. "You lay off, Talon. Just lay off. Benton's a good boy even if he is a little anxious."

The dregs of my coffee I tossed on the ground. Then I stood up. "Well, he carries a gun. When a man straps one on, he accepts responsibility for his actions. All I want you to understand is that his trouble is Benton trouble, and it need not be Balch trouble."

"He rides for me."

"Then put a rein on him," I said, a little more sharply. "If you hadn't come right then, somebody would be dead by now. Maybe several somebodies. You've got a son, and a man carries a lot of pride in a son."

"Rog can take care of himself." Balch looked up at me. "Don't tangle with him, Talon. He'll tear you apart. He's small, but he's fast and he's strong."

"All right," I said.

He got to his feet and mounted up. Then he turned, started to say something, and rode away. He was a hard man, a very hard man, but a lonely one. He was a man who believed the world had built a wall around him, and he was eternally battering at it to make breaches, never understanding that the wall was of his own building.

We moved our cattle out, come daybreak, having close to two hundred head, mostly Spur.

It was spitting cold rain when we came up to the high ground. It looked level as a floor, but I knew it wasn't, for there were canyons cut into the earth, some of them two hundred feet deep. There would be cattle in some of them.

Hinge was no fool. "Talon, you an' Fuentes work the nearest canyons, start 'em down-country, or if there's a way, bring 'em here. Ben an' me will stay by." And then he added, "Might be an attempt to stampede the stock, so we want to be on hand."

It was something I had not considered, but Roger Balch or Jory Benton might do just that. Purely as an annoyance, if nothing else.

We rode out over the plain until the nearest canyon split the earth wide open ahead of us. There was no warning. We were riding and suddenly there it was—a crack several hundred yards across. In the bottom there was green grass, some mesquite, even a cottonwood or two. And there were cattle.

Scouting the tim, we found a steep slide that stock had been using. With my horse almost on his haunches, we slid down and moved toward the cattle.

There was Indian writing on some of the rocks, and I was wishing for time to look around. Fuentes glanced at the writing, then at me.

"Old," he said. "Very old."

"You read that stuff?"

He shrugged. "A little." He glanced at me. "My grandmother was Comanche, but this was not their writing. It is older, much older."

He spotted a big Stirrup-Iron steer and started him moving. The steer didn't want to go, putting his head down at me. He had forward-pointing horns, looking sharp as needles, but I rode right at him, and after a moment he broke and turned away, switching his tail in irritation. There was a nice little pocket of our stuff here, and by the time we'd come out at the canyon mouth some three miles below, we had thirty-odd head, mostly big stuff, well-fleshed.

We opened out on a flat scattered with mesquite. There were a few cattle, and with Fuentes holding and moving what we had, I rode off to check the brands. This was Balch and Saddler stuff, with a few of the major's. I cut out a four-year-old and started it toward the herd, my horse working nicely. It was a good cutting horse with a lot of cow savvy, which made the job easier. Riding that horse, the most I had to do was sit up there and look proud.

Yet I didn't like it. We were now a good five miles from Hinge and Roper, and we should be working together.

Pushing a few head, I rejoined our bunch. "You know how to get up there?" I asked.

He pointed toward what looked like a long unbroken wall of the mesa. "See that white point of rock? Back of that. It's an easy way up."

We started the bunch, and while he kept them moving, I rode wide, checking on brands, finding none of our stock. Suddenly, half-hidden by a clump of mesquite, I came on a small fire. A thin trail of smoke was lifting but the coals were black, only a few charred ends showing a thin tracery of glowing red.

Nearby, the earth was torn up and I knew the signs. Somebody had thrown and branded a steer. There was a spattering of blood from the castration, and the earth had been chewed up by kicking hoofs.

I was turning away from the fire when I glimpsed something else— a place where a rifle with two prongs on its butt plate had been standing, tipped against a fork of a mesquite.

Tony was not far off, and I gave him a call. He cantered over. I showed him what there was, including the mark left by the rifle.

"I want to see that brand, Tony," I told him.

He nodded, and we left the herd standing while we rode swiftly around, checking every brand for a fresh one. No such brand appeared. Tony reined in alongside me. Taking off his sombrero, he shook the weight of water from it. "This one is smart, Milo. He drove it away . . . maybe miles from where it was branded."

I'd been thinking the same thing, and had been watching for tracks, but saw none.

We started on with the cattle. Was the man who branded that critter a rustler? A cowhand slapping his boss's brand on a maverick? It was no youngster, but a full-grown animal that he had cut and branded . . . A bull that was making trouble?

More than anything, I wanted to go looking. But Hinge and Roper were up on the mesa holding cattle, and we had more to drive to them so reluctantly I turned away. Meanwhile I tried to remember if I'd seen anybody with that kind of a rifle.

There were a sight of different gun types around in those days, and I could recall four or five I'd seen with those points on the butt plate, set so's they'd kind of fit against the shoulder. A Sharps of one model was fixed that way, and there was a Ballard, too. And some of the James Brown Kentucky rifles.

"You know a man with a rifle like that?" I asked Tony.

Fuentes shook his head. "Not that I recall, amigo. I have seen such rifles, but not here."

We were turning our cattle to climb the mesa when we heard a shot.

It was sharp and clear in the afternoon air, a single, flat-hard report, and an echo, racketing against the rock walls. Leaving the herd, I jumped my horse past it and scrambled for the rim. As I topped out, I saw our herd scattered a little, heard a pound of hoofs and saw a horse racing away in the distance, a wild whoop trailing back.

A second shot, close by, and I saw Joe Hinge sprawled on the ground, saw him trying to rise, then slip back down.

Roper, rifle in hand, came running. I took one glance after the fleeting rider, then raced up to the cattle and dropped from the saddle.

Joe Hinge looked up at me. "Jory Benton! Damn it, I never was fast with a gun!"

Chapter 18

"**B**en? What happened?"

He stared at me, his face flushed with anger and shame. "Why, damn it! I went over the rocks, yonder. Wasn't aimin' to be gone more'n a minute, but that dirty coyote must've been holed up somewhere, watchin'."

Ben shook his head. "Soon's I was out of sight he come up. I heard the sound of his horse and figured it was you or Fuentes. Next thing there was shootin'. Only thing I heard him say was, 'if they're buffaloed, I'm not! I'll show 'em!' And then he shot."

"Was it Benton?"

"It was his voice. I didn't get back in time to see more'n his back, but he was ridin' that blaze-faced sorrel he rode when we saw him before. I took a shot, but he was too far off and movin' too fast."

Fuentes was on his knees beside Hinge, plugging the hole and trying to make him easier. Fuentes was a good hand with a wound— I saw that right away.

"Ben, we need a wagon. You want to go for it?"

"Yeah." Roper turned toward his horse, standing a few yards off. "Damn it, I had no business leavin' him. Hell, I—"

"Forget it, Ben. Hinge is a grown man. He's the boss here. Nobody needed to stand guard over him."

"I'll kill him!" Roper said vehemently.

"Don't butt up against him, Ben. It isn't worth it. Jory's fast . . . If you do go after him, remember this. He's too fast for his own good . . . He doesn't take time. If it comes to a shooting between you, make your first shot count. I've seen his kind, and with them the fast draw is everything. Seven times out of ten his first bullet goes right into the dust in front of his target. Just make sure he doesn't get a second shot."

"The hell with him!"

"Leave him to time, Ben. His kind never lasts long. Now how about that wagon?"

When Ben was gone, we moved Joe to a place slightly below the level of the prairie. Then, with slabs from the edge of the mesa, I built a screen to wall off the wind. We covered him with his saddle blanket, and then we waited.

"One damn hothead," Fuentes said irritably. "He'll get some good men killed, blowing off like that."

"Let's make sure it isn't Joe," I said, scanning the horizon.

Unless I was mistaken, Jory Benton would ride right on back and make his brag about what he'd done. That he had beaten Joe Hinge to the draw and killed him . . . Well, Joe was going to live! He had to live! Yet it was a long way to the ranch—and a long way back with a wagon. I swore bitterly.

Yet I had an idea what would happen. Jory would go back and tell his story. If Balch was smart, he would fire Benton on the spot. But there was another chance that some of his men would be for cleaning house, finishing what they had started before we had a chance to retaliate. For that reason, I had stayed with Hinge and Fuentes rather than going for the wagon myself.

Going to my horse, I shucked my Winchester. Tony glanced at me, but offered no comment. Nor was any needed. He knew as well as I what might happen, and I think Ben Roper did too.

Gathering a few sticks, I prepared a fire for the night, glancing from time to time over the rim at the canyon below. If we were just down there . . .

Any place but this mesa top, with small concealment and no shelter.

Joe opened his eyes and looked around, then started to rise. "Take it easy, Joe," Fuentes said. "You caught a bad one."

"Will I make it?"

"You're damn right!" I said flatly. "Just take it easy." Then I said, "Joe? Think you're up to being moved? We've sent for a wagon, but I mean now . . . down into the canyon?"

He looked at me. "You think they'll come back? It was Jory shot me. Damn it, boys, he never gave me a chance. Just rode up and said if they wouldn't do it, he would, and then he drew on me."

We waited for him to continue. "Hell, I can shoot, but I never was no gunman! He just shot me down, and then Ben topped out over yonder and Benton taken off, yelling. I never figured on him shootin'.

He come ridin' up—" His voice trailed off weakly and he closed his eyes. Then they opened. "You got a drink of water? I'm bone-dry."

Fuentes picked up his canteen. He held it while Joe drank. Then Joe slowly closed his eyes. After a moment, he opened them. "I'm up to movin' boys, I don't like this here no better'n you do."

There was water down there, fuel, and some shelter could be rigged if it started to rain. And down there we could at least heat up a place for him, but keeping a fire up on the mesa in the wind wouldn't be easy.

We brought up his horse and lifted him into the saddle. Joe was a typical cowpoke. He had spent more years up on the hurricane deck of a bronc than he had afoot, so he latched onto the old apple with both hands while we led the horse down the cliff.

Glancing at him, I saw his face had gone white. But his lips were drawn thin and tight and he made no sound. There was nothing but hooves against rock and the creak of the saddles as we went down, Fuentes leading, me coming right along behind.

Once on the ground near the cottonwoods I'd seen, and among the willows, we got busy and made a bed for him out of willow boughs, leaves and such-like. Knowing there would be no buckboard wagon there much before morning, we rigged up a lean-to above him. We staked out the horses, and gathered fuel for a fire.

Hinge was mighty quiet, sometimes asleep, maybe unconscious, and sometimes wandering in his talk. He kept mentioning a "Mary" I'd never heard him speak of when he was himself.

"Be gone a while," I said, "come daylight. I'm going to gather our stock and drift it down this way and give it a start toward home."

"*Si*," Fuentes had been turning the idea around in his own head. I was sure of that. "If the buckboard comes we can bring them in."

Fuentes slept and I kept watch, giving Hinge a drink now and again, easing his position a mite, sponging off his forehead or his lips with a bandana.

Hinge was a good man, too good a man to go out this way because of some hotheaded young no-account. Mentallly, I traced Ben Roper's route as he rode toward the ranch, trying to pace him, trying to figure out when he would arrive and how long it would take him to return. We had our fire in a sort of hollow where there were some rocks, and we let it die to coals but kept it warm. It would be a comfort to Joe if he happened to awaken.

At midnight, I stirred Fuentes with a boot. He opened his eyes at once.

"I'll sleep," I said, "call me about three."

"*Bueno*," he agreed. "Do you think, amigo, that they will come?"

I shrugged. "Let's just say they will. I don't know. But if we figure it that way we'll be ready."

For several minutes I lay awake, listening. There was a frog somewhere nearby in the creek or near it, and there was an owl in one of the cottonwoods.

A hand on my shoulder awakened me. "All is quiet. Joe is asleep."

I shook out my boots in case they had collected any spare spiders, lizards or snakes, and then pulled them on, stamping them into place. Fuentes lay down and I went to the sick man. He lay with his head turned on one side, breathing loudly. His lips looked cracked and dry.

I walked to the fire and added a few sticks. Sitting down in darkness with my back to a huge old cottonwood, I tried to sort the situation out.

Balch was not stealing, nor were we. I doubted if the major was . . . but what about Saddler? I had never trusted the man, never liked him, yet that was no reason to believe him a thief.

An unknown? And was the unkown some connection of Lisa's?

What to do?

First, try to find where Lisa came from, locate her, study the situation, possibly eliminate her as a possibility.

Perhaps the next thing would be to scout the Edwards Plateau country.

From time to time I got to my feet and prowled about, listening. I stopped by the horses, speaking softly to each one. The night was very still, and very dark.

My thoughts went to Ann Timberly, and to China Benn. It was rare to find two such beautiful girls in one area. Yet, on second thought, that wasn't unusual in Texas, where beautiful girls just seem to happen in the most unexpected places.

Moving back to the small fire, I added a few sticks, then went back to the shadows at the edge of camp, keeping my eyes away from the fire for better night vision. A wind stirred the leaves, one branch creaked as it rubbed against another, and far off under the willows something fell, making a faint plop as it struck the damp ground.

Uneasily, I listened. Suddenly I shifted position, not wanting to stand too long in one place. I did not like the feel of the night. It was wet and still . . . but something seemed to be waiting out there.

I thought of the unseen, unknown marksman who had shot at me.

What if he came now, when I was tied to this place and the care of a wounded man?

Something sounded, something far off . . . A drum of hoof beats . . . A rider in the night.

Who . . . on such a night?

Again the wind stirred the leaves. A rider was coming. Moving back to the edge of darkness and firelight, I spoke softly:

"Tony?"

He was instantly awake. There was a faint light on his face from the fire, and I saw his eyes open.

"A rider . . . coming this way."

His bed was empty. As suddenly as that, he was in the shadows and I caught the gleam of firelight on a rifle barrel. He moved like a cat, that Mexican did.

The rider was coming up through patches of mesquite, and I could almost hear the changes of course as the horse moved around and among them—but coming on, unerringly. This was no casual rider, it was someone coming *here*, to this place.

Suddenly the horse was nearer, his pace slowed, but the horse still came on. A voice called from the darkness.

"Milo?"

"Come on in!" I called back.

It was Ann Timberly.

Chapter 19

She stared at me, shocked. " But . . . but I heard you were wounded!"

"Not me. Joe Hinge caught one. Jory Benton shot him."

"Where is he?" She swung down before I could reach out a hand to help her, bringing her saddlebags with her. Before I could reply, her eyes found him and she crossed quickly to his side and opened his shirt.

"I'll need some hot water, and some more light."

"We've nothing to heat it in," I protested.

She gave me a disgusted look. "Tony has a canteen. Hang it over the fire and it will heat fast enough. And don't look at me like that. I've treated wounds before. You seem to forget that I grew up in an army camp!"

"I didn't know." Tony was stripping the covering from his canteen, and rigging a forked stick he could prop it over the fire with. I broke sticks, built up the flame.

"How'd you get here?" I asked.

"On a horse, stupid. They're bringing a rig, but I knew it would take too long. So I just came on ahead to see what I could do."

She was working as she talked, cleaning the wound as best she could, using some kind of antiseptic on a cloth, after bathing it with water.

Nobody had any illusions. She might know a good deal about gunshot wounds, as well as other kinds, but doctors themselves knew mighty little, and there were no hospitals anywhere near. Survival usually meant reasonable rest and a tough constitution—and mostly the latter. Yet I'd seen men survive impossible injuries time and again.

Tony had taken her horse, walked him around a little and was rubbing him down. The horse had been running, all-out and too long.

Seeing her there bending over the fire, I could only shake my head in wonder. She hadn't hesitated, but had come as fast as a horse would carry her.

I asked about that. "Switched horses twice," she said, "at the Stirrup-Iron and at the Indian camp."

My hair stiffened on the back of my neck. "*Indian* camp? *Where?*"

"About twenty miles east. A bunch of Kiowas."

"You got a horse from *Kiowas?*"

"Why not? I needed one. I Just rode into their camp and told them a man had been hurt and I needed a horse, that I carried medicine in my bags. They never asked another question, just switched horses and saddles for me and watched me ride off."

"Well, I'll be damned! Of all the gall!"

"Well, what could I do? I needed the horse and they had a lot of them, so I just rode right in."

"They had their women with them?"

"No, they didn't. It was a war party." She looked up at me and grinned. "I startled them, I guess, and they just gave me the horse without any argument . . . Maybe it was the medicine bag."

"More likely it was your nerve. There's nothing an Indian respects more, and they may have thought some special kind of magic rode with you."

I looked at Fuentes, and he merely shrugged and shook his head. What could you do with a girl like that?

Nevertheless, we both felt relieved. Neither of us knew too much about wounds, although Fuentes was better than I. We had nothing with us to treat such a wound, and I knew nothing of the plants of the area that an Indian might have used.

After a while, she came out to where I stood. There was a faint gray light in the east, and we stood together, watching the dark rims of the hills etch themselves more sharply against the growing light.

"I thought it was you," she said. "I was frightened."

"I'm glad you came. But you shouldn't have, you know. You just lucked out with those Indians. If they'd seen you first, the story would be different now."

"Jory shot him?" she asked.

So I told her how it was, and just what had happened. "Now that you're here, Fuentes and me will ride up on the mesa and bunch those cattle again. They won't have strayed far."

"What will happen now?"

Considering that question had got me nowhere, and I'd done a lot of considering since Jory fired that shot. We could only wait and see.

"I don't know," I replied.

It could be a shooting war, and I knew how that went. It could begin with scattered gunfights, and then it could turn into dry-gulching and no man would be safe—not even passing strangers, who might be shot simply because if they were not on the shooter's side they must be on the other.

A thought occurred to me that I'd not considered before. "I rode in from the northwest," I said, "an' had no reason to think about it. But where's your supply point? This is a long way from anywhere."

"San Antonio," she replied. "We get together. Your outfit, ours and Balch and Saddler. Each of us sends two or three wagons and each sends drivers and a couple of outriders. Sometimes the soldiers from Fort Concho meet us and ride along to protect us."

"But if you didn't go to San Antone?"

"Then there isn't much. Oh, there's a stage station that has some supplies for sale, a place called Ben Ficklin's, this side of the fort about four miles. There's a place across the river from the fort called Over-the-River. There's a supply point there, several saloons, and a few of those houses that men go to. The boys tell me it's very, very rough."

If somebody was to the south of us, Lisa's people, whoever they were, must be getting supplies at one of those two places. It was possible—but hardly likely—they would go to San Antonio alone, through Kiowa and Apache country. Yet even a ride to Ben Ficklin's or Over-the-River would be rough. But suddenly I knew it was a ride I had to make.

Come good daylight, Tony and me, we cut loose from camp and headed for the high ground. A few of our cattle had already found their way down to the creek for water, but we couldn't wait on the others.

They were scattered some, but we swung wide and began bunching them. By now, most of them were used to being driven and we were going toward water. Here and there, some bunch-quitter would try to cut off by himself just to be ornery, but we cut them back into the herd and drifted the cattle down off the mesa and scatted them along the creek to get tanked up on water.

It was close to sundown before we had them down there, and Tony rode in close to me, hooked a leg around the pommel and dug out the makings. He tilted his sombrero back and said, "She likes you?"

"Who?"

He looked disgusted. "Ann Timberly. . . . The senorita."

"Her? I doubt it."

"She does. I know it. If you want to know about romance, ask me. I have been in love . . . oh, dozens of times!"

"In love?"

"Of course. Women are to be loved and I could not permit it that they linger and long for some gay caballero to come along. It is my duty, you see."

"Tough," I said, "I can see how it pains you."

"Of course. But we Mexicans were made for suffering. Our hearts accept it. A Mexican is happiest when he is sad . . . sad over the senorita, whoever she may be. It is always better to be brokenhearted, amigo. To be brokenhearted and sing about it—rather than win the girl and have to support her. I cannot think of loving just one. How could I be so cruel to the others, amigo? They deserve my attention, and then . . ."

"Then?"

"I ride away, amigo. I ride into the sunset, and the girl, she longs for me . . . for a while. Then she finds someone else. That someone is a fool. He stays with her, and she becomes without illusion, and always she remembers me . . . who was wise enough to ride away before she realized I was no hero, but only another man. So I am always in her eyes a hero, you see?"

I snorted, watching a four-year-old with markings not unlike Ol' Brindle himself.

"We are but men, amigo. We are not gods, but any man can be a god or a hero to a woman if he does not stay too long. Then she sees he is but a man, who gets up in the morning and puts his pants on, one leg at a time like any other man. She sees him sour and unshaved, she sees him bleary from weariness or too much drink. But me? Ah, amigo! She remembers me! Always shaved! Always clean! Always riding the pretty horse, twirling his mustaches."

"That's what *she* remembers," I said. "What about you?"

"That is just it. I have the memory also, a memory of a beautiful girl whom I left before she could become dull. To me she is always young, gay, lovely, high-spirited."

"No memory will keep you warm on a cold night, or have the coffee hot when you come in from the rain," I said.

"Of course. You are right, amigo. And so I suffer, I suffer, indeed. But consider the hearts I have brightened! Consider the dreams!"

"Did you ever brighten any hearts around Ben Ficklin's?"

When he looked at me again, he was no longer showing his white teeth. "Ben Ficklin's? You have been there?"

"No . . . I wish to know about it . . . And Over-the-River, too."

"Over-the-River can be rough, amigo. Only now they are beginning to call it San Angela, after DeWitt's sister-in-law, who is a nun."

"I'm studyin' on taking a ride down that way, to Over-the-River and Ben Ficklin's. Seems it might be a good idea to know who comes there, and what happens around about."

"Soldiers from Concho, mostly. Maybe a few drifters."

We cut out a couple of Balch and Saddler steers that wanted to join our bunch, and moved our stock toward the camp. When we came in sight, we saw the buckboard, horses unharnessed, and Ben Roper standing by the fire chewing on a biscuit. Nearby Barby Ann was talking to Ann.

Barby Ann gave me a sharp glance, no warmth in her eyes, then ignored me. Roper glanced at me and shrugged.

"How's the gather at the ranch?" I asked.

"Middlin'. We brung in a bunch, and we're fixin' to brand what we've got when you all come in to help."

"We'll be shorthanded to do much," I said. "Joe won't be around for a while, so there's just you, me, Fuentes and Danny."

Roper glanced at me, a sidelong look from the corners of his eyes. "You ain't heard? Danny never come back." He paused a moment. "I rode up to the line-shack to bring back any stock he'd gathered, and he wasn't there. Hearth was cold . . . No fire for days, and the horses hadn't been fed."

He kicked a toe into the sand. "I picked up a trail. He was ridin' that grulla he fancies. Follered him south maybe seven or eight mile, then I come back. Looked to me like he knew where he was goin', or thought he did."

Suddenly Roper swore. "I don't like it, Talon. I think he got what Joe Hinge almost got. I think somebody killed him."

Chapter 20

When morning came again, with sunlight on the hard-packed earth, there was no change in Joe's condition. He had been hit hard, he had lost blood, and the exhausting ride in the buckboard had not helped. Yet his constitution was rugged, and such men do not die easily.

We needed no foreman to tell us our duties. There were cattle to be moved to fresh grass, then watched over during the day, and the herd had grown in size. One man could no longer keep them in hand. Although during the early hours, when there was plenty of grass with the dew upon it, and when they'd had their fill of water, there was small need to worry.

Danny had not returned during the night, and we looked at the empty bunk, but no comment was made. Each of us at one time or another had found such empty bunks in the morning; sometimes a horse returned with a bloody saddle, sometimes nothing.

It was a hard life we lived and a hard land in which we lived it, and there was no time for mourning when work had to be done.

There would be one man less to do the work. And one man less at the table, one horse less to be saddled in the morning.

Ben Roper was coiling his lariat when I walked to the corral and dabbed a loop on the almost white buckskin I'd come to like. He glanced at me as I led the horse through the gate.

"You think he's tomcattin' around that Lisa girl?"

Both hands resting on the buckskin's back, I thought about that. "Not now," I said, " although that's likely what took him off south. Maybe he knew where she was, maybe he just went hunting. But I think he found more than he expected."

"Fool kid," Ben said, irritably.

"Well," I said, "we've all put in our time at being fools. He had

no corner on it, and he was lonesome for a girl. The last time he was
in the cabin," I continued, "he had fresh mud on his boots, and there
was mud dropped from his horse's hoofs. Made me a mite suspicious."
That was all I wanted to say.

Ben considered that. "Could be picked up in a lot of places. Lacy
Creek, maybe . . . or over east. The Colorado is too far east."

"The Colorado?"

He nodded. "We've got one here in Texas, too."

"The stolen cattle," I said, "seemed headed southeast. Do you
suppose he got wind of something?"

He shrugged. "He might have gone off huntin' that gal and stumbled into something."

"You know anybody with a rifle that has kind of prongs on the
butt plate?"

Ben considered that, then shook his head. "I seen 'em on one kind
of a Sharps, and some of the Kentucky rifles had 'em. Yeah, I know."
He began saddling up. "I've seen those marks, too."

"Ben, we've got to bait the rustler. He's hunting young stuff. Let's
leave some where he can get it, then follow him."

"Maybe," Roper was doubtful. "There's just you, me and Fuentes
now, and work enough for six—even if it doesn't come to a shootin'
war."

"Barby Ann will make a hand. I mean, she'll pitch in and help,
but we'll need more."

With our horses saddled, we went back to the bunkhouse. Joe had
been moved to the ranch house, where Barby Ann could see to him
when we boys were out.

I fed a couple of cartridges into my Winchester and carried it to
the saddle. I slung the saddlebags, then put the Winchester into the
boot. We were stalling. All of us were stalling. There was work to do
and we knew it, but we were just sort of waiting around for something
to happen.

Finally, I straddled my bronc and rode out where the cattle were.
Fuentes lifted a hand and turned back to the ranch house for breakfast.
There were too many cattle for one rider, but they were busy with the
fresh graze for the time. I rode around a mite, tucking in a few strays
that were taking a notion to wander. Then I rode up on the high ground
for a look around.

Far off to the west, there was just a blue haze hiding the cap-rock,
and from up high I could see the dim shape of some low hills against
the horizon . . . maybe twenty miles away.

There was a thin green line where Lacy Creek was, and where Ol'
Brindle seemd to hang out. It was better country for sheep than for
cattle, and coming from mountain country I was less prejudiced against
sheep than most cowmen.

Bert Harley should be back. Yet I saw no sign of movement out
there. It was a vast sweep of country. Far to the east was a line that
might be a branch of the Concho . . . I didn't know this country anywhere near well enough, and had to guess at what I didn't know . . . always a dangerous thing.

Ben rode up to me. "Rossiter figures we should start branding
when we can. He wants to get the herd out of the country before they're
scattered to hell an' gone."

"All right." I pointed toward a shoulder of hill on the southern
skyline. "What's that?"

"Flattop, I reckon. Air's clear this morning."

"You ever been to Harley's place?"

"No. As a matter of fact, Bert's never invited no visitors. Stays
to hisself. You know him. He's a good man but he's got kind of an
ingrown disposition and he just shuts people out. I don't even rightly
know where his place is. This here country's only had people in it four
or five years, you know, and nobody knows it well."

Ben continued. "Marcy explored through here, but I don't rightly
know where he went. North of here, I expect. Folks have been kind
of moving gradually thisaway, but many have been killed by Indians
and some just gave up after a couple of dry years and moved on."

He stopped to scan the horizon. "There's usually said to be six
ranches in the basin, as we call it. That's the major's outfit, Balch and
Saddler, Spur, Stirrup-Iron, Bert Harley's place, and off to the southeast there's a Mexican outfit . . . Lopez. We never see much of them.
They mind their own affairs and most of their graze is south of them."

Ben paused. "I never seen Lopez. He was here before any of us,
but from all I hear, he's a good man."

He drifted off, cutting a couple of bunch-quitters back into the
herd.

Branding that lot of cattle was a big job for three men, even if
Barby Ann helped. It would be slow, and it would mean a lot of work.
For myself, while never shirking any job, I'd no wish to tackle that
one.

Bert Harley showed up about the middle of the morning, and I
headed off for the ranch. Fuentes was there. He'd been up to the line-
cabin.

"Amigo? That shirt you wore when you were shot at? The red-checked one?"

"What about it?"

"Did you bring it back with you? Back here?"

"As a matter of fact, I washed it out one day and when it was dried, I folded it and left it under the pillow on my bunk. Why do you ask?"

"I thought that was what you'd done. Seen it there a time or two . . . But now it's gone."

Well, I looked at him, wondering what he was gettin at, and all of a sudden it came to me. "You think Danny borrowed my shirt?"

"Look . . ." he held out a dirty blue shirt that was surely Danny's. "He was going courting, no? He saw your shirt, figured you'd not care, and swapped his dirty shirt for your clean one, all red and white checkered."

Ben Roper had come up, listening. "You think somebody figured he was you?"

"Well, I was on a hot trail. I don't know which horse I was riding that day, but I believe it was a gray. If he wore my shirt and was riding a grulla . . . at a little distance?"

That was all that was said at the time.

We started the branding at daylight. Fuentes was the best man on a rope, so Ben and I swapped the throwing and branding. It was slow work with just the three of us, but Tony never missed a throw and we worked the day through. It was hot, dusty work, and most of the stuff we were branding was bigger, older and a whole lot meaner than was usual.

It was coming up to noon when Fuentes suddenly called out. "Riders coming!"

Ben turned around, glanced toward the trail, then walked to his horse and slid his Winchester from the boot. I just stood waiting. Branding or no, I had my smoker on, expecting trouble.

It was Balch. Ingerman was nowhere in sight, but Vansen and Klaus were with him.

Balch drew up close by and looked over at me. "If you're branding, I want a rep right with you."

"Fine," I said. "We're branding, so get him over here."

"I'll leave Vansen," he said.

"Like hell," I said. "You'll leave a cattleman, not a gunman."

"I'll leave whoever I damn well please!" Balch said roughly.

It was hot and dusty and I was tired. Only a moment before, we'd finished throwing and branding a five-year-old maverick that had given us trouble, and I was in no mood for nonsense.

"Balch, anybody who comes over here had better be a cattleman. And if he is, he's going to lend a hand when we need him. We haven't any time for free-loaders. Every head we've got in this bunch belongs to Stirrup-Iron or Spur, but your cattleman is free to look 'em over whenever you like. But I'd rather you'd stay yourself. I want a man who knows cattle and who knows brands."

"You think I don't?" Vansen said belligerently.

"These are cattle," I said roughly, "not playing cards or bottles."

His lips tightened, and for a moment I thought he was going to ride me down, but Balch put out a hand to stop him.

"Hunting trouble, Talon?" he asked coolly.

"We've had trouble," I replied shortly. "Benton shot Joe Hinge, or didn't you know? If there's to be any riders from your outfit around here, you handle the job yourself or send somebody who is only a cattleman, not a gunman."

Vansen swung down and unfastened his gunbelt. "You said no gunman. All right, my guns are off. Want to take off yours?"

I glanced at Roper. He had a Winchester in his hands. "All right," I said. I took off my gunbelt and handed it to Fuentes, and Vansen came in swinging.

They didn't call him Knuckles for nothing. He was supposed to be a fistfighter. There'd been bunkhouse talk that he had whipped a lot of men. I don't know where he found them.

He swung his first punch when my back was half-turned, but I heard his boot grate on gravel as he moved, and threw up an arm. He had swung a right for my face with my right side toward him, and my arm partially blocked his punch. Then I backhanded him with a doubled fist that staggered him. Turning around just as he was getting his feet under him, I beat him to the punch with a left to the face, ducked under a pawing swing and hit him in the belly with a right.

His wind went out with a grunt, and I took a step back, nearer Fuentes and my gun, which was slung from his saddle horn within easy reach.

"You better take your boy home," I said to Balch. "He's no fighter."

Vansen's breath back, he lunged at me and I stepped in, hitting him with a short right to the chin. He dropped to his knees in the dust, then to his face.

"Better get him a new name, too," I said. "Better call him Wide-Open Vansen from now on."

Balch's face was stiff with anger. For a moment, I thought he was going to get off his horse and tackle me himself, and that would be no bargain. Whatever else Balch was, my guess was that he was a fighter . . . And I'd already been warned that he was better with a gun than any of his would-be gunmen.

"I'll send a cattleman," he said coldly.

"You send him, and he's welcome. We're working cows here." I paused. "Another thing . . . Is Jory Benton still working for you?"

"No . . . he's not. That shootin' was his own idea. If he's still around, that's his idea, too."

Taking my gunbelt, I buckled it on. They had turned to go, waiting only for Vansen to crawl into the saddle, but I said, "Balch?"

He turned, his eyes still ugly with anger.

"Balch, you're no damned fool. Don't let us fly off the handle and do something we'll both be sorry for. What I said before, I still believe. Somebody is stealing your cattle and ours, and that somebody would like nothing better than to see us in a shooting war. It takes no kind of a brain to pull a trigger, but if we come out of this with anything, it will be because we're too smart to start shooting."

He turned his back on me and rode off, but I knew he was shrewd, and what I had said would stay in his mind.

As they rode away, Ben Roper turned to look at me and shook his head. "I didn't know you could fight," he said. "When you hit him with that right, I thought you'd killed him."

"Come on," I said, "let's brand some cows."

Nobody else came around, and we worked cattle for the next three days without interruption. It was hard, hot, rough work, but none of us had ever known much else, and we leaned into it to get the job done. As we branded stock they were driven over into a separate little valley nearby, where they could be held and watched over by Harley.

Each morning we were up and away from the ranch house before daybreak. And each night, when we'd packed our supper away, we wasted little time. Mostly we were too tired for playing cards or even talking. The cattle we were handling were rarely calves, but big, raw stuff that had somehow run wild on the range without branding.

Then we took a day off . . . it was Sunday . . . and just loafed. Only my loafing was of a different kind.

"I'm taking a ride," I told Barby Ann.

She just looked at me. Never, since I'd refused to accept five hundred dollars to kill Roger Balch, had she spoken to me except to reply to a question.

Fuentes was there, and Ben Roper.

"There's work to do, and I know it," I said, "and I doubt if I'll be home by daybreak."

"Where are you going?"

"I'm going to find Danny," I said.

We were shorthanded and there were cattle to hold, but the thing was eating on me, worrying me. If he was dead, as he probably was, that would be one thing. But suppose he was hurt? Lying out there somewhere, slowly dying?

Danny meant nothing to me, except that he was another human being and we rode for the same brand. But I knew the others had been thinking of it also.

Throwing the saddle on my own dun, I rode out of there when the sun was high. Topping out on the ridge, I pulled my hat brim down to shield my eyes from the sun, and scanned the country.

There had been rain, and the trail would be wiped out. Yet he had been riding a grulla and wearing my red and white checked shirt.

And he had probably been looking for Lisa, who was somewhere south and east . . . Or so we believed.

South and east was Kiowa country, Comanche country, and the land where the Lipans rode.

Even the supply wagons from the ranches crossed it only with a heavily-armed escort. And into that country I was riding . . . alone.

Chapter 21

I rode alone into a land of infinite distance. Far, far away stretched the horizon, where the edge of the plains met the sky. Yet having ridden such distances before, I knew there was no edge, no end, but only a farther horizon, a more mysterious distance.

There were antelope there, occasional groups of buffalo left from the vast herds that for a few years had covered the land, constantly moving like a vast black sea.

My dun rode with ears pricked toward the distance, for he was as much the vagabond and saddle tramp as I, always looking beyond where he was, always eager for the new trail, the new climb, the new descent.

I followed no trail, for the rain had left none. I rode my own way, letting my mind seek out, letting the horse detect. For the dun had been a wild mustang, and they are as keen to scent a trail as any hound, and as wary as any wolf. Somewhere to the south and east, cattle had been taken, and although their tracks were gone, their droppings were not.

More than that, land lies only in certain ways, and a traveling man or a driven herd holds to the possibilities. Rarely, for example, will a man top out on a peak unless looking over the land, and a herd of cattle will never do so. Cattle, like buffalo, seek the easiest route, and are as skilled as any surveyor in finding it.

The herd would go around the hills, over the low passes, down the easy draws. Hence, to a degree, I must follow there. The trouble was these were also the ways the Indian would go—until he got within striking range of his goal. Although once in a while an Indian would top out on a ridge to look around the country.

This was a land of mirage, and even as a mirage would occasionally appear to let one see beyond the horizon, man himself could be revealed in the same way. If a man were accustomed to mirages, he could often detect a good deal from them. And none knew them better than the Indians who rode this wild land north of Mexico.

The Lopez peaks were off to the southeast, and I kept them there, using them as a guide to hold direction. Right ahead of me was a creek and when I reached it, I rode down into the bottom and stopped under some pecan trees, to listen.

There was no wind stirring beyond enough to move the leaves now and again. I could hear the rustle of water, for the creek was running better since the rains. Turning east, I rode along studying for tracks, but drawing up now and again to listen and look around. It was almighty quiet.

There were antelope and deer tracks, and some of javelinas, those wild boars that I'd not seen this far north and west before. they might have been there a long time, for this was new country to me.

There were some cow tracks and, sure enough, there was a big hoofprint, fairly recent, made by Ol' Brindle. I'd learned to distinguish his track from others.

Somewhere those stolen cattle had been driven across this creek, of that I was sure. The rain might have wiped out other tracks, but where they went through the mud there'd still be tracks. It was likely that Danny Rolf had crossed along here somewhere, scouting for Lisa. And she herself had probably crossed, unless . . . unless her direction had been a blind. And when I'd left her at the creek, she might have gone off to east or west.

West? Well . . . maybe, but not likely. The further west a body rode, the wilder it grew. And the least water was toward the west. It was more open, too, for a good many miles toward the Pecos it was dry . . . damned dry, in fact.

The odds said she had gone east or south . . . But what about Indians?

And where, I thought suddenly, was Bert Harley's place?

The stage stop known as Ben Ficklin's must be forty miles off, at least.

Harley's place was not likely to be more than ten miles from the Stirrup-Iron, so it should be somewhere along this creek, or in some draw leading to it. Well, that wasn't what I was looking for.

Suddenly, not fifty yards off . . . Ol' Brindle.

He had his head up, watching me. His head high, thataway, I could have stood up straight under his horns, he was that big. He was in mighty good shape, too.

For a moment, we just sat there looking at him, that dun and me.

Then I reined my horse away with a casual wave of the hand. "Take it easy, boy," I said, "nobody's huntin' you." And I rode wide around him, his eyes on me all the way. When I was pretty nigh past him he turned suddenly, watching me like a cat.

The creek ran silently along near the way I followed, and I wove in and out among the pecan trees, occasional walnuts and oak, with mesquite mostly farther back from the water.

Suddenly, maybe a half mile from where I'd seen Ol' Brindle, I pulled up.

Tracks of cattle, quite a bunch of them, crossed the creek at this point heading south. The tracks were several days old, and there were vague impressions of still earlier drives, almost wiped out by rain and time. Starting forward, the dun shied suddenly and I saw a rattler crossing the trail. He stopped, head up, looking at me with no favor. He was five feet long if he was an inch, and half as thick as my wrist.

"Stay out of my way," I said, "and I'll stay out of yours." I reined the dun around and waded the creek. The water was just over his hocks. Following the cow tracks, I worked my way through the mesquite and out on the flat.

There, on the edge of the plains country that lay ahead, I drew up. The Lopez peaks were still east and south. More closely due south was another peak that might be even higher. They called them mountains here, but in Colorado they wouldn't rank as such. Nonetheless, this was rugged country.

The peak that was almost due south must be a good twenty-five miles away, but there was some green that might be trees along a creek not more than five or six miles off. The trouble was, once out on the plain I'd be visible to any watcher . . . There was low ground here and there, but not nearly as much as I wanted.

Scouting the banks of the creek again, I found no tracks of a shod horse. Whoever was driving those cattle must have been riding . . . Unless he was atop an Indian pony!

That was a thought.

I had thought he must have been riding on air, for there had been no tracks of a shod horse . . . or of any horse, when it came to that.

Puzzled, I worked over the ground again . . . No tracks of a horse, yet cattle rarely bunch up like that unless driven. Usually, given their own time they will walk single file.

Another thought came suddenly from nowhere. Six ranches, I'd been told, and I knew of no farms . . . Where, then, did China Benn come from?

The blacksmith from Balch and Saddler had brought her to the dance . . . Was she a relative of one of them? Somehow I'd had no such impression.

Thinking of China turned my thoughts to Ann Timberly. Now there was a girl! Not only lovely to look at, she was a girl with a mind of her own—swift, sure, always on the spot in trouble and never at a loss as to what to do. Even when it was taking a swing at me with a quirt! I chuckled, and the dun twitched his ears, surprised, I guess.

The cattle tracks were headed south, and I fell in behind. Once in a while there was a hoof print. But more than that, there was a sort of trail here, a way where cattle or something had gone many times before, and bunched-up cattle, at that.

Under the shoulder of a small bluff, some twenty feet high, I drew up in the shadow, wanting to think this out. From here on, I would be in enemy country, and not only cow-thief country.

South of me somewhere, likely close to the Lopez peaks was the Middle Concho. This was deadman's country, and I was a damned fool to be riding here.

Danny was undoubtedly dead or had left the country, and there was no sense in adding my bones to his on the plains of the Concho.

My dun started off of his own volition, wearied of standing. Yet we had gone no more than fifty yards when a wide draw cut into the one along which I rode, it came in from the northeast and I saw the tracks before I reached the opening.

Two riders . . .

Puzzled, I studied the trail.

One always ahead of the other—who followed a little offside and behind. The tracks were from last night, because I could see tiny insect trails in the sand where they had crossed and recrossed the tracks during the night.

Warily, I looked around . . . Nothing in sight. A few more tracks . . . I knew that long, even stride of the first horse: the unseen rider—and probably the marksman who had been trying for my scalp . . . The tracks were clear and definite in a few places, a horse freshly-shod not long since.

Following at a walk, I studied the tracks, tried to understand what it was about the situation that disturbed me. There were a number of places where two could have ridden side by side, but they had not.

Both horses were shod . . . it came to me with a sudden hunch. The second horse was being led!

It was pretty much of a guess, but it fitted the pattern. A led horse!

I knew there was also a rider in the led horse's saddle from the way the horse had moved.

What I needed was a definite set of tracks for the second horse. I got them when they passed some damp sand near a seep . . .

My breath caught and I drew up sharply.

No mistake . . . Those were the tracks of Ann Timberly's horse.

These were days when men lived by tracks and the average cowpoke, ranchman, Indian or lawman could read a man's track or a horse's track as easily as most eastern folks could read a signature. You saw tracks, and somehow they just filed themselves away in your memories for future reference.

I'd had occasion to follow Ann Timberly to her pa's ranch. And I knew the way that horse stepped, knew the tracks he left.

Ann Timberly riding a led horse behind the man I was sure was the stock thief.

She was forever riding the country, and she must have come upon him or his trail—and been caught when he saw her coming, and laid for her. That was a good deal of surmising, but the fact was: he had her.

For three to four years, this man had been stealing stock, preparing for something. And now he had been seen and recognized, and his whole plan could blow up in his face if Ann got away to tell of it.

Therefore, he dared not let her get away. He had to kill her.

Then why hadn't he? Because he didn't want the body found? No doubt. Killing a woman, particulaly the major's daughter, would blow the lid off the countryside. Every rider who could straddle a horse would be out for the killer.

Take her out of the country and then kill her? That made some kind of sense. Of course, he might have other plans.

Now there was no nonsense about it. I had to stay with them. Moreover, I had to stay alive and save her life, and that would take some doing.

That trail had been made yesterday evening, perhaps near to dark. They had camped . . . I'd find their camp soon. They might still be there, but I doubted it. This gent would travel far and fast.

I shucked my Winchester.

Taking it easy, I walked my horse forward, lifted it into a canter, and moved along the shallow draw, alert for trouble.

Maybe I'd come upon their camp. Right now I was seven or eight miles from the creek where I'd seen the tracks of Ol' Brindle, and twelve to fifteen miles from the line-cabin.

Topping out on the plain, I followed the tracks at a gallop, went into another shallow draw—and suddenly got smart. I stepped off my horse and put one flat stone atop another, then another alongside to indicate direction. If something happened to me, and the major and his boys started looking, they might need to know where I'd gone.

Dipping down into another draw among the mesquite, I smelled smoke. Rifle in my hands, I walked my horse through the mesquite until I could see the smoke . . . only a faint trail of it from a dying fire near some big old pecans.

A small fire . . . I could see where the horses had been tied, and where she had slept between two trees. He had slept some fifteen to twenty feet away, near the horses. Where she had bedded down . . . and I could see her heel prints and the marks left by her spurs . . . there were dry leaves all around. He had also taken the precaution to break small, dry branches and scatter them all about where he left her. So if she got free during the night, she couldn't make a move without making noise.

Cagey . . . he was very, very cagey. But I'd known that all along. Whoever the man was, he was a plainsman, a man who knew his way around wild country.

He had made coffee . . . there were some coffee grounds near the fire . . . And the dew was mostly gone from the grass before they had moved out.

They'd made a late start, but that didn't help much because the day was almost gone before I found their camp. Yet I rode on, wanting to use all the daylight I had. And before it was full dark, I'd covered a good five miles and was moving due south.

Now there was mighty little I knew about this country. But sitting around bunkhouses there's talk, and some of the boys had been down into this country a time or two. Where I now was, if I had figured right, was Kiowa Creek, and a few miles further along it flowed into the middle Concho.

This man seemed to be in no hurry. First, he was sure he wasn't followed. Second, this was his country and he knew it well. And, also, I had an idea he was studying on what to do.

When Ann Timberly had come up on him, the bottom fell out of his set-up. For nigh onto four years, he'd had it all his own way. He'd been stealing cattle and hiding them out. There'd been no roundup, so it was a while before anybody realized what was happening.

Now, on the verge of success at last, this girl had discovered him. Maybe he was no killer . . . at least not a killer of women. Maybe he was taking his time, trying to study a way out.

The stars were out when I pulled up and stepped down from the dun. There was a patch of meadow, some big old pecans and walnuts, and a good deal of brush of one kind or another. I let the dun roll, led him to water, then picketed him on the grass. Between a couple of big old deadfalls, I bedded down.

Sitting there, listening to my horse eating grass, I ate a couple of biscuits and some cold meat I'd brought from the Stirrup-Iron. The last thing I wanted was to sit, but by now Ann and the man who had her prisoner had probably arrived where they were going . . . Yet one thing puzzled me.

There'd been no more cattle tracks.

Trailing Ann and her captor, I'd completely forgotten the cattle, and somewhere the trails had diverged. Yet that was not the problem now.

With a poncho and saddleblanket, I made out to sleep some. It was no more than I'd had to sleep with many a night before so, tired as I was, I slept. And ready as I was to ride on, I opened my eyes with the morning stars in the sky.

Bringing my horse in, I watered him, saddled up and wished I had some coffee. Light was just breaking when we started on, the dun and me. And I carried my Winchester in my hands, and spare cartridges in my pockets.

It was all green and lovely around me now. Their trail was only a track or two, a broken green twig, grass scarred by a hoof . . .

Suddenly the trail turned sharply away from the creek, went a couple of hundred yards off, then swung around in a big circle to the creek again . . .

Why?

Reining in, I looked back.

There was an old trail following along the creek bank that had been regularly used, so why the sudden swing out from it? A trap? Or what?

Riding back around the loop, I peered into the trees and brush, trying to see what was there, and I saw nothing. Back at the creek where they had turned off, I walked my horse slowly along the old trail. Suddenly, the dun shied.

It was Danny Rolf.

His body lay there, maybe a dozen feet off the trail, and he'd been shot in the back. The bullet looked to have cut his spine, but there was another shot into his head, just to make sure.

He wore only one boot . . . the other probably pulled off when he fell from his horse and his foot twisted in the stirrup.

Poor Danny! A lonesome boy, looking for a girl, and now this . . . Dead in the trail, dry-gulched.

Something about the way the body lay bothered me. And studying the tracks, I saw what it was.

When Danny was shot he was *coming back!*

He had been to where he was going, and he had started home . . . And the rider who was Ann's captor had known the body was there, and had circled so Ann would not see it.

He, then, was the killer.

Chapter 22

Moving over into the shadow of the trees, I studied the situation. Whatever doubts there might have been before, there could be none now. The unknown man with the rifle had killed once, and he would kill again. Yet as he had brought Ann this far, he might be having doubts. To kill a man was one thing, a woman another.

Moreover, he was wily and wary. In this seemingly bland and innocent country, there were dozens of possible lurking places for a rifleman, and anytime I moved into the open, my life was in danger. Yet so was the life of Ann.

Ahead of me, if what the boys at the ranch had said was true, this Kiowa Creek flowed into the Middle Concho. There was a fork up ahead, and the killer might have gone either way. Yet I did not believe he thought himself followed. He had passed along this creek yesterday, and by now had probably reached his destination.

I swore bitterly. How did I get into these situations? The fact that I was good with guns was mostly accidental. I had been born with a certain coordination, a steady hand and a cool head, and the circumstances of my living had given them opportunity to develop. I knew I was fast with a gun, but it meant no more to me than being good at checkers or poker. It would have been much more useful to be good with a rope, and I was only fair.

Now I was facing up to a shooting fight when all I wanted to do was work cattle and see the country. I'd heard of men who supposedly looked for adventure, but to me that was a lot of nonsense. Adventure was nothing but a romantic name for trouble, and nobody over eighteen in his right mind looked for it. Most of what people called adventure happened in the ordinary course of the day's work.

The chances were, the killer had taken Ann on to wherever he was going, and they should be there by now. There was no time to think of Ann now . . . she was where she was and she was either dead or momentarily safe.

What I had to think about was me. If I didn't get through to where she was, we might both be dead. I could ride right out of here and summon the major and his men, but by that time it might be too late for Ann.

I was no hero, and did not want to be one. I wanted to look through my horse's ears at a lot of new country, to bed down at night with the sound of leaves or running water, to get up in the morning to the smell of woodsmoke and bacon frying. Yet what could I do?

You don't follow a man's trail across a lot of country without learning something about him, and I liked nothing I had learned about this one.

What did I know? He was cool, careful and painstaking. He had succeeded in stealing at least a thousand head of cattle, probably twice that many—*and* over a period of three to four years—without being seen or even suspected.

He had managed to create suspicion among the basin ranchers, so they suspected each other and not an outsider. He had moved around in what seemed to be a wide-open country, without anyone knowing he was around.

. . . Unless he was around all the time and therefore unsuspected. That thought gripped me. If so . . . Who?

Moreover, he had shown no urge to kill anyone until I came along and seemed to be closing in on him.

Danny had probably been shot by mistake because of the red shirt.

But wait a minute . . . Hadn't somebody mentioned another cowhand who rode off to the southeast and never came back?

The chances were, the killer did not kill unless it looked like his plan was about to be exposed. He had several years' work at stake and, just on the verge of success, things started to go wrong.

I had tracked him. Danny had come into his own country. And then Ann Timberly, forever riding the range, had come upon him somehow.

One by one I turned the suspects over in my mind. Rossiter was naturally the first I thought of, because he was a shrewd man, dangerous, and known to me as a cow thief. Nor did I believe he was as blind as he let on. Nevertheless, he could not long be away from the ranch without folks worrying, because of his blindness.

Roger Balch? A tough little man who wished to be known as such, driving to prove himself, but neither cautious nor shrewd.

It could be Roger Balch. It could be Saddler.

Harley? He came and went to his place, wherever it was. He handled a rifle like it was part of him, and he was cool enough, cautious enough, cold enough. He would, I was sure, kill a man as quickly as a chicken.

Fuentes? He had been with me too much. Fuentes wasn't a killer.

Somewhere in my memory, there lurked a face, a face I couldn't quite recall, someone I had seen, someone I remembered. Somehow, from somewhere. But that was all.

That face was a shadow, elusive, indistinct, something at which the fingers of my memory grasped, only to come away empty.

Yet it was there, haunting, shadowy . . . The odd thing was, I had the fleeting impression it was something from my own past.

Only minutes had passed since I'd seen Danny's body. The wind stirred the leaves, the water rustled faintly in Kiowa Creek. Like it or not, I was going to have to go forward.

And I didn't like it. In such a case, the waiting rifleman has every advantage. All he has to do is sight in on a spot he knows you have to pass and just wait until you ride right into his sights. When he sees you coming, he can take up the slack on his trigger. And when he squeezes off his shot, you're a dead man or damned lucky . . . and I didn't feel lucky.

Nevertheless, Ann was up ahead, and there was no way I could get around that.

Using every bit of cover I could, varying my pattern of travel when possible, I rode parallel with Kiowa Creek. Once, in a thick stand of hackberry and pecan, I watered my horse and took time to scan the country.

Right ahead of me was that other arroyo that came into a junction with Kiowa Creek to form the Middle Concho. That was the one Ben Roper had once said they called Tepee Draw. I spotted a trail climbing out of the draw pointing toward the mountain and, returning for my horse, I rode down to where Kiowa Creek and Tepee Draw joined.

A fresh horse trail went up the bank and I started up, then reined in sharply. Not a hundred yards away was a corral, a cabin, and smoke from the chimmey!

Turning my horse, I slid back down the bank and back into the thickest stand of hackberry and pecan I could find. There were some big mesquite trees there, also.

Shucking my Winchester, I loose-tied my horse and found a place in the brush where I could climb up for a look at the cabin. Nothing about the climb looked good. It was a natural for rattlers, who like shade from the sun, but after taking a careful look around, I crawled up. And there, under the roots of one of the biggest mesquite trees I'd ever seen, I studied the layout.

It was a fair-sized cabin for that country, with two pole corrals and a lean-to shed. There was water running into a trough from a spring. I could see it dropping—and almost hear it. There were a half dozen head of horses in the corral, and one of them was a little black I'd seen Ann riding. Another was Danny Rolf's grulla.

Aside from the movement of smoke and the horses, all was quiet.

What surprised me was that I found no cattle anywhere around. Signs were there a-plenty, but not one hoof of stock did I see.

It was very still, and the sun was hot. Probably the coolest place around was right where I was, against that bank, among the roots of that big mesquite and under its shade. Occasionally, a faint breeze stirred the leaves. A big black fly buzzed annoyingly about my face, but I feared to brush it away for I had no idea who was in the cabin. And even where I lay, a quick movement might be seen.

A woman came to the door and threw out a pan of water, shading her eyes to look around. Then she went back inside. I felt certain it was Lisa, but it was more by hunch than recognition, for her face had been turned only briefly my way.

If it was her, I surely didn't blame her for riding up to that box supper, nor for being scared at being away. More than likely he, whoever "he" was, had been off driving stolen cattle to wherever they'd been taken.

Suddenly, the woman came out again. And now there was no mistake.

It was Lisa.

Leading a horse from the corral, she saddled up, then she hazed the grulla into a corner and got a rope on it, then Ann's black. Mounting up, leading the two horses, she started for the trail. In so doing, she would pass not fifty feet from where I was hidden.

Sliding back, I worked around to the edge of the trail. And as she started down, I stepped out.

"Lisa?"

Her horse shied violently, and she jumped. Her face went a shade whiter, and then she was staring at me, all eyes. "What are you doing here?"

"I'm looking for the girl who rode that horse?"

"Girl?" Her tone was shrill, with a note of panic. "This is no girl's horse."

"It is, Lisa. That horse belongs to Ann Timberly. The girl I danced with at the box supper."

"But it can't be!" she protested. "The brand—"

"HF Connected is one of the brands Timberly runs," I said, "and when she left home, Ann was riding that horse."

Her face was deadly pale. "Oh, my God!" There was horror in her eyes. "I don't believe it! I don't believe it!"

"The other horse belonged to Danny Rolf, who rides for the Stirrup-Iron," I said. "At least, it was a horse he rode. He rode down here hunting you, I believe."

"I know it. He came to the house, but I sent him away. I told him to go away and never come back."

"And he went?"

"Well," she hesitated, "he argued. He didn't want to go. He said he'd ridden all day, hunting me. Said he just wanted to talk a little. I was scared. I *had* to get him away. I *had* to." She paused. "Finally, he went."

"He didn't get very far, Lisa. Only a few miles."

She stared at me. "What do you mean?"

"He was shot, Lisa. Killed. Shot in the back and then shot again by somebody who stood over him and wanted to make sure he was dead. And now that same person has captured Ann . . . and I don't know whether she's dead yet or not."

"I didn't know," she pleaded. "I didn't know. I knew he was bad, but—"

"Who is he, Lisa?"

She stared at me. "He's my brother."

Her face looked frozen with fear.

"Lisa, where is he? Where is your brother? Where's Ann?"

"I don't know. I don't believe he has her. I don't . . ." her voice broke off. ". . . Maybe . . . There's an old adobe down on the Concho. He's never let me go there."

"Why?"

"He . . . he met the Kiowas there . . . Maybe others. I don't know. He traded horses with them sometimes, and sometimes he gave them cattle."

"Where were you aiming to take those horses?"

"Over on Tepee Draw. He told me to turn them loose over there, and to start them south. I should have done it last night, but I was tired, and—"

"Where is he now? Where's your brother, Lisa?"

"He's gone. He drove some cattle south. And when he does that, he's always gone all day."

"Lisa, if you'll take my advice, just take those horses out, turn them loose, and keep right on going. Don't ever come back."

"I can't do what you ask. He'd kill me. He told me that if I ever tried to run away, he'd kill me." She stared at me. "He . . . he's been good to me. He's kind and gentle and never raises his voice around home. We always have enough to eat, and he's never gone very long. But I was afraid . . . He came back one day with another rifle and a pistol. I never knew where they came from and I think he gave them to the Kiowas. After that, I was scared."

"You didn't know he was around when Danny was killed?"

"Oh, no!" Her expression changed just a little. "I don't know that Danny *has* been killed. Only that you say so."

"He's been killed. Take my advice and get out. I'm going to look for Ann."

She stared at me. "Are you in love with her?"

"In love?" I shook my head. "I never thought of it. Maybe I am. I only know she's a girl alone and in bad trouble—if she's alive."

"He wouldn't kill a woman. Not him. I don't believe he'd even touch one. He's always been kind of afraid of women. Good women, I mean. He certainly sees enough of the other kind."

"Where?"

"That place they call Over-the-River. He goes there."

"What's his name, Lisa?"

She shook her head. "Stay away from him . . . *Please!* His name is John Baker . . . He's only my half-brother, but he's been good to me. They call him Twin."

"Twin? Why?"

"He was a twin. His brother Stan was killed up north some years back. They'd been stealing cattle. He never would tell me who killed his brother. Or how, except that it was a woman."

"A *woman?*"

"They'd stolen some cattle from her, and she trailed them. She had a couple of her boys. And that woman shot Stan. Killed him."

Ma . . .

"Please, Milo, get away from here! Ride! Do anything. But *get away!* He'll kill you. He's talked about it, lives for it. And he's killed other men in gunfights. I know he has because he's told me. And he always says, 'But just you wait! Them Talons! Just you wait!'"

Henry Rossiter had engineered the steal, but we knew there'd been four other men waiting to drive the cattle away . . . *four*.

Ma shot one, Henry Rossiter got away, and she turned two men loose in the Red Desert in there underpants with no boots. Somehow, in all the excitement, nobody ever gave any further thought to the fourth man.

Twin Baker. . . .

Chapter 23

"**D**anny . . . He was a nice boy . . . Why, oh, why did Twin kill him?"

"He's been stealing our cattle, Lisa. He probably thought Danny had tracked him down. Or maybe he thought Danny was me . . . Danny was wearing a shirt of mine."

She was frightened . . . anguished. Her teeth gnawed at her lower lip until I thought it would draw blood.

"Get away, Lisa. Get away now. Go to Major Timberly and tell him all you know . . . Go now. Don't stop for anything, or Twin may kill you, too."

"He wouldn't do that. I know he wouldn't."

"You know nothing of the kind. I said you should get away, and you must." I paused, suddenly curious. "How long have you been here, Lisa?"

"In this place? Oh . . . five months. Almost six. My father died and I came to Twin. He was in San Antonio on business. He had an address there, and I had no other relatives. He was very kind, and he brought me here.

"I loved it . . . at first. Then it was so lonely, and he'd never let me go anywhere or ride out, unless I went south. Then one day, when I was riding south, I met a drifter . . . He'd been working up north— said he hated to leave because they were having a box supper at Rock Springs Schoolhouse."

She paused. "He rode on, but I kept thinking about what he said. Then Twin left for San Antonio . . . He said he'd be gone for several days, so I decided to go."

"I'm glad you did. Now get your things and get away. If anything has happened to Ann . . . Have you told me the truth, Lisa? You know nothing about her?"

"Honest! I know nothing . . . Except he did pack some food to take away, and there is that old cabin."

She started off, and I spoke quickly. "One more thing, Lisa. Where does he keep the cattle?"

She hesitated, then shook her head quickly. "I won't tell you. Anyway, I don't know they were stolen. He says they are his. He told me he would be one of the biggest cattlemen in Texas soon."

"All right, Lisa. But ride! Don't wait any longer!"

First I had to know that Ann was not up there in their cabin. Lisa offered no argument when I took the lead ropes on the horses from her. She just stared at me, her eyes wide and empty.

I rode up to the door and stepped down. The house was empty. A large kitchen-living room, two bedrooms—painfully neat.

In his bedroom, Twin's clothes were hung neatly, his boots polished. There were a couple of store-bought suits in the closet, some white shirts, and there were three rifles. All in excellent shape, all fine weapons.

Mounting the dun, I led the other horses to the corral. No saddles.

I turned up the Middle Concho. My eyes searched for tracks. He was less careful of his trail up here. Apparently, this was a place where no one ever came. It was off the beaten path. So there were tracks, and I followed them at a gallop. Suddenly they veered and went up a draw.

On the bank of the draw, under some pecan and hackberry trees, I saw an old adobe. There was a pole corral nearby, obviously little used. Grass had grown up around the place, and the roof of the adobe was sagging. Already the outside walls showed the effects of wind and rain. It must have been very old.

Drawing up in the shadow of a tree, I studied the house. Then I looked all around. I was very uneasy, for I had a hunch Twin Baker might not be as far away as would seem to be the case. He might be inside the adobe there, or he might be waiting up behind those rocks across the Concho.

Stepping down, I trailed the reins and took my rifle. On second thought, I loose-tied my horse for a quick escape—if need be.

Somehow, Twin was tied in with the Kiowas . . . Suppose they were watching? I'd no wish to tackle a bunch of renegade Indians.

Finally, I took a chance and walked directly across to the house. The door was closed, a hasp in the lock.

I spoke softly. "Anybody there?"

"Milo?" It was Ann's voice, the first time I'd ever heard a tremble in it.

Lifting the hasp, I opened the door.

She was tied to a chair, the chair tipped slightly back so that if she struggled at all, even moved, the chair would fall back with her head in the fire.

She might then wriggle free of the chair, but scarcely without catching her hair on fire.

Swiftly, keeping my face toward the door, I cut her free. She stood up, almost fell, then tried to soothe her wrists and arms where, the tightly-drawn ropes had left deep marks.

"He said if I screamed, the Kiowas would come. He said he might trade me to them for a horse . . . He hadn't yet decided, he said."

"Do you know him?"

"I'd never seen him before. Not his face, at least. He came up behind me and warned me that if I moved, he'd kill me. And I think he would have done it. It was very dark when we got here, and he did not take the blindfold off until we were in here and I was tied. Then he went away."

Her saddle was in the corner. "Ann? I'm going to have to ask you to carry your own saddle, and to saddle your own horse. I must have my hands free."

"All right."

We went quickly out, and I carried my rifle at the ready, poised for a quick shot.

Nothing happened.

She saddled her horse and mounted. Her rifle had been on her saddle but he had left no ammunition. Fortunately, it was a .44 calibre. She loaded it with ammunition from my saddlebags.

As she did so, I took a quick look around. No man left so little sign of his presence as this Twin Baker. The only thing . . . and it might be nothing . . . had been a little dried mud near the hearth, not unlike the mud that Danny had left in the line-cabin.

Of course, there were places aplenty along the Concho and up the draws where a man might get mud on his boots.

Whatever was to be done now must be done with Ann in a safe place. But, my mother having raised no foolish children, I did not go back the way I had come. In Indian country, that could be the last mistake one made. Even Lisa might have had a change of heart and be waiting back there with a Winchester. For me.

I am not a trusting soul. All of us, me included, are sadly, weakly human. We can all make mistakes. We can all make mistakes. We can all be sentimental about a brother or sister, even when you know they are doing wrong. We can also be greedy, and I preferred not to tempt anybody too much.

What we did was take off up that draw—which pointed almost due north—then top out on the plains and continue north, staying in the open as much as possible. Liveoak Creek was on our right. Some scattered trees and brush lined it, so I kept wide of the creek with a ready rifle for trouble.

Nobody needed to tell me that Twin Baker was as good as they come with a gun. His shooting, often under adverse conditions, had been good, mighty good. That I was alive was due to a series of accidents, none of them due to my brains or skill. By this time, he must be exasperated and ready to try anything.

We rode steadily north. It was a good thirty-five miles to the Timberly ranch and Ann's horse was fresh. My dun had done some traveling but I had the grulla for good measure. So we set a good pace, moving right away from there.

Meantime, I'd had a sudden hunch, and one that might be good for nothing at all. Ann was quiet. She was undoubtedly worn to a frazzle, with the riding and the worry over what was to become of her. Now she was just going through the motions. I knew she wanted to be home and resting . . . So did I.

What worried me was that it had been too easy. We just didn't stand to have that much good luck.

If Twin Baker came up on me, I had to win the fight that was sure to take place. I *had* to win. Because otherwise, Ann would be right back where she had been.

Something else worried me, too. He had some kind of a tie-up with the Kiowas, or a renegade bunch of them, and if they spotted us they'd be scalp-hunting.

That hunch I had was no more than a hunch, but suddenly I'd begun wondering about that man who had been with Balch and Saddler the first day I'd seen them—the man who had looked familiar, but whom I couldn't find a name for.

Since then, I had seen him nowhere around, and he had not been at the box supper. Could be, I'd remembered him from a glance or two when ma and us had first came up on those rustlers. So he might be Twin Baker.

The chance was a slim one, and I couldn't see that it helped any. So maybe I had seen him? What then?

When Ann and I had ten miles behind us, I spotted a waterhole off to one side. It was likely just a place that had gathered rainwater from the latest storm, but it was a help. We walked the horses over and let them drink. Meanwhile, I switched saddles from the dun to the grulla. If I was going to have to run, I wanted it to be on a fresh horse, although as Ma had said, the dun would go until it dropped.

"Milo?" Ann's voice was tremulous. "Do you think he will follow us?"

There was no sense in lying to her, and I'd never been given to protecting womenfolks from shocks. Mostly, they stand up to them as well as a man, and it's better for them to be prepared for what may come.

"He's got to, Ann. He's got four years of stealing behind him, and a rope if he's caught. But mostly he doesn't want to spoil everything now he's so close to having what he wants. He's got to find us and kill us, but he doesn't have much more time. I just hope he doesn't get back and find out what's happened until we're safe out of the country."

"Will Lisa tell him?"

"I don't know. She may run, like I advised, but the chances are she won't. She's got no place to go, and usually a person will accept a known risk rather than blaze off into the unknown. She thinks she knows him, and she trusts in that."

With the horses watered, we started on. Now we let them walk, saving them for a run if need be, and letting them get used to having a bellyful of water.

I glanced at the sun . . . Time was running out. But if darkness came, we might not be found. Not that I had much faith in that.

Where were the cattle? Twin Baker had driven them off to the south, somewhere, and when he made such a drive he was usually, Lisa said, gone all day. Cattle would move at two and a half to three miles an hour, and he would ride back a little faster. Figure fifteen miles, and maybe less.

My eyes never stopped, yet I could see nothing but the wide plain with scattered yucca or bear grass, occasional buffalo bones and no sign at all of Indians.

Ann came up alongside me. "Milo? Who are you?"

The question amused me. "Me? Here I am. This is all I am. I'm a sort of drifting cowboy, moving from ranch to ranch, sometimes riding shotgun on stages . . . Anything to make a living."

"Have you no ambition? Is that all you wish to be?"

"Well, I sort of think about a ranch of my own, time to time. Not cattle so much as horses."

"Father says you are a gentleman."

"Well, I hope I am. I never gave much thought to it."

"He says you have breeding, that no matter what you seem to be, you came from a cultured background."

"Don't reckon that counts for much out here. When a man rides out in the morning, all they expect of him is that he can do his job—that he can ride, rope a little, and handle stock. A longhorn doesn't care much whether you know who Beethoven was, or Dante."

"But *you* know who they were."

"My brother sets store by such things, and so did Pa. Maybe I take more after Ma. She knew cattle, horses and men. She could read men like a gambler reads cards, and she could shoot."

Ann was looking at me.

"Ma sang some. Didn't have much of a voice, but she knew a lot of old Scotch, English and Irish songs she'd learned back in those Tennessee hills she came from. When she was a girl she had no more than eight to ten books. She grew up on *Pilgrim's Progress* and the writings of Sir Walter Scott. She rocked me to sleep singing 'Old Bangum and the Boar,' 'Bold Robin Hood' and 'Brennan on the Moor.' And Pa, he could speak three or four tongues. He used to quote Shakespeare, Molière and Racine at us sometimes. He told us wild tales about the first Talon to land in America. He was a pirate or something and sailed clean around the world to get here."

I paused. "A mighty hard old man, by all accounts. Had a claw for a right hand, a claw he'd made himself after he lost his hand. Came to Canada and built himself a home up on the mountains in the Gaspé . . . A place where he could see a wide stretch of sea . . . Lived his life out there, they say."

"Milo?" She was looking at something.

I had seen them, too. Riders . . . three of them, all carrying rifles.

"Ride easy now," I warned her. "Sometimes talk is enough . . . or a bit of tobacco."

"I've never seen you smoke!"

"I don't, but Indians do. So I carry a sack of tobacco, just for luck. Use it on insect bites sometimes."

We rode slowly forward, and then suddenly Ann said, "Milo . . . the man on the gray horse! That's Tom Blake, one of our men!" She stood in her stirrups, waving.

Instantly, they started toward us. They were wary of me, although two of them had ridden to the box supper with the major and Ann.

When we met, Blake wanted to know where Ann had been. After

I had explained, Blake looked at me carefully. "You know this Twin Baker?"

"Only by name and what Lisa told me. But I've an idea he's been around, under one name or another."

Then we rode toward the major's ranch.

When we rode up to the ranch-house door, the major came out. When he saw Ann, he rushed toward her. "Ann? Are you all right?"

"Yes. I am. Thanks to Milo." Briefly, she explained. The major's face stiffened.

"We'll go get him," he said flatly. "Tom, get the boys together. Full marching order, three days rations. We'll get him, and we'll get those cattle, every damned one of them!"

He turned to one of the other men who had come up. "Will, ride over to Balch. Tell him what's happened, and tell him to come on over here with some men."

"I'll ride back to my outfit," I said. "Remember, if that girl's there . . . she's done no harm. But we'd better move fast, because Twin Baker will."

Swinging my horse around, I lit out for the Stirrup-Iron, riding the grulla and leading the dun.

They were all there in the ranch yard when I rode in. Henry Rossiter, Barby Ann, Fuentes, Roper and Harley. From the look of them, I knew something was wrong.

"You got back just in time!" Rossiter said. "We're ridin' after Balch! Last night they run off the whole damn' herd! More than a thousand head of cattle! Gone, just like that!"

"Balch had nothing to do with it." I rode between Rossiter and the others. "When was the last time you saw Twin Baker?"

Chapter 24

Had I struck him across the face with my hat, the shock could have been no greater. He took half a step forward, his features drawn and old, staring up at me from blind, groping eyes.

"Twin? Twin Baker?" His voice shook. "Did you say Twin Baker?"

"When did you last see him, Rossiter?"

He shook his head, as if to clear it of shock. "It's been years . . . *years*. I thought . . . Well, I thought they were dead, both of them."

"Ma killed one of them, Rossiter. She killed Stan Baker when she got her cattle back. But it's the other one I'm talking about . . . John, I think his name was, but they call him Twin."

"We got to get Balch," he stammered. "He stole our herd."

"I don't think it was Balch," I said. "Twin Baker got your herd, like he's been getting all the rest of the young stuff around here."

"You're lyin'!" he protested. "Twin's dead. He's been dead. Both those boys . . . John an' Stan. They're both dead."

"What's this all about?" Roper demanded. "Who's Twin Baker?"

"He's a cow thief. He's the man who's been running cattle off this range for several years. He's been easing them off the range a few head at a time, keeping out of sight all the while. He's been stealing young stuff from every outfit in the basin . . . And he killed Danny Rolf."

"What?" Ben Roper said.

"Danny's dead . . . Dry-gulched, then shot in the back of the head at close range. To make sure. Maybe it was because he was wearing my checked shirt and Twin mistook him for me. But more likely it was because Danny found Baker's hideout."

"I thought he had gone girlin'," Roper muttered.

"He had . . . Lisa is Twin Baker's half-sister. She's down there . . . Or was. I advised her to get out before he killed her, too."

"John?" Rossiter said. "Twin?"

We looked at Rossiter, then at each other. He wasn't paying us no mind. He was just blindly staring off across the yard toward the hills.

So I told them about finding Danny's body, about trailing him with Ann, of talking to Lisa, taking Ann home. "The major is getting a bunch together to go after the cattle, and after Twin Baker—if he can be found," I said.

"He's a gunfighter," I commented. "Lisa said he's killed several men, and that he wanted me." I looked around at them. "My mother killed Stan Baker, his twin, when they were trying to rustle some of our stock."

Barby Ann was staring at me. "*Your* stock?" She spoke contemptuously. "How much stock would a saddle tramp have?"

Rossiter shook his head irritably, and spoke without thinking. "Barby Ann, Talon's got more cattle than all of us in the basin put together. He lives in a house . . . Why, you could put the major's house in his livin' room!"

Now that wasn't true. They were all staring at me now. Only Fuentes was smiling a little.

"I don't believe it!" Barby Ann snapped. She'd never liked me much, but then she'd had no corner on that. I didn't think much of her, either. "He's filled you full of nonsense!"

"We'd better go if we're going," I said. "But one man had better stay here." I looked over at Harley. "How about you?"

"Joe Hinge is up. He can use a gun. Let him stay. I never did like rustlers."

Rossiter stood there, a huge frame of a man, only a shell of the magnificent young man he'd been when he rode for us on the Empty. Now he was sagging, broken.

"Here they come!" Harley said suddenly. "The major, Balch . . . the lot of them!"

"Talon?" Rossiter's tone was pleading. "Don't let them hang him!"

Puzzled, I stared at the blind man. "I wouldn't like to see any man hang, Rossiter. But Twin Baker deserves it if ever a man did. He killed Danny, and he would probably have killed Ann Timberly. And he's stolen enough cattle to put you all out of business."

"Talon, you can stop them. Don't let them hang him."

Balch rode up, Roger beside him. There was no sign of Saddler, but Major Timberly was there. Ingerman was with Balch, and so were several other riders, their faces familiar.

"Balch," I said suddenly. "Recall the first time we met? Over near the cap-rock?"

"I remember."

"There was a man with you . . . Who was he? He wasn't one of your boys."

"Oh, him? He wasn't from around here. He was a cattle buyer, tryin' to get a line on beef for the comin' year. He was fixing to buy several thousand head."

"Did he?"

"Ain't seen him since. He was a pleasant fella. Stayed two, three days. Rode out with Roger a couple of times."

"He said he was from Kansas City," Roger offered. "And he seemed to know the town. But he talked of New Orleans, too. Why? What's he got to do with anything?"

"I think he was Twin Baker," I said. "I think he was our rustler."

Balch stared, his face growing dark with angry blood. "That's a lot of poppycock!" he declared irritably. "He was nobody from around here."

"Maybe," I said.

"Time's a-wastin'," Roger said. "Let's ride!"

"All right." I started for my horse.

Rossiter came down off the steps. He put out a hand. "Talon! I got no right to ask it, but don't let them hang Twin Baker."

"What difference does it make to you?" I asked. "He stole your cattle, too."

"I don't want to see any man hang," Rossiter protested. "It ain't right."

"You comin' or not?" Balch asked.

"Get going," I said. "I'll not be far behind."

Angrily, Balch swung his horse. The major beside him, they rode out—a dozen very tough men.

"They could jail him," Rossiter protested. "They could hold him for trial. A man deserves a trial."

"Like the trial he gave Danny?"

At the corral I shook out a loop and walked toward that almost white horse with the black mane, tail and legs. I liked that horse, and I would need a stayer for a tough ride. I didn't think the ride would end on the Middle Concho. Twin Baker was no fool, and he would be hard to catch.

Leading the horse out, I got my saddle on him. Rossiter started toward me but Barby Ann was trying to turn him back.

"Pa? What's the matter with you? Have you gone crazy? What do you care about a no-account cow thief? Or that saddle tramp you seem to think is such a big man?"

He pulled away from her, tearing his sleeve in the process. He came after me in a stumbling run, and when I led the horse toward the bunkhouse, he followed.

"When you were a boy," he babbled, "we talked, you an' me. You was a good boy. I told you stories. Sometimes we rode together—"

"And then what happened?" I said bitterly.

"You don't understand!" he protested. "Your folks had everything! You had a big ranch, you had horses, cattle, a fine house . . . I had nothing. Folks were always saying how goodlookin' I was. I rode fine horses. I wore good clothes. But I had nothing . . . nothing!"

I was listening. "Pa worked for it. He came into that country when there were only Indians, and he made peace with some, fought others. He built that ranch, he and Ma, built it with their own hands. They worked a lifetime doing it. And we boys helped, when we could."

Rossiter's face was haggard now. "But that takes *time*, boy! *Time!* I didn't want to be a rich old man. I wanted to be a rich *young* man. I deserved it. Why should you folks have so much and me nothing? All I did was take a few cattle . . . Just a few head!"

He put his hand on my shoulder. "Talon, for God's sake!"

"Rossiter," I said patiently, "I suspect everybody wants to have it all when they're young, but it just doesn't work that way. Pa worked, too. Worked hard. Maybe a man shouldn't have it when he's young. It robs him of something, gives him all he can have when he's too young to know what he's got. I don't know . . . Maybe I'm a damned fool, but that's the way it seems to me."

I looked at Rossiter. "Now you go back inside. There's nothing to worry about."

Barby Ann had come closer. She was standing there staring at her father as at a stranger. She had changed, somehow, these past few days. Maybe it was the rejection by Roger Balch. Maybe it was something that had been there all the time and we were only now seeing. "Forget it, Rossiter. I don't think we'll ever catch him. He's too smart."

"He is, isn't he?" Rossiter said eagerly. Suddenly, his expression became thoughtful. "Why, sure! He's got a good start. He won't try to keep that last herd, and they'll be so busy getting it back they won't get on to the others. That will split their party. My boys will have to take over that herd and start it back. Balch and the major won't have more than eight men with them . . . why, that's smart! That's thinking!"

They were words of desperation.

I got my saddlebags and threw them over the saddle, then my blanket roll. I had an idea this was going to take a long time, and I was a man who believed in preparing for all possibilities.

Rossiter, I thought, was crazy. I had not realized it until now, but he must be off his head. Nothing he said was making sense, and it was obvious that Barby Ann felt the same way.

"Pa?" she said. "Pa, you'd better come back to the house."

"He will do all right, that boy will! Have an outfit bigger'n yours someday, Talon."

"Rossiter, don't fool yourself. Twin Baker will wind up at the end of a rope, or killed in a gun battle. I don't know what you think he is but he's shown himself a thief and a murderer, and hanging's too good for him."

He stopped and stared at me, then shook his head. "You don't understand," he protested.

My horse was restless to go, as I was. Barby Ann said, "Pa? Let's go up to the house."

He pulled his arm away from her. He put his hand on my shoulder. "Talon, get him away from them. Don't let them hang him. You're a good man . . . a good man. I know you're a good man. Don't let them hang him."

Rossiter spat. "That Balch! He'll want a hangin'. I know he'll want it. And the major . . . he's just like all them army men. Discipline! He'll be for a hanging, too. You've got to stop them, Talon."

I put a foot into the stirrup and swung to the saddle, turning the horse away from him. "You're pleading for him? When he stole your cattle, too?"

"He didn't know they was mine. He couldn't have known." Rossiter shook his head admiringly. "Slick, though. Real slick." He peered up at me, squinting his eyes. "You don't think they'll catch him? You said that. You don't think they will?"

"Rossiter, you'd better go to the house. You need some rest. We'll find him, and if your cattle are still around to recover, we'll recover them."

He turned away from me, his head shaking a little. At the moment, I could feel only sorrow for the man. I'd never liked him. Even as a boy, when I'd often talked with him, I'd never liked him. There was always something shallow and artificial about him, something that was all show, all front with nothing behind it. Now the physical magnificence was gone, and all that remained was a shell.

Since joining his crew I'd only seen him inside, in the half-light of the house. And there had been a shadow of strength remaining. At least, there'd seemed to be. But under the sun, the deterioration was evident.

"Go!" Barby Ann said irritably. "Get out of here! It was a sorry day for us when you came here to work. It's you who's done this to him . . . *You.*"

I just looked at her and shrugged. "When we bring the cattle back, I'll quit. You can have my time ready. I'm sorry you feel as you do."

Rossiter turned from us. "John?" he muttered. "John. . . ."

He turned suddenly to me. "Don't let them hang him! *Don't!*"

"Damn it, Rossiter! The man's a thief! He stole your cattle, he stole from everybody in the basin, and he tried to stir up a shooting war. Why the hell should you care what happens to him?"

He stared at me from his blind eyes. "Care? *Care?* Why shouldn't I care? *He's my son!*"

Chapter 25

My horse could walk as fast as many horses could trot, and he moved right out, heading south away from the ranch. Yet I had no idea of overtaking the posse. I'd never been one to travel in a crowd, and I had noticed that too often the wrong men wind up as the leaders of groups or mobs.

It was a rough thirty-five miles and a bit more from the ranch to the cabin on the Concho, and I made a beeline for it.

Shortly before night fell, I stepped down near the head of Kiowa Creek and, without unsaddling, built myself a fire and made coffee and bacon. When I'd eaten, I loaded up frying pan and coffeepot, drinking the last of the coffee from the pot itself, and I took off toward a hollow in the prairie maybe a half mile from the creek. I'd spotted this place before, and there was a seep that didn't quite make it to the surface but did green up the grass. There I staked my horse, rolled up in my blankets and, with my horse for lookout, slept like a baby until the last stars lingered in the sky.

Moving out, I held to low ground well west of Kiowa country, and I came out of the timber on Tepee Draw on the south side of the cabin.

There was no smoke, no sign of life.

For several minutes I sat the buckskin, watching the house. It had every appearance of being deserted, and there was a plain enough trail heading off toward the southeast. Chancing it, I rode up.

The cabin was empty. Most of the food had been cleared out. Only a few shabby clothes remained, and a few cast-off utensils. There was some coffee on the fire that was still warm. Stirring up the coals, I heated it again and drank from a broken-handled cut while pacing from window to window.

I went outside. After watering my horse, I went back to the house.

462

Everything that was worth anything had been cleaned out.

Mounting up, I followed the trail southeast past the mountain, and after a few miles I reached Spring Creek.

One rider was ahead of me, riding easy. The trail was several hours hold. It was that long-striding horse again.

Twin Baker!

Southeast of here lay the San Saba and the Llano River country, and I knew almost nothing about it except from bunkhouse or saloon talk.

The next day, shortly after sunup, I rode down into Poor Hollow.

There was a crude brush and pole corral there, big enough to hold a few head for a short stay. And from the droppings, cattle had been kept there recently—as well as several times in the past.

At one side, under some trees, I found a small circle of stones where repeated fires had built quite a bed of ash. The ashes were cold, but the tracks looked no more than two to three days old.

Squatting under a big old pecan tree, I studied the corral, yet my mind was ranging back over the country. Twin Baker had evidently stolen the cattle in relatively small bunches, then drifted them by various routes to this or other holding corrals where he left them, while going back for more.

There was water from the creek and enough grass to keep a small bunch. When he returned with another lot, he'd probably drive them further south and east.

Moving out of Poor Hollow toward a prong of the San Saba, I made camp under some trees. I fixed a small bait of grub where the smoke would rise through the leaves and dissipate itself among them, leaving no rising column to be seen. It was on fairly high ground with a good view all around. My back to a tree, I studied the layout.

I saw a huge old buffalo bull with two young cows, a scattering of antelope, and a few random buzzards. Otherwise, nothing but distance and dancing heat waves. Nevertheless, I had an eerie, unpleasant feeling at odds with the beauty of the land. I had the feeling that I was heading right into a trap.

Someplace, Baker had to have a base, a place with water, and good grazing, where cattle might be held for some time. After a rest I drifted on, taking my time. This country was more rugged, and there was a good bit of cedar.

Twice I camped. Twice I came up to holding grounds where cattle had been corraled for a time, mostly young stuff, judging by the tracks and the droppings.

It was lonely country. Several times I saw Indian sign, but it was old. There were several sets of tracks, mostly made by that longstepping horse, but now I began to come on other tracks, lone riders or sometimes two or three in a bunch. All of them headed east.

Come daybreak, I was up on the hurricane deck of my bronc again, and looking down the trail . . . And it was a trail. Yet this was what I liked, riding far in a wide, lovely country with distance all around. At every break in the hill, there was a new vista, yet the apparent emptiness of the country could fool you. And wherever a man looked there were hidden folds of the hills that could hide an army . . . or an Indian war party looking for scalps and glory.

Suddenly, there opened ahead of me a lovely green valley and some buildings. From a hill, I'd seen some adobe ruins off to the north and east of where I was . . . mostly east. That was the San Saba Presidio, an attempt by the Spanish in early times to settle and administer this country. Comanches did them in, wiping out the last few priests who didn't get away ahead of time.

The buildings I now saw must be south of the old Presidio. There were only four or five, a town if you wanted to call it that—a store, a saloon, a few cabins. Some empty, some occupied. There were some corrals.

The saloon was a long low adobe building. There was a bar in it, and a lean, savage-looking man with an almost bald head. Suspenders were holding up his pants. He wore a slightly soiled undershirt, and his brows were a straight bar across his head above his eyes.

"What are ya having?" He stared at me with glassy blue eyes.

"Beer, if you've got it."

"We got it an' it's cold, right out of the springhouse." He reached for the bottle, put it on the bar. "Driftin'?"

"Sort of. I've got a liking for new country."

"Me, too. This ain't my place. I just agreed to set in for the boss. He had to go down to San Antone for a spell. Stomach botherin' him, he said, and it could be."

"Can you feed a man here?"

"If you like Mexican food. We got a gal here who can really put on the beans. We got beans, rice and beef. In the early morning we'll have eggs . . . The woman's got chickens."

He laughed. "Second batch she's had. Weasel got the whole bunch here a while back. Some folks say that man is the only one who just kills to be killing . . . Those folks never saw a hen house after a weasel has been in it. He'll kill one or two, drink their blood, and then just kill all the rest. Seems to go kind of wild crazy-like."

I agreed.

"Mountain lion will do the same thing. Kill two three deer, sometimes, eat a little off one of them and bury it in brush, then go off."

I tasted the beer. It was good, much better than I'd expected. I gestured toward the north. "Isn't that the old Presidio up yonder?"

"Sure is. Ain't much account except for holdin' cattle. Buildings and the walls make a fine corral . . . hold a might big herd, comes to that." He looked at me again. "You headin' for San Antone?"

"Sort of. But I'd latch onto a cow outfit if there was one needin' a hand. I'd rather drive cattle, if it comes to that. I'd rather just sit up there on my bronc an' let the world slide by. I got a good cuttin' horse yonder, and he knows more about cows than I do, so I just set up there and let him do the work."

"Not many outfits this far west. Away over on the North Concho I hear there's some. Never been that far west, myself," he said.

"You said they sometimes held herds in the Presidio? Any cattle up there now?"

He shook his head. "Been some a few days back . . . Just a small bunch, though. Maybe a hundred and fifty head. Two men drivin' them."

He chuckled, suddenly.

When I looked a question, he smiled and shook his head. "Beats a man how some folks get together. They come in here for a beer, just like you. One of them a real quiet man. Still face . . . goodlookin' feller, but mighty quiet. Never missed anything, though. Other feller, he was younger . . . kind of a flashy sort, swaggers it around, and you can just see he's proud of that big gun on his hip. Never saw such two different fellers together before."

"Didn't the quiet one have a gun?" I asked.

"Surely did. But you know something? You had to look two or three times to see it. I mean it was right out there in plain sight, but he work it like he'd been born with it and it was hardly so's you'd notice it."

He paused. "That younger feller, he wore two guns, one stuck behind his belt on the left side with his vest hangin' over it a mite . . . But the way he wore those two guns you'd a thought he had six. Just seemed to stick out with guns all over."

"High forehead? High wave of hair thrown back? Striped pants, maybe?" I asked.

"That's him. You know him?"

"Seen him around. Name's Jory Benton. Hires his gun sometimes."

The bartender shook his head. "He never hired it to that other man. Never in this world. That other feller, he don't need any gun hands. I seen his kind before."

"A hundred and fifty head, you say? If they're trail-broke, two men could handle them, so they wouldn't need me," I said.

"They're trail-broke, all right. He had one old cow, splashes of red an' white. She was the leader and the rest of them just trailed along behind . . . young stuff . . . three, four years old. Some yearlin's."

Taking my beer, I walked to a table near the window. The bartender brought his bottle along and sat down opposite me. "I'm holed up here until spring," he said. "Got me a dugout yonder. There's beef around, and a good many turkeys. Come spring I'll head for San Antone. I'm a teamster," he added.

We saw a man come out from a house across the way. The bartender indicated him with a nod of his head. "Now there's somethin' odd. That feller . . . He's been around here two, three days, just a-settin'. Never comes over here. Never talks to nobody but his partner. I got a feelin' they're waitin' for somebody."

He was a tall, lean, easy-moving man, with a stub of cigar in his teeth and a beat-up black hat on his head. He wore a tied-down gun and a Bowie knife and he was looking at my horse. When he turned his head and said something over his shoulder, another man came out of the house. This second man was fat and short, with unshaved jowls and a shirt open at the neck, with a dirty neckerchief tied there.

Both men looked carefully around.

"Amigo," I said to the bartender, "if I were you I'd get back of my bar and lie on the floor."

He stared at me. "Look here . . ." He hesitated. Then he asked, "They comin' for you?"

I smiled at him. "Well now, I wouldn't rightly know. But that tall gent is called Laredo, and folks do say he's right handy with a six-gun. The fat one could be Sonora Davis. Either one of them would shoot you for fun . . . Except they usually only have fun when they get paid for it."

"They lookin' for you?"

I smiled again. "They haven't said, have they? Maybe I'd better go see."

Getting up, I slipped the thong from my sixshooter. "I never did like to keep folks waiting. If they respect you enough to make an appointment, the least you can do is not keep them sitting around. You keep that beer for me, will you?"

There was no door, just the open space for one. I stepped into the doorway and walked outside.

Stopping in the shade of the awning, I looked at them in the sunlight near their door.

It was very still, and the sun was hot. A black bee buzzed lazily about, and a small lizard paused on a rock near the awning post, his little sides moving as he gasped for air.

"Hello, Laredo," I said, loud enough for him to hear. "It's a long way from the Hole."

He quinted his eyes under his hat brim, staring at me.

"Last time I saw you," I said, "you were holding four nines against my full house."

"Talon? Milo Talon? Is that you?" Laredo asked.

"Who'd you expect? Santa Claus?"

We were sixty feet apart, at least. His partner started to shift off to the right. "Sonora," I said, "I wouldn't do that. Might give me some idea you boys were waitin' for me. I wouldn't like to think that."

Laredo shifted his cigar stub in his teeth. "We had no idea it would be you. We were just waitin' for a rider on a Stirrup-Iron Horse."

I jerked my head to indicate my horse. "There he is. I'm the rider."

Laredo was good with a gun, and so was Davis, but Laredo was the better of the two. Yet I could sense uncertainty in him. He didn't like surprises, and he had been expecting some random cowhand, not somebody he knew.

"I hope he paid you enough, Laredo," I said quietly.

"Well, we didn't figure on you. He just said a snoopy cowhand was followin' along behind him. Hell, if he'd known it was you, he'd have done it himself."

"He knew. I'm sure he knew," I said.

There were two of them, and I wanted an edge. I didn't know whether I needed it or not, but I wanted it. They had taken money to kill, and they would not welsh on the job.

"We taken this money," Laredo said, "an' we got to do it."

"You could always give it back."

"We done spent most of it, Milo. We just ain't got it no more," said Laredo.

"Well, I could let you have a few bucks," I said quietly. "I could let you have . . . Let's see what I've got." I moved my right hand as if toward my pocket and when they went for their guns I was a split second ahead of them.

Sonora's gun was coming up when I shot him. Sonora was on the right. It is an easier move from right to left, so I took him first.

Laredo had been fast . . . too fast for his own good. And he neglected to take that split instant of time that can make a good shot better.

His thumb slid off the hammer as his gun was coming up, and the bullet spat sand a dozen feet in front of me. Mine hit the target.

Long ago, an old gunfighter had told me, "Make the first shot count. You may never get another."

I wasn't going to need another.

Laredo fell against the side of the house and his gun went off into the dust at his feet. His shoulder against the wall, his knees buckled and he slid down to the hardpacked earth.

For a moment, I stood very still, just waiting. It was warm, and there was the acrid smell of gun smoke. Somewhere up the street, if you could call it that, a door slammed. A woman stood in the street, shading her eyes toward us.

Slowly I crossed to my horse, thumbing cartridges into my gun. When I holstered it, I stepped into the saddle.

The bartender was in the door, looking at me. "What'll I do?" he pleaded. "I mean, what—"

"Bury them," I said. "There'll be money in their pockets, and it will buy you an easy winter . . . Take it. Keep their outfits. Bury them, and put some markers on their graves."

I pointed at each in turn. "His name was Laredo Larkin, and his was Sonora Davis."

"Where they from?"

"I don't know," I said, "but they got where they were going. They've been riding down the road to this place for a long, long time."

Then I rode out of there.

Laredo and Davis. Was I riding the same road as them?

Chapter 26

The trail of the stolen cattle turned south toward the Llano River country. The worst of it was, I'd ridden out of town without getting anything to eat, and my belly was beginning to think my throat was cut. So when I saw an adobe house up ahead, I rode up to it and swung down.

A slender young woman came to the door, shading her eyes at me. I also saw a man come to the door of the barn to watch me.

"I'd like to buy something to eat," I said. "Or grub I can take with me."

" 'Light an' set," she said. "I'll put something on."

The man walked up from the barn, a thin young man with a quick, shy smile. "Howdy! Passin' through?"

"That's my name," I said, grinning. "Seems to me that's about all I do. Pass through. Been here long?"

"Nobody's been here long. I come in when the war was over. Found this place, fixed up the old 'dobe and the corrals. Got a few head of cattle on the range, and then I went back to West Virginia for Essie, there."

"Well, you've got water, grass an' time. Seems like you won't need much else."

He glanced at me again. "Surprised you didn't eat in town. That Mexican woman's a good cook."

"There was a shooting up there, so I lit out. No tellin' when there might be more."

"A shootin'? What happened?" he asked.

"Looked to me like a couple of gunhands had been waitin' for a man. He rode into town and they had at him and came up short."

"He got them? Both of them?"

"Looked that way. I just straddled my bronc and lit out," I said.

469

We walked to the trough, where I let the horse drink, then tied him on some grass while I went inside. We sat down, and the man removed his hat, wiping his brow and then the sweatband of his hat.

"Hot," he said. "I've been down in the bottom putting up some hay."

Essie came in and put plates on the table. She shot me a quick, curious glance. News was scarce in this country, and visitors were few. I knew what was expected of me. They wanted to know what was happening . . . anywhere at all.

So I told them all about the box supper at Rock Springs Schoolhouse, about the cattle thefts up in the Concho country, and repeated what I'd said about the recent shooting.

Essie put a pot of coffee on the table, then beans, beef and some fried potatoes—the first I'd had in some time. "He grows them," she said, proudly, indicating her husband. "He's a good farmer."

"Seen some cattle been driven through here. Some of yours?" I asked casually.

He shook his head quickly. "No. No, they aren't. They come through here from time to time . . . Never stop." He glanced at his wife. "That is, they never done so until this last time . . . There was a stranger along then, flashy looking man. I didn't take to him much."

Essie's face was flushed, but I avoided looking at her.

The man continued. "He stopped off, started talking to Essie. I guess he took her for a lone woman, so I came up, and he kind of edged around her, and I seen him take the loop off his gun."

"A man with a high forehead?" I asked.

"Yes, sir. He did have. Kind of wavy hair. Anyway, I was afraid of trouble, but that other man came back and spoke real sharp to him, and this first man, he rode off. When he looked back he said, 'You wait, honey. I'll be ridin' this way again.' I heard that other man say 'Like hell you will! I done too much to keep this trail smooth. I don't figure to have it messed up by—' Then his voice kind of trailed off, but I heard the other man speak. Believe me, they were none too friendly when they left."

"The one who talked to you," I said to Essie, "is a gunman named Jory Benton."

"A gunman?" Her face paled. "Then if—"

"Yes," I said blunty. "He might have killed your husband. He wouldn't hesitate to do just that. He shot a friend of mine up north of here."

They exchanged glances.

"Those cattle," I asked casually, while refilling my cup, "does he take them to his ranch?"

"Wouldn't call it a ranch, exactly. He's got him a place down on the Llano . . . Runs maybe a thousand head . . . or more. All young stuff." He hesitated. "Mister, I don't know you, and maybe I shouldn't be tellin' you all this, but that there outfit doesn't size up right to me."

"How so," I asked.

"Time an' again they drift cattle through here. They never bothered me, nor me them, until that last feller come along who bothered Essie. Hadn't been for him, I might have kept my mouth shut. I got no call to suspicion them except that it don't seem likely a man would have so many calves without cows, always driftin' along the same route."

"How many men does he have?"

The young man shrugged. "Can't say. Most often he's driftin' only a few, an' he's alone. Sometimes it's after dark, and I can't make them out. Time or two, when I was scoutin' for game down south of here, I cut their trail. One time I looked across the Llano and saw the cattle. Seemed to me there were two or three men down there, but I was afraid they'd see me and I wanted no trouble, so I lit out."

"South of here, you say?" I asked.

"Almost due south. The Llano takes kind of a bend this way. There's quite a canyon there, and he's running his cattle in south of there. Good grass, plenty of water, and lots of oak, elm, mesquite and some pecans. It's a right nice locality."

When I'd finished eating, I went out and brought up my horse, tightened the cinch and stepped into the saddle. "Friend," I suggested, "you could make yourself a couple of dollars if you want to take a ride."

"A ride to where?"

Now I knew that cash money was a hard thing to come by in these places, and any two-bit rancher like this was sure to be hard up.

"Up north of here along the Middle Concho . . . Likely they're south of there by now, and you could meet them half way. There's a party of riders . . . a Major Timberly and a man named Balch will be leading, I think. Tell them Talon sent you, and that the cattle are on the Llano."

"Those are stolen cattle?" he asked.

"They are. But you just ride, and don't tell anybody why or wherefore. The man you had trouble with was Jory Benton, and the man bossing the move is Twin Baker . . . and he's five or six times tougher and meaner than Benton. Don't cross them.

"They'll see my tracks if I miss them and they come back this way. So don't lie. Tell them I was here, that I ate here and just pulled out. I didn't talk or ask questions. I just ate. You understand?"

He agreed.

My trail was southeast, through rough, broken country with a scattering of cedar and oak. Nor was it the kind of country a man likes to travel if he's worried about being drygulched; the country was perfectly laid out for it.

Like I said before, my mother raised no foolish children that I knew of, so I switched trails every few minutes. That horse must have thought I'd gone pure loco. Suddenly, I turned him and started due east toward the head of Five Mile Creek. Then south, then west.

I scouted every bit of country before I rode across it, studying the lay of the land and trying to set no pattern so that a man might trap me up ahead. I'd ride toward a bunch of hills, then suddenly turn off along their base. I'd start up the hills on a diagonal, then reverse and go up the opposite way. Whenever I rode into trees or rocks, I'd double back when I had concealment and cut off at an angle. It took time, but I wasn't fighting time. The main idea was to get there alive and in action.

Not that I had any very good idea of what I was going to do when I arrived. That part I hadn't thought out too well. I decided to just let things happen.

Mainly I wanted them not to drive off the cattle.

Nightfall found me under some bluffs near the head of Little Bluff Creek. It was a place where a big boulder had deflected the talus falling off the rim to either side, leaving a little hollow maybe thirty yards across. And the slope below was scattered with white rocks.

There was a cedar growing near the boulder, low and thick, and some mesquite nearby. I scouted it as I rode past. Then, stopping in a thick patch of trees and brush, I built myself a small fire, made coffee and fried some bacon. When I'd eaten and sopped of the bacon gravy with one of the biscuits Essie had packed for me, I dowsed my fire, pulling the sticks away and scattering dirt over the ashes. Then leading my horse, I walked back several hundred yards to the hollow below the boulder.

Stripping my rig from the horse, I let him roll, watered him and picketed him on the grass below the boulder. Then I unrolled my bed, took off my boots and stretched out. And believe me, I was tired.

If I had it figured right, the Llano was about eight or nine miles due south, and the holding ground for the cattle right beyond that river. That young rancher I'd sent north after Balch and Timberly had laid it out pretty good for me, and Baker was running his cattle in a sort of triangle between the Llano and the James, and just east of Blue Mountain . . . but trying to hold them between Blue Mountain and the Llano.

The moon was up when next I opened my eyes. Everything was white and pretty. I could see that black-legged horse cropping grass out there, but I couldn't see his legs at all, only his body, looking like one of those white rocks.

I turned over and started to go to sleep again, and then my eyes came wide open. Why, I was a damned fool. If they came sneaking up on me . . . them or the Kiowas . . . I'd never have a chance. They'd spot my bed right out there in the open and fill it full of lead.

Well, I slid out of that bed like a greased eel through wet fingers. I rolled a couple of rocks into my bed, bunched the bedding around it and went back into the deeper shadows under that big boulder. And with the saddle blanket around my shoulders, I leaned back and dozed again, rifle to hand and my gunbelt on.

Dozing against that rock, suddenly I heard my mustang blow like a horse will sometimes do when startled. My eyes opened on three men walking up on my camp.

One whispered, "You two take him. I'll get his horse."

Flame blasted from the barrels of two rifles and there was a roar of sound—the harsh, staccato barking of the rifles.

They stood there, those two dark figures, within twenty feet of my bed, and they worked the levers on their rifles until they shot themselves out of ammunition. I had my Winchester in my hands, pointed in their direction, and I was maybe forty feet from them.

That ugly roar of sound was to ring in my ears for many a day, as they poured lead into what they thought was me, shooting and shooting again.

I heard the horse snort, and a voice called out, "You get him?"

There was a rude grunt and the other man said, "What the hell do you think?"

The moonlight was bright.

I stood up—one nice, easy movement—taking a pebble from the ground as I did so. They had half turned, but some slight rustle or shadow of movement must have caught the ear of one of them because he looked toward me. Backed up against that big boulder as I was, he could have seen nothing or, at best, only a part of something. With my left hand, I tossed my pebble off to the right, and they both turned sharply.

"You bought the ticket," I said quietly. "Now take the ride."

My Winchester stabbed flame and knocked one man staggering, reaching for his pistol. The other turned sharply off to his left, diving for cover as he drew, but I was always a good wing shot, and my bullet caught him on the fly and he went plunging straight forward on his face.

The echoes of my shots chased each other under the eaves of the cliffs, then lost themselves along the wall.

There was then a moment of absolute, unbelievable silence, and then a voice: "Boys? . . . Boys?"

I said nothing. Somewhere out there in the night, and I could have put a bullet through the sound, was Jory Benton. The trouble was, he had my horse, and I'd no desire to kill a good horse in trying for a bad man.

So I waited . . . and after a moment there was a drum of hooves. And I was alone with two dead men and a moon that was almost gone from the sky.

I was alone, and I was afoot, and when daylight came I would be hunted down.

A faint breeze stirred the leaves, moaning a little in the cedar, rustling in the mesquite.

I thumbed shells into my Winchester.

Chapter 27

Of course, Benton had taken his men's horses, also. I had to be certain, but I was sure from the sounds that he had taken them.

Rolling the rocks from my bed, I shook it out and rolled it up. Shot full of holes, it was still better than nothing, and the nights were cold.

One other thing I did. I went to where the men I'd shot had fallen . . .

Only one remained!

So one of them was still alive, able to move, able perhaps to shoot. I stripped the cartridge belt from the remaining man and slung it across my shoulders, after a brief check to make sure he was using .44s as I was.

His six-gun was there, so I tucked it behind my belt, and both rifles lay nearby. Evidently, the wounded man had been more eager to get away than to think of fighting, and had failed to take his rifle.

Carrying both of them, I walked away, keeping to the deeper shadows, wary of a bullet.

When I was off a hundred yards or so, I pointed myself south and started to walk. There were men beyond the Llano, as well as cattle, and where there were men, there would be horses, including mine.

When I had walked about four miles or so—I figured it took me about an hour and a half, and that would come to close to four miles— I found myself in the bottoms of another creek. Maybe it was Big Bluff, I could only guess, knowing the country only by hearsay.

It was dark under the trees and, finding a place off to one side, I kicked around a little to persuade any possible snakes that I wasn't good company. Then I unrolled my bed and stretched out, and would you believe it? I slept.

The first light was filtering its way through the leaves when my eyes opened. For a moment I lay there between two big logs, listening. There were birds twittering and squeaking in the trees, and there was a rustle, as some small animal or maybe a lizard moved through the leaves. And there was the faint sound of water running.

Sitting up, I looked carefully around. Great old trees were all around, some mossy old logs, and a few fallen branches—a blowdown of three or four trees, and not much else. First off I checked the spare rifles. One was empty, the other had three shells, which I pocketed. Finding a hollow tree, I stashed the rifles there, then checked the loads on my rifle and the extra pistol.

Shouldering my bed, I crossed the creek, stopped at a spring that trickled into the creek and drank, then drank again. Following it upstream, I left it and headed for the breaks along the Llano.

By the time the sun was well into the sky, I was looking down on as pretty a little camp as I'd ever seen, tucked away in the trees with several square miles of the finest grazing in Texas laid out there in front of it. Now grass is an uncertain thing. Some years it can be good, and some years it wouldn't keep a grasshopper alive. This was a good year, and in spite of the cattle down there it was holding up.

There were a couple of lean-tos facing each other maybe a dozen yard apart. There was a fire going, with a kettle hanging over it, and a coffeepot in the coals. There were a couple of pairs of undershirts and drawers hanging over a line that ran tree to tree. And there was a man stretched out on the ground, hands behind his head and a hat over his face, napping in the morning sun.

Two saddled horses were nearby, and my horse unsaddled. My own saddle was back where I'd left it, half hidden under the edge of that big boulder where I'd started my sleep. When the time came, I could pick it up again.

For a spell, I just laid there. Another man—too far off to tell who—came from a lean-to and began stropping a razor. Evidently, there was a piece of mirror on a corner post of the lean-to, because he stood there, shaving. It was a sore temptation to dust them up a little with my Winchester, but I put the idea aside.

Studying the herd, I could see several hundred head of cattle. And although it was too far to see for sure, they appeared to be in good shape.

Now that I was here, I had no idea what to do. Before anything else, I must recover my horse—or another one—and prepare to guide the posse in when it arrived.

Easing back off the hill, I worked my way down a gully to the Llano. It was wide at this point, but not deep. Working my way down to the bank, I studied the situation with care. To attempt to get a horse by daylight would be asking for trouble that I did not want, so my best bet was to lie quiet and see what developed. I was hidden in thick brush near a huge old fallen tree, and although I could see almost nothing of the camp, I could hear voices.

Only occasionally could I clearly make out a word. Straining my ears, I heard the man who was shaving . . . At least I guessed it was him, because it sounded like a man talking while he was shaving a jowl.

". . . tonio . . . deal. Figure we should drive . . . Guadalupe River."

There was a muttered response that I could not clearly hear, then some further argument.

". . . don't like it." The voice came through louder and stronger. "He ain't alone, I tell you! You know Balch? Well, I do! He's meaner than hell, an' if he gets you he'll go no further than the nearest tree! I say we sell out and get out!"

There was more muttering. As their emotions became stronger, their voices rose. "What became of Laredo? You seen him? Have you seen Sonora? All we were supposed to do was drive some cows. Now look at it!"

There was a faint sound from upstream and, craning my neck, I saw a man stagger to the edge of the stream, fall, then saw him drinking, lapping at the water like a dog.

Lifting his head, he called out, a hoarse, choking cry.

"What the hell was *that?*" one of the men said. And then I heard running.

They came out on the bank of the stream, maybe fifty yards up from where I was hidden. They stopped, stared, then splashed across the stream to the wounded man. This was probably one of the men I'd shot the previous night.

They knelt beside him. I came swiftly to my feet, and eased down the bank into the water. Moving with great care to make no sound, I moved across the Llano.

Their backs were to me, both kneeling beside the wounded man. In a moment they'd be helping him up, trying to get him back to the camp.

Up the bank I crept. At the edge of the camp I stopped, taking a swift look around . . . Nobody was in sight. Running swiftly, I crossed the camp to the saddled horses. My horse was tied to the pole corral and I took his lead rope and one of the saddled horses, then turned the other loose and shied him off.

He ran off a few steps and stopped, looking back. I could not see the stream and could hear no sound. Leading the two horses, I walked across the camp.

There was a skillet with bacon on one side of the fire, keeping warm for somebody. I took up several slices and ate them, then picked up the pot and drank the hot coffee right from the edge of the pot.

Stepping into the saddle on the roan, leading my own horse, I went back toward the Llano. Glancing upstream, I saw that the men had disappeared from the bank. So I rode my horses across and headed north to where I'd cached my saddle.

It was no plan of mine to steal the man's horse, and least of all his saddle. Shoot a man I might, but stealing his saddle was another thing entirely. When I came back to the boulder where my own rig was, I dismounted, saddled my own horse and turned the roan loose.

Good crossings of the Llano were few, for the cliffs along each side were high and the country rugged. From the highest ground I could find, I looked north. But there was no sign of Balch or the major.

Riding west along the Llano, I found a place further upstream where I could cross over. Mounting the south bank, I worked my way back through scattered cedar and oak toward the cattle. I came upon a few scattered ones, and started to bunch them to move toward the main holding ground southwest of their camp.

The man I'd shot the night before had seemed to be shot in the leg or hip, from the way they were handling him. It was possible he could still ride.

Suddenly, I wondered.

Where was Twin Baker?

He had not been in the camp. There had been some discussion of San Antonio, and Lisa had said he often went there. Was he there now?

Keeping to the brush, trees and rocks, I worked nearer to the holding ground. As Baker seemed to have bunched and stolen the cattle by himself, these were probably just hired hands, outlaws he had picked up to help with the final drive.

Whatever had been his original plan, apparently that plan had now changed, due to the events of the past few days. The discovery of his thefts, the escape of Ann Timberly, and my pursuit—of which he was certainly aware.

Laredo and Davis had been sent to stop me, at least until Baker could get the cattle moved . . . Did he know they had failed?

It was all uncertain. And the fact that Twin Baker was not visible did not mean he was nowhere around. At any moment, he might have me locked in the sight of that rifle . . . And he could shoot!

Where were Balch and the others? Had they all turned back? Was I alone in my effort to recover the cattle?

The more I looked at it, the less I liked it.

Had Rossiter sent for his men to return? Had Twin Baker known he was stealing from his own father, among others?

From her reactions, it was obvious that Barby Ann had no knowledge that Twin Baker was her brother—or that she even had a brother. She had been aghast and confused by her father's erratic words, unable to guess what he was talking about.

Uneasily, I began to wonder if I was not alone out here. And fated to be left alone!

In the shadow of a bluff, I drew up. From where I sat my horse, I could see out over the plain where the cattle grazed, and I was not the only one bunching cattle. Other riders were out there, working swiftly, bunching the cattle, with the apparent intention of moving them off toward the southeast.

They were working the breaks on the north and west, working carefully but swiftly, and moving them not southeast, as I expected, but due east.

The small lot of cattle I'd started moved out on the plain and a rider turned toward them, then suddenly slowed his pace. I chuckled grimly.

He'd seen those cattle. Then suddenly he'd begun to wonder who had started them. Now he was approaching, but much more carefully. I held my horse, watching. He swung in behind the cattle, glancing over his shoulder as he did so. But I made no move, just watched. Reassured, he moved the cattle toward the drifting herd.

Glancing north again, I searched the sky for dust, hoping for the posse's arrival. I saw nothing.

I swore, slowly, bitterly.

My eyes looked toward the river and saw the wind move the leaves. I looked beyond the bobbing horns of the cattle, beyond the horsemen, weaving their arabesques as they circled and turned, gathering the cattle.

Maybe there was more of Pa and Barnabas in me than I thought. For when I looked upon the beauty and upon distance, I could only think how short was a man's life, with all the things to be done, the words to be spoken, the many miles to ride.

Those men were gathering stolen cattle, and I waited, trying to think of a way to recover them. The distance between us was so very, very small.

The law is a thin line, a line that divides those who would live by rules with men from those who would live against them. And it is easy to overstep and be upon the other side. Yet I'd known many a man in the west who had made that step, only to see the folly of his ways and step back.

In a land of hard men living rough lives, they found it easy to understand such missteps and to forgive.

There were the others, like Henry Rossiter, who wanted the rewards without the labor, who, to get them, would take from others what they had worked hard to gain. It was the mindless selfishness of those who had not come to understand that all civilization was simply a living together, so that all could live better.

Why I did such a damn fool thing, I'll never know. But suddenly I rode out from my shadow and into the sunlight of the plain. There'd come a time when I'd lie awake and sweat with the realization of what I'd done, but it came to me to do it, and I did. I rode right out there, and one of the riders close to me turned to stare.

The others . . . and there were three others now . . . kind of drew up and looked. But they were scattered out from one another, and too far off to make out faces.

When I rode up to him, I saw a stocky man with a barrel chest and a square, tough face.

"Point 'em north," I said. "We're takin' 'em back."

"What? Who the hell are you?"

"Milo Talon's the name, but that doesn't matter. The only thing that matters is that we point these cattle north and start them for the Concho, where they were stolen."

He stared at me. What I was doing made no sense to me, so how could it make sense to him? He was puzzled and worried. He glanced toward the others, then toward the shadows of the bluffs I'd come from, like he was expecting more riders.

"No, I am alone. The posse is still a few miles off and they won't get here for a while, so you boys get a break. That posse is in a hangin' mood, and I'm giving you boys your chance. You know who Balch is . . . Well, he's with that posse.

"To get any money out of these cattle you've got to drive them and then sell them, and you can't drive them fast and you can't sell them anywhere near fast enough."

The man looked stupefied.

"Looks to me like you've got a plain, simple choice. You help me drive these cattle north and you can ride off scot-free. But give me an argument and all of you hang."

The other riders were coming around the herd toward us.

"How do we know there's any posse?" asked the man.

I grinned at him. "You got my word for it, chum. If you don't like my word, you've got some shooting to do. If I win, you're dead. If I lose, you've still got a mighty mean posse to deal with . . . Either way, you lose the cattle. You just can't drive this big a herd with any speed, and you can't hide it."

"What the hell's goin' on?" The speaker was an older man, his mustache stained with tobacco juice. "Who's this hombre?"

I grinned at him. "Name's Milo Talon. I was just suggesting you boys could make your stars shine brighter in the heavens was you to drive this herd north to meet the posse."

"Posse? What posse?"

"A very hard-skulled gent named Balch, and with him, Major Timberly and some other riders. These are their cattle, and Balch is a man with a one-track mind when it comes to rustlers. He thinks in terms of r's . . . Rustlers and ropes."

A redheaded cowhand chuckled. "There's another r got those beat all hollow . . . *Run!*"

"Try it," I suggested, "and you just might make it. On the other hand, you might lose . . . and that's quite a loss. You win, or you get your necks stretched. Was I you, I'd not like the odds."

"You got you a point there," the redhead agreed.

"I've got another one, which I was pointing out to your friend here. There's no way you can drive a herd fast enough to get away from a posse . . . So you've lost the herd, anyway. Do it my way and you'll still lose the cattle, but the posse will shake you by the hand and thank you. Then you ride off, free as a jaybird."

"Milo Talon, huh?" The older man spat. "Well, Milo, I don't know you from Adam, but you make a kind of sense."

The redhead shook his head, grinning. "He's got too much nerve to shoot, ridin' down here to talk the four of us out of a herd of cows. Mister, you got more gall than one of these here lightnin'-rod salesmen I hear about. You surely have."

"Look, boys," I said, "conversation is all right. You boys surely do carry on with the words, but meanwhile that posse gets closer. Now

I want this herd pointed north before they see you, else my arguments may come to nothing."

"What'll we tell Twin?" asked the older man.

"To hell with him!" the redhead said. "He offered us fifty bucks apiece to drive these cattle to San Antone. My neck's worth more'n fifty bucks to me. Come on, boys! Let's move 'em out!"

They swung around, turning the cattle, stringing them out toward the crossing of the Llano.

Me, I mopped the sweat off my face with a bandana. As long as I had a Sackett for a mother, I was glad I had a smooth-talking French-man for a pa. He always told me that words were better than gunpowder, and now I could see what he meant.

We strung out the herd and pointed them north, and I rode up to take the point.

Chapter 28

Two hours north of the Llano, we raised a dust cloud on the horizon and, shortly after, the posse topped a rise and started down the slope toward us.

The redheaded puncher pulled up short. "I just remembered! I got a dyin' grandmother somewhere's east of Beeville! I'm takin' out!"

"You run now, and they'll start shooting," I said. "Hold your horses, boys. Let me handle this!"

"Last time somebody said that he was reachin' for a hangin' rope," said the redhead. "All right, mister, you do the talkin', an' I pray to God you use the right words!"

Balch and the major were in the lead, and right behind them was Ann. Riding beside her was Roger Balch.

I rode out to meet them. "Here's your cattle, or most of them. These boys offered to help with the drive until we met you."

"Who are they?" Roger Balch demanded suspiciously. "I never saw any of them before!"

"They were just passin' through San Antone. They helped me make the gather and the drive."

"Thank you, men," Major Timberly said. "That was mighty nice of you!"

"Major, these boys were in quite a hurry, and I talked them into helping. Now if you could spare the price of a drink—" I suggested.

"Surely!" He took out a gold eagle. "Here, boys, have a couple on me. And thanks . . . Thanks very much!"

"Don't mind if we do," the older man said. He spat, glancing at me. "Sure is a pleasure to meet an honest man!"

"See you in San Antone!" I said cheerfully. "I'd rather see you hanging out there than here!"

They trotted their horses away, and we started the herd again.

Ann rode over, followed by Roger. "We were worried," she said, "really worried. Especially after we saw the buzzards."

"Buzzards?" My expression was innocent.

"Father found a dead man. He had been shot. It wasn't you."

"I noticed that," I commented, dryly.

"There's been some shooting in Menardville, too," she added.

"What d' you know? Is that up yonder near the Presidio? Nothing ever seems to happen where I'm riding. Looks like I missed out all along the line."

Ann glanced at me sharply, but Roger didn't notice. "That's what I told Ann," he said. "You couldn't have been involved, because your messenger said you'd talked about the shooting right after it happened."

Fuentes had ridden alongside. "Talked to an hombre at the saloon. Said he'd never seen anything like it. Like shootin' a brace of ducks, one right, one left. Picture-book shooting, he called it."

"What about Twin Baker?" Balch demanded

"Gone. His sister said he often went to San Antonio, so that's probably where he is."

"At least we got the cattle back," Fuentes said.

"Roger said we would," Ann said proudly. "He told me not to worry. We'd get them all back, and without trouble."

"I like confidence in a man," I said.

"Father didn't want me to come," Ann admitted, "but Roger said it would be all right. He said such rustlers had little courage, and Twin Baker would probably be gone before we got there."

Seemed to me Roger was expressing himself an awful lot, and being quoted more than usual. Fuentes was noticing it, too. His eyes carried that faintly quizzical expression.

"It's the memories that count," Fuentes said. "And never stay long enough to let 'em see you just put your pants on one leg at a—"

"The hell with that," I said irritably.

When we rode into the yard at Stirrup-Iron, all was dark and still. One light showed from the ranch-house kitchen, and a horse spoke to us from the corral.

"S'pose there's any grub in there?" I suggested hopefully.

"We can look. Maybe that's why the light's burning," said Fuentes.

Fuentes and I turned our horses in at the corral and I dropped my bedroll and saddlebags down on the stoop.

There was a plate of cold meat on the table, some bread and butter, and a couple of thick slices of apple-pie. The coffeepot was on the stove, so we got cups and saucers and sat down opposite each other in silence and gratitude.

"That hombre at the saloon," Fuentes said, "spoke to me of a man who was just sort of passing by . . . riding a horse with black legs."

"He should've kept his mouth shut."

"He spoke only to me," Fuentes said. "Were they waiting for you? Laredo and Sonora?"

"Twin Baker paid them to kill a rider on a Stirrup-Iron horse, no names mentioned."

"The saloon keeper said you knew one of them?"

"Played poker with him a time or two. He was no friend of mine. He and Sonora had taken money for the job. They'd spent some of it."

Fuentes pushed back from the table. "At the poker table with Laredo that time . . . Who won?"

"He did."

"You see? Nobody wins all the time, not with girls, guns or poker."

We walked outside under the stars, and Fuentes lit a cigar. "Nobody . . . Not even you."

I looked at him.

"This time it is you who can ride away. The girl will marry the other man but she will remember you, who came so gallantly from out of the distance and then rode, gallantly, into another distance."

"Are you trying to tell me something?"

"Ann Timberly. She will marry Roger Balch. Did you not see it?"

"Two big ranches, side by side. It figures."

"And you but a drifting cowhand. You did not mention your ranch, amigo?"

"I told nobody. Nor will I."

"It is the way of things. I think we should sleep now."

"Harley and Ben with the herd?" I asked.

"Of course," Fuentes replied.

"How'd you leave Joe? Still in the house?"

"Of course." Fuentes snapped his fingers. "Hah! I had forgotten. There was a note came for you. It is in my coat, hanging on my saddle, and in the morning I will get it for you."

"Get it for me now, will you, Tony?"

"Now? But of course!" He turned away and I walked to the bunk-house and picked up my blanket roll. For a moment I stood there, feeling the night, knowing the stars. Then, very carefully, I pushed the door open with my left toe and and thrust my blanket roll into the door.

A stab of flame punched a hole in the night, and the thunderous blast of a shotgun slammed against my ears. In that same instant my right hand drew, the gun came level, and I put three bullets where the fiery throat of flame had been.

Drawing back, gun in hand, I waited.

A long, slow moment of silence, then the thud of a dropped gun. Then there was a slow, ripping sound as of tearing cloth, and something heavy fell.

The night was still again.

"Amigo?" It was the voice of Fuentes, behind me.

"All right, amigo," I said.

He came forward and we stood in the darkness together, looking from the ranch house to the bunkhouse. We had blown out the kitchen light when leaving, and no new light appeared, nor any sound.

"I have some miles to go before I camp. I'll saddle the dun," I said.

"You knew he was there?" asked Fuentes.

"There was a rifle near the kitchen door with prongs on the butt-plate," I said. "That was his fatal mistake. Leaving it there. I figured he was waiting in the bunkhouse."

"That was why you sent me away to get the note?"

"It was my fight."

"*Muchas gracias,* amigo."

At the corral I saddled the dun.

"We ride together, amigo . . . *bueno?*" he asked.

"Why not?" I replied.

He smiled, and I could see his white teeth.

The ranch house door creaked open, and an old man called into the night.

"John? . . . John . . . Twin?"

There was no answer. And there would be no answer.

Fuentes and I rode out of the ranch yard.

When morning came, and the stage stop at Ben Ficklin's was not far away, Fuentes said, "The note, amigo?"

It was a woman's handwriting. I tore it open.

I enjoyed the dancing. There will be another social soon. Will you take me?

CHINA BENN

Maybe not on that day. But on another, at some time not very far off.

RIDE THE
DARK TRAIL

To Uncle Dan Freeman,
of St. Cloud

Chapter 1

The old house stood on the crest of a knoll and it was three hundred yards to the main gate. No shrubbery or trees obscured the view, nor was there any cover for a half mile beyond.

The house was old, weather-beaten, wind-harried, and long unpainted. By night no light shone from any window, and by day no movement could be seen, but the watchers from the hill a half mile away were not fooled.

"She's there, all right. You lay a hand on that gate and you'll damned soon know she's there. She's setting up there in that old house and she can shoot."

Behind the house, the mountains lifted abruptly, steep, ragged slopes broken by ledges and dikes, covered with rough growth and dead-fall timber. Directly behind the house, only the top spread of its walls visible, lay the mouth of a canyon opening into the mountains beyond.

"Old Man Talon built that house to last, and when he built it, it was the finest house between New Orleans and Frisco. He had thirty tough hands then . . . a reg'lar army."

"How many's she got now?" Matthew asked.

"Not more'n two or three. The best of her land and the sources of all her water lie back of the house, and there's no way to get at it except right through the ranch yard. And that ol' devil ain't about to let anybody get by."

"She's got to sleep, ain't she?" Brewer asked.

"She sleeps, I suppose, but nobody ain't figured out when. Lay a finger on that gate and she'll part your brisket with a fifty-caliber bullet.

"The way folks tell it Old Man Talon figured someday they'd have to stand siege so he laid by enough ammunition and grub, too, to supply an army."

The three men eyed the house, irritation mixed with admiration, then turned to the coffeepot on their small fire.

"Flanner's right. The on'y way is to keep at her, every hour of every day and night. Sooner or later she's got to sleep, and then we'll get in. Behind that house in those canyons there's some of the finest land anywhere, watered by mountain streams and walled by mountains. No ol' woman's got the right to keep that land to herself, to say nothin' of the hundred thousand acres out here on the plains that they lay claim to."

"How come they got so much?"

"Talon was the first white man to settle in this country. When he and his partner came out here there was nothing but Indians and wild game. His partner was after fur, but not Talon. He seen this place and latched onto it, knowing that a hundred thousand acres out here was no good without water from the mountains.

"Talon and his partner built a cabin and wintered here, the partner taking all the fur, Talon keeping house and land. Come spring, the partner pulled his stakes, but Talon stayed on, fit Injuns, hunted buffalo, trapped a mite, and caught himself some wild horses.

"A few years passed by and the wagon trains started coming through. Talon had grub. He had raised him some corn, and he had jerked venison by the ton, and he swapped with the travelers for their wore-out cattle.

"He held his stock back in the canyons where he had no need for hands, an on that rich grass with plenty of water he built himself some herds. Somewhere along the line he taken off for the east and married up with this Tennessee hill woman. The way I hear it she was some kin to his old partner."

"Talon's dead?"

"Dry-gulched, they say. Nobody knows who done it."

"Is it true? Did she bust Flanner's knees?"

"Uh-huh. Flanner figured when her old man died that Em Talon would pull for the States, but she never done it. Moreover, she had her an idea Flanner had killed Talon.

"Flanner came out to run her off, and she let him come right on in. When he was maybe a hundred yards off she stopped him with a bullet to his feet and then she told him for what he was . . . or what she figured him to be.

"She said she wasn't going to kill him, she wanted him to live a hundred years, regrettin' ever' day of his life what he'd done. Then she cut down on him with that big fifty and busted both knees. Jake Flanner ain't walked a step since, not without them crutches."

The wind picked up, slapping their slickers against their chaps, and the three men began rigging their tarp to hold against the wind. It was going to be a bad night.

From time to time they turned to look at the great, gloomy old house, far away on its wind-swept knoll, bleak, lonely and harsh, like the woman who waited within.

Emily Talon leaned the Sharps against the doorjamb and peered through the shutters. Cold rain slanted from a darkening sky. Served them right, she reflected grimly, they'd have them a miserable night out there. She walked back to kindle a fire and put on water for tea.

From time to time she returned to peer through the shutters. It wouldn't be so bad if she had somebody to spell her, but the last of them died, and she'd buried him with her own hands, and now she was alone.

She was old now, old and tired. If only the boys would come home! She wanted both of them to come, but she told herself she was an evil old woman to want Milo most of all, Milo because he was a fast hand with a gun and mean. She needed a mean man now, to handle that bunch, and Milo could do it.

Milo taken after her kin. No Talon was ever that mean. The Talons were strong men, hard-working men and smarter than most. They were fighters, too, game as they came—those she'd met or heard tell of— but Milo was mean.

Any man who crossed Milo Talon was taking a risk. He was her youngest and a good boy, but he'd take water for no man. If you wished for trouble with Milo you'd best come a-shootin'.

Em Talon was tall and gaunt. Her one regret as a girl was that she fell just short of six feet. Her brothers had all been six-footers, and she'd wished to be at least that tall, but she'd fallen short by a quarter of an inch.

Her dress was old, gray, and nondescript. Her shoes had belonged to pa, but big as they were they were comfortable on her feet. Em Talon was sixty-seven years old and she had lived on the MT ranch for forty-seven of those years.

She'd been living alone in a cabin in the Cumberlands when pa came riding up to the door. A fine, handsome man he was, in store-bought clothes, shining boots, and riding a blood-bay gelding that stepped like a dancer.

He drew up outside the fence near where she was cutting flowers. "My name is Talon," he said, "and I'm looking for Em Sackett."

"What do you want with her?"

"I've come courting, and I've come a long way. I was partner to a cousin of hers out in the shining mountains."

She studied him with thoughtful eyes. "I am Emily Sackett," she said, "and you won't do much courtin' a-settin' up on that horse. Get down and come in."

She was twenty years old that summer, by mountain standards an old maid, but two weeks later they were married and had a fine honeymoon down New Orleans way.

Then she rode west beside Talon into a land of buffalo and Indians. When she rode up to the ranch house she could not believe what she saw. The house was there, larger than any other she had ever seen, even in New Orleans . . . and there wasn't even a cabin or dugout within a hundred miles, nor a town within two hundred or more.

She was called Em and Talon's name began with a T, so they took MT for a brand, now known far and wide as the Empty.

Pa was gone now, but it was many a fine year they'd had together. Pa was dead, and the man who'd killed him sat yonder in the town with two broken knees and a heart eaten with hatred for the woman who crippled him.

Flanner had hated Talon from the moment he saw him. Hated and envied him, for Talon already had what Flanner wanted. Jake Flanner decided the easiest way to come by what he wanted was to take what Talon had.

At first he tried to frighten the grim-jawed old man, but there was no fright in him that anybody ever located, so he had killed him or had him killed, sure that Em would pull out when her husband was dead. No woman could ever stand in his way . . . but there she stood.

It was cold in the big old house, and the rooms were dark and shadowed. A little of the last light of evening filtered through the heavy shutters. The house was dusty, and the air was stale and old. When a woman had to stand guard all day little time was left for housekeeping. She who had kept the neatest house in the Cumberland hills now had only a kitchen in which she dared live.

Talon had been a builder, as his family had been. He had come down from French Canada to build a steamboat for river traffic. The first of his line to live west of the Atlantic had been a ship-wright, and since then they had all been ship-wrights, mill-wrights, bridge-builders and workers with timber.

Pa had built keel boats, several steamboats, a dozen mills and bridges, and finally this house. He built with his own hands and he built to last. He had felled the timber, seasoned it, and shaped each piece with cunning hands. He dug the cellar himself and walled it with native stone, and he had prepared for every eventuality he could think of.

Looking out now Em saw the men huddled under their tarp, lashed by wind and rain. In each flash of lightning she could see something else. Every rock—a dozen at least—was painted white with black numerals on the side facing the house. The numerals represented the range, the number of yards from the door to that particular rock. Pa was a thoughtful man, and he preferred his shooting to be accurate.

Yet now pa was gone and she was alone, and her sons did not know how desperately she needed them.

She was exhausted. Her bones ached, and when she sat down she only managed to get up with an effort. Even making tea was a struggle, and sometimes when she eased her tired body into a chair she thought how easy it would be just to stay, to never make the effort to rise again.

It would be easy, too easy, and nothing had ever been easy for her.

She had nursed three children with a rifle across her knees. She had driven two cowhands back to the ranch, both of them gut-shot and moaning.

The first man she killed had been a renegade Kiowa, the last man a follower of Jake Flanner. There had been several in between, but she never counted.

They were going to win. She could not last forever, and Jake Flanner could hire more men. He could keep them out there until exhaustion destroyed her and her will to resist.

So far she had managed catnaps, which had been enough since the old often require less sleep than the young. Yet one day she would nap a little too long and they would come up the trail and put an end to her.

They would fire the house. That was the simplest way for them. They could then say the house caught fire and that she died with it. The explanation would be plausible enough, and whoever came to investigate—if anyone came—would be anxious to get the job over with and go home.

The nearest law was miles away, and the trails were rough.

Emily Talon had but one hope. That the boys would come home. It was for that she lived, it was for that she fought.

"Hold the ranch for the boys," pa had always said. Had he any idea how long it would be?

Of their six sons, only two were living when pa died. The oldest died at sixteen when a horse fell on him, and the second had been killed by Indians on the plains of western Nebraska. A third had died only four weeks after birth, and the fourth had died in a gun battle with rustlers right here on the Empty.

The two who remained were far apart in years as well as their thinking. Barnabas had wanted to go away to Canada to school, and had done so. When his school was nearly completed he had gone off to France to finish and had lived there with relatives. He had served in the French army, or something of the kind.

Milo was younger by eight years. Where Barnabas was cool, thoughtful and studious, Milo was impetuous, energetic, and quick-tempered. At fifteen he had hunted down and killed the rustler who killed his brother on the Empty. A year later he killed a would-be herd-cutter in the Texas Panhandle. At seventeen he had gone off to join the Confederate army, had become a sergeant, then a lieutenant. The war ended and they heard no more of him.

Nor had they heard from Barnabas. His last letter had come from France several years before.

Em Talon added sticks to the fire, then shuffled into the front hall to peer through the shutters. There were intermittent flashes of heat lightning, and she saw no movement, heard no sound other than the rain.

She feared rain, for during a heavy rain storm she could not hear or see nearly so well. And her watchers were snug in their holes under the rocks.

Flanner and his men were not yet aware of the part played by her watchers. Inside the gate, yet near it, there were piles of rocks gathered from the prairie and adopted as homes by several families of marmots. Quick to whistle when anything strange moved near, they had warned her on more than one occasion, and her ears were tuned to their sound.

Returning to her chair she eased herself down and leaned back with a sigh. There had been a time when she had ridden free as the wind across these same plains, ridden beside Talon, feeling the wind in her hair and the sun warm upon her back.

During those first hard years she had worked with rope and horse like any cowhand. She hunted meat for the table, helped to stretch the first wire brought on the place, and helped pa at the windlass when he dug his well.

She was old now, and tired. The long, wakeful nights left her trembling, yet she was not afraid. When they came after her in the end she hoped but for one thing, that she would awaken in time to get off a shot.

Nothing had frightened her in the old days, but then pa had always been close by, and now pa was gone.

Slowly her tired muscles relaxed. Thunder rumbled out there, and the heat lightning showed brief flashes through the cracks of the shutters. She must take another look soon. In a little while.

Her eyes closed . . . only for a minute, she told herself, only for one brief, wonderful minute.

Chapter 2

Nobody needed to tell me what I needed was a place out of the rain and a good, hot meal. Maybe a drink. The long-geared, raw-boned roan I was riding had run himself into the ground and was starting to flounder. We'd come a fur piece together, and we'd come fast. It began to look like I'd out-run trouble for the time, but then I wasn't going to make any bets until I'd seen the cards.

Lightning flashed and there looked to be rain-wet roofs off there. A cold drop of rain slipped down the back of my neck and down my spine, and I swore.

I'd no idea whose slicker I was wearing, but I was surely pleased to have it instead of leaving it with him. Anyway, he would be nursing a headache for the next few days and should ought to stay in bed.

It was a town off there, sure enough. Or what passed for a town in this country.

There were six or eight buildings that might be stores or saloons and a scattering of shacks folks might live in. Lights shone from a set of four windows. There was a "Hotel" sign over two of them, so I turned in at the livery stable.

Seemed to be nobody around so I found myself an empty stall, stripped the gear from the roan, rubbed him dry with a few handfuls of hay, and then taking rifle and saddlebags I walked up front.

Of a sudden there was a pounding of hoofs and a team came tearing around the corner and into the street, coming at a belly-to-the-ground dead run. Me, I'd started for the saloon in that hotel building and I jumped clear just in time to keep from being run over.

The driver pulled up in front of the hotel and got down, a wisp of a girl in a rain-wet dress that clung to a mighty cute shape. She tied the team and went inside.

When I fetched open the door and came in quiet she was the center of attention, all wet and bedraggled in the middle of the floor.

There weren't more than five or six men in the place. A big, blond man wearing a red shirt and a nasty kind of smile stood at the bar.

"It's that waif-girl who taken up workin' for Spud Tavis," he was saying. "Looks like she run off and' lef' ol' Spud, an' him expectin' so much of her, too."

"I would like to talk to the owner of this place," the girl said. "Please, will somebody tell me where he is? I want a job."

"Not fat enough for my taste." The speaker was a short, thick-set man with black hair. "I like 'em plump so's you can get hold of something. This one's too skinny."

Me, I closed the door soft and just stood there, liking nothing I saw, but wishing for no trouble. Three of the men in that saloon were trying to pay no mind to what was happening, but a body could see they didn't hold with it. Neither did I.

Nobody ever held Logan Sackett up to be no hero. Me, I've run the wild trails since who flung the chunk, and I've picked up a few horses here and yon, and some cattle, too. I've ridden the back trails with the wild bunch and from time to time I've had folks comin' down my trail with a noose hung out for hangin', but I never bothered no womenfolk.

"You, there," the big blond man said to her, "you come here to me."

"I'll do no such thing." She was scared but she had spunk. "I'm a good girl, Len Spivey, and you know it!"

He chuckled, then straightened slowly from the bar. "You comin', or do I come after you?"

"Leave her alone," I said.

For a moment, nothing moved. It was like I'd busted a window or something the way everybody stopped and turned to look at me.

Well, they hadn't much to see. I'm a big man, weighing around two-fifteen most of the time and most of it in my chest and shoulders. I was wearing a handlebar mustache and a three-day growth of beard. My hair hadn't been trimmed in a coon's age and that beat up old hat was showing a bullet hole picked up back of yonder. My slicker was hanging open, my leather chaps was wet, and my boots rundown at heel so's those big-roweled California spurs were draggin' a mite.

"What did you say?" That blond man was staring at me like he couldn't believe it. Seemed like nobody ever stopped him doing what he had a mind to.

"I said leave her alone. Can't you see the lady is wet, tired, an' lookin' for a room for herself?"

"You stay the hell out of this, mister. If she wants a room she can have mine, and me with it."

I turned to her. "Ma'am, you pay no mind to such talk. You just set down yonder and I'll see you have something warm to eat an' drink."

That blond man wasn't fixed to like me very much. "Stranger," he said, "you'd better back off an' take another look. This here ain't your town. If I was you I'd straddle whatever I rode in here and git off down the road before I lose patience."

Now we Clinch Mountain Sacketts ain't noted for gentle ways. The way I figure it is if a man is big enough to open his mouth he's big enough to take the consequences, and I was getting tired of talk.

Stepping over to an empty table I drawed back a chair. "Ma'am, you just set here." I walked over to the bar, and, turning to the man behind it, I said, "Fix the lady a bowl of hot soup and some coffee."

"Mister," he rested both hands on the bar, his expression as unpleasant as that other gent's, "I wouldn't fix that—"

A man can lose patience. I reached across that bar and grabbed myself a handful of shirt and jerked that bartender half over his bar.

The grip I'd taken was well up at his throat and I held him there and shook him real good a time or two and when his face started to turn blue, I slammed him back so's he hit that back bar like he'd been throwed by a bronco. He slammed into it and a couple of bottles toppled off and busted. "Fix that soup," I said matter-of-factly, "and be careful what tone you use around a lady."

That Len Spivey, he just stood there, kind of surprised, I take it. I'd been keeping him in mind, and the others, too. Nothing in my life had left me trusting of folks.

"I don't think you understand," the blond man said, "I'm Len Spivey!"

Seems like every cow town has some two-by-twice would-be bad man.

"You forget about it, son," I said, "and I'll promise not to tell nobody!"

Well, he didn't know what to do. He dearly wanted to stretch my hide but suddenly he wasn't so awful sure. It's easy to strut around playing the bad man with local folks when you know just what you can do and what they can do. But when a stranger comes into town it begins to shade off into another pattern.

"Len Spivey," the black-haired man said, "is the fastest man in this country."

"It's a small country," I said.

The bartender came with the soup and placed it on the table very carefully, then stepped back.

"Eat that," I told the girl, who looked to be no more than sixteen, and maybe less. "I'll drink the coffee."

Talk began and ever'body ignored us, only they didn't really: I'd been in strange towns before and knew the drill. Sooner or later one of them would make up his mind to see how tough I really was. I'd looked them over and didn't care which. They all sized up like a bunch of no-account mavericks.

"Are there any decent womenfolk around here?" I asked her. "I mean folks who aren't scared of this crowd?"

"There's only Em Talon. She ain't feered of nobody or nothing."

"Eat up," I said, "and I'll take you to her."

"Mister, you don't know what you're sayin'. That ol' woman would shoot you dead before you got the gate open. She's nailed a few, she has!"

She spooned some soup, then looked up. "Why, she shot up Jake Flanner, who owns this place! Busted both his knees!"

"Somebody mention my name?"

He stood in the door behind the corner of the bar, leaning on two crutches. He was a huge man, big but not very fat. His arms were heavy with muscle and he had big hands.

He swung around the bar, favoring one crutch a mite more than the other. A good-looking man of forty or so, he was wearing a holstered gun, and he had another, I was sure, in a shoulder holster under his coat.

"I'm Jake Flanner. I think we should have a talk."

Nobody was supposed to know he had that shoulder holster. There were mighty few of them around, and this one was set well back under his arm, and as the gun was small it could go unnoticed on a big-chested man like Jake Flanner.

A crippled man is smart to leave off wearing a gun. There's few men who would jump a cripple, and in most western towns there'd be no surer way of getting yourself nominated for a necktie party. So if this man was all loaded down with iron there had to be a reason.

Something about those crutches worried me, too, and how he favored one side. To use a gun he'd have to let go of a crutch.

"May I seat myself?"

"Go ahead . . . only stay out of line in case somebody decides to open the ball. I wouldn't want to kill any innocent bysitters."

"You're new around here," he said, easing himself in his chair. "Riding through?"

"More'n likely."

"Unusual for a man passing through to take up for a lady. Very gallant . . . very gallant, indeed."

"I know nothing about gallant," I said, "but a lady should be allowed to choose her comp'ny, an' should be treated like a lady until she shows she prefers different."

"Of course. I'm sure the boys meant nothing disrespectful." He taken a long look at me. "You seem to have traveled far," he said, "and judging by the looks of your horse, you've traveled fast."

"When I get shut of a place, I'm shut of it."

"Of course." He paused, stoking a pipe. "I might use a good man right here. A man," he added, "who can use a gun." He paused again. "I would surmise you are a man who has seen trouble."

"I've come a ways. And I've been up the creek an' over the ridge, if that's what you mean. I've busted broncs, roped steers, an' fit the heel flies. I've skinned buffalo and laid track an' lived with Indians, so I don't figure to be no pilgrim."

"You're just the man I've needed."

"Maybe, maybe not. You trot out your argument an' run her around the corral an' we'll see how the brand reads."

There was nothing much about this Flanner that I took to, but when a man is on the dodge with a lot of country he can't go back to right away he's in no position to be picky about folks he works for.

"I heard the young lady here mention Emily Talon. She runs the Empty outfit over against the mountain, and she owes me money. Now she's a mean old woman and she's got some mean cowhands and I'd like to hire you to go out there and collect for me."

"What's the matter with Spivey there? He looks like a man who's bit into a sour pickle with a sore tooth. He'd be just the man to tackle an old woman."

Spivey slammed his bottle on the bar. "Look, you!" He was so mad he spluttered.

"Spivey," I said, "you got to wait your turn. I'm in a coffee-drinkin' mood now, an' right contented to be in out of the rain. I'll take care of you when I get around to it an' not a moment sooner."

"There's fifty dollars in it," Flanner added, "and you don't have to shoot unless shot at. I'll even give you a badge to wear, so's it's official."

"Right now I need some sleep," I said, "and I ain't about to crawl back in a saddle until daybreak. How far's it out there?"

"About seven miles. It's a big, old house. The biggest an' the oldest around here." Flanner's eyes were bland. "It is an easy fifty, if you want it." He paused. "By the way . . . what shall I call you?"

"Logan . . . Logan will do."

"All right, Logan, I'll see you in the morning. Boys," he struggled to his feet, getting the crutches under his shoulders, "lay off Mister Logan. I want him around to talk to in the morning."

He swung away, moving easily on those crutches. He was a big man but he handled himself easily. Crippled or not, if 'n I ever saw a dangerous man, this one was. Dangerous but smooth, mighty, mighty smooth!

"Don't you do it," the girl whispered. "Don't you help them bully that old woman."

"Thought you was scared of her. Scared to go out there?"

"She shoots. She's got herself a Sharps Fifty an' she will hit anything she shoots at. They're trying to take her ranch away. It's him an' them nesters. They were Johnny-come-latelies, all trying to move in on that old lady just because she's old, alone, and got the best land anywhere around."

"Are you from here?"

"Not really. My pa was one of the nesters. Pa was an honest man but he never done well. Everything he put a hand to seemed to turn sour. He wasn't much of a manager when it came to money, and he never worked no harder than the law allowed.

"There was just the two of us. Pa picked himself a piece of prairie land and tried to prove up, but the land he plowed mostly blew away and no rain came and pa took to hitting the bottle. One night coming home he fell off his horse and come morning he had pneumonia.

"I taken a job keepin' house for Spud Tavis and his youngsters, only it turned out what Spud was hunting was a woman for himself and not a housekeeper. He got almighty mean, so I got into a buckboard and came into town."

"How old are you?"

"Sixteen. Mister Logan," her voice lowered so only he could hear, "it may sound a hard thing, but if pa had to go I'm glad it was right then. Pa was going to sell something he knew to Flanner."

"About the Empty outfit?"

"Pa knew a way in. When we first came into this country we boarded a cowhand who'd worked for her. He got scared an' quit, buffaloed by Flanner's men, but before he left the country he told pa one night about a way he knew to come into the Empty outfit from behind.

"It was an Injun trail, and he come on it one time huntin' strays. It had been used a time or two, year ago. He found some sign of that, and he reckoned it was that gun-slinging kid of Talon's . . . Milo."

"Milo Talon? He's kin to the old woman out yonder?"

"Son. There's another boy, too, only he went off to foreign parts. Seems they had kinfolk in Canada and France. This cowhand was quite a talker, and him an' pa had knowed each other back in West Virginny."

"Your pa knew about a trail into the back of the Empty? Did he ever tell Flanner?"

"I don't think so. He figured we had to pull out and we needed a road-stake. He figured he might get a hundred dollars for it, an' we could go on to Californy or Oregon, but pa never did have no luck. That horse dropped him an' he taken sick to his death."

"That cowhand, where did he go?"

She shrugged. "He taken out. That's six, eight months ago."

"What's your name, girl?"

"I'm Pennywell Farman."

"Pennywell, I've got no money to speak of. I can't send you nowhere, but we might get you to that Em Talon. She might like to have somebody to he'p out now and again."

"We'd never get in. She'll shoot you, mister. These folks been after her place, and she'll let nobody close."

My eyes taken a look around that room and nobody seemed to be paying us no mind. All the same, I knew they were trying to listen and that they hadn't forgotten us. Pennywell went to spooning soup, and I gave thought to the fix she was in.

Me, I was a drifting man, and there was nothing around here I wanted. Right now I was figuring on wintering in Brown's Hole. I had to get shut of this girl and leave her some place she'd be safe.

I'd no idea of taking Flanner's offer. That was just a mite of stalling to get trouble off my back until I could get my horse rested and a meal in me. Seemed our only chance was that old lady yonder.

"Pennywell, when that cowhand was a-talkin' to your pa, what were you doin'?"

"Sleeping."

"Now, Penny, if I'm to help you, you got to help me. I don't figure to get myself killed, and it might be you could help that old lady. Don't you recall what that cowhand said about that trail through the back?"

She gave me a long, thoughtful look. "I think you're a good man, Mister Logan, or I'd say nothing. I think maybe I could find that trail if you'd help."

Suddenly the outer door burst open and a big man stood framed in the doorway. Len Spivey turned to look, then began to grin.

"Lookin' for your girl, Spud? There she is . . . with that stranger."

When that door opened I recognized trouble. That big man was surely on the prod and he came into the room like he figured to smash everything in sight. He was big, he was wet, and he was hoppin' mad.

"You, there! What d'you mean runnin' off with my rig? I got a notion to see you jailed for stealin' horses. You git up out o' there an' git back to the buckboard. Soon's I have a drink we'll be drivin' back home. What you need is a taste of the strap!"

"I quit!" Pennywell said firmly. "I went to care for your children, Spud Tavis, and to cook for them and you, but that was all, and you *knowed* it. You got no right to come after me thisaway!"

"By the Lord Harry, I'll show you what!"

"You heard the lady," I said mildly. "She's quit you. You're no kin to her an' you've got no rights in the matter, so leave her alone."

He reached for the girl and when he did I just kind of slapped his arm away. It caught him unexpected and spun him so's he had to take a step to keep balance.

He caught himself, his features flushed with anger, and turned on me. He had a big, thick, hairy fist and he drew it back to throw a punch, but as he stepped forward there was an instant when his foot was off the ground and I let go with a sweeping, sidewise move of my foot that swept his foot over and up. He staggered and fell, hitting the floor with a bump.

He got up fast, I'll give him that. For a man of his heft he was quick, and he came right at me.

Me, I never so much as moved from my chair, only hooked my toe around the leg of the chair at the end of the table. He taken a lunge at me and I kicked the chair into his path and he came down across it, all sprawled out.

"Something the matter?" I asked. "Seems like you're kind of unsteady."

He got up more slowly, but he let his hand close over one of the broken chair legs. "Better get back against the wall," I told Pennywell, "from here on this is going to get rough."

This time he was cautious. He came toward me slowly, gripping the club in his right hand; he raised it a mite more than shoulder high and poised to strike. But this time I was on my feet. He didn't know much about stick fighting and his one idea was to bash in my skull. He struck down and hard. Blocking the downcoming blow with my forearm, I slid my right hand under and over his arm to grasp my own wrist in an arm lock. I had him and there was never much mercy in me. I just slammed the pressure to him and his hand opened and dropped the club as he screamed.

He went over backwards to the floor and I released him and let him fall. I had almost broken his arm. I could have without no trouble. He was game and he got up. When he tried to swing with his injured arm I was suddenly tired of the whole thing. I hit him four inches above the belt buckle with my left, and then clobbered him on the ear with my right. He went down, his ear split apart, gasping for breath.

"A man that can't fight shouldn't try," I commented. "He's just lucky I didn't break his fool neck."

Taking Pennywell by the elbow, I went to the door. "I'm taking this girl to a good home," I said, "but I'll be back."

Spud Tavis was slowly sitting up. "Tavis," I said, "you've got youngsters, Pennywell says. My advice is to go home an' take care of them. If you ever bother this young lady again, you'll answer to me. An' next time I won't play games."

The rain had wind behind it, lashing the boardwalk and the faces of the buildings. We slopped across to the livery stable, where I left Pennywell under the overhang and went in alone, gun in hand.

Nobody was there. I saddled up my horse, who looked almighty unhappy with me, and then mounted up. At the door I gave her a hand up and we went out and down the road. As we left I saw somebody standing on the edge of the walk, peering after me. Once out of sight and sound in the darkness we cut across a field, took a country lane, and headed for the mountains.

The trail began at a lightning-scarred pine and wound steeply up among the rocks, slick from rain and running water. After a climb of nearly half a mile we came to a huge boulder that hung over what was called a trail. It taken us nearly two hours to travel maybe a mile and a half of trail, and then we were riding smooth and in the woods a couple of thousand feet above the prairie.

Wet branches slapped at our faces and dripped water down our necks. Several times the horse slipped on the muddy trail. The horse I rode was bigger than most and powerful, but it was carrying double. After a while I got down and walked, leading the horse along.

"Logan Sackett," I said to myself, "you can get yourself into some mighty poor situations."

Here I was, slippin' an' sloppin' through a wet forest, headin' toward what might be a bullet in my fat skull, and all because of some no-account drifter's girl.

The house when I saw it looked almighty big, even from up on the mountain. It looked the way folks figure a ha'nted house might look like, standin' up there on its hill, peerin' out over the country around.

Behind it there was a long building, more'n likely a bunkhouse. There were a couple of barns, sheds, and some corrals. I could see light reflected from a water tank. It must have been quite an outfit when it was all together an' workin' right.

We walked and slid down the steep hill behind the house, and lookin' back I could see why nobody tried that way in, because it was rimmed around with cliffs two or three hundred feet high or mountains too steep for a horse to climb.

I led my horse inside a barn and stripped off the saddle. The barn was empty and smelled like it'd been empty a long time. Very carefully we crossed to the bunkhouse and I opened the door, stepped in, and struck a match. It was empty, too. No bedrolls, nothing.

A few old dried-out, worn-out boots, some odds and ends of harness and rope, a dusty coat hung from a nail.

We crossed the yard and went very easily up the back steps. The door opened under my hand, and we stepped in.

All was dark and still. The house had the musty smell of a place long closed. Lightning flashed revealing a kitchen storeroom. We tiptoed on through it, opening the door into the kitchen.

There was a fire in the kitchen range, and the smell of warmth and coffee was in the room.

The floor creaked ever so slightly as we crossed it. I could feel the skin crawl on the back of my neck, but I laid a hand on that door.

By rights we should have had a gun barrel stuck in our faces, but there hadn't been a sound. Was the old lady dead?

Gently I opened the door. Beyond was a big room, cavernous and dark. Lightning flashed and showed through the shuttered windows and the glass transom window over the door. And in that momentary flash I found myself looking across the room into the black muzzle of a big pistol. Behind it stood the old lady.

The flash, then darkness. "All right," her voice was steady, "I may be old but I have ears like a cat. If you so much as shift your feet I am going to fire, and mister, I can hit what I aim at."

"Yes, ma'am. I've a lady with me, ma'am."

"To the right of the door there is a lamp. There should still be a little coal oil in it. Take off the chimney, strike a match, and be mighty, mighty careful."

"Yes, ma'am. We're friendly, ma'am. We've just had a run-in with some folks down at the town."

Carefully I lifted off the lamp chimney, struck a match, and touched it to the wick. Then I replaced the chimney and the room was softly lit.

"Better stand clear of the light," she said quietly, "those no-accounts yonder shot two or three of them out for me."

"Yes, ma'am. My name is Logan Sackett, and this here girl is Pennywell Farman."

"Any kin to Deke Farman?"

"He was my father."

"Maybe he was a good father, but he was a shiftless, no-account cowhand. Never did earn his keep."

"That sounds like pa," Pennywell said mildly.

The hand that held the gun was steady as a rock. And it was no ordinary gun. It was one of those old-time Dragoon Colts that would blow a hole in a man big enough for your fist . . . or mine.

"What are you doin' here?" the old lady asked.

"Ma'am, this young lady taken on to cook an' care for youngsters at the Tavis place. Spud Tavis made things bad for her, an' she run off an' fetched herself into town. She came to the Bon Ton huntin' the boss to ask for a job, and some of that crowd—Len Spivey for one— they talked kind of mean to her, ma'am. She needs a lady to set with, ma'am, and somebody who will teach her the things she should know. She's sixteen, and she's a good girl."

"Do you take me for a fool? Of course, she's a good girl. I can see that. What I want to know is what kind of a man are you? Are you fit company for her?"

"No, ma'am, I'm not. I'm mean, ma'am, meaner than a skunk, on'y I never figured to be comp'ny for her, only to bring her here. I'm fixin' to ride on, ma'am, soon's my horse is rested up."

"Ride on?" Her voice grew stronger. "Ride to where?"

"I don't rightly know, ma'am, just on. Just to ride on. I been a sight of places, worked at a whole lot of things. Was Milo Talon your son, ma'am?"

Suddenly the room was still. And then she said, "What do you know of Milo Talon?"

"Why, we met up down Chihuahua way, quite a spell back, only I understood his folks were all passed on."

"He was wrong, and I'm his ma. Where is Milo now?"

"Driftin', I reckon. We drifted together, there for a while, and got ourselves in a shootin' match down Laredo way."

"Milo was always a hand. He was quick to shoot."

"Yes, ma'am, or I'd be dead. He seen 'em sneakin' up on us before I did an' he cut loose. Yes, ma'am, Milo Talon could shoot. He had said his brother was better than him."

"Barnabas? At targets, maybe, or with a rifle, but Barnabas was never up to Milo when it came to hoedown-an'-scrabble shootin'."

There was silence in the room. "Ma'am? There's coffee settin' yonder. Mightn't we have some?"

She got up, placing the pistol in a worn holster slung from her hips. "What ever am I thinkin' of? Been so long since I had a guest I don't recall how to act. Of course, there's coffee."

She started toward the door, then paused. "Young man, would you mind taking a look out yonder? If you see anybody creepin' up . . . shoot him or her as the case might be."

She lighted the other lamp in the kitchen and then carried the lamp from the big front room back to join it.

"Nobody coming, ma'am. Looks like they're holed up against the rain."

"Fools! They might have had me. I fallen asleep in yonder. Heard the floor creak as you stepped into the kitchen or somewhere. They're a lazy lot. Gunslingers aren't what they used to be. Was a time you could hire *fighters*, but this lot that Flanner has are a mighty sorry bunch."

She turned, a tall old woman in a faded gray dress and a worn maroon sweater. She looked at me, then sniffed. "I might of knowed it. Clinch Mountain, ain't you?"

"What was that, ma'am?" I was startled.

"I said you're a Clinch Mountain Sackett, ain't you? I'd read your sign anywhere, boy. You're probably one of those no-account sons of Tarbil Sackett, ain't you?"

"Grandson, ma'am."

"I thought so. Knowed your folks, ever durn last one of them, and a sorry lot they were, good for nothing but fightin' an' makin' moonshine whiskey."

"Are you from Tennessee, ma'am?"

"Tennessee? You're durned tootin', I am! I'm a Clinch Mountain Sackett myself! Married Talon an' came west an' we set up here. Fact is, a cousin of mine helped put this place together, and he was a Sackett.

He went off somewhere in the mountains and never come back.

"Traipsin' just like you, he was, traipsin' after some fool story of gold. Left some boys back in Tennessee, and a wife that was too good for him.

"Come in an' set, son, you're among home folks!"

Chapter 3

It was comfortable in that old kitchen, and old as it was the place was neat as a man could wish. The floor was scrubbed and the copper pots shone brightly with light reflected by that coal-oil lamp.

The coffee smelled right good. Even though I'd had a cup at the Bon Ton down in town, this here was better, better by a whole lot.

"They said down in town you had some hands," I told her.

She chuckled. "I aimed for them to think so. I been alone for nearly a year now. Bill Brock, he picked up some lead last time we had us a fight with those folks, and he died. I buried him out yonder." She nodded toward the area behind the house. "Figured to move him to a proper grave when the time came."

She taken a cup of coffee after she'd poured for us and then she came and set down. Her face was lined and old enough to have worn out two or three bodies but her eyes held fire. "You be Logan Sackett. Well, I d'clare! You a puncher?"

"I'm whatever it takes to get the coon," I said. "I guess I ain't much, Aunt Em. I'm too driven to driftin' an' gun play. Why, even that horse I'm ridin' yonder ain't mine. Come time to leave back yonder down the country I hadn't no time to buy a horse nor the money to do it with. This one was handy so I taken to his saddle and lit a shuck out of there."

She nodded. "I've seen it a time or two. Come daylight you go yonder to the barn an' turn that horse loose. He'll take time but he'll fetch up back home sooner or later. We've horses a-plenty here on the Empty."

"I wasn't figurin' on—"

"Don't you worry none. There's enough rooms in this here house for the whole of Grant's army, and then there's the bunkhouse. We ain't short of grub, although we could do with some fresh meat now and again.

"No reason you can't hole up here until the weather clears."

"Thank you, ma'am. On'y I was sort of figurin' on Californy. I been there a time or two and when winter comes I just naturally get chilblains. I thought maybe I'd head for Los Angeles, or maybe Frisco."

"I can pay," Aunt Em said. "You needn't worry none about that."

"I wouldn't take money from kinfolk. It's just that I—"

"Logan Sackett, you be still! You're not movin' a step until the weather shapes up. If you're worried about those folks out there, you just forget it. I can handle them, one at a time or all to onct."

"It ain't that, it's just that—"

"All right then, it's settled. I'll get you some blankets."

Looked to me like I wasn't going to see Californy for some time yet. That old lady just wasn't easy to talk to. She had her own mind and it was well made up ahead of time. Anyway, I was kind of curious to see what that outfit out front looked like.

"If I'm going to stay," I said, "I'll keep watch. You two go yonder and sleep."

When they had gone I got me a mattress off a bed in one of the rooms and laid it out on the floor, then I fetched blankets and settled in for the night.

Outside the rain beat down on the roof and walls of the old house, and the lightning flashed and flared, giving a man a good view of what was happening at the gate and beyond. And that was just nothing.

The lamp was in the kitchen and I left it there, wanting no light behind me when I looked out. After watching for a while, I decided nobody was likely to make a move for a time, so I went back and stoked up the fire in the kitchen range and added a mite of water to the coffee so's there'd be a-plenty.

Off the living room there was a door opened into what must have been old Reed Talon's office. There were more books in there than I'd ever seen at one time in my life, and there were some sketches like of buildings and bridges, all with figures showing measurements written in. I couldn't make much of some of them, although others were plain enough. Studying those sketches made me wonder how a man would feel who built something like a bridge or a boat or a church or the like. It would be something to just stand back and look up at it and think he'd done it. Made a sight more sense than wandering around the country settin' up in the middle of a horse.

Time to time I catnapped. Sometimes I'd prowl a mite, and a couple of times I put on that slicker and went outside.

There was a wide porch on the house, roofed over, but with a good long parapet or wall that was four feet high. Talon had put loopholes in that wall a man could shoot from, and he'd built wisely and well.

When I came in I sat down with coffee, and then I heard those old shoes a-scufflin' and here come Em Talon.

"Well, Logan, it's good to see a Sackett again. It's been a good many years."

"I hear tell some of them have moved up around Shalako, out in western Colorado," I suggested. "Fact is, I know there's several out there. Cumberland Sacketts," I added, "good folks, too."

"The man who helped pa had some boys back in Tennessee. I often wonder what became of him." She filled her cup. "His oldest boy was named for William Tell."

"Met him. He's a good man, and he's sure enough hell on wheels with a six-shooter. No back-up to him."

"Never was back-up in no Sackett I can call to mind. I reckon there were some who lacked sand, but there's a rotten apple in every barrel."

She was a canny old woman, and we set there over coffee, with once in a while a look out to see if anybody was coming in on us. We talked of the Clinch Mountains, the Cumberland Gap country, and folks who'd moved west to hunt for land.

"Talon was a good man," she said. "I married well, if I do say it. When he first rode up to my gate I knowed he was the man for me, or none.

"All the Talons had a gift for working with their hands, they had the love of good wood in their fingers, an' when a Talon taken wood into his hands he felt of it like he loved it."

She looked over at me. "It's like you Sacketts with your guns."

"From what they tell me you're pretty good your own self."

"Had to be. Pa wasn't always home, and there were Injuns. I was never like some. Lots of folks lost relatives to Injuns, and hated 'em because. Me, I never did. They was just something else to contend against, like the storms, the stampedes, the drought, and the grass-hoppers. A time or two I seen grasshoppers come in clouds that would darken the sun and strip bare the land like a plague." She stared off, as if calling up her memories.

"Shoot? Well, I guess yes. Gun loads was mighty scarce back yonder in the hills, and when somebody went out for meat for our family he or she was expected to come back with meat for every load taken."

She refilled my cup and hers. "Logan, I got to find Milo. This here place belongs to the boys, him and Barnabas. I'm not so young as I used to be, an' one night I'll fall asleep and those out there, they'll close in an' finish me off. I need he'p, Logan."

I shifted in my chair, feeling guilty-like. I'd lost no ponies around here. Californy was where I'd be fixing to be, and then I had to put my oar into that squabble down in town.

"I could stay on a few days," I said. "There's nobody waitin' for me yonder. Or anywheres else," I added, thinking on it. I guess since my folks died nobody had ever waited on my coming or cared what happened.

"That Flanner," I said, "he carries a gun in a shoulder holster."

"He does? Well, I reckon he carries one someplace. He's killed a few. Nobody braces him." She looked up at me, real sharp. "You seen Johannes?"

"Not to know him. There were several men a settin' in the saloon. In the Bon Ton. But I don't know—"

"Wouldn't have been him. Johannes Duckett. He's some kin to Flanner, and he's not quite right in the head, I think. Or maybe he's just strange. But he's a dead shot with a gun of any kind and he's a back-shooter . . . he'll shoot you front, back, or sideways. Mostly he cares for the livery stable."

"I didn't see anybody."

"Well, he was around there, then. Whenever he ain't there, some-body else is, and when Johannes is about you just don't see him unless he's of a mind to let you."

After a time she went off to bed and I fussed around a mite, and taken a turn outside. Pretty soon Pennywell came down to spell me and I curled up on a mattress to take five.

Daylight was coming through the shutters when I awakened, and I could hear folks stirring around out in the kitchen. From the porch I could look over that layout there by the gate, and of a sudden I started gettin' sore.

Holding an old lady like that! And shooting at her so's she didn't dare stir out in front of her own house.

Setting there on the porch in the shadows I studied the layout and made up my mind that come sundown I was going to do some moving around of my own. Californy looked bright and pretty to me and I wasn't going to leave here with those fellers out there makin' trouble for Aunt Em.

Out back I fetched a bit of corn from the bin for my horse—I guess he'd never had it so good.

Em Talon was right. They had some mighty fine stock out yonder in the fenced pasture behind the barn, so I saddled up, roped myself a half dozen horses, and brought them up to the corral one at a time. Then I stripped the gear from the borrowed horse and turned it loose.

It ran off a ways, then commenced to graze out there betwixt those boys and the house. Finally as if it taken a notion to travel, it moved off.

Leaning on the corral I studied those horses. The ones I'd picked were mighty fine stock, all wearing the Empty brand. There was a tough-looking strawberry roan that I liked right off, and a steeldust gelding with a wise look about him.

Those were good horses but they hadn't been under a saddle for months, maybe. They'd take some riding, so I made up my mind to do it.

Whilst I was puttering around I got to studying on where Milo Talon might be. If I was to get shut of this job I'd better find him . . . and that wasn't easy to do.

Milo was a man who covered country. There'd be folks in Brown's Hole might know where he was, or up in the Hole-in-the-Wall country. What I had to do was start the word moving along the trails. It might take time, but if Milo was alive, he'd hear it.

Meanwhile there was a lot to be done. I topped off those broncs, and they showed me plenty of action, but they were good stock. To make sure we'd have plenty of riding stock in case of trouble, I topped off a few others, too.

The gate to the corral was sagging and a board on the back step had come loose, so I made out to fix them up. I never cared much for such work, liking to do nothing I couldn't do from a saddle, but it had to be done.

Working around, I gave the place some study. Old Talon, who had moved in here when the Injuns were on the warpath often as not, had built with cunning. And that was what had Flanner's boys in a bind . . . he'd built so there was no way he could be got at.

Moreover, each building was like a fort, and it was easy to move from one to the other without exposing yourself to rifle fire from the outside.

There are a lot of places in the mountains where small valleys or ravines open out into the plains. Talon had found such a place and built so that there was no access except right through his ranch. Which allowed him to control the grazing in a succession of small but pleasant valleys that cut deep into the mountains.

He had located most of the possibilities for trails into the area and had blasted rock to block them off, or had felled trees across them. It was a rugged area of deep canyons, rushing streams, and wild, broken ridges.

There isn't any place that I ever saw that couldn't be got into or out of, but often it isn't easy, and nobody wants to go scouting in rough country, scrambling up rock slides and the like when he is apt to get his skull opened up for trying.

Talon had been thinking about Injuns, I figure, but maybe he'd had the foresight to know that a lot of the savages wear store-bought clothes. Anyway, he was ready . . . else his widow would have been buried deep and this place would have been cut up and divided, or taken over by Flanner.

Meanwhile night was coming on. Just to see what would happen I taken a blanket on a stick and moved it in the shadows of the porch, standing well inside.

Sure enough, a rifle blasted and a bullet went right through that blanket. Now out where they were all they'd be able to see was something moving. They wouldn't know but what it was Em Talon.

Come evening time when the shadows are long and it begins to get hard to see, I taken my Winchester and went out through the kitchen.

Pennywell stopped me. "Where you going?"

Em turned from the stove. "I just fixed supper," she said, "you set down."

"Keep it warmed up. I'll be back." I hesitated in the back door. "Those boys out there can spread it around. I want to see what they do when it's all gathered up."

Outside I moved into the shadows. Nobody ever said no Clinch Mountain Sackett was anything but mean, and me and my brother Nolan, we shaped up to be the meanest. I never asked no favors and never gave none that I can recall, not when it came to fighting.

We Sackett boys had grown up among the Indians. Cherokees mostly, but we'd known and hunted with Creeks, Chickasaws, Choctaws, and Shawnees. What I done right then any of those Injuns could have done, but I figure I did it as well as most. Anyway, I moved across that open ground, sort of filtering through the shadows, like.

There were three men settin' by that fire and I stood up and walked amongst them. I was right on them before they saw me and I kicked the boiling coffeepot into the lap of the nearest one.

The man whose back was to me started to get up and turn and I pushed him into the fire. Then I taken a swing with my rifle and fetched the next one in the belly. He went down and I walked into that outfit and never gave them a chance to get set.

Like I said, I'm a big man, but that ain't the important part. My shoulders and arms have beef on them from wrassling broncs and steers, from swinging an ax and rafting logs down the Mississippi, and I was feeling no mercy for an outfit that would tackle an old woman.

The one I'd shoved into the fire jumped out of it and turned, grabbing for his six-shooter. Well, if he wanted to play that way he could. I just pointed my rifle at him, which I held only in my right hand, and let him have the big one right through the third button on his shirt. If he ever figured to sew that particular button on again he was going to have to scrape it off his backbone . . . if he had any.

The man into whose lap I'd kicked the coffeepot had troubles enough. He was jumping around like mad and I could see I'd ruined his social life for some time to come. He'd been scalded real good and he wasn't going to ride anywhere, not anywhere at all.

The other one was on his hands and knees, gasping and groaning. I pushed him over on his back with my boot and put the rifle in his face and looked down the barrel at him.

"You ever been to Wyoming?" I asked him. "Or Montana?"

He stared at me, his face a sickly yellow like his insides must have been.

"Well, when you can get on your feet, you start for one or the other, and you keep going. If I ever see you around again I ain't going to like it."

Taking up the three rifles I busted them over the nearest rock, then threw the rest of them into the fire along with the ammunition and their tent.

Then I sort of backed off into the night and went back to the house.

Aunt Em an' Pennywell, they were on the porch watching the fire out there, and when I came up the steps I said, "You kep' my supper warm, ma'am?"

"Yes, I did. Dish it up, Pennywell."

When I sat down to table, Aunt Em she said nothing at all, but Pennywell was younger and almighty curious. "What happened out there? What did you do?"

"Like Samson," I said, "I went among the Philistines and smote them, hip and thigh." And after a good swallow of coffee, I grinned at her and said, "And one of them in the belly."

Chapter 4

The rain soaked up the ground and went on about its business, and the sun came out hot as roasting ears. When I looked out front there was nothing beyond the gate but a lot of distance. Flanner's boys had taken out, and I didn't look for them to come back.

There was work to be done around the place. No Clinch Mountain Sackett was much account at fixin' up. Our places yonder in the high-up hills always looked fit to fall apart, only they never done it. Still, it griped my innards to see such a fine place run down like it was. Besides, I was wishful to be handy if any of Flanner's outfit came back again.

After a day or two, and no trouble showing, I taken off to the meadows to find us some meat.

Each meadow was a mite higher than the last, and all told there was a thousand acres of good bottom land, the stream running from one to the other. There was a fair stand of grazing under the scattered trees that stretched back to the mountains from the edge of the meadows, stretching back to sheer walls that reminded me of the Hermosa Cliffs edging the Animas Valley near Durango.

Old Man Talon had known what he was about when he came to this place. He had water, grass and shade, hay and timber for the cutting. There were other, higher meadows, bordered with groves of aspen. He had what was needed, logs for building and shelter from the worst of the storms. Above all, he had a closed-in land where few cowhands were needed, and where he could cut hay on the meadows against the cold of winter.

Below the ranch lay thousands of acres of prairie completely dependent for water on his mountain land. That prairie would graze a lot of cattle, but all those vast acres were nothing but useless without water for stock. Who held the Empty held the range. No question about it.

At first I paid no mind to hunting. From time to time I glimpsed deer but passed them by to scout the country. Nowhere did I see any fresh sign of horse or man, and that was what I hunted, being doubtful of any ranch a man couldn't get into.

There are few things men cannot do if they have a mind to, and I had a hunch Flanner had been trying the easy way. Now he would have to come up with something else, and that was what we must be ready for. Meanwhile, riding and looking, I corraled myself into a patch of thinking.

Milo Talon was a far-riding man, and he'd be somewhere along the outlaw trail. He favored no country over another, but moved. He was a more slender man than me, lean and hard as seasoned timber, good with horse, rope, or gun, and a handsome devil to boot.

Brown's Hole stuck in my mind, and it wasn't far off. If he wasn't there it was certainly a place where a man could start the word along the wild country trails. And if I was to get shut of this place I'd have to get him over here.

Barnabas? He was supposed to be in France. I knew nothing about France or any other place I couldn't get to on a horse.

Flanner wanted this outfit and he could buy the men to take it for him. A man who wouldn't hesitate to get an old woman killed was a man who wouldn't stop at much a body could think of. If he kept on pushing he was going to make me sore as a grizzly with a bad tooth, and I didn't want that. When I get really down to gravel mad I act up something fierce, and I had enough posses hunting me here and yon as it was.

A man could live well off the country. Deer and elk were around and I'd seen a sign of bear and lion. A mountain lion swings a big circle—maybe thirty-odd miles of it—and he usually manages to live off the elk or deer that are getting on in years or are too young to escape. From time to time he takes a rancher's calf.

Living in wild country you become like one of the animals. You learn their ways, you kill what you need to live and you bother none of the others and fight shy of them. I never killed anything unless pushed to it . . . including men.

Clinch Mountain, yonder in Tennessee, was mighty sparse on topsoil, at least where we Sacketts lived. It made up for beauty what it lacked in richness. Ma used to say it offered more food for the soul than for the belly, so we Sackett boys taken to making our living with rifle and trap, but we never figured to take more then our due. We trapped a stream a year or two, then held off, let it be, and worked another one to let the first recover. There was a lot we boys didn't know, with no schoolin' to speak of, but we learned early that if you want water on the land you need beaver in the high country. They build their dams, keep them in repair, and they hold back in ponds water that would run off down the country to the sea. I never seen the sea, but they tell me it's off down the country somewheres.

Pa told us we held the land in trust. We were free to use it so long as it was kept in shape for the generations following after, for our sons and yours.

This was rugged country, faulted and twisted. It looked like it had been crumpled like a shoot of thin paper, with tilted layers whose saw-toothed edges had been honed down some by wind and rain. It would take months to learn all the canyons and hollows, rising higher and higher into green forest and finally to timberline and the gray and lonely peaks up yonder against the sky.

I'm tellin' you, man, that there was *country!*

The stock I'd seen was in good shape in spite of the fact they'd been kept in the high country, pasture Talon probably held back for the hot weather. Ordinarily up to this time they'd have been down on the flat plains, but due to the shennanigans of Flanner's boys they had to be holed up in the hills, which meant scant feed for later in the year.

On the way back I killed me a deer, dressed and skinned it, then rode on to the ranch.

When I got there Aunt Em was already looking rested. Pennywell was pert, kind of flirty when she looked my way, but I fought shy of her. She bit her lips every time she turned her back to make them redder, and I'd seen her pinching her cheeks to bring the color to them. Not that she needed it much.

If she was setting her cap for me she was wastin' time. I'm too old a coon to be caught by the first trap I see, and I'd baited too many traps myself not to recognize the signs.

We set up to table and it was fine cookin', mighty fine. I said as much and Em said Pennywell done it, so I knew they were in it together. No wet-behind-the-ears girl could put vittles like that together.

Mostly when a girl invites a man to supper her sister or her mother or some friend fix up the meal, and all she does is put on a fussy little postage-stamp apron and set the table and dish it up just like she'd done it all herself.

By the hour I was gettin' irritated. I could have been into Arizona, almost, by this time, and headed for Californy and that ocean-sea. I was out there before, but never got right where I could see it. This time would be different.

There was nothing out there but silence and the empty prairie, but I wanted them to come. I wanted them to come so's I could have it done with and be gone.

I never was much on waiting unless it was for game. I get meaner and meaner as time goes on. And I don't like being corraled. It just don't set right.

Which brought me around to thinking of Brown's Hole. Brown's Hole was a colossal big hollow set down amongst the mountains with mighty few ways to get in or out. It was a trapper's rendezvous one time, then mostly an outlaw hangout, although a few-cattlemen had wintered herds there.

There were a few horse and cattle thieves who holed up between runnin' off one man's stock and another's. Tip Gault was there. For an outlaw he was a decent sort and a man I respected. I couldn't say the same for Mexican Joe. Mexicans and me usually got along. I'd spent some time down Sonora way, and they raised some of the best riders and ropers you'll find anywhere, and some mighty fine folks. But Mexican Joe was another sort of hombre entirely. The way I heard it he'd been run out of Mexico for things he'd done, but he was a mighty mean man with either gun or knife, favoring the latter.

I'd seen him a time or two, and he'd seen me, but so far we'd never locked horns.

What I had to do was make a fast ride to the Hole and back, trying to get out without Flanner knowing I was gone, and then get back before he found out. Anybody in the Hole might know where Milo was, but the ones most likely to know or to pass the word along were Tip Gault or Isom Dart.

Gault's outfit rustled horses and cattle mostly. It was not much of a business with them. They were just out to get money enough to throw a wingding once in awhile and have eating money.

Dart was a horse thief, too, but more cautious. He'd come close to losing his hair or winding up at the end of a rope not long before and he was a cautious man. That first close shave had taught him a lesson. He'd been a slave, freed by the war, and had come west under another name. He knew everybody along the outlaw trail and would give the word to any drifter who came along. Wherever Milo Talon was, he'd hear that word sooner or later. I hoped it would be sooner. What I really hoped was that Milo would be wintering in the Hole from time to time and they might know where he'd gone.

"Aunt Em," I said, when supper was finished, "I got to ride off a ways."

"Are you pullin' your stakes?"

"No, ma'am, but we got to get word to your son. I think if I rode out of here a spell I could give the word to a man who would pass it along."

She looked up at me, Em did. That old woman was no fool; she'd lived close to the edge for a good long time and she knew things.

"You going into the Hole?"

"Well . . ." I hesitated, not wanting to lie, "I guess that's the best grapevine in the world, out of there."

"You mean Isom Dart? You tell him you're a friend of mine. We saw him through it once when he was bad hurt."

"Flanner's cookin' up something, and I hate to pull out like this, but it's got to be done."

We talked it around over coffee, thinking over the trail I had to ride. Aunt Em had been in the Hole herself, with her husband when they first came west.

"We wintered in there our ownselves," she said. "We'd heard of it from some Cherokees who held cattle there."

Pennywell hadn't much to say. She sat across the table looking big-eyed at me and making me uneasy. When a talking woman sits quiet a man had better look at his hole card and keep a horse saddled.

The old house was warm and quiet. Taking up a rifle I walked out the back door and around to the front, holding close to the wall. Nothing showed against the skyline, but probably they wouldn't, anyway.

I stood listening for a while, but the sounds seemed right and I went back to the stable, forked down some hay for the stock, and looked over the horses. Then I went to the bunkhouse and got a pair of old, wore-out boots somebody had cast off. I taken them to the house.

"Ma'am," I said to Pennywell, "I want you to put these on."

She looked at the boots and then at me. "They're too big," she said, "and too old. Besides, I've got shoes."

"You've got none that make man tracks, and that's what I want."

She put on the boots and we walked out to the gate and up where the Flanner gunmen had their camp. We walked around, leaving tracks. They'd figure mine were the big ones, but they'd surely figure there was at least one more man on the place.

Later that night I got moccasins out of my saddlebags, put them on, and went out again. That way they'd see those tracks, too.

We Sacketts were mountain folk, and that meant we'd been woodsmen before we were riders. All of us had growed up among Indians and had learned to like moccasins for work in timber country; a man can feel a dry stick under his foot and not step down on it with a moccasin. With a boot or shoe it isn't that easy to go quiet.

Time was wasting, so when I came back I turned in for an hour or two of sleep. When I woke up, I got dressed and went into the kitchen.

Em Talon was there, and there was hot coffee on the stove. "I figured you'd be riding," she said. "Nothing like coffee to set a man on the right trail."

"Thanks," I said. I taken the coffee and set down across that well-washed kitchen table. "Aunt Em, you're quite a woman."

"Always wanted to be six feet high," she said, "my brothers were all six-footers, and I aimed to be high as them. I never quite made it."

"You stand tall in any outfit," I said. "I'd like to have known your husband."

"Talon was a man . . . all man. He walked strong and he thought right, and no man ever left his door hungry, Indian, black man, or white. Nor did he ever take water for any man."

"He was a judge of land," I said, "and of women."

"We had it good together," Em said quietly, "we walked a quiet way, the two of us, and never had to say much about it to one another." She paused. "I just looked at him and he looked at me and we knew how it was with each other."

Hours later, well down the trail to Brown's Hole, I remembered that. Well, they'd been lucky. It was not likely I'd ever find a woman like that, but no matter what any man says, there's nothing better than two, a man and woman, who walk together. When they walk right together there's no way too long, no night too dark.

Chapter 5

The Union Pacific tracks lay to the north, and beyond was the Overland Trail to California. On the Pacific side of South Pass that route divided into two, the northern becoming the trail to Oregon.

Horse and cattle thieves operating out of Brown's Hole had developed a thriving business stealing stock from emigrants on one trail and selling to those on the other. Occasionally the thieves drove their stolen stock into Brown's Hole for sale the following season. The grass was good, and by comparison with the country around the winters were mild.

To the north and east lay the Hole-in-the-Wall country; north and west from there, the Crazy Mountains with the border of Canada beyond. To the southwest of Brown's Hole lay Utah's San Rafael Swell with its Robbers' Roost, and south of that, Horse Thief Valley near Prescott, and a ranch near Alma, New Mexico. This was the country of the so-called Outlaw Trail.

In fact it was a maze of trails, obvious and hidden, and along those trails ranchers or homesteaders were friendly to drifting men, asking no questions, and providing no information to strangers.

Originally most of the trails had been scouted by Indians or mountain men, and here and there they had located hideouts away from prying eyes. A drifting man might ride from the Mexican border to Canada and be assured of meals and shelter or an exchange of horses anywhere along the route.

Those who rode the outlaw trail were not all wanted men; some were tough cowhands or drifters who traveled with the seasons and had friends among the wild bunch. A few were occasional outlaws, rustling a few cows when the occasion offered, playing it straight the rest of the time.

Milo Talon was known along the Trail. As there was constant movement up and back, it seemed the best way to get in touch with him was just to ride to the Hole and pass the word.

Morning came with me a-horseback. By daylight I'd put the Empty far behind and was snaking along a trail up through the pines and skirting the aspen groves. It was a fine, clear morning with the air washed clean by rain and drops hanging silver on every leaf. Even the wild things a body saw didn't seem to mind him much, so pleased they were with the morning.

My horse and me were of a mind. We taken our time, just breathing the good air, keeping an eye out for trouble, but just enjoying it. Far off and below I seen a dot that had to be buffalo. Most of them had been killed off, but here and there small herds had taken to the mountain valleys. Maybe two hundred in the lot I saw.

Of a sudden I rode out on a grassy slope that dropped steeply off into a valley far, far below. Ahead of me and a mite higher was a thick stand of aspen, and turning my horse I skirted the edge of that grove until I came on a likely spot. Putting my horse on a picket rope, I bunched a few sticks and with some shredded bark and twigs built myself a coffee-making fire.

I'd backed up against that grove on purpose. Looked at from down below no smoke would show against the white of the tree trunks and the gray-green of the leaves. From alongside the aspen a little branch trickled down over the rocks, twisting and turning to find itself a way down the mountain. It was so narrow in places the grass almost covered it from view. Dipping up a pot of water I set her on the fire, dumped in some coffee, and waited for it to boil. With that, some jerky and a chunk of homemade bread I figured to make do.

There's no prettier place than a stand of aspen. The elk and beaver like the bitter inner bark, and you'll nearly always find them where there's aspen. There's no thing that provides more grub for wildlife than the aspen grove.

There's usually wood around. The aspen is self-pruning, and as it grows taller it sheds its lower branches, just naturally reaching for the sun. Those branches dry out quickly and make excellent kindling.

Much as I wished to be back at the ranch for the safety of the womenfolks, I didn't figure to lose my hair in the process. Stopping to make coffee was giving my horse a rest, giving me food to start a long day, but it was also giving me time to watch my back trail a little.

I was pretty sure I'd come away from the Empty without being seen, but a man can get killed taking things for granted. If anybody was on my trail I wanted to look him—or her—over before they came up to me.

Meanwhile, setting there in the morning sun and watching my water get hot was a pleasure I could take to heart. I never was one for rushing through a country. I like to take my time, breathe the air, get the feel of it . . . I like to smell it, taste it, get it located in my brain.

The thing to remember when traveling is that the trail is the thing, not the end of the trail. Travel too fast and you miss all you are traveling for.

When my coffee was boiled good and black I poured myself a cup. It was strong—take the hide off a bull, that stuff would. Fellow I punched cows with down Sonora way said my coffee was dehorning fluid . . . one drop and a bull's horns would melt right off.

It ain't true, but it does measure up. A cup of it will open a man's eyes.

Chewing some jerky, I tasted that coffee now and again, and kept an ear out for sound and one eye on my horse. That horse was wild and a wild horse has all the senses of a deer and a good deal more savvy.

Pretty soon the roan lifted his head, pricked up his ears, and spread his nostrils. I forked my Winchester around and slipped the thong of the butt of my pistol. I wasn't one to hunt trouble, although I've buried a few who did.

There were two of them, studying the trail as they rode, and they had not seen me. Holding the Winchester in my hands, I stood up slowly. At that instant my horse whinnied and their heads turned sharply as if on one neck.

"Lookin' for something, boys?" My Winchester was easy in my hands. I never sight a gun of any kind; I just look where I'm shooting.

They didn't like it very much. They were tough-looking characters, and both of them rode Eight-Ladder-Eight brands on their horses. Their horses were Morgans, fine stock, and the brands were a rewrite job if I ever saw one.

"Eight-Ladder-Eight," I commented sarcastically, "an' Morgan horses. Ain't many Morgans in this part of the country, boys, but a good man with a cinch ring and a hot fire could change a Six-Four-Six into an Eight-Ladder-Eight without half trying."

"You saying we stole these horses?"

"You did or somebody did," I said. "But if I were you boys I'd get shut of them, an' quick."

"Why?" one of them said.

"You ever heard of Dutch Brannenburg?"

"Wasn't he the one who chased those hombres from Montana to Texas?"

"Uh-huh. That's the one." I grinned at them. "You boys maybe don't know it, but he's registered a Six-Four-Six brand. You're sittin' right up in the middle of two of his horses."

Seemed to me their faces turned a shade gray under the tan. "You're funnin'," one of them said. "Why, we—!"

"Shut up, you damn' fool!" The older man was as sore as he was scared. "I tol' you it looked too damn' easy!"

"He's probably right behind you now," I told them, "and from what I hear of Dutch he wastes no time. You boys better learn to pray while you're ridin'. Dutch takes pride in his horses."

They headed off down the trail, rattling their hocks out of there. Me, I finished my coffee, tightened my cinch, and was just about to step into the leather when I heard them coming.

Dutch was a tough man. He was maybe fifty years old and nearly as wide as he was tall, and every ounce of him was rawhide and iron. There were nine in the party and they swept up there just as I turned. My Winchester was still in my hands.

They taken a quick look at me and at my horse. "You there!" Dutch shouted. "Did you see a couple of men ride through here?"

"I wasn't looking very close," I said.

He pushed his horse at me. He was square-jawed and mean. I'd heard a lot about Dutch and liked none of it. He ranched, but he ranched like he was bull of the woods. You crossed him and you died . . . I'd heard he'd set fire to a couple of rustlers he'd caught.

"You'd have been a lot smarter if you'd given me a straight answer. I think you're one of them."

"You're a damned liar," I said. "You don't think any such thing."

He started to grab iron but that Winchester had him covered right where he lived.

"You boys sit tight," I told the others. "If one of you makes a wrong move I'm going to kill your boss."

"You ain't got the guts," he said, his tone ugly. "Kill him, boys."

"Boss," a slim, wiry man was talking, "that's Logan Sackett."

A bad reputation can get a man in a lot of trouble, but once in a while it can be a help. Dutch Brannenburg sort of eased back in his saddle and I saw his tongue touch his lips. Dry, I reckon.

"You know the tracks of your own horses," I said, "and you can read sign. So don't try to swing too wide a loop. Your hide punctures the same as any man's."

He reined his horse around. "You watch yourself, Sackett," he said. "I don't like you."

"I'll watch," I said, "and when you come after my hide, you'd better hide behind more men."

He swung his horse around and swore, muttering in a low, vicious tone. "I don't need any men, Sackett. I can take you myself . . . any time."

"I'm here," I said.

"Boss?" That slim man's voice was pleading. "Those thieves are gettin' away, boss."

He swung his horse back to the trail. "So they are," he said sharply, and led off down the trail.

That was a mean man, I told myself, and a man to watch. I'd crossed him, backed him down, made him look less than he liked to look in front of his men.

"Logan," I said, "you've made you an enemy." Well, here and yonder I had a few. Maybe I could stand one more.

Nevertheless, I made myself a resolution to get nowhere near Dutch Brannenburg. Then or ever.

He had come west like many another pioneer and had taken up land where it meant a fight to hold it. Trouble was, after he'd used force a few times to hold his own against enemies it became a way of life to him. He liked being known as a hard, ruthless man. He liked being known as a driver. He had earned his land and earned his way, but now he was pushing, walking hard-shouldered against the world. He had begun in the right, but he had come to believe that because he did it, whatever he did, it was right to do. He made his own decisions as to who was criminal and who was not, and along with the horse and cow thieves he had wiped out a few innocent nesters and at least one drifting cowhand.

I'd been on the way and in the way, and only my own alertness had kept me alive. Now I'd made him stand back and he would not forgive.

The trail I'd followed had lost whatever appeal it had, so I mounted up and rode up the mountain, skirting the aspen and weaving my way through the scattered spruce that lay beyond. Somewhere up ahead was an old Indian trail that followed along the acres of the mountains above timberline. I was gambling Brannenburg did not know it.

His place was down in the flat land, and I had an idea he wasn't the type to ride the mountains unless it was demanded of him or unless he was hunting somebody.

The trail was there, a mere thread winding its way through a soggy green meadow scattered with fifty varieties of wild flowers, red, yellow, and blue.

Twice I saw deer . . . a dozen of them in one bunch, and on a far-off slope, several elk. There were marmots around all the while and a big eagle who kept me company for half the morning. I never did decide whether he was hoping I'd kill something he could share or if he was just lonely.

The peaks around me were ragged and gray, bare rock clean of snow except for a patch here and there in a shady place. Nor was there sound but that from the hoofs of my horse on the soft earth or occasionally glancing off a bit of rock.

It was the kind of trail I had ridden many times, and as on other times I rode with caution. A lonely trail it was, abandoned long since by the Indians who made it, but no doubt their ghosts were still walking along these mountainsides, through these same grasses.

Once I saw a silver-tip grizzly in the brush at the edge of the timber. He stood up to get a better view of me, a huge beast, probably weighing half a ton or more, but he was a hundred yards off and unafraid. My horse snorted and shied a bit, but continued on.

There were lion tracks in the trail. They always take the easiest way, even here where there are few obstructions. I'd not get a sight of the lion—they know the man smell and edge away from it.

It was mid-afternoon before I stopped again. I found a stream of snow water running off the ridge and an abandoned log cabin built by some prospector. There was a tunnel on the mountainside, and a pack rat had been in the cabin, but nobody else had been there for a long time.

I drank from the stream and left the cabin alone, not caring to be trapped inside a building, the first place anyone would look. I went back in a little cluster of pines and built my fire where the smoke would be dissipated by the evergreen branches above.

The coffee tasted good. I ate some more of the bread and chewed some jerky while drinking it, and I watched the trail below and the valley opening into the mountains, smoky with distance.

Two days later I rode into Brown's Hole from the east.

The Hole is maybe thirty-three or four miles long by five to six miles wide, watered by the Green River and a few creeks that tumble

down off Diamond Mountain or one of the others to end up in the
Green. It is sagebrush country, with some timber on the mountains and
cedar along the ridges.

The man I was looking for was Isom Dart . . . at least that was the
name he was using. His real name had been Huddleston . . . Ned, I
think. He was a black man, and he had ridden with Tip Gault's outfit
until riders from the Hat put them out of business.

I planned to stop at Mexican Joe Herrara's cabin on Vermilion
Creek. Riding into the Hole I had come on a man driving some cows.
When I asked about Dart, he looked me over careful-like and then said
I might find him at Herrara's cabin, but to be careful. If Mexican Joe
got mad at me and started sharpening his knife, I would be in trouble.

I was hunting trouble, but as for Joe, I'd heard about him before
and I didn't much care whether he got mad or not.

There didn't seem to be anyone about when I got to the cabin. I
pulled up and stepped down.

Chapter 6

As I tied my horse to the corral with a slipknot, I kept an eye on the cabin. Men of that stamp would surely have heard me come up, and right now they were undoubtedly sizing me up.

In those days no law ever rode into the Hole. Most law around the country didn't even know where it was or just how to get in, and they'd find little to welcome them, although a few honest cattlemen like the Hoy outfit were already there.

Hitching my gun belt into a confortable position, I walked up to the door.

As I came up on the rock slab that passed for a stoop the door opened suddenly and a Mexican was standing there. He wasn't Herrara, not big enough or mean enough.

"Buenos días, amigo," I said, "is the coffee on?"

He looked at me a moment, then stepped aside. There were three men in the cabin when I stepped in. I spotted Herrara at once, a tall, fierce-looking Mexican, not too dark. Sitting at the table with him was a white man who had obviously been drinking too much. He looked soft, not like a rider. There was another Mexican squatting on his heels in the corner.

"Passin' through," I commented, "figured you might have coffee."

Nobody spoke for a minute; Herrara just stared at me, his black eyes unblinking. Finally, the Anglo said, "There's coffee, and some beans, if you'd like. May I help you?"

He went to the stove in the corner and picked up the pot, filling a cup for me. Pulling back a chair, I sat down. The big white man brought me the coffee and a dish of beef and beans.

"Has Dutch Brannenburg been through?"

Herrara stared at me. "You ride for Dutch?"

I laughed. "Him an' me don't see eye to eye. I met him yonder and we had words. He's headed this way, hunting two horse thieves . . . Anglos," I added, "but he hangs whoever he finds."

"He did not hang you," Herrara said, still staring.

"I didn't favor the idea. The situation being what it was, he figured he could wait."

"The situation?" the Anglo asked.

"My Winchester was sort of headed his way. His motion was overruled, as they'd say in a court of law."

"He is coming this way?"

"There's nine of them," I said, "and they size up like fighters."

For a minute or two nobody said anything, and then around a mouthful of beans and beef, I said, "They'll come in from the north, I'm thinking. I didn't find any tracks in the Limestone Ridge country."

They all looked at me. "You came that way?"

I shrugged. "Joe," I said, "I'd been in this Hole two, three times before you left South Pass City."

He didn't like that very much. Mexican Joe had killed a man or two over that way and they'd made it hot for him, so he'd pulled his stakes.

I'd come in there first as a long-geared apple-knocking youngster. I'd been swinging a hammer on the U.P. tracks and got into a shooting at the End of Track. The men I killed had friends and I had none but a few Irish trackworkers who weren't gunfighters, so I pulled my freight.

"Are you on the dodge?" It was the Anglo who asked the question.

"Well," I said, "there's a posse from Nebraska that's probably started back home by now. I came thisaway because I figured I'd see Isom Dart . . . I wanted to sort of pass word down the trail."

"What word?" Herrara's tone was belligerent.

The Mexican had been drinking wine, as had the others. He was in an ugly mood and I was a stranger who did not seem impressed by him. There had been some other Mexicans down in Sonora and Chihuahua who weren't impressed, either, and that was why he was up here.

"Milo Talon," I said, "is a friend of mine, and I want to pass the word along that he's needed on the Empty, over east of here, and that he's to come careful."

"I'll tell Dart," the American said.

Herrara never took his eyes off me. He was mean, I knew that, and he'd cut up several men with his knife. He had a way of taking it out and honing it until sharp, then with a yell he'd jump you and start cutting. But the honing act was to get a man scared before he jumped him. It was a good stunt, and usually it worked.

He got out his whetstone, but before he could draw his knife I drew mine. "Say, just what I need." Before he knew what I was going to do I had reached over and taken the stone. Then I began whetting my own blade.

Well, it was a thing to see. He was astonished, then mad. He sat there empty-handed while I calmly put an edge to my blade, which was already razor sharp. I tried the blade on a hair from my head and it cut nicely, so I passed the stone back to him.

"Gracias," I said, smiling friendly-like. "A man never knows when he'll need a good edge."

My knife was a sort of modified Bowie, but made by the Tinker. No better knives were ever made than those made by the Tinker back in Tennessee. He was a Gypsy pack peddler who drifted down the mountains now and again, but he sold mighty few knives. The secret of those blades had come from India where his people, thousands of years back, had been making the finest steel in the world. The steel for the fine blades of Damascus and Toledo actually came from India, and there's an iron pillar in India that's stood for near two thousand years, and not a sign of rust.

I showed them the knife. "That there," I said, "is a Tinker-made knife. It will cut right through most blades and will cut a man shoulder to belt with one stroke."

Tucking it back in my belt, I got up. "Thanks for the grub. I'll be drifting. I don't figure to be trapped inside if Dutch comes along."

Nobody said a word as I went outside, tightened my cinch, and prepared to mount.

Then the American came out. "That was beautiful," he said, "Joe is an old friend of mine, but he's had that coming for a long time. He didn't know what to think. He still doesn't."

"You're an educated man," I said.

"Yes. I studied law."

"There's need for lawyers," I said. "I may need one myself sometime."

He shrugged, then looked away. "I should pull out," he said. "I just sort of drifted into this, and I've stayed on. I guess it doesn't make much sense."

"If I knew the law," I said, "I'd hang out my shingle. This is a new country. No telling where a man might go."

"I guess you're right. God knows I've thought of it, but sometimes a man gets caught in a sort of backwater."

I stepped into the saddle, listening beyond his voice. Nobody came from the cabin. I heard no sound on the trail.

The American pointed. "Isom Dart has a cabin down that way. He's a black man, and smart."

"We've met," I said.

He looked up at me. "They'll be wondering who you are," he said. "It isn't often a man stands up to Mexican Joe."

"The name is Sackett . . . Logan Sackett," I said and rode off. When I looked back he was still looking after me, but then he turned and walked toward the cabin door.

I trusted the Anglo. I had heard of him before, and he was a man of much education who seemed to care for nothing but sitting in the cabin and drinking or talking with the Mexicans or passers-by.

This Brown's Hole was a secret place, although the Indians had known of it. Ringed with hills, some of them that could not be passed, it was a good place, too, a good place for men like me. There were places like this in Tennessee where I had been born, but they were more green, lovelier and not so large.

My thoughts returned to Emily Talon. She was a Sackett. She was my kin and so deserving of my help. Ours was an old family, with old, old family feelings. Long ago we had come from England and Wales, but the family feeling within us was older still, old as the ancient Celtic clans I'd heard spoken of. It was something deep in the grain, but something that should belong to all families . . . everywhere. I did not envy those who lacked it.

There'd never been much occasion to think on it. When trouble fetched around the corner we just naturally lit in and helped out. Mostly, we could handle what trouble came our way without help, but there was a time or two, like that time down in the Tonto Basin country when they had Tell backed into a corner.

Riding through wild country leaves a man's mind free to roam around, and while a body never dast forget what he's doing, one part of his mind keeps watch while another sort of wanders around. My thoughts kept returning to Em Talon and the Empty.

That old woman was alone except for a slip of a girl, and you could bet Jake Flanner was studying ways to get her away from the ranch. Chances were he thought I was still around, but if he did know I was gone he'd figure I was gone for good.

Well, if I could find Milo Talon, I would be.

Right now I wanted Milo more'n anybody, but I hadn't any fancy ideas about being safe in Brown's Hole. So far most of the folks in the Hole, if they weren't outlaws themselves at least tolerated them. The

Hoys, however, tolerated them least of all, as they'd lost some stock from time to time.

From time to time I rode off the trail and waited in the cedars to study my back trail, and I kept my eyes on the tracks. I wanted to see Dart, but there were others around I'd no desire to see at all.

Suddenly I heard hoofs a-coming and I pulled off the trail. It was Dart, and he was riding a sorrel gelding. They called Isom Dart a black man and he'd been a slave, but he surely wasn't very black.

He seen me as quick as I did him. "H'lo, Logan. What you all a-doin' up thisaways?"

"Huntin' you. I want to pass word to Milo Talon. He's needed on the Empty. His ma's still alive and she's in trouble. He's to come in careful . . . and anybody in town is likely an enemy."

Dart nodded. "You know how 'tis, Logan. He's a fast-ridin' man, and he may be a thousand mile from here. I'll get word to him."

I gathered my reins. "You'd better hole up for a while your own-self. Brannenburg is huntin' rustlers."

"I never been in his neck o' the woods."

"Don't make no dif'rence. Dutch thinks he's godawmighty these days. If you ain't a banker or a big cattleman you're a cow thief."

No man in his right mind rides the same trail going back, not if he has enemies or it's Injun country. After leaving Dart I taken to the water, swam the Green and edged along through the brush, weaving a fancy trail for anybody wishful of hunting me. I backtracked several times, rode over my own trail, swam the Green again, and stayed in the water close to the bank for a ways.

When I did come out of the water I was in a thick stand of cedar and I worked my way east toward the Limestone Ridge. Turning, I walked my horse toward the gap that led to Irish Canyon, then turned east again and crossed Vermilion Creek and proceeded on east to West Boone Draw.

Most of the time I was riding in cedar or brush or following draws so that I could keep out of sight. I saw nobody, heard nothing, yet I had a spooky feeling.

There are times riding in the hills when you know you are alone and yet you are sure you are watched. Sometimes I think the ghosts of the old ones, the ones who came before the Indians, sometimes I think they still follow the old trails, sit under the ancient trees, or listen to the wind in the high places, for surely not even paradise could be more lonely, more beautiful, more grand than the high peaks of the San Juans or the Tetons or this land through which I rode.

There's more of me in the granite shoulders of the mountain or in the trunks of the gnarled cedars then there is in other men. Ma always said I was made to be a loner, and Nolan like me. We were twins, him and me, but once we moved we rode our separate ways and never seemed to come together again, nor want to. There'd been no bad feeling between us, it was as if we sensed that one of us was enough at one time in one place.

Riding out of the brush I looked across the country toward East Boone Draw. I just sat there for a while, feeling the country and not liking what I felt.

There was something spooky about Brown's Hole. Maybe it was that I couldn't get Brannenburg out of my mind. The Dutchman was hard . . . he was stone. His brain was eroded granite where the few ideas he had carved deep their ruts of opinion. There was no way for another idea to seep in, no place for imagination, no place for dreams, none for compassion or mercy or even fear.

He knew no shadings of emotion, he knew no half-rights or half-wrongs or pity or excuse, nor had he any sense of pardon. The more I thought of him the more I knew he was not evil in himself, and he would have been shocked that anybody thought of him as evil. Shocked for a moment only, then he'd have shut the idea from his mind as nonsense. For the deepest groove worn into that granite brain was the one of his own rightness.

And that scared me.

A man like that can be dangerous, and it made me uneasy to be riding in the same country with him. Maybe it was that I'd a sense of guilt around him and he smelled it.

Here and there I'd run off a few cattle from the big outfits. They branded anything they found running free without a brand, but let a nester or cowhand do the same and he was a rustler.

I'd never blotted any brands. I'd never used a cinch ring or a coiled wire or anything to rewrite a brand. Here and there I'd slapped my brand on mavericks I'd come across on the plains. By now there must be several thousand head of stock running loose on the plains that I'd branded.

Suddenly I'd had enough of Brown's Hole. I was going to get out and get out fast.

And that was when I realized somebody was coming down my back trail, somebody hunting me.

Chapter 7

When I was a small boy I often went to the woods to lie on the grass in the shade. Somehow I had come to believe the earth could give me wisdom, but it did not. Yet I learned a little about animals and learned it is not always brave to make a stand. It is often foolish. There is a time for courage and a time for flight.

There is no man more dangerous than one who does not doubt his own rightness. Long ago I heard a man in the country store near my home say that a just man always had doubts. Dutch Brannenburg had no doubts. And he had gathered about him men who had no doubts. They were not outlaws, they were just hard, cold men who rode for the brand and believed every nester or drifting cowhand if not a thief was at least a potential thief.

They had decided, when they lost the trail of the men they followed, that I must have aided them, and so intended to hang me in their place.

Had I remained on the trail they would have had me now, and as it was they were coming.

Nine hard men with a noose ready for hanging, and me alone with womenfolks over the mountain who waited for my coming.

A draw opened through brush head-high to a horseman, and I turned into it, praying to God that it was not a dead end. My horse was a fast walker, and I walked him now, saving what he had for a time of need.

No more than a quarter of a mile behind, they were working out my trail, and they'd do it, too. I hadn't an idea they would not. I was a good man at hiding a trail, but these were man hunters, cow trackers, Injun fighters. Every man-jack of them was good at reading sign.

Suddenly the canyon branched; I went up the smaller canyon,

537

followed it a couple of hundred yards, and then went to the bank and off through the cedars.

The ridge lay a half mile beyond, and I took off for it, angling up and using all the cover I could find, holding myself on a low angle to keep from their eyes as long as possible. My horse was in fine shape, and it would need to be, for I'm a big man and the trail would be long.

This was no time to lead trouble to Em Talon, so I headed off into broken country. A man who has been riding the wild trails as long as me gets a feel for them and for mountain country. Beyond that ridge up ahead were other ridges, canyons, buttes—a maze of rough country. The last fifty yards lay ahead of me and I glanced back. They were topping out at the canyon's edge, and a far-off shout told me I'd been seen.

They done a foolish thing. They started to run at me.

Being too anxious sometimes can deal a man a hard blow. They rode fast up that slope and there's not much that can take more out of a horse than that. I'd purposely walked my horse, taking it easy. I kept on walking, wanting both to save my mount and give them the idea I did not realize I was being pursued.

Then I topped out on the ridge and went over, onto a long shelf of above-timber line rock. I followed it for fifty yards, then doubled back and rode back on the far side of a V where the ridge had been the point. As they came up one side of the V, I was riding along the other side just over the ridge from them.

Then I trotted my horse. I taken our time, but I pushed just enough to get out of sight in the spruce trees before they topped the ridge. Once in the spruce trees I followed along as I was going, weaving among the trees for a quarter of a mile or so, turning downhill a few yards, then up, riding betweeen trees so close together I had to pull one leg out of a stirrup to get through, crossing bare rock and changing direction as I crossed, or doubling back.

If those boys fitted my neck into their noose they were going to have some riding to do first.

The roan I was riding had been showing me something more than I'd expected. Talon was a horse breeder as well as a builder, and if this horse was any example he was a man with talent. Judging by what Em had said during one of our sort of rambling talks, Talon had bred Morgan stallions to the best of the mustang mares he could find, and the roan seemed to have the brains of the Morgan and the all-around wild animal savvy of the mustang. Since Talon died, most of his stock had been running wild in the mountains, and this roan took to high country like it had known nothing else.

What was important now was that that horse would go just about anywhere I asked it to, and it had been teaching me that most of the horses I'd known up to now were something not to be considered in the same rank with this one.

Riding up through a bunch of cedars, I turned in my saddle and glanced back. They were maybe a thousand feet lower down, and by the way they'd have to ride, a half mile behind. Suddenly I saw a huge boulder—it must've weighed half a ton—balanced beside the game trail I'd come out on as I topped the ridge.

The boulder had tumbled down from a shoulder of higher rock and was held in place by a couple of rocks no bigger than my fist. It had probably been there no longer than since the last windstorm and maybe less. If it started to roll it was going to roll right down on them as they came out of the woods.

Stepping down from the saddle I taken a long pole, the broken trunk of a young spruce, and I jammed the end of it against one of those small rocks. It came loose and the boulder teetered. I smacked it again and that boulder crunched down on what lay ahead and beneath it.

It turned over slowly, majestically, then rolled over again, a bit faster. Right below it was a drop of about six feet and then the steep hillside. It rolled over that drop, hit hard, and then started down the slope followed by an army of smaller stuff, rocks from the size of a man's head to fist-size.

Down below Brannenburg and his men, bunched pretty well, came out of the woods. For a moment there I didn't think they'd see it, then Dutch looked up. As he looked that huge boulder hit a jump off place and must have bounded thirty feet out into the air.

Dutch cut loose with a yell that I heard faintly, and then the bunch scattered . . . only just in time.

One horse hit on a side slope and went rolling, rider and all, another went to pitching as the boulder lit with the shower of rocks coming with it, then rolled off down the slope to lodge in the trees.

I hadn't wanted to kill nobody. I just wanted to slow them up, make them cautious, but they were some shook up, I could see that.

One man had been bucked off and he was getting up, limping. A horse was running away, stirrups slopping. The others were fighting their horses, trying to get them calmed down, and they were having troubles. I just rode off around the knoll and cantered across a long green meadow toward the lip of a basin.

Before reaching it I rode across a great shelving ledge of tilted rock, knowing my horse might leave some hoof scars, but they would be few and the trackers would have to ride slow to read the sign.

There was a steep, winding trail down from the shelf into a basin that lay partly below timberline. A scattering of spruce and foxtail pine had crept up the south-facing slope, and I let the roan pick its way down through the trees.

High on a slope opposite I saw a half dozen bighorn sheep watching me. Their eyes are sharp, and they miss mighty little. A camp-robber jay picked up my trail and followed me along, hoping for some food I might drop, but he was backing the wrong card. I'd no time to stop and dig something out of my outfit.

There are folks who can't abide camp-robber jays, but I take to them. Often enough they've been my only company for days at a time, and they surely do get friendly. They'll steal your grub right from under your nose, but who am I to criticize the life style of a bird? He has his ways, I have mine. Like I say, I take to them.

This was my kind of country. I'm a high-line man. I like the country up yonder where the trees are flagged by the wind, where there's sedge and wild flowers under foot and where the mountains gnaw the sky with gray hard teeth, flecked with a foam of snow gathered in their hollows.

All the time I was working my way east, trying to wear them out or lose them, but drawing closer and closer to the MT ranch and Em Talon.

That night I made no fire. I chewed on some jerky and some rose hips I'd picked from time to time, finished the last small chunk of bread I'd brought, and ate a half dozen wild onions.

Once I'd stripped the gear from the roan I scouted the country around, rifle in hand. There was no way a body could see my camp until they were right up close, and no way anybody could approach without making some noise. I was backed up against the edge of a grove of aspen and I'd picked about the only level spot on a steep hillside.

Before daybreak I was off and riding, heading right off down the valley and paying no mind to my trail. It was rolling up clouds for a heavy rain and whatever tracks I made would soon be gone.

My grub was gone and I was dearly wanting a cup of coffee when

I sighted a ranch house trailing smoke into the rain. First off I pulled up near some trees and gave study to the place. I was a half mile off and five hundred feet higher, and the place lay in a meadow with a trail running past the gate and aspen spilling down the mountainside opposite. Circling around, I came up through the aspen and sat there five minutes or so, studying the house. Finally I decided whoever was there it certainly wasn't the posse. So I rode on in.

I walked my horse up to the house and gave a call and after a bit a door opened. The man in the door had a gun on, and he yelled, "Put up your horse and come in."

I took my horse to the stables and stepped inside. There were four horses there, three of them dry, one wet. I took the roan to a stall and rubbed him down with a handful of hay, then forked some hay into the manger for him. Prying around with a lighted lantern, I found a sack of oats and put a good bait of that in the bin for my horse.

Studying on the situation, I commenced to feel uneasy, but my roan surely needed the grub, and so did I. Slipping the thong from my pistol butt, I went inside the house. The door opened as I walked up.

There was a red-haired girl there, of maybe seventeen years. She had a sprinkling of freckles over her nose and I grinned at her. She looked shy, but she smiled back.

There were three men in the place, all of them armed. One of them, a tall, thin galoot, stooped in the shoulders, had wet boots and the knees of his pants above the boots were wet. He'd been riding in the rain under a slicker.

"Travelin'," I said. "I ran short of grub."

"Set up to the table. There's beef and there's coffee."

The other men bobbed their heads at me, the man with the wet boots slowest of all.

Now excepting that red-headed girl there was nothing about this here setup that I liked. Of course, any man might have been riding this day, but it was uncommon for men to be wearin' guns in the house with a woman—I mean, unless they were fixing to go out again.

The man who seemed to own the place was a stocky gent with rusty hair, darker than the girl's, but they favored and were likely some kin. There was that tall galoot with the wet boots whom the others called Jerk-Line.

"I'm Will Scanlan," the rusty-haired one said. "This here's Jerk-Line Miller and that gent over yonder with the seegar is Benton Hayes."

Scanlan nor Miller I'd not heard tell of. Benton Hayes a man in my line of business would know. He was a scalp-hunter . . . a bounty hunter, if you will. He had a reputation for being good with a gun and not being very particular on how he used it.

"And the lady?" I asked.

"Her?" Scanlan seemed surprised. "Oh, that there's Zelda. She's my sister."

"Favors you," I said. And then added, "My name's Logan. I ride for an outfit over east of here."

The coffee tasted almighty good, but already I was thinking of an excuse for getting out. No traveler in his right mind is going to pick up and leave a warm, dry place for the out-of-doors on a rainy night, and if I did that they'd been bound to get suspicious.

Meanwhile I was putting that beef where it would do the most good. Zelda brought me a healthy chunk of corn pone and a glass of milk to go with it.

"Lots of outfits east of here," Hayes commented. "Any pa'tic'lar one?"

I decided I did not like Mr. Hayes. "The Empty," I said. "I ride for Em Talon."

"Talon?" Benton Hayes frowned. "I've heard that name. Oh, yes! Milo Talon. He's on the list."

"List?" I acted mighty innocent.

"He's a wanted man," Hayes replied.

"Milo? He'd never break no law."

"He's on my list, anyways. Somebody wants him and wants him dead."

"Well," I said, smiling friendly-like, "don't try to collect it. Seems to me Milo Talon was kind of quick on the shoot."

"Makes no dif'rence," Hayes said. "They can be had. All of them."

"I'm sure he's not the kind to break the law," I said, still smiling. "Milo was a nice boy. Could it be somebody else wants him?"

"How do I know? He's wanted, somewhere. There's five hundred dollars on him." He shuffled through some notes from an inside pocket. "There it is . . . Jake Flanner, mayor of Siwash. He'll pay it for him or his brother, Barnabas."

"What do you know about that?" I said. Then I yawned. "I'll bunk in the barn," I said, "no use to bother you gents."

"You can sleep here." Scanlan had shot a quick look at the others before he made that offer, and he seemed a mite anxious.

"Zelda, fix Mister Logan a bed in the other room, there." He glanced at me. "You can get to sleep without us botherin' you with our talk."

I taken up my rifle and followed the young lady into the next room where there was a better than usual bed. There was no window in the room, only the door I come through.

Zelda put the light down on a table, then looked at me quickly and whispered, "You watch it, mister. I don't like that Mister Hayes. I don't trust him."

"Neither do I." I grinned at her. "But I do like you, and if I get things straightened around a mite I may just come around this way again."

She looked at me seriously. "Mister," she said quietly, "I favor a man who is willin' to settle down. I don't want to marry up with no man who rides trails by night."

"You're a hundred percent right," I said. "Can you make bear-sign?"

"Doughnuts? Of course, I can."

"Make some," I said, "and keep them handy. When I come courtin' I'll expect a plate full of doughnuts."

She went out and I taken a quick look around. The man who built this cabin built it to last. He also put in a trapdoor leading to an attic.

Chapter 8

I put a knee on the bed so's it would creak some, and then I dropped a book on the floor, hoping it would sound like a boot. After a moment, I dropped it again.

Taking the chair I tiptoed over to that trapdoor, put the chair down, and got up on it. Very carefully I put both palms under the door and lifted the least bit. Dust sifted down, and the door moved. Hadn't been opened in a long time. More than likely they no longer thought of it being there.

Easing it aside I grasped the timber with one hand, laid my rifle up with the other, then chinned myself on the edge, hoisting myself up until I could wiggle over onto the floor.

The attic was dark and still and smelled of dust. There was a faint square of light across the room that looked to be a window. Very carefully, I eased myself that way. Near to the chimney I was stopped by a voice.

"He's riding an MT horse, all right. And that's the Talon brand."

"I'm tellin' you," Jerk-Line was sayin', "that's got to be him Brannenburg is huntin'. I talked to that posse when they came to the Hoy place, an' they were sore as hell. This here gent had really run their legs off, an' then they lost him."

"Will Brannenburg pay? I hear he's a tough man to deal with." Hayes was talking now.

"We'd better ride over an' see," Scanlan said. "You surely ain't goin' to bluff him into payin' for something he never asked to pay for."

"Jerk-Line," Hayes said. "You ride over. He's at the McNary place tonight. Find out what he'll give for this man's hide. You get him to offer a good sum and we'll split fifty for me, twenty-five each for you."

544

"Why not in thirds?" Jerk-Line wanted to know.

Benton Hayes's voice was cool. "Because I'm goin' to kill him. All you boys got to do is wait an' watch."

Well, I nearly went back down that trapdoor to give him his chance, but there was three now, and if Dutch did what he'd be likely to do he'd let this man take off on his return trip, then he'd follow. Dutch liked to do his own killing . . . or see it done.

After some more talk Jerk-Line went to the door and went out. I heard him slosh through the mud to the barn, and a moment later I heard his horse pounding off down the road.

I didn't know how far he'd have to go to this McNary place, but I didn't figure to wait. I tried to slip that window at the end of the loft up or down or sideways, but she was fixed in place. Taking out my Tinker-made knife I put the point into the frame and cut deep. That there knife was sharper than a razor. It cut deep, a sliver several inches long, then another. In maybe two shakes of a dog's tail I had cut that window loose from its frame.

Easing myself out I dropped to the ground and stood flat against the wall for a minute. Then I crossed to the barn and saddled my roan. Leading her out I put her in the edge of those aspen, and then I stopped.

That Benton Hayes back there. He was bound and determined to kill me if there was money in it. Well, I wasn't near so greedy.

I walked back to the house and up to the back door. Easing it open, I saw Zelda staring at me wide-eyed. "Get your brother out here," I said.

She hesitated only a moment, then went to the door and said, "Will? Can I talk to you for a minute?"

Scanlan came to the door and stepped in, closing it behind him. "Zel? Can't you see I'm busy? Couldn't this wait?"

"Not if you want to live," I whispered.

He looked at me and that pistol in my hand, and he swallowed. "Mister Scanlan," I said softly, "you got you a fine sister here, but you're trailin' your spurs in mighty poor company. You give me that gun you got, and then you set down yonder, and don't neither of you make a move until I'm gone . . . you hear?"

He nodded, handed me his gun, and edged to the chair. I shoved his gun behind my belt and dropped mine into my holster.

"He figures to hang my hide," I said. "I'm going to see can he do it."

I opened the door and stepped through. Benton Hayes looked up.

His expression was kinda sour as he spied me standing there in the doorway.

"Mister Hayes," I said, "you was talkin' a minute ago about selling my hide for a few dollars. You said you would do the killin'.. Well, you got you a gun there, let's see you do it."

He got up slowly. He was surprised and scared at first, then the scare left him. "Why, sure. One way is as easy as another, Logan."

"Sackett's the name," I said, "Logan Sackett."

I might as well have kicked him in the belly. His face went taut with a kind of shock, then sick. He was a sure-thing killer who figured he was better than most he'd meet, but I could see he didn't think he was better than Logan Sackett.

Trouble was, he'd already started to draw.

Well, he'd started. So I shucked my old hog-leg and let 'er bang. He taken two of them through the middle button on his vest and just for luck I put another through his Bull Durham tag, where it hung from his left vest pocket.

Then I taken Scanlan's gun from my belt and throwed it free of shells. I left it there on the table when I went down the steps.

The roan was waiting and I swung into the saddle and taken out. I mean, I left there. If Dutch was going to come hunting he'd have to find his game elsewhere. My old pa was never one to let his enemy choose the ground for a difficulty. "Boy," he used to say, "don't you never side-step no fight, not permanent, that is. Just you pick the time and the place."

I taken out and rode over the mountains to where the Empty lay, and I came on her in the fresh light of morning after a night in the saddle. The roan was ga'nted and tired, but he was ready to keep going, knowing the home place was yonder.

We rode in by the back way again, and I stepped down and leaned against the door there for a minute, dead beat.

That girl, she came out the door, looking perky as all get-out, but scared too when she seen me leaning.

"*Oh!* Logan, are you hurt?" She ran to me, and caught me by the hand to look at me the better, and I was ashamed to see her stare at me so with old Em looking down from the doorway.

"I ain't hurt." Maybe my voice was a mite rough. "I've come a fur piece."

"There's coffee on," Em said, her being the practical one, "come in an' set."

When I'd stripped the gear from the roan and cared for it, I went into the house. First off, I walked through and looked out front.

Nothing.

And that scared me. Jake Flanner wasn't a forgetting man.

We set about the table and I told them about my ride, my meeting with Brannenburg, and that Flanner had put a price on her sons' heads.

She was furious. Her old eyes turned hard and she asked, "Where'd you hear *that?*"

"A man named Benton Hayes . . . a bounty hunter."

"Is he hunting my boys? Is he?"

"No ma'am, he ain't huntin' nobody. He give it up."

She looked me through. "Ah? You read him from the Book, then?"

"Well, ma'am, he had him a sheaf of papers, names of men to be hunted and the money to be paid for them, and I heard him tell those other men that Brannenburg wanted me enough to pay money for it.

"You see, ma'am, he might have come huntin' me, layin' for me like, when I was breakin' a horse or mendin' fence or somewhat. I decided if he wanted my hair he should have his chance without wastin' no more time."

"And?"

"He wasn't up to it, ma'am. He just wasn't up to it." I emptied my cup and reached for the pot. "Seems like in a new country like this, ma'am, so many men choose the wrong profession. You can't tell. In something else he might have made good."

Three days went by like they'd never been. I was busy workin' around the place from can-see to cain't-see. I even ploughed a vegetable garden with some half-broke broncs who'd no notion of ploughin' anything. I harrowed that same ground and planted Indian corn, pumpkins, onions, radishes, melons, beans, peas, and what-not. And I surely ain't no farmer.

Why, I hadn't done the like since I left that side-hill farm in the Clinch Mountains. Up there in those Tennessee hills we had land so rocky the plants had to push rocks away to find room to grow in. We used to have to put pegs alongside our melons to keep 'em from rolling down into the next farm. I heard tell of a Tennessee farm where there was two brothers each having a short leg. One had a left leg short, the other a right leg, but they worked out the ploughin' just fine. One would take the plough goin' out where his long leg would be downhill, then his brother'd be waitin' for him to plough back the same way.

On the third night we sat about the table, Em Talon, Pennywell,

an' me, rememberin' the pie suppers, barn-raisin's, and such-like back
to home. We were poor folks in the hills, but we had us a right good
time. Somebody always brung along a jug or two of mountain lightning,
and toward morning there'd be some real old hoedown and stick-your-
thumb-in-their-eyes fightin'. A time or two it would get serious and
the boys would have at each other with blades.

Mostly it was just good old-fashioned fun and yarnin' around the
pump out back of the house between dances.

All we needed was a mountain fiddler. Come to think of it we
didn't even need him. Sometimes we'd just sing our own tunes to dance
by, such as "Hello, Susan Brown!" or "Green Coffee Grows on High
Oak Trees."

With moonrise I taken my Winchester and went outside to feel of
the wind. Wandering off toward the gate I listened. For a long time
there I heard nothing but the wind in the grass and then I thought I
heard something, so I lay down and put an ear to the ground.

Riders coming up the trail, several of them. I checked the lock on
the gate, then faded back into the darkness toward the house.

They came on, quite a bunch of them. They stopped by the gate
and there was sort of an argument there.

Suddenly a board in the floor creaked and I turned my head. Em
Talon was standing there with her Sharps Fifty and she said, "Logan,
you better go inside. Those men aren't Flanner's outfit."

"How do you know that?"

She ignored that, but simply said, "I think it's Dutch Brannenburg,
huntin' you."

We heard a faint rattle from the gate, which was locked, and Em
up with her Sharps and put a bullet toward the gate. Somebody swore
and we heard them moving off a bit.

"You go to sleep, Logan," Em said. "I'm an old woman and it
don't take much. You've had a hard time of it these past days."

"This here is my trouble," I protested.

"No, it ain't. You're ridin' for me, now. I knew Dutch when he
first came into this country, singin' mighty small. He hadn't any of
those biggety notions he's got now. A man's only king as long as folks
let him be. You leave him to me."

Em Talon was not a woman you argued with, so I turned around,
went inside, and bedded down. Besides, I had a good notion they'd
wait until morning. Hanging a drifter was one thing, attacking a ranch
with the reputation the MT had was another.

For the first time in a long while I slept sound the night through and only awoke when the sunlight filtered through the shutters. Opening my eyes, I listened but heard nothing. Then I got out of bed, put on my hat, and got dressed. What I saw in the mirror looked pretty sorry, so I stropped my razor on a leather belt, then shaved.

Somebody tapped on the door. It was Pennywell. "You'd better come," she said, "there's trouble."

Picking up my gun belt I slung it around my hips and cinched up, then I slipped the thong from my pistol and went into the hall.

"What's happening?"

Pennywell pointed and held up a finger for silence.

The door was open and Emily Talon was on the porch. There were a bunch of riders settin' their horses at the door, and I heard Em's voice.

"Dutch Brannenburg, what do you mean ridin' in here like this? You never were very bright, but just what do you think you're doing? Riding in here, hunting one of my men?"

"I want that Logan, Missus Talon, an' I want him now."

"What do you want him for?"

"He's a damn' thief, Missus Talon. He deserves hangin'."

"What did he steal? Any of your horses?"

Brannenburg hesitated. "He was one of them stole my horses. We trailed two thieves an' we come on him, he—"

"When were your horses stolen?"

"About ten days back, an'—"

"Logan has been working for me for several weeks, and he hasn't been off the place until he rode over to Brown's Hole."

"He killed a man," Dutch protested. "He shot a man over west of here."

"You damned right he did." Em Talon's voice was cold. "I know all about Benton Hayes, a dry-gulching, backshootin' murderer who has had it coming for years. If he hadn't shot him, I might have.

"Now, Dutch, you turn your horses around and you ride out of here. You ever bother an Empty hand again and I'll nail your hide to the fence.

"I recall when you first come into this country, Dutch, and I recall when you branded your first stock. You've become high an' mighty here these past few years, but if you want to rake up the past, Dutch, I can tell some stories."

Brannenburg's face flushed. "Now, see here, Missus Talon, I—"

"You ride out of here, Dutch, or I'll shoot you my ownself."

Dutch was angry. He did not like being faced down by a woman, but he remembered this one, and she could be a holy terror when she got started.

"I want Logan," Dutch insisted. "That man's a thief. Why else did he run when chased?"

"You'd run from a lynch party, too, Dutch " She looked down at him from the porch, and then suddenly she said, "Dutch, do you really want him? Do you just have to have Logan?"

Suddenly wary, Dutch peered at her, trying to read what was in her mind.

"That's what we come for," he said sullenly. "We come after him."

"I've heard all about your lynching cow thieves, or them you thought were thieves, and I heard you set fire to a couple of them. All right, Dutch, you want Logan, I'll give him to you."

"What?" Dutch peered at her. "What's that mean?"

"Logan Sackett," she said quietly, "is kin of mine. We come of the same blood. I'm a Sackett, same as him, and I know my kinfolk. Now you boys believe in fair play, don't you?" she spoke to Brannenburg's riders.

"Yes, ma'am, we surely do. Yes, ma'am."

"All right, Dutch. You want Logan Sackett. I hear tell you shape yourself around as something of a fighter. You been walking hard-heeled around this country for several years now because most of these folks hadn't lived here long enough to know you when you walked almighty soft. You just get down off your horse, Dutch. You want Logan, you can have him. You can have him fist and skull right here in front of my stoop, and the first one of your boys who tries to help you will get a bullet through his brisket."

Well, I just walked out on the porch and stopped on the steps. "How about it, Dutch? You want to take me, it's like Em says. You got to do it yourself, with your own hands an' without help."

Chapter 9

Well, his face was a study, believe me. He was mad clean through but there just wasn't anything he could do but fight. Dutch sat up there on his horse and he knew he had it to do. Em Talon had laid it out for him and there was no way out short of looking small before his men, and no ranch boss of a tough outfit dares do that.

He got down off his horse and trailed his reins. He taken off his gun belt and slung it around the horn, and then he hung his hat over it.

Meanwhile I'd unslung my gun and knife and come down off the porch. When he turned around I knew I was in for trouble. I was taller than him, but he was broad and thick and would outweigh me by fifteen pounds or so. He was shorter, but he was powerful and he moved in, hands working back and forth.

I moved out toward him, a little too confident maybe. He taken that out of me but quick. Suddenly he charged, and he was close in before he did, and he went low into a crouch, swinging both hands high. One of them crossed my left shoulder and connected like a thrown brick.

Right away I knew that whatever else Dutch was, he was a scrapper. Somewhere along the line of years behind him he'd learned how to fight. He came up inside, butting his head, then back-heeling me so I fell to the ground. I rolled over and he put the toe of a boot into my ribs before I could get up and raked me with his spur as his foot swung back from the kick. He raked back and he raked deep, ripping my shirt and leaving a trail of blood across my chest. I was up then, but he came at me, and I knew this wasn't just a fight. He was out to kill me.

You think it can't be done? I've seen a half dozen men killed in fights, and there was no mercy in Dutch, nor in any of his boys. Nor in Em Talon, for that matter.

He came at me, boring in, punching, driving, stomping on my insteps when he got close, raking my shins with the sides of his boots or his spurs. And it taken me a moment to get started.

He was a bull. He had great powerful shoulders under that shirt, and he slammed in close, butting me under the chin with his head. I threw him off and he charged right back. I managed to slam a right into his ribs as he came close, but he knew where he had to win that fight, and that was in close where I couldn't use my longer arms.

He slammed away at my belly, and I taken a few wicked punches. Then I slammed him on the side of the face with an elbow smash that cut to the bone. When that blood started to show, Dutch went berserk. It was like roping a cyclone. He slammed at me and every punch hurt. He was fighting to kill, but I shoved him off, stiffened a fist into his face, then caught him with a right as he came on in.

It stopped his rush, shook him to his heels. I landed a left and then, as he crouched, swung a right to that split cheekbone that ripped the cut wider.

He hit me twice in the ribs, charged on in, head under my chin, and I tripped and went down. He came down on top of me, grabbing for my throat. I reached across one of his arms, grabbed the other, and jerked. He rolled over and I got to my feet first. I started for him as he started to roll and he lashed out at me with both spurred heels. I jumped back just in time to get a wicked slash across one wrist. Then he came up and I hit him in the mouth.

It smashed his lips back into his teeth. He came at me again and I split his ear with a left hook, turning him half around. He grabbed my arm and tried to throw me with a flying mare but I went with it and put both knees into his back. He went down hard, me on top. Grinding his face into the dust, I had him half smothered before I suddenly let go and jumped back. I wanted to whip him, not kill him.

He came up from the ground, staggered, located me and rushed. I put a left jab to his mouth, and as he came close caught him under the chin with the butt of my palm and slammed his head back.

There was no quit in him, I'll give him that. He was bull-strong and iron-hard and his punching away at my belly was doing me no good. I shoved him off, hit him with a stunning right as he tried to come in again, and then I let him come, but turned a little as he came in and threw him over his hip with a rolling hip lock. He came down hard in the dust.

"Dutch," I said, "you know damn well I never stole any stock of yours. An' you know I didn't know those two who did."

Paying me no mind, he got up on his hands and knees, then threw himself in a long dive at my legs. My knee smashed him in the face as he came in, and he fell, but he rolled over and came up again.

"You fight pretty good, Dutch," I said, "but it takes more than owning a lot of cows to make a big man. Hanging anybody you can find or anybody you don't like makes you nothing but a murderer, lower than any of the men you chase."

He wiped the blood from his face with his sleeve and stared at me. His cheek was cut to the bone, his lips were in shreds. One eye had a gray lump over it, but he stood there, his big hands opening and closing, the hatred in his eyes an ugly thing.

"You want some more, Dutch," I said, "you come an' get it."

"Next time," he said, "it'll be with a gun."

He wasn't stopped. I'd beaten him, but he wasn't through. He liked too much what he thought he'd become. He liked the feeling of power, liked walking hard-heeled down the boardwalks of the towns, liked being followed by a lot of tough riders, with people stepping out of the way.

Most of them were just being polite in spite of his rudeness, but he thought they were afraid. He liked bullying people, liked shoving them around. And he wasn't going to give it up because he'd lost a fist fight.

One of his riders spoke up. "When he comes, Sackett, he won't be alone. We'll all come with him. And we'll bring a rope."

"You do that," I said, "he'll need all the help he can get."

They turned their horses and rode away. At the gate one of them got down and opened the gate, then fastened it again. That was cattle country . . . nobody left a gate down when it was there to close.

"Thanks, Em," I said. "That could have been rough."

"It was rough. But it ain't the first time. It used to be Injuns when pa was away."

"Logan?" Pennywell tugged at my sleeve. "Let me fix up your face."

My face was bruised and battered some, although I'd no bad cuts. Dutch had been a lot more of a fighter than I figured him for and he'd battered my ribs something awful. I never said nothing even when Pennywell hurt my face, fixing it up.

Late that night, stretched on my bed, I swore softly. As if Em Talon hadn't enough trouble! I'd brought more upon her in the shape of Brannenburg. He was a vindictive man, and those who rode for him were a rougher crowd then you'd usually find on a cow outfit. Cowhands could be almighty rough, but this bunch were trouble hunters. Many of them had taken a turn at being outlaws, gun hands and whatever the occasion demanded . . . like me.

The trouble was, I'd brought them down on Em Talon.

·I never was no hand for figurin'. I've seen folks set down an' ponder on things until they saw their way clear, but me, I was never no hand at that. I'm strong and mean, but I never found no way of doing things except to walk right out and take the bull by the horns. Settin' an' waitin' rankled. I wasn't geared for it. I needed a problem where I could walk out swinging both fists. Nolan was more inclined to study on things. Me, it was always root hog or die, and that was what I needed right now.

Troubles were bunching around us. Everywhere I looked I could see it shaping up like thunderheads gathering over the high peaks. Jake Flanner was cooking up something, and now Dutch would be also.

It was right about then that I decided I'd better go right after them instead of settin', waitin', and finally getting clobbered.

Some folks take to running. Some folks hope that by backing up far enough they'll not have trouble, but it surely doesn't work. I'd ridden all over the Rio Grande, Mogollon, Mimbres, La Plata, and Mesa Verde country and what I saw was a lesson.

The Indians there were good Indians, planting Indians. For a long time they lived in peace and bothered nobody, and then Navajo-Apache tribes came migrating down the east side of the Rockies. They found a way west without climbing over mountains. Those nice, peaceful tribes along the Rio Grande were shoved right off the map. Some were killed, some fled to western lands and built cliff houses, but you couldn't escape by running. The Navajo followed them right along, killing and destroying. Had they banded together under a good leader and waited they might have held the Navajo off, but when danger showed, a family or group of families would slip away to avoid trouble, and those left would be too few to hold off the enemy.

Finally most of them were killed, the cliff houses fell into ruins, the irrigation projects they'd started fell apart. The wild tribes from out of the wilderness had again won a battle over the planting peoples . . . so it had always been.

I'd ridden through that country, I'd seen the broken pottery and the deserted villages. Farther west I'd find more of the pottery and more ruins. Sometimes you'd find where groups of Indians had merged, but it was always the same. They'd pull out rather than make a stand, and they saw all they'd built fall apart, saw their people cut down, saw their world fall apart.

A couple of times hiding out in canyons I'd come on some of those cliff dwellings. I never told nobody about them because I wouldn't have been believed. To most white men all Indians were blanket Indians. Several times I'd holed up in a cliff dwelling, drinking water from their springs, sometimes finding remnants of their corn fields where volunteer corn stalks had grown up after constant reseeding of itself.

I had a warm feeling for those folks, and sometimes of a night I'd lie there where they slept. One night I awakened filled with terror. I got up and looked out the window over the moonlit canyons and I fancied I could hear them coming, hear the wild Navajo coming out of the wilderness to attack the peaceful villages. The terror I felt was the terror they must have felt, even when they moved on they'd know it was only a matter of time.

Sometimes only a few warriors would come filtering through the canyons, killing a farmer at work or shooting his wife off a ladder where she climbed with her child. A few would come, but they'd wait around until more came, and more. Up in the cliff dwellings the people would wait, looking down, seeing their crops reaped by others or destroyed, seeing them gather there, knowing someday they would come in sufficient numbers and the floors of the cliff houses would be dark with blood. Some of the people would climb out over the tops of the cliffs and escape, some would try and be killed in the process.

It was like Em Talon. Her husband had been murdered, her hands killed or driven off. Little by little they had gone until she had stood alone against them, a tall old woman, alone in her bleak mansion, waiting for the day when she could no longer lift the Sharps or see to fire it.

I'd come drifting along, a man with no good reputation behind him. I was one of the savages, one of the wanderers. I was no planting Indian, no planter at all. I was a drifter, a man who lived by the gun. But I'd dug in here and stayed . . . now the time had come to carry it to them.

I'd had enough of waiting. I wasn't going to sit and let them bring death to me and to this old woman. I was going after them. I was going to root them out, throw them out, burn them out, or die trying. It just wasn't in me to set and wait.

Like I said, I'm no hand at figuring. It's my way to just bull in and let the chips fall where they will, but I did give thought to getting into the town unseen, and to getting away when it was over . . . if there was anything of me left.

Not even a mouse will trust himself to only one hole, so I sat back and recalled the town, thinking out where the buildings and the corrals were situated. Somewhere along the line, sleep fetched itself to me.

At breakfast Em was in a talking mood. She had been up shy of daylight, peering out through the shutters, studying out the land.

"You should have seen it when me an' Talon came west," she said. "There was nobody out thisaway, just nobody at all. Talon had been far up the Missouri before this, on a steamboat, and he'd been up the Platte as far as a boat could go. He'd seen his buffalo and killed a grizzly or two, and he'd lived and traveled among Injuns, and fit with them a time or two.

"We come west and he kept a-tellin' me of this place, and me, I was ready for it. I was a mountain gal, raised back yonder in the hills, and all that flat land worried me, nothing moving but the grass before the wind and maybe an antelope far away or a herd of buffalo.

"Then we seen this place. We seen it from afar off, standing out on the grassland with the mountains behind. Talon had left four mountain men in a cabin on the land, but they weren't needed.

"At first the Injuns just came to look, to stare at the three-story house looming above the country around. They called it the wooden tepee and sat their horses in astonishment, gaping at the house that had appeared like a miracle, for the Indians had been gone on the annual buffalo hunt when the house was built.

"When the Cheyennes rode up to see, Talon went out to meet them. He took them, four at a time, through the house, showing them everything, from the enormous stretch of country that could be seen from the railed walk atop the house to the loopholes from which shots could be fired while the shooter was safe within.

"He knew the story would be told, and he wanted them to know they could be seen a long time before they reached the house, and that an attacker could be fired upon from any place within the house."

"But you've so much furniture!" Pennywell exclaimed. "How ever did you get it out here?"

"Talon made some of it. Like I said, he was handy. The rest of it we brought out. Talon had trapped for fur, and he kept on trapping. He found some gold here and yon in the mountain streams, and he ordered what he had a mind to. We brought us a whole wagon train

of things out from the east, for Talon liked to live well, and that's the
sort of thing you break into mighty easy."

Sittin' back in that big hidebound chair I could see behind her
words. Seeing the Indians filtering back from their hunt, riding through
an area they probably only saw once or twice a year, anyway, to find
this great house reared up, staring out over the plains with the great,
empty eyes of its windows.

To them it must have been a kind of magic. It had been built
quickly. Talon was a driving man, by all accounts, and the mountain
men he had helping him were not the kind to stay in one place for long.
How many he had to help Em never said, but there were four who had
lived in a cabin on the place while Talon rode east to find his bride.
There might have been more.

Probably Talon and Sackett had framed much of the structure
before their help arrived, and certainly the plan must have been put
together in his mind whilst working on the rivers or building for other
men.

Sitting there, eyes half closed, listening to her tell it in that old
Tennessee mountain tone of hers, I found myself getting restless again.
Nobody had the right to take from them what they had built.

Me, I was never likely to build anything. A no-account drifter like
me leaves no more mark behind him then you leave a hole in the water
when you pull your finger out. Every man could leave something, or
should. Well, maybe it wasn't in me to build much, but I surely could
keep the work of other men from being destroyed.

I was going to ride into Siwash and open the place up. I was going
in there and drive Len Spivey and his kind clear out of the country.

I'd go tonight.

Chapter 10

Now I never laid claim to having no corner on brains, and most of what I picked up in the way of knowledge was knocked into my head one way or the other. What I've learned, or most of it, has been concerned with just staying alive.

Guns, horses, hitches, and half-nelson's are more in line with my thinking, but here and there just plain looking and seeing what you look at has taught me something. Also, whilst never much of a hand to go to the mat with a book, I'm a good listener.

Folks who have lived the cornered sort of life most scholars, teachers, and storekeepers live seldom realize what they've missed in the way of conversation. Some of the best talk and the wisest talk I've ever heard was around campfires, in saloons, bunkhouses, and the like. The idea that all the knowledge of the world is bound up in schools and schoolteachers is a mistaken one.

There have been a lot of men who just didn't give a damn about tending store or keeping school but who just cut loose their moorings and went adrift.

Wandering men see a lot, and all knowledge is a matter of comparison and the deductions made from it. Moreover, in any crowd of drifters you'll find men of the finest scholastic education as well as men who have just seen a lot and have been putting two and two together.

One time or another I've heard a lot of campfire talk about towns and how they came to be, and a good many sprang up from river crossings. Folks like to camp close to streams for the sake of water, but crossing a big river was quite an operation, so they'd go into camp after they'd crossed over. That is, the smart ones would. Those who went into camp to cross over in the morning often found the water so high come morning they were stuck for several days.

Rome, London, Paris . . . all of them sprang from river crossings, and usually there was some bright gent around who was charging toll to cross over. Any time you find a lot of people who have to have something or do something you'll also find somebody there charging them for doing it.

When people stop at a stream crossing they camp and look around, and you can bet somebody has set up store with things for them to want.

The town of Siwash came to be in just that way. The stream was no great shakes, but there was a good flowing spring, and a man came in, stopped his travels, and began raising sheep. A few months later a man came along headed for the Colorado gold fields, he seen that spring and knowing that water was sometimes more precious than gold, waited until the sheepman's back was turned and then split his skull with an ax, buried him deep, and planted a crop of corn and melons over the ground where he buried the sheepman.

It was the age-old conflict between the farmer and the stock raiser that probably began when Cain killed Abel. Cain was not only the first farmer according to the Good Book, but he built the first city mentioned in the Bible, and this farmer, seeing that lots of people stopped at his spring for fresh water, set up store and began selling vegetables and corn.

He would probably have done all right in the fullness of time but for a gambler with rheumatism in his hands. The gambler rode into town and stopped to watch the business. He listened to the rustle of the cottonwood leaves and the lovely sound of flowing water from the spring, and that night he brought out a greasy deck of cards. Rheumatism in the hands was spelling his finish as a gambler, but those hands still were good enough to deal three queens to Cain.

Cain hadn't seen a woman for a long time so when those three queens showed up together he overrated their value, and when the rheumatic gambler showed his four aces Cain discovered he was no longer a farmer and keeper of a store but a wanderer. The gambler wanted him out of there so he made him a present of his horse . . . and perhaps with a warning from a friendly ghost, he didn't turn his back when Cain picked up his ax. So Cain rode out into the world again, and the gambler became a storekeeper and a tiller of the fields.

He called the place Siwash. Nobody knew why, including him. The name came to him, and he used it. By that time he was selling supplies to the MT ranch, and to several others in the vicinity.

Siwash wasn't a big town. A man with good legs could walk all around it in five minutes, but you could have done the same thing with the first settlement of Troy, which also was built around a spring and on a trade route.

The gambler with the rheumatic hands was still there, and his hands were in even worse shape. The hands that could no longer deal one off the bottom or build up a bottom stock couldn't handle a gun either, so the oldest citizen in Siwash was also the most peaceful.

When Jake Flanner showed up and began quietly taking over the gambler considered shooting him until he saw what happened to several others with the same idea. So he smiled at Jake's stories and kept a gun handy just in case.

•Nevertheless, he harbored no good wishes for Flanner; he wished the man out of there, and not merely because he wanted to be top dog. The gambler's name was Con Wellington, and his hands being what they were he wanted peace. It took no wise man to see that there would never be peace where Jake Flanner was. So Con Wellington waited, listened, and bided his time, and as all things eventually came to him, he knew Flanner had been stopped cold by Emily Talon and Logan Sackett.

Logan was no stranger. They'd never been friends, had scarcely met, in fact. Logan had once sat in a poker game with Wellington, whose hands were not rheumatic at the time, but Con knew a good deal about Logan Sackett and he dealt his cards with extreme care.

He was considering some way of getting word to Logan without Flanner's spies telling of it when there was a tap on his window.

Con's mind worked swiftly. Jake Flanner or his men would come to the front door, hence if somebody came to the window it had to be an enemy of Flanner's, and an enemy of Flanner's was always welcome . . . so long as Flanner didn't know about it.

He opened the window a bare inch. "Who is it?" He was studying the background as he asked the question. It was unlikely anybody would be hiding and watching the back of his store, which was also his dwelling, but he was not a trusting man.

"Open your door," I said, and heard him mutter something from within. I'd left my horse under the cottonwoods beside the stream and had come on foot to the Wellington store.

There was a moment of movement within, and then after a bit, a door opened into darkness. "Come in then, and make it quick."

Once inside, Con Wellington uncovered a lantern. "I had an idea it would be you," he said. "There's nobody else would come to me in the night."

He sat down on his bed. It was an old four-poster and the springs creaked heavily as Wellington seated himself, leaving the chair for me.

"It's about Flanner you've come," he said abruptly. "Well, understand me. I don't like the man but he's left me alone. Granted, my business is less than half what it was, but I'm alive, and some are not."

He opened a cigar box and took one himself before pushing it over to me. He lifted his hands, gnarled and twisted from rheumatism. "I've as much nerve as the next man, I think, but with these nerve doesn't matter. I can pull a trigger if I've plenty of time . . . I could still hunt buffalo. But to pull a gun against another man? I'd not have a chance."

"It isn't a gun you'll need. It's another thing I have in mind."

Wellington looked at me sharply. "Logan, you've tied in with Em Talon . . . what's in that for you?"

"We're kinfolk. She was a Clinch Mountain Sackett before she married Talon."

"A Clinch Mountain Sackett may mean something to you. It doesn't to me."

"It means little to anybody but us," I told him. "We set store by kinfolk. We've our troubles, time to time, but when one of us is in danger, there'll be help from any who are around."

Wellington lit his cigar. "I wish my folks were like that. They were glad to be rid of me. My family had money, education, pride of family. So when I lost my money and got into difficulties they threw me out."

"It happens." I lit my cigar, too. It was a good one. "I had a hunch," I said, "that you didn't care for Flanner. Now I want you to stand aside."

"No more?"

"I'm gettin' tired of him. So's Em. Her son's comin' home but he may take a time gettin' here and I want action. I'm goin' to run him out."

"You? And who else?"

"I don't need nobody else. I figured you would know who his friends were. I don't aim to hurt innocent bystanders if it can be helped."

He looked at me, long and thoughtful, and then he said, "You know, I think you might do it." He looked at the long ash on his cigar, then very carefully knocked it off on the edge of his saucer. "Most of the people here don't like him, but right now there's not more than twenty to twenty-five people in town aside from Flanner and his men."

He named them for me, told me where they were likely to be, described a few of them. "The hotel, saloon, and livery stable, and the bunkhouse back of the stable, that's where most of his boys will be. Flanner sticks close to the hotel."

"How about that other one?"

"Johannes Duckett?" Wellington squinted his eyes. "He might be anywhere. He might be outside this minute. He moves around like a ghost."

He paused a moment. "Don't belittle the folks here in town. Jake swings a wide loop but he's left them strictly alone. He shows up at the dances, pie suppers, and the like, and he contributes to get the minister to come to town. They don't like him much, but they've little to complain about.

"They figure his business with the MT is his business. Not many folks around here knew the Talons. They kept to themselves pretty much, and then after the old man was killed Em came to town mighty seldom . . . and after a while, not at all.

"Some of them are jealous. After all, the Talon outfit is big. Most of these folks were latecomers, and none of them realize what it takes to put a big outfit together, especially when the Talons came here."

"They'll stay out of it then?"

"I expect so. Naturally, I can promise nothing except for myself."

What my next step would be I simply did not know. Like I said, I'm not long on planning. I just start moving and let things happen. The only planning I do, you might say, is to see that I don't hurt any innocent bystanders. And that was why I risked my neck to come in and talk to Con Wellington.

Suddenly I had a hunch. I wasn't going back the way I came in. If this here Johannes Duckett was laying for me it would be out back, so I'd go right out the front door.

Wellington didn't like it much, but he agreed Duckett might be lying in wait out yonder in the dark, so I went to the front door of the store.

"If they see me and ask about it, tell them I'm running scared but wanted tobacco. I'm not that much of a smoker, but they don't know that. I've seen men risk their necks for a smoke."

Wellington took down a couple of sacks of tobacco. "Just in case," he said.

The door was well oiled, and I slipped out to the boardwalk without a sound. Four long strides and I was across the street, ducking into the space between two buildings. Carefully I worked my way back to my horse.

When I was crouched down near some stumps, looking through

the brush at my horse, I saw a man come out of the trees near the road. He looked left and right, then came on. He saw the horse and I heard him give a muttered exclamation, then he reached over and pulled the slip knot I'd tied in the bridle reins. He gathered the reins and was just throwing a leg over the saddle when I heard a shot.

The roan jumped and the strange rider toppled from its back into the grass. The roan ran out of there, head high, reins trailing.

From behind me and to my left there was movement. I waited, and then a tall, thin man came out of the trees and walked down to the dead man. He struck a match, then swore.

"Wrong man again, Duckett?" I yelled into the darkness.

He turned and shot. It was one move, only I had already fired. He had shot at sound and he missed by a hair. My bullet smacked hard against something metallic, then ricochetted off into the night.

Moving swiftly, I went through the trees, angling toward the road to try to head off my horse.

There were no more shots, no sound. The moon was just showing on the trail and there was a smell of dust in the air. I walked along holding to the shadowed side of the trail, and sure enough, about of a quarter of a mile up the road I found the roan. The horse came to me when I spoke, and I petted it and talked to it for a while before stepping into the saddle.

It was near daybreak when I got back to the ranch.

Chapter 11

Pennywell was on the lookout when I came in, and when I got inside she brought me a cup of coffee. "Em's asleep," she said, "catching up on some of that lost time."

She studied me critically. I looked beat. After I'd caught my horse I'd had to hightail it for the MT, careful to leave no sign they could use, so I'd come right down the trail and through the main gate.

"Looks like you been out among 'em," she commented. "I frown on that as Em would say."

Explaining what happened, I added, "The way I figure it, Duckett spotted me when I came in and laid for me near my horse. Meanwhile some other of Flanner's men saw me in town, saw me go into or come out of the store, and got ahead of me, planning to get my horse and then me."

"But you shot Duckett?"

"Shot at him. From the sound I must have hit his rifle or a tree near him. I doubt if I did him any harm, but he came within an inch or less of nailing me. That man can shoot, an' Lordy, is he quick!"

"Teach you to go gallivanting around in the middle of the night. Wait for them to come to you."

"I'm a poor hand at waitin'. My style is to carry it to them, show them a fight has two sides."

"Do you think this will do it?"

"Well," I commented, "I've an idea they'll think twice before they open a door. They know I'm huntin' them, too, and that can be a worrisome thing."

Two slow days went by while I worked around the place. One day I rode to the hills and shot an elk, bringing the meat down to the place. I also taken my iron out to the meadows, roped and branded a couple of yearlings.

No work had been done around there for some time and it would be a rustler's dream to get back in there and find all that fine stock wearing no brands. After that I decided to carry an iron with me wherever I went on MT range.

Johannes Duckett didn't shape up like the kind of man who would sit by and let me get away with shooting at him. I knew I'd be hearing from him, with or without Flanner, and I also figured Duckett would go a-prowling for me. He was the kind who would be apt to shoot from anywhere, so I kept off the skyline, rode through the edge of the trees, kept myself out of range as well as I could when I'd no idea where the attack would come from or when.

Nonetheless I still had an idea of riding into Siwash and making myself known.

Em was on the lookout when she seen a rider coming. She turned to me. "Logan? What do you make of him?"

He was coming down the road at a walk, heading for the main gate. Through the glasses I could see he was riding a beat-up buckskin. He was a small-sized man with a narrow-brimmed hat, a speckled shirt and vest. Light glinted from his eyes so I reckoned him for glasses. He was wearing a six-shooter and he had him a rifle shoved down into a boot.

As he rode up to the gate he suddenly touched a spur to his buckskin and I'll be damned if that horse didn't just sail right over a six-bar gate that was all of five feet tall, and did it with no particular mind, sort of offhand and easy.

Em, she taken up her Sharps and that ol' gun boomed as she put a bullet right into the dust ahead of him.

The rider he just taken off his hat, held it high, and waved it down in a low bow. But he kept comin'.

I hitched my Colt into a better position and walked out front. Nobody else was in sight, and I figured to be all ready for this man, whoever he was.

He came on up, walking his horse, and about fifty feet off he drew rein and looked at the house. For a long time he looked, then he dropped his eyes to me. One eye was covered with a kind of white film . . . I reckon he could only see from one.

"You'll be Logan Sackett, I expect? I've come here to join you."

"What for?"

The man did not smile. "The word is that you are about to be run off. Flanner is recruiting fighters. I am Albani Fulbric, and my people have been fighting on the wrong side for a thousand years. I see no reason to change now."

"Can you fight?"

"With any weapon . . . any one at all."

"Well, it's gettin' on to supper time. Come in an' set and we'll talk it over."

He was an odd man with an odd name, but somehow I liked the cut of him. At table he showed himself a fair hand at putting away grub, although in size he wasn't more than two-thirds of me.

"Where'd you get a name like that?" I asked him.

"Names are how you look at 'em. My name is funny to you, yours is funny to me. Sackett—ever listen to the sound of that? Think on it, my friend."

He reached for the beef. "Now you take my name. My folks, both sides of them, come over from Normandy with William the Conqueror. One of them was squire to Sir Hugh de Malebisse and the other rode with Robert de Brus.

"Neither one of them had anything but strong arms and the willingness to use them. One was an Albani, one a Fulbric, and you will find their names in the Doomsday Book. Bold men they were and we who follow their steps are proud to bring no shame to the names they left us."

"They were knights?" Pennywell asked.

"They were not. They were simple men, smiths and the like, between wars. One of them settled in Yorkshire with Sir Hugh, and the other went off to Scotland, hard by. And one of the family later helped to put a Bruce on the throne of Scotland, although a lot of good it did either of them."

I knew nothing of foreign wars or foreign parts, and the talk when not of horses and cattle or buffalo or guns was scarcely easy for me to follow, but there was a lilt to his voice like he was speaking of magic, and I liked to hear what he was saying. The names meant nothing to me, nothing at all.

"I've heard those names," Em Talon said. "Talon spoke of them. His family came from France, and by all accounts a roistering lot they were, building ships and sailing them to foreign parts, and more often than not on voyages of piracy. It's a wonder they weren't hanged."

"Are you a hand with cattle?" I asked him.

"I am that. I'll handle a rope with any man, and my horse is good with cattle. I'll earn my keep and whatever it is you'll pay.

"That horse you see me riding has been hard used, but don't look down upon him. He's carried me into and out of much trouble, and time and again we've been to the wars. Let me put a loop over anything that walks, and that buckskin will hold it, whatever it is.

"In the saddle of that horse I'd not be afraid to rope a Texas cyclone, rope and hog-tie it, too. He'll climb where it would put scare into a mountain goat, and one time when a man holed me with a Winchester slug, he carried me fifteen miles through the snow, then pawed on the stoop until folks came to the door to take me down.

"You can call me a dog if you will, sir, but you speak ill of my horse and I'll put lead into you."

"I'd never speak ill of any man's horse," I said sincerely. "I've ridden his kind, and we've a few fit to run with him right here on the Empty."

If Albani was a fair hand at the table he was a better one in the field. We turned to and roped and branded fourteen head the following morning, cleaned out a waterhole where there'd been a slide, and checked out the grass on the upper meadows. He was a handy man with tools and not backward about using them, but I was wary. He'd not said much about himself beyond running off at the head about those old ancestors of his who came over . . . from where I wasn't sure. I'd never heard of Normandy until Pennywell, who reads a lot of books, told me it was in France and that the Normans were originally called Northmen or Vikings, and they'd settled in there where the country looked good. Well, that made sense. Most of us who came west were wishful of the same thing.

Al—as we came to call him—was as good at working on fences, too, and we tightened up the wire where it was needed, replaced a few rotting posts, and branded more cattle in the next few days. He'd been working up Montana way and in the Dakotas and had first come west from Illinois, working on the railroad, building at first, then as a switch-man.

It was the sort of story every man had to tell them days. Men moved often and turned their hand to almost anything, developing the knacks for doing things. Most men were handy with tools—their lives demanded it of them—and most men worked at a variety of jobs, usually heading toward a piece of land of their own. Some made it, some never did. In any bunkhouse you'd find men from a dozen states or territories, and men who had worked at dozens of jobs, doing whatever was needed to earn a living.

Most of them were young, and the younger they were the harder they worked to be accepted as men. No boy over fourteen wanted to be thought of as a boy . . . he wanted to be considered a man and a top hand at whatever he was doing.

The first thing he learned was to do his part. Nobody had any use for a shirker or a lay-around . . . it just made more work for the others, and such a one became almighty unwelcome awful fast. On the other hand, nobody asked who you were or where you came from, only that you stood up when there was something to be done.

Nobody thought of horses except as companions and working partners. The value of a horse in terms of money wasn't often mentioned. You'd hear a man say, "He's a damn' fine cuttin' horse." Or maybe, "He'll go all night an' the next day. Stays right in there." Or, "That's the horse I rode when I tied onto that brindle steer that time, an' . . ."

You hear folks say how horses were rough used on old-time ranches, but it ain't so. At least, they used them no worse than they used themselves, and usually a whole sight better. You'll hear folks say that horses are stupid, but they ain't if you give them a chance. A horse is like a dog . . . he needs to belong to somebody, to be trusted by somebody. Once they know what's expected of them they'll come through.

There was no word from Milo Talon, and I lay awake nights wondering what Flanner would do next. Me an' Em talked it over at breakfast, with Al Fulbric putting in his two cents' worth. The result was that I got out a team that had once been broke to harness, hitched them to a plough, and then went out and ploughed a firebreak twelve furrows wide just below the crest of the hill that divided us from town. It taken several days, but I got it done, and Al ploughed some on the other side.

Back up into the woods we scouted the country, and here and there tied onto a dead fall and dragged it into place. In other places we cut trees and felled them so they'd form a barrier to riders or even men on foot. We laid out trails through these barriers with certain logs to be lifted to let us by. It was like one of these mazes you hear tell of. If a man knew his way as we did he could ride through almighty fast, but if he didn't know the key entrance and exit he played hob gettin' through.

Fire was what we feared most. We set out barrels and filled them with water near the barns and bunkhouse, and we shot more meat and jerked it against a long fight.

Two nights later I woke up with a yell ringing in my ears. Somebody was pounding on the door and yellin' "Fire!" I grabbed for my hat and my pants, slamming the first on my head and scrambling into the others. I stamped my feet into boots, grabbed my gun belt, and ran for the door.

The whole horizon was lit by flames. They were coming right at us with a good beat of wind behind them. As I ran for the corral I heard the beat of hoofs and Al Fulbric came out on the dead run. He was in his long johns with a gun belted on, waving his rifle and yellin' like a Comanche. But across his horse in front of him he had a bunch of old sacks and a spade.

It taken me a moment to throw the leather on the roan and get into the saddle. There were sacks laid out and ready and I grabbed a bundle along with a shovel and raced after him.

We reached our firebreak just ahead of the flames. Believe me, had it not been there we'd have been wiped out, but because it was lyin' like it was, on our side of the hill, Flanner hadn't even guessed it was there.

We hit the dirt, and leaving our horses on the ranch side of the break, we ran across and went to whipping out the first inroads of flame with our sacks. We managed to fight it for a bit, then fell back after starting backfires.

The backfires burned right up to our firebreak and gave us about fifty more feet of leeway. Only a few sparks managed to blow across to the ranch side and we whipped those out or buried them with earth before they got started.

Pennywell was right there with us, and so was Em. Suddenly I turned sharp around. "The house!" I said. "They've gotten into the house by now!"

We hit our saddles on the run, Em no slower than the rest of us, and we went down the slope on the run.

As we came into the back door, a bunch of men were crowdin' into the front door and Em ran through, me behind her. Al cut around through another room.

Len Spivey was there, and Matthews, and some others. Len was grinning. "Looks like we got you! Jake thought that fire would do it."

They all had guns in their hands and there were eight of them and only two of us in sight.

They guessed right on some things, they guessed wrong on Emily Talon.

"You got nothing," she said, and she cut loose her dogs . . . only they were slugs from a big Dragoon Colt.

They couldn't believe it. They'd been sure if there was trouble it would come from me, and they paid no mind to the womenfolks, or mighty little. And they didn't even know about Al.

Em just tilted her old pistol and cut loose, and just as she fired, Al Fulbric jumped from the bedroom door with a shotgun in his hands, and somehow my old six-shooter was speaking its piece right along with them.

It was shock that won for us. They'd not expected shooting with the women there, not really knowing what kind of a woman Em was. It was shock and the time it takes a man to react. Em's first shot caught Matthews, who was closest to her, and turned him halfway around. His own gun went off into the floor just as Al cut loose with a double-barreled shotgun.

Matthews was falling, shot through the body. Another man grabbed at the doorjamb and slid down it to the floor, and Len Spivey threw himself at the door and damn near broke his neck getting out of there.

We ran to the door after them. One man turned to fire and my bullet cut him right across the collarbone from side to side. I saw him stagger and cry out, seen his shirt flop where the bullet cut it, and then I put a second one into his brisket. And then they were gone.

They left three behind. Matthews was down and dying. The man who slid down the doorjamb had taken a load of buckshot at twelve-foot range, and he was dead. A third man lay on the grass outside the front door.

They'd drawn us off with the fire as they figured, but they had guessed wrong on Emily Talon.

I might have held back myself, for fear of the women getting shot, but there was no hold-back in Em.

Nor in Pennywell.

She had got off two shots. I saw her loading up again afterwards. She was pale as a ghost when it was over, but she was thumbing two cartridges back into her pistol, and she was ready.

Man, those were *women!*

Chapter 12

There was a meanness in me. We'd come off lucky. Em had been burned by one bullet, but that was the only injury to any of us.

We'd lost some grass, but spring rains and the winter snows would bring that back. The burning left us secure from that side at least, for now there was nothing left to burn.

They'd busted through the front window. They'd tried to break down the door, but it just didn't bust that easy. They'd pried off one of the shutters and had busted through the window to get in. That was what allowed us time to get down there.

But it was not in me to sit by, so I went right outside, and saying nothing to anybody I hit the road for town. I pulled up in the shadow of a barn, saw their horses at the hitch rail of the hotel-saloon, and I walked across the street and up the steps. They were all inside, cursing and swearing and downing drinks when I came through the door, and they turned around thinking I was Flanner.

I never said yes or no, I just cut loose. My first bullet taken Len Spivey just as he closed his fist over his gun butt. It slammed him into the bar and the second one opened a hole right in the hollow at the base of his throat.

One other man went down before a slug hit me in the leg and I started to fall. I braced myself against the wall, hammered the rest of my shells into them, and then commenced pushing the empties out.

The room was full of smoke from that old black powder, and from somewhere near the bar flame stabbed at me and I was hit again.

I didn't fall. I just kept plugging fresh cartridges into those empty chambers and then lifted my six-gun for another have at them. Sliding down the wall to one knee I peered under the smoke that filled the room. I saw some boots, stabbed two shots about four feet above them, and saw a man fall.

I crawled toward the door and managed to push it open and get outside. Nobody needed to tell me I was hard hit, and nobody needed to tell me I'd done a damn fool thing to ride into the enemy camp and go to blasting.

My horse was yonder, and I crawled for him. A door opened in the side of the hotel, then closed easy like. I hitched myself down the steps into the street and using the hitch rail, pulled myself to my feet.

I was backing across the street, gun in hand, when Jake Flanner stepped around the corner of the hotel on those crutches of his. He had a six-shooter in one hand, and he kind of eased his weight on the other crutch and lifted the gun. At the same moment I saw Brewer come out of the saloon door. He had a rifle in his hands and he was maneuvering himself into position for the kill.

My gun came up. I took a step back and my boot came down on a rock that rolled under it. Weak as I was, it was all that was needed. The stone rolled, I staggered and fell just as two guns went off, followed quickly by a third.

That last had a different sound. It was a sharper *spang,* not the dull report of the forty-four. I saw Brewer stagger and go down, then crawl around the corner and out of sight.

Flanner was gone. An instant ago he was there and then he was gone.

I started to get up and felt a hand under my arm. "Easy now!" The voice was strange, but my eyes were fogging over and when I started to look around he said, "You'll have to walk. I can't carry you and shoot. Let's go."

Somewhere along in the next few minutes I felt myself getting into a saddle, and I felt the movement of a horse because every time he set a hoof down it hurt like hell.

There was a fire burning. I liked the pinewood smell. It was night and there was a roundup of stars right overhead. I could see them through the branches of a tree. My head ached and I didn't feel like moving, so for a long time I just lay there looking up at the stars.

After a while I must have passed out again because when my eyes opened the sky was gray and there was only one star left on the range of the sky. For a time I lay there looking at it and then my eyes located the fire. It was down to coals and gray ash, and over beyond it I could hear that wonderful sound of horses munching grass.

Nothing moved so I just lay there, not even wondering what had happened to me or where I was. Then I smelled something else and my eyes located it, a blackened coffeepot on the coals.

I wanted coffee. I wanted it bad but I wasn't so sure I could get to it or what I'd drink it out of. For a while I lay there, listening to the wind in the pines, and finally it began to come over me that I'd been shot . . . I'd been hit at least once, probably twice or more. Somehow I'd gotten out of town. Vaguely, I recalled a gentle voice and a hand on my arm. I recalled riding, and a hand on me much of the time. Finally I'd been tied into the saddle . . . but where was I now?

When I made a try at moving my right arm I found it was tied up somehow. My left was free.

Reaching out, my hand encountered something . . . my pistol! Well, I'd been left a gun, anyway. I could see the horses now, right yonder beyond a few scattered aspen. They were picketed and eating grass. Turning my head I saw somebody sleeping off on my left. His head was on a saddle, and he was bundled up in blankets with part of a ground sheet over him . . . but it was no type of ground sheet I'd ever known.

My right arm was hurt. Rolling to my left side a little I pushed into a sitting position. The horses looked over at me. There were two horses, one of them my roan.

Some gear was stacked on the grass near us, and two packsaddles. So this gent was a drifter. His gear looked a whole lot better than any drifter I'd ever come across, and he hadn't much in the way of spurs on his boots . . . and they weren't western boots.

When I started to twist a little I got a shot of pain through me that made me gasp, and when I gasped this sleeping man came awake sudden-like.

He was a tall man, not more than thirty, and handsome. He was one of the best dispositioned men I ever met, and he dressed neat. His outfit was all of the best, and while I couldn't make out his rifle, it was a handsome weapon.

He sat up and looked over at me. "Don't try moving," he said, "you'll start bleeding again. I had a hard time getting it stopped."

"Where'd you come from?"

He chuckled dryly. "What does it matter? I came at the right time, didn't I?" He shot me a look. "What happened in there, anyway?"

"We had us a fight. They were pushing us hard so I decided to push back. I done it."

"Did you get any of them?"

"I got two inside. I thought I got another outside, or somebody did."

"That was me. I took a shot at the man with the crutches but missed. Probably it was just as well. I'd hate to shoot a crippled man."

"Just because a man's got game legs doesn't say he's got a good disposition. That was the worst of the lot. That was Jake Flanner."

"What was the fight about?"

"Ranch out yonder," I said, "called the Empty . . . for MT. There's an old lady runnin' it . . . salt of the earth . . . named Emily Talon. Those back in Siwash were tryin' to run her out, and I got myself into the fight . . . I don't exactly know how. They hit us, tried to burn us out, and we saved the ranch, then whipped them in a fight at the house. But they'd be coming again and I got sore, them pushing an old lady that way . . . so I rode into town."

"Alone?"

"Why not? There wasn't all that many of them. And I couldn't take from them the only hand they've got."

"You look familiar."

"There's a few posters around. My name is Sackett. Logan Sackett."

"Hello, cousin. I am Barnabas Talon. Em is my mother."

Lying back on my blankets, I looked him over. He had the look, all right. He reminded me of Em, and a little more of Milo. "Heard you were in England."

"I came back. We'd received word a few years ago that ma was dead and buried. We were notified of it, and that the estate had been settled. There seemed no reason to return, so I kept on with what I was doing.

"A few months ago I was talking about Colorado with some English friends, and they commented on seeing the house, our house, and they had heard about an old woman who lived there alone.

"At first I thought it was nonsense, but it worried me, so I caught a ship and came over. In New Orleans I went to an old man who had been pa's attorney, and he told me there had been no settlement of the estate and that he had a letter from ma not two months before. So I started home."

He filled a cup with coffee and handed it to me. "My father taught me caution. I had been formally notified that the estate had been settled and ma was dead. Obviously someone had done so for a reason. Apparently the reason was to cause me to forget Colorado and whatever property we had there.

"Whoever had such intentions would not be pleased if I returned, so I came quietly, and when I reached Denver, I made inquiries. Nobody knew anything until I consulted a former deputy sheriff whom I knew. He told me that a man named Jake Flanner, who had lived in Siwash, was hiring fighting men . . . the worst kind.

"There had been a mention of a man named Flanner in ma's last letter to me, so I came along through the country passing myself off as a mining engineer. I was warned a couple of times I'd better go somewhere else, that the area around Siwash was headed for trouble.

"Just as I was riding into town you fellows cut loose in there, and when you came out I got a good look at you in the light over the door. I could see you'd been hit and you were favoring one leg, but you were still in there with that six-shooter. Then Brewer came out and he started to pull down on you so I shot him, then flipped a quick one at that crippled man."

"How'd you get my horse?"

"You told me where it was."

Well, I remembered none of that. Seems I told him some other things, too.

"You'd better keep an eye on our back trail," I warned him. "They won't give up."

"You forget that I grew up around here. I know hiding places in these hills they'd take years to find. I knew places that even pa never knew. Only Milo and me."

"I put out word for him. If he hits the outlaw trail they'll tell him."

He looked at me. "Milo? An outlaw?"

"Not really, I guess. It's just that they all know him. And he's got a way with that gun of his."

Lying there alongside the fire I told him about Em, Pennywell, and the place. I also told him about Albani Fulbric, bringing him up to date on the situation.

By the time I'd finished I was all in. I drank a swallow more of coffee and eased myself back on the blankets. It was broad daylight and I could see Barnabas was worried.

"You better mount up and head for the Empty," I said. "They'll know they put lead into me and they'll try to get to the ranch."

"I can't leave you," he said. He squatted on his heels. "Logan, I got to tell you. You're hit very hard. You took three slugs. One went through the muscles on your upper leg, and you got another one in the upper arm, but the bad one is through the body. You've lost a lot of blood." He paused a moment. "I am not a physician, but I do know a good deal about bullet wounds. I was an officer in the army of France for a while during the war with Prussia. I can't leave you."

"You'd better. Em will need you. As of me, it's going to be a long, hard pull."

He looked at me for a long time, then he went to his pack and got out some coffee and other grub which he stashed near me. He refilled my cartridge belt, and broke out a box of forty-fours. "Lucky I had these. I bought them in case they were needed on the ranch."

He squatted on his heels again. "You're about six or seven miles back of the ranch, but there's no short way across. It will take me most of the day to get there.

"Right down there is the spring. Your canteen is full and I'm leaving mine also. There's a big pot of coffee, and I'll try and get some help to you as soon as I see how it is on the ranch."

I looked around at the hills. It looked like a cirque, or maybe a hanging valley. It was a great big hollow that was walled in on three sides, or seemed to be, and maybe three hundred acres in the bottom of it. There were a lot of trees, and there probably was a lake . . . in such formations they were frequently found.

Barnabas saddled up, looked down at me once more, then rode off. And I was alone.

For a while I just lay there. The sun was in the hollow and the shadows of the aspen leaves dappled the grass with shadow. I was weak as a cat, and I just lay there resting.

How much of a trail had Barnabas Talon left? He might be a good man on a horse and with a gun, yet he could have left sign a child could read. Covering a trail is an art, and far from a simple one. I've heard of folks brushing out tracks with a branch. That's ridiculous— the marks of the branch are a sign themselves. Anything like that must be done with great care to make it seem the ground has not been disturbed by anything. A tracker rarely finds a complete track of man or beast on a trail he's following. Only indications of passage.

The spring was all of thirty yards off, but there was no flat ground nearer on which a man could sleep. It was all rocks down there. With my rifle close at hand and my horse nibbling grass a few yards away, I dozed the long day through. Come evening I added a few sticks to the fire, poured some water into a pot Barnabas left, shaved some jerky into it, added some odds and ends, and set it on the fire. Then I just lay back and rested.

You want to know something? I was scared. I never feared man nor beast when I was on my feet with two good hands, but now I was down, weak as could be, and my right arm was useless.

Later, I ate my stew and contemplated. I had no idea Barnabas Talon would get back. He would intend to, but there'd be need of him there and his first duty was to his ma. As for me it would be root hog or die, so I settled to figuring what I could do.

My chances were slim if Flanner's men trailed me down, as they would surely try to do. Despite what Talon said, I'd no doubt they could find this place, so I must find a better one . . . somewhere I could really hide.

My need for water tied me to the spring, so I commenced to study the ground, looking for someplace I could hide. There were tumbled boulders down the stream bed below the spring, and scattered branches of dead trees, piled-up rubble, and debris.

When I finished my stew, and mighty good it tasted, I took a long pull at a canteen and felt better.

Yet worry was upon me. There was weakness in me, and I'd an idea the worst was yet to come, that I might become so weak I could not move, even delirious. I'd seen men gunshot before this and knew my chances were slight if caught in a sudden shower with a fever upon me. And showers in the high peaks are a thing that happens almost every day.

I saw nothing that would help. No caves, no corners hidden from the wind . . . nothing.

Suppose I crawled into the saddle and made a try for the ranch? I'd never make it, of course. And my horse was not saddled now, and there was no way I could get a saddle on it. Yet there had to be a way.

Gathering my gear together, I rolled my bed, drank the last of the coffee, and using my rifle pulled and pushed myself up until I stood on one foot, clinging to an aspen. Inch by careful inch I searched the terrain. There was little I'd not seen in my few years and I knew about all that could happen to trees, brush, and rocks that would provide a place to hide, and I found none of it here.

Yet there was something nagging at me, something I should notice, something that worried at my mind like a ghost finger poking me. No way my thoughts took brought any clue to mind, and one by one I climbed the trees of my ideas and looked over the country around each of them. But I came upon nothing.

It came to me at last as I was hitching myself along from tree to tree toward the roan.

What I heard was a waterfall.

Chapter 13

Em Talon peered through the slats of the shutter toward the gate. Nothing in sight.

Logan should have returned by now. It was foolish of him to ride off as he had done, yet she knew how he felt, and she also subscribed to the theory that once you have an enemy backing up you must stay on top of him. "Never let them get set," she muttered.

The sky was overcast, the air still. Sullen clouds gave a hint of rain.

She went from window to window, checking the fastenings on the shutters. Pennywell had been up on the lookout atop the house and now she returned. "There's nobody, Aunt Em. The road's empty all the way to town."

"He should be back." She was talking half to herself. What would he have done? Riding in like that? She knew exactly, because it was what she would do. He had tackled them head on, horn to horn. Logan might not be the smartest Sackett there was but he was meaner than a cornered wolf, and he wasn't a back-shooter.

She pictured the town, tried to think out what he would do. And if wounded? He'd run for the hills. He would try to lead them off, like a wounded quail would do, anything to keep the enemy away from the nest. It was the instinctive response of a wild thing.

He would ride into the mountains, hunt him a hole, and wait until the time was right to come home. If he could get home.

That was the worrisome part, for he might be holed up yonder in the mountains, needing help, needing it the worst way. And the trouble was to pick up his trail a body would about have to pick it up from town, from Siwash.

Pennywell would be no good on a trail of that kind; besides, she was vulnerable. She was a young thing, and it would not do for her to be traipsing around the hills with the kind of men around that Flanner had brought into the country.

Al? She hesitated. He might be a good man on the trail, but he was new to this country, and trailing was more than a matter of following the sign a body found.

She did know the country, and she could read sign as good as any Sackett she knew of, which was better than most.

Em Talon made up her mind, and she made up her mind there was nothing to do but get ready. There was also a matter of time. She'd have to cut out from the ranch at a time when she'd not be seen, she'd have to get up there in the hills and find Logan.

She told them over breakfast. "I'll be gone a day or two. Al, you stay here an' take care of the place an' you watch over Pennywell."

"Ma'am," Al Fulbric protested, "you just cain't do that! You ain't a young woman, and those are mighty rough mountains."

"Of course, they're rough! That's why I like 'em. Son, I'm mountain born an' bred. I growed up walkin' the hills. I run a trap line before your mammy was born. As for these here hills, I've dodged Injuns all over them. I know the hideouts, and I know the mind of a dodging Sackett.

"We don't run just like other folks do, an' I know what Logan'll do, more than likely. You leave him to me. Just ketch me up that grulla mule out yonder—"

"Mule?"

"That's right. Him an' me been to the wars together, an' we can go again."

"If you say so, ma'am. A mule's not very fast."

"Neither am I. But I know that there mule and he'll take me there and bring me back, and that's what counts at my age, mister."

"Yes, ma'am. At any age."

Al walked out the back door and to the corral. He looked at the mule doubtfully and the mule looked at him. "I'd like to have this friendly," Al said. "It's the old lady's idea, not mine."

The mule put his ears back, and Al shook out a loop. He had tried to rope mules a few times, and had done it too . . . after a while. Most of them had a gift for ducking a rope., He walked out into the corral trailing his loop and studying the situation.

Behind him he heard Emily Talon. "You won't need that rope. Coley, come here!"

Without hesitation, the mule walked right to her. She fed him a carrot and slipped the halter on him while Al Fulbric gathered his rope.

"What was that you called him?"

"Coley . . . it's short for his name. Coleus. Talon named him, and Talon was a reader of the classics. The way he tells it, Coleus of Samos was the first Greek to sail out of the Mediterranean into the Atlantic."

"Well, I'll be! What did he want to do that for?"

"Seems some other folks—the Phoenicians, it was, who were some kin to the Philistines of the Bible—they had that whole end of the Mediterranean sewed up. They had laid claim to all that range, and they let nobody sail that way.

"This Coleus, he told them he got blown that way by a storm, and anyway he got through the Gates of Hercules and out into the Atlantic. And then he sailed up to Tartessus and loaded his ship with silver. That one trip made him a rich man.

"Talon favored him because he done the same. Folks said he was crazy to ride out here and start ranching in country only the Indians wanted. Anyway, Coley here, he had a way of straying into new pastures hisself, so Talon named him."

"I like it." Al Fulbric spat into the dust. "A man like that deserves credit."

"After that trip he never needed credit. He could afford to pay cash. Anyway, that's how Coley come by his name, and we've come a fur piece together, Coley an' me. We've been up the crick and over the mountain, and he'll fight anything that walks."

"That *mule?*"

"That mule, as you call him, was a jack once. They cut him, but they done forgot to tell him about it. He still figures he's a jack, and don't you borrow no trouble from him or he'll take a piece out of you."

Em Talon picked up her saddle and before Al could move to help her, had slung it in place and was cinching up. She slid her Spencer into the boot, then turned on him.

"Al, you go about your business now. I'm goin' to ride him astride, which no decent woman ought to do, but I'll have no man standin' by when I do it. You get to the house and keep a sharp lookout. They'll be a-comin', especially if they got Logan."

Al swore, spat into the dust, and walked off toward the house. When he reached the steps he turned to look back. Em was riding out toward the gate, and sure enough, she was sitting astride, and he could see a short stretch of her long-johns where they disappeared into her boot tops.

He blushed a little and turned his head away, ashamed for what he had seen. Pennywell was pouring coffee when he entered the house.

"She beats me," he said, "she really does. I'd have gone—"

"She'd not let you, and one thing I've learned about Em Talon, Al Fulbric, and that is that you get no place arguing with her. She's a notional woman, but the only notion she pays mind to is her own. When she sets her mind to something, you just stand clear."

Emily Talon was no longer young, but there was a toughness in her hard, lean body that belied its age. She had never been one to think in terms of years, anyway. A person was what they were, and many a man at forty was sixty in his ways and many another was twenty and would never grow past it.

As a small girl she had helped her father and brothers with their trap lines, and when she was ten she had one of her own. She was more familiar with the life of the forest than of the settlement, and riding away from the ranch she suddenly felt free, freer than she had felt in many a year.

She scouted back of the town, between Siwash and the hills. A Sackett hurt and hunted was a Sackett heading for the high up yonder. She knew their nature well for she was one of them . . . he would ride out and he would ride far.

As it was getting dark she came upon a trail, only it was two horses rather than one. Puzzled, she studied the tracks again. One of them had to be the roan . . . and the roan seemed to be led.

She squinted at the tracks warily, then looked all around. Nobody seemed to be watching, nobody seemed to have followed them, yet all hell must have torn loose down there in town.

Scouting farther she saw bunched tracks . . . seven or eight riders, not on the trail of the two, but hunting it.

She had to have more information, so she rode toward town. It was dark, and she was unlikely to be seen, but she knew where to go.

There had been a time when men had killed over Dolores Arribas, but the years had gone by and somehow she had found herself at the end of a trail in Siwash.

In her veins was the blood of Andalusia, but there was Indian blood, too, the blood of a people who built grandly in stone when Spain was only the hinterland of Tarshish.

She washed the clothes of the gringo but took no nonsense from him. Fiercely proud, she walked her own way in the town, unmolested, even feared.

Emily Talon knew that of all the people in Siwash, Dolores would know what had happened and that she would be willing to tell what she knew.

The mule picked his way delicately up the alleyway and around to the dark side of the stable. Em did not dismount, for Dolores Arribas was sitting on her steps in the cool of the evening, watching the clouds.

"You ride very late, Mrs. Talon." She spoke with only the trace of an accent.

"There was a shooting in town?"

"Yes. Two men are dead, two are wounded. One will die, I think." She spoke matter-of-factly, and then added, "They were Flanner's men."

"And he who done the shootin'?"

"There were two . . . one of them was Logan Sackett, but Jim Brewer was killed by another man, a stranger with a rifle, a tall, elegant man."

"Logan was hurt?"

"Yes . . . he was hit very hard . . . more than once. The other man took him away."

"I got to find them."

"You think you are the only one? Flanner looks for them, too. At least, his men look for him."

They were silent, and then Dolores suggested, "You would like a cup of tea? It is long, the way you will ride."

"I reckon. Yes, I'll take that tea."

She got down from the mule, spoke gently to it, and followed Dolores into the house. It was a small house, and even in the darkness she could feel its neatness.

"I will not make a light. The water is hot."

"Thank you."

They sat in the vague light, and Dolores poured the tea.

"Where are your sons?"

"I wish I knew. Milo, he's ridin' somewheres, but Barnabas, he went off to Europe, lived right fancy the way I hear tell. I always figured him for that, but wondered why he never wrote. Then I heard. Somebody passed word that I was dead and the place broken up."

"He would do that. It is like him."

"Flanner?"

"Of course. That way they might not bother to come back. What is there for anyone in Siwash? Except those of us who have no money with which to leave."

For a while they sat in silence, then Emily said, "If it's just money—"

"I earn my own money."

"Reckon so. Reckon you always will. I just figured that if a loan would help you to move out of this place, I could come up with it."

"Gracias. I do not think so. I will wait. Soon I will have enough, and then I shall go." She paused. "At least you were never one of those who tried to force me to go."

"No, I never was . . . nor was Talon." Emily Talon hesitated. "It was just that you were too popular, and a durned sight too much woman. They were afraid you'd take their men from them."

"I did not want them." She turned her head and looked at Em in the darkness. "You were not afraid?"

"Of Talon? No . . . one woman was all he ever wanted. One that was his own."

"You are right, but what of your son?"

"Milo? You mean you an' Milo?"

"Not Milo."

"Barnabas? I didn't think he had it in him."

"He was a good man, a fine man. I liked him. He was a gentleman."

"Thanks." Em got to her feet. "I got to be far back in the hills come daylight."

"Be careful. Jake Flanner will not care that you are a woman. Nor will most of the men he has now . . . they are scum."

"I know that Len Spivey. I . . ."

"Do not worry about him. He will not be one of them."

At the door Em paused, looking back. "Len Spivey?"

"Logan killed him. He was the first one."

Em went down the steps with care, then paused to look carefully about. At last she crossed the small yard to the mule. Dolores Arribas, standing in her doorway, heard the leather creak as she mounted.

"Mrs. Talon? I did not see it, but from what I heard I would swear that was Barnabas out there today."

Emily Talon waited a slow minute, wanting to believe it. "Barnabas?"

"He rode in at the right time. They'd have killed Sackett. Oh, he was making his fight, but he'd been hit hard and Jake Flanner himself was lining up for a shot and so was Brewer."

"And Barnabas fetched him?"

"He did. He took Brewer out, then turned his rifle, but Flanner was gone."

"That's Jake, all right. That's Jake Flanner."

"Yes, Mrs. Talon. So you be careful. Very, very careful. It is you they want, you know. Just you."

Emily Talon turned her mule toward the mountains. Barnabas was back. Her son was home again.

Chapter 14

Em Talon was a considering woman, and now she gave thought to Barnabas and his plight. He was riding into the mountains with a wounded man. He would need shelter, and he would need medical attention for Logan. The obvious place was the Empty, but if they had tried to cross the country between Siwash and the ranch they would have certainly been inviting death.

Hence they must have headed for the mountains, to lose themselves in the forest at the earliest possible moment.

Barnabas would undoubtedly try to reach the ranch, but he had never known the mountain trails as Milo had, and Logan might be in no condition to show him the trail he knew. Apparently Barnabas emerged from the gun battle uninjured, but there was no way she could be sure of that.

Talon had hunted and trapped these mountains years before any other white man he knew of, and part of that time Em had hunted with him. She knew trails where no trails seemed to be, and she knew those the buffalo used to find the mountain meadows.

When he was but ten years old she had once taken Barnabas with her into the mountains, showing him the lightning-blazed pine on the shoulder of the mountain that marked the opening of the trail to the crest of the ridge. It was likely he would remember that trail, for it had been their first trip into the mountains together, his first trip into the very high mountains. The mule's memory was good, for he had followed this trail many times and as soon as she turned him toward it, he knew where he was going.

It had changed, of course. The screen of brush that concealed the opening was thicker now, and the grove of young aspens had become sturdy trees in the passing of time, but the trail was there and she followed it swiftly. When she was well back in the forest she dismounted and screening the match with her hands, she studied the trail. There were two horses, one close behind the other, the second one probably led.

She made no attempt to guide the mule. It was almost too dark to see the trail under the trees and the mule could be trusted. At places they skirted the very rim of a canyon, a vast depth that fell away on one side. They climbed steadily.

At last, knowing she could go no farther without seeing their tracks, she got down from the mule at a place she knew. She had camped here before. There was fuel and shelter, and sounds from down the canyon carried easily to this point. Unsaddling the mule, she picketed it and wrapped it up in a blanket, leaning against the flat bole of a tree.

For a long time she remained awake looking at the stars through the trees and letting her tired muscles relax slowly to invite sleep. It was not as easy as it once was. She was old now, and her muscles grew stiff too early in the game. She thought ahead, trying to decide where Barnabas would be apt to stop.

Awakening, she watched a chipmunk nibbling at a seed he had found. For a moment she sat still just enjoying the gray light of morning. The air was damp, and she was surprised to observe that a light rain had fallen during the night without disturbing her.

She got up slowly, led the mule to the little trickle of water that came from a spring under the scarp, and dipped enough water for tea. Back at camp she kindled a fire and brewed a cup, drank it, and saddled up, listening to the sounds from down the canyon. She heard nothing, but she had not expected to. If there was pursuit it would come this morning, and by now they were breakfasting and arguing about what happened the night before. That would give her another hour's advantage.

Now she moved with greater care, studying the trail as the mule moved along. Usually she could pick up the sign well ahead—a track here, a bruised leaf there, the mark left by the edge of a shoe. They had been moving slower; obviously Barnabas was hunting a place to stop.

She rode into the cirque almost an hour later when the sun was halfway up the morning. It was right at timberline, the last of the growth giving way to the tumbled talus of broken rock that had broken off the walls and fallen down to mingle with the stunted growth and grass.

She found the place where the horses had cropped grass and crushed down grass and wild flowers where a bed had been.

One rider had ridden off by himself, leaving the other behind. That would be Barnabas heading for the Empty, which was hard to get to from here unless a body knew every twist of the trail.

But where was Logan Sackett?

She knew he had to be in bad shape, and a hunted man in bad shape would hunt a hole. He would want to be out of sight, and he would need water and a place for his horse. Em Talon scanned the country, studying every possible nook or corner tht might offer such a shelter. There were several possibilities but all came to nothing.

Logan Sackett had vanished.

Could he have followed Barnabas? It was a possibility. In any event there was one thing she could do. She could make a lot of tracks so those who might try to find him would not guess that he was hidden, as Em was quite sure he was.

Yet the cirque's high walls eliminated any possible way out on three sides. A rider or walker would have to go down the mountain. Mounting her mule again she also turned toward the open side of the cirque and walked the animal down the dim trail into the canyon.

White, slim aspens lined the trail on either side, their pale green leaves trembling slightly. Due to some quirk of temperature or wind currents this grove was higher on the mountain's slope than the aspen was usually found. The grove was littered with the long dead trunks of fallen trees, remnants of some old landslide or snowslide. She was well into the grove when she heard a sound of horses.

Drawing rein, she listened below her, below on the trail she had herself followed into the cirque.

A moment later they came into view. There were eight men, all tough men by their look. The man in the lead was Chowse Dillon, occasional cowpuncher, occasional outlaw, consistent troublemaker. They were no more than a hundred and fifty yards right down the hill, a hill too steep for a horse to climb except on the switch-back trail they followed. Yet by the trail they must follow they were a half mile away.

Em lifted her rifle and put a bullet into the dust about a foot in front of Dillon's horse. Most of the riders were undoubtedly on broncs— she had counted on that. The sudden *spat* of the bullet as well as the thunder of the heavy rifle in the confinement of the rock walls was enough.

Dillon's horse reared straight up, spinning halfway around to bump the horse behind. Instantly horses were buck-jumping all over the narrow trail and one of the horses went over the edge, rider and all, rolling into the trees and deadfalls below.

Two men unlimbered their six-guns and shot into the trees where she was, but they were shooting blind and hit nothing. The shooting only added to the confusion. Emily Talon rode calmly on down the trail she had been following, leaving them cursing and fighting their horses.

The trail was never more than four or five feet wide. Somebody was up there with a rifle and willing to dispute the trail, and nobody was eager to be the first to accept the challenge.

Yet she had ridden scarcely a quarter of a mile, winding down a steep trail, when she picked up the first sign since leaving the cirque. It was the white scar left by a glancing blow from a shoe, and it was fresh! She tried listening for the horses of the men she had seen on the trail but she could hear nothing but the tumbling waters of a nearby fall.

Em Talon did not like the place. She did not like any place that drowned the sounds from her ears. She wanted to hear . . . she needed to hear.

The falls was about eight feet wide, a fairly thin sheet of water except at bottom where it plunged among some boulders and slabs of rock. There it was a thick white burst of foaming water that then plunged off down the mountain in a series of steep cascades.

At the top of the falls trees leaned over the stream, and near the base was a mass of fallen timber, trees washed down from above, some of them with masses of roots, leaving a veritable maze.

Emily Talon contemplated her situation. Somewhere up the mountain behind her were several of Jake Flanner's men, and down at the ranch Barnabas, the son she had not seen in years, was returning home or trying to. Neither Pennywell or Al knew him, and they were just as apt to shoot as not.

Suddenly Em decided there was but one thing to do. She had to get off the mountain and back to the Empty. If Logan was anywhere about he was well hidden, too well hidden to be found while she herself was hunted. She hesitated a moment, but the mule was tugging at the reins, wanting to go on down the mountain, and she gave in.

At that moment she was less than seventy yards from Logan Sackett and he was looking right at her, trying to call. But he was too weak. His hoarse shouts could not be heard above the noise of the falls. Em Talon rode on.

Chapter 15

There I lay, weak as a cat and scarce able to crawl, and I seen that ol' woman draw up there and look down toward me. She was lookin' right square into my eyes, only I was behind the falls and could not be seen. I tried to yell out, but I could scarce make a sound louder than a frog croaking, and she heard nothing.

That she was huntin' me I had no doubt, and in the shape I was in I dearly wanted to be found. Yet she kept turning to look back up the trail and that made me wonder. A short time back I'd been asleep and something waked me. It could have been a shot, although behind that falls even a shot was muffled. Yet something on her back trail worried her, and she rode on.

Looked to me like I'd covered all sign, all right, but I'd done it too durned well. There was every chance I'd die right here, and nobody would find me or know what happened. Well, I'd not be the first western man that happened to. Many a man rode off them days and never came back . . . there was a sight of things could happen to a man that had nothing to do with guns or Indians or anything like that.

A man could get throwed from his horse and die of thirst, or he could drown swimming a river, get caught in a flash flood, fall off a cliff, get bit by a rattler or a hydophoby skunk, or cut himself with an ax. A lot of men them days traveled alone and worked alone, and if they had an accident that could be the end of them.

I'd known of three men who amputated their own legs, and a half dozen who had trimmed fingers off their own hands. There wasn't no medical corps around like there'd been during the war . . . a body just had to make out as best he could.

Now this place I'd found wasn't the only one like it. When water falls off a ledge a certain amount of it just naturally kicks back against the wall, and after years have passed that water wears away the rock slow or fast depending on the force of the water and the softness of the rock. Sometimes it will wear away until with the river cutting down from above it cuts through the rock. Then the flow will go under what had been the rim, leaving a natural arch.

The space behind the falls is often small, and in this case it wasn't far from the year when the riverbed would drop. In other words, I'd lucked out. There'd been a sight more space back there than I reckoned.

Nor was I the first to use it. Pack rats had been back there, and judging by some old droppings, a bear had holed up there one time. Getting to it had been a puzzle, but I'd found a way through the maze of old tree trunks, broken branches, hanging streamers of torn bark, and the like, and I led my horse right into it.

That horse didn't much care for it at first, but after a bit he settled down. I was all in, and I dragged my gear into a corner back from the water and laid myself out. By dark I was in bad shape. I felt hot all over and my mouth was dry. I had me something of a fever and knew I was in trouble, bad trouble.

When I saw Em I tried to call out, but she heard nothing and rode on. I was still watching when the first of the riders came into sight. They were almighty cautious, and there was eight of them. Only one of them glanced toward the falls, and he didn't seem much interested.

After a bit they rode on. I crawled back after getting a drink and passed out on my blankets.

When I came out of it again it was dark night and all I could hear was the steady roar of the falls. For a time I lay there just staring up into the darkness. My mouth was bone dry and I desperately needed a drink but lacked the energy to get over to the falls. I probably would have lay still like that forever, but it was thinking of my horse that got me to move. That horse needed to be let loose. He'd had water but nothing to eat in hours, and I might die right here with that horse tied up.

After a while I rolled over and kind of eased myself to my knees and crawled to the water. I drank and drank, and then I crawled to the horse and, catching hold of a stirrup, I pulled myself up and untied the bridle reins. Then I tied them loosely to the pommel. "You go ahead, boy," I said hoarsely. "You go on home."

You know that horse wasn't about to go? He stayed right there until I led him to the trail's opening and hit him a slap across the rump. Even then he lingered, but I'd slumped down beside the rocks. The last thing I'd done was to swing my saddlebags off the horse and let them fall to the ground.

After the horse had gone I sort of crawled back to my bed and let go of everything. It was gray light with dawn when I first opened my eyes again and I lay there knowing I had to do something. I had to think it out first, then make every move count so that my strength would last. First thing was to get a fire going. The next thing to heat water, bathe my wounds, and make some coffee. There was almighty little in my saddlebags but there might be enough to help.

There was no end of dry wood back of that fall. Some of it was driftwood, but the pack rat's nest was a bundle of dry stuff right at hand. Bundling some of it together I struck a light and got a fire going. It looked almighty good just to have it there, and once it got started I just sort of lay there and stared at it.

After a while I got into my saddlebag and got out an old pint cup I'd been toting around for years. I put water into it and then dumped in some coffee and let it come to a boil. When it had boiled enough to have body to it, I taken it off the fire and sipped a little here and there, trying not to burn my lips. That coffee surely hit the spot, and I started to perk up. After I'd emptied the cup, I boiled more water in it and set to work on those wounds I'd picked up.

Being a big, healthy sort of man I could shed hurts as well as most, better than a lot. I'd lost blood a-plenty, but what I needed now was to check out those wounds for infection. And there seemed to be none. When I'd bathed them pretty well and done the best I could dressing them, I laid back on my blankets and was soon asleep.

When I awakened I felt better. But I was worried about Em Talon. I was fearful that she'd not gotten home safe, and worried about those eight men back-trailing my horse. When that horse came up to the ranch they would think surely I was dead. Barnabas knew where he'd left me, but Em had been right there and she would have found nothing.

I checked over my guns and made ready for trouble, if trouble came. And of one thing I could be sure—where I was, trouble was not far away, dogging my heels all the way to perdition.

It was cold and damp, and for a few minutes I lay still just thinking and listening. My mouth was dry, and I felt almighty hot and tired. Although I was feeling better than I had the night before, there was just no strength in me, not even to build me a fire. I just lay there, staring into the half darkness of the cave and wondering whether I'd ever get out of there alive. Right then I wouldn't have bet any money on it.

I could hear no sound above the tumbling water, and soon I dozed off again. When I awoke I was hot and dry like before, only more so.

My mite of fire had gone out long ago and I poked sticks together and got hold of some old, dry bark from one of them; crumbling it in my hands and striking a match I coaxed a little flame to burning again.

For a while I just poked sticks into the blaze and tried to get some coals, then I put some coffee into the cup again and when it was brewed, I drank it down. Just having something hot inside me felt good.

By now most of them must have figured me for dead. I guessed I had been holed up a couple of days and nights, although it could be longer. I had to get out of this place. I had to get out in the sunlight and the air, and I had to get myself some grub. Without a horse I was going to play hob gettin' anywhere, but I could surely try. If I was to die I wanted to be out in the fresh sunlight and under the trees.

It taken some time, but I rolled my blankets, taken up my guns, and crawled for the opening, dragging my gear along.

When I first got into the air everything looked wrongside to. It was morning time and I had been sure it was afternoon. Somewhere I'd lost some time . . . a day was it, or two days? By the way my stomach felt it might have been a week.

I studied the trail that I crawled along and I found no tracks. It had rained since I'd come in, but that wasn't surprising as in the high-up mountains it can rain every afternoon and often enough does just that. Whatever tracks there might have been were washed out, and I found the same thing on the regular trail when I got to it—that trail Em had followed showed nothing at all of her mule, those who chased her, or me.

Using the low limbs of a tree I pulled myself up, favoring myself not to open my wounds, and I hitched along the trail, making no effort to hurry. I just wanted to move along. Where I was headed I surely had no idea, only I was going to come down off the mountain to where I could get some better grub.

I taken rest a-plenty, but by the time an hour was passed I'd made more'n a half mile. The river was off to my left, and a mite of a stream was flowing in from the right to join it. I stopped, laying flat out on the grass, and drunk my fill. Then I hobbled on again.

Once, afar off, I seen a deer. And a couple of times grouse flew up, or some bird resembling them. Marmots, of course, were there wherever I came up to a rock pile of some sort. After a while I just couldn't make it any farther and I moved back into the trees and found a place at the edge of a small clearing where I could stretch out in the sun. When I'd rested there awhile, I started on, keeping off the trail and taking time a-plenty. Little by little I worked my way along the mountainside toward the higher meadows back of the ranch.

The easiest way had been to follow along the steep side of the canyon and gradually work my way down. I couldn't travel but a little way without stopping to rest, and nobody was going to see me unless they were looking over into the canyon. Pretty soon the sides grew steeper and I made my way down to the streambed.

It was lucky I did so because the walls became sheer, white rock cut with many places where water had run off or with deep cracks. At the bottom the stream ran almost bank to bank, but there was an edge of sand or gravel that I could work my way along so that I only had to enter the water occasionally for a few steps.

There was a lot of driftwood, logs and such, washed down by the flash floods that happen in mountain country. After a ways I commenced to get awful tired but there was no place to set down. Suddenly I came upon a kind of gap in the wall. It was half filled with trees and such, but beyond it I could see a patch of green that had to be a meadow.

Crawling over the brush in the mouth of the canyon I found myself with a meadow stretching away before me, but I had to wade through marsh to get to dry land. Ahead of me were a bunch of grass-grown hummocks that were old beaver ponds, and higher I could see the still water of beaver ponds that likely had beavers in them yet.

Off to one side there was a grove of aspen, for the beaver never live very far from them. I sat down on a log just inside that aspen grove.

I was beat. My side ached and there was a weakness on me like I'd never felt before. I needed a camp and place where I could lie down and be safe, but the shape I was in I wasn't up to looking around. So I just sat there watching the light change. Huge billows of cloud lifted high above the mountains catching the last light. Slowly I began to peel flakes of thin, very dry bark from a long dead aspen; then I moved off the log with an effort and I began putting a little fire together.

Leaning my rifle against a tree I started cutting evergreen boughs for a bed. The heavy six-shooter on my leg weighted me down, and after a bit I taken it off and hung it on a low branch. Then I went on cutting boughs, rigging me a halfway shelter there in the aspens. Limping back, and nearly played out, I bent over to replenish the fire. I added a few sticks, dropping to one knee to do it. My breath was coming short and my head was dull and heavy. I started to rise when I heard the footfall on the moss. Just as I started to turn something hit me.

I started to fall, grabbing for my six-shooter, but it was gone. Through a haze of pain I could see the legs of several horses. I tried to get up.

"Hit him." It was Jake Flanner's voice. "Make a job of it."

Something did hit me again, and this time I fell flat out on the leaves and grass. And they hit me again and again, only there was no more pain, just the sodden brutality of the blows. The first blow had stunned me, leaving me only a shell.

Somebody kicked me in the side and I felt the warm flow of blood where the wound was torn open. My hand reached out but there was nothing to lay hold of, and after a time I passed out.

It was the rain brought me out of it. A drenching downpour that came down in buckets. The rain brought me to consciousness and to realization of pain, but I did not move. I simply laid there, unable to move, while the rain poured down, soaking me through and through. After a while I passed out again.

They believed they'd killed me for sure this time. That was my first thought, and it stayed with me. Maybe they were right. Maybe I was already dead. Maybe I was dead and this was hell.

I was wet, soaked through, but it was no longer night. It was coming up to morning although there was no sun as yet. As I lay there I began to remember other things. They had shot into me as I lay on the ground. I recalled the roar of the guns and remembered a burning stab of pain. There had been at least three shots . . . funny, how I remembered that.

If they had done that, how was I even alive? How could I realize anything at all? How could I feel? And I did feel. I felt pain, I felt weariness. I felt like just lying there to be finished with my dying. Trouble was, I was mean. Too many folks wanted me dead for me to go out of my way to please them. I opened my eyes and lay there looking at some sodden green-brown leaves and the wet trunk of a tree.

No matter what they'd done or tried to do I was still alive. I knew what was happening to me and a man who can feel is a man who can fight. It just wasn't in me to die there like a dog in the brush without getting some of my own back. Jake Flanner had come after me himself. He'd brought help, but he'd come. And now I was going after him. I'd no idea what happened down there in the valley at the Empty. Nor right at this moment did I care much. I was an animal fighting for life and I tried to roll over to get my hands under me.

I done it. It wasn't easy. I couldn't move at all on one side so I turned over, mighty careful, the other way. I got one hand under me and I pushed up until I could drag a knee up.

As I got to one knee I realized my shirt was stuck to my side where I'd been shot before. I'd been kicked there, right where my wound was, and it had bled some. All right, so I'd lost blood. I'd lost it before this, and a-plenty. They wasn't gettin' no maiden when they tried to bleed me.

I caught hold of an aspen and pulled myself up. By that time there was light enough for me to see what they'd done to me, and it was a-plenty. My shirt front was stiff with dried blood, and so was the side of it. On my left side I found a fresh bullet hole from front to back. The bullet had gone through a place where my shirt bagged out to one side, going clean through without so much as scratching me. I had a fresh scratch atop my shoulder, and I had bruises all over from the blows and kicks. On my skull I had a fresh cut and a couple of lumps.

Oh, they'd laid it to me proper, only being down like I was, lying on soft ground and grass, some of the shock had been taken from the blows. Most of it I had taken, and so I was sore outside as well as inside.

If they'd hunted for my guns in the dark they surely hadn't found them, for there they were—the rifle had fallen from the tree where I'd leaned it and was lying on the wet grass, but the pistol still hung from the stub of a branch where I'd hung it the night before when all weighted down.

My head was throbbing like a big drum, my stomach was hollow and I was weak, but there was a mad on me like nothing I'd ever felt before. Looking around I saw some broken branches, all seasoned and gray from exposure, and out of one of them and a crosspiece of green aspen I fashioned myself a crutch to spare my wounded leg. Then with my six-gun belted on and my Winchester in my good hand, I started off along that trail those riders had left.

It was plain to see where they were going. They were riding down on the back of the Empty, and they were going in for a kill. They had a lead on me, but it wasn't so much. Where they went, I could follow.

My clothes was torn and I looked a sight, but nobody offered me no beauty prizes at any time, so I kept on. My jaw had a healthy growth of whiskers, caked with mud and blood. My hair likewise. Somewhere back along the way I'd lost my hat, and my bloody shirt was ripped in a couple of places, but I was mean as a cornered razorback hog and I was hunting blood.

Here and there at a place where they had to do a switch-back descent, being a-horseback, I just sat down and slid, saving myself some time a-travelin'.

By noontime I could read their sign enough to see I was closing in. They'd stopped a while to wait for sunup, not knowing the trail or what they faced, so I'd gained a mite. As I edged up to the back meadows I expected to hear gunshots, but I heard nothing at all, and that worried me. I didn't want them killing Em Talon, and I knowed that was what they had in mind. And if they killed her there must be no witnesses so they'd kill that girl I'd taken there for shelter. And that was my affair, all mine.

That crutch was sawing into my armpit, making it sore, but I'd no choice. When I slid and crawled down through the rocks near the ranch, I still heard no sound. I could see the horses down in the corral and mine was there. So he'd found his way home, all right. The horse Barnabas rode was there also. He'd gotten into the place alive . . . or at least his horse had.

I'd come to that point of rocks up behind the place and to one side. It was a raw-backed ridge, covered with broken slabs of tilted rocks, a lot of brush, and some scattered pines. There were a thousand hiding places or shelters on that ridge and I could look right into the corrals and yard without being seen . . . I hoped.

The sunlight lay easy upon the yard. The shadows lay where they ought to lie, and the horses lazed in the corrals. There was no sign of horses that shouldn't be there.

I couldn't make it out.

By rights Flanner and his men should have arrived and should have attacked the place. Right now there should be a fight . . . or else Flanner had already taken over. But where were their horses?

It was almost midafternoon and there should be some sign of life around the place. But still nobody showed. With four people on the place somebody should be moving around.

I lay quiet in the brush and studied all the cover around. Maybe the Flanner outfit had moved in, opened fire, and now were waiting, just as I was, for somebody to make a move.

Then I saw something that didn't figure. On the back steps there was a dark patch where no shadow fell. Water would have evaporated in the time I'd been lying there, at least enough of it so's I couldn't see the stain. Water would, but blood wouldn't.

That there was a blood stain.

My side was throbbing so I wrinkled my forehead against it, scowling and squinting. My side was stiff and my whole body was sore. I eased myself down among the rocks, taking a look back and up from time to time. A body can't be too careful, I told myself. Meanwhile I kept my rifle up and ready. Still no move.

Were they all dead? Every last one of them? It didn't seem likely.

But maybe the men were inside now, abusing Em and the rest. That started me worrying, and I figured I had to get down there. Yet suppose they were deliberately keeping quiet, expecting an arrival?

Me?

They'd left me for dead, and if they hadn't believed me dead they'd not have left me at all.

Who, then?

Or was I figurin' it wrong, all wrong?

And while I waited somebody down there might be dead or dying, somebody who depended upon me.

Chapter 16

The black appaloosa with the splash of white over the right hip had a dainty, dancing step. Even the miles that lay behind had taken none of the spirit from the gelding and he tossed his head at the restraint of the bit, eager to be off and running.

The rider sat erect, holding the reins easy in his hand, a dark and handsome young man whose what-the-hell sort of smile was in odd contrast to the coolness of his eyes.

There had been changes made. Siwash had grown a little, as he could see even from a distance, and despite his seeming ease he rode with cautious eyes on the country. It was unlikely he would be remembered by many . . . quite a few years had passed.

How had Logan Sackett ever gotten into this country? He was a drifter, of course, and his kind might light anywhere. It was odd, now that he thought of it, that he and Logan, who had been friends, might also be kin. He always thought of ma as Em or Mrs. Talon. Somehow he had forgotten she was also a Sackett.

The word had been to avoid Siwash and come right to the ranch, but if trouble lay in Siwash he'd be damned if he'd ride around it.

He stopped in a hollow where the trail passed through an arroyo, and dismounting, brushed off his clothes with care. He combed his hair by running his fingers through it, whipped the dust from his hat, then stepped back into the saddle and rode into Siwash.

Several people saw him ride into Siwash, and one of them was Dolores Arribas. Another was Con Wellington.

Dolores looked once and knew him; Con looked, then looked again. Con swore softly to himself. Logan Sackett and now Milo Talon. Things were looking up around town and he might soon be back in business. One of them—even if Logan was dead, as they believed—

would be bad enough, but there was that slim young fellow with the rifle who pulled Sackett out of the soup, and now this one.

Jake Flanner should have left the Empty alone.

Johannes Duckett saw Milo Talon ride in, ride past his livery stable, and tie his horse at the hitch rail. Duckett looked long at that horse. No cowhand could afford a horse like that. Even in this country where there were many horses, such a horse could not be had for love or money.

The rider stepped down and went into the saloon, opening the door with his left hand. Johannes, who knew most of the riders along the outlaw trail at least by name, furrowed his brow with thought. Who was this man? And why was he here? Any outsider might be somebody Jake had sent for, like he had sent for others. The fact that he had gone right to the saloon without putting up his horse might be an indication. Yet it might be otherwise, and Johannes Duckett took up his rifle and walked across the street to the saloon. He entered and went to the bar, keeping the stranger on his left. In his right hand he held his rifle. Johannes Duckett had big, strong hands and he could handle a rifle as easily as a pistol, and often had.

Milo Talon walked right to the bar. "Rye," he said gently, "an honest rye, from the good bottle."

The bartender glanced at him and switched from one bottle to the other under the bar. "Yes, sir," he said. "The good rye. Ain't no better drink," he added.

He waited a minute, let Milo Talon taste his drink, and then said, "Travelin'?"

"Passin' through," Milo said politely. "Ridin' down to Brown's Hole."

"Know the place." The bartender was thoughtful. "Late in the season for much ridin' down thataway. The boys will be pullin' their freight or settlin' down for the winter."

"Maybe I'll do the same," Milo said. He downed the rye, then pointed with his middle finger to a table. "Whatever you have to eat, set it up for me over there . . . the best you have."

"Yes, sir." The bartender looked at him, hesitated, and glanced at the bar. He had seen no money. "These times, when I don't know a man the boss expects cash on the barrel head."

"And rightly so." Milo pointed again with his middle finger. "Over there, and I'm right hungry."

He went outside the door where there was a barrel of water, a wash basin, and soap and towel and washed his hands. When he came in again the bartender was putting food on the table.

Milo sat down, glanced briefly at the long, quiet man at the bar and at the rifle he carried. The man had not ordered a drink. He just stood there, seemingly looking at nothing.

The door opened and two dusty riders walked in and to the bar. "The boss wants you to fix him a hamper of grub. Make it for two days."

"All right." The bartender glanced at Milo, who was eating quietly, showing no interest in the proceedings.

Milo glanced up. "Better make it a week's supply," he said gently. "When a man's travelin' an' used to good grub he'll miss it. And he's got a long way to go."

There was a momentary pause, then all eyes turned toward Milo, who contined to eat.

"What's that?" Chowse Dillon turned around. "Who put a nickel in you?"

Milo Talon smiled. "Free advice, offered freely. When a man starts on a long trip he'd better go provided for it. I've always heard that Jake Flanner liked the good things of life. Pack that hamper, bartender, and pack a little grub for those boys, too."

"You tryin' to be funny?"

Milo smiled again. "Of course not, but on a long trip—"

"Nobody said anything about a long trip!" Dillon said irritably.

"Oh, yes, they did. You weren't listening. I mentioned a long trip." Milo finished his coffee and put the cup down gently. "Free advice, freely given. Travel is broadening, gentlemen, and my advice is for you, Mister Flanner, and all concerned to broaden themselves considerably, starting as soon as possible."

They did not know what to make of him. Dillon felt he should be angry but the stranger's manner was mild and he did not seem in the least offensive. Yet there was something in his manner . . . and the fact that he was obviously a seasoned rider.

"I don't know what you're gettin' at," Dillon said. "You're talkin' a lot but you ain't sayin' much."

"Then I shall put it more directly." Milo spoke quietly. "You've been stirring up trouble with the Empty, and we don't like it. So the fun's over, and all you boys who depend on Mister Flanner for a living had better rattle your hocks out of here."

There was a moment of silence. Duckett looked into his glass and said nothing; Dillon was taken aback by the calmness of this stranger, and worried by it. A lot had been happening that he did not like. First there was that other stranger who had pulled in to bail Logan Sackett out of his trouble, and now this man. How many more would there be? When Jake Flanner hired him he had promised it would be an easy job . . . no trouble at all, nobody but an old lady.

Dillon turned to Milo. "You're takin' in a lot of territory, mister. Just who might you be?"

"Milo Talon. Em's my ma, and you boys been makin' trouble for her."

Chowse Dillon was worried. He was no gunfighter, although he'd had a hand in a half dozen shootings, and he had pushed his weight around here and there, mostly against nesters. But there was something about this he did not like at all.

"There's only one of you," Chowse said, trying for a bluff. "You're buckin' a stacked deck."

"Stacked decks don't always turn up the cards a body would expect," Talon said mildly, "especially when I've got all the aces. I didn't come in here to lose anything, and if you'll recall, I opened the game. Of course," he straightened from the bar, "if you boys want to see what I'm holding you'll have to ante up, and the chips are bullets . . . forty-fives, to be exact.

"I'm betting," he said easily, "that I can deal them just a mite faster than you boys can, and without braggin', boys, I can say I ain't missed anything this close since who flunk the chunk."

The bartender was in the line of fire and the bartender had no stake in the game. He worked for Flanner, who paid him well and on time, but a corpse spends no wages. He cleared his throat. "Chowse," he said, "Milo Talon ain't lyin'. What you do is your own affair, but this man is hell on wheels with a pistol. I've heard of him."

Chowse had made up his mind not to push. There were other times, and he could afford to wait. This might be a job for Johannes Duckett, and not for him or the others. Duckett could do it, and he would tell him as much.

There was a coolness about the features of Milo Talon that Chowse did not care for, a coolness somehow belied by the recklessness of his eyes. Chowse Dillon was a stubborn man but he was not an overly brave one. He was dangerous enough when the advantage was his or when backed into a corner, but he had not survived this long without some knowledge of men, and if he read Milo Talon right he was not only a man who would be quick to shoot, but one who would look right into a man's eyes, laugh at him, and shoot him dead.

"I am not goin' to call you," Dillon said. "That's Flanner's affair, if he wants it. If he sends me against you, I'll come, but nothing was said about you."

"He didn't know about me," Milo replied. "Jake Flanner made his bets without having any idea what Em was holding." He chuckled. "Why, ma could whip the lot of you, guns or any other way. You boys just be glad she had that place to watch over and hadn't a free hand to come after you. When I was knee high to a short sheep I saw ma send a bunch of Kiowas packin' . . . and they carried their dead with them."

He stood back from the bar. "Sorry I can't wait to meet Flanner right now, but I'll be back." He paused. "Any of you boys seen Logan Sackett?"

"He's dead." Dillon said it with satisfaction. "Killed right out there in the street. He done tried to take the whole town by himself. And he's dead."

"Where's he buried?"

Dillon's smile faded. "Some other gent who came along helped him off to the hills, but he had lead enough in him to sink a battleship. Come to think of it, that other gent favored you, only he wore store-bought clothes, like a tenderfoot."

"He was no tenderfoot," Milo replied as he backed toward the door. "That was my brother, Barnabas. I've seen him cut the earlobes from a man at two hundred yards with a Winchester."

He smiled again. "Well, well! Barney is back! Looks to me like you boys bought trouble wholesale! My advice was good," he added from the door, "travel is downright healthy. You boys pull your freight or we'll be back into town to hang everyone among you who isn't killed by bullets."

And then he added, "And don't you count no Sackett dead until you've thrown the dirt on him. I've seen Logan so ballasted with lead you'd never believe a man could carry it and live. But he's alive, which is more than I can say for those who shot him up."

He stepped into the saddle, eyed the door, then gave a quick glance up and down the street. Con Wellington was standing up the street, watching. Con lifted a hand, and Milo waved in return, then rode swiftly from town.

Milo Talon was no fool. He knew what Flanner was attempting, knew also some of the hatred that welled up within the man, and knew he would not easily call it quits. And sheer numbers were always an advantage. He could afford to lose men and still send more into the fight . . . men of that stamp were not hard to find, and there were always renegade Indians.

If Logan Sackett was hurt and holed up in the hills, he must find him. Despite his claims to the contrary ma could not have held out alone for long. It was Logan who had saved her and saved the ranch as well.

The road to the ranch had changed little. Longingly, he waited for his first glimpse of the old house, and when it came he sighed deeply, excited to see it, to find it still standing. He had heard his mother was dead and the land scattered among many owners, but now he knew that story must have been started by Flanner himself in an attempt to keep them away by offering no reason to come back.

Johannes Duckett had stood very quietly at the bar, his beer resting on the polished surface, scarcely tasted. He had listened to Milo Talon, keeping his eyes averted after that first glance. When Milo backed to the door and went out he made no attempt to follow, for he was thinking back to his first days with Jake Flanner.

Flanner had not hired Duckett, merely suggested they ride on together, and Duckett, essentially a lonely man, had done so. Flanner was a talker, an easy, gracious talker who won most of his battles with his smooth tongue. Somehow Flanner always had money, and Duckett, who had more often than not lived from hand to mouth, had found it easier to just ride along with Flanner. Soon Flanner was suggesting things he might do, and Duckett had done them. Occasionally Flanner had said, "Here, you must be short of cash," and then had handed him a twenty, a half dozen twenties, or whatever. Johannes Duckett found himself living better than he had ever lived, and found himself with more ready cash than ever before.

Flanner had not noticed, although he would not have cared, that Johannes Duckett had few needs, but he would have been surprised at the quiet little hoard Duckett had accumulated. A man with few or no wants and a fairly steady flow of cash can gather together a nice sum, and Johannes Duckett accumulated several thousand dollars of which nobody was aware. Neither did they know where Duckett kept it hidden.

Duckett was a lean, quiet man whom some of the hands around Siwash did not consider overly smart. Others who knew him better did believe him smart, but the fact was that the thoughts of Johannes Duckett moved narrowly in only a few deeply grooved channels. He had no particular feelings about good and evil, but he had his own odd compulsions and beliefs. No amount of money or argument could have brought him to kill a child, yet he would have killed a woman without the slightest hesitation, and he had killed several. He had no moral or religious feelings about this, nor could he have explained why he did any of the things he did. He simply had no more scruples about killing a human being than about shooting a snake or a coyote.

He had no loyalty for Jake Flanner, although Flanner believed Duckett followed him from nothing but loyalty. Jake had provided a kind of traveling companion that Duckett liked. He liked Flanner's smooth-talking ways and he liked that Flanner made his life easier. Also, Duckett had decided that Jake Flanner was shrewd . . . he was a winner. And Johannes wanted to be associated with a winner.

Now for the first time he had doubts.

The doubts began when he looked at the great house on the MT. To him it was awesome, astonishing. It seemed impregnable. Emily Talon had seemed the same. In the time before the shooting started he had seen her on the trail or in Siwash and there was something about the gaunt old woman that shook him. When she looked at him he averted his eyes, and had she reason for scolding him he would have stood quietly and accepted it.

Yet he was not one to argue. Had Flanner been less full of his own plans he would have seen that Johannes Duckett was hesitant. Yet the battle had begun, and the time drew on with no decision in view. From time to time Duckett heard gossip around the town about Milo Talon and his brother. A vague feeling of unease worked itself into those deeply channeled furrows within his brain, and for the first time he grew restless.

"Ever been to the western slope?" he asked Flanner once.

"What? No . . . I never have been." Flanner was irritated. "What brought that up?"

"It's a good country, so they say. There's a place named Animas City. Down in a big park around the Animas River."

"We've got enough to do right here," Flanner replied. "Why ride away from a sure thing?"

"Is it?"

Jake Flanner was startled. He had become so accustomed to Duckett's ready acceptance of any of his ideas that the comment startled him. "Of course, it is. Once that old woman is out of there we've got the finest setup ever. We'll just move in, and——"

"There's more of them now. There's that girl, and there's Logan

Sackett, and now there's that one with the rifle who helped Logan, and some of the boys say there's another man out there."

"Look, Duck, I wouldn't be in this if I didn't know we can win and win big. When the time comes that girl will just go off by herself or one of the boys will take her. And Logan Sackett's dead. No man can soak up the lead he caught without dying. Why he must have been hit seven or eight times, and as for that other one, I think he caught some lead, too."

"You want to kill that old lady because she busted your knees."

Flanner's face grew red with anger. He stared at Duckett. "All right," he said softly, "I do . . . and I will. But that's beside the case. It is the place we want."

Duckett listened but his thoughts were on this other man . . . Milo Talon. Duckett talked little but he listened a lot, and he knew more about Milo Talon than any other person in Siwash. He knew, for example, that Milo was a lone wolf, that he was amazingly swift and accurate, and that even men known as dangerous avoided him.

The odds were piling up. From now on every shot fired would increase the risk, as there were more people to fire back. Johannes Duckett's thinking was simple. He knew that two and two made four. He also knew that where there had been one old woman on the place in the beginning, although even then some suspected there were more, there were now two women and probably four men, for he had not for a moment accepted Logan Sackett's death. Hurt, maybe, but not dead. Johannes Duckett counted the dead when he saw the bodies.

The odds had risen, and who was to say they would not continue to rise? Sackett was one of the feudal clans from Tennessee . . . who was to say the others might not ride in?

For the first time Duckett doubted the sagacity of Jake Flanner. For the first time he began to think of that money he had put away. He had enough to live as he lived for a year, perhaps two . . . and two years was an almost immeasurable distance in the day-to-day living of Johannes Duckett.

"I'm going to ride," he told himself.

Once formulated, the idea established itself in its own groove and began to develop.

Jake Flanner would have been surprised to discover that to Johannes Duckett he, Jake Flanner, meant no more than a horse Duckett might have ridden for a time. He had been a convenience over the last few years, but no more than that.

Flanner believed Duckett to be loyal to the death. Duckett considered Flanner a source of income . . . and now that source of income was endangered.

And, of course, there was the western slope of the Rockies.

Chapter 17

My mouth was dry and my head was hot—the trip down the mountain had taken a lot out of me. I crouched there among the rocks and brush and studied the layout below. I still couldn't make it out.

That spot on the back step was blood, sure as shootin'. Somebody had caught one there, and I was praying it wasn't the old woman or Pennywell. Search as I might I couldn't find anybody hid out, but they'd be hard to find until they moved . . . if they were there.

I'd lost a lot of blood and from the way I felt I knew I was worse off than I'd thought. A couple of times there my eyes kind of glazed over until I couldn't see except through a mist. Leaning over I rested my arm on a boulder and my head on my arm. My breathing was hoarse and rasping and I was sick.

Nothing moved down below, and I must have passed out there for a few minutes. When I came out of it I was still there, my head resting on that rock, but I felt like I was dying. That made me mad.

Die? With that old lady in trouble? With that girl I'd brought to the house in danger because of me? With my friend's ma down there, maybe about to get killed? And yes, I'll sure be honest with myself—a whole lot of the reason I was mad and surely determined to live was Jake Flanner. I could hear his voice again, tellin' them to do me in. All right, Jake, I said to myself. You want Logan Sackett dead. You want him dead but you're going to have to go all the way to make it happen.

So I forced my head up and slid down to a better way of sittin'; through that brush, I watched the house. Below me I could see a sort of slide through the rocks. It was too steep to walk down, but a man lyin' flat on his back could maybe drop down fifteen or twenty feet lower, if he was careful.

Easing myself around, I got my legs stretched out. With a rifle in one hand and the crutch in the other I moved myself between two bushes and under the edge of a boulder and slid, using the crutch and rifle to keep me from going too fast. As it was I stopped with a hard jolt against a slab of rock and, worst of all, I'd made some dust.

Now I was closer down. I checked my guns to be sure I had them loaded, then I felt of my cartridge belt and didn't like what I found. I had eleven cartridges left for my pistol, and in my pockets I had a couple more rounds for the rifle. This here was not going to be any long fight.

Fogged though my thinkin' was, the more I studied that layout, the more sure I was that there was somebody inside who shouldn't be, that ma and them were dead or prisoners. Surely somebody would have come out that door otherwise.

Or else there was somebody on the hill behind me.

Now that was a thought. Maybe somebody back yonder had me right in their sights. Turning my head, I peered back up the mountain, but if they were right above me they couldn't see me at all. Suddenly I saw something I couldn't have seen from where I'd been until I slid.

There was a man's body—alive or dead there was no way of knowing—sprawled in front of the bunkhouse. I couldn't see it well but it surely looked like Al Fulbric. Regardless of who it was, there'd obviously been a fight. If that was Al, and I was sure it was, then somebody would have come for him.

The day had drawn on, and the sun was warm on my shoulders, but I wasn't feeling much but the warmth and the sickness that was in me. The house and the corrals down there seemed to waver, like there was heat waves between us. From time to time I ran my hands over the rifle. It was reality, it was something tangible, something I knew. Squinting my eyes I peered down there. Somebody had to come down, somebody had to come out of the house. Then I'd know.

Suddenly my eyes caught movement, something out there on the road. Turning my head stiffly I peered, scowling, trying to see through the delirium that was in me.

It was a horse. It was a black appaloosa.

Only one man sat a horse like that, only one horse I'd ever seen looked like that. Far enough off so's I could just make him out, Milo Talon was riding up to a trap. Riding to his death from the guns that waited inside. Somehow he had to be warned, somehow he had to be told. I had no idea who was inside or how many there were, but I was sure there were too many. There'd been eight men including Flanner in the group that jumped me. Eight men in there with guns, just waiting for Milo or me.

If I fired a shot the chances were I'd never get off that slope alive. The only reason I'd made it so far was that they didn't know I was there, and if I moved they'd nail me instantly. But I knew I was surely going to do it because Milo was my friend and I wasn't about to see him shot down as he rode up, unsuspecting.

Unsuspecting? Well, maybe not. Milo never rode anywhere without being alert. He was like me, like a wild animal. He was always ready to cut and run or to fight.

He was only some three hundred yards off now, and you could bet they had him in their sights. My rifle tilted and I fired into the air. He slapped spurs to his horse, went down on the far side, and left there with bullets kicking all around him. And me, I went down off that mountain.

Nobody needed to tell me that I was walking into hell, nobody needed one word to tell me that ridge where I'd been holed up was going to be split wide open with rifle fire. If I died it was going to be gun in hand, boots on and walking, so I half ran, half slid off that hill, coming down like a madman.

I hit ground knees bent, heels dug in, with bullets kicking dust all around me. My mind was a blur but I went for that door and hit it with my shoulder. Like I said, I'm a big man and strong, and even weak as I was I tore that door loose and plunged into the kitchen. A sandy-haired man with a double-barrel shotgun was right square in front of me and I banged a shot at him, then lunged on in, jerking up the muzzle of my rifle. It missed his throat and tore his nose wide open and he screamed like a scared woman. I came around with the butt and there was a dull *thunk* as he hit the floor under my feet.

In the next room there was a sudden explosion, a yell, and I shifted the rifle to my left hand, grabbed up the shotgun, and plunged into the living room.

There were four men there and Em Talon and Pennywell lying in a corner. Pennywell seemed to have a bloody lip. I swung that shotgun around and let go with both triggers at twelve-foot range. She boomed like a cannon and the room was so full of smoke that my eyes stung with it. My head was buzzing and my knees felt like they were going to go any minute but I levered shot after shot into the smoke where those men were.

A man rushed through the smoke, six-gun in hand, his hat gone, hair wild, his blue eyes staring. I was to his right and he looked at me and swung the gun at me. I threw the shotgun at his face and followed it in. I had the rifle but I forgot it. I just taken a swing with my big right fist and clobbered him right over one of those blue eyes. His knees started to go and I taken that rifle in both hands and took a full swing at his belly with the butt. He folded like a wet sack and when he hit the floor on his knees I booted him in the face.

Staggering, I went down. My knees hit, and I lunged to get up and fell down. I tried to get up and rolled over in time to see a man come busting in from the front door. He was a square-built man in a red-checkered shirt and he had a gun. He seen me and he throwed down on me. I figured he had me dead to rights. I looked square into that pistol and knew I'd bought it, but my whole life didn't pass in front of me. All I could think of was getting up and at him, knowing I'd never make it in time.

Behind me a gun boomed, then boomed again. That man stood up on his tiptoes, his gun dribbled from fingers gone rubber, and he fell all in one piece. As I turned my head, there was Em Talon holding a big Dragoon Colt she'd had hid somewhere in the folds of her dress.

Next thing I knew Pennywell was beside me, hauling me over to the wall, and the room was quiet. After a bit there was a moan . . . and it was me. Then somebody said, "Don't shoot! For God's sake, don't shoot!" And a man, bloody and dying, staggered past me to the door.

A window opened and the smoke started to suck out and the air cleared up. Three men were on the floor, but what shape they were in I don't know. They just laid there as Em knelt alongside of me and stared down at me. "You come just right, boy, you surely did. They got Barnabas tied up and they've shot Al."

"Milo's here. I shot to warn him."

"Milo? Then they better hunt cover."

They never tried to move me. They fetched a pillow for my head and they bathed my wounds that had tore loose and after a while they fed me some broth. Part of my weakness was just sheer hunger, but the blood I'd lost had done me no good.

Of the three men on the floor two of them were dead. One of them had caught most of the shotgun blast and the other had taken two forty-fours from Em's Dragoon Colt.

The man I'd hit in the belly with the rifle butt was still alive although he was in bad shape. The others, one way or another, got out of the house and we never did know what became of them. Anyway, they were gone and there was no sign of Flanner. He'd been there, but crippled or not, he was gone before the shooting was over.

Em told me three of them had been down on their knees at loop-holes letting Milo ride up. Somebody among them knew who he was and Flanner wanted him dead. With Em and Barnabas prisoners they expected to force one or the other to sign over the MT to them.

Three weeks I lay abed, waited on by Pennywell and Em. Three weeks when I lay mighty weak and came close to cashing in. Barnabas, Milo, and Al Fulbric rode into town but the Flanner outfit had scattered.

Albani Fulbric had been shot, all right, and had him a concussion, but no more than that and a minor flesh wound that gave him no trouble.

With Barnabas and Milo around things were back to normal. Al taken it easy a few days and then he set to and worked like the hand he was. I was the only one laid up, and I was sick enough so I scarcely knew where I was or what was keeping for the first ten days.

With the return of the Talon boys the house took on a new air. It surely didn't seem like that house was too big for them. They sang and roughhoused and told stories of the years between when they had been apart. Barnabas had traveled in Europe, had served in the army of France, and he was an educated man. Lyin' there in bed I listened to the easy flow of his talk and for the first time felt envy of another man.

When I was a boy yonder in the mountains we had to walk or ride miles to the nearest school, and often enough there was work to keep us from it, and nobody to make us go when there wasn't. We youngsters tried to duck out of school whenever possible, and it shamed me to think there were now youngsters who knew more than me, who could write better and read better.

I had never given thought to it before, and I could work as well as any man, but then I began to notice men like me ending up setting by with nothing to live on while others had a-plenty. Barnabas had plenty of schooling, and even Milo had a good bit. I didn't know nothing but how to use a gun, ride a horse, and track game . . . or men.

Jake Flanner had disappeared. So had Johannes Duckett. Nobody had seen either one, and that tough lot who were hired by Flanner had all shaken the dust of the country from their hocks. The Flanner saloon and hotel had been taken over by Dorothy Arribas, while Con Wellington had opened his store full blast and was doing a good business.

But lyin' up like I was I done some thinking, and I wasn't at all sure those two were gone. A man as anxious to get even as Flanner, who'd done as much and spent as much, wasn't about to quit while losing. As for Duckett, he seemed ready to do whatever Flanner wanted.

Pennywell, she was around and about. She'd put up her hair and she was making eyes at all three of us, although the Talon boys the most. Em watched it and she was amused more than anything else. Barnabas didn't seem to be aware of her as more than just another person around, but Milo, I seen him looking her over once or twice.

Em had been to town, bought herself dress material, and was sewing up some new duds for herself. The boys shaped up the place and the cattle were loosed on the open range to get the best of the grass that was left.

I lay back in bed and stared up there at the ceiling wondering what was next for me. I never gave thought to it before, taking things as they came, but here I was laid up, mending slowly but surely, but seeing this big house around me and those folks. There was a strong feeling between Milo and Barnabas . . . brothers they were, and different as two men can be, and as boys they'd fought like cats and dogs, or so they said, but it was good to see them now. They made a team, the two of them, and between them the old Empty began to shape up.

Maybe I lay abed a mite longer than needful. It was simply that I hated to leave that old house, Pennywell and Em and all of them. My own family busted up early, going off in different directions. We had a strong feeling for kinfolk in trouble, but my own family had scattered to the winds. Even Nolan, who was my twin brother, I'd not seen in a coon's age.

But the time had come for ridin' and one morning I rolled out of bed and put on my hat. Seems like in cow country a man always puts on his hat first. I slid into my jeans, and pretty raunchy they were, although Em and Pennywell had each taken a hand at putting them in shape. My shirt was patched up—Em had wanted to give me one of the boys' shirts but it wouldn't fit no way. I was too big in the shoulders and chest for either of them.

I was on my feet and slinging my gun belt around my hips when Pennywell came in. She taken one look and called out, "Em! Mrs. Talon! Logan is up!"

Em Talon came in and taken a long look at me. "Well, I knew I wasn't going to keep no Sackett in bed for long. Come on down, son, and have you some breakfast. You need to get some red meat into you, for blood. You lost a-plenty."

"Yes, ma'am," I said, and went.

Chapter 18

For three days I did nothing but sit on the porch and look down the road toward Siwash. Everything was moving along on the Empty—the cattle were grazing on the prairie grass where they had not been able to graze freely since Flanner came into the country. The place was getting fixed up, and Em was for the first time looking kind of easy in the mind. She was sleeping all night, and so was Pennywell.

The Talon boys were out on the range most of the time, branding calves and picking up what mavericks they could find left over from the years since the Empty had been properly worked.

Me, I sat there on the porch and tried to think out what was in the thoughts of Jake Flanner and Johannes Duckett. Yet my mind kept straying down the trail to California. Soon I'd be well enough to go there. There was nothing to keep me longer. The boys were back, Em Talon was in good shape, and nobody would try to take the Empty with even Milo around. I'd seen Milo in action a time or two and knew he could handle whatever came his way.

In the three days of sitting on the porch I saw nothing to worry a man. In fact I saw nothing but grass and cows, with a few white clouds lazing it across a blue sky. On the fourth day I went out to the corral when the boys were topping off their horses. I was getting restless. Soon I'd be getting hog-fat with just setting by.

I taken up a rope, shook out a loop, and caught up that roan horse. He dodged around a bit but once the loop settled over his neck he stood by. I petted him a mite and talked to him, fed him a carrot, and slapped the saddle on him. He humped his back a mite, but by this time we'd become right friendly and he didn't feel like offering much of an argument. Anyway, I'd had it out with him before this and he knew who was boss.

Pennywell came to the door, drying her hands on a dish towel. "Logan Sackett, you must be a great big fool to try to ride in your condition. You tie that horse up and come in here!"

"Time for me to be headin' down the trail, ma'am. I never stay long in one place, and I've been around here a sight too long."

"'Rolling stones gather no moss,'" she said pertly.

"I never saw moss grow on anything but dead wood and half-buried rocks," I said, "and anyway, a wandering bee gets the honey."

"A lot of honey you've had!"

"That's because you kept your eyes on Milo," I said, grinning at her. "An' I don't blame you. He's a sight prettier than me!"

"Depends on who's looking," she said. She watched me swing the horse around. "Where you all goin'? Em's in town. She's goin' to be mighty upset."

"Who rode with her?" Suddenly I was scared. "She wasn't alone, was she?"

"Who is there? Barnabas went to the mountains after a deer, an' Milo, him and Al, they went scouting the grass in the high meadows. Anyway, Em can take care of herself."

I taken up my saddlebags and slapped them over the saddle, then my rifle. "You tell the boys I said so long," I said. "I'll see Em in Siwash."

Swinging into the saddle I taken off down the trail to Siwash. Maybe it was because I'd been sick, but I was scared. Em had gone off alone, and that was what Flanner would be waitin' for. The boys figured he'd left the country, but not me. He was a vengeful man, and she'd crippled him bad. But he'd been whipped in what he'd tried against her. Maybe he had left the country but I didn't believe it.

The roan had been in the corral for a while and he was ready to go, so we taken the trail to Siwash and I scouted for sign of Em. Most of the time I'd been watching that trail, but a time or two I'd gone inside or out back and on one of those times she had taken out for town.

In no time at all I picked up mule tracks. She was walking him along, paying no mind to anything it seemed like. Anyway, from the steps of that mule she'd been letting him make his own speed, which was a bit slower than slow. That mule had no business anywhere and he was in no hurry to get there.

Meanwhile I swept the country toward Siwash, studying for sign. Nothing and nobody. Not even a dust cloud. Overhead the sky was still a clear blue dotted with fleecy clouds like lambs on a blue pasture. The roan taken me down into a hollow, then up the other side, and I'd gone several hundred yards when it came to me that the tracks were gone . . . played out.

I rode on a mite farther, still studying for sign, but there was nothing. That old woman and her mule were suddenly leaving no tracks at all. Town was only a half mile farther so I booted that roan and we went into town a-flyin'.

The first person I saw was Dolores Arribas. "You seen Em Talon?" I asked her.

"She ain't in town. If she was she'd have come to see me."

Con Wellington came to the door, his store apron on. "She hasn't been in," he said. "I've been expectin' her."

"You," I said to them, "you find her if she's in town, I mean you go to every door. You be mighty damn sure she ain't here, because when I come back I'll be hunting mean."

Swinging the roan around I hightailed it back down the trail to where her trail wiped out. I found tracks before she reached the shallow bottom I'd crossed when her tracks disappeared, but I found none on the other side. She was gone.

She'd disappeared like she'd turned ghost or something. I could believe that of her, but not of her mule. A mule is a notional sort of crittur and that mule wasn't going to vanish . . . not before dinner time, anyway.

A quick swing up the draw, scouting for tracks, showed nothing at all. Not a turned grass blade, nothing. Then I went back to the trail and set my horse a-studying the premises. Folks just don't vanish; so somehow, some way, she'd been made to disappear . . . but how? This time when I gave study I wasn't looking for her tracks, I was looking for any kind of sign, anything at all.

I'd gone over that ground two or three times before I seen it, a straight line in the dust almost under the edge of some prickly pear and right in the bottom of the draw.

Now who would draw such a line? And for what? I studied it as I sat my saddle, and I came no nearer to guessing the cause of it. Getting down, I trailed the reins of the roan and studied the ground. There was an area about twelve by twenty that was totally free of tracks except for those made by my own horse as I rode to Siwash.

Turning down the draw I stopped and studied the sand before I taken a single step. There was sand, a few scattered rocks, and some brush, nothing much to attract the attention. Yet some of the grass was kind of pushed down, and the leaves of some sunflowers were bruised and the flowers crushed. Something had pressed them down, something heavy, but what it was or how it had been done, I couldn't guess.

Wandering on down the draw about a hundred yards, I found here and there some scratch marks in the sand like somebody had brushed out tracks. Now I'd done that a time or two myself but it never fools a good tracker because he will ask himself why the scratch marks or brush marks or whatever? You don't need hoof tracks or foot tracks to follow a trail. All a body needs are the indications that somebody passed that way, and most of the ways a man can brush out a trail show up just as well as his tracks.

The draw merged into a wider one that turned off to the southeast, and there around the corner I found where several horses had been tied . . . at least three, I guessed. There were several cigarette butts, like one of the men had been holding the horses or staying with them at least.

Up the draw I found what I was hunting—a mule track among the horse tracks as they went away. It taken no great figuring to see the mule was led. It might have been a pack mule except that Em Talon rode a mule and I knew the tracks her mule left.

Putting a toe to the track, I squinted at it, then sized up the other horse tracks one by one. Now a track of man or beast reads as plain as a signature to a good reader of sign. By the time I'd followed on a ways I knew each of those horses . . . and one of them was the horse ridden by Jake Flanner when he gave me the beating and left me for dead in the mountains.

Turning around I walked back to my roan, gathered the reins, and stepped into the saddle.

It was a long trail. They hadn't killed Em outright so it looked to be some plan of torture or ransom or something of the kind. Knowing what I did about Flanner I knew Em could not expect to get out of it alive . . . and I knew she knew it.

Fortunately, I was on the trail, and I was on it sooner than they figured anybody would be. I'd ridden the owl-hoot trail too long not to know about every dodge a man can use, and it hadn't taken me long to work out their direction. The way I surmised, they'd not expect pursuit before nightfall when Em didn't return to the Empty.

The sun was slanting down already, but it didn't look like I was more than a couple of hours behind them, and I could follow a trail like the one they now left with my horse at a gallop. The strides of their horses were longer. They were making good time now, but I could see the mule was making trouble. He was hanging back, and I hoped they wouldn't lose patience and shoot the old fellow. Em set store by that beast.

Now the route left the draw and taken off across the plains, cutting in closer and closer to the hills. It was an area I'd never seen and knew nothing about. I kept watch as far ahead as I could, knowing they might come in sight and they might also lay ambush for me. There was no dust clouds, nothing. Within an hour I'd gained on them. Some of the tracks were right fresh, but it was coming on for sundown and once it grew dark I'd lose the trail. And night would give Jake Flanner time to work on Em.

By this time the boys at the ranch would be getting restless with Em gone and me taking off like that. Pennywell would know I'd been scared for her, and the boys would come on into town to find out what had happened. Daybreak, at the latest, would see them fogging it down the trail after me—and the trail I left behind they could follow with ease.

One thing was sure. They were headed for someplace they knew. They were riding right into the hills now, not looking around for an opening, but riding toward some place they knew about. And I knew nothing about this country. The last tracks I could see were pointed into the hills, and sure enough, a canyon opened its jaws at me as I rode up. There didn't seem much chance they'd cut off to right or left, so I rode in and drew up, listening.

Now a canyon carries sound, and I did not want them to hear me. I sat very still, listening. Nothing . . . just nothing at all. A night bird cried somewhere, but that was all. I searched the gray sky where a few stars appeared for the vague trail that smoke might make, and I studied the canyon walls for a reflected glow from a fire.

Nothing. . . .

It gave me an uneasy feeling. There was a coolness coming out of that canyon, and no smell of smoke. After a bit I walked my horse a dozen yards farther and stopped just short of where the canyon narrowed down. I stepped down from the saddle and with the most careful touch ever I touched the sand. Inch by inch I worked my way across the narrow opening. Forward, then back. There were no tracks in the sand.

Leading my horse I walked back to the mouth and went off to the right-hand shoulder of the canyon. There I peered up, looking for some opening in the dark wall of the trees that would show a trail. Sometimes there is a narrow gap against the sky . . . but this time there was nothing.

On the left it looked to be the same thing, and then I caught a faint odor of something that wasn't the damp coolness of green grass, brush, and trees.

Dust. . . .

I kneeled on the ground and felt with my fingers. Grass . . . wild flowers, and then a narrow trail, and in it my fingers felt out the vague pattern of hoofs.

For a moment there I stood with my hand on the pommel, my head leaning against the saddle. I was tired . . . almighty tired. This was the first time I'd been out since I'd been shot, and it was no time to be making a long, hard ride through mountains.

Pulling myself up into the saddle I let the roan have his head. "Let's see where they go," I said quietly. "Come on, boy, you've got to help me."

He taken off up the trail. I knew he could smell those other horses, and it is horse instinct to be with others of his kind, so I had a hunch I could trust that roan to take me to them once I had him on the right trail. He started along, walking fast. Loosening the grip of the scabbard on my Winchester, I taken the thong off my six-shooter. Somewhere up ahead those men had an old woman of my own family. All right . . . the kinship was distant, but it was there, and we'd talked together, drunk coffee together, fought enemies side by each.

We topped out on a rise and I made it quick over to the other side, not wanting to leave any target on the ridge. Ahead of me was a meadow, tall grass all silver in the rising moonlight. Silver but for one dark streak where riders had brushed off the dew of night. I trotted my horse, knowing in that damp grass it would make no sound to be heard farther than the creak of my saddle.

Ahead of me was a grove of aspen, big stuff, much larger than a man was usually likely to see. I rode to the edge of the grove and drew up to the white trunks ghostly in the beginning moonlight. We were high up, nothing but spruce and timberline above us.

Something was beginning to nag at my memory, and I couldn't place it. We'd come a good distance since I picked up the trail near Siwash . . . I'd make a guess at twenty miles. I was all in and the roan was beginning to lag, but there weren't too many groves of aspen that grew to this size. Aspen start to decay at the heart when they get too big, although I've seen some that didn't.

Looking up the mountain I could see timberline up there, not more than a thousand feet above me with a thick stand of spruce in between.

There was a snaggly old tree up there that looked almighty familiar in a lopsided sort of way. And that was the trouble . . . everything looked kind of back-side to.

It came to me all of a sudden as I sat there on the roan just letting it soak in.

This was the old Fiddletown Mine country.

The Fiddletown had been a hideout for outlaws almost from discovery. There'd been several mines of the name, I guess, but this one was named by an Arkansas hillbilly who killed a man in a knife fight down near Cherry Creek. He took to the hills to hide out and discovered gold. There wasn't much gold but the country was mighty pretty, so Fiddletown Jack, as they called him, built himself a cabin and worked his mine, piling up a little gold against the time when it would be safe to come out. From time to time some friends of his holed up with him, and one of them, hunting Fiddletown's gold cache, was killed by Jack. But Jack was killed by the would-be thief's partner. After that, even outlaws shied away from the place for six or seven years, but from this moment to that somebody would hide out there for a while. I'd spent three weeks there one time . . . but that was years back. I hadn't heard tell of the place since then, and it was a way back yonder in the hills and an unlikely place to go.

I walked the roan on a couple of hundred yards and then drew up and got down. For a moment there my knees buckled and I feared I was about to fall, but I had me a grip on the old apple and I hung on until I got over the dizzy spell and the weakness.

I tied the roan there, leaving him room enough to nibble around on the brush, and then I shucked my Winchester and began to Injun through the aspens and spruce toward the cabins.

There was a bunkhouse yonder, the opening of the tunnel, a root cellar where Fiddletown had stored his moonshine, and there were a couple of old log cabins caved in by the heavy snows. It often got fourteen or fifteen feet deep through here, and deeper in the hollows. This was high country . . . more than ten thousand feet up.

First off I hunted their horses. I wanted an idea as to how many there were. I wanted that old lady out of there but getting myself killed wasn't going to help her none.

Three horses and a mule. I found them in a corral beyond the bunkhouse, but I stayed away, looking at them from a distance.

Three horses . . . was one a pack horse? Yet there had been at least three riders around the draw where they'd grabbed Em. Edging closer, and keeping shy of the corral where the horses might warn them, I worked up under the eaves of the bunkhouse. Making my way along the wall, close under the overhang of the low roof, I reached a window. It was so dirty and cobwebby I had trouble seeing through, but the first thing I saw was Em.

It gave me a lift just to see her. She was sitting up straight and tall. There was an ugly bruise on the side of her face where she must have been hit the time she was grabbed, hours ago, and there was a cut on her lip. She'd been hurt, but the fire was there, and the contempt she felt for them.

It was quiet inside and I could see none of the men I was hunting. I could make no move until I knew where every man-jack of them was. I didn't dare step into that cabin with Em in the line of fire or I'd just get her killed, and probably me, too. The worst of it was one of them might be outside somewhere on watch. If I started in he could take me from behind. My rifle shifted to my left hand while I checked to make sure my six-gun was there. It was.

Crouching down, I went under the window to look in from the other side. It was so dirty I could just barely make out one man sitting on the far side of the table from Em. He was talking to somebody else who was out of sight, so that accounted for two of them.

Em didn't seem in any immediate danger, but how could a body tell? I couldn't hear anything but a mumble of voices, but I couldn't feature them keeping her around long. Flanner wasn't fool enough to imagine he could scare the Talon boys into anything, and if he tried to get them to sign the ranch over to save their ma he'd still have them to deal with after.

Whatever he intended to do, he would do here.

I backed off from the cabin and got back to the stable. Then I began an inch-by-inch check to see where the other man was. At least to find out if he was outside the house. None of them could be made out from that window.

Nobody was in the old stable, nor in the entrance to the mine tunnel. I worked my way around the place, moving, listening, then moving again.

There was only the one door and one window in the cabin. Squatting down among some rocks, I gave study to the situation. I had to get them out of there. There was no other way to do it—and when they came clear of the door I'd have to be shooting. It was no small thing to tackle three tough, well-armed men, and I was going to give them no more chance than they'd give me. I was sure that all three of them were in the crowd that beat me and left me for dead yonder over the mountains, so I'd get a little of my own back.

They had them a mite of fire going as the night was cold at that altitude. If I could get on the roof . . .

There was no chance of that. They'd hear me right off and shoot me to pieces before I could nail even one of them. They weren't pilgrims, who'd come running outside to see who or what was up there. They'd just go to shooting right through the roof . . . I'd done it myself, a time or two. A fory-five bullet will go through six inches of pine, and that roof was nothing but poles with a thin covering of grass and some dirt.

So I went back to the stable and got me a rope off one of the horse's rigs. I taken that rope, edged around in the darkness, measured the distance with my eyes, and built me a loop. Then I stepped back and roped that pipe they had for a chimney. I gave her a good yank and it came loose and there was a yell from inside. I stepped back into the deeper shadows, then ran around to the front door.

By the time I got there that cabin was filling up with smoke and those boys came out of there a-running. The first one was a man I'd seen before but never had his name. He was a big-chested man, showing a little belly over his gun belt. He came running outside, gun in hand, ready to drop whatever showed, but I wasted no time. Throwing up my Winchester, cocking as I lifted it, I shot him right in the belly. He heard the click of my hammer coming back and he let go with a shot that exploded before he wanted, my bullet knocking him back a step where the second one nailed him.

The light went out inside the cabin and then another man came out. I fired a quick shot at the vague outline of his figure and missed, and two bullets clipped brush near me. I ran at the cabin, thinkin' of Em. I heard a bullet thud into the logs just as I reached it, and I jumped inside. The cabin was filled with smoke, but I saw Em struggling against the ropes. I couldn't really see her but I made out a dim outline that had to be her.

My knife was razor sharp and I cut her loose. "Watch it!" she whispered hoarsely. "Flanner, Duckett, an' Slim are outside."

I'd figured on three . . . and that made four. There might be another around.

"Em," I whispered, "can you crawl?"

She went to the floor near me and started for the door. They'd be laying for us outside, so I taken up a chair and heaved it out the door, then plunged out and began raking the area with rifle fire to cover Em's escape.

There were a couple of shots and then a whole lot of silence and I saw Em making for the corral. Nobody fired, so I backed up, trying to see all ways at once. The moon was getting up over the shoulder of the mountain now, so we got back against the corral's indefinite shadow and crouched there.

"You take care of yourself, Logan," Em said. "I got the dif'rence now," and she showed me the big old Dragoon Colt that she must have caught up before leaving the cabin.

The moon was shining over half the clearing now and we could see the body of the man I'd shot lying out there in the open. He wasn't dead but he was going to wish he was. I'd seen men shot in the gut before and took no pleasure in it. Nothing else moved. I studied the cast of the moonlight and decided we were all right as long as we stayed still. Leaning my Winchester against the poles of the corral, I shucked my six-shooter and waited for something to move out there.

It was almighty still. I could hear the chuckle of the water in the creek some distance off, and once in a while a horse shifted his feet in the corral. I guessed that the fire had gone out or died down because smoke no longer came from the cabin that did duty as a bunkhouse. The door gaped open, a black rectangle that suggested a place a body could hide and stand off a crowd, but I liked the open where a body could move.

You know something? It was beautiful. So still you could hear one aspen leaf caressing another, the moon wide and white shining through the leaves, and just above the dark, somber spruce, bunched closely together, tall and still like a crowd of black-robed monks standing in prayer.

And the old buildings, the fallen-in cabins, the log bunkhouse, the black hole of the mine tunnel. A bird made a noise, inquiring of the night. There was nothing else but an occasional rustling from the aspen whispering together like a bunch of schoolgirls. And me there with a gun in my hand, and Em by my side.

A voice spoke, a low voice, not over ten yards off. It was a voice I'd heard only once that I could recall, but I knew it for Johannes Duckett.

"Logan Sackett?"

I wasn't about to answer, nor to shoot until I heard him out. I had his position spotted the instant he spoke, but I learned long since not to shoot too soon or without reason. So I waited.

"This is Johannes Duckett. I am pulling out. I have had enough of this. I never wanted to shoot at Emily Talon, and I will not. This is Jake Flanner's fight."

There was a pause, during which I waited, listening to see if it was a cover for movement. Then he said, "I want to move now, and I don't want to get shot when I do."

I said nothing, but then he commenced to move, and I could hear him drawing back. The sounds slowly drifted away farther off down the hill, and then there was silence.

Two men left . . . I got up slowly, standing by the corner post of the corral, which was taller than me.

Suddenly a match flared in the cabin, a lamp was lit. I heard the tiny click of the chimney as it was fitted to the lamp again. A man moved within the cabin and we heard the thump of a crutch, but then a chair was drawn back and we heard the creak as a heavy man sat down.

"Em," I whispered, "he's gotten into the cabin."

"You don't do nothin' foolish, boy."

"There's another one, Em. I think he's out around here some-where."

"You do what you have to, son. I'll watch that other one."

"Jake Flanner is a talker, Em. I think he wants to talk to me. I don't believe he'll try killing me until he's had his say."

"All right."

I turned and walked across the open ground toward the bunkhouse. My six-shooter was in my hand, but as I stepped inside I dropped it into the holster. I had listened for sound outside, but heard nothing.

Jake Flanner had gotten to his feet and was leaning on his crutches, favoring one side as he always seemed to do. There was a pistol showing in its holster, and I knew he carried another one inside his coat. He moved his arm, letting me glimpse the butt of that hideout gun.

Why?

Every sense alert, I waited. He was the talker, not me. I was tired, dead tired. As I stood there, feet apart, hands hanging, I felt all sickish and weak. If I didn't get better soon I'd never get to California.

Suddenly Jake's voice rang out of the stillness. "You've given me a lot of trouble, Sackett. I wish you had come to work for me that first day."

"I never work for no man. Not with a gun."

"But why against me? I did nothing to you."

"I didn't like the way your boys set after that girl."

"Her? Really? But she's nobody, Sackett. She's just a broken-down nester's daughter."

"Everybody is somebody to me. Maybe she don't cut no ice where you figure, Flanner, but she's got the right to choose her man when she's ready, not to be taken like that."

He laughed, his eyes glinting. "I heard you were a hard man, Sackett, and so you've proved to be. I would never have suspected you of chivalry."

"I don't know what that means, Flanner. I only know she was a poor kid, all wet from the rain and scared from runnin', and that Spivey—"

"But that's over, Sackett. Spivey is dead. Why did you take up for Em Talon?"

"Emily Talon is a Sackett. I don't need no more reason than that."

He shifted his weight, leaning kind of heavy to one side, and that nagged at me. I don't know why except that I'm a suspicious man.

"Too bad, Sackett. We'd have made a team. You, Duckett, and me."

"Duckett is gone."

He was shocked. He stared at me. "What do you mean? You've killed him? But I heard no shot!"

"He just pulled out. He had enough, Flanner. He said he never did believe in going after Em Talon. He's gone. You're alone, Flanner."

He smiled then. "Oh? Well, if that's the way the cards fall." He moved up a little and turned a shade to one side. "Mind if I sit down, Sackett? These crutches—"

Jake Flanner hitched himself forward a little. Suddenly one of the crutches swung up and I shot him.

It was as fast and clean a draw as I ever made, but as that crutch swung up as though he were going to lay it on the table, I shot him right in the belly. My second shot hit the hand and wrist that held the crutch and he fell back against the chair, caught at it, and they fell together.

"You'd shoot a crip—?" His voice faded, but not the glow in his eyes. His crutches had fallen but his right hand was going toward the hideout gun.

There was a sudden *boom* from outside that could only be the Dragoon. "Everything's all right out here, Logan," Em said. "I taken this one out."

I just stood there gun in hand, watching him take hold of the butt of his hideout gun.

"Jake," I said, "I always wondered why you favored that one crutch over the other, and all of a sudden it come to me."

With my free hand I reached over and picked up the crutch. There was a rifle barrel right down the length of that crutch, and a grip trigger on the handle. All he had to do was swing that crutch up and squeeze her off. I'd heard of trick guns, belt-buckle guns and the like, but this one surely beat all.

His hand was drawing his hideout.

"You want another one, Jake? You're dead already, why make it worse?"

He looked at me. "Damn you, Sackett. An' damn that old lady, damn her to hell, she—"

"You were out of your class, Jake. No tin-horn's ever going to come it over a woman like that. She's the solid stuff, Jake, all the way through, and you were never anything but a cheatin' tin-horn four-flusher."

Em came in and stood by my side.

"I'm sorry for them knees, Jake Flanner," she said, "but you killed my man. You killed Talon, a better man than you could ever be."

"Damn you," he whispered, "I—"

He faded out and lay there, dead as a man could ever get, and the thing that hit me so hard was how such a man could cause the death of so much a better man like Talon.

"Em," I said, "there's nothin' more for us here. The boys will be worried. Let's mount up and ride back to the Empty."

"You look kinda peaked, son. Are you up to it?"

"If you can do it, I can do it, Em. Let's make some dust."

So we rode down the trail together, Em and me, and we met the boys a-comin' up.